The Alchemist's Lost Treasure

The Alchemist's Lost Treasure

A NOVEL

By

Lawrence Terry Liebling

First Printing 2022
First Edition 2022

Published by:
Nothing But Blue Skies Publishing.

Printed and bound in the United States of America

ISBN 978-0-96-428744-0

Library of Congress Control Number: 2022903267

Publisher's Cataloging-In-Publication Data
(Prepared by The Donohue Group, Inc.)

Names: Liebling, Lawrence, 1952- author.
Title: The alchemist's lost treasure : a novel / by Lawrence Terry Liebling.
Description: First edition. | Bedford, New York : Nothing But Blue Skies Publishing, 2022.
Identifiers: ISBN 9780964287440
Subjects: LCSH: Alchemists--Fiction. | Families--Fiction. | Crystals--Fiction. | Good and evil--Fiction. | LCGFT: Domestic fiction.
Classification: LCC PS3612.I33 A43 2022 | DDC 813/.6--dc23

This book is dedicated to my loving wife,
Carolyn and dear son, Josh.
They are this alchemist's eternal treasures.

And to a puppy named Blue, who keeps us all laughing.

Contents

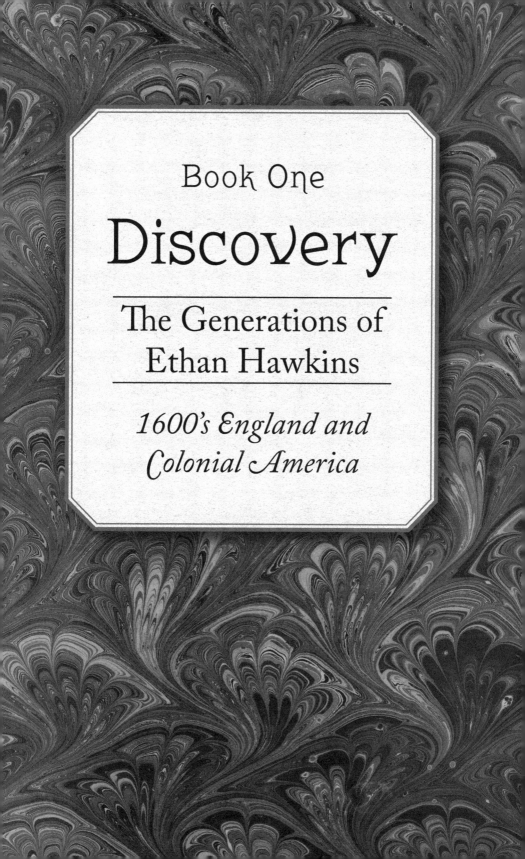

Book One

Discovery

The Generations of
Ethan Hawkins

---

*1600's England and
Colonial America*

Prologue

Cambridge, England
MAY 1691

Isaac Newton

Dear Daniel,

Saddened as I am to learn your unfortunate news of our friend and one-time protégée, Ethan Hawkins, we must not let this opportunity slip through our fingers. Your discovery requires quick action and, if I have read your letter correctly, there may still be time to change the course of events. Hence my urgent reply, which I am sending by the quickest means possible.

Should what you say be true, we may have, at long last, found the prize, the treasure of treasures, the very keystone that reveals the deepest secrets.

I regret that I cannot immediately join you. My responsibilities here detain me indefinitely. Write me when you are able to take possession of it again. Ethan's diary might hold significance as well. His formulae could be of great value. After all, it was he who found it and quite possibly the only one to have worked with it since the ancients last knew its power.

Remember, there is a great ocean of truth that lies undiscovered before us. I shall pray that what you will soon hold in your hands may reveal the beauty that lives beyond the depths of the ordinary. Though should time and events be such to prevent you from doing so, then we shall leave it all to Destiny.

Your loving friend,
Is. Newton

Chapter 1

Hunstanton, England, by the North Sea
APRIL 1674

Ethan Hawkins

"Ethan! Come quick! Elizabeth is calling for you!"

The voice, gasping for breath, swept toward a young man standing on the shoreline, gazing out toward the churning blue of the North Sea.

"Ethan, what's the matter with you? COME QUICK!"

Ethan turned to see his neighbor, Jonathan Stokes, standing on the cliff above, chest heaving as he fought to catch his breath, looking at Ethan with exasperation mixed with concern. Ethan knew why Jonathan had come to find him.

Elizabeth, Ethan's wife, was about to give birth.

I just need another moment to be alone, Ethan thought as he held the crystal firmly in the palm of his hand. As always, the stone nestled perfectly against his fingers. Other than Elizabeth, the crystal was his greatest treasure.

Jonathan looked at Ethan, wondering how to make him come NOW. While Ethan's healing skill with plants and herbs was much admired in Hunstanton, more than one local had considered whether Ethan Hawkins might be a bit off in the head. Watching him stare out at the rolling waves, Jonathan could think of no other explanation for such behavior. Certainly Ethan must know what it meant when a woman with child had reached her time.

Stokes knew. His wife, Gillian, was the village midwife, and too often she returned to their cottage with sad news. The birthing bed was as likely to end in death as in life. So why did this foolish man not go immediately to his wife? Especially after the last time. There were plenty of days ahead for keeping company with the sea.

"Ethan! This is no time for wandering!" Jonathan tried again. "Hannah Fletcher sent me to fetch you. Elizabeth's time is near!"

Despite the urgency in Jonathan's voice, Ethan was sure there were moments enough for what he needed to do. "I HEAR YOU, JONATHAN STOKES," Ethan called. "Please tell Elizabeth I will come directly."

Shaking his head, Jonathan spun around and headed back to deliver Ethan's message. He had done all he could. It was out of his hands now.

Ethan was relieved to see Stokes disappear. In truth, Ethan was far from calm. He knew too well the uncertainty of the hours to come.

It was not so long ago that Elizabeth had lost one girl babe in childbirth, and Ethan had nearly lost his dear Elizabeth too. With her feelings raw from loss and her body frail, it had taken all of Ethan's skill to bring Elizabeth back to full health.

Slowly her good nature reappeared, as did her strength, and the day came that Elizabeth told Ethan she was with child again. He felt both the joy and the fear of what it might mean.

Now Elizabeth was about to give birth, and his heart was filled with joy. Yet that feeling, so true, was joined with an equal dose of fear. Those twin emotions were separated by only a slender turn of fate. What would life bring him this time?

It was that question which drove Ethan to the shore on this morning. He wanted to quell his doubt in favor of joy and jubilation. God willing, this time it would surely be different. How could it not? He was ready with elixirs and potions lovingly prepared.

And he had the healing stone. It had worked before — it had worked when his dearest friend, Daniel Fletcher, was dying. But it had not saved the girl child. The crystal was a mystery, and had been, since he discovered it on this very shore.

Ethan's mind flew back to that moment nearly seven years ago, when he first encountered the shimmering jewel. It was a day not unlike this one, with the sun shining so brilliantly by the shore....

In those days Ethan was new to the sea. He had been born far from here, in Nottingham, though it was from the village of Woolsthorpe, in Lincolnshire, that Ethan had made the escape that brought him to Hunstanton by the North Sea.

Ethan's early life was a series of misfortunes marked by extraordinary acts of good luck. He grew up with no memory of his mother, who died in his second year. When Ethan was twelve, his father, a smithy in Nottingham, picked up his bellows one day, his muscular arms moving to and fro to stoke the coals. And then, suddenly, he stepped back, turned away from the fire, grabbed at his chest and fell facedown in the dirt — dead.

His father's tools were sold to cover the debts and Ethan, now an orphan, went to live with an uncle, his mother's brother, whom Ethan had never met. William Fleming kept a tavern in Woolsthorpe, a day's journey from Nottingham. Fleming was neither mean nor kind but a man who viewed life as an endless round of duties. Taking in his long-dead sister's child was an obligation, nothing more. In turn, Ethan was expected to do whatever he was told, immediately and without comment.

Ethan worked — and lived — in the tavern stable. Though he felt every bit as alone in the world as he was, he soon made a friend in the old collie dog that also slept in the stable and found company in the horses. For a time, Ethan thought the tavern would be his life, his father having died before he could teach Ethan the ways of the smithy.

But then a turn of fortune wrought the transmutation of Ethan's dull existence and triggered events that would ultimately bring him to his dear Elizabeth.

As unlikely as it might seem, it all began with another outbreak of the plague, in the year 1665. Soon after, the great university at Cambridge shut its doors and one Isaac Newton returned to his home at Woolsthorpe Manor. Though his education was interrupted, Newton continued his studies of the world and its forces — including his interest in the secrets of alchemy.

Joining Newton in this pursuit was Daniel Fletcher, a boyhood friend and the noted apothecary of Woolsthorpe.

It was Daniel who first took notice of young Ethan. Many a traveler was in need of a healing spirit beyond the tavern ale, and Ethan was often dispatched to Fletcher's inn for the necessary cure. Ethan was curious about the potions and ointments that revived the sick and restored the ailing. Daniel answered his many questions with a tolerance that Ethan had rarely encountered in those older than his now thirteen years.

In time, through Daniel, Ethan met Isaac Newton. The brilliant scholar was not a friendly sort like Fletcher, yet he was a fascinating presence to Ethan. Where Daniel saw promise in the stable boy, it was Newton and his sharp perception that seemed to divine Ethan's hidden gifts. Though Newton had no patience for it himself, he urged Daniel to teach the unschooled Ethan to read, write and do sums. Grateful for the attention, Ethan slipped out of the stable at night and learned quickly under Daniel's guidance.

Daniel had no wife and lived alone in his modest cottage. Sometimes when Ethan arrived, he would find Newton there, with the two engaged in the mysterious mixing and heating of metals. At first Newton was cautious around Ethan — not that the boy knew anything of alchemy. But their experiments could be deemed evildoing in the eyes of certain religious and political factions.

Eventually, as Ethan won his trust, Newton felt free to speak openly about his observations and theories. What intrigued Ethan the most in the discussions around alchemy was how to influence the course of events. Daniel and Newton wanted to know why things were the way they were, how life works — the world, both seen and unseen — and what was beyond the great boundary of death. Newton, his eyes flashing, would insist again and again, "We must find the key! There is a reason things are as they are. To find the missing ingredient is to shape the world, master the art of creation and fashion life beyond the sway of Fate." His steely passion captivated both Daniel and Ethan.

It was Newton who gave Ethan his first gift, with the command to continue improving himself by writing. Within a burlap cloth, wrapped in string, was a diary. It was thick with paper of an ivory tint and covered with rough cowhide, which made the diary feel sturdy and assured Ethan that anything he entered within would be well protected. "Be curious, Ethan." Newton's words encouraged the boy. "Life is waiting for us to explore its secrets. Each discovery startles the mind into pursuing the next."

Ethan tried to imagine his diary filled with his notes and pictures, like those that Newton created. He saw the diary getting fatter and fatter with more pages as one year turned to the next.

Ethan looked at his diary every day, even when he had nothing to record. Always he started by reading the inscription: *The Diary of Ethan Hawkins.*

The opening sentence was a thank-you to Isaac Newton for the diary. The next was a thank-you to Daniel Fletcher for his knowledge of healing.

The first years of Ethan Hawkins' diary were filled with stories of Isaac Newton. Ethan marveled at Newton's ideas, trying to feel and understand the strange, unseen powers and energies that Newton described.

"Everything vibrates with its life-force." Newton said. And Ethan could practically feel the force that pulled him down and kept him attached to the earth, just as Newton said was happening to everyone and everything.

Then there was Newton's looking glass that made the heavens come so close, it filled Ethan with awe and ignited his inner vision of a world beyond the place he knew.

In this way, nearly two years passed, with young Ethan gaining in knowledge and friendship, particularly with Daniel Fletcher. Yet Ethan grew more restless too. He hated the tavern and his uncle's constant demands. After his nights of inspiration with Newton and Daniel, considering the vast possibilities of the world, his own existence felt so small and limited. He was as much a captive in the stable as the horses within.

Then the day came that Newton announced he was returning to Cambridge. The worst of the plague was over, the university had reopened its doors and he could continue his studies once again. Ethan was saddened to write in his diary of Isaac Newton's departure from Woolsthorpe. But it planted a seed in Ethan's mind — he could leave too.

Through Newton, Ethan had also learned of the New World, to be found across the wide ocean: America. True, Newton said this land was filled with disease and wild natives that massacred Englishmen. But Daniel also knew of it, and he called it a land of freedom, too far away for the king to bother with.

Ethan could now read and write. He was learning the healing properties of plants and metals, and the mysteries of alchemy. He would find his way to this place and discover what might be there for him.

When Ethan disclosed his plan to Daniel, his friend did not try to stop him, as Ethan expected. Rather, Newton had also inspired in Daniel, now past his twenty-sixth year, a desire for opportunities that he could not find in Woolsthorpe. America, with land for the taking and crops that flourished, also called to Daniel. He could grow his healing plants and continue all of his endeavors undisturbed.

And so the two made plans to leave together. They would walk east, to the coast, to the North Sea, for neither had ever seen a great body of water. And then they would book passage on a ship, or so they expected. In truth, neither was certain of how to get to America.

At last the night came that Ethan wrapped up his diary and a small stash of food and snuck away from the stable for the last time, giving the old collie a chunk of bread in thanks for her friendship. He found Daniel holding a bundle of potions and herbs and what little money he had made from selling his few belongings. Naturally, they could not know what was ahead of them, but they had the confidence of the young and were sure they would find their way....

The hot sun on his face momentarily awakened Ethan from his memories. He took several deep breaths, tasting the salty air, and then gently smiled at how his life had shifted so dramatically from the time long ago of his father's death. *If you could see what's become of me, Father. You would surely not recognize the man I am. I have discovered great mysteries and I have this!*

Ethan slowly uncurled his fingers and opened his hand to reveal the crystal stone. It was the discovery of the crystal that changed everything beyond what Ethan could imagine. And with that very thought came the familiar vibration of the crystal and the diamond light in the palm of his hand.

The stone was a constant wonder to him, cut in an unusual geometric shape, with angles here and there, and terminating in points at both ends. Ethan could only guess how it came to be that way. It caught the sun's waves in an array of sparkling light that flashed a brilliant white. Yet in his closed hand it was a blue-white light that made his skin glow, as it had that day, beside the sea, when Daniel was so ill....

After they left Woolsthorpe, travel was hard, with unending rain. What started as a cough from deep within Daniel's chest developed swiftly into a raging fever. By the time they reached Hunstanton, he was hacking blood.

A kind family named Morgan took Daniel into their cottage, the mistress and her daughter, Hannah, being able nurses. By morning,

Daniel's fever created a delirium that terrified Ethan. Powerless to help his friend, he was sent off by Hannah to find solace by the sea.

As he walked along the shore, his mind was churning. *What if Daniel should die? Can I make it to America alone? What is to become of me?*

The horizon rose up before him, and he sensed his life was at a crossroads. *What should I do now?* That question repeated to the rhythm of the waves.

Ethan's life had turned as surely as night turns to day. His mind had brightened beyond his father's forge and his uncle's stable. Yet here he was again, in a place of great uncertainty.

It was then that he noticed something glistening in the water as the waves washed back to the sea. The chatter in his mind stopped and his curiosity engaged. Bending down for a closer look, he beheld a luminous crystal that reflected every color of the rainbow. *Was it a diamond?*

He quickly picked it up and closed his fingers around the stone. As it pressed into his palm, Ethan's hand lit up in the blue-white light. The crystal began to vibrate and Ethan instinctively closed his eyes to feel its full measure. As he did, his mind was illuminated by the shining glory of the brilliant white light.

A wave of warmth rolled over Ethan and his heart began to beat loudly, as though for all the world to hear. His breath deepened and he seemed to breathe in the very sunlight. Enthralled, his sense of himself — his awareness — expanded, as if there were no boundaries to keep him contained.

Just as quickly, the feeling passed. He still held the crystal, but it was quiet now. A blue shadow shaded his hand and cold seeped into his skin.

Even so, the experience had been vivid. As Ethan watched the crystal flash with glints of color from the sun, the words came to him with a start — *philosopher's stone*. The alchemist's tool, changing the lowly to the magnificent; the stone of perfection, with the secrets of life and the power to heal.

Could it be? He remembered a conversation between Newton and Daniel back in Woolsthorpe, and Newton's words:

*"All elements hold their own vibration, a unique sig-
nature be it silver or gold, or even rock or crystal. These
elements are alive, bursting with life-force. Though they
seem inert, they are anything but. We must know their life-
force, make it available, malleable, to suit our purpose. We
must find the elixir of life, the perfection of the universe
that opens our awareness to the world beyond this world
and to the secret mysteries of life itself."*

Ethan opened his hand and stared at the crystal and wondered
what mysteries had Newton meant? Could this crystal help him see
the world as Newton did? Could it reveal what to do next? Or might
its purpose be to solve the mysteries of illness and suffering? Was that
why it had come to Ethan?

He rubbed the crystal between his hands, his curiosity rising. And
then, in a voice that wasn't his own, came the words; *By the grace of this
light, may you have complete healing.*

The refrain became louder and louder and Ethan knew what he
must do, and he jumped to his feet.

When he returned to Daniel, who was still blazing with fever, blood
dried on his lips, Ethan approached his mentor and friend. In one
hand Ethan held the stone so tightly he could feel it digging into his
palm. With his free hand he entwined his fingers around Daniel's limp
hands. In a gentle but fearless voice — a voice that was his own and yet
not — he spoke the words that came to him from beyond: *By the grace
of this light, may you have complete healing.* As he recited the phrase over
and over, his hand with the crystal began to glow.

A few days later, Daniel was well.

From that moment on, otherworldly notions filled Ethan's thoughts.
When no one was around, the stone silently spoke to his mind in a
language, not of words but of feelings, which came to him as a lightning
flash and guided his mind and his heart. There was a hidden world
of unseen energies — a world Ethan first learned of from Newton.

Now Ethan was being shown the fabric of life that held the world together — the very structure of creation. And even more remarkable to Ethan sometimes, when he held the stone, he felt those forces flow through his body.

Ethan never told anyone about the stone — not Daniel, not even Elizabeth. Only in his diary did Ethan divulge the stone's existence and his understanding of it. He had come to believe that if it were indeed the *philosopher's stone*, it was meant to be revealed only to him.

The crystal ended Ethan's thoughts of a new life in America. His destiny was here, in this village by the North Sea. Once Daniel fully recovered, he too was content to go no farther. A romance bloomed between Daniel and Hannah Morgan, and within the year they were married.

So both built fresh lives. Whereas Daniel came to the village near death, he was soon much in demand for his knowledge of healing, an irony that he greatly enjoyed. Ethan learned more of Daniel's methods and practices in the healing arts, and continued his own exploration of alchemy. And always, Ethan had the crystal and its power....

"Ethan! You must come now!" Jonathan Stokes had returned, this time with an even more insistent tone.

Now Ethan needed no further prompting. But as he turned away from the sea, sunlight reflecting off the crest of the waves caught his attention and bade him to look one last time. Staring at the glistening water, his heart leapt at the sight of his own future. Not so much a vision of scenes to come; rather, a knowing that he and his progeny were on a great adventure — a journey that would span the ages and come to rest in a time unlike any other.

Holding the stone tightly, his heart lit with joy, Ethan ran to be with his dearest Elizabeth. For it was in her that Ethan had found his greatest happiness ... his perfection, his *truest* treasure.

Chapter 2

Elizabeth Hawkins

With each thrust of pain, Elizabeth grew more anxious. *Where is Ethan? He's been gone for such a long time.*

The first pains had come early that morning, as the light began to warm the horizon over the North Sea. When Elizabeth told Ethan this was certain to be the day, her dear husband had held her tightly, promised her all would be well, kissed her lips and then rose from their bed to go down to the shore, as he did most days.

To ensure Elizabeth would not be alone, Ethan had gone first to the Fletcher cottage to inform Daniel and Hannah, and explain his intention to go down by the sea. Hannah arrived not long after to check on Elizabeth's condition. She remained by her side, leaving only to prepare the noontime meal for Daniel and their children, Jacob, Isaac and baby Annabelle, all in her husband's care. "Daniel is good at watching Annabelle, but oh, he lets the boys get into such trouble!" Hannah chuckled.

Elizabeth loved and envied Hannah Fletcher. Birthing children seemed so effortless and natural for Hannah. Not so for Elizabeth. And she wanted desperately to have a child, to give Ethan a child.

"Hannah, did you see Ethan's beautiful rose garden?" Elizabeth's

15

pain had subsided for the moment. "He planted them the day I told him I was with child."

"Yes dear, they are sure to be lovely when they bloom in June." Hannah sat by Elizabeth, holding her hand.

"Ethan explained that roses are a sign of wondrous events to come and herald great new beginnings…. I'm sure that's true enough. But that Ethan thought to do it means everything to me."

"Rest now, Elizabeth, you need your strength," Hannah instructed.

"Oh Hannah, I know they will bloom so full. Not only red roses, but white and pink as well." Elizabeth continued.

With the urgency in her voice, Hannah knew that Elizabeth, and Ethan, saw the roses as assurance that this child would live and blossom too.

"That's enough talk for now. You really must take care," Hannah announced, determined to guide her friend safely through this moment.

Elizabeth breathed in deeply and soothed herself, preparing for the next surge of pain. She closed her eyes and tried to see Ethan's face — the way his brown eyes looked so intently into hers, as though checking to be sure she was still there. Even in her discomfort, Elizabeth smiled, recalling the first moment she had seen those eyes.

It was some time after Ethan and Daniel Fletcher had settled in Hunstanton. Daniel had married Hannah Morgan and had quickly become a trusted apothecary and healer.

Elizabeth, like her mother, was a seamstress in the great manor house of Hunstanton. One day a visitor arrived from London and, shortly thereafter, took ill. Though the last terrible plague had ended some years before, no one who knew the history of that hideous scourge ever believed it was truly gone. So when the visitor sprouted spots and then collapsed, the household was in terror that the plague had returned.

Daniel Fletcher was summoned, with Ethan at his side. Elizabeth was ordered to bring rags to the sick room. It was Ethan who answered her light tap on the door and then held her eyes in his until she blushed, stuffed the rags in his arms and backed away with a smile.

After the visitor recovered from cowpox, not the plague, life in the village returned to its previous pace. But for Elizabeth and Ethan, everything had changed. Within the year, they were married, and they had scarcely begun sharing the same bed when Elizabeth was with child.

But holding onto the unborn had proven to be very difficult. Twice Elizabeth endured the sudden slipping away of her hopes and happiness. And then the last time, when she finally dared to believe they would be blessed with a precious babe.... It had taken so long to recover her strength after the tiny girl emerged, quiet and still.

Another wave of pain ... Elizabeth's eyes darted around the room, searching for Ethan.

"I'm here." Hannah took her hand. "Let's see how this little one is coming along. He's going to be a big one, by your size. And that's good, Lizzy. That's a sign of health."

Elizabeth hoped it was true. Still, the pain ... surely she must be dying. Surely she was being cut in two.

She closed her eyes again and willed herself to think only of Ethan, her husband of five years. Together five years and no children.... *Please, God, this child must live,* Elizabeth prayed. *Whatever I must endure, the child must live.*

Ethan had held her tenderly when she told him she was again with child. She had wept with joy and yet there was the nagging fear. Ethan had wiped her tears and assured her that this time they would have a strong and healthy son. He and Daniel had mixed potion upon potion to bring her through her term, helped as well by Hannah's steady vigilance and common sense.

Although Elizabeth was certain the babe was coming too early, there was fight in this child. She could feel it. That was a hopeful difference from before.

In truth, throughout these many months, Elizabeth had felt confusing premonitions about the being within her. She had many questions, some disturbing, about who she was bringing into the world.

Sometimes the child seemed a gentle soul, filled with the light of the moon and stars, peacefully resting inside her. Yet, at other moments, a wild child seemed to stir within, an untamed force unable to find quiet or comfort. Now, as the child was soon to be born, she prayed for the child of light.

At last Elizabeth heard familiar footsteps. She opened her eyes, thankful that her husband was home. "Oh, Ethan!" It was all she could choke out, as tears of relief and pain made parallel paths down her cheeks.

Ethan kissed away the salty tears and his touch was a gentle stroke that momentarily eased her agony. "My girl, my dear girl, I'm right here," Ethan whispered.

"It will soon be my time Ethan. This very day our lives will surely change." Elizabeth's eyes meet his.

"I'm ready for whatever comes." Ethan assured her. "There is so much ahead of us."

"I wish only for our happiness." Elizabeth said almost as a prayer, still taking in his gaze.

Now Hannah Fletcher took command. "Kiss her again and then be gone with you," Hannah demanded. "I need you to go to the Stokes' cottage and fetch Gillian." The midwife would soon be needed.

All through the evening Elizabeth Hawkins struggled to give birth, first to Jeremiah and then, on his heels, a twin, Benjamin. Though they were small, each arrived well formed and, with a loud wail, registered his complaint at being brought from *there* to *here*.

Exhausted by the ordeal, Elizabeth drifted in exultant haze as Hannah and Gillian tended to the newborns. When Elizabeth felt the babies in her arms, their warmth heralded the triumph of their birth. Ethan stood beside her, his face full of amazement and joy.

"Look Ethan, there are two of them. Two sons. Are you happy?" Elizabeth beamed in soft hues of gentle grace.

"More than I can even say." Ethan's heart danced with delight.

At last, God had blessed them — twice blessed them — with children. As Elizabeth's senses cleared, she recalled the premonitions before her babes were born and her confusion about the contrasting forces she had felt within. But gazing on her swaddled sons, they were surely both beings of light. It was her fear that had created the feeling of darkness. Surely, it was only her fear.

Chapter 3

Hunstanton
APRIL 1674 – DECEMBER 1675

Elizabeth & Ethan, Jeremiah & Benjamin

Despite her joy, Elizabeth was slow in recovering from childbirth. Thankfully, it was the exhaustion of caring for twins, not sorrow, which plagued her this time.

And yet, it was more than sleeplessness and the near-constant needs of two infants that nagged at her. Elizabeth could not avoid recalling her strange bewilderment, when she had sensed two very different souls within her.

As they grew, it was clear that Benjamin was the child of light. He smiled and cooed and seemed rarely to cry. Even then, his tears were usually brought on by the wails of protest coming from his brother. To Elizabeth, Jeremiah too often seemed inconsolable and she worried that he bore a troubled spirit.

And as more months passed, Elizabeth arrived at the awful conclusion that perhaps she was to blame. Was Jeremiah being punished for her sin, *the sin of indulgence?* She had begged God to give her a healthy child. It had been her prayer morning, noon and night. Now, Elizabeth feared, had the Devil heard her too? Was that how she came to birth two boys? They did not carry the magic of having the same face, as Elizabeth had seen in some children born together. Benjamin had Ethan's dark eyes and full lips, while Jeremiah's eyes had flecks of gold. And there was a pucker in Jeremiah's chin that Ethan recalled from memories of his father's face.

Before the twins were born, Elizabeth never shared with Ethan her concern about the dueling spirits she had sensed within her. Now she would not diminish Ethan's happiness by speaking of her fears for Jeremiah. She kept her worries in her own heart.

For his part, Ethan's delight in his sons was complete. True, growing up alone, Ethan had no idea that babies were so noisy and messy. Their little cottage was no longer the neat, quiet home he and Elizabeth had shared. But Ethan cared little about that. He had lived in a stable — he knew what mattered.

With each new day, Ethan took more pride in his boys, who were lively and robust. Though they emerged tiny, they had the good fortune to be born in the spring, when warm days led to warmer ones, and the air was clear and clean. With all of nature alive and thriving, so too were his boys.

And since the day his sons were born, whenever he held the crystal stone it seemed to glow with an even brighter light. Ethan felt right with the forces of the world.

But in time, Ethan's happiness began to diminish as concern for Elizabeth grew. The roundness of her body as she carried her babies had quickly given way to a thinness that disturbed Hannah Fletcher, who was forever encouraging Elizabeth to eat. When the next winter arrived, the bitter gales off the North Sea gave Elizabeth a perpetual shiver. No amount of clothing or blankets could warm her sufficiently.

As Jeremiah and Benjamin approached their first birthday, Elizabeth remained frail and Ethan began to worry in earnest. He realized with much sadness that Elizabeth did not have the constitution to bear more children, and he very much feared what another pregnancy would do to her.

On many nights while she slept, Ethan would gently hold her hand, which was rough from constant work, though he hardly noticed. Ethan would trace the blue lines beneath her skin and wonder what new potion he might mix to boost her blood and bring her life-force to full strength. Often Ethan would take his diamond crystal in his other hand, willing the light to glow and its warmth to vibrate through him, to revitalize his dearest Elizabeth.

But now the stone was silent, as it had been through their every loss before. That silence made Ethan confused — and then furious. He did not understand the stone's power. Why had he found it — or, as he came to believe, it had found him? *Why does it sometimes give me such shining wisdom, such clear understanding of what is needed and how to heal, but not always?* That was maddening. Why did it help him feel and harness the unseen forces — and then turn mysteriously lifeless?

On the day of their birth, the stone had glowed to announce his sons. And they had survived and they were thriving. But their mother was not, and surely they needed their mother. Why would the stone not help Ethan, especially now, to aid his dearest Elizabeth?

As the stone's silence persisted, Ethan's frustration and fury gave way to uncertainties that sparked disturbing conclusions. Was he living a preordained fate? Was the future set in cold stone? Was the promise of alchemy — to fashion one's life guided by free will, beyond the sway of fate — an illusion?

The turmoil within him unsettled Ethan. Strangely, and yet not so, it was Elizabeth who could calm him. On some nights when the crystal would not speak, Ethan could not stop himself from reaching for Elizabeth. He needed the moments of oneness — the ecstasy of pleasure. She eagerly accepted him, as she always had.

Still, Ethan knew full well how babies came and he struggled with what might befall Elizabeth because of his passion. After each time, Ethan began to repeat the same prayer: *Heavenly Father, let not our union bring forth another child.*

He also turned to his old friend, Daniel Fletcher, who offered preparations for prevention, but made no promises. Daniel offered understanding too, for he knew the intimate bond of husband and wife and could appreciate how deep love could complicate desire.

Other things can complicate love as well. Elizabeth wanted so much to give attention and affection to both her sons equally. Yet Benjamin was so much easier to care for, to tend to — yes, easier to love. Jeremiah squirmed and squawked, always wanting to move, even when he was distressed and Elizabeth wanted to soothe him. Benjamin nestled so comfortably on her lap and in her arms, rarely resisting her touch.

Most heartbreaking to Elizabeth were the times when Jeremiah stared at her as she held Benjamin. Could he feel a deeper bond forming between his brother and mother? When Elizabeth prayed for her sons, it was Jeremiah she spoke of most. Her guilt dug deeper and deeper into her spirit.

As Jeremiah and Benjamin's second autumn approached, Elizabeth recognized a host of familiar signs, which she tried to keep hidden from Ethan. Then, almost overnight it seemed, her belly was a gently rolling hill giving shape to her loose dress. At the sight, Ethan was a burst of feeling — guilt at his lust, concern for Elizabeth's health and, he could not deny it, excitement at the obvious: Elizabeth was again with child.

"Why did you not tell me as soon as you knew?" Ethan asked one night. Elizabeth sat before the fire, mending clothing by the light. She paused, her head still bowed over her work.

"Oh, husband, you know my troubles, and …," Elizabeth hesitated, then continued, "Hannah told me that you confided your guilt and fears to Daniel. Do not be angry with her, or with Daniel. I was glad to know."

Elizabeth paused again, a blush that was more than the fire's warmth spreading over her cheeks. "Ethan, I know we do not speak of this, of our pleasure in each other, but I feel it too. And I believe this is God's blessing on our union. Be not afraid, my dearest. I love you deeply and I love the sons we have made together. Have faith that, God willing, we have made another child who will bless our lives." And then, with a wry smile, she added, "But a girl baby this time."

Now Ethan's prayer was for Elizabeth and a healthy child. But he could not shed all his doubts. And as the days unfolded, despite himself, his fears magnified.

As he had discovered long ago, the stone revealed life-forces and energies to him, even though it was not perfect knowledge and often a puzzle to decipher. Yet Ethan's experience told him a truth he did not want to know. It was an awareness deep within him that came from years of working with the crystal. No matter how hard he pushed the feeling away, it always came back stronger and stronger. Elizabeth had not the life energy to create more children. And Ethan suspected that she felt it too. It had been there from the beginning. Benjamin and Jeremiah were miracles.

That reality was soon painfully clear. Elizabeth had felt the quickening — the fluttering movement that confirmed a living child was within. It was not as great as she remembered, but there had been two babes with Benjamin and Jeremiah, she reasoned. And she expected more activity as time went on.

And there was — for a short time. But then, to her growing panic, the kicks and taps began to diminish until, just before Christmas, all movement ceased. Yet with the holiday upon them, Elizabeth could not, would not, destroy Ethan's happiness. Silently she prayed for the child to live, for the movements to return. Fervently she prayed, on her knees when Ethan could not see her.

They had their Christmas Day together, Elizabeth and Ethan, Jeremiah and Benjamin. And though Elizabeth felt no answer to her prayer, she felt no warning either, nothing that told her to hug her babies extra tight and her dear husband too.

On a bitterly cold night some two days before the new year, not long after they had gone to bed, Ethan awoke to Elizabeth moaning in pain. By candlelight he could see the blood spotting her woolen gown.

He knelt on the floor beside her and pressed her hand into his. When her eyes opened, Ethan thought she had revived. "Feel my strength, beloved," he murmured in her ear.

Elizabeth, barely able to grasp his hand, slowly turned her head to face him, and she filled his eyes as ever. "I will always be with you, my love — always with you."

"Yes, always!" Ethan answered, tears welling and wetting his cheeks.

There was no response.

He moved the candle over her. The blood on her gown had spread.

"Oh Elizabeth, forgive me!" Ethan sobbed. He repeated the words over and over, as though an antidote for her pain.

"Elizabeth, don't leave me!" Ethan pleaded, feeling the panic rise.

Still she did not respond.

Frantic now, Ethan ran for the stone. *He must try again.* Surely it would work in Elizabeth's own hand.

His mind racing, clouded with fright, he placed the crystal ever so carefully in the center of her palm and folded her fingers over it. Her hand felt warm, though she rested in perfect stillness.

He waited for a sign — something that would tell him the stone was working. He closed his eyes and spoke aloud: "Shine the light of healing grace upon her. Do not forsake her, do not forsake me, in our hour of need."

"Ethan…."

He was sure he heard Elizabeth's voice, distinct yet fading. He opened his eyes, willing her to be awake and smiling at him in the way he loved.

But she remained in a deep sleep. He wrapped his hand around hers, desperate to feel her warmth, to feel the stone vibrating. Instead, he felt a coldness settling into her body. He placed his face next to hers, waiting for her breath on his cheek, but … nothing….

"ELIZABETH, ELIZABETH!" He took hold of her shoulders, trying to shake life back into her.

"God no! NO!"

Grief thundered through Ethan, flooding his eyes with tears. He began to cry, then weep. His chest heaved and he struggled for air as he screamed out, "DAMN YOU! DAMN YOU!" In the next instant, as his anger swelled into howls of agony, he was joined by the cries of his sons.

Ethan looked down at his fingers, still wrapped around Elizabeth's own, still grasping his once precious stone. Tenderly he unwrapped her fingers from around the crystal and wept again at how hard he had to tug to release the stone from her stiffening grip. Ethan patted his wife's hand in his familiar way and then staggered to the cottage door.

As he tore open the latch, he looked at the gem in his hand. How could he have thought this treasure equal to his Elizabeth? *Philosopher's stone! I curse the day I found you.* Ethan felt the bile of disgust in his throat. *SATAN'S STONE!*

As the words screamed and echoed in his mind, Ethan threw the stone with the vengeful strength of the mad, cursing aloud, "GO BACK TO THE HELL FROM WHENCE YOU CAME!"

Benjamin and Jeremiah were now wailing in terror, their sobs filling the cottage. Ethan turned toward Elizabeth and walked numbly to her, his fury spent. Barely aware of his own thoughts and movements, he picked up her lifeless body, holding her close. "WHY?" he whispered, again and again, in a rhythmic lament as he gently rocked Elizabeth.

The boys' screams intensified and Ethan stared in disbelief. His Elizabeth was gone. The terrible sight of her dead body would haunt him always.

"WHY? WHY?" Ethan sobbed again as he dragged himself away from Elizabeth, to tend to his now motherless sons.

The very next morning, and even though the ground was beginning to harden from the December cold, Ethan took his axe and tore out the rose garden he planted for Elizabeth, all the while thinking how foolish he had been to believe in the hopeful future he'd promised them both.

Chapter 4

Hunstanton
APRIL 1689

Ethan, Jeremiah & Benjamin

A new king and queen … like much of England, Ethan celebrated the crowning of William and Mary and, perhaps more than many of his countrymen, was thankful no blood was shed in bringing them to the throne. Since the loss of his dear Elizabeth and their unborn child nearly fourteen years earlier, Ethan knew too well how life could slip away as blood flowed thick and red. So he had cheered mightily at the word that James II had fled England and there would be no battles that might rage on from year to year and ensnare his growing sons as soldiers.

Ethan had also welcomed the news that his long-ago mentor, Isaac Newton, was elected to Parliament. It was a Glorious Revolution, indeed, to have the brilliant scientist making decisions for the country.

On the day that he heard of Newton's appointment, Ethan had set aside his work and indulged in a review of the early entries in his diary, starting with the inscriptions thanking Isaac Newton and Daniel Fletcher for it. His notes from his life in Woolsthorpe were a powerful reminder of the world of ideas, of mystery and unending possibilities that had been opened to him by Daniel, and especially by Newton.

Observing their explorations of alchemy had taught Ethan the secret art's true meaning and purpose. His diary was filled with reflections on the nature of alchemy as far more than simply finding the key to turning base metal to gold. And through his years in Hunstanton, perfecting the art of creating elixirs and other physical remedies, Ethan came to understand that, at its core, alchemy is the belief in wisdom and truth that springs from the headwaters of life, a mysterious force that nourishes and renews all with love and compassion — a force so powerful that it arises within all things and surrounds all things.

The diary was also the one place where Ethan had poured out his wonder and excitement at the diamond crystal and its powers. Here he had detailed how the stone worked and how it worked upon him — the knowledge of the world he absorbed when the crystal glowed in his hand.

Now there was scant mention of the stone in Ethan's diary. It was primarily a record of his life with his sons and his enduring longing for Elizabeth. There was an occasional rant of bitterness at the crystal's failure to save her or, on more tempered days, regret at having thrown it away, lost forever, along with his dear wife.

Ethan's sorrow and mourning over Elizabeth's death had taken him to the edge of unending despair. Were it not for Daniel Fletcher and Hannah too, Ethan's life, and his sons with him, might have sunk permanently into the dark night of the soul.

Daniel had gently guided his friend out of the darkness until Ethan felt the warmth of light and life again. It was then that Ethan reconnected with his life's purpose — the alchemist's way — and dedicated himself to his boys and their well-being.

Despite Hannah's efforts to persuade him, Ethan chose not to seek a new wife. His devotion to Elizabeth remained steadfast. As his deep grief lifted, he found sustenance in his memories of her — in the wonder of their moments together, and their legacy shared through the lives of Jeremiah and Benjamin.

So Hannah taught Ethan how to care for his sons — to be mother and father — and he raised his twin boys as best he could.

Now nearly young men, Jeremiah and Benjamin remained as distinctly different as they had been since birth, and before. Jeremiah had a sharp mind, easily acquiring information and recalling the slightest fact on a variety of interests. With a muscular build, he was already as strong as a grown man. Quick to anger, easily stirred by jealousy, he was known as a fearsome fighter. Yet Jeremiah was also courageous and sensitive to injustice, toward others as well as himself. Had Elizabeth lived, she would have seen in many ways the troubled spirit she feared. But she would have recognized a noble soul as well, one who would fight for what he believed.

Just as he was as a baby, Benjamin was a far gentler spirit than his brother. Where Jeremiah was drawn to the pounding sea, Benjamin flowed easily with the rhythms of the fields and woodlands around Hunstanton. Benjamin listened to and could speak the language of the natural world. Deer, birds and small animals alike were at peace in his presence. Benjamin often seemed far away in his imagination, uninterested in learning the ways of men.

Ethan loved his two boys, and they loved him. When he looked upon their faces he thought of Elizabeth. Their eyes were her eyes to him. Their deep black hair was her hair. For Ethan, her memory was a part of every day.

But memory, if held too tightly, can stifle the life before you. And so it was at times within the cottage of Ethan Hawkins and his sons. Even as he had learned to live without Elizabeth and risen from his sorrow, memories of her could still work upon Ethan, sinking his heart and mind into a twisted world of melancholy that would last for hours, even days.

Even so, it was through that experience that Ethan had come to learn a certain wisdom — that life is like a river, a steady flow of experiences that come toward you and then move on. When he felt despondent, he allowed himself to feel its power and give it space to run its course. And each time the melancholy passed, Ethan emerged stronger.

The affect on his sons, however, having no memories of their mother to guide them, was a potent mix of bewilderment and confusion. When Ethan's eyes turned vacant, Benjamin would seek out the friendship and comfort of Daniel Fletcher, who saw in him many of the same qualities as Ethan the stable boy. Benjamin displayed a similar curiosity and interest in the ways of healing that had long ago brought his father to Daniel's cottage in Woolsthorpe.

By contrast, Jeremiah had no one to turn to. Unlike Benjamin, he wasn't close to Daniel. And when Ethan drifted into a stupor, Jeremiah faithfully remained beside his father, stirring the fire to keep Ethan warm. But Jeremiah was perplexed by his father's despondency and in bearing witness to his father's distant sorrow, Jeremiah felt truly alone, which made him jealous of his brother's friendship with Daniel.

In those times Ethan, Jeremiah and Benjamin were not a family but three struggling souls adrift, moving away from each other.

But there was something else. When Ethan stared blankly into the fire, it was not only Elizabeth who filled his mind. It was also the stone. He recalled every moment spent with it. He could see the crystal's white diamond glow and feel its warmth in his hand, so that Jeremiah would watch his father rub his empty palm and wonder why.

Yet the stone had failed him — even betrayed him. When he encountered those memories, then Ethan would feel again the madness of the moment after Elizabeth died and rage again at "Satan's stone."

Once the bouts of melancholy passed and Ethan's mind was clear, he recognized anew it was not the stone that had failed. It had brought him wisdom, which he would welcome again. And every so often he would search for his lost gem, hoping that it would call to him. But it remained hidden.

The stone was indeed hidden from view … hidden deep underground. That fateful night, when Ethan, in his grief-fueled fury, had thrown the crystal with all his crazed might, it had landed in the soft ground and tall grass beyond the cottage. Then the full force of the winter rains and snow arrived, and soon the stone was buried by layers of snow that, come spring, melted into a thick ooze of mud. Little by little the crystal sank below ground, until it was tangled in the far-flung roots of an old oak tree. There it remained, an ornate obstacle to the grubs and worms that worked the soil. Its properties of light and warmth were lost in the dark and clammy underworld. And so the crystal was silent, from one year to the next, for what might well have been an eternity.

But the history of the crystal was not complete. It was yet to have a second act in the life of Ethan Hawkins.

In the same month of April that Jeremiah and Benjamin passed their fifteenth birthday, a violent storm swept in from the North Sea. The rain beat on the soil, soaking it deep into the ground, and the wind swirled and screamed so that Ethan, Jeremiah and Benjamin huddled against the strongest wall of the cottage. When the storm was at its fiercest, a furious gust of wind caught the aging limbs of the old tree and, with a roar, lifted the tree, ripping it from the ground. The wet earth gave way easily and as the web of roots tore loose from soil that had secured it for centuries, great clumps of dirt rose with it. The grubs and worms from deep below were suddenly surface dwellers, as were the rocks and sticks and stones dislodged by the force.

Ethan's crystal was returned to nearly the same spot where it had landed those many years before. As the rain washed away the layers of mud, the crystal flashed in rhythm with the lightning that streaked the sky.

Chapter 5

Hunstanton

MAY 1689

Ethan, Jeremiah & Benjamin

For Ethan, spring was harvest time for the tender plants that he used in his remedies. Before the thick grasses of summer covered the ground, it was also the chance to mine the minerals that were other ingredients of healing.

In addition to teaching both Jeremiah and Benjamin to read and write when they were boys, as they grew older, Ethan began teaching them the healing arts. Jeremiah had little interest in or patience for the sick, although as the stronger and faster of Ethan's sons, he was the one dispatched to deliver urgent remedies to anxious villagers.

Ethan saw in Jeremiah his own father, working at his forge, and considered whether Jeremiah might be better suited to the life of a smithy. Yet when Jeremiah complained at the suggestion of becoming a blacksmith's apprentice, Ethan did not insist, as was his fatherly prerogative. Rather, he would wait to see how Jeremiah's life took shape — what innate gifts Jeremiah would bring to the world.

Benjamin easily connected with the elements of the natural world, of all matter of flora and fauna around him. He was a willing student, eager to identify, decipher and experiment with the elixirs his father created to heal.

So now it was some weeks after the storm that uprooted the old tree and all three were foraging beyond the cottage. Jeremiah was watching Benjamin, as he often did, looking for the same plants and wanting the same silent nod of approval from their father. Suddenly Jeremiah noted a change in Benjamin. Something different occupied his brother's attention.

"What have you found, Benjamin?" Jeremiah called, as he ran to his side.

Benjamin did not answer. He stood perfectly still, eyes closed, his hand clenched tightly.

"Benjamin, what's in your hand?" Jeremiah asked more definitively.

Still Benjamin did not move. Jeremiah gave his brother a shove, yet Benjamin did not respond. His eyes remained closed and he was humming a low tone.

Aware now of the commotion, Ethan watched Benjamin with growing wonder. Light was seeping through Benjamin's fingers.

"WHAT'S THAT?" Jeremiah shrieked, as he too saw the light.

Ethan ran to the boys.

"Look, Father!" Jeremiah called.

Ethan's attention was already on the light shining from Benjamin's closed hand. Rays of gold, violet, blue and green seemed to burst from between his fingers. The boy looked to be in the grip of a trance.

In a flash of both gratitude and dread, Ethan knew Benjamin had found the crystal. There was only one object that could throw off light in that fashion, though the intensity was greater than Ethan remembered it.

Now his inner ear detected the vibration of a soft, soothing sound emanating from Benjamin's closed hand. Soon Benjamin's voice was harmonizing with that sound.

"Father! What is it?" Jeremiah was shaking his arm, as Ethan too seemed to be slipping away.

Then Jeremiah was pulling at Benjamin's fingers. "Give that to me!"

Before Ethan could stop him, Jeremiah had yanked the glowing crystal from Benjamin's hand. The stone immediately began to dim.

A ray of sunshine caught the stone and it sparkled. Jeremiah's heart jumped and he began to smile. In the next instant, a cloud blocked the sun and the crystal lay dull in his hand.

Jeremiah looked down at his hand and then to his father. He closed his hand around the stone, certain he must cover it to make it glow. Jeremiah held the stone tightly, waiting.

Benjamin watched his brother struggle.

"IT'S NOT WORKING!" Jeremiah screamed in frustration.

Jeremiah tried again, holding the stone even tighter and shutting his eyes as Benjamin had done. *Nothing. No light, no sound.* Jeremiah felt only the stone's cool surface and sharp edges.

"TAKE IT!" Jeremiah threw the stone on the ground and stormed away in the direction of the sea.

Something within Ethan dared not move. He could only stare at the stone that he had discarded years ago, just as Jeremiah had now.

Benjamin silently retrieved the crystal and it glowed again in his hand. Then Ethan held out his hand and Benjamin passed the stone to him. The stone lit up in Ethan's hand too, although not as brightly.

"Father, you can make the crystal work!" Benjamin's eyes were wide with amazement and delight.

Ethan nodded, then looked about quickly, thankful that Jeremiah was not in sight. "Come inside and I will tell you more of the stone. But do not speak of this to your brother or to Daniel Fletcher. You must promise." Ethan spoke in a hoarse whisper, the emotion of the moment having stolen his voice.

Sitting inside the cottage, with his back to the door, one ear cocked for Jeremiah's return and ready to hide the crystal inside his pocket, Ethan held the stone and wondered how to explain its mysteries to Benjamin. He had never spoken of it with anyone — only in his diary. As Ethan had come to believe of himself long ago, so he believed now that the crystal had found Benjamin. It was no accident that he had discovered it, and not Jeremiah.

As Ethan shared the history of the stone with the son his mother had called the child of light, the son with the troubled soul walked beside the sea, feeling troubled indeed. Though he was stronger and smarter than Benjamin, Jeremiah had always sensed the qualities that mattered to his father were the ones he lacked. He felt it now, in a surging stream of jealousy that sent him splashing into the frigid waves. His brother could make a stone light up and he could not. What would their father think?

If the stone would light for Benjamin, why would it not light for him? Jeremiah began searching among the smooth white stones that collected on the beach. He picked up those that were most similar to the crystal, willing one to glow in his hand — to confirm that he too had the magic within.

Again and again, he heaved a cold, damp stone into the rolling surf, until he collapsed by the water's edge in anger and exhaustion, numb now to the waves soaking him, adding droplets of the salty sea to the salty tears upon his face.

That evening, after a dinner in near silence, Ethan ordered both sons to the loft they shared in the small cottage. He did not want their watchful eyes upon him as he considered what to do with the stone. Was it truly the all-powerful philosopher's stone, as he had first believed years ago? Or was it some kind of devil's stone, as he had last concluded?

Even now, Ethan was not certain. Should he keep the stone for Benjamin? Would it give this boy, whose oneness with the world was already apparent, the full glory of its powers?

Yet, ultimately, the stone had not brought Ethan happiness. Would it do the same to his sons — be a curse upon them? Should he take it far from the cottage and bury it deep in the ground? Should he return it to the sea?

Ethan knew that Benjamin had the gift of alchemy, perhaps even stronger than his own. Jeremiah had yet to display the gift, nor the inclination to learn its ways. Ethan knew that he must not let this crystal come between them. The stone was a mystery to him, one that perhaps was better left for someone else, in another time and place, to decipher.

Up in the loft where they slept, neither brother was sleeping. They lie with their backs to each other, both thinking of the stone. Benjamin longed to hold it again, to feel its strange warmth and vibration. And Jeremiah wondered again and again why it was silent for him and when he might have another chance to make the stone work, as it had for Benjamin.

Jeremiah was sure his father had kept the stone; although when he returned from the sea, wet and shivering, his father and brother were quietly engaged in sorting plants they had gathered earlier. Ethan had relieved Jeremiah of his usual duties to help prepare their simple meal and instead had ordered him to sit before the fire, lest he become ill.

Though Jeremiah had the hardiest constitution among them, he was grateful for his father's concern. He wanted to ask about the stone but had dared not. He was not yet prepared for what the answer might be. Tomorrow, he thought, as his eyes began to close. He would ask tomorrow. There must be a way. He was so much stronger than Benjamin — how could he be denied the stone's power?

Perhaps it was the emotion spent by the sea, but despite the turmoil within, Jeremiah was the first of the household to find respite in sleep. When Benjamin heard the familiar rhythm of his brother's slumber, he slipped down from the loft.

Ethan sat before the fire. From the flashing glints of light emanating from his hand, Benjamin could see that he held the stone. "The crystal, Father!" Benjamin began in an eager whisper, holding out his hand. "Let me."

Cautiously, Ethan looked toward the loft.

"Jeremiah sleeps," Benjamin whispered.

"Then we must keep it that way," Ethan answered. "Come close."

Benjamin sat crossed-legged on the floor beside Ethan, his eyes glued to the crystal in his father's hand.

"First," Ethan began, "tell me again what you felt, what you saw and heard, when you found the stone and held it in your hand."

Benjamin's voice carried the wonder of that moment. "Everything around me — the plants, the sky, the air I breathed — had its own light glowing in many colors. And everything seemed to be flowing in a river of light and sound, even those things that should be hard and solid."

"What did you hear?"

"Oh, Father, it was singing … like this.…"

"Shhhh!" Ethan hissed. "Your brother!"

Benjamin struggled to quiet his voice and excitement. "Father, when you found the stone, was it the same for you?"

Ethan nodded, not yet willing to describe his own first moments with the stone.

"Why didn't it work for Jeremiah?"

Ethan slowly shook his head. "The stone decides to whom it speaks."

"I want to hold it again, Father. It is like being in a palace of light!" In his eagerness, Benjamin's voice rose again.

Above them, Jeremiah stirred.

Despite Ethan's worry, Benjamin's words brought back powerful memories and his eagerness overwhelmed the voice of caution in Ethan's mind.

"You will," he whispered. "Patience, Benjamin. We will work together with the stone."

"And Jeremiah. He can try again," Benjamin confirmed.

"My son, it is better that you not tell your brother of this."

"But why?" Benjamin asked in confusion. His father had never before told him to keep a secret from his brother. He'd thought the command earlier that day, to not speak of the stone, was only because Jeremiah was so upset. "He's never to know about the stone — how you found it and how it works? Why?"

Ethan felt his own emotions rising. "It will never work for Jeremiah!

It will only distress him!" Then, more calmly, "Benjamin, I am your father. I know best."

"And Daniel?" Benjamin asked. "He can't know either?"

"No. It is better that only you and I know of the crystal. We do this for Jeremiah. Remember that." Ethan was firm. "Now, to sleep with you. Tomorrow I shall send your brother to the village and we will work the stone again."

For a moment, Benjamin hesitated. He recognized the unfairness of excluding Jeremiah in this way. But his boyish excitement at his discovery — at his ability to do something his brother could not — banished his uncertain thoughts. Instead, he jumped up to hug his father with words of thanks.

"Enough of this. To bed with you," Ethan chuckled, returning his son's hug. Silently, Benjamin went back up to the loft.

Ethan nodded slightly as the boy climbed out of sight, the parting smile he had given Benjamin quickly fading.

Still, the decision was made. The crystal had returned for a reason. He could not discard it again.

The next morning Jeremiah could hardly contain himself. "Where is the stone, Father?" He asked as soon as his early chores were done. His voice clearly signaled the turmoil the crystal had triggered within him.

In that moment, when Jeremiah confronted Ethan, for the first time in their lives, Ethan chose one son over the other — and he lied in doing so. "While you and your brother slept, I have taken the stone to the shore and flung it back into the sea," Ethan announced. "There will be no more talk of the stone — not now, not ever."

The sternness in Ethan's expression was upsetting to both sons. Benjamin wondered whether his father had changed his mind about teaching him the ways of the crystal. Jeremiah protested loudly, "Father, I wanted another chance to make the stone glow!"

"It is an unnatural crystal," Ethan stated. "It's best it should drift away out under the sea, lest it cause heartache to us all."

He kept his voice calm, hoping that Jeremiah would hear his words as wisdom spoken from a father's concern. "I have done what is best for all." And in his heart Ethan believed he had — by giving one son an opportunity and shielding the other from hurt.

Jeremiah was quiet then. Satisfied that neither he nor Benjamin could have the crystal, he made no further objections.

But it was now Benjamin who protested. "You have thrown the stone away? How could you, Father?"

"We will speak of this no more!" Ethan commanded. "Jeremiah, you are needed to take a basket of plants to Daniel."

"Could I not go?" Benjamin asked, wishing to quell his confusion with a visit to Master Fletcher's home.

"No, I need you here. There are herbs and minerals to be gathered." Ethan understood Benjamin's confusion and was secretly relieved at his protests, for it was sure to seem more natural to Jeremiah that the loss of the crystal would upset his brother too.

Then, in a statement he knew to be true, Ethan held out his arms to both of his sons. "You are my dearest treasures. There is none greater than my love for you, than our love for each other."

Together the two sons looked upon their father, each nodding in agreement.

Ethan saw sadness on Benjamin's face, yet knew he would soon replace it with joy when he again produced the crystal. And he saw relief on Jeremiah's face and felt the pang of guilt for his deception.

But there was more within Jeremiah's heart that Ethan failed to see. There was joy in the belief that his father had thrown the stone away *for him,* so that it would not separate the brothers, separate father from son.

At that moment, Ethan misunderstood the son who always seemed the stronger, who didn't seem to want his father's guidance as much as Benjamin. In fact, Jeremiah desperately wanted reassurance that his father did not think less of him because he couldn't make the crystal glow, as Benjamin had. Ethan had not read the deeper signs of Jeremiah's aching need, and one since birth, for love and acceptance.

Satisfied that his father had gotten rid of the crystal, Jeremiah set off that day to find Master Fletcher. With his brother gone, Benjamin took his first steps toward releasing the full power of the jewel that flashed with fire at his touch.

Chapter 6

Hunstanton
OCTOBER 1689

Ethan, Jeremiah & Benjamin

In the months that followed, as spring became summer, and then fall, Ethan and Benjamin worked with the stone. Ethan taught Benjamin the techniques that he had once learned and were recorded in his diary.

He explained to Benjamin that everything in the universe vibrates its own signature and has its own life-force, and that from the One come the many, each humming its own unique name.

"The crystal helps you to hear each distinctive tone — the appellation that the Good Lord bestowed when it was created," Ethan explained. "And if an object is in distress, not vibrating at its optimal pace, the crystal lets you hear that too. By noting the vibration of any object at any given time, you can establish its qualities and energies. The crystal guides you to find the tonal responses required to move the object back to its ideal sonic state, returning it to its original blueprint and evolutionary destiny."

Ethan also shared lessons from his studies long ago with Newton and Daniel. "Everything originates from a master plan in the spiritual planes that exist beyond the physical world. The planes take the shape of geometric patterns, held together by swirling energy, each object according to its design."

These explanations, as well as Ethan's demonstrations of how the stone worked, enthralled a wide-eyed Benjamin. Soon he could not only match the tones that Ethan produced, but also describe the geometric shapes and swirling vortexes surrounding an object in his mind. This mastery convinced Ethan that Benjamin's skill with the crystal foretold great tidings for his son.

At first, keeping the stone a secret from Jeremiah was a challenging task for Benjamin, and he spoke his mind in a way he rarely did with Ethan. "Father, it makes my heart ache to hide the stone from my brother. Can't we show him? Give him another chance to feel its powers?"

Ethan was somewhat surprised by Benjamin's loyalty. Their different interests and personalities had always seemed to separate them. "It must be this way," he explained. "Only great harm could come from Jeremiah finding out."

For his part, Jeremiah, believing the crystal had been discarded, softened his demeanor in the months that followed. He was quicker to respond when his father gave him a task, showed more interest in Ethan's potions, and felt as if a great burden had been lifted from his shoulders.

Ethan noted the change in Jeremiah and swore Benjamin to secrecy again and again. He demanded that Benjamin must never use the crystal alone, out of his presence. These were the conditions that Ethan set, knowing it was essential that Benjamin adhere to this solemn oath.

In this way, eliciting the complicity of Benjamin, Ethan hoped to control both sons. He wanted to harness Benjamin's desire for the crystal's secrets. And he wanted to protect Jeremiah from a stumbling discovery that the stone lie not among a bed of shells in the sea, but in a wad of cloth in his own home.

Chapter 7

Hunstanton
JANUARY 1690

Ethan, Benjamin & Jeremiah

For the first time in well over a decade, as Ethan welcomed the new year in his diary, he once again wrote with excitement about his experiences with the crystal. Since Benjamin had found the stone, Ethan arose every morning eager to feel its warmth and pure vibration radiating in the palm of his hand. It comforted him far beyond what he expected.

He was also astonished to find that the blue-white glow felt even stronger than it had years long ago. The crystal infused Ethan's elixirs with a greater strength and purity than ever before, and the demand for his remedies grew. He became widely known beyond Hunstanton and often traveled long distances to administer his prized potions.

It was not only his increased acclaim as a healer that gave Ethan deep satisfaction and confirmed that his decision to hold onto the crystal had been the right one. Mentoring Benjamin and watching his son's gifts develop filled Ethan's heart with great pride. In passing on his legacy, Ethan felt his life had a new purpose.

And as he had predicted when he first observed Benjamin with the stone, indeed, Benjamin's abilities were well beyond his own. With each lesson Benjamin's skill grew tenfold. When Ethan imagined Benjamin's future, his mind took flight conceiving extraordinary possibilities. Benjamin might have the brilliance of Ethan's long-ago mentor, Isaac

Newton. His own son might one day be as revered as the great man. That was Ethan's hope, humbly and honestly inscribed in his diary.

And so, as described in his diary, the last decade of the 17th century began in the household of Ethan Hawkins and sons. As Ethan portrayed it, life was good. Moreover, as the year proceeded, he included a mention of his hopes that by keeping the stone, although he had done it for Benjamin, Jeremiah's power to use it might somehow develop too. Someday, perhaps, both sons would know the wisdom of the crystal.

Yet decisions made with the best of intentions can create consequences that are unforeseen and unintended. Notwithstanding Ethan's exuberant diary entries, an undercurrent of struggle was born the day the crystal was unearthed and with Ethan's decision to keep it.

The presence of the stone and his crucial lie to Jeremiah kindled a constant state of unease in Ethan's mind. How could he corral the changes unleashed by the stone? How to protect his sons — to keep the truth from Jeremiah while satisfying Benjamin's eagerness to test the stone?

Over time, the excitement and wonders of working with the stone dissolved Benjamin's guilt. As he was pulled in more and more by the crystal's warmth and vibration, his sympathy for his twin diminished, and was replaced by growing resentment. Jeremiah was the reason Benjamin could not have more time with the stone. He wanted to be free to work with the crystal anytime, anywhere.

Benjamin kept those feelings hidden from his father, for he knew Ethan would disapprove. Though they were so different, their father had always encouraged his sons to get along.

Thus, the true situation of the Hawkins household was far less promising than the diary described. One brother was deceived and the other was eager to deceive more.

And the father, who meant well at heart, was unable to recognize the damage being done. Though if Ethan had truly listened to the wisdom of the crystal when it glowed in his hand, he would have heard the warning — that the path he was following would surely lead to tragedy.

None could know it then, but by the end of that fateful year, and continuing into that momentous decade, the Hawkins family would be changed forever.

Chapter 8

Hunstanton
AUGUST 1690

Ethan, Benjamin & Jeremiah

Perhaps it was inevitable that the deception Ethan tried to manage would eventually unravel. The undoing began on a sizzling summer morning. The weather had been unusually hot for weeks. Soon after the sun was up, the cottage was already baking.

Up in the loft, Jeremiah woke early from the heat and settled on a cooling swim before he began his chores. Benjamin pretended to sleep as he heard Jeremiah slip down the loft steps, and then unlatch the door and quietly step outside. Benjamin knew his brother's habits. At this hour he would walk leisurely to the cliffs overlooking the sea, and then race down the path from the nearest cliff and into the surf. After his swim, he would walk along the shore for a time. Jeremiah never said as much, but Benjamin suspected he was looking for the stone … the jewel that Jeremiah believed his father had thrown away.

As soon as Benjamin heard the door close, he scrambled down from the loft to wake his father. "Father, Jeremiah has gone for a swim and a walk by the shore. Let us work with the crystal while he's away."

"I see you have become a keen observer of your brother's ways," Ethan responded.

"He swims almost everyday," Benjamin answered defensively.

Ethan arose from his bed and retrieved his diary from inside the rough straw mattress where he kept it hidden. "Before we work with the crystal we need to review our last session. Do you remember how we infused the crystal's vibration into the elixir for a cough? You begin with the mullein plant and…."

"Father, we don't have time!" Benjamin interrupted. "Please let me hold the crystal. Jeremiah will be back soon."

"No, Benjamin. First things first. You must learn how to use the crystal to create the remedies recorded in the diary. We start with the diary — today and every day. Beginning with a review is an important step in understanding how the crystal works."

Ethan knew well the desire the crystal invoked and the dangers of impatience. "You must understand that for every action, there is a reaction when using the crystal," he explained.

At that moment, Ethan could not know how prophetic his statement was. Reluctantly, Benjamin sat next to his father as they looked over Ethan's diary.

Jeremiah made his way quickly to the shore, happy to be away from the stifling loft he shared with Benjamin. He eagerly tore off his clothes, stripping down well before he reached the shoreline. Without hesitation, he dove into the surf, finding relief in the cool sea water.

As his body moved rhythmically with the waves, his mind began to drift. That his father threw away the crystal stone, perhaps in this very spot, was a comfort to him. But his thoughts of the crystal persisted. Why had it not worked for him? He scanned the seabed, spotting glistening stones and shells of every shape and size. Could the crystal find its way to him, in this very instant, right beneath him?

But he knew better. Such things were fantasy.

When Jeremiah was sufficiently cool, and sensed from the sun's position that it was time to begin his chores, he swam back to the shore, retrieved his clothing and started back. Surely his father and brother would be awake by now, probably preparing the morning meal.

As Jeremiah reached the cottage, he caught a glimpse of Ethan and Benjamin through the slats of the wooden door. They were sitting side by side, looking at something. *What are they doing?* he wondered, as some of the old suspicion and vulnerability stirred underneath his skin.

Quietly, Jeremiah pressed his face to the door, his eyes fixed on Ethan and Benjamin. He noticed how intent their father was, vigorously explaining something to his brother. In the next moment the two were laughing, sharing an ease that Jeremiah seldom felt with his father. *If only I could hear them.* Now he put his ear in an open space and concentrated on their voices. "Remember, Benjamin, embedded in the light are the healing codes...."

They were studying something. *Was it a book?* Memories of sitting beside their father in that same way, learning to read. *But why?* Benjamin knew how to read.

Jeremiah shifted his body to see and hear better and, as he did, the door creaked loudly.

At the sound, Benjamin and Ethan scurried to hide whatever it was they were looking at. Jeremiah could only see their movements, not the object or where it was hidden. But he had a sick feeling that this object, this book, was not meant for him to know about. His heart began to sink.

But he quickly regained his composure, stepped away from the cottage, and pretended to be just arriving. His father and brother must not suspect what he had observed. He commenced to humming and was singing in full volume as he entered the cottage: "*Have her wash it in yonder dry well; Parsley, sage, rosemary and thyme, Where ne'er a drop of water e'er fell. And then she'll be a true love of mine.*"

"Ah, Jeremiah, lad, I see the morning agrees with you," Ethan remarked.

"So it does Father, thanks to my morning swim in the sea."

"Shall we have a meal together, boys?"

"Let's, Father," Benjamin agreed, keeping his demeanor as calm as he could.

As they ate their meal, Jeremiah's heart began to race. *What are they hiding?* he wondered over and over. *And if it be a book, where is it?*

Jeremiah could only brood alone and in silence. In the days that followed his early swims brought no other opportunities to catch his father and brother together in anything other than their usual activities. Yet something was very different. His father and brother were holding themselves apart. He was sure they were masking their true intentions, and it caused him to feel more alone than ever.

Then, finally, a chance to find out. Ethan was called to a nearby hamlet where there was a serious accident that required his remedy for burns. It was not unusual in such situations for Benjamin to accompany his father and for Jeremiah to remain home, to complete the day's chores.

In the past, Jeremiah often watched Benjamin leave with a tinge of envy, wishing to have the same time and connection with their father. But this time he didn't care that he was left behind. He had a single purpose. *What were they looking at together?* He must find it — and now he would have hours to search....

There were but a few books in the cottage, and the same small collection remained where it had always been. Jeremiah looked through each volume, searching for new passages underlined or secret messages slipped in between pages. *Nothing.*

Next he searched about the cottage, focusing on his father's workspace. He was careful not to disturb the plants and vials. But it was soon clear there were no objects he was not familiar with, nothing with writing, no hidden books.

What was it? Where was it?

Jeremiah stepped back and surveyed the room, his sharp eyes looking for a clue. *Nothing.*

Then he noticed it. There, beneath his father's bed — more straw than usual from the mattress was scattered on the floor. *Why?* Jeremiah went to investigate.

Sitting on the bed, Jeremiah patted the mattress ... *nothing ....* *nothing....* And then he felt *something... solid... shaped like... a book.*

With little effort, Jeremiah extracted the object from inside the mattress. He recognized his father's diary. He had seen him writing in it, though not in a long time. Still, it belonged to his father, filled with his remedies and not to be touched. He and Benjamin had always known that.

Part of him knew he should return the diary to its hiding place. But it had always been on the shelf with the other books. Why was it now hidden in his father's mattress? Both he and Benjamin knew of the diary. And if this *was* the mysterious book that his brother and father were looking at together why were they hiding it from him. Couldn't he see it too?

Jeremiah fingered the cover's rough leather and opened to the inscription inside: *"The Diary of Ethan Hawkins."* There were the names of Daniel Fletcher and Isaac Newton, the great scientist that his father had known as a boy. Many times he had heard Master Fletcher and his father speak so fondly of their time together with Newton.

Now Jeremiah began flipping through the pages. There were lists of plants and minerals. Next to each were odd symbols that meant nothing to him.

Then he saw it — the first mention of *the crystal.* Jeremiah read with wonder, but a growing foreboding too, of how the stone had come to Ethan from the sea, its mysterious powers, the knowledge it gave him — and how he had thrown it away on the night of their mother's death.

The entries changed in character as Jeremiah continued. They were mainly about him and Benjamin, and their father's great longing for their mother.

Then he flipped forward in the diary, looking for mention of the crystal. The first statement, written in May of the previous year, was not a surprise to Jeremiah: *"The crystal has found its way back to me. My son, Benjamin, has found it unearthed by an uprooted oak tree."*

But what followed made his eyes widen in shock and despair. He read of Benjamin's gift with the crystal, how quickly he was learning its wisdom and of predictions for his brother's future, as glowing and glorious as the crystal itself. Tears blurred the words as he read of his father's hope that *"someday the crystal might still speak to Jeremiah as well."*

But how could that ever happen? His father had lied. He had assured Jeremiah that the crystal was thrown into the sea. But instead, he was working with Benjamin — in secret. *Lies! Lies! And more lies!*

It is an odd thing about deception. Even for those who have accepted a concocted story because they want it to be true, there comes a moment when both the deception and the real truth are suddenly visible. For Jeremiah, that moment came next in a fury of jealousy. The implications were clear. He had always suspected he was second to Benjamin in his father's eyes. But now he knew for sure and that realization was like a knife thrust into his heart.

"Oh father, WHAT ABOUT ME!" Jeremiah shrieked, and a rush of tears cascaded down his cheeks. And he began to cry himself out of tears.

His shoulders slumped as he attempted to take deep breaths, trying to recover from the ghastly meaning of what he had read.

The certainty that his father had kept the stone, that his father and brother had conspired to keep the stone from him, made Jeremiah suddenly ill. He ran outside and as far as he could from the cottage before the contents of his stomach spilled out onto the tall grass.

Then he stumbled back inside and fell onto his father's bed, feeling sick and numb and beyond forlorn. Why had his father lied?

The question echoed through his mind as Jeremiah's thoughts began spinning around in his head. His father had not chosen him. *HIS FATHER HAD CHOSEN BENJAMIN AND THE STONE.*

Those words were a lightening strike that killed Jeremiah's joy for living even as it revitalized him with new purpose: to enact revenge for the betrayal visited upon him by his father and brother.

He returned the diary to its straw home and cleaned up every bit of evidence that the mattress had been touched. And from that day onward, the web of deceit that had been spun around the stone expanded. Jeremiah was determined to catch his father and brother with the glowing crystal. Like a predator waiting to pounce, he watched their every move.

Now when Jeremiah was given an errand to do, he set off and then stealthily returned, to spy through the chinks in the cottage walls. At times there was nothing to see. His father and brother were simply going about their usual routines.

But there were other times when Jeremiah's stealth was rewarded. Pressing his ear to a wall, he could hear his father explaining the stone this… and the stone that….

With each passing day, Jeremiah grew more disturbed. An inner voice continued to spill venom into his mind and heart. That he had always felt apart from those closest to him had been most cruelly confirmed.

Revenge, indeed, became the one thought that consumed his days and allowed sleep to come at night. The image of his father and brother, prostrate before him, begging forgiveness for deceiving him — betraying him — was all that could soothe his throbbing temple and quiet his heart when its hammering made him gasp for air.

He would crush the stone before their eyes! The thought of his power in that moment was the only antidote for the ache that made Jeremiah double with pain, as real as any injury he had ever endured.

Chapter 9

Hunstanton
JANUARY 1691

Benjamin & Jeremiah

Benjamin began the new year reflecting on the previous one and how with each passing day he had grown more frustrated with his brother and his father too. He was consumed by the crystal and the glory of its light. And it drove him to despise Jeremiah, for it was his brother's fault that he was forced to keep the crystal and its power a secret.

He also bristled at Ethan for holding him back. Benjamin longed to be alone with the stone. He had his own notions, separate from his father's, about how to use the crystal and he yearned to try them out. Where once he appreciated Ethan's interest, now he wanted to be free of his gaze. Benjamin felt trapped, hiding his gift from his brother and finding intolerable his father's plodding pace.

The rising turmoil within the home of Ethan Hawkins was perfectly captured in the fitful dreams of his sons.

One frigid night, in particular, held a reckoning for Benjamin. In his dream, he was alone on the deck of a great sailing ship. In his palm was the diamond crystal stone. His eyes were filled with stars that revealed the fullness of a silent night. Benjamin marveled at the glistening world about him. The ocean waves danced with moonlight and the air sparkled with swirling stardust.

Then the image gave way to another, as a cold wind descended from the north and bolts of lightening crackled in the distance. Without warning a storm was upon him, tossing Benjamin about. He struggled mightily, covering his eyes from a torrent of rain that relentlessly fell from a flashing sky. All the while he held onto the crystal stone tightly in his hand.

Suddenly a strange gale, one that seemed directed at him alone, blew Benjamin into the water. His grip loosened and the diamond crystal was gone. Panicked, he dove to the ocean floor. There, he saw the crystal and, as he reached for it, the earth parted, swallowing the stone. Benjamin watched helplessly as the rip in the earth closed, sealing the crystal's fate, lost forever.

He bolted straight up, wide awake. *It was only a dream, just a dream,* he reassured himself. *A nightmare — that's all it was.*

Staring at the ceiling, still half asleep, he tried to make sense of it. *Alone... a great ship... a storm ... Where's Father? ... Jeremiah?... The crystal stone gone?*

Benjamin took a few deep breaths and steadied himself. His mind was quieter, yet the experience of losing the crystal was deeply unsettling. Was it an omen?

He began looking around the room. Jeremiah was sleeping. He looked down from the loft to the floor below, where his father was also fast asleep.

I must get away with the stone before it is lost to me forever. That thought, a tiny seed of an idea, planted itself in Benjamin's mind. The glowing crystal was his destiny. Like his father before him, he had come to believe that the stone had chosen him. His father had his chance and threw the stone away. Now it was his turn to unlock the crystal's secrets.

I must be alone with it, hold it without Father's meddling. That thought moved from Benjamin's brain to his feet. He quietly got up and made his way down from the loft. The room was lit by a full moon seeping in through the window. The fire was glowing in red embers now. Cold air snapped at his face and his senses felt alive.

Looking down on his sleeping father, he remembered Ethan's

admonition never to use the crystal without him. *Well, Father, it is as you commanded, you are here.*

He made his way to Ethan's worktable, for the tool his father used to pry open a piece of the hearth. Hidden there was the crystal, wrapped in a cloth. Neither Jeremiah nor Ethan stirred.

Benjamin carefully removed the crystal, which immediately began to glow and vibrate at his touch. He placed it in the palm of his hand, took a deep breath and remembered his father's instructions: *"Place your fingers around the crystal … let your fingertips rest on its face … let its power flow."*

Benjamin took another deep breath … and then another … and the light of the crystal moved into his fingertips … and then his fingers … his entire hand … and then up his arms. Soon his whole body felt illuminated by the crystal's energy. He could feel the pulse of the crystal flowing through him, infusing his life-force with greater strength.

Everything became clearer. His body was accepting a new surge of energy and his senses were opening wider than ever before. With each breath, the feeling became deeper and fuller. He felt himself expanding. He closed his eyes, waiting to feel the crystal's full power inside his mind….

Instead, he heard a rasping cough and the moment melted away in a fit of panic. *His father! Quickly, before he wakes! Hide the stone!*

With rapid and precise movements, Benjamin returned the crystal to its hiding place and scurried back up to the loft. It was only a flash of feeling, but he had experienced what it would be like to have the crystal to himself, unencumbered by his father and brother.

Benjamin vowed to have that feeling again.

At the same time up in the loft, Jeremiah too had a dream, one that revisited him over and over again since the day he found his father's diary, some five months before. The dream always began with Jeremiah running joyfully in a sun-drenched field of tall grasses and wild flowers. So swift was he that his feet lifted from the ground and he was flying. Higher and higher he went, the sun warming his face as he streamed through soft, billowy clouds. No one was more content in that moment than Jeremiah. His life was full.

Then he heard voices coming from below and he was drawn back toward the earth. As he glided lower, he saw Benjamin standing on a high hill overlooking a lush valley. Benjamin's face shone with great satisfaction and his arms were raised toward the sky. As Jeremiah flew closer, he could see that Benjamin's hands were shimmering with the diamond light of the crystal stone.

He landed beside Benjamin and, instantly, his father appeared. Cupping his hands around Jeremiah's ear, Ethan whispered, "See, your brother is as gifted as Newton himself! Even more!"

Jeremiah was stunned, yet he tried to answer. "*Father, give me a chance with the crystal.*" But when he opened his mouth, no words could come out. All the while, his father smiled and pointed at his brother, saying, "I am so proud of my son, Benjamin."

Each time, Jeremiah awoke from the dream with a start. Each time it inflamed his hurt and fury more and more. There was a tipping point, and Jeremiah was coming perilously close to reaching it. His mind raced. *What to do? What to do?* To confront his father seemed impossible.

His feelings for Benjamin now approached hatred. And this night, as he awoke from his dream — Jeremiah imagined a new scenario for his revenge. His father was on his knees, begging his forgiveness. But now his father also banished Benjamin from the cottage and the village too. Only Jeremiah was his true son, "the gifted one," his father proclaimed. Benjamin would be shamed and disappear.

How to make that happen? Jeremiah wondered over and over. *How?*

Chapter 10

Hunstanton
April 1691

Ethan, Benjamin & Jeremiah

As their seventeenth birthdays approached, both of Ethan's sons had mantras in their head — one for freedom, one for revenge — and plans on their mind. Now, the many months of false errands and falsehoods were coming to an end, as the deceptions of the three Hawkins men finally came to a climax.

It happened one afternoon, as the promise of spring floated in a balmy breeze that blew in from the sea — a phenomenon that defied nature, as the still-frigid sea should have cooled the air, not warmed it. Jeremiah was first to throw aside his ax, where he had been chopping wood, with the intention of running to the cliffs and then down to the sea.

Benjamin and Ethan had been gathering wild herbs. Seeing Jeremiah and feeling the same call of the sea air, Ethan followed, lifting his face to the sun, still powerfully drawn to the shore that had bequeathed the magic stone so many years before.

As his father and brother made their escape from the afternoon's duties, Benjamin was beside the uprooted tree, where he had found the crystal and still searched for new gifts that might await. And now Benjamin held back, recognizing his chance to claim a greater prize. He watched until he was certain that neither father nor brother had changed direction and was making a quick return.

Benjamin dashed into the cottage and to the hiding place that concealed his jewel. He scrambled up the loft with the crystal in hand. Already it glowed a mesmerizing white light in his palm. Instantly, Benjamin was transported far beyond the tiny loft.

Jeremiah too was transported ... for a time. With long, powerful strides he sprinted toward the cliffs. He turned a moment to look behind him and saw his father following at a leisurely pace. But Benjamin ... there was no sign of his brother.

In a flash Jeremiah knew that Benjamin had stayed behind for THE STONE. The impact of that realization brought his senses to full alert and his mind spun an instant plan. Instead of going to the sea, he would speed up out of sight — his father was familiar with that and think nothing of it. Then he would double back to the cottage.

Oh, to catch Benjamin with the stone! Jeremiah could feel power surging within him. *Finally, his moment ... to have the stone; destroy it! ... Throw it back into the sea! ... Watch his father and his brother.... See their humiliation.... Hear their cries for forgiveness....!*

Perhaps he and Benjamin would fight for the stone. Jeremiah had never struck his brother — not with the hatred that consumed him now. They had wrestled and exchanged minor blows now and then. But, ah, how he wanted to feel his fist exploding into Benjamin's face, pounding his body, making his brother feel pain ... the kind of hurt he had endured ... left out ... alone ... unwanted.

Jeremiah raced back to the cottage, waves of jealousy pulsing through him. As the cottage came into sight he slowed his pace, covering the final distance with careful steps, to be sure nothing might give him away. He watched for the strange light, certain his brother — and the stone — were within his grasp.

It took only a step inside the cottage for one brother's jealousy and the other's obsession to collide in an explosion of fists, oaths, sparks and fire. The light of the stone gave the loft a ghostly glimmer and the humming tones confirmed Benjamin's presence above.

In a torrent of movement, Jeremiah was across the cottage, up the loft steps and atop his brother, twisting the stone from Benjamin's hand. Jeremiah's weight crushed him and Benjamin felt searing pain as his fingers were bent back nearly to breaking.

Reaching out blindly, Benjamin grabbed a hunk of Jeremiah's hair and then felt another burst of pain as Jeremiah's head slammed into his own. Benjamin fell back as the room spun. Jeremiah's legs pinned his arms as a fist exploded first against one cheek and then the other. Benjamin tasted blood and saw spasms of light as the blows continued.

With all his might, he kicked out with his legs, upending Jeremiah long enough to slip out from under him. *The stone!* Jeremiah had dropped it to make full use of both fists. Benjamin grabbed the crystal and scrambled down from the loft.

But Benjamin was no match for his swifter and stronger brother. Jeremiah jumped from above, tackling Benjamin as he ran by their father's bed, a serendipitous turn no doubt saving both from graver injury. The force of Jeremiah upon him knocked the stone from Benjamin's hand. Even as he reached out to find it, Benjamin felt a thrust of pain cut across his head as Jeremiah's fist pounded his temple. Then the pain seemed to dull and he felt only a throbbing ... and then nothing....

Jeremiah stared at Benjamin, who had ceased to move. He never imagined Benjamin having such fight within him. *Had he killed his brother? What might their father do?*

Those horrid thoughts momentarily registered. Yet so driven by rage was Jeremiah that in the next instant their effect gone.

There! The stone! Jeremiah saw where it had rolled on the floor and ran to retrieve it. He paused, and then squeezed the crystal inside his closed hand. *Would it respond this time?*

It was silent, just as before, and now he was desperate to destroy it. Jeremiah had longed to do it in full view of his brother and father, to hear their cries begging him to stop, pleading for his forgiveness. But he could not wait. *Now! Do it now! Destroy it!*

But where? How? Jeremiah had always imagined throwing the stone back into the sea. His father and brother chasing him ... he racing ahead and then halting by the shore ... a mighty wave rolling forward.... And then, as the wave rushed back, he would pitch the stone into the surf and the stone would ride away gone forever....

Jeremiah's knees collapsed as his body suddenly began to tremble uncontrollably. *Where was his power?* He crawled to the hearth, cold and shaking. He looked back at Benjamin, still motionless on their father's bed.

Then love, hate, anger, sadness, jealousy, hurt — a full heart of emotions poured forth through every artery, sharpening his mind and restoring his strength. Jeremiah looked at the smoldering embers just inches away. *Fire and brimstone ... brimstone ... stone ... the stone!*

A roaring fire was surely the means of destruction for the stone that had come from Hell. Jeremiah stacked up log upon log until flames crackled and snapped, sparks popping and bursting in showers that threatened to expand the fire beyond the stone hearth. When his face was seared by the heat, a sign of the fire's destructive power, Jeremiah threw the stone where the flames leaped highest. His heart beat wildly as the stone began to glow. *Oh, that it would melt away or be blackened forever, no light ever to escape again!*

As he watched the fire, now flaming with an eerie blue light, Jeremiah felt the calmness and comfort of the cottage he had known all his life. As boys, Jeremiah and Benjamin had played by the hearth as their father worked in the healing craft he loved. To have those moments again, content together.

But then those memories turned. Ethan mixing his potions and just Benjamin by his side. Only Benjamin had found favor with their father and comfort from him. *No more!* Jeremiah vowed as the fire raged.

Fatefully, while lost in thought, Jeremiah failed to notice his brother stirring or the frantic shouts from outside.

"BENJAMIN!" Ethan's voice rang out. "BENJAMIN! Where are you? The fire! There's too much smoke from the chimney!"

In that brief moment, and before Ethan came hurrying through the door, Jeremiah could only focus on the fact that his father had not called his name, only Benjamin's.

Ethan took in the roaring fire and Jeremiah by the hearth. "Jeremiah! What are you doing? Why does the fire burn so strongly? Where is Benjamin? My God …!"

As Ethan spoke, he saw Benjamin, head bloody, struggling to rise from his bed. *What had happened?* Instinctively, Ethan knew … *the stone!*

"Jeremiah, what have you done?" Ethan ran to Benjamin, gently helping him up as he coughed out blood that had pooled in his mouth.

Jeremiah looked at his father and then at the stone, which now glowed bright orange and red in the fire.

Benjamin opened one eye, the other on its way to swelling shut. Light moved in strange patterns about the room and it took several seconds for Benjamin to realize the light coming from the hearth. *What was happening?*

As his dazed mind cleared, Benjamin recognized Jeremiah before the fire — and then memory flooded back.

"Father … he has … the stone!" Benjamin cried out. He felt his body try to lunge toward his brother, but strong arms were holding him back.

"NOOOO!" Ethan roared. "NO MORE! Tearing at each other like Cain and Abel!"

Benjamin could not be silenced. "OUR STONE! He's thrown it into the flames!"

Jeremiah felt the words "our stone" like a double blow. It was not only the stone that would not speak to Jeremiah, but also the bond with his father that had been denied to him.

"Jeremiah?" Ethan turned, looking into his other son's eyes.

Full of hate and hurt, Jeremiah simply smiled.

Now it was Ethan who came face to face with his own actions. The consequences of deceit came hurling toward him.

Benjamin watched the grin that mocked his father and himself, a grin that filled him with a loathing that brought every nerve to life and strength to his limbs. He shook off his father's grip and rushed toward his brother. "Jeremiah!" he screamed. "I HATE YOU! Look what you've done!"

Ethan surprised both his sons by the speed with which he came between them. Tossing each on opposite sides of the fire, Ethan grabbed the nearest tool, a poker, and tried to fish out the stone from where it had fallen between two logs.

"YOU DECEIVED ME!" Jeremiah shrieked.

Ethan glanced at Jeremiah, then put his head down as he maneuvered the poker to push the stone clear of the flames.

In seeming to ignore Jeremiah, Ethan pushed his son into a greater frenzy. Springing to his feet, Jeremiah screamed out in anguish. "DO YOU HEAR ME, FATHER? I know what you did! YOU LIED TO ME! You gave Benjamin the stone!"

Overwhelmed by the realization of the mistake he had made, Ethan wanted only to end this scene that made his heart feel near to breaking. "We'll talk about it later," Ethan said softly.

"NO! WE'LL TALK ABOUT IT NOW!" Jeremiah had never spoken to his father so boldly.

His own nerves stretched taut, Ethan's anger was swift. "I'll not have your impudence! You've done enough damage, Jeremiah!"

"It is you — and Benjamin!" Jeremiah spat out his brother's name. "YOU have done the damage! YOU kept the stone from me!"

Here it was, what Ethan had feared. *How to explain?*

"You must understand, Jeremiah," he began, mustering all the composure he could. "Benjamin has a gift with the stone."

"And you love him more because of it! You've always loved him more!" Jeremiah accused.

Then, launching the final salvo, Jeremiah exclaimed, "YOU SAID YOU THREW THE STONE AWAY! AND I THOUGHT YOU DID IT FOR ME! Not true, not true! You made it a prize, FOR BENJAMIN!"

Ethan reeled in shock, feeling the magnitude of his ignorance. He had misjudged his more difficult son. He was far more tender than Ethan had understood. He must find a way to put things right.

"Jeremiah, you know not what you speak. The stone is mine. It is my possession, not your brother's. The stone was my first treasure long ago. Forgive my weakness. I could not part with it again."

Forgive … Jeremiah wanted his father to ask his forgiveness, yet what he was saying was just more lies.

"Your stone?" Jeremiah sneered. "Then why, Father, did I find my brother today on the very spot where I sleep, hands wrapped around the stone? Did you not hear him say 'OUR STONE'?"

Ethan looked toward Benjamin and knew the truth. Benjamin had defied his warning never to use the crystal alone.

Seeing the stunned look and then the waves of sadness cross his father's face, Jeremiah could at last taste revenge. Whatever the agreement had been, Benjamin had deceived their father. Now Ethan too knew the pain of betrayal. And Benjamin — surely his deception would make him the favored son no more.

Jeremiah eyed the crystal that still lay on the hearth where Ethan had pushed it out of the fire. *Another chance to destroy it, perhaps this time with Father's blessing!* Jeremiah sprang to his feet and grabbed a set of heavy tongs from the wall. Waving the tongs above his head, he stepped closer to the crystal.

"Let me take the stone, Father. Let me send it back to the sea! You must hate it now as much as I do!" Jeremiah lunged for the stone, screaming, "GIVE ME THE STONE!"

"NO! THE STONE IS FOR ME!" Benjamin screeched, as he tackled Jeremiah. The two collided with a mutual groan and fell back on the dirt floor.

"STOP!" Ethan commanded as his sons rolled about, punching and kicking each other. Ethan reached out and grabbed for them both, attempting to halt their fight. But he lost his grip and stumbled backward, his head smashing against the heavy stones of the hearth wall.

Ethan staggered at the impact and his eyes ceased to focus from the jarring of his brain. He fell forward, taking another blow as his face struck more stone. Blood poured from a wound above one eye and a deep gash in the back of his head.

Jeremiah was the first to see his father down. Horrified, he immediately let go of Benjamin, who followed his brother's gaze and then understood the panic on Jeremiah's face. Both sons stared in terror as Ethan lay motionless on the floor, the life draining from him with each passing second.

Finally, Benjamin grasped the gravity of the scene and his mind prodded him to action. He grabbed a cloth from Ethan's worktable and, with Jeremiah's awkward help, wrapped his father's head to staunch the bleeding. He watched, waiting, willing his father to open his eyes, to speak, to demand of Benjamin why he took the stone, why he breached his trust. But there was nothing.

Ethan's breathing was shallow and his face ghostly white. Then a low rattle came from his chest. Even as his soul prepared to leave his failing body, Ethan wanted to speak, to tell his sons … *love each other.…* Instead, there was a quiet rush of air, like a sigh, and then a stillness.

Benjamin understood, even as Jeremiah continued to gape at their father, holding his limp hand, seeming not to comprehend that Ethan was dead.

Fearing his more powerful brother, Benjamin saw his moment to act. Jeremiah sat facing the wall, looking away from their father's bed. Forgotten in the battle over the stone was an equally great treasure — Ethan's diary. Benjamin knew this would be his only chance to retrieve it.

He slowly stepped away and moved carefully to Ethan's bed. Kneeling at the foot, watching Jeremiah for the slightest sign of movement,

Benjamin pulled out the diary, wrapped in rough cloth, as straw fell in piles on the floor. He stuffed the diary inside his shirt. There was no time to consider anything else; and besides, he had no possessions of any value.

He only needed the jewel, which was now rightly his. Quickly Benjamin scanned the floor, searching for the crystal. Whether from the fight or Ethan's fall, it had rolled a distance from the hearth.

Jeremiah had not moved. Head bowed, he sat beside their father, blood smeared on his clothing. Absently, Benjamin wondered what his brother was thinking and wished he could ask.

Benjamin moved noiselessly past Jeremiah, fingers extended to scoop up the stone. He yelped inside as he felt the still fierce heat of the crystal, then quickly wrapped it in one end of the burlap that held the diary. Benjamin noted that the crystal did not glow at his touch. *No doubt the fire was to blame.*

Then Benjamin felt his brother's eyes upon him, watching him … wordless … motionless. He stopped, waiting for Jeremiah to pounce, for the blows that might mean his own death. Yet Jeremiah still did not stir.

Benjamin began to inch toward the door.

His heart crumpled as he took in his father, dead on the floor, and his eyes filled with tears that made all around him a watery blur. Silently begging his father's forgiveness, Benjamin cautiously undid the latch.

The door opened with the slightest creak. A final glance at Jeremiah, whose face hid all emotion, and Benjamin was gone.

He was free.

Chapter 11

Hunstanton
APRIL 1691
The same day

Benjamin & Daniel Fletcher

In the fading light of a cool spring afternoon, Daniel Fletcher sat by his hearth, gazing into a waning fire in need of a new log. He appeared still, yet his face bore the stunned expression of one who was reeling. Inside, his heart was about to burst.

Ethan Hawkins, his friend of twenty-five years, next to Hannah and his children the dearest person in his life, was dead. The news had buckled Daniel's knees, sending him sinking down into his chair. He sat there now, absorbing the chilling truth; his friend was gone.

Steadying himself, he rose slowly and moved to comfort Benjamin Hawkins, who had delivered the news. Daniel's shock at Ethan's death was magnified by Benjamin's appearance. He had taken an awful beating. His face had multiple cuts, with large bruises, and one eye was swollen shut. His shirt was torn and stained with blood. But it was Benjamin's haunted look that gave Daniel an awful premonition: the heartbreak that had befallen the Hawkins family with Elizabeth's death, and before, had played out again in unimaginable tragedy.

"I loved your father like a brother," Daniel said softly, as he wrapped his arms around Benjamin.

Until that moment Benjamin's anguish pumped through his veins without relief. In Daniel's compassionate embrace, Benjamin could feel his father's presence. Tears pooled in his eyes and rolled down his cheeks.

Daniel shifted his hands to Benjamin's shoulders, gazed upon his face and asked, "Tell me, lad, what happened? How did your father die?"

Benjamin's mind filled with uncertainty. What could he say? Should he show the crystal to Daniel? Describe the wonders it revealed to him? Explain about Jeremiah's jealousy? The secret he and his father tried to keep?

Part of Benjamin wanted to tell everything, to relieve himself of his guilt. He longed to explain his actions that had unintentionally led to his father's death. Daniel would understand. Daniel would forgive him.

But what if Daniel insisted that he throw the crystal back into the sea, to end what seemed a curse upon the family? Benjamin could not take that chance. Not yet.

"It was an accident…." Benjamin launched into his explanation without revealing the crystal in his pocket. "Jeremiah and I were fighting. Father tried to stop us. He fell and hit his head on the stones, the hearth…."

Benjamin's tears fell faster and harder now as images of that terrible scene, the blood, the stillness, all replayed in his mind. "I was afraid of Jeremiah … afraid he would kill me. I ran."

Daniel listened, considering possibilities. "Benjamin, are you certain about your father? Could he have been only knocked unconscious?"

Benjamin shook his head. "No, Master Fletcher. I …," Benjamin sobbed. "I heard his last breath. It will fill my ears forever! Then he … did not move."

His hopes dashed, Daniel could feel his own heart grow heavier with grief. *Poor Ethan,* Daniel thought. *His last moments witnessing his beloved sons tearing at each other!*

Memories of Ethan's double joy at his twin boys' birth nearly seventeen years earlier flashed into Daniel's mind. He thought about the heartache that had come before, with the babies lost to Elizabeth and Ethan. Then the agony Ethan endured after Elizabeth's death and his vow to raise his sons alone, sustained by her love. They were together now. Ethan had returned to his dearest wife. It was the one note of comfort to ease Daniel's overwhelming grief.

How could it all have come to this? Daniel longed to weep, to let his grief pour from his body and soul. But he knew he could not let his mourning take full bloom in front of Benjamin. He had many questions that needed answers — chief among them, what caused Benjamin and Jeremiah to come to blows — and only a clear head would do now.

First, though, he must tend to Benjamin. He had always been Ethan's bright light. It pained Daniel to see Benjamin so shaken, his face growing pale and his eyes so dim.

Daniel built up the fire to warm Benjamin and then carefully cleaned his wounds. He wished Hannah were there; her tender touch would soothe Benjamin. But she and the children were away, visiting her sister in the nearby village of King's Lynn. Jacob, their eldest son, now a capable young man of twenty-one, had taken charge of their travel.

When Benjamin was bandaged and had been braced with a cup of ale, Daniel asked his most pressing question: "Where is Jeremiah?"

"I … I don't know," Benjamin replied.

"Where was he when you left?" Daniel tried again.

Benjamin hung his head. He could not look at Daniel. "With Father."

Daniel winced. What happened that Benjamin would leave his father's side? Benjamin had always been Daniel's favorite. He didn't want to think of Benjamin as dishonorable. Still, Jeremiah was stronger and far more brooding and unpredictable. And clearly, Benjamin had taken serious blows from his brother.

"What made you so fearful of Jeremiah that you would leave when your father was…," Daniel paused, pained to say the word, "dead?"

Then another pause as Daniel searched Benjamin's face for clues. "Lad, what happened?"

Benjamin looked down at his swollen hands to avoid Master Fletcher's stare. *What to say? What to reveal?* Benjamin could hear the ticking of the mantel clock and Daniel waiting for a response.

As the minutes passed by in silence, reluctantly Benjamin could see that there was no other way. Daniel knew them all too well. But what he didn't know of was the crystal. Only the truth could explain the accident that had killed their father.

"It was the stone ... the crystal. The one Father found then lost. I found it again. It spoke to me, not to Jeremiah. He hated me for it. We fought over the stone."

Daniel felt the dread of one who was about to learn a secret that could shatter his image of his dearest friend. "What stone is this? Where did your father find it?"

"By the shore, here in Hunstanton. It was long ago, before Jeremiah and I were born, before he met our mother. He said it saved you, Master Fletcher, when you were very ill. He never told you ... he made me swear that I would never tell you."

Daniel closed his eyes, trying to take in Benjamin's confession. *What is this I'm hearing? It was Hannah who saved me as I lie near death. Surely it was her kind heart that bound my wound.* He was profoundly puzzled. *What had Ethan found? What crystal could this be?* Yet in his heart he knew. *It must be true, or Ethan would not have said it.*

"Benjamin, if this crystal led to your father's death, I must know more."

So Benjamin told Daniel all he knew. How his father found the stone ... how he used it to formulate potions ... and how it amplified the sound and light of an object. Benjamin also vividly described his experiences with the crystal — how when he held the crystal, it produced inner visions of the most extraordinary kind.

Daniel listened, trying to push away disturbing feelings that were rising within. He had taught Ethan everything he knew. *Why,* he wondered, *had Ethan never confided in him — shown him the treasure he had found?*

Yet long adept at keeping his emotions in check, Daniel set aside his own bewilderment and hurt. There was plenty of time — years ahead — to consider Ethan's reasoning. At the moment, Daniel wanted to understand more about the mysterious crystal and how it led to Ethan's death.

"Why did your father throw this healing crystal away?" Daniel asked. "Do you know?"

"Yes. When Mother was dying, Father used the crystal to try to save her. But it failed him and Father thought the stone was cursed. Even though it gave him healing powers and knowledge to help others, when he needed it the most, the crystal brought only pain."

Daniel shook his head in despair. *Had the tragedy of Elizabeth's death set in motion this cataclysmic ending?*

"And how did you find the stone again?" he asked.

"After a storm," Benjamin answered. "I found it by the base of an uprooted tree."

Again Daniel shook his head and wondered. *Was this chance or fate? Why had such good fortune, yet also misery, been visited on Ethan Hawkins?*

"Do you have the stone, Benjamin?"

There it was, the question that Benjamin knew was coming. And without hesitation, he chose to avoid it with a half-truth. "Jeremiah tried to destroy it. I never saw him so angry. He flew into a rage. He said if I hadn't found the stone, none of this would have happened."

Daniel Fletcher was a gifted alchemist, and over the years he had become a biblical scholar as well. He knew the deepest meanings of the canonized scriptures. But one need not know the secrets embedded in the holy books to recognize the jealousy at the center of the stories of Cain and Abel, Jacob and Esau, Joseph and his brothers.

Had Benjamin and Jeremiah, so different in temperament, become another terrible tale of brother against brother? Had Ethan seen this and been unable to stop it? Daniel was grasping at the fragments of Benjamin's narrative, trying to piece together what had occurred, when his concentration was shattered.

"Master Fletcher, open the door!"

A pounding fist and familiar voice shook the silence between Daniel and Benjamin.

Chapter 12

Hunstanton
APRIL 1691
The same day

Jeremiah & Daniel

"Master Fletcher!" Again the pounding from outside.

Daniel watched as Benjamin's face turned pale at Jeremiah's voice. Daniel motioned for Benjamin to go into his workroom — a space with no windows that Daniel used to conduct his experiments in alchemy, away from prying eyes.

Then the voice again, but less demanding and, if not pleading, nearly so: "Please let me in. I'm looking for my brother. I know he would come to you."

As Benjamin moved out of sight, Daniel called out. "Jeremiah, is that you? Be patient. I am coming." Then Daniel looked carefully for any telltale signs of Benjamin. Satisfied, he opened the door.

"Master Fletcher, my father is dead!" Jeremiah wasted not a moment in idle greeting before announcing his dire news. His tone was flat, yet his eyes were rimmed with red. Daniel could see cuts on his face and bruises blooming, proof that Benjamin had delivered some blows, though had still gotten the worst of the fight.

Daniel also recognized Ethan's cloak wrapped around Jeremiah, which sent another shockwave of grief rolling through him. "Oh dear God, Jeremiah, this cannot be!"

The raw emotion and appearance of unrehearsed distress from Daniel momentarily stunned Jeremiah. "But Master Fletcher, you must know this already!" he insisted. "Benjamin must be here, and surely he's told you. There is no one else he would seek out but you! He knows you are his friend!"

Daniel felt the unspoken condemnation ... that he had not been the same friend to Jeremiah. He knew that the decisions he made now would impact Jeremiah and Benjamin for the rest of their lives. He could no longer help Ethan, but he might keep his sons from truly becoming Cain and Abel — if it were not too late already.

Certainly, he could protect Benjamin. That was within his power. But perhaps he could also protect Jeremiah, from the inner demons that were surely trying his soul.

He must keep them separated. And he must convince Jeremiah to trust him. Ironically, the only way to do so was to lie.

"No, you're very much mistaken," said Daniel, reaching out to comfort Jeremiah, who instinctively pulled away. As he did the cloak fell open, revealing Jeremiah's shirt smeared with blood. From the quantity, Daniel was sure it was Ethan's and grimaced at the sight. Still, he stepped closer to Jeremiah, to prove his concern.

"Your brother is not here. He must be distraught and looking for solace. Perhaps he has sought sanctuary in the natural places he loves. But come. Sit down. You must tell me what happened. I loved your father! How could he be dead?"

In his sorrow and hurt, Jeremiah wanted comfort too. Yet he had always known that Benjamin was Daniel's favorite. "I don't believe that Benjamin has not come to you. Surely he has told you *his* story. So very well, now I will tell you *mine*."

Jeremiah sat in the same chair that Benjamin had occupied not five minutes before. Hunched forward, Jeremiah spoke in halting words and phrases. "We fought. Father tried to stop the fight. He…," Jeremiah paused, his voice breaking with emotion. "He fell by the fire … on the stones … he was bleeding. We tried to help … Benjamin wrapped his head. But then…." Again Jeremiah's voice broke. Unable to continue, he hung his head, letting Daniel narrate the ending.

"He fell on the hearth? Hit his head? Is that it?" Daniel confirmed.

Jeremiah nodded in silent agreement. Then, in the next instant, he seemed to throw off his sadness and his eyes flashed with anger.

"They deceived me!" Jeremiah erupted, pounding one fist into the other. "Father and Benjamin — they lied to me! Father said he threw the stone away, threw it back into the sea! I thought he did it FOR ME! Because I could not work the stone. IT WOULD NOT SPEAK TO ME! BUT FATHER LIED! He saved the stone for Benjamin! It was always Benjamin he loved!"

Jeremiah had told much the same story as Benjamin, and Daniel felt the agonizing truth of it. But there was a new detail — that Ethan might have lied to Jeremiah for Benjamin's advantage.

There was no denying that Benjamin would be the easier son to love. Daniel had always preferred Benjamin. And here he was now, deliberately lying to Jeremiah to help Benjamin.

Had Jeremiah been deceived and treated unjustly by his father and brother? Could there be truth in his grievance?

And yet, in his admiration for his dead friend, Daniel struggled for another explanation. He did not want to believe that Ethan had chosen Benjamin in a way that had so wronged Jeremiah. Surely Benjamin was the victim of his brother's jealousy. Surely Jeremiah had misunderstood Ethan's intentions.

Too agitated to remain sitting, Jeremiah suddenly jumped up from the chair, losing his balance and falling against the table nearby. He grabbed the empty tankard that Benjamin had drained of ale and threw it against the hearth. The force dented the metal as it clanked and clattered onto the stones.

Those actions strengthened Daniel's argument that Jeremiah was mistaken, that his brooding personality had brought on this devastating tragedy. This brother was powerful and menacing in his anger. Had he not just demonstrated those very qualities?

As Daniel remained silent, Jeremiah felt the old man's distrust. "You don't believe me, Master Fletcher! And I don't believe you! I know Benjamin is here!" In a rush of movement, Jeremiah raced toward the door of the windowless room where Benjamin was hiding.

"STOP!" Daniel yelled with all the force he could muster. "DO NOT OPEN THE DOOR!" Then, softer, "I have important work within. That room is to stay quiet and dark. You must not let in the light."

Jeremiah paused mid-step, then obeyed. Despite his unchecked fury, Jeremiah recognized Daniel's authority, this man who had been his father's closest friend. He turned to look at Daniel, still certain that Benjamin was near. *Why wouldn't Master Fletcher admit it?*

As Jeremiah continued to scan the room, Daniel understood the danger of Benjamin's situation and why he had run. The dented cup was proof enough of what Jeremiah might do were he to find his brother. Daniel had seen it before in the village, caring for those on the wrong end of a jealous tirade. But this was more than a momentary outburst. Daniel feared that Jeremiah's jealousy was so deeply rooted, that his loathing for Benjamin could not be controlled.

Whatever the truth — or the deception — might be, Daniel was convinced that he must help Benjamin escape his brother's wrath. He must do what he could to safeguard Benjamin's life. He must do this for Ethan. If it meant more lies to Jeremiah, then he must tell them. When Benjamin was safe, then, if he could — if Jeremiah would let him — Daniel would try to help him too. For now, he must calm Jeremiah and get him to leave.

Daniel said no more, waiting for Jeremiah to abandon his search. When he again dropped into the chair, Daniel spoke in a soothing voice. "Jeremiah, let me clean your wounds and exchange your shirt for another. You do not want to wear the blood of your father."

"Leave me be, Master Fletcher."

"All right, Jeremiah," Daniel conceded. "But where is your father's body? We must give him a proper burial."

"I did not leave him where he fell, as my brother did!" Jeremiah said bitterly.

Then, once again, Daniel observed Jeremiah's mercurial nature as he slipped from fury to private grief. "I washed the blood from his face," Jeremiah continued, "and carried him to his bed. He lies there now."

"Jeremiah, you have treated your father well. Go home and swim in the sea to cleanse yourself. It will soon be time to return your father to the earth."

Though he hung his head, Daniel could see tears welling in Jeremiah's eyes. "But what of Benjamin?" His voice carried the depth of a brother's hurt and a lifetime of feeling forsaken. "He has a share in Father's death!"

Daniel listened with a sympathetic ear, yet he also recognized an avenue for Benjamin's escape. "Jeremiah, your brother may be long gone, on the road to somewhere, afraid to return. You are much stronger. No doubt he was no match for you."

Watching Jeremiah, trying to gauge his reaction, Daniel continued. "If he has run away, then he shall pay a heavy price, for he shall have no proper opportunity to bid your father farewell. He shall have nothing of your father's to remember him by…."

"Oh, but he will!" Jeremiah interrupted, his tone turning ominous. "Benjamin took the crystal stone and the diary. He has Father's greatest treasures!"

Another surprise for Daniel, who regretfully surmised that his understanding of what had transpired between Ethan, Jeremiah and Benjamin was far from complete. Daniel knew of Ethan's diary, of course. But Benjamin had not admitted to having it, and more importantly, to having the crystal stone.

Even so, Daniel was sure his course was right. He must protect Benjamin from his brother's madness, lest next time it could be fatal.

"Jeremiah, let us not think on those things now," Daniel began.

"Master Fletcher, if you help my brother, you will make an enemy of me."

Daniel had no doubt that Jeremiah fully meant what he said. There were strong emotional currents at work, all coursing through an ocean of subjective truths and half-truths. Amidst all the uncertainties, Daniel realized that his ability to help Jeremiah would be greatly compromised by helping Benjamin. But Daniel saw no other way.

"You have had a great shock. Go home now. We are not enemies, Jeremiah. Let me help you. I shall come with herbs to place around your father's body and we will mourn him together. We shall bury your father in the morning, with or without Benjamin."

Jeremiah gave the room a final sweep of his eyes and then nodded silently. Wrapping the cloak about him, he followed Daniel to the door, pausing again outside before heading back in the direction of the cottage.

Daniel watched with relief as Jeremiah departed. This child of Ethan, so different from his father, was overflowing with emotions that burned hot and dangerous like a volcano spewing lava.

It was also plain to see that he was deeply pained by his father's death. Daniel felt deep sympathy and pity for Jeremiah.

Even so, as he closed the door, Daniel immediately began plotting Benjamin's escape. But when this time was behind them, Daniel vowed, he would do more to make a friend of Jeremiah — to be a friend to him.

Chapter 13

Hunstanton

April 1691

The same day / The next morning

Daniel & Benjamin

Daniel waited some time after Jeremiah left to be sure it was safe and then signaled Benjamin to come out from the workroom. Daniel noticed the book clutched tightly in his hands as he emerged. Clearly, Benjamin had heard Jeremiah reveal the diary.

"May I see it?" Daniel asked.

Benjamin held out the diary, and as Daniel accepted it, he rubbed a hand wistfully over the cover. "I remember the day I gave this to Ethan, when he was even younger than you. I can still see the excitement on his face."

Daniel looked upon the inscription and thumbed through the pages. "No time now, but one day, if the fate allows, I would like to spend time reviewing your father's notes."

To Benjamin's relief, Daniel handed the book back.

"You must leave here," Daniel declared. "Jealousy blinds your brother and I fear more tragedy will befall you both. You must seek a new life away from Hunstanton — perhaps from England too."

Freedom! It was what Benjamin had wanted for so long. And now Master Fletcher, nearly as close to Benjamin as his own dear father, was telling him to seize it and go.

Yet, when Benjamin had imagined being free to use the stone at will, he saw no farther than the cottage he knew, the familiar hearth and loft.

"But if I leave Hunstanton, where would I go, Master Fletcher? And if I left England…?" Benjamin couldn't imagine that possibility.

"Did your father ever tell you that he and I were bound for America when we arrived here?" Daniel asked.

"Yes, you became ill. And when you recovered, you and father decided to stay." Benjamin paused, uncertain whether to bring up the stone again, but then continued, "That's when Father found the crystal."

"Ah, Benjamin, I would like to understand more about this crystal. But we haven't much time. I will arrange passage for you by ship, to sail to America."

Benjamin began to take in the immensity of what Master Fletcher was suggesting. "But that's so far!" Benjamin exclaimed. "Couldn't I stay in England somewhere?"

Daniel could recognize the conflicts within Benjamin — wanting freedom, yet safety and comfort too. "Benjamin," Daniel said gently, "there is a madness that drives Jeremiah to find you. I fear it burns too deep. A sea voyage would make it more difficult for him to follow you."

Intuitively Benjamin knew the wisdom of Master Fletcher's words. His brother had fought like he meant to kill him. And though unintentional, he and Jeremiah were the cause of their father's death. It was doubtful that any amount of time would heal the gaping wounds left in each of their hearts.

"But I haven't any guineas for a voyage," Benjamin stammered. "It must cost a great deal."

"I have a friend, a sea captain." Daniel retrieved the letter he recently received. "As fate would have it, he sails again in the weeks ahead. There is not much time, as you must make your way to Deal, in Kent, where his ship, *The Sutherland Rose,* docks now. I shall write a letter of introduction that you can carry to Alfredo. Yes… Captain Alberto Alfredo will help us," Daniel pronounced. "He will help you get to America."

"Who is he?" Benjamin asked cautiously.

"Alfredo has sailed to the heavens and back!" Daniel laughed, patting Benjamin on the shoulder for reassurance. "He is not only a sea captain but has mapped the stars and can read the subtleties of the natural world. He has sailed many times to America and knows many secrets of that new land."

"But will I understand him? He does not sound English."

"Alfredo carries the proud name of his ancestors in Napoli, but he is English through and through. He is an acquaintance of the great Newton, like your father." Daniel's eyes took on a faraway look — a momentary daydream of a different time.

"Enough of this. We must complete our plan and I must go to Jeremiah. He expects me with herbs for your father's shroud. We must not make him suspicious," Daniel advised.

"And," he continued, "I think it best that you not stay here, even with Hannah and the children away. Let us not tempt fate further, lest you be discovered somehow. I will give you some food. Find a place in the fields or woods to hide for the night. Then come to me very early in the morning, before the sun rises. When I return later, from your cottage, I will write the proper letter to Alfredo to arrange your passage. You can be on your way tomorrow, as your brother and I bury your father. Jeremiah will be in my sight and it will be safer for you."

"I cannot see my father buried?" Benjamin's voice was near to weeping.

"How, lad?" Daniel responded. "To hide in the shadows? The risk is too great. You must find your own way to say goodbye."

Still Benjamin lingered. "What will I do in America? How will I live?"

"Your father was teaching you the ways of healing — and perhaps the art of alchemy too?"

"Yes, Master Fletcher, he was — both."

"And it was my understanding from your father that you have much promise. You must apply those lessons. Your brother also said you have the crystal stone in your possession…."

Benjamin began to protest, determined to hold onto his story, but was silenced by Daniel's raised hand. "I know not the complete truth, but there is no more time for discussion. Let me give you some bread to hold off hunger and then we both must depart — you to a hiding place and me to Jeremiah. If your brother returns here and finds you, I fear there could be two burials in the morrow! On my love for your father, I will not let that happen!"

Benjamin took the bread with a nod of gratitude. Yet guilt and grief weighed him down. He felt comforted next to Daniel and loathe to be alone. "But I wish I could see my father one more time!" Benjamin wept.

Daniel's own eyes began to tear at the reminder that Benjamin, though on the verge of manhood, was yet a boy, and now an orphan about to brave the world.

"There are no boundaries to love. Keep the image of your father here," Daniel tapped his temple, "and with you here," signaling his heart. "He will help you find your way."

With his own heavy heart, Benjamin accepted Daniel's words. At the same time, Benjamin questioned how he could ever have been so unhappy with his father, so determined to be free, to have the stone to himself. Now he was free and the diamond crystal was his. And he felt more alone then he ever had in his life. He had gained his freedom but lost his father — a terrible bargain with yet unforeseen consequences in the darkness of a future night.

"Off with you to the woods and streams. Mother Nature will give you comfort," Daniel assured Benjamin with another embrace. "Come to me before sunrise. Rap once on the door. I will have everything ready for your leave-taking."

∽

If the dead can view those they leave behind, Ethan Hawkins would surely have departed this world in deep sorrow at the sight of his two sons, separated by anger and fear, each enduring a long, lonely night — Jeremiah beside his father's body, feeling its coldness seep into his own; Benjamin shivering on the ground, familiar with the night sounds but longing for the hour before dawn. All their lives were now rent asunder by a spinning wheel of actions and consequences.

The morning was still dark when Daniel heard the light rap on his door. Benjamin appeared pale. His torn and bloody clothes were now covered with dirt, leaves and pine needles from his hours of hiding.

"Did anyone see you?" Daniel asked.

"No, Master Fletcher. I was very careful," Benjamin replied.

"Good," said Daniel. "Then let's be quick. The sooner you are on your way, the better for all of us."

As Daniel disappeared into the windowless room, Benjamin felt a rush of emotion, thinking about his father and Master Fletcher, of their many moments of good cheer together. It made him realize how much he would miss Daniel's presence in his life.

Master Fletcher reappeared with a small knapsack and some clothing. "Here," he began, "I have prepared some things for you. There is food — bread and dried meat — and all the coin I could spare. Put these on." Daniel held out a clean shirt and pair of britches, worn but still serviceable. "It won't do for you to travel looking like that."

"But those are Jacob's!" Benjamin protested.

"So they are. You are close enough in size. They will fit you well enough, and Hannah will sew him others."

Daniel took his own cloak off the peg by the door. "And take this. You will need protection from the elements, especially aboard ship."

Though wary and frightened, the hours alone in the woods confirmed for Benjamin that there was no other option but to leave. He felt deeply grateful to Daniel. And in his gratitude, he had determined to be honest as well.

"Master Fletcher, you have shown me kindness all my life. I cannot leave now with deceit between us. What Jeremiah said is true. You know I have the diary. I have the crystal stone too. I started the trouble that led to Father's death."

His head bowed, Benjamin tapped the bulge inside his shirt where the diary and crystal were concealed. Then he raised his head and squared his shoulders, realizing that he was about to go off into the world and had to accept his shame like a man.

"I disobeyed Father," Benjamin continued. "He told me never to use the crystal without him. But I took it when Father and Jeremiah were off by the sea. Jeremiah caught me with the crystal. And then we fought. I've told you the rest. That was all true."

"And you took the crystal and diary? After your father had died?" Daniel asked quietly.

Benjamin paused, remembering that moment. "I did. I could not leave them behind!"

"Why didn't you tell me that you had the crystal when you came to me yesterday?" Daniel's voice was still calm, though inwardly Benjamin's revelations were having a deeply unsettling effect.

"I was afraid you would make me throw the crystal away … return it to the sea. I know it seems cursed, yet its wonders are so great, Master Fletcher! I feel certain I can use it for healing and knowledge in the way it was surely created."

A noise outside the cottage made both Benjamin and Daniel freeze. The noise came again … a scratching. Daniel shooed Benjamin into the special room and then carefully opened the cottage door. A minute later he called Benjamin back by the fire.

"Just a raccoon, looking for a last scrap before hiding for the day," Daniel explained, relief audible in his voice. "But we were lucky it was only a hungry raccoon. We must not tarry much longer."

Before Benjamin left, there was one last thing for Daniel to do. "Please show me the crystal. I must see it for myself."

Uncertain yet unable to refuse, Benjamin produced the stone. When he dropped it into Daniel's outstretched hand, the crystal immediately glowed with light. Benjamin watched and listened, recognizing that Daniel's ability to experience the crystal was perhaps as powerful as his own.

Daniel felt waves of light roll through him. He could feel Earth's life-force rise up into the soles of his feet and climb through his legs. He took slow and easy breaths as the wave entered his spine and flowed into his heart. Then he felt the top of his head open to the heavens. Light poured into his mind and streamed straight into his heart.

It all integrated in the most sublime way — from below, the life-force of Earth; from above, the heavenly light; and in his heart, his own life-force… And then the experience passed.

Daniel held out the crystal, still feeling its awesome power. "Benjamin, this stone is indeed a wonder," he explained. "I understand its obsessive hold and why your desire for it challenged the reason within you, as well as your duty to obey your father. But be mindful. That unchecked desire is part of its affect. It amplifies the state of your emotions — both good and bad — and it can enhance the turmoil that emotions stir."

In experiencing the crystal, Daniel had gained insight into its nature. Now he clasped Benjamin's shoulder, wanting to be sure the young man was listening. "The stone may have seemed dormant in Jeremiah's hands, yet I think it was anything but. It likely intensified your brother's state of mind, his jealousy and rage, when he realized he had been deceived."

As he spoke those last words, Daniel made no effort to hide his displeasure at the deception he had come to believe. Then, more carefully, he spoke again. "Perhaps it's best to leave the stone with me, Benjamin. If it falls into the wrong hands, great damage can be done."

Daniel gazed at Benjamin, watching for his reaction. As he remained silent, Daniel continued. "Let's weigh the circumstances further. We also have to consider that even though your father instructed you in the crystal's use, you are still very new to the world of alchemy."

Benjamin appeared to listen, yet Daniel's suggestion had stunned him, so that all his thoughts focused on keeping the crystal.

"It is true that I am not as experienced as you in healing and alchemy, Master Fletcher," Benjamin began. "But I have learned much about the stone through the fire of my experience. It is meant to be in my hands. It is my legacy. Father believed it to be true. It is why he kept the crystal instead of giving it back to the sea. It is bequeathed to me to unlock its secrets, whatever they may be. Search your feelings, Master Fletcher, and I am sure you will sense it too."

Daniel could not deny that truth. Clearly, Ethan had wanted Benjamin to have the stone. And Ethan had never revealed the crystal to him, Daniel recognized — though he wondered what would have happened if he had.

Daniel nodded in consent, watching Benjamin smile for the first time since his father's death. No doubt Benjamin had a gift with the stone and Ethan had seen it. But all the same, Daniel feared Benjamin's youth and this powerful tool, and was compelled to offer words of advice.

"I believe this crystal can extend your intent. But it may also reflect your inner state of mind. As a healer and alchemist, it can bring you great reward," Daniel affirmed. "It is surely a special crystal with properties I have never seen. It seems to have the power to enhance inner vision, showing the light of worlds beyond. I am equally certain that it has other attributes, which my limited time with it have not revealed."

Then Daniel finished with another word of caution. "Benjamin, I believe this is a legacy from your father that you are meant to have. But you must be on your guard. The stone has already spawned great harm. Your father is dead. You and your brother are about to be separated, likely forever. Stay pure of heart when you seek the power of the crystal. And let it not fall into the wrong hands or more tragedy could result."

Benjamin sat in silence, realizing the seriousness of Master Fletcher's admonition. "I'm sorry. I've disappointed you."

"Benjamin, my lad, just remember my warning. Honor your

father — honor me — by using the crystal well all your days. And remember your brother not with anger but understanding. He has struggled far more than any of us know."

Daniel was feeling his own regret over Jeremiah, but there would be time enough to correct that. As light began seeping through the cottage windows, the task at hand grew more urgent: Benjamin must be on his way.

"Let us not postpone your departure further," counseled Daniel. "The village day begins and it will not do for you to be seen and a report to reach Jeremiah. There will be no stopping the wagging tongues today, as word of your father's death spreads."

Benjamin quickly changed his clothing while Daniel packed the crystal and diary into the knapsack. He added a handful of seeds from the herbs and other plants that he used in his remedies, wrapping them carefully for Benjamin's long journey. It was a gift to a fellow alchemist, Daniel reasoned. Wherever Benjamin might land, alchemy was in his stars.

Daniel felt a melancholy descending as Benjamin prepared to leave. Seeing Ethan's diary brought on a sudden longing for his own youth — for the days he had spent with Isaac Newton and Ethan, when their path into the future was still full of possibilities. Now Ethan's journey was complete and Daniel's own felt far closer to the finish than ever before.

As Benjamin shouldered the knapsack, Daniel held out a rough map that he had drawn. "This will help you find your way to Deal. If you get lost or need direction, look first for a man of the cloth or a tavern keep. They can best be trusted. And stay off the roads until you are beyond King's Lynn," he added. "There is less danger of being seen by those who know you."

In Daniel's other hand was an envelope. "This letter to Captain Alfredo will secure your passage on *The Sutherland Rose* and his help when you reach America. Guard it well, Benjamin. And follow Alfredo's instructions and listen to him carefully. I know him to be an honorable man and he will guide you well."

Benjamin accepted the letter and map, feeling the excitement of his journey beginning to stir. Yet it was also with deep sadness that he asked, "Will I ever see you again, Master Fletcher?"

"If you return to England someday," Daniel stated honestly. "My time for a voyage to America is past. But you shall live in my heart always, Benjamin."

"Thank you," Benjamin whispered, as he returned Daniel's embrace. "I shall never forget you."

"Nor I, you," Daniel replied. "I have asked Alfredo to write me of your arrival in America, but send me your own message through him, if you can." Then, with a final hug, "Now Godspeed, Benjamin, Godspeed."

Tears clouded Daniel's eyes as he watched Benjamin disappear into the gray morning. "May you find *your* destiny in the New World," he whispered.

Now Daniel's thoughts turned to Ethan and that he would bury him this day. "Oh Ethan, my dearest friend," he spoke aloud. "If only you had confided in me about the crystal stone, perhaps this whole desperate heartbreak could have been avoided."

Then, pausing, Daniel considered the power of fate and concluded, "Or perhaps not."

There was one more urgent task. Daniel took out quill and parchment and began to write a letter to his confidante and fellow seeker, Isaac Newton. He must inform Newton immediately of the crystal, the ultimate alchemist's prize — a treasure beyond measure — one that had eluded them from the beginning of their search, when he and Newton first embarked on their journey into alchemy.

What Daniel had not told Benjamin about the crystal that young Ethan Hawkins found was Daniel's suspicion that it had risen from deep within the earth and was the alchemist's crystal of legend, imbued with creative life-force. It was truly an extraordinary object. Enclosed within the crystal were the highest sonic octaves used to seed the heavens — a celestial symphony by which the word of the creator formed all things on the earth and in all universes.

In his letter to Newton, Daniel also must confess that he had let the crystal go, for its destiny rode alongside Ethan's son. Indeed, as Benjamin himself understood, the task was his, both his burden and legacy.

Daniel feared that Newton would never forgive him for letting such a treasure out of his possession. But then again, Newton had not held the crystal and seen the truth, as Daniel had — that its future resided with someone and somewhere else.

Chapter 14

Aboard *The Sutherland Rose* to America
JUNE 1691

Benjamin Hawkins & Captain Alberto Alfredo

"Do you know the stars, lad?" Captain Alberto Alfredo asked as he approached Benjamin Hawkins, standing on the quarterdeck and observing the night sky. Alfredo's olive skin announced his Mediterranean heritage. His once-black hair was streaked with white and gray, though his body, stocky and muscular, was still as steady on a rolling deck as when he first went to sea twenty-five years before.

"Not like this, sir," Benjamin replied, giving a slight bow to the commander. "I have seen the stars from the shore of the North Sea back home, but they seem different here, out over the ocean. There are so many more of them and they're brighter. I've never seen such a sight." Benjamin spoke quietly, carefully watching the dark eyes of Captain Alfredo.

How quickly life had changed for Benjamin. Gone were his aimless walks in the woods and fields, listening to the familiar sounds of nature. Instead, now he was thrown into a different world, a whirlwind in which his very survival depended on his ability to quickly decide if someone was foe or friend. Every moment held the possibility of turning volatile. No longer protected by his father, Benjamin needed to sharpen his wits and use every ounce of strength to make it through the day. It was a necessity that he rapidly gain his sea legs, for now he was living among men hardened by the harsh life of sailing the high seas. Working with the crystal was a dangerous proposition and there was little time for sorrow and regret to creep into one's thoughts.

But most important, Benjamin deemed it crucial that he learn how to read Captain Alfredo. It didn't take long to discover that the captain signaled his mood with his eyes. He was fearsome when angered, and while Benjamin had not felt his wrath directly, he had seen the captain's eyes snap with fire.

Tonight, though, Captain Alfredo's eyes caught the twinkle of starlight. Benjamin was relieved and delighted, for the captain had promised a conversation between them. But a ship was a demanding mistress, and so Benjamin had spent no time alone with the captain since the day he was ushered to Alberto's quarters, with the letter from Daniel Fletcher in hand.

"Such beauty above, so vast and unknowing, yet exhilarating," Alberto observed, lifting his face to the sky and prompting Benjamin to do the same. "I trust your work is done and Master Hardy has released you?"

"Oh yes, Captain, sir," Benjamin was quick to respond. He had found the cook, Master Hardy, for whom he was now cabin boy, to be a man of ill humor and no patience. The previous cook's assistant, a boy of twelve called Jelly, had fallen overboard and drowned on the last voyage to England. Listening to Master Hardy growl, Benjamin wondered if poor Jelly had jumped to free himself of the miserable man.

Indeed, it took a strong constitution to work beside the cook. He bore a sickly odor, though his foul temper was even harder to stomach. It was understood that Benjamin's time in the galley was limited only to the crossing to New York and that blessing, Benjamin had come to suspect, was encouraging Master Hardy to rain double terror on him. Still, Benjamin kept his sights set on America and tried as best he could to follow the cook's orders and stay out of his way.

"Thank you, Captain. I hope I can repay your kindness." Despite Master Hardy, Benjamin meant what he said. The money from Daniel

Fletcher had not covered the entire cost of the passage. With the ship in need of a galley hand, Alfredo had offered Benjamin the chance to work off the rest.

"Just do as Master Hardy says and obey without question. The ship's cook is commander of his galley. We are fortunate that Hardy is better than most," Alfredo spoke, with grim satisfaction.

Then he turned his attention again to the stars overhead. Alberto Alfredo never felt more humbled than when looking up at the glory of the night sky or more sure of divine presence in the world. "The sky is lit with the delight of God's heavenly bodies," he said aloud. "So too each of us lights our way through our time on this earth. Your father's light shown brightly, did it not?"

"It did, Captain. It did for me…," Benjamin paused, "and for my brother too. Did you know my father, sir?"

"Not well, lad. I recall him as a young man, though not as old as you, when I was visiting Fletcher and Isaac Newton in Woolsthorpe, in the plague year. But any man who holds the high opinion of Daniel Fletcher must be worthy."

"Master Fletcher was a good friend to my father," Benjamin agreed, "and to me." A sudden sadness took hold of Benjamin as he thought of his father and the life he had known in Hunstanton. "My father taught me a great … a great deal …," Benjamin sputtered. He caught himself from speaking further and looked away, embarrassed at the emotion in his voice.

Alberto Alfredo was a complex man of many contrasts. Despite the hardships and hard characters that were part of a life on the sea, Alfredo's heart remained open and full of compassion. He had grown wise from his vast experience, not only as ship's captain but as one who navigated the waterways of a bold and daring life. He had traveled to distant lands and observed people and places seldom seen by ordinary men. His life had given Alfredo an uncommon capacity to understand others, including this young man that he had taken on as a favor.

"The memory of loved ones lingers throughout our time," Alfredo said, clasping Benjamin on the shoulder. "We are the better and the greater for having had them in our lives."

Benjamin nodded silently. From his first moments onboard he had promised himself to keep his emotions in check, fearing them a sign of weakness. But the captain's words had come as a surprise and touched the simmering feelings just below the surface. Now he was determined not to speak again until the stirring of unshed tears could pass.

Alfredo read Benjamin's posture and let him be. He saw no failing in the young man's feelings for his father. Above all, Alfredo honored relationships of family and friends. It was that knowledge of Alfredo that had made Daniel Fletcher certain the captain would help him with his plan to protect Benjamin. Many years before, Daniel had saved Alfredo's life.

Alberto Alfredo and Daniel Fletcher had first met on the doorstep of Fletcher's cottage in Woolsthorpe. Alfredo leaned heavily on the arm of Isaac Newton, both covered in Alfredo's blood. Alfredo and Newton had been classmates at Cambridge. When Newton came home to escape the plague, Alfredo soon followed, to enjoy his friend's hospitality.

Alfredo had none of Newton's brilliance but instead, and in abundance, Alfredo had an eye for adventure and a zest for life to match. He also had a courageous aura about him that made him alluring to both men and women. Newton, despite his taciturn nature, found pleasure in Alfredo's company.

On the night that Daniel would make his acquaintance, Alfredo and Newton were in a tavern. Alfredo was flirting with the serving girl, who was also attending two oafs at the next table. Wanting the girl's attention all to themselves, without warning, one lunged at Newton with his fists, as the other caught Alfredo with his knife. At first it seemed the damage was only a stunned blow for Newton and a nick for Alberto — until blood gushed from Alfredo's wound. As the louts ran, Alfredo wanted to make chase. But seeing Alfredo's face turning pale, Newton carried him directly to Daniel Fletcher.

Later, when Alfredo was recovered, Daniel explained how close to death he had come. Had the thrust been a bit higher and stronger, the long knife would have torn into Alfredo's heart. Still, it took all of Daniel's skill to save him, and it was months before he could travel again.

When Alfredo bade goodbye, he proclaimed his lifelong indebtedness to Daniel. Over the years Alberto had made good on that promise several times over — and now again with Benjamin.

"Captain Alfredo? Sir?" Benjamin's voice, once again steady, interrupted Alfredo's silent reflection. "May I ask you, sir? Master Fletcher said you have sailed to America many times. How did you become a captain on the ocean?"

"Ah, Benjamin. It was for many reasons. I have the sea in my blood, as my ancestors sailed the great waters of the Mediterranean, although I'd not thought of a sailor's life when I met Isaac Newton at Cambridge. But when I returned from Woolsthorpe, where I met your Master Fletcher, the plague still raged and the university was closed. England was at war with the Dutch, and having learned to read the sky from Newton, I signed on with Sir Christopher Myngs. They called him a pirate, but he was a brave man."

Benjamin could read in Alfredo's eyes a distinct pride in recounting this history. He nodded, wanting the captain to go on.

"In time I earned my own ship," Alfredo explained. "Not in the Crown's own navy but with the likes of those that were bringing folks to the 'New World.' That's what they call it. Did you know, Benjamin, that New York was once New Amsterdam? But we chased the Dutch out, we did! Now it's New York … and will be forever!" Alfredo laughed, still showing the bravado that over the years had made him a favorite of some and a target of fury for others.

"And America … New York…?" Benjamin began.

"That's enough for one night, no more questions," Alfredo declared. "But I leave you with this. See that star?" He pointed to the sky. "That is no star, but the planet Jupiter. Seeing it on one's maiden voyage is an auspicious sign indeed. It is a messenger from the heavens, lad. Be watchful; keep your wits about you. It's a difficult crossing, but if you mind yourself, what you learn will serve you well in America. Now, I've duties to attend to … and you'd best to bed."

"Yes, Captain," Benjamin answered obediently. "Good night, sir."

Alfredo nodded in response as he turned and walked away, to confer with the officer on watch.

Confident he was out of sight of Captain Alfredo, Benjamin moved behind one of the great masts, the sail fluttering above. He looked out at the horizon. The waves shimmered in the moonlight and the stars danced on the surface of the water. It seemed impossible that only weeks before he had met Captain Alfredo and not long ago had been living with Father and Jeremiah in the only place he had ever known. Now he was alone on this vast ocean, on his way to what would surely be a new world.

Facing the night, Benjamin softly whispered, "Oh Father, if only I had known what trouble I would put us all through…. I would never have …. What have I done? Please forgive me!" Benjamin swallowed hard, choking back his tears. A boy turning man, never knows the moment when it comes.

A few moments passed, then Benjamin looked down at the water cresting against the side of the ship. He placed his hand in his pocket, firmly griping the crystal inside his palm, and welcomed the familiar vibration. After its silence following his father's death, the stone had slowly begun to speak to him again.

Gazing again out over the water, he spoke again, "Father, where have you gone? How I wish I could hear your voice — to look upon your face. How I wish you were here with me now!"

The breeze picked up and caught the sail above. The salty air filled Benjamin's nostrils and he lifted his face toward the sky.

"Where have you gone, Father?" he asked again. "Where have you gone?"

A gust of wind caressed his cheek and filled his ears, and he waited for an answer…and waited…and waited….

Chapter 15

Hunstanton
July 1691

Jeremiah Hawkins

The quiet of the cottage drove Jeremiah nearly to madness. His days had always been filled with the sounds of life with his father and brother — waking in the morning to his father's sniffles and snores; hearing his brother stirring next to him in the loft or, when Benjamin awoke before him, listening to him preparing the breakfast porridge below. His father always signaled the start of the day with a rap on the table just as breakfast ended. "All right boys, there's work to be done." Then later, after the day's work, when night had fallen and supper finished, his softer voice filled the cottage. "It was a fine day, boys, and there's a full day for us tomorrow, so to bed with you now."

Although the easy relationship between Benjamin and his father had irritated Jeremiah like an itch under the skin that can't be scratched, their conversation was the background hum that had confirmed to Jeremiah that he was not alone in the world.

But not now.

In the months since his father died, Jeremiah's world was one of churning turmoil. He could not make sense of it. The ground beneath him had opened up and swallowed whole the life he used to know. He dwelled in a netherworld of dark emotions that led from anger to sadness to self-loathing, and back again.

Even the cottage, the home he'd known all his life, seemed a foreign place. The loft where the fight with Benjamin began was filled with shadows of that terrible day. And the hearth where his father fell, and the bed where his father lie in death until carried to his grave, were even more haunting to Jeremiah.

One day, in desperation, he took an ax to the bed and chopped it to bits so small they looked like kindling. Then he built a fire in the hearth and fed it the pieces until it roared and the heat made the sweat pour from him. He threw everything that had belonged to Benjamin, his clothing and the few other possessions that were his, into the blazing fire too. Jeremiah watched until it flamed out, leaving nothing but a smoldering pile of ash. And when the ash was cool enough to touch, he scooped up great handfuls, filled a wooden bucket and sent them into the North Sea, to drift away and be seen no more.

Later, disgusted by his own stink and filth, Jeremiah cleansed himself in the freezing seawater. He rubbed the brine on his skin until it glowed red. He felt the sting of salt in every cut and scrape on his body and it seemed right. No pain was more than he deserved.

Though the law, backed up by the consensus of the village, had deemed the death of Ethan Hawkins an accident, Jeremiah knew better. His own dark heart was to blame. It was a feeling that had sunk deep into his skin and never left him, not even for a moment.

In the first days after his father died, Jeremiah had born the condolences of those who loved Ethan, as well as those more curious than sad. Over and over, he was called on to relate how his father died and he hid no detail except one — the crystal stone and the deception that had triggered his fury. In his telling, he fought Benjamin out of petty jealousy and speculated that Benjamin had run away out of fear. Jeremiah even announced his willingness to accept punishment for his father's death. It was a remarkable turn of events for one who had always felt unfairly treated.

The local folk who knew the history of Ethan's sons and their opposite personalities found Jeremiah's story riveting and had no doubts about its validity. Only Daniel Fletcher knew the whole truth and vowed to himself never to tell another soul what really happened. Instead, he championed Jeremiah, admitting he saw Benjamin before he ran and that both brothers gave the same explanation of Ethan's death. Daniel testified to Jeremiah's grief and made the case that this Hawkins son had assumed a kind of tarnished nobility in shouldering the blame for a family tragedy. Daniel's voice carried weight and it became the common view that Jeremiah had been punished enough by his own violent temperament.

The benevolence of the village in sparing Jeremiah became a kind of sentence, nonetheless. Aware of the prying eyes and loose tongues that followed him, Jeremiah burrowed into the cottage, even as the days grew longer and warmer, and suffocated in its silence.

Only Daniel Fletcher attempted to see Jeremiah. Daniel had helped Benjamin escape for the good of the two brothers. Now he wanted to help Jeremiah escape from what appeared to be the twin torments of grief and guilt.

But in the aftermath of Ethan's death, Jeremiah was convinced — and rightly so — that Master Fletcher had done more for Benjamin than he would admit. And with Daniel's steadfast refusal to acknowledge what he knew of Benjamin's whereabouts, Jeremiah wanted nothing to do with Daniel. Each time he came to visit, it ended with the same refrain.

"Master Fletcher, leave me be!" Jeremiah's voice, hoarse and bitter, responded to Daniel's knock on the cottage door.

"Jeremiah, let me in. You know I grieve for your father, as you do. Let us grieve together."

"Go away. Do your grieving at my father's grave."

"Jeremiah, I am not your enemy. Can we not be friends?"

"Tell me where my brother is and we shall be friends."

Thus was the conversation — if it could be called as such — between them until one bright July day, when Jeremiah responded to Daniel's knock by slowly opening the door.

"Come in, Master Fletcher." Jeremiah's voice had a hollow sound.

Daniel braced himself as he entered, for he knew not what to expect. He saw that Ethan's bed was gone. But other than that, the cottage looked much the same. Ethan's various jars and baskets of herbs were all in place, as though waiting for him to use.

Jeremiah's person was clean. Although his hair was now below his shoulders, it was pulled into a tail at the back of his neck and tied with a strip of cloth.

"Thank you for receiving me," Daniel began.

Jeremiah motioned for him to sit at the table and Daniel complied. Without a word, Jeremiah set out some dried meat and poured each a cup of warm ale.

"Jeremiah, you and I are not enemies."

Daniel studied Jeremiah, wishing he could read his expression more clearly, for the natural shadows in the cottage revealed Jeremiah only in half-light.

Jeremiah had one thing on his mind. "Master Fletcher, where has my brother gone? Have you come here today to tell me?"

"Why, Jeremiah? What is your purpose in seeking Benjamin? You must know I will not help you find him if you intend to do him harm."

The jealousy that was never far below the surface rose within Jeremiah. *"Just like Father!"* he replied, giving emphasis to each word. "You come here pretending to care, wanting to help. When really it's about protecting Benjamin! That was Father's way and now it's yours. Well, I want my father's crystal, and his diary too. It is my right as much as Benjamin's. If I have to dispatch Benjamin to the heavens — or to hell — to get them, so be it."

Inwardly, Daniel felt the frustration at his inability to reach Jeremiah.

Outwardly, he displayed only earnestness. "Jeremiah, let us walk down to the sea together. Feel the salt air and talk about all the good you felt for your father. I beg of you, Jeremiah, if not for yourself, then for your father's memory, let go of what has transpired between you and Benjamin. Free yourself from your jealousy and hurt. Leave that all behind you."

Leave behind … Daniel's words faded as Jeremiah heard the echo of his father's voice, telling him to understand his brother's gift with the stone.

In his mind Jeremiah could see his brother creeping off with the crystal and the diary while their father was dead on the floor, blood dried on his face, his hair matted with blood. Yes, Benjamin had left Jeremiah to bury their father, to face the village and answer the questions about how Ethan came to die.

"Forget? And how would I do that?" Jeremiah asked, eyes popping and voice bristling with anger. "Do you know what you ask? Have you some potion that will blot out Father's death from my mind? Wipe away the knowledge that you helped Benjamin get away and won't tell me where?"

He paused, as though waiting for Daniel to speak. Then Jeremiah continued, his voice more ominous. "I have lived my life in the shadow of my brother — the 'good' son to my father. How am I, as you say, to 'leave all that behind'? I would need to be like a fool who is knocked in the head and wakes up with no memory of *who I am* and *what my life had been!*"

Jeremiah punctuated his last words with a bitterness that was not lost on Daniel. Though Jeremiah exhibited the dangerous quality of a cornered animal that has bared its teeth, Daniel was determined to hold his ground. "Do you think I only cared for Benjamin? Don't you realize I care for you too? I hear the loathing in your voice — the loathing for yourself."

"Stop!" Jeremiah raised a hand, longing to push away a conversation he wanted no more of, now or ever.

"I know you blame yourself as much — maybe more — than you blame Benjamin for your father's death," Daniel added. "I know you believe in your heart…."

"Master Fletcher!" Jeremiah gripped a knife from the table. "I warn you. Leave me be!"

"I have no fear of you," Daniel said with a deliberate calmness. "I will take my leave, though not because you raise your knife to me. I can see you are a greater threat to yourself."

Jeremiah appeared to grasp the knife tighter as Daniel continued. "Let go of your anger, Jeremiah. Your brother is gone. Somewhere he is on his way to a new life. You can do the same."

Daniel got up to leave and made his way to the door, feeling Jeremiah's eyes on him. Daniel had spoken with a good deal of self-assurance, but he was far less confident than he appeared. When he reached the door, he paused. "Good-bye, Jeremiah." There was no reply.

Then, as Daniel touched the latch, he felt Jeremiah's breath on his neck. In a frenzy of movement, he was spun around, with Jeremiah's one hand instantly around his throat, the other hand holding the knife against Daniel's belly.

"Sorry *Master* Fletcher, I will wait no longer," Jeremiah hissed. "I must know where Benjamin is!"

Daniel could see a burning glare in Jeremiah's eyes. But he was determined not to shrink from speaking a truth he hoped would bring Jeremiah back to reason. "Is this not the same rage that you felt for your brother and father? THINK JEREMIAH of how your father died. Do you wish to repeat the deed?"

Then with relief, Daniel could feel his words had struck home. He looked into Jeremiah's distant eyes — what would he do next?

Jeremiah loosened his grip around Daniel's throat as his gaze fell away toward the hearth.

Daniel had momentarily stayed the seething emotions that had guided Jeremiah's hand, and now he took a chance. "Let me help you

through this." He spoke with compassion, placing his hand around
Jeremiah's wrist that held the knife.

Jeremiah shook off Daniel's touch, dropping the knife on the floor
and backing away from Daniel. "Leave me now, Fletcher. I can no
longer bear the sight of you. Leave me be!"

"Please, Jeremiah…," Daniel started to speak.

"Go!" Jeremiah interrupted, his voice still menacing.

Jeremiah's last words drifted in the air, a sense of defeat filling the
cottage. Daniel reached his hand out to him, but Jeremiah turned, his
back facing into the hot, silent abyss — the prison cottage that was
now his home.

With nothing more to do or say, Daniel opened the door and left.
Outside he felt revived by the fresh air and a cool breeze coming from
the North Sea. "I have done all I can," he whispered aloud.

Yet looking back at the closed door, he felt his own utter powerlessness. With all his skill as a master alchemist and healer, he was helpless
against the foe that had a hold on Jeremiah. No herb or potion in his
collection of remedies could soothe Jeremiah's spirit or cure the heartache that had cursed the Hawkins family.

And at the moment, all that heartache — of the young orphaned
Ethan whom Daniel had first met, of Elizabeth's agony at her lost babies,
of her untimely death and now of Ethan's own — all seemed pooled
within the twin son who from birth had appeared a troubled soul.

Chapter 16

Aboard *The Sutherland Rose*
AUGUST 1691

Benjamin & Captain Alfredo

The perils of crossing the wide ocean to America were many. Each voyage was filled with unexpected challenges. The specter of ongoing hardships haunted even those with the most hopeful dispositions. And though rapidly changing circumstances were an accepted probability for anyone onboard the great ships, life often hung by strained fingertips gripping tightly to the edge of certainty. The endless trials and unknowns stressed even the most physically resilient. Strange intrigues often roamed the decks, above and below.

Still, these were the circumstances in which Captain Alfredo thrived. His crossings were many and he had gained a reputation as a superb seafarer, guiding cargo and passengers to safe harbor even under the most dire conditions. He was considered a fair and just captain, although he tolerated no challenge to his authority.

It was Alfredo's way to always maintain a clear head and keen eye during each voyage. He took pride in his acute powers of observation, in reading the winds and the sea, as well as watching over his crew. He was ever alert to warning signs of scheming, odd alliances and misplaced loyalties that plagued the most experienced captains.

But sickness can undo anyone, and such was the case for Captain Alfredo. Nearly two months out from England and he lie in his quarters, weak, his body in misery and burning up with a fever that tossed his mind into periods of delirium. The illness had quickly swept through his vessel, with most of the crew and practically every passenger sick as well.

Benjamin too had the sickness come upon him. As the hour had turned from midnight to morning, he felt the first wave of nausea. His experiences with his father, traveling from Hunstanton to other villages to heal victims of spreading disease, taught him how to quickly create remedies from whatever was available.

On his walk to Deal to meet Captain Alfredo's ship, Benjamin had collected plants that he knew were medicinal. Now he went to his store of dried specimens for meadowsweet to attack fever, and bayberry root bark and catnip for the debilitating biliousness in his stomach. From the galley Benjamin gathered cinnamon and dried rhubarb and ground all into a powder. Then he made it into a solution, adding apple cider vinegar in a large mug of rainwater and vigorously mixed it together.

Lastly, as his father had taught him, he placed his crystal in the solution. He positioned his hands around the mug and closed his eyes. He envisioned diamond shapes forming in the solution — perfect geometric configurations that he perceived as a sign that his remedy had the necessary balance and pure potency to cure the mysterious illness sweeping through *The Sutherland Rose.*

Yet even in that moment, Benjamin had a startling insight. He wondered if the images he saw were an observation of the remedy coalescing, a true gift in and of itself, or was there something more extraordinary happening? Was he, with the aid of his father's crystal, manifesting the treatment with the power of his own life-force — with the power of his intent? Was this some new gift through the crystal that was now coming to his attention?

As much as he wished to explore the possibility, Benjamin had not time. He must drink the solution to protect from the illness getting worse.

And once he had, and the symptoms disappeared and he felt restored, Benjamin was eager to find Captain Alfredo. He had to convince the captain that his remedy could help others recover too and stem the tide of the illness gripping the ship.

Unaware that the captain was also ill, Benjamin first searched on deck for Alfredo and then wove his way below deck to the captain's quarters. It was bold of Benjamin to seek out Alfredo, but it was providence that propelled his legs forward.

"Where do you think you're off to, laddie?" Benjamin's steps were halted by a sailor twice his size.

"I must see the captain right away."

"Captain's taken sick. I have strict instructions no one's to see him."

"But I can...."

"Move along, boy! You have no business here. Be gone with you before I tell Master Hardy you have time on your hands. I'm sure he'll be pleased to fill it for you."

The very thought of Master Hardy made Benjamin wince. He quickly retreated without saying another word.

But as Benjamin walked away, he remembered and could feel his father's ardent resolve — that to heal the sick was a mission to embrace fully without hesitation. He became more determined than ever to see Captain Alfredo. His mind began to churn. *A good dose of valerian.* Benjamin had that among his plants too. *That would put this hulk out where he stands.*

The rest of the day Benjamin tried to go about his chores. But an eerie sense of doom wafted through the ship. No one had died from the illness, but some seemed terrifyingly close. And there was something else disturbing. The men that were not affected by the sickness were picking through the belongings of those that were, taking anything of value. Benjamin dared not interfere. But though this was his first voyage, he was sure something sinister was adrift.

It was then that Benjamin began to take note of who among the crew were ill. First Mate Johnson, Master Hardy, and eight others who were making their first voyage with Alfredo, were not affected. Officers that had sailed with Alfredo many times — and most loyal to him — were wasting in their bunks. It seemed unlikely it was mere coincidence.

That night Benjamin zigzagged through the maze of cabins and storage compartments below deck to Captain Alfredo's quarters. As before, the same mate stood guard.

"Master Hardy sends this ale for you." Benjamin watched as the guard thirstily drank the solution of ale and valerian root that he had prepared. He felt calmer than he thought he'd be.

"How is Captain Alfredo?" Benjamin asked.

"You've done as Master Hardy sent you to do. Now move along," the guard answered with a shove.

Undeterred, Benjamin found a place to wait for the potion to take affect. He must rescue Captain Alfredo from the captivity in which he was being held. In that moment, Benjamin surprisingly thought about Jeremiah and how steadfast and headstrong he was. It occurred to him that perhaps some of that quality had rubbed off on him too.

He hid under the steps leading to the quarterdeck, and when he thought sufficient time had passed for the valerian to work, he ventured back to the captain's door. The guard was asleep across the threshold, snoring for air. Watching the mate for any movement, Benjamin slipped by and enter Captain Alfredo's cabin.

There, Alfredo tossed uncomfortably in his bed, wrestling with the evil spell that illness had cast upon his body.

"Captain Alfredo, wake up!" Benjamin tugged at his arm. Alfredo moaned and muttered incoherently.

"Here, Captain, you must drink this!" He lifted Alfredo's head and helped him take in the solution of herbs that had cured Benjamin of the sickness. At first Alfredo spit it up. But with Benjamin's firm insistence, he began to drink the rest. "That's it, Captain. You must finish it."

Benjamin anxiously waited for the plants to do their work.

For the rest of the night, Benjamin stood watch over Captain Alfredo. Now and then he would peek outside the door, to ensure the valerian still worked on the sleeping mate. Eventually, near first light, Benjamin dozed off. But as morning came streaming through the cabin's bow window, his face was awash with a new day.

He immediately looked over at the captain, whose eyes were fluttering from the sunlight. Alfredo lifted his head and, spotting Benjamin, asked in surprise, "Hawkins, what are you doing here? Why aren't you in the galley? What's happened?"

"Do you not remember? You've been ill, Captain Alfredo — most of the crew and the passengers too. Only Master Hardy, First Mate Johnson and a few others are well."

Alfredo instantly grasped the possibility before him. Mutiny by gun and knife might be more common, but poison could work as well. "Why are you not sick, Hawkins?" he asked suspiciously.

"I have a cure. A remedy I learned from my father and Daniel Fletcher. It brought me back to health and has helped you too. I gave it to you last night. It is why I am here."

"Suspected foul play, did you? Good instincts," Alfredo nodded. "Thank you, lad. No doubt this sickness is no accident. Now tell me all you've seen. What else is amiss aboard my ship? I need to know."

Benjamin described what he had witnessed. "And they are rifling through the belongings of those that are sick," he added.

"I've seen plots before. Mutiny is always a threat as our crossing gets closer to shore. We carry more then just passengers, Benjamin. We haul much valuable cargo seldom seen in America. Our holds are filled with silver coin and a whole host of spices — pepper, cloves, cinnamon and nutmeg. If I know anything about the sea, I know that Johnson and Hardy surely have a ship waiting to remove my cargo and run my ship to ground, whilst the lot of us lie dying from the cook's devil deed. It's piracy of the worst kind."

Alfredo paused, his mind devising a plan, then spoke again. "Let us have a plot of our own, Master Hawkins. Go and make me another draught of your potion. I must fully regain my strength. And be careful that Hardy does not see you. Then you must make as much of your remedy as you can carry and bring it here to me," Alfredo directed. "Together, we must give it to the crew. I need as many men as we can muster to retake the ship before Johnson and Hardy have time to act. Then you will help the passengers with your remedy, as many as you can."

"There's more, sir," Benjamin added. "I can put the men who follow Master Hardy to sleep." Benjamin quietly opened the door to reveal the guard. He was still dozing, though his stirring about warned that he would soon wake. Benjamin quickly explained the valerian-tainted ale he had given the mate.

"Ah, Benjamin Hawkins, you are a wonder!" Alfredo declared. "It was my lucky day to bring you aboard this voyage! But be off now! There is much to do and it all depends on you."

Benjamin was exhilarated to be so important to Captain Alfredo's success. But there was something else. He felt his father and Daniel's faith in him and his abilities. They saw in him great possibilities as an alchemist and healer. Life was filled with circumstances, some foreseen and others unexpected. To know that his actions could effect the world in such a beneficial way filled him with purpose. And he knew too that the crystal, which had caused such upheaval, could be put to good use when directed with the proper intent.

With his strength fully regained, Alfredo resumed control and rallied his crew. Too groggy from the valerian to fight, Hardy, Johnson and their disloyal followers were easily locked in the ship's brig. Alfredo's fierce, commanding presence made clear who was once again in charge.

As it turned out, Hardy had intentionally poisoned the ship with tainted meat he had brought aboard for that purpose. Hardy's scheme, with the first mate's backing, was well on its way to succeeding, if not for Benjamin.

Captain Alfredo praised Benjamin's courageous actions. He had saved Alfredo's life and others onboard as well. And he had prevented the ship's takeover.

"We will arrive on shore tomorrow, lad. Many of us would surely be dead were it not for your skill and quick actions. You started this voyage indebted to me by my allegiance to Daniel Fletcher. Now it is I who am eternally grateful to you and yours."

Though Benjamin welcomed Alfredo's attention and commendations, the events aboard *The Sutherland Rose* had a greater meaning for him. That he might have atoned in some measure for the deeds that led to his father's death was Benjamin's greatest wish.

"And now that we are about to make landfall, there is another matter at hand," Alfredo asserted. "Though I believe in your capacity to heal, you have no means to begin a practice and you must make your way in this often savage land. As thanks for what you have done, I have an offer that could suit the both of us."

Captain Alfredo's face had a glow about it as he continued. "Up the great Hudson River, I was granted five hundred acres of land in payment for services to the Crown. It has been my hope, when my sailing days are over, to settle there. I believe that five years hence may be that time. I need someone to start preparing now for my eventual arrival."

Alfredo went on and explained. "Benjamin, if you will work the land for me, planting crops and grains to sell, you can also cultivate the plants that make your remedies. When five years are finished, there will be twenty-five acres that are yours. You'll need to build a cabin for yourself, as there is none. It will be hard work, but you will be a free man, indebted to no one, and not a servant, like most who come here without means. Accept my offer and you'll soon be able to establish a healing practice. There is much need for your cures. You will see that."

Benjamin was stunned by the offer. For most of the crossing Master

Hardy had worked him to the point of exhaustion. He'd had little time to contemplate his fate in the New World. And when he did, it always ended in uncertainty. Since his father's death he had lived on the edge, glad enough to be surviving each day and waiting for the next. He had assumed that was the way it would be.

"I know not what to say, Captain. I'm humbled by your offer."

"Then it is settled. I will write you a letter of intent to present to the authorities should you be questioned, to ensure the authenticity of our endeavor. Rest assured, lad, life has just taken a good turn."

The two shook hands, sealing the bargain between them and a bond of friendship forged in the fire of trial and triumph.

His path set now, Benjamin counted the days until he would catch his first glimpse of New York. Even as his excitement grew, Captain Alfredo's offer gave rise to new worrying questions that weighed on Benjamin's mind. Could he manage the land and fulfill Alfredo's expectations? What if he failed? He was still alone in the world, far from the home he had always known.

Each night, as he strained to see a shadow of land, Benjamin looked up to the sky, be it filled with stars or clouds, hoping to feel at ease with himself and the new world he was about to enter. Always there was the same question that had stayed with him since the beginning of his voyage. *Where have you gone, Father?* And now he asked, *please give me a sign that you are watching over me.*

Night after night, the warm wind rustled his hair but offered no comfort — until the last night of the voyage, when a sailor high up in the crow's nest called out, "Land, ho!"

It was then that a gentle breeze filled Benjamin's ears with a sweet sound that reached deep within and stirred his heart: *Benjamin, I am here. I will always be here.*

The crystal in his pocket glowed. Benjamin could feel its light and visions of his father appeared in his mind's eye. Then a whisper again: *Benjamin, I will be with you always.*

Like many around him, Benjamin knelt on the deck in thanks. He welcomed the new world beyond, certain he was not alone.

A son's prayer answered; a father's message delivered.

Chapter 17

In America, the Hudson Valley of New York
OCTOBER 1691

Benjamin Hawkins

From the highest point on Alfredo's land, Benjamin gazed upon the autumn landscape marking the magnificent valley in which he now dwelled. His first months in America left him nearly as much in awe at the transformation of his own life as he did at the breathtaking changes all around him. The natural world was ablaze in extraordinary color, just as he felt his own future, his destiny, was emerging more brightly, more fiercely, here in the New World.

So much had happened to Benjamin since leaving his home in England. Since his dramatic role in foiling the plot against Captain Alfredo, he was filled with an emerging new sense of himself and had come to realize he was no longer just a young man attuned to the rhythms of nature, but now was firmly planted in the dominion of men.

His triumph aboard *The Sutherland Rose* gave him faith that he could fare well in the shifting sands of daily life in a largely unsettled world. And for good reason, considering the skill and initiative he had shown in a perilous situation. In turn, those qualities awarded him with good fortune indeed. Unlike most who came to America at that time, he had a letter of introduction and legal tender to start him on his way. When the ship at last docked in New York, the growing port city and gateway to the English colonies, Benjamin was eager for the adventure ahead.

Alfredo had further shepherded his immediate arrival, arranging for Benjamin to travel up the great North River — some called it the Hudson — with two fur trappers. Then, eventually, he would have to make his way on foot to Captain Alfredo's land.

The trip would be long and demanding, and Benjamin would have to keep his wits about him at all times. As he prepared to bid Alfredo goodbye, Benjamin grasped that he was alone in a way he had never been before. He had not his father or Daniel Fletcher or Captain Alfredo at his elbow to guide him. He would have to be just as cautious as he was on the ship, choosing his associates wisely and not revealing too much about himself. At all costs, he had to keep the crystal stone a secret. He knew from his experience with Jeremiah, and even with Master Fletcher, that the lure of the stone and the jealousy it could provoke were all too real.

During the journey on the great river, Benjamin observed the trappers closely and concluded they were honest men who said little and inquired even less. They had a reverence for nature that was new to Benjamin. While he felt oneness with the natural world, they displayed knowledge of a more practical kind. From them Benjamin quickly learned how to exist on what food and water the river offered. He saw how they read the river's currents and the wind and sky, to know when to seek quieter waters or shelter on the shore. And as they moved up the Hudson, Benjamin discovered how to listen to the language of the river. Its vibrancy filled his soul with the majesty of this new land.

In time, Benjamin left the trappers to continue, now completely on his own. With each passing day the trail grew more challenging. He had never known so many long hours hearing only his own voice. It gave rise to mixed emotions: He felt himself alive like never before, but he felt lonely at times too.

What a joyous day when Benjamin reached Alfredo's land grant, where he was met by wild grassy meadows and deep, dense woods of oak, elm and chestnut. High rock outcrops gave way to streams and ponds teeming with fish and beaver. His eyes were filled with panoramic beauty — a rich bounty of good and plenty.

Benjamin always knew there would be difficult circumstances ahead — of that he could be assured. Now that he had finally made it to Alfredo's land, he needed a plan. And so it was that Benjamin met his closest neighbor, William Clark, a journey that took him a full half day. Like the seaman he was, Alfredo had explained that Clark lived "under the North Star, lad — travel due north to find him!" And that was the path Benjamin followed.

William Clark, his wife and their young sons were a friendly lot. Alyce Clark fed Benjamin a hearty plate of rabbit stew when he arrived and the family insisted he join them for their evening meal and bunk in their barn that night.

The next morning, as Benjamin looked around the Clark farm, he saw a modest place but one with a feel of great promise. Could he do the same?

"It takes a lot of sweat to clear this land," Clark declared, firmly letting Benjamin know he was in for a challenge.

But Benjamin had come so far and knew there was no turning back now. If he went back to New York, what would he do? Be a servant, a laborer? Follow someone else's orders day and night? No. Opportunity was right in front of him. All he needed was the will to persevere.

"After five years of clearing and farming, Captain Alfredo promises me my own land," Benjamin confirmed.

"That's fair," Clark stated.

"I don't know much about farming," Benjamin admitted. "All I know is plant remedies, which I learned from my father."

Alyce, who'd been listening, nodded and smiled. "That's a wonderful thing to know. And to have a neighbor who knows cures!"

After spending the last few days with Benjamin, Clark made a judgment of the young man before him — he was confident and earnest and not the sort to just run off. So he made him an offer. "Look,

Benjamin, life in the valley is hard. Having a good neighbor is worth it's weight in gold. Let's resolve to help each other. You help me here on my farm and I'll teach you what I know while we work. Then I'll help you plant some winter wheat. And we'll build you a decent cabin. You help me, I'll help you, it serves us both."

Then Clark gestured toward the sweep of land before them, glowing red under the setting sun. "Benjamin, this here is the future. Don't let it go."

Clark was good to his word and Benjamin immediately set about the task at hand. He cut down trees, providing himself with a rough shelter. With the money from Captain Alfredo, he bought a horse, a wagon and an old wooden plow. Clark schooled Benjamin in planting winter wheat, and together they managed to clear and sow enough land to produce a decent crop — with luck — in the spring. By the fall there was even a small new barn to house the tools and horse.

Yet the prospect of farming the land offered a host of challenges, not least of which was the hard physical work of clearing the trees and stumps to create more land for planting. It would take years to make a thriving farm, and on plenty of days it took every ounce of fortitude that Benjamin had to continue.

But he had a larger vision that kept him moving forward — and he had the crystal. With each new moon Benjamin planted the seeds that Daniel Fletcher had provided, the alchemist's cornucopia of herbs that would serve as the basis for Benjamin's remedies. He also gathered native plants, using the diamond crystal and his intuitive power to read their life-force and determine their potencies. He ground them into powders and then cataloged their potential uses in his father's diary — his diary now — waiting for the moment when they would be useful.

Benjamin marveled at his vast experiences over the previous few months. Including his newfound ability for compounding remedies through intuitive cues that came in lightening flash and engraved themselves on his mind. They had grown stronger and more frequent from the first moment they appeared on Alfredo's ship when he fashioned the healing formula that saved Alfredo, the crew and passengers.

And more than ever, his connection to a crystal that spoke to him in a language beyond words made him realize how unlike other men he was. Somehow, through an act of grace, he was given attributes and abilities that were highly uncommon. He could cross the threshold beyond normal sight and could dwell in an unearthly place of diamond crystal light and healing. Yet he also understood there was a shadow world of hurt and fear that lurked close by, one he had already experienced. He had to learn how to navigate the thoughts and urges that could veer him off course.

It was not only his intuition that was expanding. As he worked the land, Benjamin noticed that he was developing a more physical nature — one that reminded him of Jeremiah. His arms and legs were bigger and stronger, and his lungs must have grown as well, for he seemed to take in more air when he breathed and his heart pumped harder to keep his body running.

As he took stock of himself and his situation, he felt ready and able to take on what would come. And though it was the least of his worries now, it crossed his mind that should he ever meet Jeremiah again, he'd offer a far bigger fight.

Chapter 18

Jeremiah
1691

In the months since Daniel Fletcher had made his last visit, Jeremiah had become more and more isolated. No new vistas spread before him. His only visitor the vast sea pounding against the cottage walls as the seasons moved toward the storms of winter.

Now truly alone, night after night Jeremiah sat at the table where he and Benjamin had taken meals with their father all their lives. As the hours drained away, he felt increasingly powerless to stop the emotional arrows of guilt and remorse, of revenge and self loathing from ripping into his heart. Over and over he declared himself responsible for his father's death and over and over again he imposed the same sentence — exile from all that was good in the world.

Every day he'd ventured out of the cottage to hunt for food, and always, no matter how far he might wander, he ended up by the uprooted oak tree where Benjamin had found the stone. He would stare at it, his anger building, and cursed the ground for bringing his father's crystal back into their lives.

This filled his days and nights until one evening after returning to the cottage, a new feeling took hold. Piling dried pieces of cut wood in the hearth, he made a fire and watched it catch, all the while asking himself over and over again, *Why did this happen...Why did this happen TO ME?*

Feeling utterly forsaken, Jeremiah sat in his father's chair as the flames grew hot and high. He watched the flickers and sparks, staring deeper and deeper into the silhouettes cast at the back of the hearth. There as if etched on the wall an image of his father appeared.

Ethan was sitting by the fire gazing at the glow in a melancholy stupor, as he sometimes did. Though his father never said, Jeremiah wondered now, in his own deep loneliness, if his father had been thinking of his mother all those times, trying to make sense of losing his wife, his dear Elizabeth, the mother that Jeremiah had no memory.

And then just as quickly the imaged disappeared. Jeremiah rubbed his eyes, and again looked for the image of his father in the back of the hearth, willing it to come back. But it was gone.

The fire still aglow, shot hues of red upon the walls of the cottage. Jeremiah closed his eyes seeking relief. Taking a deep breath, his mind unexpectedly filled with the vision of wild roses, so lush and full.

And then there was a sudden scent of roses thick and heavy, spreading across the room. Jeremiah opened his eyes now trying to find the source. It seemed impossible since he hadn't brought any flowers into the cottage — their scent and color too joyful for his aching heart.

Nevertheless, with each breath the bouquet became stronger and stronger. And Jeremiah felt compelled to close his eyes again. Immediately more images of roses filled his mind as spinning vines sprouted everywhere, growing down his arms and his legs and enveloping his heart. Then tiny red roses emerged from the vines and their petals flew wide open. *What magic is this?* he wondered.

Red roses flowered everywhere. And then pink roses and white roses too. Jeremiah let himself feel their softness. It was the first moment in months that he allowed himself to feel anything other than hardness… and then a new vision appeared.

Descending from above, a woman in long flowing robes materialized in his mind's eye. She had a sash of roses across her waist and a garland of roses upon the crown of her head. She stood strong and true. She proudly held out a gilded winged staff that shimmered with streams of golden light like a beacon. Steadfast, Jeremiah waited expectantly.

Then, arms wide, as though embracing him, she looked down at Jeremiah lovingly and called out for all the world to hear, "BLESSINGS TO YOU."

Jeremiah was astonished at the message and his heart leapt with an explosion of joy. *What could it mean?*

Then an unwanted thought, of his brother. And the obsession that fueled Jeremiah now swiftly intruded. Was it not always Benjamin who was blessed, always the favored. Did this apparition come to the cottage expecting to find Benjamin, only to taunt Jeremiah in his torment?

He bristled at the notion of thinking of his brother. He wanted only to find him and for the sword of justice to strike him down for his misdeeds, and that he suffers as much as Jeremiah. And with that thought darkness converged around his heart and in his mind once again.

The robed woman and her gilded staff disappeared and his imagination was now filled with roses and vines, though this time, one by one the rose petals fell away and only thorns began to grow. And each thorn stabbed at his skin and threatened to sink deeper and deeper. And to save himself, his heart closed tighter, and tighter still, until the last bit of light was covered with shadow.

Chapter 19

The Hudson Valley
June 1692

Benjamin Hawkins

Benjamin had made it through the long winter. Aside from William Clark and his family, he rarely saw others, except for an occasional trapper or other frontiersman traveling through. When he had time before the heavy snows arrived and after, on warmer winter days, he had roamed Alfredo's five hundred acres, familiarizing himself with every hill and dale. There, in the forests and meadows, he found a world of wild enchantment and contentment too. With creatures large and small, flowers and fruits of every kind, America was bountiful beyond what he had known in England.

When his mind grew quiet, he could feel the vibration and see the color that surrounded everything. Benjamin lived in two worlds. One was rooted in the rich ground of the earth, and the other hovered beyond the sight of ordinary men, emblazing all things with light and life. And for the moment, Benjamin felt that he had found his place in this solitary and, for him, idyllic world.

By spring he could harvest his winter wheat and plant more acres of fresh tilled soil in more newly cleared land. And as the seeds of his medicinal plants sprouted and bloomed, he could add to his expanding collection of remedies.

On a warm June morning, with the sun brightening a clear blue sky, Benjamin was drying marigolds, preparing them as a remedy for pain relief, when William Clark, along with Alyce and their young sons, rode up in a wagon brimming with belongings.

"Good tidings, neighbor," Benjamin welcomed them.

"And greetings to you," called out William Clark, rolling his wagon to a halt.

"Where are you off to with such a heavy load?" Benjamin asked, sensing trouble.

"Haven't you heard, Hawkins?"

"You're the first folks I've seen for weeks."

Alyce poked at her husband. "I told you we had to be sure he knew!"

"What is it?" Benjamin repeated, certain now that something was wrong.

"The French are massing — sending an expedition down the river, trying to drive us out of the valley again," Clark explained. "And they have the natives all stirred up — the Mohicans and Delaware. The last time they came through it was hell to pay. You don't want to be here when any of them arrive, French or Indians!"

Benjamin stood quietly, taking in this disturbing news.

"Time's a wasting, Benjamin. Gather some things, get your horse and ride with us to the fort," Alyce urged.

Yet Benjamin wondered how he could leave. He was resolved to settle Alfredo's land and that meant safeguarding it too.

It was as though Clark could read his mind. "Benjamin, come away with us now. It'll serve no purpose to stay. You cannot stop raiders alone, and you'll be no good to anyone dead," Clark reasoned. "Besides, in a few weeks the French will have spent their foolishness. They cannot sustain their presence here in the valley. More and more of us Englishmen arrive every day."

Reluctantly, Benjamin could see the wisdom in his neighbor's logic. He gathered a few belongings and rode off with the Clarks. Looking back at the neatly plowed field, the cabin and barn, he prayed they would all remain, untouched, when he returned.

∞

Their destination was a British fort some forty miles north, in the upper reaches of the Hudson Valley. Their travel was laborious and nerve-wracking, but thankfully uneventful. When they arrived they soon realized that they were far from the only ones seeking refuge. The fort was buzzing with people anxiously moving about.

"Where should we settle ourselves?" William Clark asked the soldier at the gate.

The guard looked them over with a quick eye and determined they were indeed farmers getting out of harm's way, and not French spies. "Over there," he pointed. "Lieutenant Richardson … he's in charge of the settlers."

As they rode toward the lieutenant, Benjamin took in all the activity. He had been alone for so long, the sights and sounds of so many people were at once welcome and overwhelming.

"Lieutenant Alan Richardson, at your service." Richardson spoke formally, tipping his hat briefly toward Alyce Clark. "Any news of the French expedition? Any sightings?"

"All was quiet where we passed through," William Clark quickly responded.

Richardson nodded, and Clark extended his hand as he introduced their small party. "I am William Clark, my wife, Alyce, our boys Henry and Isaiah, and this is Benjamin Hawkins, our neighbor."

"You may expect your stay here to be brief. We intend to push the French back before they arrive," Richardson declared. "Hitch up in front of that building yonder and put your mark in the registry inside. Miss Catherine Steward runs the trading post and will see to it your presence is recorded. Then find whatever place you can."

"Thank you, Lieutenant, much appreciated," Clark nodded.

Several steps behind William, Alyce and their boys, Benjamin was the last to enter the trading post that was now doubling as a welcome station for farmers and trappers seeking safety from the French. At first Benjamin didn't notice the young woman who was helping this one and that one, bustling about the room. But as he stepped up to write his name in the fort's registry, he looked straight into the eyes of Catherine Steward, who held out the quill pen, asking him to sign. He could feel his legs go weak.

Catherine couldn't help but notice her affect on the young farmer. But as the daughter of a British colonel, she was too well bred to show it.

"That's right, sir, fill your name in. We must have a full accounting," she said.

"I'm Benjamin Hawkins," he announced, though he made no movement to write his name.

"Fine, Mr. Hawkins. Just fill in your name or make your mark."

Her soft voice brought Benjamin back from his stupor. He realized he'd been staring at the young woman and his face blushed shades of red and pink.

"Here, Mr. Hawkins." Catherine pointed to the spot where Benjamin should write.

"Thank you," Benjamin mumbled as he shyly signed and then stepped away. "I'm Benjamin Hawkins," he repeated, unable to think of anything else to say.

"You have a fine script, Mr. Hawkins. I am Catherine Steward. Good day to you." With a curtsy and a demure smile, she moved on to the next task to find and complete.

Benjamin seemed unable to move, his feet firmly planted on the rough boards below. Belatedly, he made a slight bow in the direction of the departing Catherine Steward.

"Let's go, lad. We need to get settled," Clark chuckled, clearly amused at Benjamin's reaction to the pretty Miss Steward.

Before they could exit, the lieutenant filled the doorway. Alan Richardson was a strapping man, commanding in every sense of the word,

bold and courageous in a land that required such attributes. His movements were true to the nature of a man that knew what he wanted and
how to acquire it.

"Miss Steward, how goes it here?" Richardson made a deep bow as
he walked up to the young woman. "So many new arrivals. How many
men have we within the fort?" he asked.

Catherine's curtsy to Richardson was deeper than the one she gave
Benjamin, and she smiled, clearly pleased to see the officer. "Some fifty,
Lieutenant," she replied, "plus the women and children."

"Ah, Miss Steward." Richardson took her hand delicately. "You've
been a flurry of activity for hours. Let someone else tend the registry.
The colonel would not want you to outdo yourself."

"Thank you for your concern," Catherine replied, allowing her hand
to linger in the lieutenant's before properly withdrawing it. "But like
my father, I am happy to serve."

Then, aware of his own place in the fort's command and the need
to attend to his duties, Richardson bowed again to Catherine, who
curtsied in turn, as he left.

Before the Clarks practically pushed him outside, Benjamin watched
the two carefully and could see that the lovely Miss Steward appeared
very interested in the lieutenant. He felt an emotion welling within
him that was disturbing: jealousy.

Benjamin and the Clarks were unhitching their horses as Lieutenant
Richardson stepped up to speak with them. "Where are you from?"
he asked.

"Forty miles south of here, in the prettiest country you ever did
see," answered Clark proudly.

"Let's hope everything settles down, and before too long, so that
you'll be back home again." With that, Lieutenant Richardson gave
the party a sharp nod. He was about to move on when he noticed
Benjamin's attention was distracted elsewhere.

Catherine Steward had emerged from the trading post and was walking toward a courtyard. Benjamin took in her every movement in a show of interest that did not go unnoticed.

A familiar feeling washed over Benjamin. It rose up through his body and raced straight for his heart, which began to thump faster. Benjamin wanted Catherine Steward, just as he'd wanted the crystal.

As he gazed at the lieutenant, it was as if he felt his brother's presence, the obstacle to overcome. It began to grip him as before.

Yet Benjamin was no longer the obsessive boy determined to have the stone and freedom. He had learned hard lessons from his own fateful actions. Now eighteen, he had grown into manhood from his experiences, and his higher mind steadied his more earthly passions. He reassured himself that providence would lead the way. If he and Catherine Steward were to be together, it would come about only through hearts of mutual connection and yearning.

What Benjamin didn't know was that Lieutenant Alan Richardson intended to marry Catherine Steward. In fact, once this French threat was passed, he planned to ask her immediately, certain her father would approve.

Though thoroughly confident of himself, Richardson had been fully aware of the eyes of Benjamin Hawkins on "his" Catherine. And though he wasn't completely sure, he thought she seemed unduly interested in this stranger.

Richardson would brook no competition. The lieutenant's thoughts turned dark. *I must watch this stranger. His leaving cannot happen quickly enough. Perhaps his departure might even be hastened. Yes, in these troubled times, I think that can be arranged.*

Chapter 20

At the Fort, Upper Hudson Valley
JUNE 1692
Day One, evening

Benjamin & Emma Wells

That night Benjamin and the Clark family made their encampment together, with Alyce insisting that Benjamin join them in the supper she'd prepared. Afterward, as Alyce put the two young Clark boys to bed, William and Benjamin joined other men in discussing the French threat and the likelihood that the fort might be attacked. As oaths and concerns, as well as promises of bravado, were exchanged, Clark introduced the exploits of Benjamin Hawkins.

"This lad stopped a mutiny!" Clark declared. After which the assembly listened raptly to Benjamin's tale of the nefarious incident aboard Captain Alfredo's ship, and how he had made his remedy, without mention of the stone.

"By God, this young man can take care of himself!" Clark crowed. "Good to have him living near me. Now if only he could give his sleeping potion to the French and we could all go home!"

Shortly thereafter, with the uncertainties of the day to come, the men disbursed and Clark announced his intention to turn in. Benjamin was far too restless and decided instead to walk about the fort. Overnight it had become the home of nearby settlers and frontiersmen, along with the English regiment.

Campfires blazed on the ground, while stars dotted the darkened sky like diamonds across the night, anchored by the light of a full moon. As he strolled about, nodding to the many others who were too on edge for sleep, wondering where the French were, Benjamin's mind was filled with pictures of the day's events, and especially of meeting Catherine Steward.

"Young mister, give us a moment, if you please." Benjamin's pining was suddenly interrupted by a woman's voice.

"Are you speaking to me?" Benjamin asked hesitantly. He looked in the direction of the voice, which seemed to be coming from a campfire.

"Yes, over here." Now Benjamin could see the outline of a woman silhouetted against the canvas of a covered wagon.

"That's a good lad, give us a hand. Be a fine fellow and get me two chairs from my wagon and bring them to me here by the firelight. And that barrel too — roll that over."

Benjamin did as the woman asked.

"That's right, lad, we'll set up here." She took the first chair from him. "My name is Emma Wells." Benjamin tipped his hat.

Emma Wells was a magnificent looking woman in her thirties, with a dark complexion and deep green eyes.

"And what is your name, good fellow?"

"Benjamin Hawkins."

"Be the fine man that you are, Benjamin Hawkins, and come sit awhile and keep a lonely woman company."

"I really should be…," Benjamin stuttered, searching for an excuse to continue his walk and rekindle his thoughts of Catherine.

"Now, now, a cup of ale will calm the roaming spirit that has taken control of your feet."

Benjamin laughed at Emma's astute observation. "Aye," he agreed.

She retrieved two mugs, opened the barrel tap and poured out an ale for each of them.

"Thank you," Benjamin said as he took a mug from Emma. He waited for her to take the first sip.

"Have you been in America long?" she asked, returning to her seat opposite him.

"Since summer last. Though I haven't noticed the time go by. I've been working the land since I set foot here. What about you?"

"Near ten years. I had a husband once. But he died 'bout three years ago."

"I'm sorry."

"No matter, he left me this wagon. I've been moving around ever since."

"It must be hard being a woman alone out here, traveling and all."

"I make out all right. Earn a good living while I'm at it."

"What is it you do?"

"You're drinking it — my own brew. The fort's full of settlers. My wagon's full of ale." Emma smiled, and the two clinked mugs. "Here's to drinking the French away!" Emma proclaimed.

After a few more sips in silence, Emma spoke again. "Where do you hail from Master Hawkins?"

"Hunstanton, in England. By the North Sea."

"Did family come with you? A mother, father, brother — a wife, perhaps?"

"No... all gone ... my father, mother...." Benjamin thought about Jeremiah and how it was between them now. "No, no family. No wife yet."

"Hmmm, I see — all alone in this new land. Lots of opportunity," Emma said.

Benjamin barely noted Emma's words. He was looking into the fire, memories of his father and brother beginning to take hold. He shook himself, trying to cast off the painful images of the past.

Benjamin's deep thoughts and troubled expression were more than apparent to a keen observer like Emma Wells. From a purse dangling around her waist, she took out a deck of cards and began to shuffle them. "Like to know your future?" Emma asked.

Her movements caught Benjamin's attention, and his thoughts returned from the fire's glow and his dreams of Catherine Steward. He suddenly could feel the crystal in his pocket begin to warm.

"Well, yes, sure, why not." he answered, "but do be kind."

"These are cards of divination. *Carte da trionfi,* cards of triumph." She spoke with a hint of intrigue, suggesting there were secrets soon to be revealed.

A day ago Benjamin might have had no interest in Emma's cards. But a day ago he had not met Catherine Steward.

"Let us see what the cards have to say about you." As she vigorously shuffled, Benjamin watched her hands skillfully move the cards to and fro, weaving them together and then apart.

"Say nothing, Mr. Hawkins," Emma instructed. "Rather, think about what you would like to know about your future."

Benjamin closed his eyes and a hundred images appeared.

Then Emma softly spoke into the night. "I ask the cards to tell me of this man. He sits before me young and full of life. What will become of him?"

Benjamin could feel the crystal growing warmer still, and Emma sensed something was very different about this young man.

Images of the sun and stars entered Benjamin's mind. He saw swords and chariots, and a tower by a turbulent sea. Then what appeared to be an angel was blowing a trumpet and there was a great wheel, with a woman who was blindfolded at its hub.

"Let us see what we will see." Emma's voice, in a low whisper, announced a beginning. "Open your eyes."

Benjamin did so, and before him were cards spread out on the barrel top, arranged in a pattern. To his amazement, some of the very images that had danced in his head appeared on the cards facing him now.

"Slowly the world turns," Emma spoke in low soft tones. "May what we see in the cards help this young lad journey through this world, and beyond."

Benjamin was mesmerized by her voice. It was as if she had undergone a sudden transformation, becoming a different person than the one who had first greeted him.

Emma began examining the cards. "My dear Mr. Hawkins, each card holds unique significance. The sequence is important too. Here is the first card. Look at is closely. What do you see?"

Benjamin studied the card and then spoke. "It's a young man walking close to a cliff. The sun is shining and he has a staff thrown over his shoulder, with his belongings attached."

Emma raised her eyebrows, acknowledging the discerning observation of the young man before her.

"He is an adventurer off to see the world," Emma began. "The cliff is the unknown. But see his face, how he smiles? And his pose is open. He is full of energy."

Benjamin instantly thought about himself and his journey across the sea. That he had stepped into the unknown, uncertain of his fate. Yet he had landed safely from his voyage with his prospects brighter than when he started.

"Yes, Benjamin, you are an adventurer, a seeker," Emma confirmed, and then continued. "See now the second card. A man in a chariot struggles to control two horses pulling in opposite directions. They represent conflicting impulses within you, Benjamin. Good and evil, courage and cowardice, love and hate…*shadow and light*. You have experienced each of these recently, have you not?"

Benjamin nodded as his thoughts flashed back to his father and brother, and to Alfredo and the plot aboard ship. He placed his hand in his pocket and wrapped his fingers around the diamond crystal.

"As you continue through your journey, Benjamin, there will be struggles. But if you learn to steer the middle path, my young friend, you have what it takes to win the day."

Benjamin did not respond, yet he sensed the truth of her words.

"The third card symbolizes your arrival at your current situation. A man runs away with seven swords. Seven is the number of completion, so this event has occurred. You have become separated from your home and family, those you love. You are running away from a secret. But see how the man smiles? You are happy with your escape. Yes, Mr. Hawkins, you are indeed an interesting young man."

"I'm just another settler seeking refuge from the French, Madam Wells," Benjamin answered, not wanting to reveal himself.

"No, Mr. Hawkins there is much more to you than meets the eye."

Emma gave Benjamin a piercing look. Not with suspicion, not in accusation, more in admiration. Then she continued. "Let's look at the next card."

Benjamin followed her finger, hovering over the spread of cards, to the fourth in the row. "Ah, the great wheel. Your story is coming into focus. Something of great importance has happened to you recently, something very unexpected. It has swept you up and moved you."

Benjamin's first thought was Catherine Steward — unexpected, indeed.

"Look at your life, Benjamin," Emma continued. "See the events as threads woven together to bring you to this point. Know that a great opportunity to take responsibility for your life and your fate is at hand. It may seem that life has tossed you about, but you have the power to determine your destiny. Look not to outside forces; look within to power your days. You are a remarkable young man, in touch with a multitude of inner resources that can assist in manifesting a reality beyond the convention of our time. And this is your moment. You have arrived at a great turning point. Choose your path wisely."

Now Benjamin took a deep breath. Could he really decide the course of his life, control the very outcome? Was it possible to live a life not subject to the whims of others or the prevailing winds of the world?

Emma motioned toward the next cards. "Here, these can serve as an instructive guide. The first picture is a young, dark-haired man. He is a magician, dressed in white and a scarlet cloak. With wand in hand, he points heavenward as he stands beneath an arch of red and white roses. There is a flash in your eyes, my young Hawkins. I saw it the moment you sat down. You have a great alchemy within you. Look into the eyes of the magician. Can you feel his power flowing through your veins?"

Benjamin felt for the reassurance of the crystal stone in his pocket as he looked at the magician's eyes. Emma watched closely as Benjamin appeared to slip into a trance. There was a light about him. She had seen this light only once, around her mother, a great wisdom teacher of the village in Europe where Emma grew up.

Benjamin closed his eyes and his mind was ablaze with a vision. The eyes of the magician loomed before him. He looked deep into those eyes and saw an inner light that grew stronger and stronger, an undeniable stream that flowed through the magician. As though a bolt of lightening had illuminated his mind, Benjamin understood: *The eyes were not the magician's but his own.*

Yet as he looked still deeper, it all became dark, and like an eclipsed sun, flames of fire ringed the darkness. Benjamin wanted to look away, afraid he was in some evil place. Then, in the next moment, out from the darkness came streams of light that again filled his mind until it was as bright as the sun. There was light in the darkness. The darkness was light. Facets of colored light sparkled everywhere. It was as sublime a place as he had ever been. And there he recognized his own internal source, and it enveloped him with peace and knowing.

"Come back, Mr. Hawkins," Emma called, and Benjamin awoke with a start. "You left us for a time, yes?" Emma's eyes were searching his.

Benjamin briefly felt woozy, but his head and vision quickly cleared. Yet he would not admit what he had experienced. "No ... no, you're mistaken .... I'm just a might sleepy from your ale."

"I think not," Emma corrected. "There is a deep well within you. It is a powerful gift that offers many rich rewards. Remember, my friend, look toward the middle path. Use your gifts wisely."

Benjamin had difficulty focusing again. Part of him was ready to leave Emma Wells. There were shades of discomfort in her words. She could see through him. Nothing he might say — or deny — would fool her. Yet he also felt the need to stay — to learn if the gift he had known since the day he found the crystal might have a higher purpose than he had ever imagined. Yes, he wanted to know more.

Silence passed between them, each feeling the moment.

Now Emma looked at the next card. "Well, well, I wondered if this card would appear. Is there a young woman in your life?" Emma asked.

"No," Benjamin quickly answered, even as the image of Catherine Steward immediately entered his mind.

"In this card a man is standing next to a woman, above them the personification of an angel. Here we have the card of choice that involves great significance. The road of life diverges, and the decisions made at this moment will resound down throughout time."

Emma closed her eyes and took a deep breath, and then immediately opened her eyes. "Indeed," she confirmed, "one of unique consequence. Be wise, my handsome friend, when it comes to affairs of the heart. Your choice will echo through the rest of your life."

Benjamin listened intently as she issued her warning about a future decision and he wondered who Emma Wells might really be. What had she seen in her mind's eye that he had not imagined in his own meditations? What powers had she?

"Your cards do intrigue me, Madam Wells," admitted Benjamin. "Please tell me more of what you see."

"The cards are but possibilities, lad," Emma laughed slyly. "The choices are yours. Remember always that you are the captain of your destiny. But let us see what we can glean from the remaining cards. There are but three."

Emma described the next image. "A man stands, shooting eight arrows into the air at once."

"Eight arrows at once? Shot from a single bow? What could that mean?" Benjamin was more curious than ever.

"It is time for you to move boldly forward," Emma explained. "There is much that propels you into the future. Inspiration is yours. Be not afraid. Dive into the unknown and let your fertile imagination chart your course. The images that come to you are worlds you are meant to explore and inhabit."

With all his responsibilities on Alfredo's land, and with the opportunity to have his own land eventually, Benjamin had given little thought to other possibilities for his life in America. Now he read the arrows as symbolizing other paths that could be open to him.

"Here we have the next-to-last card. She is a priestess who sits between columns that hold up a veil, beyond which are the secrets of life yet to be revealed. Be prepared to be reborn. The springs of the deepest wells of intuitive wisdom flow from your soul's light. Scale the heights of inner light and journey to the sun and stars, and there find beauty and truth."

Emma's eyes sparkled in the firelight. Watching her, Benjamin wondered if she were seeing his inner world, the lights he saw when he grasped the diamond crystal.

"And now, my dear Mr. Benjamin Hawkins, the last card. An older man, an accomplished man, sits comfortably after a lifetime of work. He is assured that his creations are valued and his gifts to the world are riches for future generations to enjoy. So too are the possibilities for your lifetime. The choices are yours."

With that, Emma Wells closed her eyes a final time and put her hands over the cards. She began to sway as she made sweeping motions in the form of figure eights.

Benjamin did not move. When Emma first offered to read the *carte da trionfi,* he thought it a bit of fun. But now he was captivated.

Finally Emma's hands stopped. She took one last deep breath, opened her eyes and stared directly into Benjamin's own. "Young Hawkins, you have been given many unusual gifts. Open your heart and mind to beyond the boundaries of ordinary thought, and the miraculous will be yours."

For a few uncomfortable moments, Benjamin was speechless. But soon his tongue regained its agility. "Madam Wells, thank you. I will heed the wisdom of your cards."

"That is well, Master Hawkins. You are a master of choice, so chose your destiny wisely."

"I will," Benjamin smiled.

Emma smiled in return, nodding at his words. "Good, good. Let us celebrate your destiny with more of my ale."

The next morning he awoke to a strong hand on his shoulder. "Wake up there, Hawkins! 'Tis a new day." William Clark stood over Benjamin, who was rolled up in a blanket beside a burnt-out fire.

Benjamin looked around for Emma Wells. There was no trace of her. Then he realized he was back in the encampment with the Clarks, though he had no memory of returning last night.

"Come along, lad. Lieutenant Richardson has ordered a meeting of all newcomers. Apparently our time here is not to be spent in idle mischief."

Benjamin was only half listening to William Clark. Even as he tried to shake off sleep, his mind was immediately filled with Emma Wells. Was she real? He was certain she was and eager to see her again to confirm his experience.

Now he thought of his father, who had always taught that everyone and everything are but mirrors reflecting where one is on the path of life. Who was Emma Wells and what was the meaning of their time spent fireside, divining Benjamin's life?

"Did you see a wagon there?" Benjamin pointed in the direction where he had meandered off after leaving Clark the previous night.

"No, can't say I did." William responded. "But we have to get a move on, Benjamin, the meeting is about to start."

Benjamin dusted off his clothes and was set to follow when he saw a card at his feet. Without question, it was one of Emma Wells' *carte da trionfi. Emma was not a dream.*

Benjamin picked up the card and began to study it. The card depicted a pastoral scene, with a waterfall rushing off a cliff into a still pool below. A daytime sky was dominated by a star surrounded by twelve smaller stars. A woman and a man stood in the foreground at the water's edge. The woman poured water from a container. The man held a book in one hand and pointed to the cliff above with the other.

It was not one of the cards that Emma had read. Benjamin was sure of it. But he let the image penetrate his mind and stepped into the scene. It was very familiar to him, and yet he was certain it was a place where he had never been. Then, with a start, it dawned on him that he was visiting his future. It was such an odd sensation, as if somewhere in time the future existed as a place to roam, as real as if it were the present.

"Let's go, Benjamin!" William Clark's impatience brought him back to the present — the fort and the French threat. "We can't keep Lieutenant Richardson waiting!"

Chapter 21

At the Fort
JUNE 1692
Day Two

Benjamin, Catherine Steward
& Lieutenant Richardson

Lieutenant Alan Richardson was in fine form that morning, his commanding presence plain to see as he addressed the settlers, men and women, gathered before him. His charge was to keep order among those fleeing the French and the native tribes that threatened. And order was exactly what he would have.

Richardson held the interest of most of the group, who were anxious to hear out the lieutenant and know the plan for the day. But when it came to Benjamin Hawkins, the lieutenant's directions fell on deaf ears. As he and Clark joined the gathering, Benjamin's attention was drawn to Catherine Steward, who was standing on the steps of the trading post, just above Richardson and facing the group. For Benjamin, there was no one else present.

Catherine recognized the shy young man from the previous day and gave him a welcoming nod. Benjamin smiled, thrilled that she acknowledged him.

"You there, what's your name?" Richardson growled.

"Benjamin Hawkins, Lieutenant."

"You're late, Hawkins. No one will be allowed to tarry in the service of the Crown. His Royal Majesty, The King, is extending his protection."

Richardson was certain it was Catherine that had elicited the happy look on Hawkins' face. Whatever he had in mind, the lieutenant wasn't going to allow it.

"You'll find my willingness to meet my obligations second to none, Lieutenant," Benjamin responded boldly. The sight of Catherine Steward gave him an unexpected confidence.

"Hawkins, I'm sure you're quite an able fellow, and that being the case, we need your assistance."

"At your service, sir."

"Well then, that's the spirit. We need to clean the privies and make space for more, and I'll bet you're just the man for the job." Richardson would allow no one, especially a bumpkin, to put a crimp in his plans to wed Catherine Steward. What better way to knock down this would-be rival a peg or two.

But Benjamin was not as disturbed as Richardson had hoped. "Lieutenant, allow me to make another suggestion. I am a man of the healing arts, as was my father, and brought my knowledge with me from England. I'm sure with all these people crowding the fort, I can be of better service."

As Benjamin spoke, the crowd began to part and Colonel Steward stepped forward. Catherine made her way to greet her father, and the colonel and Richardson exchanged crisp salutes.

"Yes, Lieutenant." The colonel spoke with a deep, gruff voice. "It is a much better idea to survey this lot to determine their skills before handing out assignments. Take this man, for example. Why have him cleaning the privies? No doubt our physician, Dr. Elsberry, is overwhelmed by the influx of settlers. I'm sure he could use an assistant."

"But Colonel…," Richardson spoke softly, trying to catch the colonel's ear.

"Now, now Richardson, it's time to break this up."

"Yes, sir…," Richardson complied. The colonel gave him no choice but to agree. Still, he would not forget Benjamin Hawkins for shaming him, in front of Catherine and all these folk. Another strike against Hawkins, another reason to find a way to put him in his place.

And another strike against the colonel in Richardson's mind, even though he was Catherine's father. Colonel Steward had embarrassed Richardson more than once, and the lieutenant felt that Steward never treated him with the respect he had earned. Richardson also considered the old man soft and filled with an English pomposity that didn't suit the new frontier. It was he, the lieutenant, who made sure the fort ran smoothly, with little help from the pretentious commander.

Colonel Steward paused to give Catherine a gentle kiss on the cheek and then moved on. Richardson dismissed the settlers with orders to return to their encampment, where soldiers would come promptly to inventory their skills. Then the lieutenant would give out assignments.

Benjamin bid William Clark goodbye and went in search of Doctor Elsberry. Along the way, he came upon Richardson. "Lieutenant," he asked, "can you tell me where I can find the physician?"

Richardson shrugged his shoulders. "He may be anywhere. You'll have to look. You're a smart fellow. I'm sure you'll find your way."

"I'll do just that," Benjamin agreed. But once he saw the lieutenant had moved on, he had another thought and returned to the trading post. Even more settlers were arriving and he was hopeful to find Catherine inside, helping as she had the day before.

"Good morning, Miss Steward."

"Good morning, Mr. Hawkins. I see you are quite the nimble fellow. It takes some verbal agility to get yourself out of the most unpopular of tasks." Catherine gave him a sly smile and they both laughed.

"I thought I could be put to better use, considering my talents."

"I'm sure you did … and besides being a healer, what other talents do you have?"

"Well, I've become quite a decent farmer, or so it appears from my first crop."

"And do you like being a farmer?"

"I like being close to the earth, and farming is honest and necessary work. But I prefer being a healer, like my father."

"And where is your father?"

"He's gone, left this world… too soon."

"Oh dear, I'm so sorry, Mr. Hawkins," she said in a voice filled with sympathy.

"Benjamin. Please, call me Benjamin."

"Oh, I couldn't, Mr. Hawkins. I don't know you," Catherine responded with discretion.

"Pardon, Miss Steward, I meant nothing by it…." Then, changing the subject, "I was hoping you could tell me where I might find the doctor. I would like to make his acquaintance."

Despite her position as the commander's daughter and her fondness for Richardson, Catherine found herself enjoying the attention of this young man. "Of course, Mr. Hawkins. I'll be happy to show you myself," she offered. "As fate would have it, I need to go near Dr. Elsberry's quarters."

As the two walked together, their path crossed that of the lieutenant, who was conferring with scouts newly returned to the fort. Furious at what he observed, though required by duty to remain with the scouts, Richardson swore silently to rid himself and Catherine of this intruder. Benjamin Hawkins' moment would come.

That night Benjamin and the Clarks sat around the evening fire, wondering when they could go back to their lives. Before too long, Benjamin, after a long day and the previous night's uncertain sleep, decided to turn in early.

∞

About the same time, Catherine Steward and her mother, Jane, were deep in their own conversation. Colonel Steward was off with Lieutenant Richardson, checking the sentry posts to ensure the fort was secure.

"Does Lieutenant Richardson have designs on you?" Jane Steward was quizzing her daughter for information again.

"Yes, Mother, that is quite apparent."

"Well, a young woman could do worse."

"Richardson is a decent enough fellow. I'm just not sure…," Catherine answered, her voice trailing off. She knew her mother did not view love as necessary in marriage.

"The lieutenant has prospects, Catherine. You will not be a girl forever. And the Colonel and I would enjoy some young ones around."

"Oh, Mother!" Catherine cried in embarrassment. Even so, mother and daughter smiled silently as each considered the future.

Strangely though, Catherine also found herself thinking about Benjamin Hawkins. There was something about him. She couldn't explain what it was, but he had captured her thoughts nonetheless.

Colonel Steward returned, satisfied with the reports that all was quiet in the immediate countryside. Wife and daughter kissed him good night as he settled before the fire, his usual place to sleep when the fort was on high alert.

Chapter 22

At the Fort
Day Three
JUNE 1692

Benjamin, Richardson & Catherine Steward

Treachery operates in many ways and a well-placed coin — or *franc* — can cause allegiance to change with a full purse. Even as the soldiers eyed the settlers to ensure none was entering as a French spy, within the fort a plan was underway. Cut off the leadership, frighten and confuse the common soldiers, and the fort would be suddenly vulnerable despite the solid stockade walls.

In the wee hours of his third day at the fort, Benjamin was jolted awake by a rumble of shouts: "FIRE! FIRE!" The word spread as fast as flames.

Benjamin jumped up, gathering his wits. An orange glow lit the black night over the fort.

"Come quickly, Benjamin!" William Clark handed him a bucket, and they ran off in the direction of the fire.

They were among the first to arrive. Two buildings were ablaze, one with the roof engulfed in flames, the other billowing smoke.

"Form a line men!" a soldier directed. They passed off their buckets to be filled and began dousing the flames.

"My mother! My father!" It was Catherine Steward screaming, face smudged with soot and tears. She pointed toward the house that was not yet in flames. "Save them! Save them!"

At that instant Lieutenant Richardson emerged, carrying Jane Steward in his arms.

"Father is still in there!" Catherine yelled.

Dazed from the smoke and his rescue of Mrs. Steward, Richardson looked at the colonel's quarters, flames now licking the roof. He hesitated.

In those seconds, another body raced past the lieutenant. Benjamin was on the front step. "Be quick, lad!" Clark hollered.

Benjamin looked back and saw Catherine, frantic, her eyes pleading with him to save her father. Benjamin went into the burning building.

Richardson quickly gathered himself and followed, knowing he could not be outdone by Benjamin Hawkins.

Inside the smoke was thick. Richardson could just make out Benjamin trying to lift Colonel Steward, who was passed out in a chair by the fireplace. He took a step to help Benjamin, who was staggering under the colonel's dead weight.

Benjamin got the colonel standing, only for him to fall back into the chair. The minutes were ticking as Benjamin tried again, with no greater success.

Richardson froze, not in fright but in recognition of the opportunity before him. He could rid himself of this would-be hero and, at the same time, be done with the colonel, with whom he was so often at odds. He had saved the mother. Surely Catherine would marry him without question.

As the smoke grew thicker, Benjamin watched the fire threatening to circle around him. And out of the corner of his eye, he spotted Richardson standing nearby.

"Help me! I need your help!" Benjamin called out.

Richardson did not move.

Everything was catching now, the fire eating toward the door and a wall of flame coming at Benjamin. He looked down at Colonel

Steward and slapped him hard across the face. "Wake up, wake up!" he shouted.

Another glance at Richardson, who was moving toward the door, leaving Benjamin and the colonel to fend for themselves.

"Richardson, you coward!" Benjamin screamed. The lieutenant disappeared into the smoke.

Before the smoke enveloped all of them, Richardson took a last look at Hawkins and the colonel, and concluded they were doomed.

With one more attempt, Benjamin grabbed Colonel Steward by the shoulders and shook him. "COME ON! COLONEL! We must get out of here!" As he spoke, Benjamin could hear the crash of wood falling. There was little time left.

He slapped the colonel, making a final attempt to rouse him. Then, with all the strength he could muster, Benjamin pulled the colonel up and threw the man's arm across his upper back. As he did, Benjamin saw Steward's eyes flutter open.

"SIR! Can you walk?"

"I think so," the colonel coughed, still semi-conscious but now able to assist in his own escape.

Even so, Benjamin had to drag the colonel forward, step by step.

"Don't leave me!" A voice moaned in the smoky darkness as Benjamin and the colonel reached the door.

It was Richardson, lying on the floor close to the entryway, felled by a burning beam now pinning his legs.

Benjamin could not stop to help the lieutenant. He pulled the colonel out to safety, where several soldiers took him from Benjamin's side, with Dr. Elsberry ready to attend to Steward.

Then Benjamin turned back toward the open door, flames now licking the frame and smoke surging out. William Clark ran to stop him, grabbing Benjamin and blocking his way. "You cannot go back inside, Hawkins!"

"We have to get Richardson!"

"He's done for, Benjamin! There's nothing more to do!"

And in eerie confirmation, barely a second later, the roof caved in with a thunderous crash. Benjamin nodded and collapsed.

The plot was uncovered, the culprits hanged and Colonel Steward thankfully recovered. Word soon reached the fort that the French had been thwarted further north. With their forces subdued, the native threat calmed as well. Within a week, the settlers were leaving, returning to their homes.

But for Benjamin, the whole world had changed yet again. In the days that followed the fire, he and Catherine grew closer. At first it was profound gratitude that made her welcome his visits enquiring after her father's health, her mother's and her own. But soon they were taking long walks and stirring each other's hearts.

As it turned out, Jane Steward would soon have no more worries about her daughter being wed — and then, in due course, of a little one to enjoy.

Chapter 23

Hunstanton
June 1692

Jeremiah Hawkins

On a cool, foggy night, a drunken Jeremiah Hawkins, cursing his life, staggered out of a tavern and onto a jagged dirt road. And as he had many times before, he expected the road to bring him home. Week after week, month after month and over a year had gone by since his father's passing. And like this night, he spent the coin he earned to drink away his sorrows.

Needing a livelihood to subsist, Jeremiah had turned to the sea for work. Though he could read and do the sums his father had taught him, it was his brawn that served him now. The men fishing the North Sea welcomed his powerful muscles for hauling in their nets.

He was still as defiant and withdrawn as when his father first died. But so were many of the men he sailed with. Jeremiah made no effort at friendship and received none in return. And whatever his life might have been before his father's death, his life now was one of difficult, dangerous work and the tavern — when the ghosts of the cottage drove him away.

The folk of Hunstanton left him alone. Even Daniel Fletcher gave up making the trek to the cottage. Now and then, Hannah sent Jacob with a basket of food she prepared and with instructions not to knock but to leave it outside the door. Though she pitied Jeremiah, she also knew his temper.

Although she could not see inside his home, let alone his heart, Hannah Fletcher was as correct in her assumptions about Jeremiah Hawkins as one outsider might be about another. He was as miserable as a human being could be.

Time might heal for some, but for Jeremiah time only magnified the horror of his last day with his father and brother. The fight with Benjamin replayed over and over in his nightmares. His father tumbling backward, falling ... falling ... until suddenly Ethan's head slams onto stone. Then a fountain of blood drenches the scene. Yet through it all, there was Benjamin, the favored one, stealing their father's diary and crystal, running away.

Night after night he awoke from that same dream, wracked by guilt and gnawed at by a fury that went on and on.

On some nights, sleep would not come at all, and Jeremiah cowered on the floor, haunted by sounds and shadows that filled the cottage.

So he drank to numb his mind. He whored to calm his body with momentary explosive release.

But nothing lasted. Nothing helped.

On this particular evening, with a thick mist creeping in from the sea, flashes pierced the dark from the lighthouse at Hunstanton burning bright. It was the kind of night when a beacon was all that stood between safety and oblivion.

Each drunken step took Jeremiah closer to the cottage. Situated as it was near the cliffs by the sea, one needed to walk with care. But his foot got caught in a thicket of rose vines. And with a twist of his ankle, he stumbled.

"This is shite!" he yelled, trying to get up but stumbling again. "SHITE!"

He raised his fist to the sky, ready to take on the heavens. And then providence sent its beacon from the lighthouse above the cliff and made Jeremiah naked to the world.

He managed to get to his feet and screamed, "I'M STILL HERE! YES, I AM... STILL HERE!"

The light went dim, as it did when in need of more coal. For Jeremiah, it was a denial of his presence, of his very existence, of his repeated cry for help. His appeal was being ignored.

Standing alone in the silent night, the cool air cleared Jeremiah's ale-fogged eyes and steadied his stumbling feet. But his legs would take him no farther. And in that moment, with the dying of the lighthouse beacon, Jeremiah recognized that he was like the boats at sea in danger of being pounded upon the rocks — his life was being crushed.

Tears welling in his eyes, he reached out into the night, to the one source he still believed in. Though his lips moved, his plea spoke from his true heart, in words that had never come before:

"Something has hold of me, Father! It won't let me go! It's growing stronger than I am… suffocating me…. A thick darkness is wrapping around my heart. Oh, Father, I have tried to understand what I am supposed to do! How to make amends. But the pain and the sadness never end. The voice in my head always proclaims me guilty, good for nothing…. Oh, Father, help me!"

Jeremiah stretched out his arms, pleading into the darkness, his voice now loud and piercing. "WHAT IS TO BECOME OF ME?"

Yet the silence of the night gave no discernable answer.

Then the light again, bright again, the coal replenished. Jeremiah let it fill his eyes and his mind was illuminated with unexpected clarity.

There is nothing for me here except the specter of memory. Step out of the cottage, close the door and leave the ghosts behind.

That he could do so — that nothing held him to this spot — was suddenly so apparent.

And what of Benjamin? Have I stayed because someday he might return?

That likelihood was also abundantly clear. He had remained in Hunstanton, in the cottage, because he expected that day to come.

And what would I do then? Seek revenge?

It was the burning desire that fueled his days — but to what end? He was hardly into manhood, and he was spent.

No. I need to escape, just as Benjamin has escaped. But to where?

In the days to follow, the idea planted that night took root. Jeremiah was determined to leave quickly. If he lingered, he might change his mind, for human nature being what it is, the cottage never seemed so dear to him as when he planned to abandon it.

Nevertheless, before June had given way to July, Jeremiah collected what he thought he must take, including his father's ale mug and cloak, and all the coin he had not drunk away.

He closed the cottage door behind him with a prayerful wish for the ghosts to remain inside. Then he walked the familiar steps to the edge of the cliffs blooming with roses. He scanned the scene, willing his mind to tuck it away where he might call it up when he needed a soothing reminder of what had been, in his first eighteen years, "home."

Then he turned toward the road heading south, into the unknown. And he walked for days, hugging the seacoast, certain he could not go too far adrift if the North Sea was always in view.

It was this path that brought Jeremiah to Deal, to the very seaport from which Benjamin had sailed for America the previous year. It was an irony unknown to Jeremiah. And all the better that it was, for had he known the vast difference between his brother's prospects, then and now, and his own, it could only have done more to harden the layers of grievance, and of grief, that were a shell around his heart.

Chapter 24

Deal, England
July 1692

Jeremiah Hawkins, Abigail Briar & Bess Hays

Stumbling from side to side, Jeremiah fell into a familiar rhythm, one step in front of the other, leaning forward, barely staying on his feet. He hadn't traveled very far when he felt his head explode in pain. Then another thump, and Jeremiah knew that treachery was upon him.

A drunken man alone, with the strength and heft to be a worthy seaman in the King's Navy, was an easy mark and a profitable target of thieves in a bustling place like Deal. Many a sailor was pressed into service in the back alleys of Deal. Simple to whisk him from street to ship before he sobered up to his new situation.

So Jeremiah found himself fighting three large and brutish men. He fought valiantly, shedding one attacker and then another. But his drunken state made it hard for Jeremiah to stay on his feet. Again and again, after landing a hard swing, he found himself falling to the ground, where he was a less-able opponent. And each time, to save himself from the misery of life on a British galleon, Jeremiah managed to get back on his feet. But the longer it took the trio to subdue Jeremiah, the more determined they were to capture him.

Abigail Briar and her younger sister, Bess Hays, were startled awake by noises from the alley below. They were growls or groans. It was hard to be sure.

"What is it?" Bess asked in fright.

"Could be a dog. Or some other creature turned loose," Abigail suggested. "God knows what comes in on these ships from godforsaken places! Let's look. No other way to know."

Abigail scurried out of bed and opened their one small window. Immediately the stink of the alley filled the room.

A guttural chorus rose up clearly now. Not animal sounds but human; a man in pain, his groans interrupted only by deeper moans.

"What should we do?" Bess whispered, still huddled in bed.

Bravely, Abigail put her head out the window to see below. Three men were kicking what appeared to be another man, helpless, lying on the ground.

Enraged, Abigail yelled into the night. "LEAVE HIM BE!"

"Abigail! What are you doing?" Bess whispered in alarm, throwing the blankets off and jumping out of bed to join her older sister. "They'll see *you!*"

Bess pulled Abigail from view as the three men looked up, searching for the voice coming from above them. In grim silence they looked at each other, and then at the motionless body.

The trio were maneuvering arms and legs to carry the man away when the voice boomed out again. "I SAID LEAVE HIM ALONE!" Abigail shouted firmly.

This time another window flew open in another room.

The three men swore, realizing their moment to capture this drunk without the risk of getting caught had vanished. One last kick to convey their anger at a missed opportunity, and then they swiftly disappeared down the street and into the night.

"I'm going down to help that man!" Abigail announced as she quickly lit a candle and began to change out of her nightgown.

But Bess hesitated. "We don't know who he is or what he did."

Abigail shook her head. "I don't care. That man needs help. Are you coming with me or not?"

"Oh, Abby!" was all Bess could say. She adored her older sister — except for the streak of fearlessness that seemed foolish for a young woman completely on her own.

Within minutes Abigail and Bess were by Jeremiah's side, trying to rouse him.

"Poor dear man, looks like he's hurt badly," Abigail surmised. Even in the dim lantern light, they could see the cuts on his face and blood drying around his mouth. His breathing was raspy and when Abigail knelt beside him, an accidental tap on his side made him yelp in pain.

"Get some water and cloths, Bess," Abigail directed. Then she took the palm of her hand and caressed his stumbled cheek. "Easy now, don't move, I'm here to help."

Jeremiah's first instinct was to try to get up, but his throbbing head made him submit to Abigail's tender touch.

"There, that's better, let me help you," she confirmed, now gently stroking his forehead.

Jeremiah blinked his eyes and looked up drowsily at Abigail.

"My name is Abigail Briar."

"I'm…J-e-r-e-…."

"No, don't try to speak."

Jeremiah looked into Abigail's strong and steady eyes and had an unexpected sense that he was safe.

"Is he all right?" Bess asked anxiously, having quickly returned. She handed a cloth to Abigail and placed a pail of water beside her.

Soon the cool water was reviving Jeremiah as Abigail washed away the blood. She wrapped the wet cloth around his head, to soothe the lumps growing from the pounding he'd received.

"Help me up," he requested, willing himself to stand. "Help me … please."

Abigail placed his arm around her shoulder as Bess did the same, and they got him to his feet, with Jeremiah wincing in pain.

"Now," Abigail declared, "let's get you away before more trouble arrives."

Like Jeremiah Hawkins, Abigail and Bess Hays had known their share of life's difficulties. Both their mother and father perished in an outbreak of cholera that also took the rest of their siblings. Abigail was only thirteen then, and Bess, eleven. They were poor and on their own, but they swore allegiance to each other. No matter what happened, they would always look out for the other.

At fifteen, Abigail wed Miles Briar. Bess naturally came to live with them, for Abigail would not have married otherwise. Briar was also from lowly stock, but he was an enterprising young man. He had heard that the English colonies in America were a place where men could get land and where those like him, without family or formal schooling, could make a decent life. Many soldiers remained in the colonies when their service was done.

So Briar volunteered to be a soldier and to fight the battles of King William's War in the New World. He expected that in a short time he would send for Abigail and Bess, and then all three would make a new start in America.

Briar's friend, Henry Rogers, was a soldier in the company too. He had taken a shine to Bess on his visits with Miles and Abigail. He was eager for his own prospects in America — and with Bess.

That was two years earlier, when all was hopeful. But before they could join Miles, he was dead, killed in a battle, in a place called Quebec, by the hideous French. Henry Rogers wrote with the news.

It was October, in 1690, when Miles died, along with the dream of America.

Abigail had not known Miles as a husband long enough to mourn him deeply, though she saved the money he had left them for sailing to America, and she thanked him daily for that pocket of security. Together the sisters added to it through whatever honest work they might find. Neither could do more than barely read and write. But Abigail had taught herself sums, to keep from being cheated, and she managed every coin they earned and spent with equal care.

Henry Rogers continued to write, a few letters a year, enough to show he'd never lost his designs on Bess.

He'd finished soldiering and become a fur trapper. His letters were full of derring-do and, in time, descriptions of his success as fur trader on the Great Hudson Bay. Abigail and Bess immersed themselves in Henry's tales of America.

Then his last letter had been more serious. He was looking to expand his opportunities in the booming city of New York. Soon he would have a store to run. Why not come and join him? If they made their own passage, he would be waiting in New York.

Abigail was certain this was meant as a marriage proposal for Bess. Her practical side reasoned that women must be scarce in the colonies. But a woman could do worse than Henry Rogers.

She and Bess filled each other's heads with promises of a new life in America. They counted their guineas and arranged to cross the ocean, sailing from Deal.

Now their departure had been delayed, and they had taken the cheapest room in the cheapest inn to wait. And on their second night, they found themselves assisting a young man far too badly beaten to go off on his own. And so, in short order, they were nurses to that man, named Jeremiah Hawkins, who was taking up their bed.

Chapter 25

Deal

AUGUST 1692

Jeremiah, Abigail & Bess

Hour by hour, day by day, in the weeks that followed, the Hays sisters brought Jeremiah back to health.

Abigail cared for Jeremiah with a tenderness he had never experienced. Though not much was said between them, in that silence the turbulent storm that had raged in Jeremiah's soul was quieted by her soft grace. Such gentle goodness in another took him by surprise. *How is it possible after all I've done that this woman is so kind to me?*

Bess also took her turn making sure Jeremiah was fed and his wounds tended to, but she was always relieved to release those duties to Abigail. Bess found Jeremiah's presence more than a minor annoyance. Mainly, she wanted to go back to the way it had been — to having her sister to herself.

The sailing date was moved yet again, keeping Abigail and Bess in Deal and giving more time for Jeremiah to recover. As his strength returned, his guarded nature was more apparent. At first his broken ribs made it too painful for much talk. But as they mended, and as Jeremiah remained reluctant to join in their conversations, the women wondered what were the dark secrets that this man they sheltered held so tightly.

Nevertheless, whenever Abigail looked into Jeremiah's worn face, she could see his youth hidden behind a rough coarseness that dug deep into the surface of his skin. When her eyes came to rest in his, she perceived the pain and sorrow of a decent soul unhappily caught in a drama that had blown his life off its axis. Her heart stirred with sympathy and concern. *This man is in pain,* she concluded. *He carries a heavy weight. What could have happened to him?*

The one topic that elicited the interest of the taciturn Mr. Hawkins was the sisters' plans for America. He made no secret of listening and one day, finally, he asked to know more.

"So, you are off to the New World," Jeremiah asked.

"Yes, we are looking for a new start," Abigail confirmed.

"You have no kin you leave behind?"

"Bess is all I have," Abigail smiled, and then winking, "and she is restless and looking for adventure."

"She is teasing!" Bess blushed.

Abigail laughed. "What about Mr. Henry Rogers?"

"You know someone in America?" Jeremiah asked.

"Indeed, Bess has a friend, Henry Rogers."

"He is your friend too!" Bess was turning redder still.

"Yes, he was a friend of my husband. A fur trader. He will help us in America." Abigail had briefly mentioned Miles Briar once before, when she explained her widowhood to Jeremiah.

Then, feeling embarrassed, Abigail suddenly announced, "I must go and see if the *Esmeralda* is ready to set sail." She was glad for this daily errand and ran off to check on their ship.

In truth, Abigail realized, she was uncomfortable speaking of Miles with Jeremiah Hawkins. She could not help the strong emotions building inside her for this man that she and Bess had rescued. Abigail had not experienced such longing since Miles. And with each passing day she found it more and more impossible to ignore.

She began to hope for more delays, to have more time with Jeremiah Hawkins.

For his part, Jeremiah also hoped for more delays. He had known women, but with Abigail the feelings that warmed his body moved him in a way he had never experienced. As he listened to the plans for America, he too felt the allure of a new life.

An idea started to take shape in his mind.

The day came that Abigail returned with the news they had long expected: The ship would sail the next morning.

Jeremiah waited until Bess left the room, to fetch an afternoon pot of tea, to speak. "I thank both of you for your kind hearts."

Abigail's eyes glistened with tears at his words. "What will you do now, Jeremiah?" He had divulged so little about himself, but even so, Abigail felt invested in his well-being. "Have you any family?"

"No, none that keeps me here in England."

Jeremiah wanted to say more, but didn't know how to tell her what he was thinking. Instead, he turned the subject to their voyage. "Will you and Bess be safe aboard ship?" he asked.

And then, before he realized what was happening, he spoke his true mind and heart. "I wish I could accompany you... to be sure of your safety. But I have no money to make my way to New York. And you and your sister have already been so generous."

In the silence of the next seconds, the world turned.

Abigail, speaking with mock formality, asked: "Mr. Hawkins, are you proposing a business agreement?"

Jeremiah couldn't answer. In his mind, he was transported back to the night by the lighthouse, and he could hear his own words echoing: *I need to escape.... But to where?*

And now he knew. And he told himself: *I cannot let this moment go by.... It may be my only chance.*

"Yes," he mumbled. Then, finding the fullness of his voice, he stated his case. "If you would stake me the passage, I will work off my debt in America, no matter how long it takes. Traveling across the sea is long and arduous. I can protect you and Bess against any darkness you may encounter on your journey."

Now it was Abigail whose words met the moment, proclaiming the true yearning of her heart. "I have to admit the thought of you coming with us has crossed my mind. Bess and I have been on our own, making our way for such a long time. But I can see a certain advantage to you joining us. So I'll agree to it, Mr. Hawkins. This can work well for us all!"

But Jeremiah continued, as if Abigail's response hadn't registered. "I promise that I will be of service to you and your sister, will earn every penny that you lend me, and…."

Abigail started to laugh.

"Why are you laughing?" asked Jeremiah, now confused.

"Jeremiah, you needn't be so serious! I will talk to Bess. I'm sure she will welcome your protection, as I do. And when we reach New York, a strong worker, such as yourself, will help us establish ourselves."

The two of them smiled, each realizing that what had just transpired could never have been expected only mere weeks ago.

But contrary to Abigail's hopeful expectations, those of her sister were quite the opposite.

"You did what?" Bess glared. "Sorry to tell you, Abby, I have my doubts about Jeremiah Hawkins. And you know that. He says so little. We know nothing about his background, or his character," she argued.

"Actually, Bess, we DO know his character!" Abigail insisted. "He's considerate. He returned our bed to us the moment his ribs could tolerate the floor. And he's honest. Not one pence has gone missing from our pockets!"

Still, Bess was unmoved. "He hides something, Abby! You know it. You've said it yourself!"

"Oh, let's give him a chance," Abigail pleaded. "He said he would do whatever we ask. He's a strong man and we could use someone like him, especially on the voyage and when we get to New York."

Bess paused, mulling over her sister's logic.

"This is our coin, our security," Bess countered. "What if Henry Rogers is not there when we arrive in New York? We will need every penny."

"AND we will then require Jeremiah Hawkins' protection all the more," Abigail reasoned.

"But we have managed alone without him! And what if he leaves the ship and leaves us too?" Bess challenged. "We could not stop him!"

"Bess, I do not believe any of this will happen! Dear sister, you mustn't worry so!"

Then, shaking her head from side to side, Bess relented. "For your sake, I'll agree. But I will be watching him very closely. I hope you know what you're doing. The moment he falters, I promise, you'll not hear the end of it."

"Thank you, dear sister!" Abigail gave Bess a bear hug, her signal of resolve. "And I promise *you* that all will be well!"

Abigail prayed it would be. She was confident that she understood Jeremiah. She knew nothing about his life, and yet she felt she knew *him*. There was the deep hurt in his eyes and it stirred her. She saw in him a man who was raw and vulnerable, and he aroused her sympathy and her passion. She knew not where it would all lead, yet she felt the hand of providence and was ready to follow.

Chapter 26

Aboard the *Esmeralda* to America
SEPTEMBER 1692

Jeremiah, Abigail & Bess

Captain John Walters was as meticulous as they come. A master of the Atlantic crossing, he ran a disciplined ship and took his authority from maritime law and the king himself. He was the first and final arbiter of all disputes aboard his ship, the *Esmeralda*. But he had a reputation for fair and steady judgment, and Abigail and Bess were glad to sail with him.

Nevertheless, believing in the old adage about safety in numbers, they were also pleased that their fellow passengers included members of a Christian sect seeking religious freedom in America.

Though the voyage across the ocean was known to be long and arduous, the day that Abigail and Bess sailed from England, their spirits were buoyed by the notion of a fresh start. Jeremiah also felt a sense of renewal, yet his life's experience told him to be wary and on constant guard.

He never forgot his obligation to Abigail and Bess. They had watched over him while he recovered, and now he watched over them. He was especially attentive to Abigail, but Bess' well-being was also his concern. For her part, Bess was still uncertain of Jeremiah and kept him at a distance. He took no offense. No matter what, he viewed the safety of Abigail and Bess as his unwavering responsibility.

Soon after departure, Bess caught the eye of one of Captain Walter's sailors, Jack Moore. With much of the crew a scruffy lot, Moore stood out as broad shouldered and handsome.

Perhaps because she was unhappy with Jeremiah's presence, or more precisely, with Abigail's growing interest in him, Bess allowed herself to answer Moore's greeting one day with a shy smile. Jeremiah caught the exchange, and having spent enough time around sailors in Deal, knew he'd better pay close attention to Bess' whereabouts.

The seas were serene for the first weeks of the voyage. Bess went every day to seek the fresh air above deck, always with Abigail and Jeremiah alongside. Then the weather turned, the wind grew and the seas swelled. Abigail became seasick and stayed in her berth below deck. Now Jeremiah was torn between helping Abigail and staying watchful of Bess.

The rolling waves bothered Bess not at all. She had grown more comfortable aboard ship and bolder too, spending more time on deck alone. She even chatted with Jack Moore now and then. He remarked on her "sea legs," which Bess took as a compliment, though she was not sure what it meant. Certainly he could not see her legs beneath her long skirt.

Though she knew men could be treacherous, she felt at ease with Moore. She even began dreaming of romantic possibilities.

Then one particularly dreary night, with the sea churning and without the benefit of moonlight, Bess slipped up to the deck. She wished to escape the foul smell, for Abigail was not the only sick passenger. And if she might catch a glimpse of Jack Moore, that would make the fresh air even more pleasant.

Moore was on deck and now he saw a possibility. "You should not be up here. A storm is coming. Let me help you below."

Once there, he offered to show her where the great stores of cargo were kept. Bess had no desire to return to the putrid passenger quarters quite yet and so she agreed.

Bess might be more familiar with the ways of the world than many young women her age, but she was still ill-prepared when things took an unexpected turn. She had no sense of where they were when Moore suddenly grabbed her. His hands were searching for her breasts and his mouth trying to cover hers.

Then a second man appeared out of the shadows. He startled them and Moore momentarily eased his grip, giving Bess a chance to pull away and look for a means of escape. Her instincts had sharpened and alarm swept across her face.

"I want to go back. I …!" Bess stuttered.

But the second man, a sailor named Sikes, was even more sinister. "Come on, be a good lass and let's have a time of it," he sneered.

Moore nodded, signaling his willingness to share his "catch" and the two men laughed.

Sensing great danger, Bess turned to run.

"Not so fast." Moore reached for her arm.

Bess screeched, hoping to be heard.

Sikes grabbed her from behind as Moore started to lift her skirt. She kicked out at Moore as she bit the hand that was trying to cover her mouth. She chomped down on a finger and let out another scream.

"BESS, IS THAT YOU?" A booming voice rolled forward. Her eyes lit up with recognition.

She twisted away from Sikes and Moore long enough to answer. "I'm here! Jeremiah, I'm here!"

Jeremiah quickly appeared and immediately saw the trouble Bess was in. "Let her go," he announced, his voice forceful but calm.

Sikes and Moore both eased their hold enough for Bess to break away and run to Jeremiah's side. She clung to his arm as he spoke to her softly. "You're safe. Come with me now."

"Mind your own business, mate!" Moore sputtered. "We's just showin' the lady around."

"Bess, and her sister Abigail are my business," Jeremiah countered, "and you best not interfere." But as they turned to leave, Jeremiah felt a strong hand grasping his neck.

With lightening fast reflexes, he grabbed the hand of his attacker. Moore yelped as Jeremiah bent his fingers backwards. Then Jeremiah grabbed Moore's other hand, and with a sharp twist one way and then the other, broke his wrist for good measure.

Sikes sent his fist flying toward Jeremiah's face, only to be met with a well-placed thrust to the groin from Jeremiah's knee. Then Jeremiah took hold of the sailor's shirt, pulled it over the man's head and threw him to the ground.

Both men were doubled over in pain. Any doubt about who was in full charge of the situation was dispelled. Though as Jeremiah and Bess moved away, Moore grimaced, "This is not the last of it."

Jeremiah returned and bent down to hiss in Moore's ear. "If I see you speaking with Bess or with Abigail — with any woman on this ship — I will not show the restraint I have today." To be sure the message was heard, he repeated the same in Sikes' face.

When Abigail learned what had happened, she immediately went to the pastor who was leading the Christians to warn his people about the crew. Together, they went to Captain Walters to demand proper punishment for Moore and Sikes.

True to form, Captain Walters, master of his ship, ordered Moore and Sikes to be flogged, though only in front of the crew, and given duties that kept them away from the passengers. Tensions between the crew and passengers ran high during the remainder of the voyage, but thankfully they reached New York with no further incident.

Now Bess only took air on deck in the company of Jeremiah. And from that day forward, their relationship changed. Bess apologized, to Jeremiah and to Abigail, for having doubted him. She now saw him as protector and friend.

Abigail's feelings were deepened by the experience. That her sister might have been injured, raped, even murdered — that she might have lost her sister — made her aware, anew, of how deeply she loved her. That Jeremiah had saved her dearest sister made Abigail feel not only gratitude, but more than ever, a certainty that her destiny and Jeremiah's were bound together. She began to think about how she might let him know.

Then one morning, more than six weeks since leaving Deal, as the sun burned off a thick mist, a yell from the crow's nest bellowed out through the ship: "LAND AHOY!"

Abigail and Jeremiah were topside, and like others, they ran to the side of the ship and peered into the distance. "Jeremiah, look, the New World at last! What a welcome sight."

Abigail turned and smiled at Jeremiah. As he faced her, he found expectant eyes pouring into his. She kissed him on the cheek and hugged him, a familiarity she'd not taken before. He instinctively put his arms around her shoulders and held her tightly.

Neither was content to sanctify the moment with a simple kiss on the cheek. She reached for his lips as he reached for hers. Their hearts stirred with tender longing.

That very evening, after Abigail and Bess were asleep, Jeremiah took a silent walk on the deck. The day would soon come when they would leave the ship and touch the sweet firmness of the good earth again. Looking out to shore, with stars twinkling above the coastline, Jeremiah thought about the life he had left behind.

Everything was changing rapidly. It had been only a few months since Abigail and Bess had saved him in the back alley in Deal. Then came the events aboard ship, and his heroics rekindled an important understanding about himself: he had a strong impulse to know and do what was right and just.

He thought about Benjamin and his father. He recalled his emotions, raw with jealousy. He replayed the tragic results, as he had done so many times before.

Moments passed, the quiet landscape slid by and Jeremiah felt a strange sense of release. Though he knew those memories, those emotions, still lived unresolved within him, yet the cottage, the lighthouse on the cliff and the old tree with the crystal in its roots — they were all far away from him now.

And here, with a new world beckoning, Jeremiah felt the wheel of fate turning. It occurred to him that the storm that had raged inside him for as long as he could remember was quiet. He felt his life cast anew — that he was landing on the bright shores of rebirth. Where it would lead he could not know, but a faith awakened inside him and spoke to his open heart: *Behold a new time awaits.*

Chapter 27

The Hudson Valley
OCTOBER 1692

Benjamin & Catherine Hawkins

The wedding of Benjamin Hawkins and Catherine Steward was full of military pomp and circumstance of the best that frontier life would allow.

Jane Steward had been insistent. "Catherine, we must take a trip to the city of New York, to purchase the very finest fabric for a proper wedding dress." And so mother and daughter had made the journey in August, by boat and by carriage. And though both knew London and its elegant shops, they were duly impressed with the goods to be found in New York.

On the day of the ceremony, Jane and the other officers' wives made sure that Colonel Steward's daughter and her groom were married with the pageantry befitting not only the colonel's rank, but the warmth and good cheer felt toward Catherine by one and all. An arch of swords marked the end of the ceremony and a new life for Benjamin and Catherine Hawkins.

Benjamin had never felt more right with the world. A deep sense of peace settled inside of him. The pressure to understand the significance of his life and pursue some grand purpose fell silent, at least in this moment. Now he looked forward to seasons to come with the wife of his dreams on his arm.

And Catherine felt simply as light as a feather, filled with joy and grace.

Yet, as the glow of celebration faded, the task of beginning a life together began. Jane Steward begged her daughter to remain at the fort. She even spoke to the regimental physician, Dr. Elsberry, about taking Benjamin on as an assistant.

And Elsberry, impressed with Benjamin's skill as a healer, was more than willing. It was Benjamin's calendula recipe for burn salve that had helped to restore Colonel Steward, and other victims too, following the traitorous fire.

But as Benjamin explained to a distraught Mrs. Steward, he had to get back to the land that Captain Alfredo had entrusted to him. He was eager to lay claim to the acres that were set aside for him, even as he kept his agreement to cultivate Alfredo's woods and streams into a prosperous estate.

Fortunately, both Catherine and Colonel Steward understood and admired Benjamin's commitment and determination. He vividly described to Catherine all that Alfredo's land had come to mean to him. In the year Benjamin had lived there, he'd formed a bond with the forests and meadows of those five hundred acres. They called to him. He was a part of that land, as it was now a part of him. Its life-force flowed through his veins, and in return, he gave it sustenance. There was an alchemy present, with new discoveries and new visions yet to be.

And there was something else more practical. Benjamin knew this land could be home in a conventional sense, where he and Catherine would happily raise a family.

And so the week following their wedding, Benjamin and Catherine said their good-byes. Tears ran down the cheeks of both mother and daughter, each promising frequent visits.

As he left the fort, Benjamin considered how his world had altered since arriving with the Clarks a mere five months before. He had not felt acutely alone before meeting Catherine. In fact, he had always enjoyed his own company. But now, with her by his side, he realized how grateful he was to no longer live by himself. Love, so different from what he had known, bloomed in his heart and its inescapable fragrance filled him with happiness.

So their journey began good-naturedly, telling stories about their early lives as they continued to get to know and appreciate each other. Catherine described her life in England and what she loved about the comparative wildness and freedom of America. She had no siblings, for the two born after her had died of illness as babies, and she described her desire to have a large family — five children, at least.

Benjamin excitedly told her again of his adventures with Alberto Alfredo, and how he had come to live and work on Alfredo's land.

For hours they daydreamed together about their lives going forward. Yet as the trip wore on, Benjamin grew ever more quiet. And it didn't take long for Catherine to notice.

"What's the matter, Benjamin? I see you have become lost in your thoughts. You know you can share them with me."

Benjamin barely knew where to begin. "I have to tell you a few things about my life that you do not know."

Catherine laughed softly. "I am sure there are more than a few things I do not know about your life, Benjamin!"

He gave her a quick smile and went back to gazing at the road ahead.

Though only eighteen, Catherine was a young woman of exceptional poise, with remarkable intuitive sense about the world and the people around her. Seeing that her light-hearted comment didn't lighten his mood, she became intent on encouraging her husband to unburden himself. "Please, Benjamin, you can tell me anything."

Acknowledging his new wife's heartfelt openness, Benjamin began to relax. It was time to share the feelings that lurked in the shadows of his past.

"I told you my father is dead and my mother too. But I did not tell you that I have a brother, and he is alive, in England, in Hunstanton," Benjamin explained.

Catherine's face registered her surprise, but she only squeezed

Benjamin's arm, to encourage him to go on. When a few minutes of silence had passed, she asked quietly, "Is there more?"

Benjamin took a deep breath and nodded. "Jeremiah and I were so jealous. One day it erupted into a terrible fight. We were rolling around on the ground, punching and kicking each other with such force that one of us would surely soon be dead. Father tried to stop us. He fell...."

When Benjamin could not continue, Catherine put her arm around her husband. "It was a tragic accident," she gently consoled.

"I know. But if we were not fighting, my father would still be alive." Benjamin looked at Catherine with such sadness, but with relief as well in finally revealing what had happened.

But Catherine was curious. "What had you to be jealous over that made you fight with such fury? Benjamin, you are not that way. I know you are not."

And then Benjamin told her of the storm that uprooted the old tree when he was fifteen — of the discovery he made and how it had come between him and Jeremiah, even more than the differences that had always been there.

Benjamin pulled on the reins to stop the horse. It was time to tell Catherine. For the first time, he showed her the diamond crystal stone.

"As an alchemist, my father taught me many things about the natural realm. This crystal was his before it was mine. It served him well — until it failed him, when my mother died. It serves me, Catherine. When I hold it, it brightens my mind and enables me to peer deeply into the world beyond this world."

Catherine stared at the stone, uncertain what it was and how to understand the powers that Benjamin described. Then he placed the diamond stone in Catherine's hand and put his hand around hers.

The crystal began to glow.

"Can you feel it?" he asked.

Catherine took a deep breath. "I do."

Benjamin's thoughts streamed to the cottage in England — to his father and brother, and Daniel Fletcher, and the last time someone else had experienced the crystal. Could Catherine's knowledge of the crystal create a problem? That was something that worried him all along.

Thankfully, Benjamin decided not hold anything back from Catherine now. He did not want any darkness between them, and so he told Catherine of the feelings that stalked him in showing her the crystal stone.

Catherine looked upon his face, saddened that Benjamin was dismayed.

"I'm glad you spoke of all this with me," she assured him. "But my dear Benjamin, have no fear. I live not for a stone, but for the love I have for you and for the life we'll make together. Once I chose you, the light in my heart was lit, like this crystal that glows in our hands."

With those words, all the tension that furled around his brow eased. And Benjamin knew that it was no longer the crystal stone that made the world seem bright, but the love now kindled in his heart, the fountainhead of all life.

Catherine released the stone and Benjamin returned it to his pocket. He reached for the reins, to continue their journey, but Catherine stopped him. She took his hand and placed it over her heart. Then she took her own hand and placed it over his heart. "*This* is truth, and the window to all things good in this world, and in any other."

They held that moment, and Benjamin and Catherine knew each other deeper than before. A portal to their souls was unsealed and they looked into the full measure of their unending spirits.

Benjamin acknowledged his bride as an alchemist in her own right. Not in the way of he and his father, or of Daniel Fletcher and Isaac Newton. No, a different sort: Catherine knew the alchemy of love.

Chapter 28

Colonial New York
OCTOBER 1692

Jeremiah, Abigail, Bess & Henry Rogers

At last, the *Esmeralda* sailed into New York Harbor. Abigail and Bess left the ship, eyes ablaze with wonderment. Henry Rogers was waiting for them as they came down the ramp, for he had met every ship arriving from England since he received Abigail's letter that she and Bess would come.

But Jeremiah lagged behind in leaving the ship. The image of his brother appeared fleetingly before him, as if he were close by. It was the same feeling Jeremiah remembered as a boy, whenever he and Benjamin would know what the other was thinking without saying a word.

Could Benjamin be here in America? The thought was more than a question. They had both grown up with their father's story of his intended voyage to America. *Surely much has happened since I last saw him,* Jeremiah considered. *Would he be the same? Am I?*

Jeremiah allowed himself to sink deeper into this moment that was alive with emotion. So much had passed between the brothers. And while the angst, the jealousy, the anger, the blame still resided inside of him, yet another strong feeling stirred within Jeremiah. Abigail had reawakened his capacity to love. And despite the strife between him and Benjamin, in his own way, he had loved his brother when they were children. Were they to meet again, what emotions would come to the fore?

"Jeremiah, what's keeping you? Please come join us," Abigail called out.

She looked up at him eagerly from portside and Jeremiah felt his heart expanding with joy. Thoughts of Benjamin evaporated as he turned his attention to Abigail and Bess, standing with a man who must be Henry Rogers.

Yes, Jeremiah allowed himself to believe, *a new day in a new world.*

Henry Rogers was truly delighted to see Bess and Abigail at last. But what of this man traveling with them? Was he a rival?

"So who is this handsome fellow?" Henry asked with more than a passing interest, even before introductions could be made.

Abigail was quick to speak. "This is Jeremiah Hawkins. He has been most helpful to us both. I cannot imagine what the voyage would have been like without him." Abigail did not waver in her praise, even as she thought it best not to reveal Bess' incident aboard ship.

"No, it is I who am indebted to Abigail and Bess," Jeremiah corrected. "They made it possible for me to come to New York."

Before Rogers could comment on that startling admission, Bess spoke up. "We looked forward to getting every one of your letters," she smiled shyly. She was eager to change the subject from the voyage and to show her gratitude for the opportunity that Rogers had presented.

In turn, he was pleased by Bess' thoughtfulness. And her pleasing face and quiet manner reminded Rogers of why she had appealed to him before.

"The potential in commerce that I wrote you about has only grown," he confirmed. "Having those with me I can trust will enhance all of our prospects. We have much to discuss! If you follow me ladies, I have a room for you above the shop," Rogers explained. "Hawkins, there is a spot in the back, amid the inventory, where you can bed."

Jeremiah watched everything with a keen eye. He had sensed that

Rogers was leery of his presence, and while the man was cordial enough, Jeremiah's protective stance toward Abigail and Bess would not give way with a few happy words. Jeremiah would not rest easy until he could gauge Rogers' plans and whether they were truly honorable.

That being said, Jeremiah was excited to be in New York — to be in America! His life had shifted so markedly that where the wheel of fate would land him next he could not guess. For now, the back room of Henry Rogers' store suited Jeremiah just fine.

Their first weeks together in New York were spent with a watchful Henry Rogers assessing Jeremiah Hawkins, and a watchful Jeremiah assessing Henry.

It did not take long for Jeremiah to gain a sense of Henry Rogers, as the man had the gift of gab. For Henry, walking down the street was one continuous conversation, shaking hands with one person, exchanging pleasantries with another. It mattered little what the topic, Henry had an opinion and was willing to share it. Easy to smile and with a quick wit, Henry was charming, naturally using his way with words to develop trading partners. Commerce was the backbone of New York life, and with impeccable timing, Henry Rogers had put himself in the right place at the right time.

As the weeks passed, Jeremiah grew confident that Henry was indeed earnest, sincere and true to his word. The opportunities Henry had envisioned for Abigail and Bess in his letters were real. Henry's general store was a hum of activity and the sisters quickly became an integral part of its success.

Bess blossomed in the store. She lost some of her shyness as she discovered her capacity to engage customers in pleasant conversation, sharing her advice and impressing them with her knowledge of every item that lined the shelves.

Abigail revealed her own talents. Her skill with numbers was extraordinary. She could calculate the cost and profit of an entire order in her head. And in what seemed an instant, she could recall who owed what and when it was due. That Abigail was so capable made Jeremiah admire her all the more.

And Jeremiah too was an invaluable asset. Not only for his brawn, which was considerable, but also for his ability to spot trouble and diffuse a difficult situation. He became a surprising steady hand and just arbiter of disputes in Henry Roger's general store — which at times could be fierce especially over the exchange of money and goods.

With Bess, Abigail and Jeremiah so able in managing the store, Henry Rogers could expand his reach, buying and selling in markets all over the city. In time, he even began regular visits to other nearby colonies, locating goods and services to offer his customers that his competitors could not. And with greater success, Henry was more than generous in sharing the profits with his three "partners" — if not yet legally, surely in spirit.

Thus, Jeremiah was thriving in New York in a way he never could in England. It would not be long before he could earnestly begin paying off his debt to Abigail and Bess.

In only one way did he seem to stumble upon reaching New York. Somehow, he had lost his bearings when it came to Abigail and the promise of love.

Chapter 29

Colonial New York
FEBRUARY 1693

Bess & Henry, Abigail & Jeremiah

Though Jeremiah was having his difficulties, love was not alluding all at Henry Rogers' mercantile. Time and circumstance can change many matters, but others become solidified. In England, Henry indeed had an eye for Bess, which was fully rekindled upon seeing her again. And Henry's eager welcome had put both sisters at ease.

Whatever Bess had anticipated, she revealed little even to Abigail. The voyage to America had a strong impact on Bess — not only the harrowing incident but also seeing Abigail's fondness for Jeremiah. By the time they had reached America, Bess had reconsidered her own prospects. Henry Rogers was now at the top of that list.

Just as working in the store awakened a livelier side of Bess, the same was true for Rogers. He seemed so different from the person that Bess remembered back in England — or perhaps it was she who was different now. It was plain that Bess and Henry enjoyed each other's company. They were always laughing together in animated conversation. And though Bess had never been one to react to teasing, she and Henry both delighted in a silliness that amused themselves and others too.

As the new year arrived, it seemed only a matter of time before Bess and Henry would wed.

∞

Abigail was delighted for her sister and relieved too. But Abigail had another motive for wanting to see Bess settle down. Knowing her sister was happy and could not only survive but thrive in this new land, Abigail was free to completely turn her attention to her own happiness.

Reading Jeremiah's response to her wasn't always easy. Nothing further had happened between them since their kiss aboard ship. He had again become so formal. Yet Abigail was certain of his interest in her. His kiss had told her everything. She searched for a way to let Jeremiah know her feelings for him.

For his part, there was no doubt that Jeremiah wanted to be with Abigail. However, once in New York, he was determined to concentrate all his efforts on taking advantage of the opportunity before him. His debt weighed heavily upon him, and he reasoned that he must get out from under it before he could rightly pursue Abigail.

Still, he worried that if he delayed too long, would she find another? There were far more men than women in New York, this city of traders like Rogers and newcomers like he. Jeremiah couldn't help but notice that many a man's eyes followed Abigail's attractive shape as she went about her business.

Jeremiah had felt her in his arms. The memory was still clear and powerful for him. But with each passing day, that moment on the *Esmeralda* seemed farther away. Jeremiah was becoming more and more confused about what he should do.

Fortunately, as time passed, Abigail felt less and less confusion about the state of things with Jeremiah. Her longing for him had only grown, about which she had no shame. She was determined to uncover his feelings for her, once and for all.

So in the fifth month since their arrival, on a frigid winter night, Abigail slipped out of bed. She had waited until Bess, in the next room, was certain to be asleep. Then Abigail silently descended the stairs to the shop below. She glided across the cold floor, careful not to disturb a single item despite the pitch-black darkness, and continued out to where Jeremiah slept. Looking upon his face, her heart warmed with tenderness. Ever so quietly she slid under the covers beside him. He began to stir.

"Shhh," she whispered in his ear. "I've come to be with you."

Jeremiah started to speak, but she put her fingers to his lips. Then, without a word, she cradled his face, kissing his forehead, his cheeks, his lips. He could taste her sweetness and took her in his arms to draw her closer. She could feel his power and sighed, "Slowly."

Then she kissed his neck and shoulders with soft caresses, and Jeremiah closed his eyes. He had never bedded a woman who cared for him and offered tenderness and affection. Nor had he known a woman with passion rising. She stroked the length of his body and her ardent touch warmed Jeremiah and aroused his passion even deeper.

As they joined in one, she breathed into his ear, "I love you, Jeremiah." He opened his eyes, searching her face for the meaning behind the words. She gazed into the light shining from his eyes, and said again, "I love you, Jeremiah Hawkins."

Knowing it to be true, he heard himself say, "I love you too." With that promise, his fears and uncertainties, a lifetime of pain, began to slip away.

That night, the two were wed in everlasting devotion to each other — a heavenly bond beyond the laws of man. And by the time spring arrived in New York, following the marriage of Bess and Henry, Abigail and Jeremiah had pronounced their union before the earthly law as well.

For any that doubt the power of love to heal, there could be no better proof than Jeremiah Hawkins. He had lived all his life with the certainty that he was not good enough — not as a son, for his father had favored Benjamin; not as a brother, for he had been jealous of his twin; not good enough to light the diamond crystal.

Over and over again he had doubted himself, and that doubt had been an open sore that would not heal.

But here he was with Abigail — an angel, soft and loving, yet lion-hearted with courage and wisdom beyond the measure of most men. Yes, here he was with Abigail, and to her, he was more than enough — he was everything.

Chapter 30

The Hudson Valley

AUGUST 1693

Benjamin Hawkins

As they joyfully made their life together on Alfredo's land, Benjamin was ever thankful that he had confided in Catherine. He intuitively recognized that if he had left the crystal a secret, it would eventually stand between them.

And soon there was more joy. Catherine was with child! In the months that followed, the light of love between Benjamin and Catherine grew only stronger. And on the day in early August when her time came, Benjamin rode for Alyce Clark to assist with the birth, remembering his first trip to the Clark farm two years before. He had seemed so young then. Now he was a husband and soon to be a father.

Awaiting the arrival of what would be his first son, Benjamin walked the fields near the cabin, feeling the fullness of his life. His mind was not only on his dear Catherine, but on his father as well. With a mixture of happiness in his heart and longing for his father's presence, Benjamin silently addressed the billowing clouds and the sunlit sky.

Now I know how you felt waiting for Jeremiah and me to come into this world. I too am to become a father this very day! Everything will change yet again.... My only wish is that you were here.

He smiled, imagining how delighted Ethan would be if he could witness the birth of this child. But there was another matter Benjamin wanted to tell his father.

The crystal's light grows weaker and weaker each time I hold it. I know the same thing happened to you. But still it comes as a surprise…. Life, Father, seems to be like that.

And so it was, not long after Benjamin revealed the stone to Catherine, it began to dim in his hand. When he learned of the child on the way, and in the months that followed, the stone's light faded even more, until the day he raced to get Alyce, and it was completely mute in his pocket.

Indeed, the crystal's time with Benjamin appeared to be over. At first it saddened him. The stone had introduced him to the field of diamond light. Yet he also noticed that as the crystal's influence was weakening, his own power was growing. His connection to his own inner light had multiplied tenfold.

The crystal was a teacher stone, and perhaps its greatest gift to Benjamin was to awaken him to the light at the core of his being. And now another gift — in its silence, the crystal was showing him it was time to let it go.

As he thanked the crystal for serving him well, he remembered what Emma Wells had said to him that night at the fort, at the end of the blessed day when he first met Catherine: *"You are a remarkable young man, in touch with a multitude of inner resources that can assist in manifesting a reality beyond the convention of our time. And this is your moment. You have arrived at a great turning point."*

And so, indeed, it was a turning point. Yet Benjamin felt calm and confident of what was to come. The crystal was dormant and no longer lighting his way. He looked skyward and the summer sun warmed his face. He raised his arms and took in slow and steady breaths. With each inhalation, diamond light filled him. Images of a river of tiny diamond droplets flowed through his body, lighting every part of him.

He rode this current of radiance deeper and deeper inside, and discovered himself anew.

And then his attention was pulled back out into the world as Alexander Steward Hawkins, named for Catherine's father, screamed his presence far and wide. In that fateful moment, Benjamin accepted completely that his time with the diamond crystal had ended.

A few days later, as Catherine and the new babe slept, Benjamin wrapped the stone, along with Ethan's diary, in the burlap cloth. He put both in the knapsack that Daniel Fletcher had given him for the journey to America. Then the knapsack went into the bottom of a trunk in which Catherine stored her wedding gown, ready for a daughter someday.

Perhaps, when he was grown, Alexander would take up the crystal and feel its power as a healer, like his father and his grandfather Ethan. Benjamin knew not what might come next for the stone.

He only knew that his destiny had brought him to a new world; that, together, he and his beloved Catherine had arrived at a new life, creating new life as well. Now, bolstered by Catherine's alchemy of love, Benjamin would harness his own inner power — a gateway opened by the crystal's light and glorified within his being.

And the diamond crystal knew its time with this worthy being was over. The crystal had opened a cosmic doorway and Benjamin Hawkins had walked through.

Seasons come and seasons go, and everything is measured in due time.

Chapter 31

Colonial New York
APRIL 1694

Jeremiah & Emma Wells

It was a proud day for Jeremiah Hawkins when a new sign went up on a storefront in colonial New York City: *Rogers & Hawkins, General Mercantile.*

The year before, at his own wedding, Henry had promised Jeremiah and Abigail a partnership if the store continued to grow. They had put in tireless hours to ensure the store's success, and it was booming, thriving like never before.

But Henry's motives were far from altruistic. He had big dreams that went well beyond his general store. Henry had the golden touch in the world of mercantile trade. As raw materials and native goods flowed from the colonies to mother England, Henry made himself part of the deal-making in New York. And while the store was a center of that activity, Henry's business prospects were expanding far beyond even his earlier sights. With the need to travel greater distances to the Southern colonies, it made sense to make a formal partnership with the two people — besides his darling wife, Bess — he trusted most.

As Jeremiah and Abigail looked up at the store's new designation, they beamed with pride. For Jeremiah it was an outward sign — in every meaning of the word — of the transformation that had begun in Deal, edged farther aboard the *Esmeralda* and continued apace in New York.

While there were always twists and turns from day to day, in large measure, Jeremiah was now willing and able to glide along in wonder, where the flow of life eases downstream in boundless joy. After a lifetime of feeling *less than,* he had come to understand that no one could define who he was, *unless he allowed it.* From that moment on, he was determined to be his own master. And with that, he felt more and more released from the tether that chained him to his past.

Yet, not completely, for Jeremiah was soon to observe his twenty-first birthday. Then it would also be three years since his father's death and the last time he had cast eyes on his brother, for that day, despite all his mighty efforts, could never truly be forgotten, though it was now submerged below the din of everyday life.

On a fine April morning, not long after they raised the new sign, Jeremiah was carrying boxes and barrels of provisions out to the main floor of the store. A ship rumored to be full of pilgrims was expected in the harbor. Suddenly he heard a commotion outside, where a group of men and women were congregating in front of the store.

"I'm going to see what the fuss is all about. Perhaps there's news of the ship!" Jeremiah called to Abigail and Bess, who were busy stocking the shelves and envisioning a store full of new customers.

"Yes, husband, but do hurry back," Abigail answered. "There's much work to be done and I fear we're not ready!"

Jeremiah walked out and waded into the thick crowd. As he made inquires about the ship's whereabouts, he noticed the large gathering around a woman seated by a barrel. Across the top was a set of picture cards. She had a man, and the crowd, enthralled by her description of the meaning of each card.

She became aware of a young man joining the circle and shifted her gaze to him. Something about him seemed familiar. Her mind flashed: *Do I know you?*

In some unfathomable way, Jeremiah picked up her thought.

Then she noticed the sign: *Rogers & Hawkins.* Now she knew.

Ignoring the crowd, Jeremiah walked directly up to her. He felt an overwhelming need to speak to this woman.

"Hey fella, wait your turn!" someone yelled from the crowd. Jeremiah ignored the plea and held his place in front, watching the woman read the cards of the man seated before her.

Jeremiah was intrigued, though he quickly recognized the woman's trade. There were others like her who came through the city. They told fortunes, or offered other entertainment, to draw a crowd. The real business was selling homemade brew and handicrafts. Like many a peddler, no doubt she traveled from Massachusetts Bay to Pennsylvania to New York and back again, making a living selling good cheer. Jeremiah knew that he would have to wait until she was through accommodating those who would spend their coin.

When at last the crowd thinned out, Jeremiah approached her. "Can I help?" he asked, as she loaded her wagon.

"I can manage," she replied. "But what is your name?" She gave his face a piercing look.

"Jeremiah Hawkins."

"Hawkins. I thought as much. I trust you know mine by now. You've been watching for some time. Did you get an eyeful?"

"The sign says *Emma Wells* and you've been very entertaining."

"Would you like me to read your cards?"

Jeremiah shook his head.

"What then? You have something in mind."

"Have we met before?" he asked.

"No, but if you are the Hawkins of that sign," she said, pointing, "as I'm sure you are, you are the second Hawkins I have met. It was near two years ago, far up along the Hudson, when the French were stirring up trouble. He'd come to the fort for shelter, like the others, the settlers and farmers. His name … let me think … it will come to me…."

Emma closed her eyes, waiting for the name to appear.

In the silence that followed, Jeremiah knew it was Benjamin. He recalled his arrival in New York and the uncanny sense that Benjamin was near.

"Ahh!" she cried. "It will not come to me!"

"Benjamin," Jeremiah said quietly.

Emma had shrewdly watched and listened for how Jeremiah said the name. The markings of a turbulent life lined this young man's face. "Yes, it was *Benjamin.* He was running away from something that had happened to him, from someone he feared. Was he running from you?"

Jeremiah thought for a moment. Indeed, Benjamin had run away to escape his wrath. But something else was true as well.

"The man you met is my brother. And yes, he was running away from me. But I too had reason to run. The two of us, born at the same time, yet so different, both needing to escape from each other and from what we had become."

Then Jeremiah told Emma about his father, about Benjamin and about the crystal stone. Of everything that came before the fateful day when jealousy and greed turned brother against brother, and of the furious fight that ended with their father's death.

Emma not only read cards, she also read people. She looked upon Jeremiah with compassion and saw the broken heart he had endured. But she also saw a man filled with vigor, reclaiming his life. She had seen the same in Benjamin, who was restoring himself from the emotional barrage that had befallen all of them.

As an intuitive, Emma knew that certain life events coalesce around specific moments as turning points in time, and they reveal crucial elements about individuals. It was not coincidence that she had met these two brothers, each escaping from his past.

Emma had the ability to rise to a state of being, perched high above, where vision is limitless — a perspective that originated beyond time. Providence had led Benjamin and Jeremiah Hawkins to her.

"I am sorry that life has struck such a severe blow to you and your family. I do not know where your brother resides," she spoke truthfully, "but I know he is nearby."

She continued, watching for Jeremiah's reaction at her next words. "Look for further signs of your brother's whereabouts. Meeting me, Jeremiah, is but the first sign that you and Benjamin will meet again. And when you do, it will be up to the two of you to determine the nature of the circumstance — to exchange accusations and fists once again, or to experience reconciliation."

Jeremiah tried to envision a reunion with Benjamin. What would he be like? What had happened to him? And did he still have the crystal stone?

The turn of many seasons had transformed much about Jeremiah. But could he be sure his jealousy and his bitterness were cleansed from his heart? There was much that was right in his life, yet could he be sure this unresolved injury did not remain a poison that would slowly eat away at his happiness?

Imagining Benjamin before him, his mind flickered to his father. As Jeremiah looked at the sign above the store, now bearing his name, he yearned for his father to see it too — to know the good fortune that had come his way.

Without speaking, Emma reached out and grasped his hand.

"Madam, thank you. When I first saw you, I knew something significant would come of meeting you."

"Jeremiah, life gives us clues. All we need to do is see them."

Then, from among her wares, Emma retrieved a silver box bearing an image from a *carte da trionfi*. The lid depicted a woman standing by a pond, one foot in the water and the other on land. Above her were stars.

It was the same image as on the card that Emma had left for Benjamin at the fort. At that time, she thought it represented something that would happen, or perhaps a place to come, in Benjamin's life. Now she felt it represented something the brothers would experience together.

Though they were so different in nature, there was something about their relationship that struck her. Each brother had brought out the vulnerability in the other. It became a hidden strength that allowed their need for love to flourish. And it might draw them close again one day. If, in that moment, they reached for the tender place inside reserved for the other, a precious gift might be revealed.

"Here, this is for you. A remembrance of this occasion," Emma said as she held out the box.

Jeremiah could see that it was finely made. "I couldn't. It's too costly," he protested. "I have no surplus coin to offer for it."

Emma pressed the box into his hands. "It is my pleasure to give it to you. Now make me happy, Jeremiah Hawkins, and accept it graciously. And when you see your brother, and I trust you will someday, show him this box. Together, you will know what to do."

Emma Wells did not know all that the future might bring. Her gift, great as it was, saw the shadows of what might be — different paths possible that spread out ahead. Even so, some certainties were clear. She had seen something extraordinary in Benjamin. Now she saw the same in Jeremiah. The Hawkins' story was far from finished.

"Thank you, Emma," Jeremiah answered, holding the box firmly. "Will I see you again?" he asked.

"Only time will tell…. Let me leave you with this. I have learned many things in traveling the countryside, reading the cards. Contentment comes from being happy with who you are. Look toward your heart's desire for the guidance you need."

Jeremiah nodded and shook Emma's hand. He watched until she had climbed aboard her wagon and drove on toward the next stop on her journey.

Abigail found him then. "Who was that?" she asked. "You were gone so long."

"Forgive me, dearest … but I am not quite sure," Jeremiah replied. As they walked back to their store, his arm around her waist, he began telling Abigail of all that he had learned from Emma Wells.

Chapter 32

Cambridge, England
APRIL 1694

Daniel Fletcher & Isaac Newton

"It's been so long, my dear Isaac! It's so good to see you again. Thank you for taking the time from your busy day." Daniel Fletcher was excited to be with his old friend and to see him at the university where Newton had achieved such success.

"Fletcher, if I cannot make time for you, who can I? But you must tell me about this experience you had — a visitation you say?" Newton was also happy to see Daniel, but his mind, ever pressing, wanted to know immediately what was so urgent. What was so important that Daniel needed to see him in person.

"First, allow me to introduce my eldest son," Daniel explained, presenting Jacob, who had traveled from Hunstanton with his father.

"Yes, of course, Jacob." Newton extended his hand. "Your father has described you often in his letters. What a fine young man you are." Then, pointing each to a chair, Newton returned to his primary concern. "Now Fletcher, tell me your news about the Hawkins stone."

Daniel had a twofold reason for making the trip to Cambridge. He wanted his son to meet Isaac Newton, for Daniel could see a blossoming gift in Jacob's intuitive abilities. Yet even more critical, he needed Newton's assessment of a most unusual experience that he dared not relate in a letter. It pertained to their roles as alchemists and their mutual quest to understand the world and man's task in it.

Daniel's visitation was indeed connected to the Hawkins stone. With Newton leaning forward to catch every word, Daniel launched into his retelling of a most extraordinary story. Thus it began.

"One silent evening, I was sitting by the hearth, the family all retired, when a gentle rap came upon the door. Expecting no one, I was startled, but quickly went to answer the knock. When I opened the door, no one was there. I took a few steps outside and looked around. There was no sign of man nor beast, though strangely, on a cool night, I felt a warm breeze rush by me.

"Satisfied no one was about, I returned inside and closed the door, yet I immediately noticed that the atmosphere in the room had changed. A marked calm filled the air. As I went back to sit by the fire, there, in my chair, was the image of a man glimmering in light.

"You can imagine my astonishment. He had the most unusual glow about him. I could see that his life-force extended far beyond his body. He was bathed in a golden light and from his chest came luminous particles of diamond light. I have seen many life-force auras, but this was so unlike anything I had ever observed. His body flowed with crystal light. Prism colors of red and blue, purple and green glimmered in such pure quality, it was like he was made of shining gemstones.

"Then, Isaac, the specter gazed upon my face and started speaking in mellow, rhythmic tones of a land and a journey he had made.

"'Master Fletcher,' he said, 'I come from a land far away to be with you this night. I have traveled from high in the Himalayan Mountains, a place of wonders known to few people from the West. Like you, I was born in the English countryside. As a young lad, I journeyed to many places seeking truth. My quest, to know the alchemy of who I was and my place in the world. After many years of endless searches, which only momentarily satisfied my longing, one day my inner voice led me to the Himalayas, to Tibet and a monastery by a lake. There I met a holy man with whom I had the briefest audience.'

'Then Isaac, the specter voice *suddenly changed*. And it was as if the holy man was speaking directly to me. His voice was strong and commanding, yet sweeping in it's compassion. These were the holy man's words:

> "*Liberation comes when you free yourself from all earthly conditioning — the expectation your world places upon you. It is a pattern of thought that has been planted inside you by those who came before. There, beliefs are codified and passed on to you as your own. But they are limiting. Now you must expand your mind and heart and know the truth. Peer deep within to find who you really are. The creator of All That Is and his creations are One, not separate in any way. The creator and we are One, made from the same substance, the same life within the One life. The Eternal Being that occupies all space and all time, all universes — Was, Is and Will Always Be, without beginning and without end. There is only The One. There is nothing else — and this is our being. Look inside your heart, for there resides the portal of all truth and beauty, and all that you seek. Find the destiny that resides within.*'

"'Master Fletcher,' the specter addressed me again but was now back to his own voice. He began detailing his experience while listening to the holy man: 'As he spoke, I could feel the words reach into the center of my soul, and something shifted. My mind was clear, free of fear, doubt or questions. My heart was filled with wonder, and it was as if I were standing at the threshold of the eternal. It occurred to me that the holy man's very words loosened the bonds that had chained me to a karmic reality that had outlived its purpose. Yet, I had no idea of what to expect next.'

"'I was given a guide for my trip down the mountain,' the specter continued. 'Yet in traveling down a footpath, a sudden mudslide washed away the trail, separating me from the guide. I was not injured, nor was he, or so he called out to me, but we could not make our way back to each other. He shouted to me to double back. There, he said, I would find a fork in the road that would lead off the mountain another way. But when I reached that point, it too was swept away by the heavy rains. I was left to blaze my own trail.'

"'I had walked a distance when I came upon the entrance to a cave. I was about to pass it by when I saw a light flickering from deep within. My curiosity was overwhelmed, and I walked inside. And as soon as I entered, I felt an intense vibration that pulled me further into the cave. The light grew stronger, and I could see that I was in a tunnel-like structure. As I continued to walk deeper into the cave, I was suddenly in a chamber with a vaulted ceiling. At the very top was a vast shaft of light that opened to the sky and bathed the room in sunlight. I could see massive crystals. The very walls were crystalline.'

"'A ray of light illuminated one side of the cave. It was glowing in diamond light, with a shimmer that was hypnotic, and I was drawn to touch this glistening wall of radiant light. I placed the palm of my hand on it and could feel the power of the whole cave enter my being. I felt the petals of my heart unfurl and the top of my head opened to the sky. My mind expanded, unlocked from any constraints, and I found myself transported to another place, a cliff overlooking the sea.

"'There, on the shore, is a young man wading into the water. I see him stop to pick up a jewel that has washed up from the sea floor — a crystal, which comes alive in his hands. I see his life-force expanding beyond his body. He stands transfixed by the discovery of another world.'"

∞

Daniel paused, allowing this detail to sink in. "Isaac, you know of whom the visitor speaks." Newton nodded, signaling his understanding and encouraging Daniel to continue with the specter's description.

"'Then I am carried to another time and another scene. I am on the cliff above the shore again, but now the man in the water is beside me, though he does not know I'm there. He has the crystal in his hand. He is gazing into the future. The generations unfold before him. He watches two brothers, his sons. Providence speaks to them in tones that instruct what they must do. They stand at the ready. And the man who is their father dissolves into illumination, for he now dwells in the light of the everlasting present.'

"'Finally, a third image emerges. I am in a different place. A new light fills the mantle about me, and I am who I will eventually be — a very uncommon form, changed from the being that sits before you. I am with a man of older age, guiding him, as I have others, to the higher worlds. He looks toward me for explanation why he has found himself in an unfamiliar place. I know this man from somewhere. He is very familiar to me but for the moment I cannot place him. But I know someday I will.'

"'Then all the images fade into pure light and sound. I am in stillness, yet my mind is filled with a message: *Live your destiny, Keeper of Light.*'

"'The journey back to England has been long and arduous, with other twists and turns. But I have been guided here to be with you. The crystal cave that I stumbled upon, the young man holding the crystal by the sea, his sons, the old man to guide — you and I, friend — we are all bound together in a dance of the ages.'"

As Daniel finished the specter's story, all three men sat back in their chairs.

"I was speechless, Isaac!" Daniel exclaimed. "Much I could not understand, but I grasped the stranger was describing Ethan and his crystal, perhaps its origin and future events."

Newton remained silent, taking it all in. Then he spoke, but only a question: "Tell me, did anything happen after that?"

Daniel nodded. "The visit was near ended. The specter stood, thanking me for the warm fire. As he moved toward the door, I asked, 'What is it you want of me?'

"And he answered, 'The future is to be written. Search your heart and find your place in it. God has given you a song to sing. It is a song that never ends. All that changes is where you sing and in what octave.'

"Then the man left. I went back to the fire and allowed myself to take in what had just occurred. My dear Isaac, I believe this visit was the sign I have been looking for. Even as I sent Benjamin away for his own protection, I reasoned that it was not an end. I am certain now that Ethan's crystal has not fulfilled its purpose."

Isaac Newton had listened intently to his friend and knew the truth of Daniel's story from the sincerity of his voice. "There is no doubt your visitor was describing something significant about the crystal. Indeed, Daniel, there is much we do not know, but you have been given rare insight into the higher realms. I know not where else this story will lead — except for this, my good man. If you be up to it, you must make your way to America."

"Yes, I thought you would say as much," Daniel replied. "The difficult choices will come once I find Benjamin and the crystal. Isaac, do you think the specter's visit is an indication I should convince Benjamin that his time with the crystal is over? Is the crystal my destiny — our destiny — now?"

Newton held up his hands and shrugged, signaling his uncertainty. "Daniel, this diamond crystal is far more mysterious than it seemed in those brief moments you had with it. The crystal has its own destiny — one that appears connected to every Hawkins, to their generations, and in some unfathomable way, to your mysterious traveler, with his tales, premonitions and visions of the future. I cannot say whether you should take possession of the crystal, as I once believed. You must decide in the moment. Be wise and look for divine counsel. And should you return with it, we'll have our time together with the crystal. It may indeed be the very key to all we have sought."

Daniel reached out to clasp Newton's hand in quiet thanks. From the moment his ethereal guest had returned into the night, Daniel had known he must cross the great ocean to Benjamin Hawkins. Yet the journey, at his age of nearly sixty years, was arduous to consider. He had sought Newton's advice to be sure of this sign and that there was no other way.

"I will sail with Alfredo. He will know where Benjamin resides," Daniel explained.

"Ah, yes, our friend Alberto Alfredo, a man with the stars in his eyes," Newton confirmed. "Your Jacob must accompany you, for he too has that curiosity. Has he a wife to object to the voyage?"

Daniel and Jacob exchanged knowing glances. "He has no wife," Daniel chuckled, "though my Hannah will scold and worry about the both of us!"

Newton stood, giving Jacob a light tap on the shoulder. "Then it is settled! You will go with your father to America. I have something for your journey." He disappeared into the next room, returning swiftly with a telescope, one of his own design, which he handed to Jacob.

"Use this well, Jacob Fletcher," Newton directed. "Gravity explains the movement of the planets, but it cannot explain what — or who — sets them in motion. The heavens abound with truths, all waiting to be discovered. Be a wise explorer."

With that advice, Daniel and Jacob Fletcher bid Newton a fond farewell. They immediately made their way back to Hunstanton, to prepare for their passage to America — there to find Benjamin Hawkins and the diamond crystal.

Chapter 33

Daniel & Jacob Fletcher &
Captain Alberto Alfredo

With a sense that their journey would yield the unexpected, Daniel and Jacob Fletcher were off for the New World. It was the advent of summer and the best season for sailing. But even so, there was no way to know what might be ahead. Once they left port, certainty gave way to the unanticipated, which could shift even the best-laid plans. To Jacob, that was part of the excitement. But Daniel was wary, especially when considering what he would find once they reached the colonies in America.

Luck had been with the Fletchers, for Daniel's letter to Alberto Alfredo came back with excellent news. The captain planned yet another voyage to the colonies, leaving England from Deal, with New York the destination. His ship, *The Sutherland Rose,* would depart before the middle of June, if there were no unforeseen delays. Daniel considered the irony of sailing to America to find Benjamin in the very ship that had taken him there.

When Daniel returned from his meeting with Newton, in Cambridge, he had only a few weeks to rest and prepare for the ocean voyage. As expected, Hannah was greatly distressed at his going, though relieved that Jacob would be with him. Daniel promised to return to England, sailing with Alfredo if all went well, to arrive before the new year of sixteen ninety-five.

Daniel and Jacob reached Deal with days to spare. At the hour of departure, they were comfortably settled aboard ship, and went topside to see the crew lift anchor and set sail. For Daniel, it was a moment marked by a sudden rush back in time.

"It was nearly thirty years ago that Ethan Hawkins and I were bound for America. So much has happened. Yet it feels as if those days were but an instant ago," he confided to Jacob. "How I wish Ethan were here with us, to see this!"

Jacob looked at his father, yearning for his friend. "Whenever you speak of Ethan, it is with such love. You have kept his memory alive in your heart ever since his passing."

Daniel wore a sad smile as he replied. "Indeed, I have, Jacob, and always will. When you find someone in this world that you care for and who cares for you, it is a relationship to cherish. And when that person is gone, a hole in your life appears — one that can only be mended by filling it with loving memories."

A warm breeze caught the sails and the ship cut through the water at a stirring clip. Father and son felt the excitement of their adventure beginning.

"There, Father… watch the sails. Is Ethan not here with us?" Jacob asked. "Is it not his breath that fills them with air and sends us on our way?"

Daniel had come to know his son's perceptions to be insightful, yet to hear this wisdom struck him with newfound appreciation for Jacob. With a fresh twinge of sadness, Daniel considered the tragedy of Ethan's sons — and by contrast, his good fortune in the children he called his own.

∞

Quiet seas made for an easy voyage and gave Daniel time to clear his mind. One bright morning, bathed in sunshine, he walked about the deck, stopping now to gaze upon the sparkling water. It danced in diamond light as far as the eye could see, until it touched the horizon and flew up to the sky.

Inhaling the salty air, Daniel recalled the morning that Benjamin showed him Ethan's stone. It was as if Daniel were holding it again. He closed his eyes, and breathing in deeply, his senses filled with life flowing around him. His mind flew open to the wind, and he felt his very being encompass the entire ocean and the sky.

With his heart beating a gentle rhythm, Daniel perceived the uniqueness of his own life. Each breath became deeper and deeper, as if his whole body was breathing... his skin, his organs, his bones. His ribs were like gills, bringing in breath to light up his heart.

But it was not simply air that he took in. He was imbibing the diamond light that skipped along the water and sparkled on the waving crests. With each inhalation, life-force streamed through his body in waves of light. It was unlike anything he had experienced before. No thoughts, nor concepts, nor images entered his mind. There was no past, no future, only that moment and his spirit.

He wished he could hold on forever... but then it was gone. The waves, the light, the breath from beyond this world ... all disappeared to a place where he could not travel. But he came away knowing the purity of his spirit — a lesson he suspected the crystal might teach — and an unfolding beyond what he had previously imagined.

Daniel's inspirations came in the dazzling light of day, but for Jacob, the stars held untold mysteries to unlock. He used Newton's telescope on every clear night, and each time he peered through the lens, viewing the stars so close was like magic. Often Alfredo would join him to take a turn with the telescope, for it was a wonder to the old seaman too.

Nighttime, when his duties were lighter, was also when Alfredo could join Daniel and Jacob for conversation and ale. The captain was pleased to be taking his old friend to the New World, and many hours were spent telling old stories.

Alfredo was aware that Daniel's purpose in making the voyage was to see Benjamin, and he described what he knew of Benjamin's life in the New York colony. Alfredo repeated the tale of how Benjamin came to farm his land. And though Daniel and Jacob knew the details, he reveled in the retelling of Benjamin's derring-do aboard *The Sutherland Rose*. Daniel was also impressed by Benjamin's heroics at the fort and most surprised to learn that he was married and had a young son.

"Little did I realize, when I sent Benjamin to you, that he would become a prince of the Hudson Valley and find his beloved as well," Daniel teased.

"I had no part in finding him a wife, though she is a lovely lass," Alfredo laughed in return. "But seriously, settling virgin land is dangerous and no easy task. He does me a favor as much as himself."

Daniel nodded. "No doubt 'tis true. I'm anxious to see Benjamin and his handiwork, farming your lands. After his father's death, I felt an obligation to Ethan to protect his sons from each other. Benjamin and his brother were teetering at the edge of oblivion."

"Benjamin never speaks of a brother. Is he older? Younger?" Alberto asked.

"Jeremiah is his name. They are twins, though they do not carry the exact likeness," Daniel explained.

Alfredo registered his surprise. "What of Jeremiah? Where is he?"

Daniel shook his head, lamenting his inability to guide Ethan's other son. "Jeremiah left Hunstanton two years ago — vanished."

"And no word of him?"

"No word. Nothing. After he mourned his father, he was left with such fury burning inside. He could well be dead, for he drew his knife on me and might do so to another. God rest his soul, if that be true."

Alberto saw the sorrow in Daniel's eyes. "Ah, Fletcher, he might have a better ending than you know. Providence is a most mysterious phantom that yet transforms the most cunning mind and the hardest heart," Alfredo observed.

"Indeed. I hope you are right," Daniel replied.

"Will you come with us to see Benjamin — and check on your land?" Jacob asked.

"Perhaps. I will know more after we arrive," Alfredo explained. "My return cargo is to be mainly beaver pelts, so sufficient inventories are needed to make the voyage to England profitable. If the warehouses are not full when we make landfall, then no doubt there were will be ample time to travel inland."

"It would please me to spend more time together," Daniel stated plainly.

Alfredo responded with a broad smile. "It would please us both! The ale rolls down the tongue easier when we enjoy it together."

Chapter 34

Colonial New York
AUGUST 1694
First week

Daniel Fletcher & Jeremiah Hawkins

Steady winds and no major storms meant *The Sutherland Rose* was entering New York Harbor by the first days of August. Alfredo maintained that Daniel Fletcher had carried the good luck with him. Upon docking, Alfredo learned that it would be nearly October before he might expect his cargo of furs to fill the ship and pay for the return voyage. But all the better, for not only could he travel with Daniel and Jacob to meet Benjamin, but they could return with him, to England, and Daniel would easily keep his promise to Hannah, to see her again before next year.

Fredrick Nichols, Alberto's able first mate, stalwart and trustworthy, would keep watch over the ship while they were in New York and the captain was away up the Hudson. When the time came to sail, Nichols would ensure *The Sutherland Rose* had its full complement of crew. Not that it would be difficult. Morale was high on Alberto's ship. With the English colonies growing, new markets were expanding, and ships and crew were much in demand. And sailing with Captain Alfredo, an expert navigator, was considered fortunate indeed. He was among the most sought-after captains, sailing the trade routes, carrying people and goods to and from Europe and America.

Daniel, of course, was delighted that Alfredo would join Jacob and him in their trek up the Hudson, and who better to be their guide.

The party wasted no time in preparing for their reunion with Benjamin. They would need horses, a wagon, guns and gunpowder, and food and ale for the journey. Alfredo knew from his ship's quartermaster that Henry Rogers' store was reliable and sold fairly priced provisions. Now he set off with Daniel and Jacob for Rogers' mercantile, and then straight away to find Benjamin.

When they arrived the sign above the store immediately struck Daniel. "Rogers & Hawkins," he recited. "Hawkins? Alberto, could this be Benjamin?"

Alberto waved away the thought. "No! How could it be Benjamin? 'Tis another Hawkins, that's all. Do you think every Fletcher is a relation?"

With that they entered the store. A most capable-looking woman was present to greet them. "Hello, and what shall you have?" she asked.

In the same moment, from the back room a voice rang out in song.

"Don't mind my husband's singing. Our daughter is born three months today and he is all beside himself with celebrating," she explained.

"The world favors the light-hearted, isn't that right, Daniel?" Alfredo responded.

The singer was undeniably English. As Daniel looked around the well-stocked room, his mind was still on the Hawkins connection. Could it truly be a mere coincidence?

"Might I ask your name, madam?" Daniel asked.

"Abigail Hawkins."

"Are you the Hawkins of the sign?" Alberto asked.

"Yes, my husband and I."

"And his name?" Daniel asked.

"Jeremiah"

"From Hunstanton, in England?"

"That's right."

Daniel looked at Jacob, who mirrored his father's astonishment and concern. Jacob was well aware of Jeremiah's threats and had been relieved when he had vanished from Hunstanton.

Jacob stepped closer to his father and could feel his fists clenching, notwithstanding the calm demeanor of the woman who claimed to be Jeremiah's wife and the carefree birthday song that still filled the air.

"Come out here, Jeremiah," Abigail called to her husband.

The singing stopped and then a muffled voice, which grew clearer as it came closer. "My dearest Abigail, if you want me to finish stacking these wares, best leave me to it…." Jeremiah was still speaking as he appeared in the doorway.

"These gents seem to know you from Hunstanton," Abigail explained.

"Daniel…," Jeremiah's voice was barely audible as the blood ran from his face. He flashed back to the last time he had seen Fletcher, in the cottage, holding a knife to Daniel's belly, demanding he reveal where Benjamin had gone.

More than once Jeremiah wished he could return to that time — could replay the day that his father died, and that instead of returning to the cottage and finding Benjamin with the crystal stone, he had gone to the sea to swim.

Now he wished that Daniel Fletcher had never entered his store, or that he and Abigail had been on an errand and it was Henry and Bess receiving them. Whatever had brought Daniel Fletcher to him, Jeremiah wanted no part of it. His life was moving forward. He did not want to be pulled back.

Then he recalled his meeting with Emma Wells and her prophecy. From the stunned look on Daniel's face, he had not come to America to find this Hawkins. Surely his presence in New York was because of Benjamin — which meant his brother was near.

A revolving mix of emotions swirled in Jeremiah's head. He felt shame for his violent and drunken past. He was a better man than that now. The jealousy that had made him nearly mad with rage had faded, as if it never happened.

But it did happen. And seeing Daniel Fletcher standing there, Jeremiah could feel it stirring again. Those memories could too easily bring him back to his father lying dead on the floor and Benjamin running away. It was a place that ripped his heart out and shattered his mind — a place he had hoped never to visit again.

Jeremiah looked at Abigail, whose face was calm, yet he could see worry forming in her eyes. He had never told her the depth of his pain, but she had always known it and had accepted him, warts and all. What higher love was there? It was something that filled his days with gratitude and made him love her all the more. He wished he might sweep her up at this moment and the two of them might disappear.

Instead, Jeremiah slowly extended his hand toward Daniel. What else could he do? He hoped Daniel would accept his offer, get what he came for and then leave — and Jeremiah could go back to his new life.

Daniel Fletcher eagerly grasped the open hand and then, after an awkward pause, he placed his other hand on Jeremiah's shoulder. Daniel could feel Jeremiah's muscles tense, even as he accepted a tentative embrace. An unanticipated exchange silently swept between them, an acknowledgement of those who are connected by bonds that are indefinable.

As they let go of each other, neither Jeremiah nor Daniel were able to speak. Abigail, who could feel their emotions, broke the silence. "I am Abigail, Jeremiah's wife," she reintroduced herself.

Daniel then did the honors for his party, first introducing Alberto Alfredo. Jeremiah remained silent as Daniel presented Jacob to Abigail, and then himself. "Jeremiah's father and I were the closest of friends. I loved Ethan dearly."

Abigail immediately placed Daniel, knowing the story of the crystal stone, of Benjamin and of Ethan's death.

Then Daniel addressed Jeremiah. Unable to wait any longer, he needed to know. "Jeremiah, how did you come here — to America, to New York? Did you come to seek out Benjamin?"

Jacob listened intently to his father's direct but honest words, wondering what Jeremiah might say. He'd always had sympathy for Jeremiah, though he kept it to himself, for Benjamin was clearly the favored son of Ethan Hawkins.

Abigail began to speak, but Jeremiah stayed her voice with a light touch on her arm. "When I left Hunstanton I followed the coast to Deal, and there providence brought me to Abigail and her sister Bess, who is married now to Henry Rogers. I sailed with them, in debt to them, for opportunity here in America."

Daniel and Alfredo exchanged knowing looks at the mention of Deal — that Jeremiah had followed nearly the same tracks as Benjamin.

Jeremiah rarely showed affection in front of others, but now he took Abigail's hand, clearly displaying his love, but also in need of the source of strength they drew from each other.

"I did not come to find Benjamin. But I know he is here. I knew it the day our ship entered the harbor. I felt him near. And then I received another sign, a few months ago. But I've never sought him out."

Daniel didn't know what to make of this man that looked like Jeremiah Hawkins, but whose nature seemed so changed. Even so, memory made Daniel cautious. "But where do you believe your brother to be?" he queried.

Jeremiah laughed. "So you test me still, I see?"

Daniel started to protest, then saw the honesty in Jeremiah's face and knew he must be honest as well. "Can you blame me, lad? You and I have been at odds for some time."

"True enough. The Jeremiah of those days may still reside within me, but he no longer controls my every thought. By God's grace, I've landed on the shores of happiness, and with the love of Abigail, who saved me from ruin. I had a choice. Carry the weight of sorrow upon my shoulders and allow the poison of revenge to flow through my veins, or let go and live the light of a new life. Thus I have been blessed."

Daniel was struck by Jeremiah's sincerity. "So you have," he agreed, bowing to Abigail in respect.

"I have something to show you," Jeremiah stated, then moved swiftly to the stairs, toward the rooms he shared with Abigail.

"You see, Mr. Fletcher," said Abigail, moving to reassure Daniel, who couldn't help but be captivated by this gracious woman and her obvious love. "Truth cannot be denied. It rings clear from the heart. Whatever you may recall of Jeremiah, his life is different now."

Then Jeremiah reappeared, holding a silver box.

"This was given to me by a woman, Emma Wells, a reader of cards and peddler of wares who entertained a crowd outside our store, on a warm day in April. It was she who told me of Benjamin. She had met him some two years ago, at a fort up along the Hudson, where he had gone with other settlers to escape a French force. She gave me this box and said someday Benjamin and I would meet — and together we would know it's meaning and what to do."

Jeremiah laid the box on the counter, to give the others a closer look. "It is indeed most beautiful," said Daniel, as he inspected it. Then he noted the perplexed look on Alfredo's face. "What is it?"

"This image … the waterfall, the pool of water, the rock outcrops … I know this place!"

"You've seen it in your travels?" Daniel asked, expecting to hear a tale of darkest Africa or some tropical isle.

"It is on my land," the captain confirmed.

Daniel immediately recognized the implication. "Jeremiah, I have come to find your brother," he admitted.

"Of course you have. I knew it the moment I saw you. And does it have to do with my father's crystal stone?"

"It is about the stone."

Jeremiah looked away and said nothing.

"Benjamin lives on Captain Alfredo's land.... Come with us...," offered Daniel. The words that escaped his lips surprised everyone, including himself.

But none more than Jeremiah, who raised his head and looked squarely at Daniel, expressionless, his eyes unreadable, even as emotion churned inside of him and a thought took hold: *A chance to see Benjamin again. Ah, the look on his face....*

Chapter 35

The Hudson Valley
August 1694
First week

Benjamin & Catherine

Catherine Hawkins watched her husband's rhythmic breathing as he slept next to her. Admiring his kind face, her heart was full of love for him; for the life they had together; for little Alexander, about to turn one; and for the babe that kicked inside of her.

But Benjamin's sleep had been fitful for the last few weeks, and she worried. Something was disturbing him. There was a burden he had yet to share.

Catherine heard Alexander stirring. Though she hated to wake Benjamin, it was time. The sun was up already. She kissed his forehead and whispered, "Good morning."

This was the latest Benjamin had slept for months. He was usually awake before sunrise, not only to accomplish all that he needed to do, but also to fill his senses with the newness of night turning to day. Every morning he looked forward to feeling the power of life renewing itself. He'd breathe it in deeply, willing it to flow through his veins.

"I love you, Benjamin Hawkins…," Catherine purred, nudging him again.

A soft smile formed on Benjamin's lips. "How are you today?" Waking to Catherine gave each day a peaceful start. He placed his hand on her belly.

His touch was reassuring, but it tickled too and she giggled. "I'm fine, and this child is fine. Now it's time to get up! Alexander will be awake and demanding breakfast any moment."

"Just let me linger a while longer with you." Benjamin took Catherine in his arms. She closed her eyes and they gently rocked back and forth.

"I knew the first instant I saw you that the heavens had unlocked the gates to happiness," Benjamin murmured. Catherine opened her eyes, and her light came pouring into his.

Unlike most days, when the earth called to him with all the work to be done, after a fine morning meal, Benjamin took his coffee and went to sit outside. He allowed himself to enjoy the finest beans that William Clark had brought back from a visit to New York.

Benjamin looked out upon the fields of corn and wheat and felt satisfied that he was fulfilling his pledge to Alberto Alfredo. He was certain the captain would agree.

And he should know soon. A letter from Alfredo had arrived from England in the middle of July. As was the captain's habit, he wrote whenever he planned a voyage to the colonies and might journey up the Hudson, to see Benjamin and the land.

But this letter carried the stunning news that Daniel Fletcher would be with Alfredo aboard *The Sutherland Rose* when he next arrived in New York, which was expected to be in August. Daniel's son Jacob was making the journey too. It was clear their purpose was not to settle in America. Alfredo included Daniel's intention to return to England before winter storms made the crossing even more perilous.

They were all were eager to see Benjamin, Alfredo wrote. He would accompany Fletcher and son, if he could, or they would make their way with a guide.

But why would Daniel Fletcher be coming to America? And why didn't he write himself? Instinctively Benjamin reasoned it had to be about the crystal stone. Was Daniel coming to take it from him? Did he want it for himself or for his friend Isaac Newton?

Only something that extreme would explain why Daniel, at his age, would board a ship for a voyage that could be perilous, and would take two months or more, even if the weather was favorable.

Benjamin felt conflicted. To see Daniel Fletcher again, the friend who had helped deliver him to a new life — and to his beloved Catherine's love — made his heart swell with gratitude. But how would Daniel respond to the news that Benjamin no longer worked with the crystal? That the object Benjamin had coveted, around which was so much heartbreak, now sat silent in the bottom of a chest, on hold for the future, like Catherine's wedding dress?

Daniel would be shocked, no doubt. Yet he could see it as a fateful sign. He knew the crystal had stopped speaking to Ethan, and now it grew dim in Benjamin's hand too. Would Daniel feel all the more empowered to take the crystal, because Benjamin's time with it was done?

And yet, was it? What if some day he wanted the crystal in his hand again, or needed it to heal Catherine, Alexander, this babe or others to come, even himself?

No, I must deny Daniel's request, as I did years ago.

But if he was coming all this way for the crystal, he must have a good reason. Daniel was sure to be more determined to take it away.

What to say to Daniel — and how he might respond — preyed on Benjamin's mind. He also feared what Alfredo might think of him if he refused Daniel. And was Jacob coming simply to protect his father? Though Benjamin was hardy and strong, he blanched at the thought of another fight over the crystal.

As the days grew closer to when he might expect Daniel to arrive, Benjamin grew more and more anxious. In truth, he breathed a sigh of relief each day that no visitors appeared on the horizon.

Chapter 36

Colonial New York
AUGUST 1694
Second week

Jeremiah & Daniel

Since Daniel Fletcher had appeared at Rogers & Hawkins, General Mercantile, Jeremiah had struggled with what to do next. Should he accept the invitation to travel up the Hudson to see Benjamin?

Yet, just as he'd felt when he first saw Daniel, Jeremiah still feared dredging up the past. Why, when he was so happy?

But the woman, Emma Wells, had said that he and Benjamin would meet again.

Even so, was he ready for that meeting? Was this the right time, or should he wait?

Hearing a prophecy of a someday meeting with Benjamin was one thing. But knowing that he could meet Benjamin *in a matter of days* was quite another.

How might he respond if he saw the crystal in Benjamin's hand? Would he be jealous again? And what did he want from Benjamin? Did he still need for his brother to explain himself, to ask Jeremiah for forgiveness?

∞

From the first mention of joining Daniel Fletcher to meet Benjamin, Abigail could feel Jeremiah's uncertainty.

For days, as the Fletchers and Alfredo made their preparations, Jeremiah and Abigail talked of what to do.

"Jeremiah, if you go to your brother, it can be a gracious and noble gesture," Abigail proposed. "Your brother needs to see you, to know how you feel — to know who you are. Your world was broken, and now it's not. Your life, our life, is filled with far more joy than sorrow. To leave your brother with a memory of yesteryear is not fair to him, or to you."

Jeremiah shook his head. "You speak of fairness. But was my father 'fair' to me? My brother 'fair' to me? Why should I worry whether I am 'fair' to him?"

Abigail reached out to hold him tenderly. "No, dear one, they were not fair. But *you* can rise above — *you* can go beyond. What others do — even your own folk — need not rule your actions."

Calmed by her touch, Jeremiah felt his anger subside. But his agonizing indecision still loomed. "I know you are right," he agreed. "Yet doubt is an uncompromising master."

Now Abigail faced him with hands on hips and determination enough for them both. "Go or not, you are not bound to any master, Jeremiah Hawkins, including the pains of the past! You are as much your own captain as Alberto Alfredo. Believe it, my love."

As for Daniel Fletcher, no sooner had he issued his impromptu invitation that day than he wished he had kept silent instead — at least until he had a clearer understanding of Jeremiah's true disposition. In the moments after, he was unable to read Jeremiah's face or tell from his eyes what emotions he was feeling. And that concerned him.

But what was done, was done. Daniel could only wait for Jeremiah

to make up his mind, as he, Jacob and Alfredo made their preparations
to travel inland — and discussed the possibilities of the meeting between
the Hawkins brothers.

Though Daniel saw and felt the changes in Jeremiah, the brothers
had been such a volatile mix. What would happen if Jeremiah saw
Benjamin again? Would he revert to his bitter and jealous nature?

"What if he is violent again?" Daniel asked, remembering the sharp
point of Jeremiah's knife. "And what if Benjamin has more fight in him
now? Might your first mate, Nichols, come with us? There's a man who
could crack a head. He and Jacob would keep order."

Alfredo waved away the suggestion. "Nichols is needed aboard ship.
It remains up to us, Daniel, to make sure that if Jeremiah decides to
journey with us, he and Benjamin do not come to blows."

Daniel tried to image all the possible outcomes. Yet he was also distressed by an even deeper concern. Yes, Daniel was bothered by what
might happen between the Hawkins brothers, but it was the influence
of the crystal that was beyond prediction. How would Jeremiah react
to the allure of Ethan's diamond crystal stone. Daniel had held it only
once and he could easily recall its power. How might his own Jacob
respond, or even Alfredo?

With his invitation to Jeremiah, Daniel had spun the wheel of
fate and now he was left with an eerie question. Had he set in motion
another tragedy?

As the hours passed Daniel still could not settle his mind. Then
unexpectedly, from a wiser place, Daniel felt the hand of Ethan resting on his shoulder. For the moment, it eased his mind. He knew not
whether Jeremiah would take him up on his offer. And he had no way
of knowing whether it would turn out well. But his mind rested in its
place as he heard the words; *it will be what it will be.* And even though

in the moment how everything would play out was beyond his control, he knew he had no choice but to let it be and accept that it would unfold in the course of time as it was meant to be. It was up to Jeremiah now.

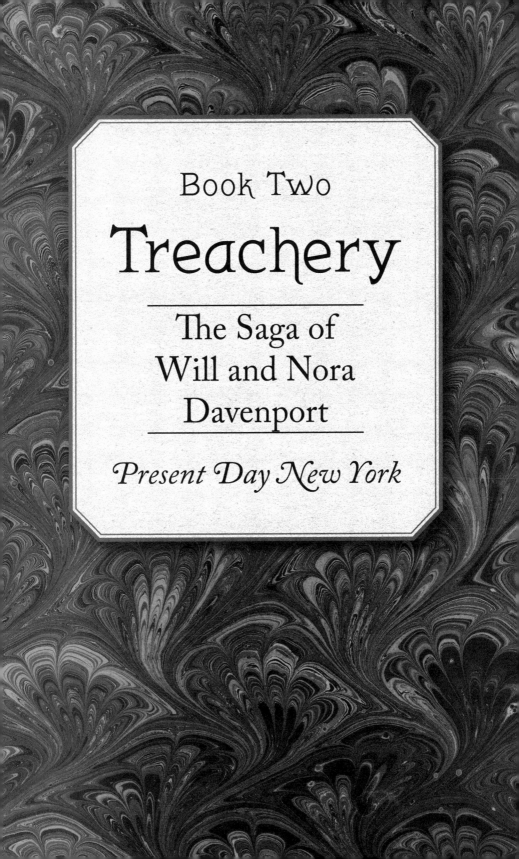

Book Two

Treachery

The Saga of Will and Nora Davenport

Present Day New York

Prologue

Ken Davenport

"Did you see this yet?" Molly McQuire bounded into the office, her high heels rhythmically tapping the floor. She raced over to her boss, sitting behind his desk, and jammed the front page under his nose.

Ken Davenport's face registered initial confusion at Molly's dramatics, so unlike her usual discreet arrival.

Then Ken rocked back in his chair, bracing himself, as Molly pointed her finger at the headline of the story in the lower left column. "Here!" she said urgently.

Simmering frustration immediately gave way to full-blown worry for his brother as Ken took in the words: *NOTED COSMOLOGIST AND JOURNALIST WIFE MISSING.*

"Damn it, Molly!" he swore. "Cooper thought he could keep this out of the news!"

Ken's friend, NYPD detective Jack Cooper, had tried but there were clearly limits to what he could do. And of course, Ken himself could not stop the university from reporting an explosion in an office on campus. The situation was spinning out of control.

"What the hell did Will get himself into this time?" Ken muttered, giving the desk a hard pound with his fist. He'd been concerned ever

215

since his telephone call with Will the day before — a call that was abruptly cut off as they talked, no doubt from the blackout.

But then Will had disappeared. No messages, no calls, nothing, not even when cell service was restored. There was a growing knot of worry in the pit of Ken's stomach.

He began scanning the article in *The New York Times*, now and then jabbing a finger at an offending sentence.

"*Dr. Will Davenport, a noted scientist, and his wife Nora Martin, an award-winning freelance journalist, are missing following an explosion at the Upper West Side university campus where Dr. Davenport was reportedly using an office to work on a forthcoming book. Neither is believed to have been in the office at the time of the explosion. The couple, who moved from California to New York in recent weeks, are wanted for questioning. Repeated efforts to locate them have been unsuccessful, leading the police to declare them missing....*

"*NYPD detectives investigating the explosion would not comment on the nature of the blast or materials recovered from searches of the damaged office and the couple's Westchester home. At a news conference held at police headquarters, Commissioner Holloway declined to speculate on whether the blast was connected to the blackout yesterday affecting New York City and the metropolitan region....*"

Ken jumped to a paragraph near the end of the piece:

"*Although Dr. Will Davenport is not affiliated with the university, his brother, Dr. Kenneth Davenport, is a professor of geology there. A call to Dr. Kenneth Davenport was answered by a research assistant, Molly McQuire, who stated that Professor Davenport was concerned about his brother and sister-in-law, but had no further comment.*"

Ken frowned, taking a deep breath to settle his mind. "Well, there you go, Molly, your name in the paper. Even spelled correctly. No McGuire with a G, for once." Molly gave a half-hearted smile, which Ken acknowledged with a wink.

The police would surely want to interview him. In fact, Ken wondered why he hadn't already received a visit from the NYPD. He guessed Cooper had something to do with the delay.

"No matter what they say here in the paper, certainly NYPD, probably FBI and Homeland Security too, all suspect Will had something to do with the explosion *and* the blackout. Molly, my brother is in a lot of trouble…a lot of trouble…."

Molly looked for a way to soothe Ken. It distressed her to see him so upset. She adored him, and ever since an office romance blossomed between them, she couldn't help her growing affections. Molly knew she was falling in love and worried she'd get hurt — another research assistant bedded by her divorced professor.

For his part, approaching forty and having been stung by a seemingly idyllic marriage turned ugly, Ken was taking his relationship with Molly slowly. What the future would bring he couldn't say. Yet with great tenderness and affection, Molly had eased his loneliness not long after his wife served him with divorce papers out of the blue. For that he was grateful and wondered, now and then, about the possibility of loving again.

But all that would have to wait. Ken's pressing issues were multiplying. "Will's not the only one in trouble," he revealed to Molly. "I called in a number of favors to get him that office. Let's just say there are some very unhappy people walking around this building!"

Ken returned to the article, stroking his chin, a sign he was deep in thought. He was trying to solve the puzzle of what evidence the police might have — and what Cooper might be able to tell him — and the even bigger puzzle of what made his brilliant, yet misguided sibling become so deeply involved in someone else's business.

"Maybe some media attention will give Will a chance to get his side of the story out?" Molly offered hopefully.

"I wish that were so," Ken mumbled wistfully. "But I'm afraid what Will really needs now is time to put the pieces together and prove his innocence."

Ken's voice trailed off as he stared again at the headline, shaking his head and rubbing his forehead in the way he did when he was deeply perplexed. He took comfort only in the fact that Nora was apparently with Will. She was as steady as they come and always had her husband's back.

But Ken Davenport didn't know the half of it — of what both Will and Nora had stumbled into and been ensnared by since arriving in New York only a short time before. Nora had pursued a story that had boomeranged. And since first learning about a letter from Isaac Newton, Will had been chasing after the lost diary of a Newton associate and possible 17th century alchemist named Ethan Hawkins. The diary was invaluable for its history — and, possibly, something more. Most significantly, it was stolen property.

And now Will was in even deeper trouble, tied to a plot to subvert the city's energy grid. And not to be overlooked, a body with two bullet holes in the torso had been found in Will's temporary office.

Suddenly frustrated again at his own powerlessness, Ken fumed aloud. "I told that damn brother of mine he was sticking his nose in where it didn't belong! I told him don't get involved in that whole diary thing. Keep your priorities straight and focus on writing and publishing your book!"

That Will might not be able to clear himself was Ken's rising fear. Will could be many things — reckless, careless and admiringly fearless — but he was no saboteur and certainly no murderer. Yet a mountain of circumstantial evidence was building against him, and unless things turned around in a hurry, the momentum toward guilt would soon take on a life of it's own.

"Now the shit has hit the fan!" Ken sputtered. "And I can expect a call from Long Island at any moment. What the hell am I going to tell them?"

Molly knew "Long Island" was code for Ken and Will's parents. "When they call I'll answer. I can say you're in a meeting," she suggested. "That'll give you more time — and maybe to hear from Will?"

"Thanks, kiddo, but my folks will need to hear from me." Ken looked at Molly, feeling truly glad for her presence and wanting in that moment to tell her so. "Mol ...," he began, when a light tap on the office door startled him into silence.

They eyed the closed door as an envelope slid under and across the floor. Molly stifled a yelp as Ken jumped to his feet. Both stood still, listening for retreating footsteps. There was not a sound.

Ken stepped gingerly toward the envelope, which bore his name in a messy script. As he slowly picked it up, he thought how ridiculous he was going to feel if this package was some cowardly grad student's late research data.

Ken eased open the envelope, scanned the paper inside and then rushed to open the door, amazing Molly with the speed of his movements. The hallway was empty.

"What is it?" she whispered and moved by his side as he read the letter again, more slowly now.

> *Ken,*
>
>   *Nora is with me and we're both OK. Tell your detective friend Cooper we're innocent. We think the proof may be on the body they found in the office. And sorry, bro. Hope you're not in trouble too.*
> *Love you,*
> *Will*

Ken was relieved to hear from Will, but no less worried and apprehensive. What was going on? Why didn't Will say where he was?

"What's with the mystery, Molly?" Ken grumbled, angst giving way to irritation. "Why didn't he come right out and tell me what Cooper should look for? It's always reading tea leaves with Will!"

Chapter 1

Will Davenport

"*IF YOU SEE SOMETHING, SAY SOMETHING.*"

Ever since 9/11, Metro North railroad played the same sometimes blaring, sometimes barely audible, recorded message to commuters making their way from points north to Grand Central Station on the East Side of Manhattan.

Will Davenport shuffled up the station steps to the platform for the train to New York, juggling his briefcase in one hand, a cup of coffee bought from a station vendor in the other, and a laptop computer over his shoulder. It was all he could do to keep everything in balance, willing the coffee not to spill all over him. His legs were not pumped yet with their morning dose of caffeine. Knowing no one, having moved recently from Los Angeles, Davenport traveled alone.

For his maiden commute, Will had given himself ample time to get to the station and find parking. Granted, it was Tuesday, but he assumed there'd be as many people as on a Monday morning. Then, just as he was thinking he'd timed it well, an announcement crackled over the station loud speaker: *"The 7:31 express for New York is running ten minutes late."* Will glanced at his watch: 7:20. *Damn! Twenty more minutes to wait! And late the first day!* he thought. *Maybe I should just drive in from now on.* He certainly wasn't intimidated by traffic, especially after a lifetime of navigating California highways.

Yet thoughts of what to expect today — and the days ahead — gave Will plenty to think about, and before he knew it the train was pulling into the station. He became caught in a primal rhythm as his fellow commuters pressed toward the doors, waiting for them to open.

Will always marveled at crowd behavior. While people came in different sizes and shapes, the herd seemed determined to fill the same space.

As he entered the train, he was jostled by an oblivious — or obnoxious — young man with a backpack slung over his right shoulder that gave Will and others a good whack. The guy was rushing from the seat he'd been occupying to a row that had just emptied of people getting off the train at this stop.

What an idiot, Will thought, and stared at him, waiting for an apology. A seasoned commuter took a more direct approach: "Hey, watch it with that backpack!"

The man ignored Will and everyone else, and jumped into the empty row swinging the backpack off his shoulder and clutching it close to his chest.

"Great, my first New York weirdo," Will mumbled to himself.

The train was far more crowded than he expected. Clearly, if he planned to commute by rail, he would have to perfect his ability to spot choice seats.

Will ventured up and down the aisle and was about to go into the next car when he saw a place open in a four-seater — two seats facing each other.

The trio of women already there appeared to know one another. As Will approached they were all frowning at him, and he had a moment of indecision. *Do they recognize me?*

But not wanting to stand for the next fifty minutes, Will decided this was probably as good as it gets. The women displayed their annoyance and gathered the various items they had placed on the empty seat and reluctantly made room for Will. He slid onto the seat and tried to settle himself. The threesome, resigned to the intruder, ignored him as they resumed their conversation.

Will looked around, getting his bearings. He was facing into the car, which gave him a clear view of his fellow travelers.

He quickly noticed the young man who had jostled him sitting a few rows away. He was still clutching his backpack like he was holding on for dear life. He was also fidgety, alternately patting the backpack and rubbing his eyebrow with his other hand. *That guy looks awfully nervous*, Will thought. *What the hell's he carrying, anyway?*

The possibility sent adrenaline surging through Will. Could there be something dangerous inside — say, a bomb? Boston, Madrid, London, Paris … plenty of reminders that it could happen. Will looked at the other passengers near the man, but no one else seemed the least bit disturbed. *Hmmm, am I the only one paying attention … or am I just being paranoid?*

As Will continued to watch the backpack guy, he was relieved to see him quiet down. He still seemed odd and uncomfortable to Will's California sensibilities. *But,* Will thought, *perhaps this guy is just Exhibit A of the famous New York pace and brusqueness.*

With a slight shrug of his shoulders, Will relaxed into his seat. Better to use the forty-five minutes or so left of the trip into Manhattan to do some real work, rather than play amateur detective.

He pulled a folder of notes from his briefcase for the book he was working on — his redemption, he hoped — but found it impossible to concentrate. His eyes roamed the car again and then out the window. As the express train whooshed by station after station, and the tall trees of Westchester morphed into the tall buildings leading the way into New York City, Will closed his eyes and replayed the events that had led him to this day.

∞

What an odyssey was the career of William Conner Davenport, Ph.D., cosmologist. He had gone from obscure college professor to the media darling of science pop culture, appearing whenever an expert was needed to explain a scientific discovery in simple terms.

Cosmology — the study of the universe — was his area of expertise: how the universe started, how it evolved and humanity's place in it. But he could talk on so many topics — astrophysics, quantum physics or even down-to-earth biology. Will had a genius for explanation. He could deliver a complex discourse and actually make it understandable and relevant to most anyone interested enough to listen. And that made him sought after, first at California Union, the small, elite private college where he had taught physics, and then by the news producers and national media programming chiefs in need of a science star.

It had all started innocently enough, appearing on local television in Los Angeles. That he stood out as a natural — at ease, articulate, handsome in an old movie star way — was obvious. Soon he was making appearances on national broadcasts, including CNN and MSNBC. When he was booked on the *Today* show and garnered record audience approval for a science guest, his celebrity status skyrocketed.

Will was never the bookish scientist ossifying in a lab. Fundamentally life energized him and the mysteries of life challenged him. It was that spirit he conveyed to audiences of all ages.

His on-camera charm was discussed in broader circles. Entertainment executives saw him as a double bonus: personality and good looks. There were conversations with cable networks about serious science programs, and other concepts too that were clearly aimed at ratings, such as Will as *Galaxy Cowboy* or *Universe Hunter*. Network suits flattered Will that he could be as well known as the late, great Carl Sagan.

It was heady stuff for a thirty-two-year-old who had never imagined such attention — and couldn't deny it was fun to be fawned over. In fact, that may have been what got him into trouble. He allowed himself to become "a personality" — oh, hell, he'd welcomed it! — followed on Twitter and invited to celebrity events packed with reality and other stars whose greatest talents were self-promotion. Will's rise was applauded at California Union for the reflected glory it offered the campus — though his integrity was also inevitably questioned by the grumblers who argued he'd taught little and published less compared with many scholars.

"Jealousy is such an ugly quality." That was how Nora, his wife, explained his circumstance, when his reputation had cascaded over the cliff of notoriety. Or, that was her explanation once the initial shock and fury were behind her.

When the fateful turn occurred, Nora was home in California and Will was in New York for a week of guest spots leading up to the first solar eclipse in decades to be seen across the country. He was exuberant at how well his appearances were being received — and then he'd gone to an exclusive "eclipse" party. That was the start of a different kind of eclipse — a shadow that would fall across his once-promising career.

Will was still sleeping off the whiskeys that had gone straight to his head, when Nora, in California, was checking her newsfeed.

What followed was a conversation he was certain he would never forget.

Through bleary eyes, he saw "NORA" on the phone's display as her distinctive ring tone reverberated through his brain.

"Hullohh…." The remnants of a boozy night were obvious in his lifeless voice.

"Will?" Nora's voice, hesitant and uncertain. "Are you alone? Tell me the truth!"

"Alone? Who would I be with?"

As those words made their way to Will's foggy brain, Nora had already launched into a soliloquy, giving him a well-deserved earful.

"I woke up to a picture of you that looks like you'd be anything but alone! Who was at this party, anyway? I thought they were all 'scientists.' You didn't tell me the guest list included the most nationally celebrated Party Girl around! You know what I'm looking at right now?"

Will didn't answer.

"It's you from last night, lips locked with her… her hand is practically on your goddamn crotch!"

Nora's fury had the affect of sobering up Will — fast.

"Nora, it's nothing…."

"It might be nothing to you, but I've got news for you, it rates as something out here…. Jesus, Will, the whole campus is talking about it…."

As proof, Will could hear the telltale sound of Nora's text alerts chiming away.

"Thanks a lot, Will — I just got a 'I'm concerned, Nora!' text from my mother…. Oh, and this is lovely — a text from the gossip wing of the faculty spouses, asking if I'm 'doing okay.' Well, that's just fine. Do you have any idea what a mess this is about to become?"

Will's memory of the previous night was a jumble. He reached for his laptop, needing to see for himself what Nora's fuss was about.

There he was, clearly on display under "entertainment news" — and a video too. He clicked and cringed as he saw himself, arm slung casually around Party Girl, slurring through something he was trying to say about the wonders of the universe. Then Party Girl interrupted him with a big kiss, which he appeared to make no effort to avoid.

Then a flash of memory: her tongue inside his mouth, her hand caressing his thigh. Yes, it had happened.

"Will, are you there?" Nora was shouting into the phone.

"Yes," he answered weakly. "I was watching."

"See why I'm so upset? How could you let HER kiss you like that?"

Nora's voice was angry, but more devastating to Will, he could hear the underlying tones of hurt and disappointment. He'd been an idiot. What could he do?

"Nora, I'm so sorry, honey. I don't know what happened to me last night. You're right. But the kiss meant NOTHING, Nora. You have to know that!"

Now Nora didn't answer.

"I love you, Nora. You have to believe that!" he pleaded.

"But how could you have been so careless? To get smashed at a party swarming with paparazzi!"

"I'm going on the wagon today!" he pledged. "God's honest truth."

She managed a deriding tease. "Sure you are." Her tone was somewhat lighter as her worst fears were apparently eased.

He'd been relieved to hear something closer to her usual banter. "I love you, Nora! I do. You know I do! I'll make this up to you, sweetie, I promise!"

And then Nora's prophetic statement: "I just hope this is the end of it, Will."

Of course, it wasn't. Will had not understood the risks of celebrity. While he might be an expert in the forces of the universe, he had no conception of the momentum of an unflattering photograph and unchecked video in cyberspace. Once the celebrity machine had him, it wasn't letting go. And it was about to grind him up into pieces.

He had tried to make amends. He wrote a letter of apology to the California Union dean and college president, which, per their agreement, was made public. But the apology ultimately backfired, giving entertainment sites a new reason to post the offending images and update the story all over again.

Then Party Girl refused to deny the rumors of a romance with Will, which created a whole new crop of stories. It was all innuendo, much of it silly stuff about star gazing together. But it was the kind of publicity that's not associated with credible scientists or science show hosts. The respectable media outlets stopped calling; the offers disappeared.

And Will was feeling a definite chill from the California Union administration. His media "personality" had become a problem. Many of his students were clearly more interested in his on-camera experiences than his science expertise. It was embarrassing and it brought the knives out from those who were just waiting for the right moment to cut Will down to size.

It was then that Nora, who had done her best to forgive him, attributed his troubles to the jealousy of less dynamic colleagues and an administration unwilling to ride out the storm. But to Will, the meeting of lips in New York was a nuclear explosion. He felt helpless to stop the chain reaction that was turning his professional prospects into radioactive dust.

With Nora's agreement, he resigned his position at California Union. He would start over, he decided. So he closed his Twitter account, took down his Facebook page, changed all his phone numbers and stayed out of camera range as best he could. Basically, he would wait to be forgotten so that he could begin what he needed and longed to do: regain his scientific integrity.

He'd never lost his dedication to science. Now he just needed to prove it.

Will opened his eyes again, relieved to be on a commuter train, seemingly an anonymous New Yorker. *Why did I let myself get so carried away back then?* He tried to shake off the memories of that dark time.

In New York, he hoped to be able to reinvent himself. But more importantly, he felt he needed to regain Nora's belief in him, her complete trust in their future. Sure, she had forgiven him; they had worked hard to get through the mess he created. But he had recklessly planted the seed of doubt in their relationship — something that hadn't existed before. He could only hope that the days ahead would give him the chance to make it up to her. And he promised himself again, *You'll see Nora, I'll do what it takes to make this right.*

The train rocked back and forth, jogging Will's thoughts. He turned his attention to his research for the book that was central to reclaiming his good name. But before he began reading, he made a quick check on the backpack guy, who was looking out the window, his fingers drumming away on the bag.

That guy still looks nervous to me, Will concluded. *What the hell is he carrying in that backpack?*

Chapter 2

WESTCHESTER, NEW YORK
MARCH 5
7:15 A.M.

Nora Martin Davenport

Nora Martin Davenport, on her second cup of coffee, stood staring out the window. At least ten minutes had passed since she watched Will slowly pull out of the driveway and head toward the train station. She was feeling lonely already, wishing Will had waited till tomorrow. But he had already delayed his first day. He had planned to go in yesterday, but they'd agreed that spending Monday doing settling-in errands together was a priority.

So here it was Tuesday. And she was alone, in a strange house, strange community, strange part of the country — and deep in thought, trying to make sense of how their lives had turned upside down. *Why has this happened to him… to us? Where is the life I planned — career, marriage* AND *children?*

Those questions hung in the air, unanswered.

Then with another a sip of coffee came more practical thoughts: *Why didn't I take Will to the train station? Now I'm left without a car!*

Not that it really mattered. She intended to stay home today and continue the tedious job of unpacking. Yet she was a California girl who'd learned to drive even before she was old enough for a license. They'd crossed the country together, expecting to get a second car after they established themselves. But now Nora realized she wanted it ASAP.

Looking out at the dreary March landscape certainly didn't help her mood. *Why did we leave California in the winter? What a miserable time to move East!*

If they were still living in New York next winter, they'd go back to California for a week or two or more, she vowed — or to any place where the sun could still be counted on to shine.

Nora noticed her own reflection, her dark green eyes staring back at her, asking, *What's next?* Nothing was predictable anymore.

The move to New York had certainly been the furthest thing from what she expected. But it became a necessity. They really had no choice.

Those had been rough days....

It was right after Will left California Union College. He had made the deliberate decision to fly under the radar while he focused on restoring his reputation as a serious scientist. But as days passed into weeks and then months, Will was doing more than staying out of sight. He was beginning to disappear.

Nora recalled the first time she came home from a day of interviews for a story she was pursuing in her work as an investigative journalist. Will was unshaven, still not dressed, looking despondent and roaming around from room to room.

"What have you been doing?" She'd tried to keep the alarm she was feeling out of her voice.

Will's dull reply: "Nothing."

"Any leads today? Did you follow up on that grant?" she asked.

"No."

"But isn't there an application deadline coming up?"

"What's the point? Another rejection letter?" Will's voice took on a sharp edge.

"Well, what about your research?"

"What about it?" He was clearly tiring of Nora's prodding.

"Did you make any progress today?"

"How many questions are we up to? Ten? Twenty? When's this question and answer game going to end?"

Nora had resented his sarcastic tone but rather than respond in kind, she had used all her considerable willpower to stay calm.

"Have you had anything to eat?"

"No. I wasn't hungry."

Nora refrained from asking any more questions and decided to let him be. Then that night she undressed, got into bed beside Will and held him tightly, saying, "It's going to be all right, Will. I promise." Exhausted, they drifted off to sleep. In the morning, feeling more refreshed and wanting the reassurance of intimacy, she'd initiated sex. Afterwards, Will had seemed restored. They had a hearty breakfast, which Nora took as a sign that her tenderness had helped him to see past his hopelessness.

But it was not the last time that Will languished moving aimlessly through a day. A frequent chorus of "What's the point?" and "They're not interested in me" and "It won't come through" convinced Nora that her once-bold husband, so willing to meet the world head on, had lost his confidence.

It was a development that took her completely by surprise. In fact, it was the last thing she expected from Will. He had always been so daring, taking on challenges without a second thought. Now to see him so downhearted seemed unnatural, and with her inability to shake him out of it, she felt increasingly despairing herself.

After all, it was his zest and enthusiasm that first attracted Nora to Will. She was charmed by his warm, easy smile and by his hazel eyes that gleamed with a dancing light infused with his spirit. Though that was not to minimize the magnetic pull she felt for him physically. He was thin and muscular, and all through their first dinner together, she could easily visualize her body wrapped around his. And as those things often go, it was this vision on both of their parts that really got the ball rolling.

Their destinies crossed as guests on a local LA cable news show. Both were there as experts to discuss deficiencies in California's electrical grid: Will to explain the physics of energy and to theorize on possible natural causes that might contribute to future power problems, and Nora by way of her investigative reporting. At the time she had garnered attention with a controversial exposé in *LA Living* magazine. In the aftermath of a rash of power outages that swept through California, authorities had been at a loss to explain the cause, nor could they guarantee it wouldn't happen again.

It was Nora's intrepid digging that disclosed a patchwork system delivering power was awash in payoffs and corporate espionage. Later, as the full story of how energy was manipulated to drive up prices was uncovered, her article was cited by the national press for early discovery of the real story behind the blackouts. When Nora and Will appeared on the LA news show, she was still in demand to argue the finer points of her reporting.

Nora loved their "how we met story." Will got caught in traffic, arrived late and was ushered to the green room, to be added to the discussion after a commercial. Feeling upended at missing his scheduled entrance, Will watched the conversation in progress on the monitor and was further distracted by an extraordinary woman with deep green eyes and shoulder-length brown hair. She was in verbal combat with an electric company executive, determined in her argument.

Will remembered being cued to go on and suddenly feeling unusually nervous. In fact, when he came onto the set and was introduced to Nora, he feared he might give away that his immediate thoughts were not on her qualities as an expert. Anxious to recover and gain an air of professionalism, Will gave both Nora and the utility exec a brief nod, then forced himself to focus before the commercial ended and the segment continued.

For her part, Nora recalled having a momentary feeling that Will was undressing her with his eyes. But then he seemed completely proper. During the discussion, he was animated and confident, explaining why solar storms could easily disrupt communication devices and even the energy grid itself.

"It's not a matter of *if* a massive solar storm could knock out the power grid, but *when*," Will had argued. "Someday a massive blast of geomagnetic particles from the sun will destroy hundreds of high-voltage transformers, the backbone of our electrical grid. We are woefully ill-prepared. Imagine no power for weeks, months, possibly years in some areas. The outages here in California were a blessing in disguise. The entire country would be wise to heed the warning."

Although Nora thought his explanation was a bit apocalyptic, Will intrigued her. He seemed intelligent but not arrogant and attractive but not vain, which were reasons enough, especially in LA, to want to know him better.

Their awkward chitchat after the segment led — eventually — to a mutual acknowledgment that they were hungry.

"Ms. Martin, interested in grabbing a bite to eat?" Will had asked.

"I really should be getting home," Nora declined. She really was tired that night — and, besides she didn't want to seem too interested.

"Well, then, could you recommend something quick near here?" Will replied, still hoping to convince Nora to join him.

"There's a bar and grill a block away that has fabulous burgers," Nora responded.

"Great! Can you show me the way? I'm buying!"

Nora had laughed, pleased with his persistence. How could she refuse? she'd answered. To hell with feeling tired — a burger and beer were just what she needed.

In truth, she didn't believe in all the silly "rules" on dating and relationships. Will Davenport piqued her curiosity and she wanted to know him better.

And get to know him she would. Somehow, after dinner — well, maybe it was the beer that flowed to the table — they were sharing the same bed.

Their stumbling start quickly developed into a steamy romance that, contrary to what they both initially expected, never fizzled. On an October evening in 2014, Will and Nora were married.

During that time, their careers continued to build. Nora had her writing. Will kept teaching and garnering more and more television time. He loved the attention, to be sure, but he also hoped that celebrity would help deliver more research grants his way.

The arc of their ascending lives held such promise, such excitement. They both could feel the momentum. It was an exhilarating time, theirs was to be a boundless, bright future.

And then it all began to unravel. Will's star crashed hard.

Still, peering through the window of her temporary new home, Nora felt far more than three thousand miles away from the life she knew and the place, California, she loved.

How did it all go so wrong?

That question always initiated a rush back in time to 2018. First it was the embarrassing photos and the video that played online endlessly. And then the speculation that Will was actually having an affair with Party Girl. Nora had never referred to her by name. To do so would give the whole incident a legitimacy she refused to acknowledge. Certainly this woman felt nothing for Will and he felt nothing for her. It was that bedrock belief that enabled Nora to ultimately put it behind her.

But even so, *How could Will have been so careless, so hurtful?* was a mantra that still played in her head. Nora was an attractive woman, no question about it. But she was no bombshell — never tried to be. *To have a baby-voiced, silicon-filled bitch rubbing her cleavage against her husband, creating a scandal to keep herself in the headlines — was humiliating.*

And it was impossible for her to hold herself back in the immediate aftermath. She let Will know exactly how she felt. "You can't imagine how embarrassing this is! Facing our friends, my family! And when strangers recognize me, I can see it in their eyes — comparing me to her!"

Of course, it was far worse for Will, who was stared at and pointed out by seemingly everyone everywhere. But she was not inclined to be sympathetic or generous.

He tried his best to explain and apologize. "I'm sorry for what I've put you through. Everything happened so fast. She just up and kissed me! If I could snap my fingers and take it all back, I would."

Even now, Nora could still feel the sting every time she envisioned the picture of Will's drunken kiss. *Why is that image still in my head?*

Yet as time went by, and with their usual openness, they worked their way through the inevitable minefield of bruised feelings and doubts about the future.

"Nora, my life began the moment I met you. Thinking that I hurt you like this is killing me. I give you my word," Will pleaded, "I'll never put you through anything like this again."

And for Nora, there was no one else but Will. In the tender moments that followed, their love deepened. They were both vulnerable and they found comfort in each other. Still, there were days when anger overwhelmed Nora and she wondered whether she was being completely honest with all of her feelings, with Will and with herself.

∞

Nora was roused from her thoughts by the chimes of a nearby church, which rang every hour from morning to early evening. Nora was finding that she didn't really mind — especially on days like this, when she needed a kick to get going. When the bells hit eight, she chastised herself for wasting nearly an hour essentially feeling sorry for Nora Martin, displaced Californian.

"Come on, get with it!" she spoke aloud. "You've had your mental cry. Enough."

Unpacking their belongings was taking forever. Nora was now determined to finally get it all behind her today.

Chapter 3

GRAND CENTRAL STATION, NEW YORK
MARCH 5
8:50 A.M.

Will Davenport

Will's train slowed and the conductor announced, *"Harlem — 125th Street."* They were in the city, one stop before Grand Central Station. A few people got up and stood in the aisle, waiting to disembark. At this hour, most people where headed to midtown, so the exodus was light. Will noticed that the guy with the backpack was among those who were getting off. *Good riddance to you!* Will thought.

The train glided into the station and the doors opened. Passengers left and then a few entered the train from the platform. Most of the newcomers stood near the doors for the short ten-minute ride to Grand Central.

The train resumed motion and soon entered the tunnel below bustling Manhattan. Will stuffed his book notes back into his briefcase. As other passengers began to stand, he did the same. He started to shuffle toward the doors, and there, to his astonishment, gazing out the dark window, was another man, this one older than the first, but who appeared to be holding the exact same backpack!

Was he certain? *Yes.* He was a scientist for God sakes. Observation was second nature to him. *The backpack was black with a brown leather label, front pocket unzipped, same yellow-lined paper just visible inside the open pocket.*

Will looked away, trying not to be obvious. But when he looked again, the man was staring in his direction, a deep scowl on his face.

What the hell is going on? As casually as he could, Will turned away a second time and tried to assure himself he was being ridiculous. Still, in the minutes it took to reach Grand Central, Will's imagination began to fly.

Not that his imagination going wild was unusual. Since he was a boy, Will's mind had been alive with vivid imagery, as well as a fount of questions. This aspect of Will's personality had been a source of constant frustration to Ken, his older brother, who considered Will a flamboyant nuisance monopolizing their parents' attention.

Yet Will's imagination and endless questions served him well as an adult in his chosen field. It drove him to understand the nature of the universe and made him determined to figure out how everything works — from the way the solar system spun around the galaxy, to how the fabric of reality came to be.

To match his vivid imagination, Will had the heart of an adventurer. Though more recently, as the loner he'd become, he'd had few opportunities to act on this natural impulse.

Now Will was about to get reacquainted with his wilder side. His desire to know and his sense of discovery were about to merge.

"Grand Central Station — next stop, Grand Central Station — take all your personal belongings — last stop, Grand Central Station." With that announcement, everyone joined the dance to leave the train. Laptops and tablets were tucked into bags, briefcases snapped closed, jackets came off hooks and people gathered their newspapers to toss in the recycling bins on the platform.

As more passengers poured into the space by the doors, Will was pushed against the opposite side of the car from the guy with the backpack. The second the doors opened, the man was racing up the platform toward the track exit. Will made his way out of the train as quickly as he could, his eyes locking on the bobbing backpack.

Grand Central on a weekday rush hour smacked Will square in the face. Why he chose a setting of ultimate confusion to follow a stranger with a backpack, however suspicious, when he had his own clear and completely unrelated destination, was a demonstration of Will's best and worst traits — wanting to know and the thrill of chasing the unknown.

They had arrived on Track 36, on the far end of the upper level. Will, still tracking the backpack, could see the ramp straight up ahead that led onto East 42nd Street and expected the man to steer for it. Instead he stopped, as if deciding which way to go. He turned around and Will could make out the stranger's face.

Will knew from his own experience that guilt was like strong garlic that seeped out from the pores. It made you assume everyone could smell you and was aware of your every move. This guy was hiding something — and it had to be in the backpack.

Will saw two of NYPD's finest patrolling the station. What could he say? *Follow that man. Trust me — he's guilty. Smell the garlic!*

When the man turned left and headed across the jammed main terminal, Will sprinted in the same direction, his natural agility enabling him to weave among the commuters studying the track information on the high boards or tourists admiring the famous ceiling of constellations. Lots of people were moving fast, even running. Will hardly stood out.

Follow him… see what he's up to…. Will had a brief daydream of immediate redemption, hailed for thwarting a bomb plot.

The man entered a corridor lined with shops that exited out onto Lexington Avenue. *Where is this guy going?*

Up ahead, Will saw him step inside the open door of a luggage shop. Will stopped too, pretending to admire a watch in the window of a store on the opposite side of the corridor.

Then a fresh wave of people pushed past Will. When the corridor cleared, the luggage store was empty. Will quickly looked left, then right — not there. *Where did he go?*

Will stood for a moment, debating. Should he run outside, to see if the backpack was in sight? He could go find those cops and describe his suspicions. Then again maybe it was best to take the steep stairs up ahead that went down to the subway and be on his way.

But before Will could make up his mind, a voice behind him was hissing in his ear: "Hey, asshole! You following me?"

Chapter 4

Will Davenport & Izzy Rhodes

"I said, are you following me?" the voice repeated in a muted growl.

Will spun around and was looking directly into the eyes of his suspected would-be bomber, the man with the backpack.

"Nothing of the sort. Now get out of my face." Will was calm but stepped forward, to signal he wasn't about to be threatened.

"Better not, ASSHOLE!" the stranger demanded, and then deliberately started to back away.

Will might have let it go if he'd taken a moment to think it through. An actual bomber would not want to draw attention to himself. But the adrenaline was still surging though him, and without considering the potential danger — a definite Will trait — he blurted out, "Who you calling an asshole, ASSHOLE? And what's in the backpack? You hiding something?"

With that, in a calculated move, the man stepped forward toward Will. "None of your business, jerk!"

If he expected this "do-gooder" to back down, the guy had not accurately sized up Will. Instead of retreating, Will stood his ground, continuing his verbal challenges. "Yeah, well you know what they say, asshole, 'If you see something, say something.' Right? Well I see something."

241

Now the standoff prompted tourists and even a few commuters to pause. Two strangers going at it was hard to ignore — the kind of ancient show that always draws a crowd.

Izzy Rhodes, proprietor of The Great American Timepiece, rushed out to see what was causing the uproar. His burly six-foot-five-inch frame towered over the two men. "What's going on out here?" Izzy demanded. "Gentlemen, this is a place a business. If you have a beef, take it elsewhere. You're chasing away all my customers."

The addition of Izzy drew an even larger crowd. "This is crap!" the young man with the backpack said in disgust, looking around. Then, in a more sinister tone, lowering his voice, he addressed Will. "If I were you, I'd mind my own business, pal."

With that he backed away and ran toward the subway entrance, flying down the broad staircase. Anyone who might follow would have seen him pull out a Metrocard, slide through the turnstile and then calmly join the thick of commuters at a fast walk, headed toward the long hallway to the shuttle trains to Times Square.

"That's it folks, shows over," Izzy announced to those still gathered in front of his store. "Unless any of you are in need of a fine timepiece, in which case, come on in." Izzy swept his arm dramatically toward his open shop door and went back inside, hoping others would follow.

With nothing left to see, the murmuring crowd melted away and Izzy went back inside.

Will remained in front of the shop as his pumping heart was slowing to normal. Had he let his imagination get away from him? Why had he chased that guy? He certainly didn't need anymore headlines — *Mad Scientist Chases Stranger!* — and especially now.

Will's thoughts were broken by someone suddenly beside him. "Sir, I noticed you admiring my window before you were accosted. May I show you something? I have many fine watches!" Seeing Will's continued presence in the corridor, Izzy Rhodes had re-emerged.

Izzy raised his bushy eyebrows, inspecting Will closer. "You certainly look very familiar to me. Have we met?" Then, feeling a moment of awkwardness and being naturally inclined to put everyone at ease, Izzy offered an answer to his own question: "Perhaps you've brought in a watch for repair?"

"No, I'm new to New York," Will responded. "I have a-kind-of-typical face," he added, attempting to explain away why he might appear familiar. "I was just getting ideas for my wife's birthday." Will had no intention of revealing his past or his just-completed pseudo-detective adventure. "That guy threw me. I don't like being accused."

"Of what?" Izzy asked.

"Nothing." Will realized he was saying too much. "Sorry for the ruckus… I should really get going."

"Not to worry," Izzy replied. "Let me formally introduce myself and give you a proper welcome to New York. The city is not all rude characters like that one." Izzy nodded at the phantom man and backpack, now long gone.

"I'm Isidor Rhodes. Everyone calls me Izzy. I'm the owner of this fine store." He held out his arms to present his pride and joy.

"Will Davenport."

"Pleased to meet you, Will Davenport." Izzy extended his hand and Will reciprocated.

Then Izzy, ever the pitchman, couldn't resist. "Are you sure you don't want to come inside and take a moment to look for that watch for your wife's birthday?" he asked with his trademark grin. "I just put up a pot of coffee in the back. I'll treat you to a cup." Izzy gestured for Will to follow him into the store.

Why not? Will thought. Truth be told, he was feeling a bit undone from following the man on the train. He decided to give himself a few minutes to feel more together before resuming his commute. The train had been delayed; the subway might be too — good reasons to explain a tardy arrival. "Thank you, Mr. Rhodes. You know what, I would love to see some watches for my wife."

"And I have the perfect selection," Izzy promised, guiding Will inside. "But call me Izzy. An absolute must for shopping in my store."

Izzy led Will to the counter and took out a tray that displayed the very latest styles in women's watches and started to describe each one to Will.

But with no real interest in watches, Will quickly lost interest and his attention started drifting away. He was thinking about the man with the backpack. Had he been reckless again? Brought on the confrontation? Was he courting trouble, as he'd done with Party Girl?

"So Will…may I call you Will?" Izzy's voice suddenly brought him back to the moment and Izzy's pitch.

"Yes, of course. But I really must be…."

"Time… what a concept…," Izzy interrupted, eager to launch into his favorite soliloquy. He recognized that Will Davenport was not ready to buy a watch. However, Izzy was an master at cultivating would-be customers with his stories, determined to leave an impression that made them remember him when, as he liked to say, "the time is right!"

Now Izzy continued his philosophical wanderings. "Who came up with 'time' anyway? My grandfather, God bless him, was obsessed with its fleeting nature. He was fond of saying, 'You can't hold onto even a second of time." Izzy held out his hand, spreading his fingers wide. "Poof, gone!" he added, hoping for dramatic effect.

Will nodded, wanting to be polite, but thinking of his own time and the need to get moving.

"How about that cup of coffee?" Izzy suggested.

"Thanks, but I really should be going," Will explained, stepping back from the counter in the direction of the door.

But Izzy wasn't through with his oration. He made another sweeping gesture toward a display of antique watches, drawing Will's eye, as intended. "See these, Will," Izzy began. "My grandfather originally specialized in these old watches — beautifully crafted railroad time-pieces. But he had other interests as well. He had a passion for historical artifacts — not only objects, but books and letters — anything that could chronicle the human saga, all in an effort to examine and explain what our lives are all about."

Will paused now. Exploring the meaning of life was his passion too.

"My grandfather passed the business onto his two sons, my father, Elijah Rhodes, and my uncle, Samuel Rhodes," Izzy continued. "Each gravitated to a different part of the business. My father loved watches and equated watch movements with the movement of the earth around the sun, keeping a record of human history. Uncle Samuel was engrossed in artifacts, going on digs, and became an expert authenticator. They both ran this business together, though it was not quartered here at Grand Central. That's more recent…. Those two were not only brothers, they were dear friends."

Izzy's mention of brothers was another reminder to get going. He was scheduled to met Ken, his frequently irritating and older brother this morning, and he had tarried long enough.

So half listening, he looked for the moment to extricate himself, when he was snapped back to attention by one of the best-known names in science. "Newton?" Will's eyes widened. "Sir Isaac Newton?"

"Yes," confirmed Izzy. "One day the brothers were sent a copy of a letter written to a 17th century …, well, I guess you might call him a country healer, by the name of Daniel Fletcher. The exciting part — the letter was written by Isaac Newton. Actually, my father and uncle were offered a collection of correspondence between Newton and Fletcher. They were friends and, according to the letters, had practiced alchemy together!"

Will was all ears now. Newton! He knew of Newton's dabbling in alchemy, but who was this Fletcher? *What if Izzy has the letters still?* Will's curiosity was stirring.

"I'm a scientist," Will announced. "As you can well imagine, untold stories of Isaac Newton fascinate me. Did your father and uncle acquire the letters? Did you ever see them?"

Izzy shook his head and his ready smile faded, wiped away by memory. "The seller was in Colorado. This was in 1979. I was only twenty-five."

By Izzy's changed demeanor, Will could tell the story was headed toward an unhappy ending.

"My father grew up in the city on subways and buses," Izzy continued. "He was never a good driver. As it turned out, the mountainous roads were much too much for his New York City driving habits. He was going too fast and lost control. My father and uncle … neither of them ever wore seat belts. They both died instantly," Izzy sighed, "the only blessing."

Will could see that even after all these years, Izzy still felt the pain of his father's death. Will thought of his own father and mother, thankfully alive and well, not far away from New York, on Long Island. And his brother, Ken….

"I'm sorry. That must have been tough, Izzy."

A moment of silence fell between them. Then Will took a deep breath. "I've stayed long enough. I really do have to head out. Thanks for your time, Izzy — and no pun intended."

Izzy nodded, his eyes slightly moist. He swallowed, to clear his voice of emotion. "Of course. I don't want to hold you up any longer — time is money in this city! But Will, as a scientist, there's more to the story that I think would interest you."

Will had picked up his briefcase, but he then set it down again. *Let this decent man have his memories,* he thought.

"As you can see, I took up the reins from my father and uncle," Izzy resumed his story. "Moved the shop to Grand Central in the 1990's. And here I still am, decades later. Along the way all these timepieces have become more to me than just products to sell. The nature of time and the boundaries that measure our lives have become my passion."

Will looked closely at Izzy. There was something engaging about this man. With an unusually full head of curly gray hair for a man of — Will did the math — about sixty-seven years old, Rhodes suddenly gave off a glowing appearance. Will's curiosity was piqued.

"What happened to the collection of letters between Newton and Daniel Fletcher?"

Izzy shook his head. "Lost. The car caught on fire. We assume they burned up. But there was one letter that survived. It was left in my father and uncle's hotel room. How it came to be there didn't make sense to me. I guess we'll never know what really happened. I still have that one letter, though."

"BRRRRINNNG! BRRRRINNNG!" It was Will's cell. The ring tone mimicked the shrill jangle of an old phone.

"Ah, that tone brings back memories," Izzy laughed. "You'd better get it. I've been keeping you too long."

Will answered to a familiar impatient voice. "WHERE ARE YOU? It's almost ten!" He turned so that Izzy could not see the mix of irritation and sheepishness that was surely on his face.

It was his older brother Ken on the phone. Ken, who was never late. Will had meant to be on time …. He knew Ken was trying to help. But damn it! He didn't want a watchdog or a warden.

"There were train delays … I'm in Grand Central…." Will tried to keep his voice low. He didn't want Izzy to hear either.

"Okay, I understand. Got it. You have a lunch meeting AT NOON. I'll be there soon, promise." Will knew Ken was pissed. Not a good way to start, especially since Will hadn't seen his brother since arriving from LA. And of course, given what Ken had arranged….

Will turned back to face Izzy Rhodes with as much nonchalance as he could muster.

Izzy had busied himself rearranging watches, to appear oblivious to Will's tense call. Yet Izzy was anything but unaware.

"I truly hope I haven't held you up, Will. I can be too loquacious

— particularly with good company." Izzy extended his hand toward Will. "And to express my appreciation, stop by tomorrow and I'll have the Newton letter to show you. I think the scientist in you will find it fascinating. Newton and Fletcher are corresponding about alchemy and some hush, hush discovery — one that Newton was extraordinarily excited about."

Will started to form a dozen questions and then stopped. "You're right, Izzy, I am intrigued. And thanks, I'll be here first thing in the morning. I'd love to take a good look at that letter!"

He extended his hand to Izzy, who took it in both of his. "What a pleasure, Will! I'll have the letter — and that cup of coffee — waiting for you."

As Will left the shop, a customer entered, whom Izzy greeted with a loud, "Good day!" Will paused for a moment, wondering if this fellow would get the same life story that Izzy had just shared with him.

More importantly though, was the Newton letter real? There was no way for Will to know except to return and take a look.

He jogged down toward the subway entrance and asked the gods of the subway to get him to Ken's office in record time. He'd call Nora from there. Will longed to tell her of his morning adventures but thought better of it. His derring-do with the backpack guy might worry her.

And better to wait to describe his meeting with Izzy Rhodes. If the letter was authentic — and offered an unknown Newton discovery — what might that do for his career? With that possibility to ponder, Will's juices were flowing again.

Chapter 5

Ken & Will Davenport

Ken Davenport paced the hall of the eleventh floor outside his university office on the Upper West Side of Manhattan, waiting for his brother to arrive. It was irritating to waste his time like this; however, Ken was not taking any chances that Will might get lost wandering around, looking for his office. Now Will was late and Ken had to be downtown by noon. Molly McQuire, his assistant, was out of the office, prepping for a research presentation. Expecting his brother any minute, Ken had no choice but to stand here and wait.

Being irritated by his younger brother was not new for Ken. They were the quintessential opposites. Yet obscured by his impatience was Ken's deep concern for Will. It was Ken who had insisted that Will and Nora get the hell out of California after seeing the weight of the world fall on his brother's shoulders. Will, as stubborn as ever, had refused to listen.

So Ken turned his attention to Nora. "I've been trying to get our boy Will to come to New York," Ken had begun. "A change of pace is what he needs, and you too, Nora. You've got to talk some sense into him. Lots of advantages coming East. You can work from anywhere. And Will can write that book he's been talking about forever."

Nora had been grateful but unsure, at first. "I don't know, Ken. Your brother is really down. If California sunshine can't shake his mood, I don't see him making great progress on his book working from a place he doesn't know, insolated in a house and neighborhood he doesn't know. I'm not sure the East Coast is the answer."

It had taken a few more calls, until the day Ken came up with the right proposition. "Look, Nora, I can hook him up with an office here in our department. I've got enough clout for that. I'll keep an eye on him. He can write from here. Get the energy of the city. And Manhattan's the publishing capital of the world."

Nora saw the possibilities and warmed to the idea. "Ken, that sounds pretty good!"

And now that he had Nora's attention, Ken was happy to elaborate. "I think it's just the ticket to get him out of this, Nora. Have his book published, then he could go on tour. I'm sure there will be questions from the press, but at least he'll be able to tell his side of the story. And who knows, after he gets rehabilitated, he might find a professorship somewhere in New York."

That was then. At this moment Will was late and Ken had his own schedule to keep. *Damn it, Will! Can't you do what's expected, for once?*

As soon as that thought entered Ken's mind, the elevator doors opened.

"Look who we have here. Dr. Davenport, I presume?" Ken's tone was annoyed, yet he was also relieved at Will's arrival.

"And who's looking for him?" Will smiled. Having Ken annoyed with him was part of landing in the familiar presence of his older brother.

Both reached out and half shook hands, half embraced.

It was the first time Ken was seeing Will since he resigned his college post. "Well, you seem to be in decent shape. I expected you'd look like shit after what you've been through," Ken assessed, giving Will a poke in the arm.

At that moment Will wanted to tell his older brother that until recently he really *did* look like shit. And felt like shit, too. Something inside him wanted Ken to know that sometimes in the middle of the night he still felt deeply troubled about what had happened. That what he was going through had unleased emotions he had never experienced before. That even now he'd awaken from a sound sleep only to feel the onset of unaccustomed angst that arrived in the form of worry and sorrow that descended like phantom shadows — emerging from some dark place, surrounding him, until there was a thick coat of uncertainty clinging to his skin. Will worried these shadows were changing him, and that left him unsettled — unable to anticipate who he was becoming and what would happen to him next.

And that was the real rub. Like never before Will sensed that everything in his life was subject to change without warning. Joyful enthusiasm could be around the corner, but something unwelcome could appear just as easily. Where before he felt so assured, on firm ground, now he felt anything but. And no matter how he turned things in his head, Will came to understand that there were no guarantees in life.

And then there was his continued guilt and shame of what he was doing to Nora — to their marriage — dragging her down into his own special meat-grinder. He had plunged their relationship into a deep crevice and though they had worked hard to find their way back toward each other he couldn't help but feel that something was left unresolved. Over and over again he vowed to himself he'd make it up to her. But he wasn't quite sure how. And yet he promised himself and was determined to find a way. Ironically it was that unwavering commitment that signaled to him he was coming out of the miasma that had encased him for far too long.

Even so Will mourned the loss of the light of his old life. A life that was practically trouble free, and upon reflection now, even carefree. But as he desperately wanted it back, in his gut he knew that ship had sailed — that he was in uncharted territory now, in need of a new map — if one even existed. That old life was then and this was now.

Still, even as these nighttime visits persisted, Will was growing tired of holding on to all the disquieted feelings. He was especially feed up with his self-pity — and he took that as another good sign that he was shaking himself free.

All of that was what he wanted to tell his brother. But that wasn't the nature of their relationship, at least not now. And so… he didn't say anything.

"Where the hell have you been? I thought you'd get here over an hour ago."

Will shrugged off the annoyance. "I told you on the phone. Train was late getting to Grand Central…. You don't look half bad yourself, by the way. Mom said you've settled everything and the divorce is behind you."

"Thank God that's over with."

Ken went silent for a moment. But then quickly returned to grilling Will. "Hey, how could it take you so long to get here? Was the train *that* late?"

"No, I stopped at a watch store in Grand Central. Just getting ideas for Nora's birthday."

Ken looked on, waiting for more explanation. "As I recall, Nora's birthday is in September."

"Just planning ahead. And besides, I've been a New York commuter for all of a few hours!"

Ken decided not to push it. *Give him a break. He probably needed some time to himself.* Then aloud, "We'll make a New Yorker out of you."

Will's morning encounter with the backpack guy came to mind. *I think I just had a taste of that brashness.* But he intended to keep that experience to himself for now.

"Don't be saying that to Nora. She's still the original California Girl," Will laughed. "Come on, let's see this office you've been crowing about."

Ken pulled the key from his pocket and guided Will down the hall.

"OK, this can definitely work," Will said as they entered the room. There were huge windows facing west, with a view of the Hudson River.

"Impressive, right? Think this can inspire your writing?" Ken asked.

Will nodded emphatically. "I'd say so. How'd you pulled this off?"

"It's the office of a colleague who's away doing research. So it's not yours forever. I'll find you another place when she returns. There's always somebody in our department who's off in the hinterlands. That's the nature of geology — no pun intended. Generally people don't mind if somebody camps in their playground for awhile," Ken explained.

"Just don't break any windows, little brother," he added with a smirk. As a kid, Will's daredevil activities frequently concluded in broken glass or broken bones.

"Don't worry, I won't!" Will laughed. "Seriously, Ken, thanks." He stretched out a hand to shake.

"Aww, come on." Ken ignored the hand and gave Will a warm embrace. His brother's capacity to frustrate him might be enormous, but Ken was relieved to have Will in New York, where he could help. Now he hoped his brother could right himself.

Will returned the hug. He knew his big brother meant well. He just hoped that Ken wouldn't be a big pain in the ass by watching over his shoulder every second. It had been years since the brothers had been on the same coast, let alone in the same place daily.

Ken broke the silence. "Hey, listen, I heard from Dad last night."

"Let me guess. Checking up on me."

"Would you expect less? He said he hadn't heard from you since you and Nora got in."

"I know. Did you remind him I've been a little busy?" Will grinned, aiming to hide his guilt. "What did he have to say?"

"The usual. He reminded me to be sure you remember his three E's."

Ken and Will recited together: "Explore, Experience and Express."

Will grimaced in mock displeasure. "Does he realize that we're both pushing forty, and not fourteen?"

"When it comes to the E's, Will, we'll be forever fourteen."

Both paused, thinking of Robert Livingston Davenport's watchwords, his advice to his sons as they grew. "Go out there boys and *explore* the world, take in the *experience*, live it fully, *express* what you learn and share it with others."

Will walked to the window to survey the view. "What else did he have to say?"

"You know he's just back from Brazil — another buying trip for amethysts. The museum is redoing their mineral exhibition and contacted Dad. He sold them a fifteen-footer. Take a look at this." Ken produced his phone and a photo of the largest amethyst geode that Will had ever seen.

"I thought Dad was going to slow down?" Will asked. "I thought Mom was insisting?"

"Not a chance. When they moved here because of all the business from the museum, it was like Dad began Act Two. And now with a 25,000 square foot warehouse filled with fossils, minerals and crystals, he's busier than ever. It's all in his blood, anyway."

"I guess yours too, bro," Will added.

Ken was a respected scholar in one of the leading geology departments in the country and a consultant to one of the most prestigious natural history museums in the world. Despite their differences in temperament, Will was deeply proud of his brother's accomplishments.

Ken gave Will a light pat on the back. "Hey, we both have science chops from Dad. He influenced *both* of our careers."

Will's science confidence had taken a hit, and rebuilding it was part of Ken's mission.

"What about Mom? How's she doing?"

"She's concerned about you," Ken replied. "Wanted me to make sure you're eating and exercising. I told her not to worry."

"She remembers Nora, my wife, the super healthy eater, committed exerciser since birth? No potato chips in this Davenport household!"

In truth, Will was well aware of his mother's concern. He had talked with her often during his Party Girl fiasco. Olivia Davenport had her own set of axioms she sought to pass onto her sons. At the height of Will's difficulties, she urged him to "find the courage to be at peace with yourself and love the person you are. And keep in mind, though this is a dark time in your life, believe that all things are possible — including that this will pass and better times await."

He understood what she was saying, though believing it was one thing and living it was quite another.

"Now that you're in New York, I think they're expecting a visit soon," Ken noted. Seeing Will's eyes rolling, he added, "Look, I promised Mom I'd mention it."

Will didn't need to be reminded. "I know, I know. Don't worry, getting there is next on my list. Nora, too. We'll see them, I swear."

Reading Will's mood, Ken decided it was enough parent talk. "Okay then, let's get you set up here. Are you ready to get to work on that book of yours?"

"I've already started," Will confirmed, "and now that I'm here, I'm ready to pick up the pace full throttle." Will knew he sounded a bit defensive but he was fully aware of Ken and Nora's concerns for him. He was determined to move forward, to get beyond the feeling that he was being handled. And this was as good a time as any to show Ken that he wasn't just going through the motions to placate his family's fears.

"I've been thinking about this for years, Ken. Even when I'm not actively thinking about *it*, I'm thinking about *it*. It plays like background music — always there."

"Don't you think it's time you enlighten me as to what *IT* might be?" Ken asked, actually surprised he didn't know what Will was writing about, especially since Will was always talking about working on a book.

"What's the one area of life that science always shies away from?"

"Ken looked at his brother knowing he needn't respond — that Will would supply the answer in short order. Ken only hoped that it wasn't going to be too long winded…. And right on cue Will went into his spiel.

"It has always troubled me that science hasn't handled the matter of human consciousness very well. Forever dodging questions like, how do we become self aware? And where does our awareness emerge — what's its source? Where does it reside inside us — in our brain? Could it be integrated throughout our whole body? Or could our consciousness come from beyond our bodies embedded in our life stream?

"We simply don't know the answers to any of this. And what irks me is that scientists pursuit for answers have been rather feeble. We have pretty much given up on doing comprehensive research within a scientific framework on this matter, leaving it largely to the domain of philosophy or religion or even spirituality. Yet in my opinion, this is the most powerful and deepest mystery of all." Will finished with a flurry, satisfied that he had aroused his brother's curiosity.

Ken saw the light in his brother's eyes as he spoke — a spark he often envied. But he feared that Will had dug himself such a deep hole that it would take a herculean effort to climb out. Yet Ken was determined to fan the flame of that spark if he could. And he had a hunch about how. Will always responded to a challenge.

"And you plan on changing all that?" Ken found his voice egging his brother on.

"Absolutely! Think of all the areas of science this reaches. It's every-thing. It's my core belief that only in understanding the nature of awareness can we understand where we come from, who and what we are, and why we are here, and the promise held in human destiny."

"That sounds like a pretty tall order dude."

"It wouldn't be worth anything if it wasn't." Will was surprised that he felt himself standing on solid ground.

"You sound like the old man. Always stretching beyond the

boundaries, forever challenging the safety of prescribed margins that keeps the world neatly in a box."

Ken and Will both looked into the distance conjuring up their father, and that quality in him that they both admired. Robert Livingston Davenport had a persistent, inquisitive mind, forever curious and penetrating, always questioning what was possible.

Then Ken mused. "Remember that time when Dad said to walk barefoot and feel the earth's vibrations is to really understand the miracle of our lives. That all of life, every space is teaming with energy. And energy was life, and if you paid attention it had something to say." Both Ken and Will admired their father's willingness to extend his imagination beyond what most people thought of as feasible. It was this reach for the stars trait that Will had inherited. And while Ken appreciated that quality he had more of their mother mixed in his make-up. She had the uncanny ability to discern when a go slow approach might be more in line.

Will grinned at the thought of their father's ways. "And don't forget his prime directive: spend time outside everyday. And especially on those golden sunny mornings. Let those rays soak in the skin, at least for a little while. They recharge your battery, and put a smile on your face. Plants aren't the only ones that need photosynthesis. We need to absorb light too, you know. Remember that the body is electrical."

"Well, Will, he said that because he spent so many days exploring caves and was happy to see the sun again," Ken added, prompting the Davenport brothers to share a laugh.

Then Will turned back to the subject of his book. "No doubt Dad helped shape my thinking. But honestly Ken, consider the possibility that everything we come in contact with is filled with awareness — a wisdom about its own origin and existence. I cannot help but think that on some level there is a dynamic exchange of that information. And that has to influence our consciousness in some way. That's what my book's about.... How life effects us on a moment to moment basis. From the foods we eat, to how long we sleep, how we move, to the people we meet — even to the music we hear. Ultimately, I want to explore how all of these factors, and more, affects our DNA and how we evolve. I think it's a fascinating and important subject to delve into — and could be an important book. At least I hope so."

Ken nodded. "Certainly there's plenty to chew on. And as Dad would also say, 'Good luck to you.'"

In that moment Will wanted his brother to truly understand how much he appreciated the opportunity that Ken had arranged. "Seriously, exploring the nature of consciousness, from where it derives — and resides — and how different states of awareness impact our lives, has been my deepest passion ever since I knew I was going to devote my life to science. I've always considered its sway on all of my experiences, not only in the lab but in everyday life. This is to be my life's work. Expressing in layman's terms how the nature of our conscious awareness influences us."

"There you go, Will. Dad's famous trio strikes again: explore, experience, express."

A quick knock on the office door distracted Will's thoughts as Molly McQuire popped her head inside.

"Hey, Ken, I'm back.... Is this your brother, Will?" Molly inquired. She had spoken with Dr. Will Davenport but they'd never met.

"Molly, come in! Yes, meet my brother," Ken said with a broad smile, walking toward his assistant to usher her into the room.

Will noted Molly's red hair, deep brown eyes and shy smile. And, unmistakably, Will could feel a connection between his brother and Molly. It was not overtly personal, but it was not simply professional. And immediately Will felt something simmering between these two. He'd ask Nora. She'd talked with Ken a lot over the past six months. Ace investigative journalist Nora Martin would have all the details.

"It's really great to meet you in person!" Molly was saying. "If there's anything you need ...."

"Great to meet you too," Will responded, offering a warm handshake. "And thanks. I'll let you know."

Molly gave Ken the lightest tap on the arm. "Are you coming back to the office after you're finished downtown?"

"Yes," Ken said dryly.

Will noted the change in his brother's voice. It seemed he was trying to cover up for his eager greeting when Molly first appeared. Will felt more certain than ever that his instinct was correct.

"Welcome again," Molly called as she left, closing the door behind her.

Ken allowed no opportunity for questions or comments about Molly McQuire. "Okay, Brother, I'll leave you to it. I've got an appointment downtown with the NYPD."

"Thought you said it was a lunch meeting," Will recalled. "Salami and stolen diamonds? Helping out again?" He knew that Ken occasionally served as an expert on cases involving gems and the like.

"Very clever! Nothing wrong with your memory. Yeah, my buddy Cooper. You'll have to meet Jack now that you're in the city. Great guy. Been a detective for thirty years. I'd invite you today but it's work — and confidential. We'll find another day for a real lunch. Coop knows some great burger joints."

Will gave Ken a playful shove. "No problem, get going. And, really, I mean it … thanks for doing this for me." Though they were famous for their brotherly squabbles, Will was indeed grateful to have Ken by his side.

"And great to meet Molly, by the way," Will added, his poker face squarely in place.

Ken acknowledged Will's thanks with another half embrace. "Good to have you here … and I mean that. Call me if you need anything."

No sooner had he left then he reappeared with a key in his hand. "Here, to the office. Almost forgot. Turn off the lights and be sure to lock up, even if you go out for a short time. I don't know what it was like at Union, but locked offices are the rule here."

Will listened to Ken's footsteps recede down the hall. The mention of California Union triggered his innate defiance. *I don't give a shit about California Union or their damn rules....*

But Will wasn't about to let those bad memories get the best of him. Instead he was resolved to settle in and get started.

But first he needed to call Nora. He punched in the numbers of her phone. No answer. No doubt she was busy unpacking. He sent an "Office fantastic!" text. She'd be pleased to see that message.

With that taken care of, Will opened his briefcase and pulled out the same notes he'd tried to read on the train. He placed his laptop on the desk, looked around the room, and announced aloud: "Here I am. Official new start."

He immediately thought again of the three E's and, inexplicably, Izzy Rhodes popped into his head. *A letter written by Isaac Newton. Now there was something to explore. Newton so brilliant, well beyond the nature of his time.... Fascinating....*

Then Will retrieved his phone and hit a number in his contact list.

There was an answer on the first ring. "Hello Dad, it's me.... Yeah .... I'm in my new office in New York...."

Chapter 6

Nora Martin Davenport

Nora was making good progress with the unpacking until she spotted a box marked, **Nora's Magazine Files.**

Though she had all of her articles archived in cyberspace, there was something magical about holding an actual magazine with her work inside. It gave her an unexplained satisfaction.

It was Will who insisted that box come with them, rather than go into storage, where in all likelihood it would be buried, never to be seen again. "Someday I'll read these to our children," he declared.

"And they'll be very effective for putting them right to sleep!" Nora teased.

Still, she was proud of her writing, and never more so than when she reread something from several years back and could honestly say, "Damn that was good!"

Now, in a moment of nostalgia, Nora unsealed the box, picked up a 2015 issue of *LA Living* and started to flip through the pages. She smiled, remembering a time in her life that was exhilarating. She loved the adrenaline rush of digging deep into a story to find a hidden secret. *What I wouldn't do to have that feeling now!* She thought.

With the next turn of a page, a photo caught her attention. *What's this?* Three men at a gala event. Nora immediately recognized U.S. Senator Tom Broderick, Republican from Oklahoma. Broderick was a ranking member of the Senate Committee on Science, Space and Technology. A few months before Party Girl landed in Will's lap, he had testified before that committee.

And there, next to Broderick, was freaking JASON DEWITT! She'd seen that name and face enough for a lifetime! As far as she was concerned, DeWitt was obsessed with Will.

The third man she didn't know. He was identified as Victor Strong, founding member of a private investment group, in Boston.

At the moment it was DeWitt that interested her. What was his connection to Broderick?

DeWitt, you son of bitch! Nora had a sudden desire to take the scissors she'd used to open the box and jam them into the photo of Jason DeWitt!

It was certainly tempting, considering the damage that DeWitt had done to Will's already compromised reputation. It wasn't long after Will left California Union that stories accusing him of plagiarizing research showed up on social media. And then another rumor, claiming he padded his resume. The Twitter account was somebody's pseudonym — they never figured out who it was — but these were serious accusations, and they hit their mark. The damage to Will's name in the world of science was dangerously close to irreparable.

To Nora, this smear campaign was a coordinated effort to disgrace and discredit Will, and her investigative radar lifted into high alert. The fallout was out of balance with Will's Party Girl indiscretion.

It was then that DeWitt, an MIT professor, denounced Will's credentials as an expert in the sciences. DeWitt referenced the false tweets and, as an MIT luminary, he made them credible, although he was careful to always reference them as "alleged" accounts.

But he didn't stop there with his swipes at Will. "Professor Davenport, with his interest in the influence of the moon and sun in our lives, is more astrologer than scientist. Perhaps he should do astrological readings at the celebrity parties he attends and leave serious science to those of us with discipline and integrity."

DeWitt had made those comments on the record, in response to a reporter's questions about Will's rising-then-falling science media stardom. DeWitt never stopped using Will as the poster boy for why, in his words, "science and entertainment do not mix" and how "pure science could not be reduced to the simple feel-good explanations of one Will Davenport."

Nora still fumed at DeWitt's sarcasm and his science snobbery — and still puzzled over his motivation for targeting Will. They'd never even met that Will could recall. Yet, DeWitt seemed to take particular delight in Will's fall from grace and, while he was at it, to provide a few strong kicks to the groin.

It broke Nora's heart to see Will dragged through the mud. She admired his devotion to science and to what science could bring to the world.

But to DeWitt, Will was disdainful of the scientific standards and practices to which DeWitt subscribed. He considered Will a loud mouth, stoking the public airwaves with new theories that skirted the boundaries set by those more credentialed, in search of his own self-aggrandizement.

That was another reason Nora despised DeWitt. She hated his bombastic rigidity. By contrast, Nora was proud of Will's open-minded approach to science. He enjoyed roaming the fields of philosophy, religion, and Eastern and Western spirituality. Will understood how some of these ancient traditions endeavored to explain the origins of life, just as today's modern physics attempts to do. He had an unquenchable desire to explore how seemingly separate disciplines were connected in a broader tapestry.

And she loved Will's imagination and his capacity to see the pure elegance of the universe. How many times had they sat together under a twinkling night sky as Will described Earth as the home of humanity, spinning in a sea of cosmic forces. His curiosity focused on how energy from planets and stars, from galaxies far away and from particles of unknown origin all affected the evolution of life on Earth.

In fact, Will was his most passionate self when discussing the mysteries of consciousness and the origin and makeup of the vast potential of the human heart and mind. Nora prayed that this move to New York — the book Will was writing and the chance to work on it in the vibrant intellectual atmosphere of Ken's university — would restart those conversations.

Damn you DeWitt! Somehow he seemed as much to blame for Will's downfall and their years of struggle as the infamous Party Girl incident and its aftermath.

Nora gave another long look at the photo of Dewitt, Broderick and Strong. She never gave up totally on solving the puzzle of DeWitt and why he went after Will with such venom. But the leads had been slim to none. She now questioned, *How did I miss this photo…? What brought DeWitt and Broderick together at a tech event in Silicon Valley? Was this a random meeting that a photographer just happened to catch? Or did DeWitt know Broderick at the time Will testified?*

Nora's gut began churning, a sure sign she was on to something. Will's Congressional testimony had been contentious. And his chief antagonist was Senator Tom Broderick.

Nora was thrilled for Will that day, in early April 2018. She recalled the cherry blossoms were still in bloom when they arrived in Washington. And there was all the pomp and circumstance of testifying before Congress. She sat behind him throughout his testimony, happy to appear the supportive spouse that she was.

Will stayed laser-focused on his key concern. He'd explained it to her as he prepared his testimony, aiming to find the right words.

"Nora, this may be my only chance to make them listen. The

developments in science are going too fast. They're outpacing our ability to understand the effects on us individually, and our culture as a whole. Congress is ignoring the growing risks involved. No one knows where gene editing will lead or whether artificial intelligence will help us or control us. And the Internet is already a hornet's nest of hackers causing chaos, with the potential of getting exponentially much worse at any given moment."

And so Will testified.

"Mr. Chairman, honorable members, thank you for inviting me to testify today. As a scientist, I'm proud of all the advances that have been made in science and technology through the centuries. In the last ten years alone, the speed of our discoveries and the technologies developed have been extraordinary. Advances in biology, chemistry, physics and machine intelligence are on pace to transform and revolutionize our world — not once, but every few years.

"Yet it comes at a cost. We are in danger of allowing our creations to take over our humanity. The ultimate goal of science is to free us, to help us fulfill our untapped potential — and that goal is in real danger. I fear there will be unintended consequences that we do not see.

"There is potential for the forces that seek to use science to control the levers of power, to also control our beliefs and dictate the way we live our lives."

"Now is the time to err on the side of caution. We must develop ethical guidelines that ensure safe and appropriate applications of all technologies, and specifically those such as gene editing and artificial intelligence that have the greatest capacity to impact the evolution of the human race. We must be vigilant, for humanity is at stake."

The room was hushed as Will finished speaking. Then the individual committee members began asking their questions.

When it was Senator Broderick's turn, he began with what sounded like a mocking gesture of thanks. "Professor Davenport, we thank you for your *very dramatic* testimony." Broderick had paused, to ensure the meaning behind his exaggerated tone was conveyed. Then he continued, "You mentioned that technology comes at a cost, and that is very true. Yet, can we not say that every advancement has produced winners and losers?"

Will recognized a rhetorical question when he heard one. He sensed that Broderick had no intention of taking this hearing seriously. Still, Will was determined to press forward. "Yes, Senator, but we all lose when we fail to apply some common-sense parameters."

Broderick fired back, saying, "The market has always balanced out excesses and weighed the benefits. Indeed, your own 'survival of the fittest' applies, does it not?"

"We must think of the greater good, Senator. This committee must explore and address ethical restraints to ensure public safety."

"Professor Davenport, this Committee frowns upon those demanding we do this or that," Broderick replied in a huff. He had assumed his well-known contentious demeanor.

Will was undaunted. "Senator, it's not my intention to lecture the members, but rather to warn. I'm not saying our machines aren't important and necessary, miraculous even, but when they start to control us, we give up a part of our humanity. We are already addicted to our devices — that's commonly acknowledged. But that addiction is being manipulated and could get far worse."

Broderick showed no signs of being swayed. "I appreciate your concerns but I'm of the opinion that market forces are better watchdogs than government, or even scientists turned Cassandras."

Will was just as steadfast. "The lightening speed of technological change happening now is like nothing we've ever seen. If we are not careful, we may find ourselves in a world where our personal freedoms are greatly diminished."

With a grand wave of his hands, Broderick engaged in his own theatricality. "We are at a difference of opinion, Professor Davenport. In all candor, I think it is you, sir, and those of your class that will enslave us with your suggestions of more regulatory oversight."

Will made a final argument, less to Broderick than to what he hoped were more balanced thinkers in the room. "Consider my testimony when you're in a car that's been hacked and you've lost control. Or when "bots" are spreading rumors about you on social media. And what worries me most is less what's in the public eye than the developments behind the scenes. A tsunami is coming. You cannot say you have not been warned."

By now Broderick appeared to be barely listening. Nora could feel her own full fury at the memory of his dismissive last words. "Duly noted, Professor Davenport, thank you." His condescending tone was unmistakable.

Nora remembered Will's frustration, how most of the committee members appeared to be going through the motions, showing a false concern and an equally false intention to act.

Unsatisfied, Will wrote an opinion piece repeating his warnings that were published in *The Washington Post*. Immediately, he was making the rounds of the evening cable shows, where he made the case for high-tech ethics and morals to the skeptical and cynical.

Some three months later, in August 2018, "The Kiss" occurred. Whatever credibility on ethics and morals Will had went out the window.

Angry as Broderick's condescension had made her, at the time Nora wasn't suspicious of him. He struck her as just another senator, in Congress too long and having heard one too many opinions he disagreed with.

But now, after seeing the photograph, Nora wondered if there was more to Broderick's performance that day. Had Will made some powerful enemies? How *did* DeWitt, Broderick and this Victor Strong know each other — and for how long? *What was their connection?*

Though Nora had resisted leaving California, the New York City area was an excellent base for her professional work as a freelance investigative journalist. And now, for the first time she considered that with DeWitt near Boston — Strong too — and with Broderick in D.C., this move might even have been providential. If there was something to be found that might explain DeWitt's animosity toward Will, and Broderick's too, come hell or high water, Nora was determined to find it.

"If you think you can mess with me and mine, you got another thing coming!" Nora called out dramatically. "I hope you can hear me in Boston and on Capitol Hill! Fair warning!"

Of course, Nora could not solve the DeWitt-Broderick puzzle with just a photo, but it was a start. She put the magazine aside and went downstairs, to make another pot of coffee.

She had left her phone charging downstairs and was surprised to see the time was 12:21. There was a text from Will.

She could read his excitement in the brief "Office fantastic!" message. *Thank God he's off to a good start.* What a relief.

It was not only his life that had been turned upside down. Will's career plunge had forced them to delay starting the family they both wanted. It was her writing that had been paying the bills. But at thirty-seven, she was getting worried. She wanted to have a baby. In six months she'd be thirty-eight. She knew plenty of women had babies at forty or after. But the risks got that much higher too.

"Office fantastic!" She read the text again and returned it with "Fantastic, sweets!" and a blowing kiss emoji.

Then Ken's words echoed through her mind … "book tour" … "tell his side" … "professorship in New York"…. Those possibilities had seemed so far away …? So too was having a baby … but now …? Were their fortunes about to turn around? *Might this be the time? Might this be the place?*

Those prospects made Nora feel joyfully reckless.

She marched to the bathroom to retrieve her birth control. There was something she'd long wanted to do. Today was it!

Despite the gray drizzle, Nora slipped into her coat and boots and went outside to the fenced-in backyard.

The wind came up suddenly and whipped her hair against her face. *How appropriate,* she thought. *Just as I'm throwing caution to the wind!*

Praying it was a sign of good luck, Nora tossed her birth control up to the sky in a half-assed fertility rite. She laughed at the ridiculousness of her gesture, and then picked it up and marching Sousa-like to the garbage can and ceremoniously tossed it in.

But a moment later, as the wind turned biting cold, the exhilaration of the moment had passed. Nora retrieved the package from the garbage and went back inside. Perhaps, on second thought, it was foolish to choose this unpredictable move to New York as the time and place to get serious about getting pregnant.

Returning to the window, Nora noticed a patch of sunlight breaking through the clouds. Though her spiritual beliefs were as muddled as the gray sky, she willed herself to see those rays as surely a good omen — for Will and for the two of them together.

Later, when she gathered up the last of the packing debris, her birth control was buried deep within the things to toss in the trash…. No more vacillating. Decision made. Certainty be damned. It's time.

Chapter 7

Izzy Rhodes

It was lunchtime and Izzy was ready for a break. He'd had a busy and eventful morning. Now he opened the door to the private office beyond the public shop and called to Malcolm Thornberry, his watch repairman and sometime salesman, to take over. Lunch hours were when people often brought in watches for service. Having his watch repair expert at the counter made perfect business sense to Izzy, and he reasoned it was the perfect opportunity to give Malcolm his chance to shine.

Izzy retreated to his back office, where a bookshelf filled three quarters of the back wall. He was hungry all right, but his usual turkey sandwich would have to wait. There was something more pressing he needed to do.

He reached into the middle shelf, turned a latch and then slid away the bookcase, which revealed a hermetically sealed, temperature-controlled, floor-to-ceiling safe. Doing an instinctive quick check to be sure no one was watching, Izzy spun the tumblers and opened the safe. Inside were some of his most prized watches, as well as invaluable artifacts that generations of Rhodes family members had collected.

Izzy removed one item, carefully preserved in a protective casing. Then he closed the safe door, though did not lock it. He would only

270

keep the Newton letter out for a bit. He wanted to read it again, think again on its contents, more than three hundred years old.

If Will Davenport reappeared tomorrow, … if Izzy still felt as sure about him, he would show Will this letter, get his impressions from its cryptic words. Will might be someone who was familiar with Newton's world.

Meeting a young scientist named Will Davenport was no coincidence. Izzy was sure there was a reason why the odd tussle between Davenport and the menacing-looking fellow had taken place in front of his store. Izzy believed events and people that cross our paths are mirrors that reflect profound inner personal truths yet to be revealed. What life sweeps before us is chock-full of meaning. Each so-called chance encounter is an exercise in the perfection of a reality that is mutually woven by the players — that life is a cosmic dance choreographed by an otherworldly part of ourselves.

Izzy's intuition told him that Will Davenport was a good man. That's why he had invited Will back to take a look at the Newton letter.

But Izzy hadn't told Will the whole story about the Isaac Newton letters. He didn't tell Will his suspicions that it wasn't just a car accident tragically caused by his father's bad driving. Something had compelled his father to drive so fast and so recklessly. Izzy also believed that the Newton letters his father and uncle had purchased may have not burned up in the car. He didn't have proof — just a feeling. Yet his sixth sense told Izzy the truth of that long-ago accident was still to be found.

It wasn't Izzy's tendency to tell the story of his father's death to just anyone. He usually kept things close to the vest. But there was something about Will Davenport. Izzy had that odd feeling people get when they sense having known someone prior to just meeting. He felt a definite affinity with this younger man who, for all the world, reminded Izzy of his sons. And thoughts of them, and of his dear wife Agnes, were never far away.

Izzy put the Newton letter aside and closed his eyes. In the silence of one moment to the next, he let himself drift away and welcomed a

whispered invitation to travel down the pathways of yesterday, back to
Agnes and what happened.

When Izzy was twenty he married his sweetheart, Agnes Brodman.
She was eighteen. They were kids, full of optimism about their future
together. They both wanted a family. Within a year Agnes and Izzy had
their first son, Jacob, and three years later, Robert.

At that time, The Great American Timepiece was located on West 86th
Street, in Manhattan. Izzy happily worked in the shop with his father
and uncle. It was a neighborhood store, though people came from all
over the city too. For Izzy, it offered him the opportunity to meet and
greet people from all walks of life. He loved to strike up conversations
with customers, find out where they were from, discover interesting
tidbits about their lives and their families.

Then suddenly, his father and uncle were gone and the shop was
Izzy's to run. Now he was at the store all hours and Agnes was caring
for two lively young boys, ages one and four, mainly on her own. It
was a stroke of much needed luck that an apartment also on West 86th
Street became available — the same place Izzy still called home. It only
had two bedrooms; Jacob and Robert always shared a room. In those
days, the shop was forever in financial flux and though, at times, there
were plans for a larger home, it never came to be.

Yet, in truth, the tight space never mattered much to Izzy. He was
gone all day and often well into the evening. On occasion, Agnes
helped at the store, and being so close, she could easily bring the boys
with her. Jacob had always been far more interested in the shop than
Robert. That was clear even when they were little.

But most of Agnes' time was spent raising her boys. And once they
were both in school, she volunteered daily at a nearby soup kitchen on
Amsterdam Avenue. Agnes had a huge heart and it ached for anyone

down and out. At first Izzy had tried to discourage her. Many homeless were mentally ill and could be violent. But Agnes would hear none of it. And over the years nothing happened to Agnes at her soup kitchen, except that she was honored as "Outstanding Volunteer" nearly every year.

No, the soup kitchen had not been the problem. The soup kitchen did not take Agnes away. It was war ... and then senseless tragedy.

After the terrorist attacks on September 11, 2001 Jacob joined the army. It was a shock to Izzy and Agnes. Jacob was twenty-seven. He worked with Izzy at the store, by then in its current location. In fact, it was Jacob's idea to move the store to Grand Central, as the station became a bigger retail hub in the late nineties.

Izzy had begged Jacob to consider another way to show his patriotism. Yet Jacob had been steadfast. As he explained to Izzy and Agnes, he felt an obligation to serve. There were others he knew that were going, and Jacob felt it was his responsibility to go too.

Izzy feared for his oldest son from the moment they hugged goodbye. When Jacob was sent to Afghanistan, Izzy feared for him even more. When he returned Izzy prayed the danger was past. But Jacob still had two more years of active duty. And then came the war in Iraq, in 2003, and Jacob was on the push toward Baghdad.

Yes, Jacob was honorable and brave. There was a Purple Heart to prove it, awarded posthumously.

Losing Jacob was the first blow. But losing Robert too — unimaginable.

Ambulances fascinated Robert from the time he was a toddler. Other children might dissolve into tears at their wailing sirens and flashing lights weaving through traffic. Not Robert. He stood mesmerized on the sidewalk or raced from window to window to catch one flying along West 86th Street. That passion never died. Robert had one goal — become an Emergency Medical Technician. And he did, and he was a damn good EMT. He had to be, to work in Manhattan for over a dozen years. "The whole city is one big emergency," Robert would say.

His life was his team and the city. Then, when he was thirty-one, he met a young woman from New Jersey. He was swept away by love — and then, just swept away.

Izzy blamed Robert's EMT instinct to help, to save. It was at the Jersey shore, three teenagers — stupid kids … no, not stupid … unlucky — caught by a riptide, a fearsome, ferocious sweep of water.

The boys went under … and then Robert too, trying to pull them back. It took a day for his body to drift back ashore. Izzy had "identified the body" — just the way they said it in the crime shows. But this wasn't *a body*. It was *his son*.

Another hero son eulogized for courage. Agnes and Izzy had raised such fine, brave young men. But that was little solace to them. Never again would they be able to share a meal together, laugh about silly things, argue about the state of the world, or feel the warm embrace of hello and goodbye hugs and kisses.

At fifty-five years old, Izzy had lost both his sons. His father was dead; his mother long dead too.

Agnes' parents were still alive and they managed to attend Robert's funeral. But the accumulated tragedy of losing both their grandsons, and the obvious toll it took on Agnes, their only child, seemed to bring the Brodman family crashing down. Within a year, Agnes' father was dead of a stroke. Her mother was gone nine months later.

By then whatever strength Agnes had mustered to care for her ailing parents was completely spent. For a long time she wouldn't leave the apartment. She sat by the window and stared, numb to the world, unable to make sense of the cruel blows she had been dealt. At other times she talked to Jacob and Robert, as though they were little boys again.

Izzy had The Great American Timepiece and he poured what was left of his heart into running it. In the end, it was his salvation. It gave him a purpose and people to be with. And the constant comings and goings in that grand place, Grand Central, were a daily reminder that life goes on … that it must.

∞

As if on cue, Izzy's cell phone rang: LUCY. Izzy hit speaker.

"Izzy, are you having your lunch? I hope there's no mayonnaise lathered on that turkey sandwich! Remember your cholesterol!"

Izzy smiled. Lucy Webster, his most trusted assistant, but more than that, a surrogate daughter and when she was playing food cop, number-one pain in the ass.

"Nothing to worry about, Luce — cholesterol still normal. And no, I haven't gone downstairs yet for my sandwich."

"Why not? Izzy! You know you can't skip lunch again!" Lucy's concerned voice was both irksome and endearing.

"Lucy, Lucy. I'm fine. I'm going out shortly. Why are you calling?"

"Just checking in. This stupid car repair is taking forever! I'll be there soon. But I wanted to be sure you eat, okay?"

"Luce, relax, all is fine." Izzy managed his calmest voice. He knew it was second nature for Lucy to watch over him and the store. "And, need I mention again the nuisance of a car in the city? Why you hold onto that car I do not know."

"Iz, I know you don't believe me, but a car does come in handy! Look, I'll see you later — and I can close up tonight, so you can get home earlier."

Lucy… always thinking of him. "We'll see when you get here," Izzy answered.

"Ohh-kayy, Iz …ciao!"

"Bye, Luce." Izzy watched his screen go dark and laughed for the millionth time at Lucy's signature signoff. She always ended her calls with *ciao,* yet she'd never been to Italy. She'd never had a boyfriend who was Italian. But she did love her pasta.

Izzy and Lucy Webster. *We're such a pair, the two of us,* he thought.

It was in 2012 when he hired her to be an aide to Agnes.

Izzy stared at the photo of his dear Agnes on his desk. Yes, that was a tough time… and the beginning of his years of gratitude for Lucy.

∞

The financial crisis of 2008 was really hitting hard by 2011. Izzy was working double time, doing the watch repairs and sales, to keep the store from becoming another casualty.

One of Izzy's favorite customers, Audra Green, suggested Lucy. Audra was a big exec in a venture capital firm. She had a commanding manner — Audra was used to being in charge — but she had the same big heart as his Agnes. Audra knew of Izzy's tragedies and of Agnes' decline.

"Izzy, you're here at all hours. I know because I'm in the city at all hours too! But you've got to get someone to be with Agnes. Find a young woman to keep Agnes company. Get Agnes outside again. I'll see if I can find someone to recommend."

A week later Audra had Lucy's phone number and resume. "She's twenty-two, the niece of my assistant," Audra explained. "Just out of college with no jobs to be found! I've met her — she's sharp, lots of energy. Lucy Webster."

Audra had tapped her manicured finger next to the boldface name on the resume. "Call her! She's just the person Agnes needs — and you too." Audra had squeezed his arm and then *click-clacked* off in her towering heels.

"As they say," Izzy chuckled aloud, "the rest is history."

Lucy was the perfect companion. Agnes never stopped grieving for her sons, but with Lucy's help, she started to rejoin the world.

At least for a time she did. Two short years later and one day Agnes collapsed. Within minutes, she was gone. Her huge loving heart was still.

It was a blood clot, the doctor said. But it was Izzy's rock-solid belief that Agnes had died of a broken heart. At only fifty-eight, loss had shattered Agnes.

Now Izzy was left alone in the world in a way he never expected. No wife, no sons. The life he had built with Agnes was over. Izzy came home at night longing to open the door and see his Agnes inside. Instead Izzy's life became coated with agony — something that would have broken most people.

Yet, like a phoenix, Izzy rose from the ashes of so much tragedy. In part it was his extraordinary constitution. But it was also his ability to bury his hurt so deeply that no one could touch it, not even Izzy. And then, over time and ultimately in a very large way, he had Lucy Webster to thank.

After Agnes died, Lucy continued to come to the apartment once a week to clean and stuff his freezer with food. But Izzy recognized that Lucy needed a real job. Once again, Audra Green in her towering heels stepped in.

"Izzy, what are you talking about? If you'll feel bad to lose Lucy, then hire her here! You could use another person. At least give her the option. She might be thrilled to learn the watch business!"

Lucy became as indispensable to Izzy as she had been to Agnes. In that first year after Agnes' death, Izzy mourned his wife the only way he knew how — by absorbing himself in work. And with Lucy learning the business beside him, Izzy gained an able assistant, and over the days to come she became like a daughter, ever watchful, making sure Izzy had what he needed to resume his life.

Izzy eyed the clock. It was well past one. Time for that sandwich.

He gave the Newton letter another admiring glance and returned it to the safe. It would be interesting to show Will Davenport and to get his reaction. But even more than that, Izzy expected exciting news tomorrow. Very exciting news.

If everything unfolded according to plan it would be a big day for Izzy Rhodes. All his efforts over the last few years — his raised hopes and his disappointments — would have all been worth it. The next few hours could offer him long sought-after answers to questions that endlessly hung over his head. Just a little while longer that's all it would be — just a little while longer.

Chapter 8

Justin Morrow

Justin Morrow was stewing. The job, to retrieve the package, was all but done. All he needed to do was deliver it and collect his money. Still, he was worried.

Yes, he'd made his getaway from Grand Central by subway. But to make sure there was no more trouble and that he wasn't followed, as he had been earlier, Justin had taken a roundabout route to his destination. First traveling downtown into Brooklyn, and then transferring at Atlantic Avenue, his favorite busy hub, to the subway that would take him back into Manhattan and uptown on the West Side.

The job had been compromised — and he had himself to blame!

Sure, Ike Jackson, the ass, had nearly derailed the handoff at 125th Street. He was supposed to be by the door, so he could be first off the train. It was to be a simple greeting of friends who hadn't seen each other in awhile. Holding the backpack in his hand by the strap, Jackson was supposed to just put it down, the two would hug, and Morrow would pick it back up. Simple, with no one the wiser.

Instead, loud enough for anybody to hear, Jackson practically shouted, "I don't think anybody noticed me."

Right, dude. Morrow was sure Jackson's nervousness showed. That put him on alert as he entered the train at 125th street. The guy who followed him in Grand Central must have spotted Jackson's jumpiness on the train.

And then Justin had made Ike Jackson's bungling worse. Obviously the guy in Grand Central was some do-gooder who thought Justin had a bomb.

But by getting in his face, Justin had blown his cover. Yet the guy had not followed him into the subway. That at least was a good sign.

That was it for Ike! No more jobs! If that asshole had kept his cool and followed the goddamn directions, on a crowded morning train, the do-gooder would never have noticed a thing.

Morrow spat on the sidewalk in disgust. And this was supposed to be a piece of cake assignment. Swipe an old book from some old guy, an antiquities dealer. Nothing more, nothing less. Make it look like a simple robbery. No one gets hurt. The client had been insistent. No violence.

Justin brought in Lorena Hamilton, his sometimes accomplice, to do the actual theft. A woman of a thousand faces, Lorena's disguises were her stock-in-trade. And she was the perfect temptress, using the oldest trick in the book. A little hair and makeup, a low neckline, push-up bra and the old timer was an easy mark. "Steal what you can — wallet, cell phone, keys — along with the book," Justin instructed. "Don't make the book look like the target."

They'd staked the old man out together. Learned his routines backwards and forwards. They debated — do it on the street or in his shop? Lorena had dressed up in one of her many wigs and visited the shop. "Full of junk, babe," she'd reported. "A rat trap, for sure. The street will be simpler — easier to pull off." But how would they know when he had the book on him?

Lorena gathered her supply of disguises and made a few return trips to the shop. The old guy had an assistant she was getting "friendly" with, she told Justin, to find out what he knew.

Bingo. Loose lips, as they say. The assistant bragged about a "very important historical find." Lorena had inched closer, touching the assistant ever so innocently and begging for just a little peek. "Sorry," he'd said, clearly disappointed he couldn't oblige and get rewarded by Lorena in return. "The boss is keeping it with him."

It happened on a quiet street on the East Side of Manhattan, where the old man lived. That he didn't park in a garage made it all possible. Justin laughed thinking about it. Trying to save a few bucks and loses something worth, well, who knows what. When Lorena called to confirm she had it, she'd used her code for mission accomplished: *Pop's asleep. He's resting comfortably.* Translation: The old guy never knew what hit him. And Lorena was fast. Chances are he couldn't even describe her.

Yes, Lorena was smart. She could follow a plan and think on her feet. Whatever the situation dictated. And she was clever. She was the one who thought of using the backpack exchange on the train. She reminded Justin that electronic surveillance was everywhere. With cameras hidden on almost every building and with the advanced state of facial recognition it was better to break up the line of sight of there comings and goings. Who knew how connected this antique dealer was — he could have detective friends in the NYPD. No need to give the cops any advantage. Better have them guessing…. And besides her brains Lorena was especially good with her hands. A necessary art in their line of work…. Yes, indeed, Justin thought, smiling. Lorena is *very* good with her hands. *And in plenty of ways.*

As planned, Lorena had hopped on the first train to Westchester. She had a girlfriend in Brewster, way out there, that Lorena could stay with anytime. The friend never asked questions. She had her own schemes going. Worked out great when they needed an overnight between handoffs.

That morning Jackson met Lorena near the Brewster station. There was an early train into the city that would be packed. Lorena had reported in from Brewster at precisely seven o'clock that Jackson was on his way.

Justin and Lorena agreed to meet at the usual place when it was all done. Would Lorena be there yet? Justin certainly hoped so. He needed Lorena to unwind. He couldn't get the guy that followed him out of his head. Had he screwed up?

Reassuring himself, Justin patted the backpack on his shoulders. The bundle was secured in a simple padded envelope inside. The package looked like no big deal, just in case NYPD chose this day for their now-and-then random searches of backpacks on the trains and subways.

That part was perfect. But when he got on the train at 125th street and saw the guy staring at him… New Yorkers don't stare directly. That's how people get into trouble. And that was Justin's first tipoff. The guy recognized something.

When Justin popped off the train, his instincts screamed the guy was following. He tried to ditch him and when he couldn't, he took a chance. He thought he could "turn the tables" and make the guy look like an asshole for following him. Stun the guy and that would be that.

But Justin hadn't anticipated a shouting match that would draw a crowd…. When the old man at the watch shop got involved, he saw it was a good time to escape.

Stop thinking about it! He wanted to shout at his own brain. He was safely away. And he'd feel even better after he handed off the package to the client.

Speaking of the handoff, Justin pulled out his burner phone, looked around and, with no one was in sight, hit the number. He waited for the beep to record and announced, "Systems go."

That was the code to confirm Justin had the item in hand. Now he'd wait to hear back on the burner.

He hoped it would be soon. He couldn't wait to get the money. He didn't give a damn what it was, but he had to wonder what was so important about an old book that this client was paying twenty-five thousand freaking dollars for a simple heist. Maybe he needed to take a look at this thing. Maybe twenty-five grand wasn't enough….

Justin smiled as he turned onto West Ninety-Seventh Street and walked toward West End Avenue. He was grinning as he climbed the stairs to the building and pulled out his key to the street door. His worries about Jackson's screw-up, the guy following him and even his own carelessness, were behind him now.

Was this a bigger score than he thought? This could be their best job yet. Lorena would love it.

Chapter 9

WEST 97TH STREET, MANHATTAN
MARCH 5
1:15 P.M.

Justin Morrow & Lorena Hamilton

One turn of the key and the door of Apartment 5D popped open. Justin glided into the entranceway, slid the backpack off his shoulders and tossed his keys in a tray on the table beside the door. For the last seven years this was his safe house, a convenient sublet and place to lay low if need be, or like now, to wait for further instructions.

"Finally! Okay Morrow, I've been waiting long enough. Get your ass in here!" Lorena's voice came from the bedroom.

A smile swept across Justin's face, and he began unbuttoning his shirt as he slipped off his shoes. His breath quickened in anticipation.

Lorena met him in the doorway of the bedroom, wrapped in a towel. Steam still wafted from the bathroom shower. Her hair was wet and she had a fragrant smell.

With just the sight of her, Justin could feel his manhood beginning to throb. He pulled off the towel as he pulled her toward him and they kissed deeply, hungering for each other, as they always did.

Lorena sighed and Justin danced her toward the edge of the bed. She did the honors on the last button of his shirt, and gave it a tug to help it fall off his shoulders. In the next moments, as they stretched out on the bed, Lorena began to peel away Justin's pants, her feet guiding them off his legs.

Then he slipped his hands under her, stroking the back of her thighs. Using the tips of her extravagant fingernails, Lorena ran her fingers up and down his spine, whispering in his ear, "Don't stop."

Kissing her neck, Justin followed a familiar path to her breasts. It was something he knew would excite her. In the moments that followed, they explored each other's bodies, which only increased their appetite.

Then in a pause, Justin caressed her womanhood and Lorena moaned with acceptance. She took hold of him and rhythmically guided him, slowly at first, then allowing him to move at will. With each thrust their passion built. On and on, deeper and deeper still, delaying, delaying... until the moment they felt the same explosive pleasure. Then they collapsed in mutual exhaustion.

"Babe, that's why we work so good together," Lorena murmured. It was her theory, often repeated. Over time, Justin had come to believe she might be right.

With long deep breaths, they allowed waves of contentment to wash over them.

"So give me the details … how it all went down." Justin, up on one elbow, was ready to get back to business.

Lorena sighed and slid herself close to Justin. "Not yet."

She pulled him back down on the bed and began to stroke him provocatively. Justin was eager to oblige. She straddled his body, pinning him to the bed, her fingers interlaced in his. With the tip of her tongue she touched each of his nipples as he grew within her. There was no need for delay this time. Each was pulsing with feeling and for the second time in minutes, they were groaning in mutual pleasure.

"See, babe," Lorena whispered, eager to confirm her theory yet again.

She swirled her exquisitely long nails around the ample hair on Justin's chest. "Now you just close your eyes, baby, and I'll tell you a little bedtime story about how an old man lost his favorite book in the whole wide world."

Lorena's voice had a seductive note that made Justin smile with anticipation of what would follow "the story." Easy marks and easy money were great aphrodisiacs.

Justin listened with increasing pleasure as Lorena described her every movement. When she laughed at how she'd made sure her jacket was open to reveal her cleavage, Justin couldn't resist interrupting to enjoy a taste of those luscious breasts.

"Grandpa was so helpful!" she laughed again as she described pretending to trip and falling against him. And then how, when it was over, Grandpa was rewarded for his kindness by the theft of his wallet, cell phone and package.

"So you ditched the wallet and his cell?" Justin was ready to cut to the chase, working through his usual after-job checklist.

"Course, babe."

"What'd he have on him?"

"Couple of twenties."

"Keep 'em. Go fix those fancy nails of yours … after." Justin nuzzled Lorena's neck. "You're right — we do work great together. You're a pro, Lorena. Let's see what else those talented hands can do."

Justin guided Lorena's hand to get the action underway. Three times in an hour — just one of the fringe benefits of this job.

She straddled him again and the momentum was building when, suddenly, Lorena screamed, "My bracelet!"

Justin opened his eyes. "What?"

Her body turned rigid. "It's gone! My bracelet! I know I didn't take it off! Oh my God, it's missing!"

Justin grimaced in irritation and frustration. "What are you talking about?" he asked impatiently.

"I had some trouble getting his wallet." Lorena had intended to keep that detail to herself. "What if I lost my bracelet then — and he found it?"

To her surprise, Justin was still perfectly calm. "What are you worried about? Even if he went to the cops, they can't trace it back to you."

Lorena could tell that Justin didn't remember the bracelet. He'd be far more concerned if he did.

The bracelet was from her father, from Tiffany's and it was engraved with a swirling, twirling *Lorena.* He'd given it to her for Christmas. Lorena had learned everything she knew about grifting from her dad — her talent for disguises and the ability to know when to disappear.

Damn! Lorena was sure Tiffany's kept good records. Probably a video of every purchase. *If the old man has half a brain,* she thought, *he'll see where it's from.* She had to find out where the bracelet was! *I have to go back,* she thought. *He could try to track down the buyer.*

Lorena was sharing none of this detail with Justin. Instead, she offered the quick plan that came into her head. "Look, babe, I got an idea. I'll dress myself up in a brand-new look and check out that shop. If he did find it, maybe he'll just try to sell it."

"Forget the goddamn bracelet!" Now he was upset — pissed at Lorena's coitus interruptus and whining over what he assumed was a cheap bauble.

Before he could continue his objection, Justin's burner cell rang. "It's the client!"

Justin put the phone on speaker as a high-pitched voice filled the room. "Meeting is set for the day after tomorrow — Thursday, at noon. Bring the package to Teterboro Airport. Take a rider service — not a taxi, not your car. At the gate, say you are Mr. and Mrs. Stanton coming to meet your *uncle.* The plane tail number is N827QS."

Lorena was taking notes on her phone. "Did you get that?" Justin whispered.

The voice repeated the tail number. "Be sure you have it. Security will require it at the gate. And be there by noon. Day *after* tomorrow."

The voice clicked off automatically.

"It's a recording, right?" Lorena confirmed. "That's smart."

Justin nodded. "This guy's no idiot. But *shit,* we got to wait another day! I thought we'd be done tomorrow."

Lorena snuggled up to Justin, pressing her breasts against chest. "What do you say to my plan, baby? I could do it this afternoon."

Justin pulled Lorena to the bed, excited again by the feel of her naked breasts against his chest. "What plan? Forget it! You're not going anywhere, today or tomorrow. We're sitting tight together, right here!"

Then he began stroking Lorena, who responded in kind. "You and me, we're gonna be busy! Gotta … look … at … the … book," Justin panted. "See … what's … in … it…."

Lorena straddled him, their favorite position. Moving back and forth, back and forth, she watched Justin's face for her cue to moan in tandem. Lorena's mind was not on sex. She was thinking of another prize.

She'd go to that shop, before they had to meet the client. Maybe it was risky, but she had to get that bracelet back. If it was at the old man's shop she'd find a way to get it back. If it wasn't, she could find out what happened to him after she robbed him. This whole thing could go south in a hurry. It was well worth a visit. She'd convince Justin — and she knew just how to do it.

"Hmmm, babe," she purred. "Let's do it again…."

Chapter 10

GRAND CENTRAL STATION
MARCH 6
8:00 A.M.

Will Davenport & Izzy Rhodes

Will had returned to The Great American Timepiece. In fact, he had taken an earlier train than yesterday, so he could have plenty of time with the Newton letter and still get uptown to his new university office before Ken started tracking him down.

Each morning Izzy insisted the shop be opened by 7:30 sharp, to insure he was fully prepared for the commuter rush. And today he was delighted, though not surprised, when thirty minutes after he arrived, Will Davenport walked through the door.

"Good morning, Mr. Davenport!" Izzy's voice boomed in welcome. "Let me guess! You've come for that cup of coffee and a peek at the Newton letter I promised to show you."

"If the offer still stands." Will didn't want to seem too presumptuous.

"Indeed, it does. Please wait here." Izzy went into his office to retrieve the letter from the safe. Then called to Malcom to escort Will to the office. Lucy had called to say she was battling a cold – no doubt caught at that drafty car repair shop — and would be late.

With a grand gesture, Izzy ushered Will to his private office and offered him his desk chair. Then he placed the Newton letter before Will.

At first Will just stared. Then with reverence he lifted the letter with his hands. Took in the date, May 1691, each numeral of the year sixteen hundred and ninety-one written with a flourish. He took in the script, the signature — both familiar from documents he had seen printed in books. But he had never *held* a Newton letter. He had never seen the script firsthand, the fine, brown lines of ink. *Remarkable!*

He turned his attention to the actual words, though he still couldn't believe he was reading *private correspondence from Isaac Newton.*

> *Dear Daniel,*
>
> *Saddened as I am to learn your unfortunate news of our friend and one-time protégée, Ethan Hawkins, we must not let this opportunity slip through our fingers. Your discovery requires quick action and, if I have read your letter correctly, there may still be time to change the course of events. Hence my urgent reply, which I am sending by the quickest means possible.*
>
> *Should what you say be true, we may have, at long last, found the prize, the treasure of treasures, the very keystone that reveals the deepest secrets.*
>
> *I regret that I cannot immediately join you. My responsibilities here detain me indefinitely. Write me when you are able to take possession of it again. Ethan's diary might hold significance as well. His formulae could be of great value. After all, it was he who found it and quite possibly the only one to have worked with it since the ancients last knew its power.*
>
> *Remember, there is a great ocean of truth that lies undiscovered before us. I shall pray that what you will soon hold in your hands may reveal the beauty that lives beyond the depths of the ordinary. Though should time and events be such to prevent you from doing so, then we shall leave it all to Destiny.*

Your loving friend,
Is. Newton

It was hard to take it all in at once. Will would have to reread it several times to get its full significance. But for now, he focused on one passage in particular: *"... we may have, at long last, found the prize, the treasure of treasures, the very keystone that reveals the deepest secrets."*

He knew that Newton had practiced alchemy at a time when it was outlawed in England. That alone explained why Newton was hiding any direct reference to whatever had been found.

"What do you think, Will?" Izzy interrupted.

"This is fascinating, Izzy! But it's difficult to decipher without knowing more about this Daniel — who did you say he was?" Will paused.

"Fletcher. Daniel Fletcher."

"Right," Will continued, "and Ethan Hawkins too. He must have been a contemporary of Newton, but I've never read anything by or about him."

Izzy nodded. "Yes, a mystery isn't it? But of course, even a great man like Newton would have acquaintances unknown to history."

Will pointed to the passage that intrigued him. "But this implies something that Fletcher and Newton, maybe Hawkins too, had long explored together. They must have been more than acquaintances."

Izzy listened, encouraged by Will's obvious interest.

"Problem is," Will continued, "this letter raises more questions than it answers. Though that's pretty typical in science. But, for instance, was it a physical object? Or a formula of some sort? Whatever it was, did Fletcher get ahold of it? Sounds like he had it and then lost it. So where was it? Did someone else have it? Who?"

Will loved a puzzle and this one had his mind churning. "And what about Hawkins?" he posed. "This reads like something happened to him. Had he been imprisoned? If he was also an alchemist, perhaps he was discovered and arrested. And what of his diary and the reference to formulas?"

Will looked at his watch — it was nine o'clock already. *Damn!* He had to get going.

"Anything else, Will? Any more thoughts?"

Will nodded emphatically. "Izzy, my brain's swirling with thoughts! It's a scientist's dream to come upon something like this. I can't thank you enough for showing it to me — for trusting me."

He stood and held out his hand to Izzy. "I'd like to research this further — Fletcher, Hawkins, Newton the alchemist. There may be a scientific discovery here that's been missed. Alchemy is shrouded in myths."

Izzy grasped Will's hand with genuine affection. The same instinct from his first meeting with Will returned, including a sense of connection to Jacob and Robert.

"Come back tomorrow morning," Izzy urged. "We can discuss this further."

"Deal," said Will, offering another handshake to confirm. As they dropped hands, Izzy gently patted Will's arm.

The gesture moved Will unexpectedly. Strangely, he felt a strong kinship with Izzy Rhodes.

A short while later, as he walked down the corridor toward the subway, Will stopped to send Nora a text. "Come in and meet me for dinner. Let's have a night on the town. We owe it to ourselves." Will was clearly excited at seeing and holding a centuries old letter written by Isaac Newton. He had the sudden sense of anticipation — that the door to the unexpected was wide open.

Chapter 11

Lester Edwards

Nora Martin Davenport had a nose for digging out the truth. That's what made her a good investigative reporter — a quality Lester Edwards planned on using. Her reputation as a hard-nosed journalist, willing to scale whatever obstacles were put in her way, would work in Edwards' favor.

He also loved deception, as long as he was the one doing the deceiving.

Edwards scrolled down to the "D's" on his contact list, then he hit dial and waited.

One ring ... two ... three. "Come on, lady," Edwards whispered. "Answer the damn phone."

"Nora Davenport."

"Hello? Excuse me, I was looking for Nora Martin, who wrote those extraordinary articles about the electrical grid scandal. Do I have the right person?" Edwards asked, sounding oh-so-flattering and polite.

"Oh yes ... yes ... this is Nora Martin. I ...um ... Davenport is my married name...."

Edwards listened and smiled. Perfect. She was stumbling, probably embarrassed at not answering with her professional name. He couldn't ask for a better start. He liked to have the upper hand.

"Who's calling, please?" Nora asked and waited for a reply.

"Listen, I'd rather not say yet. But I need your help. I have a story that will make your exposé on California corruption look like child's play."

"And what would that be?" The reporter in Nora was always ready. Edwards could hear her voice change to steady and alert.

"I have information about an elaborate plot to sabotage the power grid — to knock out power plants, first here in New York, and then up and down the entire eastern seaboard."

Silence and then, "Why call me? You should be calling the FBI."

Edwards expected Nora to be shocked. Instead, her no-nonsense posture surprised him. He decided to soften his approach.

"Look, Ms. Martin, the people involved only want their side heard. They care about the planet. And they care about the people on it. I think it's possible, *if YOU can get their story out to a wide audience,* it will stop them from taking drastic action to get their point across. This is a delicate moment. If I go to the FBI — or you do — it could push them to act immediately."

Silence again. *I bet her wheels are turning on this,* Edwards chuckled inside. "Ms. Martin, if you meet with me, I'll explain everything."

A few more seconds of quiet and then her voice, unreadable. "Where are you located?"

"I'm in the city — Manhattan. I know you've moved to New York, Ms. Martin. Your husband too."

More silence. Edwards could imagine Nora thinking this out, wondering how he knew they'd come east.

"Ms. Martin. Nora. Can I call you Nora? You have sources. I have contacts. Information travels. You don't need to be concerned about me. But I've got a story for *you.*"

Edwards smirked at his own cool lies. *Damn, he was good.*

"OK, but it has be somewhere very public."

"Of course. Lunch. I'm sure you'll be interested once you hear what I have to say." *Yeah, bitch, you'll be very interested,* Edwards repeated in his mind.

"You have to give me evidence. Bring me a name or a document that I can follow up with. I don't go on wild goose chases."

Very professional, Edwards thought. She was primed. "Of course, Nora. I have evidence. If it's not good enough, I'll get more."

"OK, when do we meet?

She was hooked. "Can you do tomorrow?"

"Tomorrow works."

She's eager. Good. "Al Dente's. Great Italian on West 14th Street and Eighth Avenue. Noon?"

"Fine. Noon."

"Do you know the place? I can give you directions." *He willed himself to play the nice guy to the max.*

"Not a problem. I'll find it. You forget, I am an investigative reporter." There was a hint of amusement in her voice.

Good, she was relaxing, letting her guard down.

"One thing." Her professional voice again. "I do need to know your name."

"Of course, Nora. Happy to tell you now. It's Reed — Jack Reed. The table will be under my name."

"All right, Mr. Reed…."

"Call me Jack, Nora. Please."

"JACK … tomorrow at noon."

Edwards waited — let her end the call. It was a quirk but symbolic. He always held on. The other person was the one to let go, a sign of surrendering.

When the screen faded and he could see Nora had clicked off, Edwards felt satisfied.

Yes, he loved the game. And, when this was over, he was going to be a wealthy man.

Chapter 12

Izzy Rhodes

This was the day. At any moment Izzy expected to hear important news. He had gone to great lengths and expense to pull this off and it meant everything to him.

For the second day in a row, instead of taking time for lunch, he chose to stay inside his office. As Malcolm took up duties behind the store counter, Izzy retreated to his private space. He again went to the safe, though this time he withdrew an accordion folder stuffed with papers and clippings. Izzy brought everything over to his desk, as he'd done a thousand times.

First he took out the newspaper accounts of the accident in Colorado and the deaths of his father and uncle. As he always did, he tried to read between the lines, to understand what was happening that night and why his father was a madman behind the wheel. And the feeling again … the sixth sense … that the police explanation wasn't the whole story … that the Newton letters his father and uncle had gone to collect were not ashes but somewhere to be found. Still Izzy hadn't any proof. Only a feeling … and he trusted his feelings. In hindsight that's probably why he made the trip to Colorado four years ago.

As Izzy reread the decades-old newspapers about his father's death, he fingered the smooth planes of the chunk of quartz anchoring a pile of papers on his desk. He had brought the stone back from the Rockies. It was a powerful reminder of what happened to him there.

The memories of that time were resurfacing full force now and he found it impossible to quell the swirling premonitions in his mind. He recognized that his life seemed to be teetering on the edge of great change. He felt pulled toward what he was sure was an important truth. Instinct told him that the events unfolding right now were revealing a tightly wound secret, and one he had sought ever since that otherworldly day in the Rocky Mountains.

It all started on the second anniversary of Agnes's death, in 2016, when Lucy Webster had convinced him to take a vacation. "Malcolm and I will look after the shop. Just get away for a while. Get a different perspective on life." And so he did.

Something drew him to Colorado. In one of their last conversations, his father had extolled the beauty and magic of the Rockies. "The mountains take your breath away, Izzy. Colorado is one place you shouldn't miss." So, in a way, Izzy was taking a trip his father wanted him to make.

He found that the hotel where his father and uncle had stayed was still in business, so he booked a room there. Lucy didn't try to hide her disapproval. "Getting away is supposed to help you relax! Why would you want to stay there? It'll be upsetting. Why do this to yourself?"

But Izzy was insistent. And maybe it was the mountain air, or perhaps the sense of his father and uncle's presence, but soon after arriving, he chose to take in the same mountain vista that they would have seen, from the same road they would have traveled, on their fateful drive.

For years, from one tragedy to another, Izzy had buried his emotions, unknowingly letting them build to a catastrophic force. That night after returning to his hotel room, Izzy began to feel seismic stirrings that were soon jolting him with the full weight of the multiple tragedies in his life. Each loss was like a blow — his father, uncle, Jacob, Robert, Agnes — as well as his dear mother, so stoic after his father's death, and Izzy's champion until dementia stole her away.

Izzy had collapsed onto the sprawling king-size bed, feeling ashamed at the sobs he could not stifle and the flowing tears that soaked the pillow under his head. Without the blessed buffer of The Great American Timepiece, Izzy was defenseless against his own grief. Wave after wave of emotional strife broke upon the shoreline of his unguarded heart. He was naked to the world and Izzy could not console himself.

Why, oh why did this happen to me? Poor Agnes… and my boys… oh my boys! They all left me… Dad… Mom… I'm so alone.

And then a vision flashed in his mind so brightly it startled him. His sobs subsided as a phantom impression pushed its way forward. The image of his brother, Levi, momentarily appeared. Levi was angry, his face distorted in pain. He was arguing with a faceless person, and a sense of foreboding rushed through Izzy.

He and his brother Levi were not close. Far from it. Levi lived in Boston and their relationship was marked by long bouts of silence, when neither sent an email, let alone picked up the phone.

But Izzy seldom even thought of Levi, and he was quite sure Levi seldom thought of him.

So why should Levi appear to him now? Particularly as he endured an emotional upheaval that was ripping through his heart? Perhaps it was a reminder that his only remaining relative was an estranged brother. That other than Lucy Webster, he was truly alone.

After a night of fitful sleep, Izzy awoke the next morning ready to leave Colorado. He'd had enough of "getting away." But changing his flight would cost a bundle. If he could wait two days, it would be cheaper. In the end, frugality won out.

With time to kill, Izzy decided to take a day-trip bus tour of the "Majestic Rocky Mountains."

The next morning Izzy was on the bus, and after a few short stops to see the mountain peaks from different perspectives, the group got the promised opportunity to hike on their own. The guide gave out maps and asked everyone to synchronize their watches. Naturally, Izzy was precise to the second. They were instructed to return no later than an hour and fifteen minutes.

Izzy was sixty-three at the time and in excellent physical shape, thanks to his daily walks in New York. He chose one of the shorter trails and set off quickly on his own. He wasn't looking for company.

Even so, he quickly realized that following a hiking trail was not like a trot up a Manhattan avenue. The landmarks were not nearly as clear. Soon he was looking at a stream that was not on his map. Yet unconcerned, Izzy delighted in his discovery and sat down on a boulder, watching the water rush along. He then noticed a curious white stone in the water and reached to pick it up. Though marked with angled ridges, it had flat areas that were exceptionally smooth. Izzy dropped it into his pants pocket. *Souvenir,* he thought. *A hard rock for a very hard trip.*

Izzy grinned at his own grim humor. A few deep breaths and he was feeling more at peace. He pictured the history beneath his feet and those who had walked there before — Native Americans, pioneers, miners, mountain men. He tried to envision himself in their place.

Izzy began to feel hungry and dug into the backpack that Lucy had given him for the trip. He had ordered a sandwich and bottled water from room service, which were inside, along with candy for his ever-present sweet tooth, a New York Giants football hat and a thick paperback of James Michener's *Centennial,* about the settling of Colorado.

He sat in the sun on a boulder by the stream, put on the hat and pulled out the sandwich, roast beef, which looked inviting. Izzy wasn't far into the sandwich when he heard a sound behind him. *Damn!* he thought. No doubt it was other hikers from the tour. His solitary reverie was about to end.

But a second sound made him more curious. Izzy looked around — to see a black bear looking at him!

All his senses came alive. His first instinct was to run, but his legs wouldn't move. He watched the bear sniff the air and wondered if, in fact, other people might be nearby. Should he call out?

Then he heard another noise that silenced him. Two black cubs emerged from the brush. Though Izzy knew little else about bears, he knew a mother would defend her cubs to the death. He was in real trouble.

Izzy had no idea what to do except to try to get away. He walked backwards slowly, trying to scrunch up his tall frame. He carried his backpack like a shield — and when, as he feared, the bear began to charge, he threw the pack with all his might. It hit the bear square on the nose. And in a stroke of good luck, the combined weight of the full water bottle and thick paperback were enough to stun her.

Seeing the bear stop momentarily gave Izzy his chance. Turning, he ran for as long as he could until, winded, Izzy slowed to a walk. Thankfully, there was no sign of the bear. She and her cubs were probably munching on his sandwich and the candy in his backpack.

Izzy's heart was pounding and he felt a sharp pain in his left knee. It had been seriously bruised in a taxi accident years ago — his one trouble spot with arthritis. Trying to catch his breath, Izzy limped to a patch of grass and sat down awkwardly. His right shoulder hurt as well; perhaps he'd pulled a muscle when he lobbed the backpack at the bear. He hadn't thrown an object with that kind of force in years.

The fear, exertion and pain made Izzy's head spin. *Why did I come here? Stupid!*

Izzy's eyes moistened and he quickly squeezed them shut, trying to cut off the tears before they became a cascade down his face. "God, what's happening to me?" Izzy whispered aloud. He felt utterly defeated.

Izzy tried to rise. He wanted out of this place, out of these mountains, out of this state. But the throbbing pain in his knee forced him back down. *What an old fool I am!* He thought angrily. *What a ridiculous old fool!*

Then the calf muscle in his left leg began to spasm. The pain was impossible — until the right calf muscle spasmed too. Then the pain was excruciating. He felt as if he was losing consciousness. He tried to steady himself, even to rise. But the pain was too much and he collapsed onto the ground.

There he was, flat on his back in the grass, in agony, the sun glaring in his face, eyes closed and his heart sinking into gloom. He thought of Agnes and the blood clot that had killed her. Was that the pain in his legs? Might he die alone, here in this wilderness?

Exhausted and longing for relief, Izzy felt himself letting go.

In seconds all of his thoughts drifted away. His whole body was floating higher and higher in a cloud of rarified white light. He could feel his arms and legs moving freely, his heart softly beating. Comfort and peace overcame him and the emotional aches and physical pains of his sixty-three-year old body were gone.

"Where am I?" Izzy whispered aloud as he floated higher still. There was nothing but white all around him.

Am I dead? Or dying? Izzy thought. And then he remembered the bear. "Did she catch up with me?" he asked aloud. Though he could not see the kind of rips and tears he would expect from a bear's teeth and claws.

Now the white around him was beginning to fade and clear. Izzy could see images that were out of focus. He rubbed his eyes a few times. *Where were his glasses?* he wondered. Perhaps they were lost in the grass where he had been, or was still.

Yet Izzy wasn't afraid. Indeed, fear was noticeably missing. He felt a lightness within him. As his eyes began to focus, he was astonished at the sight. He was looking at a meadow of tall green grass, and in the distance upon a hill was a building with huge columns, glistening in blue light. It was like a palace of light.

"Dear Lord, what's that?" Izzy asked.

There was no answer. For all the world, it seemed to Izzy that he was alone, but he felt none of the loneliness that he'd known before.

Now he took a deep breath and felt a rush of pure light flowing through him. His mind brightened and all his senses heightened. His vision opened in a way that he had never experienced. Everything was illuminated in pure, deep, shimmering colors and he was hearing tones in harmonic octaves that he could only classify as *sweetness.*

Izzy's curiosity took hold, and with a burst of exhilaration, he rushed toward the building glowing in the distance. The green grass of the meadow appeared soft and flowing, a velvet carpet before him. But when he reached down with a sweep of his hand to feel its softness, it wasn't solid at all — rather light particles arranged as blades of grass.

As he continued to walk, getting closer to the columned structure, what looked like undulating waves of blue stardust radiated from the massive building.

Izzy entered a magnificent hall. There were rooms to the left and right, each with an open threshold that beckoned him to enter. *Where in the world am I?* he thought, and the question echoed through his mind.

At the end of the hall stood a vessel on a pedestal. As Izzy approached, the vessel glistened with a light so bright that Izzy could not make out the object. He reached out and tried to touch it, but there was nothing to hold. His fingers went straight through the light.

Izzy took a step back and gazed. Light emanated from so many angles and in so many colors that his mind seemed to stop, awestruck by the scene. And now the light was filling him. He stood motionless, listening to his heart beating a soothing rhythm. With each throb came the feeling, "You are not alone."

Izzy felt a connection to life that he'd never experienced before. His heart aglow, a profound sense of tranquility wrapped around him. He felt safe, and he felt free.

It lasted but a moment. And to his sadness, when the feeling had passed, he was still tethered to the questions he had asked so many times. *Why? Why was his life so filled with loss and pain?*

Then the light grew brighter until he could not see. Yet he could still feel the light enveloping him as he entered a higher world. A wellspring of wisdom, a knowing, not in words but in feelings, descended around him. And in the next moment, knowledge pierced his understanding and the answers to his questions came.

Izzy could see an order to life — an evolution of unending patterns of beauty and truth that reveals a divine reality in everything and everywhere. He recognized that the events in his life were not haphazard, that all human endeavor has a purpose and all human drama is a creation of a higher realm, not divorced from one's choosing. He grasped that a still, silent part of everyone knows itself as eternal.

That profound understanding now made Izzy think once again about the drama of his life and its purpose. He thought about his father, Agnes, Jacob and Robert. Were their souls bound with his through time?

Though he could not answer with certainty, one thought, one feeling brightened his heart and mind — a knowing that each of their lives had been a gift to him, and there was a choice to make. He could lament their loss for the rest of his life, or frame anew the memories of their time together. Not by burying his pain; rather, by mindfully allowing the love they shared to flower in his heart, and by celebrating who they were.

And with that insight, a flurry of joy came over Izzy. He basked in a field of gratitude, fully allowing it to nourish him.

Yet even in this place where his heart beat out answers of comfort, an unexpected longing appeared. There was one thing that Izzy could not shake: the mysterious circumstances of his father's death.

Then, as though from very far away, Izzy heard a voice calling to him. It grew louder and, as it did, he could feel a hand, heavy on his chest. "Mr. Rhodes! Are you hurt? Mr. Rhodes!"

"No!... I'm not ready... I need to know how my father died!" Izzy spoke aloud as another voice floated through his mind: *"Come to know Ethan Hawkins…. find his diary and learn what you seek…."*

"Mr. Rhodes, are you all right?"

As Izzy opened his eyes, he touched his face. His glasses. They were there, on his face. It took another groggy minute to recognize the guide from the bus tour, kneeling, his hand on Izzy's chest. Izzy also took in two younger men in uniform.

"Mr. Rhodes," the guide tried again. "Mr. Rhodes, are you hurt?"

Izzy struggled to recall where he was and why he was on the ground. Then, "a bear…," he mumbled.

The guide looked up at the two men, and then nodded. "Yeah, we know about the bear. That's why these rangers are here. Did you run from the bear, Mr. Rhodes? You *never* run from a bear."

Having determined Izzy was, miraculously, not injured, the guide and rangers awkwardly hoisted him up. "Do you feel steady, Mr. Rhodes?" the guide asked.

"I'm fine now," Izzy said, shaking off the younger men's grip. Izzy put his hands in his pockets, in a studied effort at nonchalance. He felt the stone from the stream, his souvenir of this incomprehensible trip.

With the other men around him, Izzy walked along in silence. The sun flickered through the leaves, forcing him to blink, imprinting flashes of light on his closed eyelids. For an instant, Izzy remembered the light. *Was it just a dream?*

Then *Ethan Hawkins* streamed into his thoughts. And Izzy remembered more … *Hawkins diary….*

Izzy looked at his rescuers and imagined their response if he told them of the dream he was recalling more clearly with each step. *Best keep this to myself. I'll think on this all later, when I'm back in New York.*

∞

That was four years ago, and ever since Izzy could easily bring himself back to that moment when he could feel his heart beat out a rhythm of comfort and joy — a knowing that all is well. The stone he found in the mountain stream — the quartz crystal on his desk — had come to represent the wonder of what Izzy experienced on the mountain. Yes, it could have been a dream. But Izzy was far more sure that it was a moment when he pierced the veil of ordinary time and space, of the earthly plane.

It was a cleansing experience — a washing away of so many of the whys about his life. He had plumbed the depth of his emotions, emerged with new insight and found peace in the memory of Agnes, Jacob and Robert.

But his father's accident was another matter. It remained unfinished. There was something he was meant to solve.

Izzy was certain that the voice telling him to find Ethan Hawkins' diary was an experience that was more than a dream.

Ethan was his ancestor. Izzy had grown up knowing that connection. He remembered his father and Uncle Samuel animated at the mere mention of Ethan Hawkins. They felt that Ethan was an important figure of the 1600's whose contribution was lost to history. And they were determined to set the record straight.

At the time, that mattered little to Izzy. Youth being youth, his attention was focused first on sports, and then later, on girls and rock and roll. Even when he went to work in the shop with his father and uncle, he was always amused at their fascination, really obsession, with family history. *Dad and Sam are at it again, trying to tie the pieces together.* And Izzy would smile to himself, *at least it keeps 'em out of trouble!*

But then, when they went out to Colorado, their search turned all too real. What had his father and uncle come to know? What had they learned in Colorado before they died? They had gone to purchase the Newton letters, but had they obtained more?

Izzy had returned from Colorado with one goal in mind — to find the Hawkins diary. His sole clue was the one Newton letter. Newton and Fletcher had recognized the diary's value in solving their mystery.

Now it could be the answer to Izzy's mystery too: how and why his father and uncle died. *"... Find his diary and learn what you seek."* The voice in the mountains was a constant echo.

He engaged Ian Hillenbrand, a dealer in antiquities and artifacts hunter, though Izzy was always on the trail of the diary as well. Years went by with few leads. And now, finally, a bolt from the blue gave Izzy a miraculous chance to secure the diary of Ethan Hawkins.

He had not told Will these details. He had wanted to see what Will might know about Fletcher, about his relative Ethan Hawkins, what Will might see as significant in the letter. When Will comes tomorrow morning, as Izzy was sure he would, then Izzy would reveal his connection to Hawkins. And more ... he would have the prize to show! Ethan Hawkins diary.

A quick knock on the door and then, "Izzy, you in here?" Lucy Webster peeked her head inside.

"Lucy! How are feeling?"

"Okay."

Izzy could hear the hoarseness in her voice. "Did you go by Hillenbrand's gallery?" he asked eagerly. "Anything from Ian?"

Lucy eyed Izzy to check his mood. In truth, she was feeling lousy, but only partly because of her cold. She had unsettling news. And seeing Izzy with the Colorado clippings was only going to make it more difficult.

"He's not there, Iz. He never showed up, not at the gallery. Joe Farady, you know ... that quirky assistant of his, said Ian was working at home, or that's what he thought. He was kind of vague. But the guy's got a weird personality. More importantly, Ian's not answering his phone."

A pall came over Izzy Rhodes. For the past four years, Ian Hillenbrand had been reliable, always present when expected, always available on the phone.

Why would Ian disappear NOW? Why hadn't he called?

Intuition told Izzy that Ian was in trouble.

Something's not right.

Chapter 13

TWO DAYS BEFORE

2:00 P.M.

Ian Hillenbrand

"Hey! Are you all right?"

A knock on the window and a woozy Ian Hillenbrand, draped over the steering wheel of his Audi A6, felt a terrible throbbing in his left temple. Then another knock, this time a little louder, and Ian struggled to open his eyes.

"Are you all right?"

Ian flopped back in his seat with a deep heavy sigh.

"Do you need help?"

Walking to my car... someone asking for directions ... that pretty woman... great big eyes.... The cobwebs in Ian's mind kept his fragmented memory from piecing anything together.

Another knock and this time Ian roused enough to look into the faces of two young men, looking through the passenger-side window.

What's happening? His eyes fluttered open and then shut again. He took a deep breath, filling his lungs to capacity. Then in a burst of lucidity ... *the diary!*

Ian's heart jumped. *Where is it?*

Now one of the men slowly opened the passenger door, asking, "Do you need an ambulance?"

Ian's memory was coming back. The diary ... *in the back seat?* Ian twisted to look. Nothing.

The two young men were staring at him intently. One of them had said something about an ambulance. The last thing he wanted was to be forced to the hospital.

"No, no, I'm fine now," Ian called out. He remembered a peppermint candy in his pocket and dug it out for effect. "Just a little trouble with my blood sugar. Takes a minute to work," he explained as he popped the candy in his mouth. His blood sugar was fine, but he hoped the ruse would send these two on their way.

The Good Samaritans still looked skeptical. "You seemed pretty out of it," said one. "Sure you don't want to get checked-out? We can put you in a taxi."

In truth, Ian was feeling sicker by the moment. The diary was gone. His gut told him the pretty girl with the big eyes had done it.

"Truly, thank you for your concern. You've been most kind but I'll be fine." He had to get away from these two so he could think.

"If you're sure." The men spoke almost in unison.

Ian nodded emphatically. "Don't let me delay you further."

"Okay, good luck." The two men closed the passenger door and walked on.

Ian watched them in his rearview mirror to make sure they continued up the block. When they were well away, he frantically began checking the car. He looked under the seat on the passenger side. *Nothing.* Then he searched the floor in the back. *Nothing.* Ian's heart sank.

"SHIT! SHIT! SHIT!" Ian sputtered aloud. *Shit* might be a mild vulgarism for most people. To Ian, it signified the worst.

He paused, collecting his thoughts. *What to do?* He instinctively went for his phone, thinking he should call someone. He fumbled inside his coat pocket. *Where the hell is my phone?* He began searching all his pockets again. *Crap! Not my wallet too!*

For a fleeting moment, he weighed whether to get the police. But what was the NYPD going to do? Ian knew the city's finest would give no priority to a stolen phone and wallet, especially with only a few bucks inside. He didn't even have a bill of sale to prove he'd had the missing diary. It had been a cash deal — money for diary.

But there could be fingerprints, he realized. *Maybe the girl was part of a team working the neighborhood? Maybe the cops would get on it. Maybe the wallet and phone were what the thieves were after? Maybe they grabbed the package because it was there?*

No, this was no street robbery. His gut told him that too. Ian tried to recall the details. The girl approached him for directions and then tripped, falling against him. Ian had a mental flash of her jacket falling open and looking down at her lovely full bosom. She complained of feeling light-headed, and he invited her to sit in his car for a moment, until she felt better.

Now he remembered leaning in, placing the package in the center console. Then he helped the pretty woman into the car ... and another memory of her breasts suddenly up in his face, as she nearly pulled him into the car with her. He had straightened himself up quickly. He would never take advantage of a woman that way!

Then he had gotten in on the driver's side. He had turned to look at her ... suddenly, the smell of ammonia, so strong ... and ... nothing .... until the two men knocking on his window....

"She wasn't sick! Jesus! Her boobs all over me! How did you fall for that?" Ian looked at his own red eyes in the mirror as he spoke aloud. Why hadn't he recognized what was happening? But was she after his wallet and phone — or was it the diary?

Ian wished the red eyes belonged to someone who knew the answer. And then, "How am I going to tell Izzy?"

For the last four years all he and Izzy ever talked about was finding the diary of Ethan Hawkins.

Ian's first urge was to start the car and drive to his antiquities shop. Go upstairs, talk to Joe, his long-time assistant. He and Joe could sort this out. Joe was an odd guy, but good at seeing the sunny side of things. Right now Ian needed something or somebody to remove the sense of doom descending around him.

But even telling Joe wouldn't bring the diary back. The bottom line was, he was going to have to face Izzy.

But the diary was important to Ian too, and not only because of what it was. He leaned back in his comfortable car and considered how his long history with the Rhodes family had come to this.

Elijah and Samuel Rhodes, Izzy's father and uncle, had been among Ian Hillenbrand's earliest clients. They took a shine to the young upstart who didn't hesitate to follow every lead, explore every barn and climb through every outbuilding he could find, looking for the rare and unusual. Ian had a knack for locating obscure early American artifacts, which he brought to Samuel for authentication.

The Rhodes brothers were impressed with Ian and bought many of his finds. In fact, countless mugs of beer were raised in celebration of a momentous discovery the three of them shared. And when Ian wanted to open an antiquities shop, they offered financial assistance as well. Ian was eternally grateful for their friendship. So when Elijah and Samuel died in the car crash, Ian had mourned their loss deeply.

And privately, Ian wondered if there might be more to the accident than bad driving. At the time he was not close to Izzy, or to his brother Levi, and Ian never voiced his suspicions. But even then, still young in the business, he had come to recognize the ruthless side of the high-stakes game of artifact hunting. Down through the centuries, obtaining rare and valuable historic treasures was like a siren's call to those who caught "the fever." Bolder and more dramatic exploits were often demanded to satisfy the insatiable hunger for the next score. The allure of possessing the past was all-consuming for some, and the credo of *all's fair in love and war* ruled the day. It was an infectious passion, mostly unseen by the general public.

Still, Ian loved what he did and he hated to think it could be as cutthroat as it was.

After Elijah's death, Izzy and Ian had lost touch until, out of the blue, Izzy had come to him for help in finding the Hawkins diary. It was then that Ian learned that Izzy too had always suspected there was more to his father's accident.

If finding the diary was a mission for Izzy, it was for Ian too. If it could help solve the mystery of his mentors' deaths — what a perfect closure that would be!

Ian had begun the search by explaining to Izzy that, for a serious collector, it was paramount to amass an anthology so prominent, the collector would be considered a preeminent authority on a particular object, personage or given time period. It was an advantageous and envied position from which to deal.

There was also the issue of forgery. Serious collectors had to ensure their finds were the real deal, and a lot of money went into that process. Ian knew firsthand. A lucrative part of his business was authenticating objects. He'd learned much of what he knew from Samuel.

Ian suggested they put out word that the diary of Ethan Hawkins, a contemporary of Isaac Newton, had been found and was for sale. Their description of the diary was sparse — only that it contained entries of an important nature to Newton's work.

Ian surmised a teaser like that would be enough to flush out interested buyers — and anyone who had the actual diary. There was a good chance the owner would contact Ian to challenge his claim, which could be an opening to view the actual diary, or to admit their scheme and offer to buy it. As Ian explained, every transaction was different. They'd see who and what came forward and then decide their next step. It was a strategy that Ian had used successfully many times.

Certainly there were buyers who came forward, but no one to challenge the diary. Izzy was impatient and Ian was often required to go to the store in Grand Central, or Izzy's living room on West 86th Street, to recount again how previous hunts had taken even longer.

Then, about four months earlier, Ian received an email from Susan Elliot, a nurse at an assisted-living home in Ohio. She was writing at the request of a resident, eighty-three year old Timothy Fletcher. He had the *real* diary of Ethan Hawkins, she conveyed. He was a descendent of Daniel Fletcher, a friend of Hawkins and his sons, and a confidant of Newton. The diary had come down to Tim through the generations of Fletchers. Any other diary was a fake.

Susan Elliot also included information that Tim Fletcher no doubt did not intend to share. His family had dumped him in the facility and, ever since, he had no contact with them.

Fletcher was proud that he had cared for the diary all his life and was determined to secure its future. Susan was his favorite nurse and the only one he trusted.

What a stroke of good fortune! When she mentioned Daniel Fletcher — Ian knew, of course, of Izzy's Newton-Fletcher letter — it all made sense. Ian was confident the diary was authentic. Yes, he'd have to confirm it, but the chances of a forgery were slim.

When Tim learned that Izzy was a Hawkins descendent, he needed to meet him. How his family came to have the Hawkins diary was lost to the din of history. What he did know from family lore was that his role was to ensure the diary's safekeeping — until the moment would arrive, the situation would present itself, and he'd know exactly what to do. And that time had come. Ian and Izzy made plans to fly to Ohio and meet Timothy Fletcher.

Then the wheel of fate spun again. Fletcher fell and broke his hip.

They pushed back their trip a month as he recovered. Then Susan called. Tim was gone — a massive stroke. Complications were a common hazard of breaking a hip, she explained.

Tim had wanted to meet with Izzy, and if all went well — if Ian authenticated the diary, as expected — to hand over the diary, no strings attached. After Fletcher died, Susan Elliot was anxious to make the exchange quickly.

But then her husband got wind of the situation. He saw a once-in-a-lifetime opportunity. A never-before-heard-of diary, with references to Isaac Newton, would fetch a fortune. He wasn't about to let it go for nothing.

Susan Elliot had been devoted to Tim Fletcher. But now, as she explained to Ian in a long and tortured email, she was powerless. Certainly she was embarrassed by her husband's demands, but she was not about to lose her marriage over this. She asked for Izzy to understand — and to make an offer.

Ian tried to negotiate a finder's fee of ten thousand dollars. That offer resulted in an angry call from the husband and a demand for ten times the amount. That, in turn, incensed Izzy, who saw his family legacy held hostage.

Now Izzy joined the next call with the husband. "You're nothing but a charlatan and a slacker trying to squeeze every last cent you can," Izzy shouted into the phone. "You greedy bastard, I won't give you a dime!" To which the husband replied along the lines that Izzy too was greedy, and that it would be easy finding someone willing to pay what the diary was worth.

The stalemate continued until eventually, between Ian and Susan, who at last put her foot down with her husband, they agreed on twenty thousand in cash. But it was conditional. Ian would have to come alone to make the transaction. Izzy was not welcome.

And so Ian had made plans to drive to Ohio, to avoid the inevitable questions by airport security about a suitcase full of cash.

Izzy continued to want to go along, promising to stay in the background. But Ian worried that Izzy's emotions would get the better of him, and he'd inevitably throw a monkey wrench into the exchange. At last Ian convinced Izzy to stay home.

So Ian had made the trip to Ohio, authenticated the diary and began the return trip the next day.

Ian looked again at his tired red eyes in the car mirror. How was he going to tell Izzy? After four years of searching and waiting, four months on pins and needles, Ian had the diary in his possession for only some forty-eight hours.

Whoever took the diary — what was the motive? The millions a diary with references to Isaac Newton might fetch?

But who knew Ian had it?

Again, Ian went over what had happened. Maybe he was wrong. Maybe it was a simple robbery by a street-hustling gal. She'd probably toss the diary — not even know what it was!

Ian felt sick and exhausted. Pangs of guilt rolled through his stomach. He could not face Izzy. He couldn't face himself. He had been careless — he let his guard down and the diary was gone.

He needed to go back home and lie down for a while. Think through what to do next. He had some time. He had called Izzy from Ohio, when he had the diary, but not when he first arrived in New York.

Once he took possession of an object, it was Ian's process to take photographs and video so its features could be documented for historical reference, as well as safeguarding the information. He knew when he got back from Ohio he'd need a day or two to examine the diary. He was meticulous and wanted to do it in peace, without Izzy hanging all over him.

Even though Izzy had agreed to wait to get the diary until he was done, Ian recognized Izzy wasn't going to be able to stay away once he knew Ian was back. So he kept his arrival quiet.

And now he was glad he did, and not only for the obvious reason. Ian had unexpectedly found something interesting in the binding of the diary — a cryptic message that would heighten the excitement of finding the diary and the process of interpreting its passages.

Of course, all that was moot, now that the diary was stolen.

In assessing his situation, Ian realized his vague timetable could work to his advantage. He had promised to have photos for Lucy, Izzy's assistant, to pick up at the gallery, but he hadn't said which day.

He had the time he needed — mainly to get his nerve up to tell Izzy. And he had one more move up his sleeve. If somebody was after the Hawkins diary, he might find evidence online. *There were dark sites where requests were made. Do that first. Look for a clue.* If something came of it, maybe he wouldn't need to deliver bad news at all!

The street empty, Ian opened the door and shifted to get out. *Yes, he'd go home to think — and investigate.*

In his eagerness to get away from the scene of the crime, Ian didn't notice the thin silver bracelet he'd been sitting on. It was too delicate for his ample derriere to feel.

But had he looked, he would have seen a swirling, twirling engraving of *Lorena*.

Chapter 14

Downtown Manhattan
March 6
8:30 p.m.

Will & Nora Davenport

"You've got to taste this pasta, Will. It's the best carbonara I've had since Italy!"

They were dining at Al Dente's, on West 14th Street. Nora was accustomed to mysterious phone calls from potential sources, but she made it a rule to never meet a stranger at a place she didn't know. And since Will had suggested she come into the city for dinner, it made sense to check out the restaurant where Jack Reed wanted to meet.

Will's desire for a night out — and Reed's call, strange as it was in ways — had made Nora feel more hopeful than she had in months. There was the thrill of an important story, if Reed panned out. There was also her discovery the day before of the DeWitt-Broderick tie, possibly something with a Victor Strong too, and how it might all lead to finding the truth about the hit-job on Will's career. She could feel the old spirit of adventure returning for both of them — being open to new possibilities again.

And then there was her own declaration that it was time to make Baby Davenport. With that particular goal in mind, Nora suggested a splurge: getting a hotel and staying over. Conceiving *in* New York City — what a perfect confirmation it would be of the rightness of their move here.

Yet, for now, Nora had decided to stay low-key on everything. She had no intention of bringing up DeWitt or Broderick until she had some time to poke around. And Nora knew Will worried about the unsavory sources she sometimes met. Reed didn't seem unsavory — yet — but to avoid probing questions, Nora only mentioned a possible story lead and meeting tomorrow as further argument for staying in the city tonight.

Mainly, she wanted to celebrate their new start. As she alternated between forkfuls of pasta and sipping a fine cabernet, she listened to Will recount his exhilarating experience of holding and reading the Newton letter. In turn, Will had fully explained how he came to meet Izzy Rhodes. Though Nora was a little surprised — and somewhat concerned — at his chasing down a suspicious guy with a backpack, it further reminded her of the old Will.

Well into dinner, Will was still chatting away about the letter and what it might mean for his research and book. "Nora, I would love to have some more time with it — crosscheck that time period in Newton's life."

Will gestured as if he were still holding the letter, and Nora could not help but grin, to see him so animated.

"What?" he asked, registering her laughing expression.

"Nothing," she replied. "Just happy to see you happy. Go on…."

Will smiled in return, acknowledging Nora's observation, and then continued where he left off. "Newton was a great thinker and I'm sure there were theories he proposed that are buried, just waiting to be rediscovered. Too often people look at historical facts as settled, but from my experience what happened in the past is more vital and alive than it appears. New information is forever materializing, breathing new life into what we thought we knew."

Nora loved when Will put on his science hat. Apparently his happiness was also from being on a college campus again.

"When people say New York City is electric, they're not kidding.

This city makes me feel amped up!" he roared, rising above the general noise level of the packed restaurant.

Will's eyes were shining as he spoke, which made Nora's face light up too. "It's so good to see and hear you so excited again," she repeated, feeling the soothing effects of Will's brighter spirits, not to mention the free-flowing wine.

"I feel more alive than I have in a long time," Will agreed, his faith in the possible returning.

"I think we can make a good life here, Will."

He reached across the table to offer his hand, which Nora eagerly accepted.

"So much has happened," Will spoke reflectively now. "Our lives got so messed up, derailed so fast and from out of nowhere. I was choking on my own feelings. My mind was so clouded with doubt, unable to see a way out of anything."

Nora nodded. "Will, I know…."

"Before you respond, I want to tell you something," he interrupted. He wore a comforting smile and she could see something different in his eyes.

"When I was lost, stumbling around in the dark regions of an uncharted netherworld, there was always a light to see me through the darkness. You were, *are,* that light. Who knows what tomorrow will bring, but I want you to know I'm forever grateful that you are my partner on this big, crazy, wonderful ride."

Tears glistened in Nora's eyes.

"You can speak now. I'm finished," Will teased. Nora could only squeeze his hand with a warmth and strength that told him everything.

They lingered in contented silence until their waiter reappeared with the dessert menus.

"How about it?" Will asked. "Sweets for the sweet?"

Nora met his smiling eyes with a twinkle in her own. "Hmmm, I'm thinking we skip dessert here. I've got a different kind in mind. Let's head back to the hotel."

Will was signaling the waiter for their check before Nora could finish her words. "I like your thinking, Mrs. Davenport!"

Chapter 15

Will & Nora

"Wake up, it's time to make a baby," Nora whispered in her husband's ear.

"Isn't that what we did last night? Make you a baby?" Will answered sleepily.

"Yes, indeed. But that's the fun of it. You get lots of practice in the process…." Nora nestled next to him, first kissing his shoulder, then his neck and then his ear.

"Oh, you've done it now," Will replied, eyes still closed and enjoying Nora's advances.

"And what's that, Mr. Davenport? What have I done?" She stroked the hair on his chest and then proceeded to explore lower.

Will reached for Nora, fully engaged. "If it's a baby you want, it's a baby you'll get!"

With arms and legs intertwined, Will and Nora embraced in a rhythmic dance, rocking back and forth until the breathless moment that flashed them into ecstasy, then echoed into gentle waves of quiet afterglow.

"Oh darling, that was delicious," Nora sighed, snuggling as physically close as one human can to another. Then, after a pause, "But…."

319

Will was savoring his post-sex calm, taking a few slow breaths, when Nora's *but* registered.

"BUT?" He knew her well enough to know there was something on her mind.

Nora paused again, weighing if she should continue.... Yes, she had to know now.

"Will, it's your choice of words. You keep saying, 'make YOU a baby,'... 'if it's a baby YOU want.' But this is what you want too, isn't it? I know I surprised you with my 'ritual'...."

Nora had revealed the tossing up and tossing out of her birth control after their lengthy "dessert" last night. Will had been surprised at the timing, to say the least.

But once Nora had shared her worries about age, as well as the karmic good spirits she was feeling about this time and place, Will had seemed to agree. Now, with his ambiguous choice of words, she wondered if he was really on board.

"It's just so important, Will. I want us to be together on this," Nora concluded.

Will looked into Nora's face, her eyebrows scrunched in concern, and gently kissed her forehead, nose and lips. "I'm sorry, Nora. I wish I had the *right* words to tell you how much I want a child too. You've had to carry the financial burden for some time and I've hated every minute of it. I guess that's *my* worry. What if this book doesn't sell? But if you're ready, sweetie, so am I."

They kissed tenderly and then lay back in silence, clinging to each other in hopeful dreams of the months to come.

"I wish we could stay here all day," Nora sighed.

"I know," Will replied. "But I must get my writing brilliance underway," he laughed, "and I want to walk over to Grand Central and see Izzy Rhodes this morning. Get another look at that Newton letter before I take the subway uptown."

"Well, you best get going then!" Nora gave Will a gentle push as he got out of bed. "I'm going to camp here until checkout and my lunch meeting. Maybe we can ride back together on the train this evening."

"What's this meeting again?" Will asked absently as he headed for the shower.

"It's exploratory. He might be a whistleblower. Promising a big story."

"Not another wild goose chase?"

"Got to go to know."

"So you tell me, Ace!" Will saluted his star journalist as he closed the bathroom door.

Minutes later, showered, shaved and ready to leave, Will gingerly sat next to Nora, now on her laptop in bed, and gave her a lingering kiss. "Goodbye, madam! Perhaps we can do this again sometime."

She returned the kiss seductively. "No maybe about it, Mr. Davenport! Sooner than you think."

"Good luck today, Ms. Martin…."

Nora chimed in as they spoke in unison: "Be careful and stay in touch!"

Chapter 16

Will & Izzy Rhodes

Will walked in sync with the morning crowd, the energy of the city again assuring him that his life was on the move once more. At Times Square, he joined those turning left onto the famous 42nd Street. As he crossed Fifth Avenue, West 42nd Street, of Broadway legend, became East 42nd, with its best-known icon, Grand Central Station.

Shortly thereafter he entered the terminal and continued briskly toward The Great American Timepiece. The store was in sight when he spotted Izzy Rhodes, rushing out and then pausing to lock the door.

"Izzy!" he called out. *Where's he going?* Will wondered. *And what about the letter?*

"Oh, Will! You'll have to excuse me. I know I asked you to come by, but I have to leave immediately. Something's come up."

Damn! Will tried to mask his disappointment. "I don't want to keep you. Of course, another day. I've been thinking about the letter non-stop — and Ethan Hawkins and Daniel Fletcher. Maybe tomorrow?" Will extended his hand, to shake on the arrangement.

Izzy offered his hand in turn. "I'm sorry, Will. I'm all out of sorts."

Though they barely knew each other, Will could see that something was very wrong and Izzy was extremely distraught. "Can I help?"

322

Izzy was touched again by the sense of connection with this man. He decided to take a leap of faith and extend his trust in Will.

"When I met you yesterday, I was waiting to hear from Ian Hillenbrand, an antiquities hunter. The Newton letter is just the beginning. The diary of Ethan Hawkins, Will — Ian and I have found the diary! Ian traveled to Ohio to get it, and I expected to have it by now. But the last time I heard from Ian, he had the diary and was getting ready to come back to New York. That was days ago. I haven't heard from Ian since and he should have been back long before now!" As Izzy spoke, his voice revealed both his frustration and worry.

"Perhaps he wants to surprise you with it?" Will suggested trying to inject a sense of optimism, even as he was astonished that Izzy was actually on the trail of the diary and had not revealed that fact yesterday, when Will examined the Newton letter.

"No, that's not Ian," Izzy shook his head. "He's not one for surprises, and he knows I'm not either. I'm going to his shop now. Find out for myself. Malcolm or Lucy, my assistant — you haven't met her yet — will be here soon and can reopen. I can't wait another minute!"

Izzy took a deep breath and looked at Will with determination in his eyes. "It is essential — *essential* — that I get the Hawkins diary."

Will felt again the unexpected kinship with Izzy. He wanted to help, and not only for the scientific finds that might be contained in the diary.

"Why don't you let me come with you?" Will offered.

"If you have the time now, I wouldn't mind another set of eyes and ears. It's ten blocks south on Madison Avenue. Fastest to walk at this hour. I'll explain as we go."

Will's thoughts raced... *a diary... about Isaac Newton! You couldn't keep me away. Of course I have the time!*

Outside the sidewalk teemed with people, but Izzy's long stride and Will's quick pace got them swiftly across 42nd Street and headed south. On their journey toward East 32nd Street, Izzy related the abridged version of his trip to Colorado four years earlier.

With the street noise and their frequent need to weave around people and obstacles, Will wasn't sure he caught every detail. But the main points were clear. Over his life, Izzy had suffered excruciating loss — father, mother, wife, two sons.

Putting himself in Izzy's place, Will shuddered at the mental image of losing Nora and the child they were trying to conceive.

And a near-death experience in Colorado had heightened Izzy's suspicions about his father's fatality and fortified his resolve to find out what really happened. The diary somehow was critical to solving that puzzle.

Again, Will's empathy registered with Izzy, who felt a wave of gratitude for the younger man's presence by his side. There was no time now to say more. But when things settled down, Izzy would tell Will the true nature of his connection to the diary of Ethan Hawkins — that Ethan was his ancestor — and his father and uncle were not only hunting the Newton-Fletcher letters in Colorado, but they had hoped the letters would lead them to the diary... and it's potential secrets.

Describing his dramatic experience reminded Izzy of his celestial visions in Colorado. In recent days those images kept returning as a persistent recurring dream. Mystifying as they were, the Colorado experience had also left Izzy with the strange ability to feel the flow of life through the palms of his hands. He'd heard that people who practiced tai chi or yogic breath could feel waves of energy — life-force, they claimed. But he didn't practice anything like that.

Izzy had told no one about this new development, not even Lucy. He had just come to accept it as another way he could perceive the world — a new heightened perception — as real as hearing or seeing.

Still, Izzy wanted to understand what it all meant. Perhaps Will Davenport could help him solve this mystery too. As a scientist, Will might have insight into different planes of awareness and the physics of realities beyond our world.

Will and Izzy were crossing East 34th Street now, easily keeping step with each other as they hurried toward Ian Hillenbrand's shop. Each in his own way had powerful reasons to hope that the diary of Ethan Hawkins — which, centuries ago, had been the intense focus of two other men, Isaac Newton and Daniel Fletcher — was waiting up ahead.

Chapter 17

East 32nd Street and Madison Avenue
March 7
9:45 a.m.

Will & Izzy

At East 32nd Street, Izzy signaled Will to stop. "We have to cross here and head over to Madison," Izzy explained. "Ian's shop is in an old building, on the second floor. Nothing fancy. You'll see — it looks like a crowded antiques store. But Ian's got fascinating finds. I just hope he's there and my diary is with him!"

Will reached out to give Izzy a reassuring pat on the arm. *What might they find, indeed?* Izzy's brief description of the history of the diary search had raised Will's doubts that there was a simple reason for Ian Hillenbrand's silence. *Stay alert,* he reminded himself. The amateur detective in Will was at it again.

They crossed Park Avenue South and continued west. Will could see the Empire State Building in clear view, but no time to take in the details of that iconic symbol of New York. Izzy had picked up the pace. They were getting closer.

Traffic was moving uptown on Madison Avenue. "We'll cross and then it's just over on the other side," Izzy shouted amidst horns and sirens.

He guided them toward the entrance to a small lobby. Will jumped ahead to open the door for a young woman in oversized sunglasses about to exit. Her coat was open and Will took in her tight V-neck sweater and cleavage pouring out. She gave him a sly smile as she brushed by and then turned toward Fifth Avenue.

Izzy charged inside, pausing only for the required security check. "Come on, let's not bother with the elevator," he urged, rushing toward the stairwell door. Will was amazed at Izzy's speed up the stairs. Within seconds they were on the next floor. At Suite 222, Izzy rang the buzzer, keeping his finger in place until a groggy Joe Faraday, Ian's assistant, opened the door.

"What happened, Joe? Where's Ian?" Izzy put a long arm around Faraday's shoulder as they entered the shop. Will looked around at a space stuffed with objects.

Faraday was rubbing his face, as though forcing himself to focus. "I don't know where he is, Izzy. Or the diary. But that woman. She wanted a bracelet. I bent down and she put something under my nose. I got hazy...."

Suddenly, his eyes widened. "Jesus, she's the same woman that's been hanging around here, asking a lot of questions! They're wigs — she wears wigs! Makes her look different. Oh, dear God, no! I'm sorry, Izzy. She's got to be the same person I mentioned the diary to the other day!"

Izzy let out a deep sigh, as if he'd been holding his breath for days. "Somebody's got my diary, don't they?" he groaned. "Where the hell is Ian?"

Joe gave his face another rub. "Look, I don't know, Izzy. Honestly. He emailed a couple days ago. Said he was busy photographing the diary and didn't want to be disturbed. Not answering his cell."

Will was picturing the woman he'd held the door for minutes earlier. "Sorry to interrupt," he addressed Izzy. Then, to Joe, extending his hand, "I'm Will Davenport. What color was the women's hair today?"

"Red."

Will awkwardly put his hands up to his chest. "Ah, you know, endowed?"

Joe wasn't getting it.

So much for euphemisms. "Breasts. Big tits?"

"Oh yeah!" said Joe with an enthusiasm that made Will certain they had the same person in mind.

Will had one foot out the door as he spoke. "We just passed her downstairs leaving the building! Izzy, she could have something to do with the diary! Let's find out!"

Izzy hesitated. "It's too late — she could be anywhere."

"Worth a shot!" Will pulled at Izzy's coat.

Izzy nodded and put away his doubts. "Joe, go to Ian's place. Make sure he's okay. AND TELL HIM TO CALL ME!"

With Will in the lead now, they backtracked to the stairwell and flew down the stairs. Racing out the main door, Will turned right. "She was headed toward Fifth Avenue."

As they rushed quickly up the sidewalk, Will glanced at his watch, doing a quick time estimate. "It's about ten o'clock. I think we were inside about ten minutes."

Izzy slowed his pace to catch his breath. "Ten minutes! She's not likely to be window shopping, Will. This is a lost cause. Have you ever tried to chase someone in this city?"

Will thought, *Grand Central, the other morning, rush hour and I kept up, no problem.* The man who loved adventure was in his element once again.

"Come on, Izzy!" urged Will. "Let's not give up so easily. You never know!"

Chapter 18

Will, Izzy & Lorena Hamilton

At that moment, Lorena Hamilton was emerging from a shoe store on West 32nd Street just off Fifth Avenue. If she had to break a heel — *this goddamn city and its potholes,* she frowned — at least it was near a Bargain Shoes store. She paused in front of the glass outside the store to admire her reflection, now wearing Jimmy Choo knockoffs for a mere twenty-nine dollars and ninety-nine cents!

It had taken more time than she would have liked to find her size in black. But she would have lost more time trying to hobble around on a broken heel. The red pair on display were beautiful — she might come back to get them later — but she couldn't wear anything that flashy to meet this high-end client.

Lorena's cell rang as she crossed the street. It was Justin.

"Where are you? Did you get the bracelet?"

Shit, no point in lying. "No luck, babe. But I had to try."

"Jesus, Lorena...!" She could hear the controlled fury in Justin's voice. "Just GET HERE."

"Babe, I'm going into the subway. Taxi'll take longer. I'll be there in twenty."

"Look, I'm leaving at 10:30 when the car comes. You're not here, too bad. I don't get you and your idiot obsession with that bracelet. No one would ever make the connection."

Lorena had stopped listening. She didn't care. She had to try. She'd been careful. She was always careful. Always wore gloves — no fingerprints. Changed wigs enough so she always looked different — except for some assets. Looking down at her cleavage, she smiled.

"Babe, I'm going to lose you," Lorena lied. Enough of Justin's complaining. "I'll call when I get off the subway at 96th Street. You can meet me there and I can hop right in the car."

Lorena began to run. More accurately, to walk as fast as she could. There was no such thing as running in four-inch heels. She'd get the B train at Herald Square. There was an entrance right on West 32nd and Broadway. That would get her uptown to West 96th Street. It was still a long walk over to West End Avenue. *Justin can pick me up in that car,* she thought.

Getting there quick was what mattered. Lorena was sure Justin meant it. He *would* leave without her and she wanted to be there. If any bonus money was in the works, she wanted her fair share. After all, she'd lost her Tiffany bracelet!

"There she is!"

Will and Izzy had crossed Fifth Avenue when they saw a red-haired woman leaving a store. She stopped to look at herself, giving them a priceless few seconds to confirm it was the same woman.

"It's her!" Will repeated! "Same hair, coat, and gloves…." Will remembered too what the coat, still open, was covering.

They paused, waiting to see where she would go. She was on her phone now, talking at first but then, it seemed, mainly listening.

"Maybe she's getting instructions?" Will whispered.

She was walking west, slowly, but then, once the call ended, much faster.

"Where could she be going?" Will asked.

"Could be Penn Station on Seventh Avenue. We've got to keep up with her!" Izzy replied. "Really crowded over there. Commuters and shoppers!"

Damn, why are these avenues so long! Lorena swore silently as she hobbled along. Jimmy Choo knockoffs were shitty for walking fast. *There it is, finally! Broadway.*

She fumbled inside her purse to find her MetroCard before she entered the subway. Faster that way. She tried to remember how much was left on the card and prayed that when she slid it through the turnstile reader, she wouldn't get the dreaded INSUFFICIENT FARE. She couldn't waste time in line with clueless tourists to refill her card.

Minutes later, Lorena was carefully making her way down the stairs of the subway entrance. A guy climbing up with a big rolling suitcase whacked into her. "Watch it, asshole!" she yelled. Lorena hated this station. All these cheap morons with their crap headed to Penn Station. "Take a taxi, jerk!" she added, to further register her annoyance, then immediately laughed. *Good riddance, buddy!* Had to be a tourist. Anybody else would be giving it right back.

Through the turnstile — *thank you, Jesus!* Lorena ran toward the sign that pointed to the B train straight ahead.

Izzy was the first to recognize Lorena's destination. "She's taking the subway. She just took out a MetroCard. Watch — there's an entrance on Broadway."

Will pulled out the card he'd purchased just two days before. "Here, I've got plenty of rides."

They saw her turn and descend out of sight as the seconds to cross Broadway ticked down. "Run!" Izzy called. "We gotta catch her!"

With only moments to spare, they bounded across Broadway and followed Lorena down the subway stairs. They reached the turnstile in time to see her direction.

"Looks like she's taking the B…though it could be the D train, also." Izzy kept his voice low, despite the noise of the shrieking trains and voices all around. "Got to see if she's going uptown or downtown."

Will kept his eyes trained on the red hair, just as he had the bobbing backpack in Grand Central. She turned toward the uptown platform. "Uptown! Iz, she's going uptown."

Standing on the platform, Lorena leaned forward, hoping to see a train's headlights in the dark tunnel. The schedule board said a train in two minutes, but many was the time she'd stood on a platform cursing as the promised minutes on the board didn't change, even as the minute hand of her watch ticked away. *Not today, please!* she asked the gods of the subway.

"There. See her?" Will nudged Izzy as they took the last step down and reached the platform. "If the train's crowded, maybe we can get in the same car with her."

Izzy shook his head. "Can't take the chance. She could suspect we're following her. We'll get in the car next to hers. Stand by the door and watch to see where she gets off."

The minutes flipped to zero as the flashing board signaled the train's arriving. Seconds later Lorena joined the general confusion of people getting on and off the train. As she pushed her way inside, she didn't notice the man getting onto the next car who had opened the door for her as she escaped Hillenbrand's shop not long ago, or the older, taller man with him. Lorena was quick to grab a seat.

To her relief, there were no delays. The train moved swiftly through the tunnel and the station stops, seven in all, were brief. Lorena stood when the train departed West 86th Street and moved to the door. She wanted to make a fast exit at her stop. It was 10:18. She had twelve minutes.

In the next car, Izzy nudged Will. "West 86th — this is where I live, near Amsterdam Avenue. I wonder how far up she's going?"

Two minutes later they found out.

Lorena was pulling out her phone as she headed up the stairs. "Babe, I'm here."

"Lorena?" Justin's voice crackled.

Shit connection! "Hold on! I'm almost on the street!" she shouted.

"Where ARE you?" Justin's irritation came through loud and clear now.

"I'm on 96th Street and Central Park West." Lorena enunciated each word. "Pick me up here."

"No can do. Car's not here yet. Gonna need to save time. Start walking."

"Prick!" Lorena shouted, though Justin had already hung up. *Shit!* Why had she bought these shoes?

Will and Izzy were a few steps behind Lorena but close enough to hear her side of the conversation. "Going someplace with somebody," Will whispered. Izzy nodded. With fewer people on the street in this neighborhood, they had to follow more carefully.

Izzy pulled out his phone and hit Lucy Webster's number. "Luce… yes, I'm fine… I'm *trying* to speak quietly…. Lucy … it's okay…. Stop talking for a minute! Let me speak!"

Izzy lowered his voice back to a whisper as he continued. "Are you still home? Great, get your car. Yes, *your* car. Leave now. I'm on West 96th. Come down Broadway…. Luce, no time to explain. I need you to pick us up…Yes, us. Name is Will Davenport… you'll meet him… now quick! Speed, Luce … it's the diary!"

Izzy hung up and turned to Will, "Thank God, Lucy's only twelve blocks from here!"

"Your assistant, right?" Will kept his eyes on Lorena as he spoke.

"Yes." Izzy made no attempt to explain the chaotic conversation with Lucy, whose over-concern could be exasperating. Instead, he was feeling doubt and defeat creeping in again. "Will, what if this woman doesn't have the diary? What if we're wrong about her? What then?"

"We'll find out soon enough," Will reassured him.

Will's words could not have been more prophetic. Almost simultaneously, Izzy's phone buzzed: Joe Farady's number. Izzy answered to hear Ian Hillenbrand's voice.

"Iz, it's the woman! Young, pretty — she stole the diary from me! My wallet, phone too! Joe told me how she cased the shop — it has to be her! She got me with chloroform, like she did Joe."

Will could hear Ian's voice. He was now deep in apology for keeping the theft from Izzy.

"Izzy!" Will whispered, gesturing for silence. The woman was answering her cell.

Nodding, Izzy attempted to end the call from Ian. "Later. We'll talk it out later! … We're following her…. Yes!... I'll call."

Up ahead, still oblivious to the fact that she was being followed, Lorena answered Justin's call. "I'M COMING!" she shouted. "Almost to Amsterdam…. I'm still on Ninety-Sixth! The car's not there yet? Why don't I wait for you on 97th ? You can pick me up there… ALL RIGHT! I AM WALKING! YOU'RE A PRICK!"

This time Lorena made sure Justin heard her choice description. That he was making her walk the rest of the way made her all the more irritated. But she was also relieved that Justin wasn't going to be able to skip off without her to meet the client.

Another avenue later, at 96th and Broadway, Lorena turned right to head up one more block. "I've got the worst blisters!" she grumbled aloud. "Shit!"

Will and Izzy hung back on 97th Street and Broadway, watching Lorena walk-limp up the block, headed toward West End Avenue. "Will, you follow her! I'll stay here and wait for Lucy," Izzy instructed, and gave Will his telephone number.

Will slowed his pace as Lorena called out to a young man pacing the sidewalk near the end of the block.

I don't believe it…! Will's eyes went wide as he recognized his backpack nemesis from Grand Central. Quickly Will stopped and pulled out his phone. Head down, he appeared to be searching for directions as he called Izzy. "They're on 97th just before West End. She's with the guy I argued with in front of your shop!"

Will watched as a car pulled up in front of the building and both the man and the red-headed woman swiftly got inside. "Hurry!" he added urgently. "They're leaving now!"

Then a stroke of luck. They hit a red light at the end of the street. As they waited, Will sprinted close enough to read the license number. Head down, as though he was just sending a text, he punched DIGGBY9 into his phone. Then his jangling ring tone. It was Izzy.

"I'm with Lucy. We're almost to you."

As Izzy spoke, the car pulled up beside Will, who jumped into the back.

"They went toward the river!" Will announced. "It's a blue car. I'll watch for it."

"Step on it, Lucy!" Izzy shouted. "And this is Will Davenport."

"Hi, Will," Lucy smiled into the rearview mirror. "Nice to meet you. It's my first car chase. How about you?"

Will grinned in return. "Mine too."

Then, as she deftly sped up through the yellow light, Lucy gave Izzy a quick glance. "Now aren't you glad I have a car in the city? All your complaining about my 'needless' car!" she teased.

"Yes, Lucy. I was wrong. Will, let me reintroduce you to Lucy Webster, the most determined driver in New York."

At that moment Will caught sight of the blue car. "Lucy, that's it. That car over there! See it?" he shouted.

Lucy turned onto Riverside Drive heading south and then quickly maneuvered to get behind the blue car.

"Good job, Luce!" Izzy reached over and gave her a light pat on the arm. "Will, this is my golden girl!"

"Let's hope, Iz," Lucy replied, her tone more serious now. "I wish we knew where they were going."

Izzy gestured toward Lucy's GPS. "Can't you use that thing to find out?"

Lucy shook her head. "No, Izzy. You have to know where you're going. Then it helps you get there."

Listening to their back and forth, Will got an idea. "Hey, let me make a call."

Chapter 19

West Side Highway, Manhattan
March 7
10:50 a.m.

Will

"Hey, Ken." Will wanted to sound relaxed and at ease, no hint of excitement in his voice.

"Where are you? I thought you'd be here first thing. Too much wine celebrating with Nora last night?"

Will could hear a fringe of irritation in Ken's voice. The "responsible" brother worried about the "spontaneous" one, as their mother had described them growing up.

Here goes, Will thought. "I'm doing some important research. But listen, I need a favor. Can you call Cooper to run a license plate number for me? Maybe get a GPS reading on a car?"

"Whoa, hold on a second, slow down! You're in New York for all of ten minutes and you're running a license plate? What kind of research is this?"

"This could be a really big break. Key information. Just the right hook my book needs. I'll explain everything to you later."

"You gotta give me more than that, kid."

"Can you just do this without giving me the fifth degree?"

"As a matter of fact, no," Ken responded, his voice now highly irritated. "Coop is going to ask me why you need the info, and I'm not about to tell him that I don't have a clue."

Will could feel his impatience rising. It was the same Ken who had disapproved of his curious exploits as a boy. Yet he had no choice but to remain calm. He needed to convince his brother without provoking a fight — or getting Cooper and the police involved, asking a lot of questions. He only wanted to use their high-tech computers.

"Look, Ken, I have a line on some critical information. It could be a real coup! I just want to be sure this source is on the up and up. I met him for coffee this morning. He gave me the broad details and then said he was headed to Westchester to make the necessary arrangements and was going to meet me back in New York. But with everything that's happened, I want to be sure he's not giving me the runaround. So can you help me out?"

Will surprised himself that he was able to come up with a plausible, though vague, explanation on the spot. He hoped Ken was buying it.

"Okay… yeah, now I understand." Ken's tone changed, sounding less reluctant. Will sensed he'd used just the right argument — one that made his brother's protective instincts kick in. With his reputation so compromised, no doubt Ken recognized that Will could be an easy mark.

"Text me the license number, I'll call Cooper," Ken was saying. "He owes me from the other day. Sit tight. I don't know how fast I can get back to you."

"Thanks, brother." Will clicked off as Izzy asked urgently, "Is he going to help us?"

"Yep, Iz, he is." Will looked at Izzy optimistically. They were on a chase that was building a momentum all its own.

Not five minutes later, Will's cell rang. Izzy looked at him expectantly.

"My wife," Will explained quickly, followed by a cheery, "Hi honey!"

"Where are you? I thought I'd hear from you by now."

Will paused, wondering what he should say to Nora. She expected him to be at his new office. That he was in a car, tracking a mysterious redhead, was not news he wanted to share or, he was certain, that Nora would want to hear. Fortunately, she was bursting with questions, giving Will some welcome extra seconds to think.

"Did you see the Newton letter again?" Nora continued. "Really, what a fascinating coincidence to meet this Izzy, and for him to have a letter from Isaac Newton!"

"You know, honey, as a matter of fact ..." but before he could finish his explanation, Will's cell registered another call: Ken.... "Nora, sorry, dear, hold on a sec. I'm getting a call from Ken...."

"Ken? You're not at the university?" Nora asked, clearly surprised.

"It's okay. Research for the book. Hold on and I'll explain. Umm, better yet, Nora, I'll call you right back."

Will clicked over to Ken, hoping his abrupt response was not raising Nora's suspicions too much. He'd heard the instant curiosity in her voice. Being married to an investigative reporter could have its drawbacks.

"Hey, Ken, that was fast. What did you learn?"

"Cooper came through, little brother. The car's registered to an Adam Longwright. Looks like he has a chauffer's license, works for a company that makes frequent runs to Teterboro Airport. That's mainly for private planes. Is that your guy? Cooper tracked the GPS signal. He's going to New Jersey. It's definitely not in Westchester."

"New Jersey! Teterboro Airport!" Will deliberately repeated the destination, for Izzy and Lucy's benefit. He nodded triumphantly at their relieved faces as Ken continued to talk.

"Yes! Most likely this guy is *not* on the up and up, Will. He's not going Westchester. Something isn't adding up. Did you contact him, or he found you...?"

Ken was getting warmed up to all the possibilities. Will had to get him off the phone and get back to Nora before she called again.

"No, colleague in California set it up. I'll text him to find out more about this guy. Look, Ken ... thanks...."

"I wouldn't meet this Adam Longwright again," Ken added, making sure his daredevil brother got the message. "Sounds fishy. Could be somebody trawling for something on you."

"I hear you, Ken. Really, thanks. I owe ya one. I mean it!"

"Whatever you're up to, Will, be careful."

"Always!" Will laughed, trying to defuse the concern in Ken's voice, yet knowing full well that his brother's eyes were rolling at that response.

"Hey gotta go, Ken. Nora's on the other line. Thanks again!"

As Will ended the call, he glanced at Izzy and Lucy. "Sometimes ya gotta do what ya gotta do," Will said, hoping to explain away his fibs and exaggerations.

"I understand, Will," Izzy nodded, adding a wink. "Lucy does the same thing to me."

"Izzy!" Lucy briefly took one hand off the wheel to give him a mock punch in the arm.

Will was swiftly back on the phone with Nora, doing his best to explain himself. "I'm still with Izzy Rhodes. I'll tell you all about it later. It's important — has to do with the Newton letter!"

"Okay, my Man of Mystery," Nora teased. Though she was curious, hearing the excitement in Will's voice made her heart sing. That quality had been missing for so long. "I've got to go too … check out and head to my meeting."

"Right, your meeting with that new source," Will recalled. He'd forgotten in the furor since meeting Izzy at Grand Central that Nora was tracking down a lead. "You be careful, Ace!"

"Always," she replied. "You stay out of trouble too."

Too late for that, Will thought, as he hung up and turned his attention to Izzy, Lucy and the blue car up ahead.

The backpack guy and the redhead were on their way to Teterboro Airport — to fly away? Or meet someone?

Chapter 20

Will, Izzy & Lucy

With Will off the phone, Izzy could finally give voice to his excitement. "Lucy, head to Teterboro Airport, and let's find my diary!" His hope was rising again.

Lucy's driving was masterful in keeping pace with the blue car. When it showed no signs at midtown of exiting for the Lincoln Tunnel to New Jersey, Lucy was quick to anticipate the route. "They have to be headed for the Holland," Lucy explained, referring to the tunnel to New Jersey that was farther downtown. "Could get tricky going into the tunnel. We might lose them."

"Even if we do, Lucy, the airport is fairly small. And if there's another blue car, not to worry, we have the license number," Izzy answered, strangely calm given the stakes.

Inwardly Izzy was far more anxious than he appeared. He was thinking about his father and uncle and what, God willing, he might soon learn about their fates. Both had felt a kinship with the past. Izzy didn't understand it at the time. But now, in the hunt for the diary, he too could feel the magnetic pull of his family legacy. And Izzy could feel the power of resolution, which he hoped would come soon, with the diary recovered and ultimately the mystery of his father and uncle's fatal accident explained.

Will could see from Izzy's silent stare forward that he was deep in thought. Will was thinking too, in particular of how quickly he had become invested in Izzy's quest. Probably it was the scientist in him. Every scientific inquiry involved mystery, and this was a good one. And it was moving fast, as if Newton's laws of motion were accelerating events.

However, soon their literal acceleration was slowing as signs for HOLLAND TUNNEL came into view. The blue car was weaving back and forth between lanes, taking advantage of any opening to move closer to the tunnel entrance.

"Looks like they're in a hurry," Lucy observed. "Wonder if they're running late."

"Could be, Lucy. Maybe they're meeting someone," Will suggested. "How long do you think it'll take us to get to the airport?"

Lucy shrugged. "Traffic's always the wild card."

Though he remained silent, Izzy's thoughts flew. *Who has the diary? Is it the trio up ahead? Are they about to fly away with the diary or hand it off?* Most critically, Izzy wondered, *Can we get to Teterboro in time to find out?*

At last they were going through the tunnel. The blue car had zipped far ahead of them and as they exited, it was nowhere in sight.

"Damn! I don't see the car," Lucy complained.

"Keep driving, Lucy," Izzy instructed. "Just keep following the signs for the airport."

"Izzy and I will watch for the car," added Will.

As the miles to Teterboro ticked down, the blue car failed to reemerge. Then they were taking the exit for the airport.

"There's the entrance, Izzy. Where do you think we should go?" Lucy's voice was tense. "Should I just drive around? Should I park?"

Izzy shook his head, the enormity of the moment descending. They were here — the diary might be within reach. But how to find it?

Chapter 21

Levi Rhodes

Levi Rhodes leaned back in his thickly cushioned seat. The ride on the Gulfstream V was as smooth as silk. The flight attendant informed him the plane would arrive earlier than expected.

Looking down at the time on his Rolex, Levi could only hope that completing this transaction would go as well. He mentally checked each step of a plan that, out of necessity, was hastily thrown together. It was his habit to orchestrate life to the finest detail, but not this time. Uncertainty was now an inescapable and unwelcome companion.

Levi closed his eyes, willing himself to sleep. A brief nap would be helpful after another restless night. But his iron control was failing him. His mind refused to quiet and he drifted back through a host of events, many of which he would erase from his memory, if he could.

There was the startling call two months ago from Gabriel Hornsby, a relentless collector with unlimited wealth and an unlimited appetite for what he wanted to acquire. Decades ago — another lifetime, it seemed — Levi had vitally important dealings with Hornsby. But it was an association that thankfully he considered long dead and buried. Yet, when Hornsby's call came in, Levi's mind instinctively flashed bad news.

"Levi, why didn't you tell me that the Hawkins diary has been

343

located and is for sale? The dealer is Ian Hillenbrand in New York. My contacts tell me his client is Isidor Rhodes. If memory serves, he is your brother, no?"

Hearing from Hornsby was surprise enough. But his news stunned Levi. *Izzy buying the diary of Ethan Hawkins?* It was the last thing that Levi wanted to hear.

How did that idiot brother of mine stumble onto the diary? The timing couldn't be worse for me!

Levi's brain was spinning as Hornsby waited silently on the phone. The sly bastard was trying to gauge Levi's reaction. *Typical Hornsby maneuver,* he recognized. *Uncomfortable silence — make the other guy reveal more than he intended.*

But Levi was on guard. He knew to be careful about what he said to the likes of Hornsby. "Yes, Isidor is my brother, and no, I had no idea he was interested in the Hawkins diary. But I'm sure, Gabriel, you did not call simply to ensure I was informed of my brother's activities. What can I do for you?"

Hornsby laughed, relishing the game at hand.

"Well, Levi, here we are again, you and I. We both made out pretty well the last time we did business together."

"True enough," Levi replied dryly. He knew what Hornsby wanted. It was just a matter of waiting for him to get to the point.

In the next sentence, Hornby confessed. "I want the diary, Levi. I could contact your brother or Hillenbrand directly. But based on our past, I thought you might intercede on my behalf."

There it was. Hornsby was forcing Levi's hand. Hornsby knew two vital details about Levi — that he had some dark secret that would guarantee a personal interest in the diary. And that if he made Levi aware that his brother, of all people, was on the verge of getting the Hawkins diary, Levi would be extremely motivated to intervene, get it first, and sell it to Hornsby.

Levi assessed the situation. Hornsby kept his collections private, only showcasing choice items to impress his ritzy friends with his prowess. If Levi could secure the diary, Hornsby would keep the transaction quiet and Levi could go on with his life — and Izzy would be none the wiser.

"Let me look into it, Gabriel, and I'll get back to you."

"Of course," Hornsby replied, fully understanding Levi's cryptic words to mean the diary would soon be his.

Levi had needed a plan and quickly. He could not go to Izzy or even Hillenbrand directly. He had to get to the diary seller first. And then after a few discreet inquiries, he learned it was too late for that.

The only way now was to "obtain" the diary once it was back in New York. A few more inquiries and he had the right man — Justin Morrow, a smooth operator known for his care and efficiency. He had an attractive female associate that made the perfect cover for the meeting today: a young couple visiting their uncle of means, who was passing through.

Levi had been careful to keep his identity from Morrow. Nothing must lead back to Levi. He'd offered plenty of money, to be sure the job got done quickly.

He'd been relieved to get the message that Morrow had the diary. Yet ever since, Levi had wondered at Izzy's reaction. No doubt he was furious at losing the diary. Levi could imagine Izzy, like an angry bee, buzzing about that old watch shop.

That shop on West 86th Street — Levi could see it in his mind, and then a different image of Izzy in the shop. It was another memory Levi tried hard to forget. Izzy's face contorted in anguish at the death of their father and uncle.

Then a flood of other images, long suppressed, threatened to spill out. Levi squeezed his eyes tightly shut, like a dike trying to keep the memories at bay.

It wasn't spite that propelled Levi to get the diary away from Izzy, though there was some of that. Izzy had been the favored son, following in their father's footsteps. And like their father and uncle, Izzy came to be obsessed with the "family legacy," even though, like Levi, he'd cared nothing about some ancient ancestor when they were growing up. It was after their father died that Izzy's obsessions became full blown. And it irritated Levi to no end. But more than that, it was one of many reasons why he'd kept distant from Izzy.

Now his brother's meddling had brought the whole affair full circle. Except for that one Newton letter still in his possession, Izzy would have no evidence with which to pursue his obsessions. It would all be over.

For Levi, it was time to erase the past and ensure that the truth would go with him to the grave.

"Mr. Rhodes...." Levi opened his eyes. Had he drifted off? The flight attendant was beside him. "We're landing, Mr. Rhodes."

Levi looked out and was surprised to see the tarmac getting closer. He looked again at his Rolex: 11:50. He hoped Morrow would be there.

He felt the slight thump of the landing, and looked out as the terminal building grew closer. No sign of anyone waiting. *Damn! Perhaps they're inside....*

The plane came to a quiet stop. The flight attendant opened the door. *Where are they?* Levi irritation began to build. *Goddamn it, for what I'm paying! Morrow should be here ... hell, he should be guiding in the goddamn plane himself!*

Levi's instructions to the pilot had been to expect to be on the ground for a short time. And he'd made it clear to the flight attendant that he required privacy. He would greet his guests himself. No service was needed. The attendant had already gone into the cockpit to wait.

It was noon. Levi stood up. He had no intentions of going into the terminal. But perhaps he'd stand at the door.

He wouldn't mind the fresh air at that. He suddenly felt exhausted. When this was over, he'd have to get a decent night's sleep.

Chapter 22

Izzy, Will & Lucy; Levi, Justin & Lorena

"There it is!" Will shouted. They were passing a terminal identified as SIGNATURE FLIGHT SUPPORT. The blue car was parked in front.

Lucy took a hard right into the terminal area. They could see the driver was still in the car. The back seat was empty.

They parked a distance away, in front of a chain-link fence, with the tarmac beyond. "What's our plan?" Will asked.

Lucy was opening her door as she spoke. "I'm going into the terminal to see what I can find out about who's coming and going from here." She hustled off at a walk-run without waiting for a reply.

Will noticed activity out on the tarmac. There were two planes with stairs deployed and lights on. "Izzy, look over there," he directed.

At that instant, a man appeared from inside one plane. He stood at the top of the stairs, but he was positioned in shadow and Will could not make him out.

"Izzy, there's a guy on the plane." Then, seconds later, "Look!"

Will needed to say no more. Walking toward the plane was the guy from Grand Central, the backpack on his shoulder, and the young woman, no longer a redhead. Blond hair just touched her shoulders.

348

For the briefest moment the man stepped forward, now fully visible, and gestured to the couple. He was nicely dressed, an executive type.

Will felt Izzy stagger and reached out to grab his arm. Izzy held his chest, as though he'd been hit with a force. "What's the matter, Izzy?" Will asked urgently.

Izzy was frozen in place, watching the pair climb up the stairs, the man standing above them, seeming to extend no greeting. Then the man turned and disappeared back into the plane and the couple followed him.

Something had shifted dramatically. "What is it?" Will asked again.

Izzy's voice was strained, as though his vocal chords were being crushed. "That's my brother…."

"Your brother?" Will was incredulous.

"Yes. That's Levi!"

Will studied Izzy, who stood motionless, stunned. Then, as Levi, the backpack guy and the woman disappeared within the plane, shock turned to action. Izzy locked his fingers onto the chain links of the fence and shook it with all his strength, his voice booming out, again and again, "LEVI! LEVI! LEVI!"

A red light flashed, and within seconds, a guard came out of a nearby building. "Sir, step away from the fence."

Izzy ignored the warning, continuing to rattle the fence as the red light whirled. "THAT PLANE! We need to get to that plane! MY BROTHER IS ON THAT PLANE!" he shouted.

"Sir, stand back! You're not authorized to be here!" the guard responded, raising his voice. "If you don't leave now, I'll be forced to…."

"That won't be necessary." Will recognized an unwinnable confrontation brewing and the need to get Izzy away. He put his hands on Izzy's shoulders and pulled him back from the fence. "Let's see if there's another way to get to the plane."

∞

Inside the aircraft, unaware of the commotion outside, Levi pointed Justin Morrow and his companion toward seats. There were no introductions. Levi intended for Morrow and his pretty associate to know as little about him as possible.

"The package, please," Levi instructed.

Justin fished into the backpack and then handed over a silver box containing the diary. Levi was intrigued by the detailed image engraved on the cover. It was a pastoral scene featuring a waterfall rushing off a cliff into a still pool of water below.

"Well, look at that," Levi said aloud. He'd never thought much about the diary, what it might look like or that it might be contained in something so beautiful. He gazed more closely at the scene in silver. A star surrounded by twelve others dominated a daytime sky. A woman and a man in the foreground stood at the water's edge. The woman was pouring water from a container. The man had a book in one hand and with the other, pointed to the cliff above.

Without further comment, Levi opened the lid and stared at the weathered diary. He felt an undefined nostalgia, which surprised him. *So this is what Father and Uncle Samuel were after. How would they have felt to hold it, as I do now? How would Izzy?*

"It's not an ordinary diary," Justin interrupted, seeing an opportunity. "We checked it out, of course, just to be sure, you understand." Levi looked up, eyes fixed on Justin. "Interesting how this guy knew Isaac Newton — you know, the scientist."

Justin paused, then made his move. "Considering the value, we think a bonus is in order."

Levi Rhodes was not one to be pressured. "I'm fully aware of what's in the diary," he lied. But Levi also appreciated a job that appeared well done. He was, as yet, unaware of Lorena's colossal mistake that had led Izzy to the gates outside. At that moment he was not going to fuss over a few extra dollars.

From his suit jacket, Levi pulled out his eighteen-karat-gold money clip bulging with hundred dollar bills. Carefully, he counted out ten and handed them to Lorena. Repeating the action, he handed another ten to Justin.

"There. Your bonus." Levi met Justin's stare with an equally cold one. "And here is the payment, as agreed."

Levi opened a briefcase and handed Justin two manila envelopes. "Twenty-five thousand, in hundreds. It's all there. Count it if you must, but do so quickly. The plane is ready to take off."

Izzy and Will had made their way inside the terminal and were a tag team trying to convince the manager to let them on the plane. Lucy had joined them and was holding Izzy's arm, urging him to calm down.

"We have to speak to someone on that plane!" Izzy demanded.

"I'm sorry, gentlemen, you're not authorized to go beyond this point."

"At least send a message to the plane!" Will insisted.

"MY BROTHER IS ON THAT PLANE!" Izzy shouted. "I MUST SPEAK TO MY BROTHER NOW!"

Izzy's voice echoed through the terminal. People waiting for their planes or to greet those arriving turned to stare. This was not a scene that Signature officials would approve of and the manager knew he had to make short order of the disturbance.

"Please lower your voices," he urged. "Wait here. Let me see what I can do."

The phone next to Levi's seat, connecting passenger to pilot, quietly rang. "Sir, there's an urgent message from the terminal."

"Go on," Levi replied, assuming it was a scheduling concern.

"They say your brother is here and wants to see you."

Now it was Levi's turn to be dumbstruck. But from years of practice as a high-stakes roller, he promptly mustered his poker face and voice of authority.

"That's not possible. We have a schedule to keep. I'll have to see him another time. Relay that message and prepare to leave."

Watching Levi, Justin and Lorena both recognized trouble. Justin quickly stuffed the envelopes with cash inside his backpack and stood. Then he grabbed Lorena by the hand, preparing for a quick exit.

With a swiftness that astonished Justin, Levi was out of his seat and gripping Justin's arm. "You screwed up. HOW?"

To Lorena, Levi's controlled fury was chilling. She wracked her brain. *How?* Her gut told her it was going back to Hillenbrand's to find her bracelet. That had been a mistake. *But how? Who? Couldn't be the guy in the shop. He was a fool. Security in the building didn't give a shit.*

Then the two men who had opened the door for her as she left Hillenbrand's building popped into her head. *Jesus!* She'd flashed her boobs at the one guy ... let him get a good look. *Who were they? Was that it?* They'd come for the diary ... and she'd made herself memorable!

Justin immediately suspected Lorena, though he had no intention of revealing as much. "Let go of me, asshole!" he responded, shaking off Levi's grip. "You've got what you paid for. We're going!"

Levi stared at Justin with contempt. "Yes, I've paid, and I'll be generous by letting you keep it. Now do *exactly* what I say. Get off the plane at a normal pace. Turn back toward the plane, smile and wave. Then exit by the gate to the left. DO NOT go through the terminal. Get back in the car and go to the closest Jersey Transit station. Return to New York by train and then make yourself scarce. Understood? If anything happens, I KNOW WHO YOU ARE, so don't test me."

Justin nodded. There was nothing more to say. *Get away* was the only thought on his mind.

Moments later they were down the stairs, turning, smiling, waving.

With the smile still plastered on his face, Justin growled at Lorena. "You idiot! You and that goddamn stinking bracelet…."

Lorena took Justin's insults in silence. Wait for later. She knew how to soothe his anxiety. Back in the car, she gave him a preview as she rested her hand fully on his crotch. Even as Justin pushed it away, she could feel him respond.

"I have something I've been dying to do to you," she whispered, giving his ear a provocative nibble.

"We're going to Newark, to the airport," Justin directed the driver. "Which terminal?"

Lorena leaned back and smiled, her hand once again massaging Justin, feeling him grow.

"Airport Hilton," Justin replied. "We've got to pick up our luggage."

Justin leaned over, whispering to Lorena as he discreetly slid his hand under her sweater, feeling her warm breasts. "We'll get out at the Hilton and pretend we're in the wrong place. Then we get a taxi to whatever swank hotel is closest. And then you can show me how sorry you are!"

"Oh, I'll make it up to you!" Lorena gave Justin's ear another nibble. "Then, let's go to Hawaii! I'll make it a paradise for you, babe!"

A few hours later, spent from sex, with a new roller bag filled with necessities bought at the hotel boutique and the twenty-five thousand lining their pockets, Lorena and Justin boarded a flight for Los Angeles, with a connection — destination, Honolulu.

Chapter 23

Levi

With a deep breath Levi took a long hard look at the diary on his lap. As always, forever resourceful, he had done what he needed to do. He had secured the diary of Ethan Hawkins. But what now? His brother Izzy was just outside the plane.

Once before, long ago, he managed to stave off complete ruin. And he'd been rewarded handsomely — though at such a steep cost.

He had shouldered the burden then, and because of it his career in finance took flight. Everything that followed coated his life in the attention and riches he had longed for. He gained a reputation as a sharp, no-nonsense trader and eventually caught the eye of Charles Goodwin, a principal in one of Boston's oldest brokerage firms, Strong, Price, Applebaum and Goodwin.

Soon thereafter, Levi's rise turned meteoric. His mathematical brilliance led him to develop computer modeling for newly emerging markets in exotic trading instruments. Handpicked by senior partner Victor Strong, Levi created the firm's derivatives department. His bonus money was obscene, especially once he became the firm's star player.

The biggest feather in his cap came when Levi guided the firm through the financial meltdown that began in 2008. Analyzing market conditions well before anyone knew what was happening, he anticipated the collapse. And not only didn't the firm and its choice clients lose money, Levi doubled down on positions and made a killing for the partners and for himself too.

Yet for all his business success and increasing wealth, Levi was not fortunate in his personal life. He'd had two wives, two divorces and no children.

His first marriage was to a Boston Brahmin who loved the social limelight. But in those days Levi was driven by blind ambition, working away hour after hour at the office. Eventually, Wife Number One grew tired of his outsized commitment to the firm and found the excitement and attention she craved in a series of affairs. Levi was nobody's fool. With the handwriting on the wall, he was not about to be the cuckolded mate. Still, their divorce was kept quiet and amicable, the best for both of their reputations.

His second marriage was much the same. Levi was planted in his corner office around the clock, leaving very little time for a home life. Wife Number Two, less jaded than the first and more committed to her marriage vows, nonetheless found the loneliness intolerable. She filled the hours with good works, becoming a champion for underprivileged women. Eventually, her activism extended to her own situation. She left the marriage, with her terms being that Levi provide the money to start a foundation. In time, and as Levi continued to donate to her foundation, they at least became friends again.

After that, and as he gave up on the idea of children, Levi concluded he was not meant for marriage. Instead, he became known for his young and beautiful girlfriends. It felt good to have a gorgeous woman on his arm when he went out. And his lovely ladies enjoyed his gifts and showed their appreciation. But if one got too serious, she was gone, replaced by another.

Mainly, Levi lived for the game — outdoing the other guy and leaving the table with all the chips.

Now, once again, his place at the table was full of chips. All he had to do was cash in. But first....

Levi lifted his head, wondering how much time had passed. He had drifted off. It was happening more and more lately. Ever since he heard from Gabriel Hornsby his memories began revolving unceasingly in his head. He was beginning to fear that if he couldn't control their incessant appearance and the emotions they conjured, he'd become stuck in a time warp unable to find his way out. He was determined to firmly root himself in the present again. The lack of sleep wasn't helping. *I need to get some goddamn sleep!*

A quick glance out the window and he could see they were still on the tarmac. He picked up the phone to the pilot. "What's the holdup?" he barked. "Let's go! I've got a meeting in Boston this afternoon."

It was true. Gabriel Hornsby expected him at five o'clock for cocktails. There would be a toast and then a transaction and then Levi would leave a richer man, but more importantly, free of a burdensome past.

"We're waiting for clearance to take off, Mr. Rhodes," the pilot explained.

"Then get it! What the hell am I paying you for?" Levi roared, fearful if they stayed a moment longer, he wouldn't be able to control the outcome.

A minute later, the pilot rang again. "I'm sorry, sir. The terminal manager is asking to speak with you. It's about the man ... your brother. You can see him by the door...."

Now when Levi looked out the window, he could see the six-foot-five frame of Izzy, fully animated, pointing to the plane. Next to him was a young woman who looked familiar. Yes, Levi remembered, he'd met her at Agnes' funeral.

There was also a man with Izzy who seemed vaguely familiar. Yet what struck Levi most was the man's age. He looked to be in his late thirties, about the age that Izzy's sons would be were they alive.

Then the younger man put his arm around Izzy's shoulders. He appeared to be trying to calm Izzy.

Something in that gesture awoke a seed of sorrow within Levi. He had no children, although when he was younger he always imagined he would.

But Izzy had had two sons and both were lost. Levi could only guess at the pain that had caused Izzy. He'd never spoken to Izzy about it, had never tried to comfort him beyond hollow words.

Levi was not usually prone to being moved by emotions. But the last few weeks had been a different story. Unwanted feelings had seized him from the dark recess of his mind. And now seeing the younger man with Izzy stirred a sympathy for his brother that Levi didn't expect. A good therapist might have told him that his sudden sentiment for Izzy and the cruel fate that took his sons away, was a measure of Levi's own guilt at the deep hurt that he had caused his brother.

Then Levi thought about how he had deceived Izzy before — and now was about to do so again. His brother, whose path was so very different from his own. His brother, so steeped in the family history and legacy — just like their father and uncle.

With a grimace, and needing to stave off the emotional explosion he feared, Levi acknowledged the inevitable. It was over. He was trapped. The only way was to let fate — his and Izzy's — take its course.

He picked up the phone. "Link me to the terminal manager. And shut down the engines," Levi announced. "My brother will be coming aboard."

Chapter 24

Izzy & Levi

Izzy had insisted that Lucy and Will come on the plane, too. It was not only that he was buoyed by their presence, Lucy had no intention of letting Izzy go alone. Her protective instinct was in overdrive.

Levi agreed. It was a small concession. At first he braced for his brother's wrath, but then a calm came over Levi. There was nothing to do but come completely clean, and let the chips fall where they may.

The first moments were awkward. The brothers faced each other, keeping their distance.

"You have the Hawkins diary?" Izzy asked.

"I do." Levi walked to where the silver box sat on a cushioned seat. He picked it up slowly and held it out to Izzy, who received it with reverence.

The moment hit Izzy with an intensity that forced him to sit. He paused noting the detailed image on the silver box, and then removed the lid. There it was. He opened the worn leather cover and then opened to the inscription announcing *The Diary of Ethan Hawkins*. It seemed a miracle that it was at last in his hands. The image of his father and uncle flashed before his eyes.

Izzy stood again, wanting to leave, yet overwhelmed with emotion.

He looked at his brother and struggled to speak. "Levi, what's this all about?"

Levi waved to the seat opposite and took his own. "Sit back down, Izzy. This will take a while." And then Levi began to explain.

"Forty years ago, I was just starting out in the markets, taking big risks, trying to make a name for myself. I made a play with other people's money that quickly went south. I had to act fast or be ruined. I needed cash and, with nowhere else to turn, I asked Dad for help.

"Do you remember that day I came to the shop on West 86th Street, looking for Dad? I said I needed to talk to him right away. You told me he'd flown to Colorado, with Uncle Samuel, to track down letters written by Isaac Newton and wouldn't be back for a few days. And then you gave me the number of their hotel."

Izzy was listening with mounting dread. His father and uncle made only one trip to Colorado. Levi was talking about when their father died.

"I called Dad that night. I told him my situation and was totally honest. I was dealing in precious metals then. I explained my investment strategy and why I was sure it was still viable. I just needed a little more time for the market to turn, and that required an immediate infusion of cash. He was quiet; I could hear him breathing. In my heart I knew he was going to say no, and he did."

"You know that he and Mom envisioned a different life for me. They disapproved of my decision not to pursue a career in music. Dad never missed an opportunity to tell me that I wasted my Julliard scholarship and my talent — my future as a cellist."

Izzy would not let this unfair portrayal of their father go unchecked. "You were a prodigy, Levi! You were twice blessed! Brilliant at math, brilliant at music! What father wouldn't encourage a son with such talent?"

"And I worked hard to be the cellist he wanted me to be! I did it for him!" Levi insisted. "But I didn't want to be stuck in some orchestra, eking out a living for the love of music. That's what he wanted for me.

He wouldn't admit it, but I think he refused me the money to teach me a lesson — that finance was a cut throat business, uncertain and shady, and ultimately soul crushing. That's why he wouldn't help me. Even so, I wasn't giving up that easily. I couldn't. I flew to Colorado to make my plea in person."

Izzy felt the shock of this confession sink in. He didn't know Levi had gone to Colorado.

Levi could read Izzy's face and his silence. "Yes, I was there, at the time of their deaths."

A feeling of horror was growing inside Izzy. He had found the Hawkins diary, and now his sixth sense told him he was about to discover what else he'd been searching for, and it would change his life. He braced himself for what would come next.

Levi rubbed his face, readying himself to reveal what he had always feared. "Do you want anything to drink — a whiskey?" he asked. Perhaps alcohol could help buffer them both.

"No," Izzy choked out. "Just go on. You went to Colorado — then what?"

"When I got to the hotel they'd already completed the transaction. They had the letters from Isaac Newton to Daniel Fletcher, all organized in a black portfolio. They were in their room, celebrating…."

Like a dream come alive, Levi was transported back more than forty years to a set of scenes that he would undo, erase, change in every way possible, if he could. It was all like a movie that he was watching, yet starring in, with his father and Uncle Samuel as well. And so it played out, complete with dialogue. Each character expressing thoughts and feelings that the camera recorded for all time, and for all to see.

"Levi, what are you doing here?" Uncle Samuel answered the knock on the room door. "Come celebrate with us! Look what we have — letters from Isaac Newton."

Elijah walked toward Levi with arms outstretched. "Levi, come look!" With even greater cheer he put his arm around his son's shoulders and led him to the table where the letters, in a protective portfolio, were open for inspection.

For Elijah and Samuel Rhodes, the letters were valuable in their own right. But more importantly, they hoped the letters would lead them to the Hawkins diary. Finding information about their ancestry was in their blood.

"Here, listen to this, Levi!" Elijah pointed to parchment with pale brown script as he read aloud: '*You speak of a great radiance that glows in diamond light so profound, one need only experience the presence of this wonder to understand the glory of the world. Our friend, Ethan, has found a great treasure.*'"

"It sounds like someone fawning over a beautiful object, or a beautiful woman that Ethan's in love with," Levi mused.

"Not at all, not at all," Samuel corrected. "That is Newton speaking to Daniel Fletcher in an alchemist's code, to keep prying eyes from making sense of their discovery. It's to hide their practice of alchemy. This is truly an astonishing find."

Elijah turned to another page of the portfolio and this time gently extracted the letter. "Imagine, we can hold Newton's very thoughts in our hands! Here he speaks of a diary belonging to 'Ethan.' Surely that must be Ethan Hawkins, our ancestor. His diary, God willing, will be our next great find, and then…."

Levi only appeared to be listening as his father spoke. His chance was slipping away. He felt a rising desperation. "These letters must be worth a fortune!" he interrupted.

"No doubt, Levi, no doubt. And we paid a pretty penny for them too," Elijah nodded.

As his father continued to study the letter, so mesmerized by it, something within Levi snapped. The frustration of his situation was suddenly too much to bear. "If you could afford to buy these letters, why can't you lend me the money I need?"

Elijah gently placed the letter on the table and stared at Levi. He was stunned and embarrassed that he would speak so boldly in front of Samuel.

"The two of you could use some time alone," Samuel accurately observed. "I'll be at the bar in the lobby."

Levi barely waited for his uncle to close the door behind him. "Dad, listen to reason."

"We've discussed this, Levi. I gave you my answer. You know my feelings."

"But I don't! Why? Because you don't approve of the life I've chosen?"

"Oh, Levi, I only wanted, and still want, the best for you. But yes, I would prefer a *rich life* for you, not one that is only about *the pursuit* of riches."

"Well, I decided my path some time ago."

"Indeed, you did. And now you have to live with that choice. You've made your bed, Levi. Now you have to lie in it."

"I hate when you drag out that old cliché."

"Cliché or not, I have made my decision. Now I'm going clean up a bit and then let's go find your uncle and have that drink." Elijah patted his son on the back — a father's attempt to ease the rejection — and then walked into the bathroom and closed the door.

Levi stood motionless, feeling the heat rising in his flesh. If he couldn't get the money from his father, he was finished. He started to clench his fists. His breath quickened and his nostrils flared. He strained to think … *What to do?… What to do?*

Panic took hold as blood rushed through his veins, faster, and then faster still. His eyes darted around the room, at the walls, the ceiling … no answers.

Then his sight settled on the portfolio containing the Newton letters. The world stopped.

Could he? They would be worth a fortune to the right buyer! But the letters were more than money to his father and uncle….

I'll make it up to them! Levi promised himself. *I'll pay them back when I've hit it big! I'll make copies so they can continue their search!*

Then, as if a switch was turned on, the world sprung into action again.

Levi closed the portfolio and tucked it under his arm. The letter alluding to Ethan's diary remained on the table. Somewhere in his addled brain, Levi recognized that his father had forgotten to return the letter to its sleeve. Perhaps leaving that one letter would help later, in making amends. No time to return it to the portfolio anyway.

He moved swiftly to the room door and slowly opened it. He was turning the knob when his father's voice shouted from the bathroom: "Levi, do you want to freshen up?"

Startled, Levi paused.

Go … now! The dark side of Levi's consciousness demanded.

"Levi, did you speak to Izzy? I called the shop but missed him."

His father, still talking, had no idea what was happening with his younger son … what was about to happen….

GO! Levi crossed the threshold and soundlessly latched the door.

"Levi?" He heard his father call again, before he raced toward the elevators.

Come fast! Levi demanded, and an elevator obliged. He entered, standing quietly, yet smiling with a nervous, giddy delight, feeling the excitement that comes from taking an uncalculated risk.

But he was far from home free. Placing the portfolio under his coat, he prepared for the elevator to reach the lobby. He must walk straight to the hotel doors, at a natural gait.

There was Samuel, head down, swirling the ice in his drink.

Uncle Samuel, Levi prayed. *Please don't look up.*

Elijah emerged from the bathroom, expecting to find a brooding Levi. But he was gone.

Baffled, Elijah scanned the empty room. Perhaps, to soothe his disappointment, Levi had gone to join Samuel for a drink.

In the next second, Elijah's eyes focused on where the portfolio had been.

"Good God!" he screamed. Even as he ran to the table and recognized the letter — the one he had removed to show Levi — he grasped his son's thievery.

Elijah staggered to the bed. His legs felt weak. *How could Levi do this?*

Then, as the moments passed, fury surged through Elijah. "Damn you, Levi!" He clenched his teeth and growled, "Steal from your own father!"

Without stopping to grab his coat, Elijah ran from the room, leaving the Newton letter behind.

Samuel Rhodes was stirring his vodka and tonic, musing about the great scientist Isaac Newton — and wondering what might be happening upstairs.

Then from the corner of his eye, he saw a familiar figure moving through the lobby. It was his nephew. *Where is Levi going?* he thought. *What happened with his father? So much for our celebration drink!*

Samuel got up from his seat and watched Levi exit through the hotel doors. Then, through the large windows, he saw Levi sprinting toward the parking lot. *Was he leaving?*

Now Samuel walked swiftly toward the doors and followed Levi outside. Surely he could talk sense into Levi, into Elijah. Whatever this was, it could be resolved!

Evening had fallen while Levi was inside the hotel. He fumbled for his keys, then struggled in the shadows to unlock the car door. Finally, he jumped in.

He saw his uncle leaving the hotel, waving, moving in his direction. *Go!... It will be all right. You'll make it up to them.*

Levi quickly started the car, sped out of the hotel lot and away.

Realizing there was no turning back, he floored the gas pedal and drove as fast as he could down a dark, moonless, empty road. He had to get to the airport, fly home, sell the letters, raise the capital he needed. Afterwards, he'd figure out a way to make amends and hopefully earn his father's forgiveness.

Levi looked in the rearview mirror. *Road's empty. No one's behind me.*

But he had to assume that his father and uncle were following him, or would be soon.

Elijah stood alone in the elevator, shaking his head at his son's stupidity.

What in the world does Levi think he's going to do? Hold the letters ransom until I change my mind?

Yes, he might try to sell the letters. That no doubt was his plan.

But I know all the dealers that Levi could possibly go to with the letters. I'll make a few calls. He's not thinking straight!

As he entered the lobby, he saw Samuel through the glass, running toward the parking lot. He rushed to join him.

"Sam, he took the letters!" Elijah's voice was low but urgent.

"Oh my God, no!" Samuel was stunned but quickly understood. "That explains it!" Samuel whispered. "He's in his car. He's gone! We've got to try to catch him!"

Elijah was suddenly reminded of the Newton letter still on the table. "Jesus, he left one letter. It's in the room! Should we get it?"

Both brothers froze. "Screw it!" yelled Samuel. "No time! We'll get it later."

"Damn him!" Elijah dipped into his pockets. "OK, I've got the keys. Let's go!"

Elijah got behind the wheel as Samuel jumped into the passenger side. "Where do you think he's going?" Samuel asked. "The airport?"

"Where else?" Elijah replied, his voice quieter now and filled with unmistakable sadness.

For a time, the brothers drove mainly in silence, their conversation primarily about remembering the route to the airport. The hotel was far from the bustle of Denver and the road they traveled carried few cars.

"Sam, watch for tail lights. It could be Levi," Elijah directed.

"I have been, Eli. But we may not find him. He had a head start."

"He can't just run onto a plane. We'll catch him there."

Samuel had been waiting to ask, but now he needed to know. "Eli, what is this all about? Why on earth would Levi do such a thing?"

For the next few minutes, Elijah explained his son's request, his own refusal and what appeared to be Levi's extreme desperation. "These letters are your legacy too, Sam. I can't tell you how sorry I am that this is happening."

Samuel leaned over and patted his brother's arm. "We'll get the letters back. *And* we have to help Levi. If he is this desperate, Elijah, we *must* help him. Lessons can wait."

Elijah nodded at the wisdom of his brother's advice.

Tragically, Levi sped down the same dark road, unaware that the act of taking the letters had changed his father's mind.

Had he only turned around and returned them…. But it was something Levi could not know, and so he drove faster and faster, recalling the route back to the airport as he went.

Then in a moment of confusion, he took the wrong turn. The unfamiliar scenery signaled his mistake. He turned around and was soon back on the road, headed in the correct direction.

But those minutes lost were fateful.

Up ahead, a car coming from a secondary road turned onto the main road. It had only a driver and it took off with amazing speed.

"Eli, look! That's Levi!" Samuel shouted. "Hurry!"

Elijah gripped the steering wheel and sped up too. His gut told him it was indeed Levi and he felt an immediate relief. "Thank God! Now we can stop this mistake before it goes too far and ruins all of our lives."

Lights appeared — two dots in Levi's rearview mirror. The car was coming fast. Instinctively, he could feel it was his father and uncle, chasing him.

He scanned the road ahead. *I have to put distance between us. I cannot let them catch me.*

"Damn it!" he yelled. The car roared forward. Levi watched the speedometer climb toward one hundred miles per hour. He had never driven so fast.

Then a curve! Levi's heart thumped as he barely stayed on the road. Up ahead the flashing lights of a train crossing came into view. He could hear the train whistle but the gates were not yet down.

His thoughts burned uncontrollably fast. *I've got to get across now!* They were so close. If he had to stop, his father and uncle would catch him for sure.

Some primal passion was pushing Elijah. *Get the letters back. Get Levi on track.* That hopeful rhyme echoed in his head.

He barely managed the same sharp curve that had challenged Levi.

Up ahead he saw the train crossing and saw Levi speed across. Immediately the gates began to lower.

"We can't make it!" Samuel shouted. "STOP!"

Elijah slammed on the brakes. Then, suddenly, a loud *bang!* as a tire blew, careening the car out of control.

In his panic, Elijah turned the wheel wildly, which set them in the path of a tall, majestic and oh-so-sturdy tree.

At the last moment, the car turned so it hit on the side toward the gas tank. With metal grinding and sparks flying, the car exploded.

The saving grace, the local coroner would report, was that both Elijah and Samuel Rhodes had surely died instantly from the impact. They were gone before the flames reached them.

Levi crossed the tracks and then slowed, watching the gates go down and knowing he could now make his escape. By the time the train passed, he would be far out ahead of them....

As he kept watch of his father in the rearview mirror, he saw the car suddenly convulse out of control.... Then the train began to pass, blocking his view.... An instant later he heard the sound of a crash and then a terrible explosion. Through the spaces between the train cars, he could see roaring flames.

And then, his most heinous crime, he continued to drive on, as though unaware.

He could not save his father or his uncle, he reasoned. He knew they must be dead. Get to the airport and get on a plane. Return to New York, seemingly oblivious to their fate.

No one ever found out about his presence in Colorado. Of course it was a different world then, before security cameras and people's phone cameras tracked everyone's comings and goings.

Levi looked at Izzy's face, waiting for his reaction.

Izzy sat back in the seat, struggling to absorb what he had learned. "My God, Levi, you killed them! How could you?"

"It was an accident, Izzy! I didn't mean for it to happen!"

"Even after *that*, you sold the letters?"

"I HAD TO! I needed the money. I knew you'd never understand! I knew you would only care that they were gone! Izzy, I've had to live with the horror and shame all these years."

Izzy stood, his face red with anger. "You? What *you* had to live with? I've lived with the tragedy, compounded by not knowing what happened! Father's death left a hole in my life — and one that got larger and larger with each loss that followed! Damn you Levi! How in God's name can you live with yourself?"

Then Izzy reached down and took the silver box holding the diary. He held it carefully in one hand, as he touched the raised images with the other. "This diary, our ... *my*... family legacy ... this is all I have left! And now what, Levi?" he continued. "Now you need more money? Is that why you sent those two goons to steal the diary from Ian Hillenbrand?"

"No, Izzy! The same person I sold the Newton letters to called out of the blue. He got wind that you had found the diary and he wanted to buy it."

"What did he do? Blackmail you?" Izzy scoffed.

"Of a sort," Levi explained. "He knew I couldn't take the chance that he would tell you about the letters."

"Well, you need not worry about that anymore."

Levi's voice turned uncharacteristically plaintive. "We're still brothers, Izzy. Let me make this up to you."

"No, Levi, it's too late. You might be used to buying your way out of trouble, but you can't do it with me."

"Izzy, please listen to me, I...."

Without another word, Izzy turned around to Will and Lucy, nodded toward the exit, and all three left the cabin and descended the stairs in silence.

From the window, Levi followed Izzy's slow walk to the terminal and watched the trio disappear inside. He had gambled and lost. How much was to be determined. Had he lost his brother forever?

Minutes later, Levi checked his watch as the plane became airborne. It was almost one o'clock. He would return in plenty of time to keep his five o'clock appointment with Hornsby. Better to tell him of this unexpected development in person.

Levi went to the bar in the back of the plane and poured himself a shot of whiskey. He needed a drink. Then, refilling the glass, he walked back to his seat, hoping the booze would help him relax.

What's that? He spotted something on the floor. *Can't these assholes keep this plane clean?* Then he realized it wasn't trash.

Levi bent down and picked up what appeared to be parchment, with fading brown ink. *A poem?* It must have fallen out of the silver box! There was no indication of the author. *Did Ethan Hawkins write this? Must be.*

Levi spent the next few minutes reading and rereading the poem.

"Fletcher knew it, Newton too." That line played in his head. *What was "it"?*

He raised his eyebrows. *Interesting!*

Levi needed to see all of the Newton-Fletcher letters immediately. He would arrange it with Hornsby tonight. Surely the promise of a different prize would intrigue the old goat into cooperating. But more importantly, this poem might be key, an unforeseen development indeed. Levi had always been adept at spotting opportunity.

Maybe all isn't lost!

Chapter 25

DOWNTOWN MANHATTAN
MARCH 7 12:25 P.M.

Nora Martin Davenport &
Jack Reed/Lester Edwards

"So this is the famous Nora Martin." A well-chiseled man addressed Nora as he sat down at the table at Al Dente's Restaurant, nearly a half hour late. "I'm Jack Reed and it's a pleasure to meet you," he said, extending his hand.

"Thank you for waiting," he continued, giving her hardly an opening to speak. "Please do excuse my tardiness. You were most understanding in responding to my text that my previous meeting had run long. When I called to ensure our table would be held, they told me you had already arrived – 11:55. Yes, punctual, professional and more attractive in person, if you allow me to make such an observation."

Nora's skin crawled. She had given his hand a firm shake, to let him know she meant business. Now her gut told her to hear Reed out and then leave as quickly as possible. "Mr. Reed, I'm here for information, not flattery. Shall we get to it?"

Point of fact, Jack Reed, aka Lester Edwards, had not been late at all. He'd been watching the restaurant and saw Nora enter. It was part of his game: let her wait, build up her interest and see how she would respond to his being "delayed."

"You claimed credible information about a conspiracy that could plunge the New York City area into darkness," Nora began. "And you said that time was of the essence."

Reed picked up his menu. "Not yet, Mrs. Davenport ... ah, Ms. Martin."

"Look, do you have something for me or not?" Nora had no intentions of breaking bread with Reed.

"Please, I fear we've gotten off on the wrong foot. Can I order you a drink?"

That offer made her only more wary. She needed to find out if there was a legitimate story here. A drink was out of the question.

Nora had ordered a small bottle of sparkling water while she'd waited. Now she tapped her glass. "No, thank you. I'm fine."

"I'll have one, if you don't mind." Reed signaled to the waiter. "Bourbon on the rocks."

A hefty drinker at lunchtime, she noted. Nora was feeling less and less comfortable with Jack Reed. This was most likely an effort to smear some associate. She expected Reed to start hurling unsubstantiated accusations at any moment. She'd encountered that before.

"Listen carefully, Ms. Martin." Reed lowered his voice to a near whisper. "What I'm about to tell you could get us both killed."

Nora had heard that line too. It produced none of the fear that Reed might have expected. Instead, she shifted forward in her seat and signaled her readiness to listen.

Reed paused as his drink was delivered. "I'll have the sirloin, medium rare," he instructed the waiter.

"Nothing for me," Nora spoke as the waiter looked in her direction. She fully intended to be on her way before Reed's meal arrived.

"Let's get to it, Mr. Reed," she urged.

"Ms. Martin, I promised you lunch. But if you prefer, gnaw on this." Reed took a strong sip of his bourbon. "There is a group called People for A Green America. They go by PAGA. Their stated goal is to create awareness for energy independence based on clean energy.

Actually, they're a bunch of well-heeled baby boomers, classic 1960's style environmentalists, who have joined together with a cadre of young millennials."

Nora wasn't impressed. "There are dozens of left-of-center groups."

"I'm not finished."

Nora detected an edge to Reed's voice. He didn't like to be interrupted or contradicted, she suspected. *Well, that's too damn bad, Mr. Reed.* She stared fearlessly into his steely eyes, waiting for him to continue.

"Some of the group have grown impatient working within the system. They're inspired by the radicalism of the '60's and how it focused public attention. Now this radical, more militant arm of PAGA has found a like-minded financial backer."

Reed paused for another sip of bourbon, draining the glass. "As we speak, a five-member team is preparing a coordinated attack on the energy infrastructure of the United States. They're starting on the Eastern Seaboard with an attack on New York. Their goal is to cause massive disruption through continuous acts of sabotage."

Nora purposely showed no emotional response to this highly disturbing information. From practice, she was skilled at zeroing in on a story for its credibility. "But what do they hope to achieve beyond chaos?" she asked.

"To demonstrate some half-baked notion that the whole system – our modern way of life – exploits the planet. But here's the bigger conspiracy. The financier who's backing this group of agitators chairs a cabal of right-wing ideologues."

Reed paused, wanting that information to sink in. Nora simply nodded, encouraging him to go on.

"So why back a bunch of leftists?" he continued. "To completely discredit the global warming alarmists and clean-energy movement – to show them all as wild-eyed anarchists ready to inflict harm on the country, just to prove their point. But the truth is, these environmentalists don't want to hurt anybody. It's the other side that does – they're the ruthless lot. By setting up attacks where the chaos will inevitably lead to people being injured or possibly even people killed, they want to push public opinion against all alternative energy solutions. Safeguard their investments, once and for all."

Nora had heard enough. "Okay, let me stop you here. I won't just take your word for it. I asked for evidence. What do you have?"

"Ms. Martin, you shouldn't depend on my word alone," Reed answered smoothly. "I'd be disappointed if you did." He took out a cell phone and opened to a video, then slid the phone across the table. "Take a look at this. I recorded one of PAGA's planning sessions."

Nora took the phone and pushed play. It was a video of five people around a table. They were pouring over what looked like diagrams.

"What are they looking at?" she asked. "I can't tell from this."

"Schematics of the generators that power New York City. They have schematics for dozens of cities."

"Mr. Reed, this is not evidence. This is again your word for what it is. This scene could be completely staged. I need original source documents or verified copies of documents that I can look at independently. And copies from both sides – PAGA and those you say are manipulating PAGA members. Frankly, if what you say is true, you're describing very high stakes – a war within a war. Whose side are you on?"

Reed pulled out his wallet. "I don't mind admitting that I'm on my own side." He removed a check for one hundred thousand dollars, which he waved before Nora. It was issued to Jack Reed from Falconer Energy Industries and signed by Jason DeWitt.

Nora knew her face registered surprise as her head began to swim. Could this be the same *Jason DeWitt that denounced Will? It was not a common name…!*

Reed was staring with the slightest smirk on his face. "I thought you might recognize DeWitt."

After a moment of awkward silence, Nora regained her composure. "I do recognize the name. What's Falconer Energy?" she asked calmly.

"Just a little Jason DeWitt family business that supports all things oil. DeWitt is the man behind the whole plot – pushing PAGA while setting them up."

Outwardly, Nora tried to take that revelation in stride. Inwardly she felt another jolt of surprise. Yet to prove DeWitt was a criminal and somehow had ensnared her husband would be an especially satisfying kind of justice.

But first things first, she needed to pierce the smug armor of this informant. "And you? Who's Jack Reed?"

"I'm what you might call the fixer – the go-between the radicals and DeWitt. I pass on the instructions and the money to carry out the plan."

Nora leaned in closer to Reed. The restaurant was getting louder and she wanted to be sure he could hear the skepticism in her voice. "Given what you're doing – and the stakes if you're caught – a hundred grand doesn't seem nearly enough. And why are you telling me? Guilty conscience? Patriotism?"

Reed responded with an oily smile. "You can say all that – and what I might get from a grateful public for exposing the plot."

He was being clear about his self-interest and hope for personal gain, which from Nora's experience many whistle-blowers were not. That honesty was a point in his favor. But even so, Reed's story wasn't completely adding up. There had to be more that he wasn't telling her.

But with DeWitt's possible involvement, she couldn't walk away. She had to see what this was about. Of course, it could all still be phony. Reed could easily find out Will's connection to DeWitt. The check could be forged. Reed might be trying to blackmail DeWitt. Anything was possible, Nora had learned over the years.

"Why not just go to the police, or to the FBI?" she asked, eager to hear his logic for not doing the obvious.

"Frankly, Nora, if I can call you that. And call me Jack, please...."

"Mr. Reed will do fine," she interrupted.

"So professional," he smiled in mock praise. "But, Nora, you said it yourself – the stakes are high. I'm knee deep in this whole mess and I'm going to need immunity from prosecution."

"Okay, but why me? Why not go to a lawyer?"

"I don't trust lawyers," Reed scoffed. "I've seen them bungle too many deals. No, I need someone who's a trusted conduit to the public. You'll make sure my story gets out and you'll make sure I'm seen as a hero. That will put needed pressure on the FBI to give me the deal I want. In exchange, I'll give you the exclusive rights to the WHOLE story. This is an exposé of a lifetime, Nora. There's a lot more to it and a lot more to expose about the people behind it."

Despite her doubts, she could see Reed's point. He wanted to control events. That was all fine but she wanted to make it abundantly clear there was one thing he couldn't control.

Nora assumed her most steely manner. "Let's be clear, Mr. Reed. *If* I decide there is a story to write, *I decide* how you are portrayed. *I won't* guarantee you will be a hero. *I will* report the facts."

She watched to see how he would respond. He could well have motives that he wasn't telling her. Plenty of people had unsavory motivations. Reed might be one of many she'd met over the years.

"Nora, far be it from me to write your story. Let me say, I'm confident I will be the hero once you have all the facts," he smiled, waving his hands in a grand gesture and bowing his head to her.

It was hard to tell if Reed was a jerk, a grifter or something more sinister. Nora wanted to wrap up this interview. "You've got to give me more for a story," she declared. "To start, I want to meet someone from PAGA – at least one of the five conspirators."

Reed's lunch arrived, her cue to leave. "You'll get back to me, Mr. Reed," Nora confirmed, "to arrange the meeting."

Reed nodded as he took her hand. "It's *truly* been a pleasure," he murmured.

Nora hated shaking hands with someone she didn't trust. She made it brief, then left the table. Once she was out of Reed's sight, she quickened her steps, anxious to leave the restaurant.

What a creep, she thought as she headed for the subway uptown. With the afternoon air brisk and refreshing, she decided to walk to Grand Central instead. The exercise would be a welcome antidote to her thirty minutes or so with Jack Reed. And there were plenty of trains back to Westchester.

Time would tell whether Reed would be a useful creep. Time would tell whether she would be writing a story – or going to the police. If there really was something to this plot to take down the New York City electrical grid, she had no choice but to pursue it.

For now, she needed proof of whatever this was. She needed to find out who Reed was, including his name. She didn't believe for a minute he was revealing his true identity. And, she must find out if and how DeWitt might be involved. *To take DeWitt down! How delicious that would be!*

Should she tell Will about any of this? She debated as she walked. He had a lot on his plate. And she needed to get a firmer grip on whatever this was. No, she would wait to tell him. First, make sure it wasn't a wild goose chase. Be certain it was real.

Chapter 26

Izzy, Will & Lucy

As Will followed Izzy and Lucy down the stairs from the plane, he saw that Izzy's grip was tight on the railing. It didn't take a science genius to realize that the older man was reeling. Not only had Levi arranged for the theft of the Hawkins diary from Ian Hillenbrand, he had admitted to stealing the Isaac Newton-Daniel Fletcher letters decades ago. And he had been instrumental in causing the accident that killed his father and uncle. Levi had lied to Izzy, repeatedly. In fact, Will wondered, had he told the truth now?

Will recalled the scene from moments ago, watching the brothers and thinking about the tragedy that had befallen them. The scientist in him couldn't help but observe the human condition being played out — how people throw themselves into the fire of experience, into situations both challenging and pleasing. And how each circumstance, if recognized, can become a stepping stone toward a fuller understanding of oneself and one's place in the world. Will wondered how the drama between Izzy and Levi would unfold.

For her part, Lucy was seething at Levi's deception. *Izzy's own brother!* She was determined that Levi would never hurt Izzy again.

As they reached the tarmac, Izzy looked up at the plane. He could see Levi in the window, staring at him.

"This way, please." A guard was gesturing for them to walk back toward the terminal and the way out.

Will put his hand on Izzy's shoulder. "Come on, Izzy. We're done here."

Izzy hung back for a moment and took a last look at the plane. "Damn you! Damn you, Levi!" he whispered, even though his brother's face had disappeared from the window. "I never want to see you again!" Izzy's voice, still a whisper, broke on the last words.

Lucy and Will were quickly beside Izzy, guiding him inside, through the terminal and then outside, toward the car.

Izzy opened the front passenger door and got in, as Lucy and Will did the same. They exited the airport in silence.

Lucy was first to suggest that they call Ian Hillenbrand with the good news. "He'll want to know, Iz," she insisted.

"He can wait, as he left me waiting," Izzy replied coldly.

In fact, at that moment, Izzy was feeling a deep exhaustion. He longed to return to the shop, to sit quietly in his back office and go through the diary, page by page.

As they drove on, he studied the image on the silver box and tried to imagine how his father would have felt and what he would have done first upon receiving the diary.

Izzy's thoughts were disturbed by Lucy's cell phone ringing.

Lucy checked the ID. "Iz, it's Ian. Come on, you've got to talk to him sometime."

Without waiting for Izzy's okay, Lucy accepted the call. "Ian, you're on speaker. We're driving back to the city," she explained. "We've got the diary."

Izzy shot her a look of disapproval, which Lucy ignored.

"Thank God!" Ian shouted. "Izzy, are you there? Please understand. I did not know how to tell you."

Izzy grimaced, unwilling yet to let go of his annoyance with Ian.

"He hears you, Ian," Lucy confirmed.

"Who stole it?" Ian asked. "Was it that woman … pretty one…? Joe told me she cased the shop and.…"

"Ian," Lucy interrupted. "Later. We'll fill you in later."

"Oh … okay.… Did you get everything?" Ian's tone was concerned. "The silver box, the poem, the diary?"

"POEM?" Izzy's voice filled the car.

"IZZY! Yes, a poem. I found it in the binding of the diary. It was not signed. I placed the poem on top of the diary in the box."

Izzy opened the box and carefully removed the diary. There was nothing in the silver box. He opened the diary and delicately flipped through the pages. Nothing.

"Damn it, Ian!" Izzy's frustration was immediate, and then his fury. "How could you be so careless? You let them steal the diary! Now what, a missing poem!"

"Does it matter, Izzy, really?" Lucy asked gently. "I mean, you have the diary. It's just a poem."

Then Ian's voice again, concerned and contrite. "I'm afraid it may matter, Lucy. The poem may be needed to understand something very important. It was far too long to memorize, but I recall these lines: *'Fletcher knew it, Newton too.'* And here's what makes the poem so important. There was something about the Hawkins family and unlocking a secret to find a treasure."

Will listened to the conversation, staring over Izzy's shoulder at the lid of the silver box. Though he felt for Izzy in his distress, Will was intrigued and energized at the idea of a secret known by Newton and Fletcher. What could it be? A discovery made through their practice of alchemy? Or one of a more cosmological nature? Was it a secret lost to the present … or was there a treasure for the Hawkins family yet to find?

He was pulled back to the moment by Ian's voice, even more animated now. "I just remembered another line: *'A man and a woman stand at the threshold'* — look at the picture on the silver box!"

"Picture? What are you talking about, Ian?" Izzy asked, still annoyed and feeling helpless.

Will leaned forward excitedly. "The box, Izzy! There's a man and a woman on the lid of the box."

"Who's with you?" Ian asked, curious about the unfamiliar voice.

"Ian, this is Will Davenport," Lucy explained.

"He's a scientist and expert on Newton," Izzy added, intending to zing Hillenbrand for his carelessness.

"Not an expert," Will corrected, "but I'm willing to bet there may be more clues here. Clues on this box, in the diary and, Izzy, in the Newton letter you have."

Izzy turned around to look at Will. For the first time in hours, his eyes were bright with excitement. "Yes, my letter! We can start with my letter … though I've read it so many times. But now, to read it with the diary in hand…."

Ian echoed Izzy's exhilaration. "Call me as soon as you get in!"

Lucy and Will exchanged glances in the rearview mirror, waiting for Izzy to respond.

"Ian, check all your contacts. You've got to track down the person my brother sold the Newton-Fletcher letters to — we've got to see those letters too!" It was Izzy's familiar commanding voice, a sign that he was rising from his funk.

"LEVI stole the letters back then?" Ian's voice was incredulous. "The diary now too?"

Lucy quickly answered for Izzy. "Yes, Ian. We'll tell you everything later."

Undaunted now, Izzy returned to his new purpose. "Yes, Levi had the letters — he sold them, Ian, in 1978. I know it's been decades, but see what you can find."

"I'm on it, Izzy!" Ian declared. It was a way to be in Izzy's good graces once again.

"There's a puzzle from generations ago to solve for sure," Will confirmed. "It is always possible, Izzy, you already have what you need," he added optimistically.

Will and Lucy could feel Izzy's mood shift again as he heaved a great sigh. "Yes ... or it may be essential to get those letters. I left that plane intending to never speak to Levi again... but if I have to, I will."

Chapter 27

DOWNTOWN MANHATTAN
MARCH 7
1:00 P.M.

Lester Edwards

Lester Edwards laughed as he watched Nora Martin Davenport walk away from his table at Al Dente's. She might loathe him — he could tell she did — but with this meeting and their handshakes, she had fallen into his web. Now it would be easy to implicate her — and her hubby, Dr. Will Davenport, on record as openly critical of how the U.S. electrical grid was managed, of the dangers of unchecked artificial intelligence and of unbridled biotech….

The Davenports are in for their biggest surprise. I'm about to unleash one of my masterpieces! If they thought his first career crash and burn was something, they haven't seen anything yet. This time Nora gets to join him!

If everything worked as planned, in the rush to judgment that always follows such events, Will and Nora would even be suspected among the bombers.

Edwards had accomplished everything he'd set out to do. He had laid the trap well. And by showing the check to Nora, signed by DeWitt, he had his insurance policy against DeWitt, who was a master at slipping away and hanging the blame elsewhere.

Not this time. Edwards was not about to take the fall if DeWitt had any wild ideas, like thinking of Edwards as a liability if things didn't go according to plan. By putting Nora Martin on DeWitt's trail, if DeWitt threatened him, Edwards could feed Nora information and expose all of DeWitt's underhanded activities.

He was good, Edwards smiled, impressed by his own conniving. *Better than good,* he thought. *A goddamn genius!*

To celebrate, he ordered a rich Brunello, just what he needed to really enjoy the sirloin!

Edwards took his time now, savoring his meal and the very last sip of the wine. He liked the finer things in life and he had no guilt over how he acquired them.

An espresso to finish, and then he paid the check and left Al Dente's, calculating how long it might take him to cover the twenty blocks from 14th Street to Penn Station at 34th Street. He was getting a three o'clock Acela train to Boston for a seven o'clock meeting with Jason DeWitt.

He knew the broad-brush strokes of DeWitt's master plan and expected to learn more. There was the role that Will Davenport would play, for example. Already discredited in the scientific community, Davenport's past observations about the vulnerability of the nation's electrical grid could be manipulated to seem like veiled threats. And that made Davenport ideal for DeWitt's purposes.

Edwards' work today — or, more accurately, his alter ego, Jack Reed's — had set up Nora Davenport to set up her husband. Edwards loved the symmetry of it. He assumed DeWitt would too.

Edwards admired DeWitt's cunning. But trust him — not a chance. In fact, Edwards trusted no one but himself. He was sure DeWitt already saw him as dispensable when the job was done, and Edwards had no intention of allowing that to happen.

He easily made the train and stretched out comfortably in a quiet car. He ordered a drink for the ride. A nap would ensure he was sharp for his meeting with DeWitt. Soon the steak, the alcohol and the gently swaying train had lulled Lester Edwards, aka Jack Reed, to a comfortable sleep.

Chapter 28

BOSTON
MARCH 7, 2019 PRESENT DAY
7:00 P.M.

Jason DeWitt & Lester Edwards

What Lester Edwards did not know about DeWitt's scheme was virtually everything. Edwards was a sideshow, as was the plot to implicate Will Davenport. It was the shiny object to hold the world's attention, while Jason DeWitt pulled off the heist of the century.

DeWitt and his hand-picked team at DeWitt Technologies, his primary company, had secretly designed and built a quantum computer, which was completely operational. That this monumental feat had been accomplished in secret was also to DeWitt's purpose. He knew that others were hard at work developing their own quantum computer. But being first gave him a head start that would pay off in unimaginable ways.

It was the encryption codes — that was the coup — protecting everything from the banking system to classified government documents. With his achievement, current codes would be obsolete overnight. As the first to develop new codes to protect vital information, *everyone* would be forced to come to him. Whoever controlled the power and speed of an operational super computer would control the world.

Levi Rhodes, through DeWitt's association with Victor Strong, was the mathematical mastermind who developed the necessary quantum algorithms. Levi had been "borrowed" for the project and done masterful work. But, like Edwards, Levi didn't know the extent of DeWitt's plan. And while Levi's contribution had been invaluable, now his frequent questions about when they were going public with what he considered his crowning achievement was an irritant. But it mattered little. Soon all his questions would be moot.

Until then, DeWitt was counting on Strong to get Rhodes in line. Everything and everyone had to be in place for DeWitt's most ambitious scheme yet.

Jason DeWitt was Boston old money. His chairmanship at the Massachusetts Institute of Technology — MIT to the world — gave him the perfect perch from which to recruit top talent for his business interests. And those interests centered around energy.

The DeWitt family had long been heavily invested in oil production and pipeline infrastructure. They were also among the first to invest in fracking, extracting natural gas or oil from shale. To the DeWitts, those who controlled energy were kingmakers, in every sense. And with powerful corporate friends, contacts in federal and state governments, and shills in the big media conglomerates, the DeWitts had been kingmakers for the better part of a century.

There was the occasional DeWitt humanitarian, but for the most part, they were a ruthless family over generations, willing to manipulate anyone with their money and power, all with the goal of achieving more of both. To the DeWitt bloodline, money and power meant freedom. The more power you could accumulate, the more freedom you had to control life — not only your own but everyone else's too.

But kingdoms can be lost as well as won. About the time that Will Davenport had reached the pinnacle of his science stardom, the world oil prices were beginning to plunge to record lows. Jason DeWitt, by this time totally in charge of all family companies and blinded by the family's longtime love affair with black gold, was certain prices would rise. He put together an investment group that placed a huge bet on the oil options market.

The gamble was a miserable failure. His associates lost vast fortunes and DeWitt managed to survive — barely. But he lost the dominance he craved, his true life's blood. DeWitt was desperate to regain his reputation as a brilliant strategist and the confidence of his moneyed peers.

And that's how the trifecta of computer, crisis and codes evolved. Manipulating world markets was the game, the high-speed quantum computer his instrument and a blackout his cover. The blackout would expose the need for his quantum computer to protect the entire information infrastructure with encryption codes that could not be hacked. Even more sinister, DeWitt planned to use the crisis to gain a financial windfall. His teetering fortune and influence would be restored beyond anything he'd ever known.

But he needed a pawn and, as DeWitt put it, "Davenport picked himself." It began with Davenport's criticism of the security of the electrical grid. Then he had married Nora Martin, whose uncovering of corporate espionage in California power companies had implicated a DeWitt subsidiary. And finally, once Davenport became a science celebrity, he enjoyed the perks, which made him vulnerable.

When the time was right, Edwards acted as DeWitt's sharp instrument. Like a fine scalpel, he removed the life that Davenport had known and left an empty space.

The unique qualities of Davenport husband and wife made them perfect. So DeWitt had watched and waited, and then pounced. First using Edwards, and then publically denouncing Davenport's science credentials every chance he could, to ensure Will Davenport would never recover.

∞

Lester Edwards, rested from his long train nap, arrived at DeWitt's office in Cambridge a good ten minutes early for their seven o'clock meeting. Edwards was eager for a quick meeting with DeWitt, whom he disliked as much as he assumed DeWitt disliked him.

DeWitt's assistant greeted Edwards, explaining that Professor DeWitt was on the phone and would come out shortly.

Then the assistant left to do some task — to make copies or some such thing, Edwards assumed. Whatever it was, he was pleased to find himself alone in the outer office.

Ever the slick article, Edwards edged toward DeWitt's office door to listen in on what he might hear. He was not disappointed. DeWitt was on a call that was anything but pleasant.

"Do you hear me, Strong? We're up to our eyeballs. There is no other option but to go through with what we planned. We're talking about people who aren't used to being screwed with — starting with me. And one last thing, Victor. No surprises. No side deals. Let it play out and everyone comes out smelling like a rose. But if I go down, I'm taking the whole house of cards with me."

DeWitt was playing hardball, which Edwards appreciated. But he could hear something in DeWitt's voice that gave away the man's concern. There was a hint of desperation that signaled DeWitt and his cronies were in dire straits. Millions if not billions were probably at stake. Some very influential and powerful people would go down in flames unless DeWitt was successful.

Edwards grinned gleefully at this extraordinary stroke of luck. He was certain he could use this information to his advantage, when the time was right. However, he had to manage everything carefully. The fact that he wasn't meant to know any of this made his position more profitable, but also extremely dangerous.

DeWitt's call ended abruptly and Edwards made a quick return to his chair. A moment later, he was in DeWitt's office. In less than an hour, Edwards emerged, having given an optimistic report, for which he was rewarded with a check for two hundred and fifty thousand dollars. He knew it was pocket change to DeWitt — but there was more where that came from.

Edwards liked the idea that when his handiwork was finished, the power in the world would change and most people would never know it. That simple fact was to be enjoyed. And even more to be savored, he would end up a wealthy man — and that meant freedom.

In fact, Edwards thought, *here in the city of liberty, why not let freedom ring?*

Indeed, his return to New York could wait until tomorrow. Edwards headed for his favorite five-star Boston hotel and an evening with a high-class hooker in a luxury suite. He'd earned it — and, he reasoned, there were hard days of work ahead.

Chapter 29

Izzy, Will & Nora

A week had passed since Izzy obtained the Hawkins diary and learned Levi's 40-year old secret of thievery and death in Colorado. Securing the diary had solved the mystery of his father and uncle's deaths, although in a way Izzy could not have imagined. His emotions were reeling from what was revealed and it was proving impossible to wrap his head around what it all meant.

And yet now there was another mystery to solve. The diary had come to Izzy along with a new quest — to realize an unfulfilled family legacy — some secret was buried long ago and Izzy had the distinct feeling that the past was reaching out to him. He was determined to find whatever "it" was and keep faith with generations that came before him. There was something left undone, and intuitively Izzy felt it as a karmic debt to be released through him. He sensed if he could push through the slings and arrows of this difficult time, a hard-won freedom from an unresolved collective past was at hand.

It was also a week since Will, by Izzy's side, got his initial view of the diary. It offered a fascinating journey back in time — the diary of an unknown alchemist, started *because of* Isaac Newton and containing *firsthand descriptions* of Newton developing his most defining theories. As a scientist it was the opportunity of a lifetime. But he also found himself captivated by Ethan Hawkins the alchemist. Ethan had used the natural world — herbs, plantings and minerals to heal the sick and injured. And there was this crystal that Ethan had found. It seemed to be at the center of everything. What was that about? With his curiosity at its apex, all the synapsis in Will's brain were firing up with excitement to find out.

For Nora, it was a week of follow-up and anticipation. She had waited daily to hear again from Jack Reed — to get confirmation of a meeting with a member of PAGA, People for A Green America. If Reed disappeared, as would-be sources sometimes did, it was only proof that his information had been false or certainly suspect. Nonetheless, Nora was far from idle. She had researched Reed, who thus far had no history. Most likely the name was indeed an alias. She had spent time investigating PAGA, with few results so far. But the lead that had borne fruit was Jason DeWitt's signature on the Falconer Energy check. She had not yet shared her DeWitt explorations with Will. She thought him too busy. But more honestly she needed to learn more before she wanted to open that door.

So Izzy, Will and Nora, each with a different purpose, were all waiting for the next developments in the stories they pursued.

That Izzy was churning emotionally from the thunderous developments in his life seemed inevitable. As he went through the diary and understood the terrible rift between the Hawkins brothers, Benjamin and Jeremiah, he could feel the parallels with Levi. *How could he ever trust Levi? How could he forgive him?*

Lucy Webster, with the best of intentions, encouraged Izzy to talk it out. It was classic, vigilant, always protective Lucy. "Izzy, I know you're hurting. Even though you and Levi haven't been close, it had to be awful to find out he was responsible for your father's death."

But Izzy resisted. "I appreciate what you're trying to do, Lucy. But I'm not ready to talk about it."

Still, Lucy was insistent. "Just remember what happened when you went to Colorado. Why let it build up to that point again, so that your emotions come pouring out?"

"Look Luce, there will be time later to sort this all out about Levi," he explained. "Right now I'm putting everything I have into this diary and uncovering what my gut tells me is mine to solve." It was all certainly true, but really Izzy wasn't so sure he was ready to face the consequences of his rising feelings of anger and hurt, and questions of why it had all happened and ultimately for what purpose.

Since recovering the diary it had become suddenly a formidable challenge to come home to West 86th Street and his apartment, with its world of reminders of his wife and sons.

On this particular night Izzy was frustrated and he had given in to Lucy's request that he go home early to rest. His sleep had been fitful for the past week and exhaustion was catching up with him.

Yes, the diary was a font of information, including the existence of a crystal that was imbued with power that Ethan somehow harnessed. But what was Izzy supposed to do with all this information? It began to weigh heavily on his thoughts and emotions. Was he wasting his time? *Haven't I been through enough?* Izzy's willpower was waning.

The moment Izzy opened the apartment door, he was tempted to turn around and return to Grand Central. The apartment felt so empty, no one to greet him, to give him solace.

What he wanted more than anything else was to hear his dear wife's voice. To ask her advice. And so he spoke into the night. "Agnes, I miss you so very much." He let that statement fill the air, half expecting a response. "I wish you could come to me, help me understand what is it I need to do?" Somehow it felt good just to ask.

Then he addressed his father. "I have it Dad. The diary. It's as remarkable as you and Sam thought it would be. You can rest in peace now."

Izzy paused, letting his thoughts settle. Then, as if replying to his own lament, he spoke aloud to Agnes, to his father and to a divine presence he sensed was watching over him. "I've always struggled to become aware of who I am, to know the meaning of my life. It seems we're all put in unique circumstances, in relationships that have us grappling with who we really are. Do we create these situations to learn how to navigate our relationships — to explore all the aspects of ourselves in this lifetime on earth?"

He paused, taking stock of his feelings. But no matter how he parsed his thoughts he still couldn't make sense of what Levi did. "... how *do* I reconcile that? What am I supposed to learn from this experience with Levi, from the twisted emotions that made him do what he did? What am I supposed to do ... think ... feel... about him now?" Izzy pleaded aloud. "Dad? Agnes?"

In the quiet of the apartment, Izzy waited again. In his heart he knew that dark thoughts take you to dark places, he had been there before. But still, where these new circumstances with Levi would end up was beyond his ability to know.

And then from his own inner voice came a response. It was a simple understanding, really: *What will be with Levi is what will be. Let it go for now, and find peace in that!*

Izzy felt an immediate calm that amazed him. He was willing to release himself from his need for instant answers and accept the hand of fate and how it might eventually work out with his brother.

It was a surprising turn away from his earlier ferocious anger. It was not so much that he suddenly forgave Levi. More so, it was Izzy's trust in that inner voice, a guiding spirit that somehow was always there in the quiet, waiting to be heard beyond the din and distraction of "everyday life." If there was some shared past for Levi and him to unravel together, then Izzy would trust in the signs he would receive and let it come to pass.

A simple ease entered Izzy's body and he was certain that tonight he could sleep. He fixed himself a bowl of soup, and then he headed to bed, remembering to send Lucy a text, to assure her he was fine, before he turned out the light.

Will was getting a later train than usual. It would be after eight o'clock when he got home. But he'd spent many mornings that week pouring over the diary with Izzy and Ian Hillenbrand. This had been a day for considering how the puzzle of the diary might inform his manuscript. He felt on the trail of a new chapter in the life of the great Isaac Newton. How exciting that would be, after all these years, when accepted history of Newton's biography was seen as complete, to uncover a new vein of information.

And what could Will actually discover about Newton? There was the line of the poem that alluded to a secret Newton knew. What else might the poem reveal when they could learn all the words?

The diary was already a fascinating picture of Newton — his practice of alchemy and the discovery of his laws of nature, as described by the young Ethan Hawkins. Even that Newton and his friend Fletcher had taken an interest in a stable boy. It made Newton, this greatest of all scientists, more flesh and blood. For Will, so aware of his own human foibles, it created a connection to Newton, the risk taker. In all his studies of Newton's theories, Will had not felt that before.

But there was one entry that intrigued Will more than anything he'd read so far. Ethan Hawkins had recorded Newton's ideas about gravity, including that it's more than just a force holding us to the earth.

"Newton's eyes lit up like never before as he asked Daniel and me, 'What if gravity is but a quality of Earth's life-force, an attribute of her being? What if this gravitational force is her life vibration? And it connects us to her and, in so doing, we influence and are influenced by Earth as a sentient being, full of an undefined awareness, yet to be discovered. There is so much life on Earth — is she not alive too?'"

What an astonishing concept! After rereading the entry several times, Will was eager to investigate this theory.

And he knew who to see to discuss it further. Not only was a visit to his parents overdue, but also with his father's years of experience exploring and excavating great crystal caves, buried deep within the earth, his insights would be invaluable. If Earth were "alive" as Newton wondered, were not signs to be found in those very objects that his father knew so well?

Thoughts of his father brought Will to thoughts of Izzy. There was something about him that was ageless. Izzy knew things about life that others did not.

Will was also coming to feel that his introduction to Izzy at this time, after everything that had happened, could be one of the most fortunate events in his life — perhaps even a crucial turning point — and not only for what the diary might mean. He was sure Izzy had something to teach him. He had lived through enormous suffering. His hardships reminded Will of a quote from the Greek playwright, Aeschylus. "And even in our sleep, pain which cannot forget, falls drop by drop upon the heart, until in our despair, against our will, comes wisdom through the awful grace of God."

To Will, Izzy had an aura lit with wisdom and self-awareness that surely had come in part from dealing with his pain. These circumstances appeared to be an integral part of his journey. And he shouldered it with a grace that Will wished he could emulate.

With the station platform coming into view, Will thought with gratitude of Nora, who no doubt was still working but probably pausing about now to open a bottle of wine, ready to greet him with a glass. It was Nora who saw him through his own difficulties. How lucky he was to have her.

Exiting the train, joining the exodus down the stairs, he headed for the parking lot, eager to be home. Yes, a glass of wine, dinner and then perhaps early to bed, to try again for Baby Davenport....

Nora popped the cork early on a bargain bottle of red. For fifteen bucks, it was great for every day. And with the March days and nights so cold to her California girl self, the warmth of the red wine was welcome.

She was sipping a glass when she heard her text alert. Probably an update from Will, confirming he was on the train.

But no — finally! It was Jack Reed: *Meeting set up. Tomorrow morning at 10, Brookfield Place, downtown, in café court. Come alone.*

"Son of a bitch!" Nora responded aloud. "So he didn't fall off the face of the earth after all."

She texted a one-word response: *Confirmed.*

She was ready — game on. As she began preparing one of her super-healthy salads for dinner, paired with fish for brain food, she went through her questions for the meeting.

Nora looked at the time, calculating that Will would be home soon. She took another sip of the red. She was cautiously excited — the story could still go nowhere. But, perhaps, tomorrow might offer another lead about Jason DeWitt. If only she could bring DeWitt down ... if only Will's book would be published and successful....

She had no signs yet of being pregnant, but ... on the heels of what felt like a promising development ... a perfect night to try again.

Chapter 30

Izzy

Izzy had quickly drifted off into a deep sleep and, as one day ended and the next began, he was in a state of lucid dreaming about the diary.

In his dream he was studying Ethan's entries, reading the wide range of formulae based on essences of floral and mineral compounds. Using their intuitive processes and heightened by a crystal stone, Ethan and son Benjamin had discerned the vibrational core of hundreds of natural elements and used them to heal the sick. Then suddenly Agnes appeared, still alive, cured by a formula that Ethan had given her. Izzy was overjoyed at the sight of her. Looking directly at him, she began, *"Izzy my dear, you must listen very carefully...."*

But before Agnes could complete her message, Izzy was startled awake. He immediately checked the clock on the nightstand. It was precisely two o'clock in the morning.

From habit, he got up and went to the bathroom. Then briefly considered going to the kitchen for some white wine cooling in the refrigerator, but instead, opted to return to bed, hoping to go back to the same dream and see Agnes again.

Within moments, Izzy was drifting off again and felt himself being elevated from his bed into a cloud of rarified white light. A blissful feeling overcame him as he floated higher and higher. Harmonic chords of music filled his ears in a symphony of pure pleasure. *Have I died in my sleep?* he wondered.

"Izzy, you are not dead." A soft yet distinct whisper filled his ears.

"Who's there?" Izzy asked, surprised that he wasn't alone. "And where am I?" he called out, as the feeling of floating slowed.

"You are in the space between the place you know and a time beyond time," the voice answered.

Then the white around him began to fade and in the distance he could see someone approaching. Slowly Izzy's eyes began to focus and he was astonished at the sight. Everything was illuminated in pure, deep, shimmering colors. He was looking on a meadow of tall, green grass and, in the immediate background, what appeared to be a building with huge columns, glistening in blue light.

It was the exact place from his dream in Colorado! That was four years ago. But why was he here again?

Though his question was unspoken, Izzy immediately heard an answer. "Behold the quantum storehouse of light frequencies, the very substance by which everything on Earth is created. Welcome again to the celestial Palace of Light."

And then the voice took form. A being cloaked in a mantle of light, with a soft angelic face, was beside Izzy, speaking. "Isidor Rhodes, you have been granted the rarest of opportunities."

Izzy stood in silence and then reached out his hand in greeting. As he did, he noticed that his own hand and arm were aglow, and he began to laugh.

"Okay, what the hell is this all about?" Izzy asked in his usual straightforward way.

The form smiled at Izzy's directness, then explained. "There comes a time in each being's eternal lifetime that he or she comes to know the higher worlds. This is your moment, Isidor. You have suffered much, but now you have been given a gift — a glimpse into the world beyond the earthly plane."

It took a moment for Izzy to grasp the meaning. "So you're saying I'm dead, right?"

"No, Isidor. Your life in the earthly realm exists and will continue. Come now and experience the light of another world."

Again Izzy needed a moment to think. "But if I'm not dead, then where am I?"

"Do you not recall, Isidor? Then let me show you," said the voice.

Izzy nodded, his curiosity guiding his way. Of course he remembered his Colorado dream. But then he was alone and now he was with an angelic dream-being.

"Please tell me your name, so I know what to call you," Izzy requested.

The form made a slight, formal bow. "I am The Keeper of Light, tasked to keep order within the spectrum of created light. I teach those who are ready to use the living library of light and sound, so they may fulfill their destiny. On a wave of ions, your soul has traveled through the drama of many lifetimes to reach this zenith. All is ready for you."

"Are you sure you have the right person?" Izzy joked lightheartedly.

The Keeper of Light smiled, amused at Izzy's question. "No mistake, Isidor."

The Keeper motioned to Izzy and the two walked side by side through the meadow. Izzy looked down at the green grass, which appeared soft and flowing, a velvet carpet before him. As he had on his first visit, he reached down with a sweep of his hand to feel the grass. And as before, it was not solid but light particles arranged as blades of grass.

They continued to walk, getting closer to the columned structure. Izzy noticed undulating heat waves radiating from The Keeper's shoulders giving the appearance of wings. Within the wings were wispy tendrils of vibrating colors.

Izzy and The Keeper now approached the massive building, which glowed in blue stardust. "Enter, Isidor," The Keeper beckoned. "Enter the Palace of Light and behold the universe."

As they entered a magnificent hall, Izzy recalled again different rooms to his left and right, each with its own entrance. The Keeper raised his arms and beams of light emanated from his palms. At the same moment, Izzy felt a tingling sensation in his hands. Then Izzy noticed a pulse of light emanating from The Keeper's chest and everything before him lit up in swirling particles of blue and green light. A wave of contentment enveloped Izzy.

"This is the source of the higher octaves of light," The Keeper explained. "God has created all things from harmonic light seeds. Open your mind, Isidor Rhodes, and find beauty in understanding truth. All things physical have an origin in the sound of light. Each object is a thought crystallized from the holographic properties of light. It takes what appears to be solid form and shape through geometric patterns."

As Izzy recalled more and more from his previous visit to the magnificent palace, The Keeper continued. "Here in the Palace of Light, we have the seed sounds of all living things ever created."

The Keeper pointed to the room in front of them, which was filled with ethereal containers. Izzy entered the room and surveyed the vessels. "Isidor, what you find here will illuminate your understanding of the world — of every aspect of it — and open your mind and heart beyond what you have ever known."

The Keeper pointed to a vessel labeled "Essence of Rose" and continued. "The Palace of Light is a living library of all creation. This sonic rose seed, for example, is made of light and represents *the idea* of the plant. It is the seed of every rose that ever existed or ever will exist. Imbedded in this seed is the harmonic code that resonates the essence and structure of a rose. The light of the rose in its highest octave radiates a sound that the human ear — at present — cannot perceive."

Izzy slowly nodded. Though he couldn't imagine how, he understood The Keeper's explanation. Izzy put his ear next to the rose vessel and, indeed, could hear nothing.

Then, with a wave of The Keeper's hand, he opened Izzy's ethereal ears to the sound of the rose. Izzy was struck by the beauty of the melody, which was heighted by the signature fragrance and color of a deep red rose. Awed, a tear formed in Izzy's eye and fell down his cheek.

"You see, Isidor, there is more to the world than you ever imagined."

Then The Keeper led Izzy back into the Great Hall and toward a crystal sitting atop a pedestal. "In every moment the universe is a song sung by God, the Being that is the Only Being — is, was, will be always. This is the ethereal form of the most precious harmonic crystal of all. It resonates with the echo of God's thought, singing the creation of the universe."

Izzy shook his head in astonishment. The implications of what the crystal held made him speechless. *Could it vibrate the voice of God?*

The Keeper watched Izzy, pleased by his understanding. "Yes, Isidor, this is the sound of the entire fabric of the universe, undifferentiated. Embedded in that sound is the sonic key of every individual aspect of creation — and in every individual aspect is the ALL."

Then The Keeper pointed to another crystal. "Now let me show you why you are here. This crystal holds the light of Earth's *self-awareness*. All things have a spiritual life that unfolds in an evolutionary spiral through time. There are moments when that spiritual essence ascends to another plane of existence."

The Keeper opened his arms wide, as though holding all. "The physical earthly plane is ready for such a time. It is the sons and daughters of the divine — humankind — that as stewards of the good Earth assist in her transformation. And, in so doing, they facilitate the ascension of humankind unto a higher octave of existence as well."

As The Keeper paused, Izzy took in a deep breath, anticipating what he would hear next.

"That time is now, Isidor. Earth has seen the dawning of humankind — the human spirit embodied in human form — and has sustained that life over time. So too the human race collectively shares its spiritual power and light with Earth. Each unfolds according to its destiny, learning from the other."

Izzy had continued to listen with a level of comprehension that surprised him. Somehow knowledge and understanding, like light, flowed around and through him in this place. Only one key question seemed beyond his grasp to answer: *What does this have to do with me?*

Once again The Keeper heard his thoughts. "Isidor, it is time for *you* to come into full awareness of the beauty of your true nature. Each person has a destiny as an individual expression of the divine. Transformation is at hand for you and many others. Claim your destiny and unlock the secrets of the universe that reside within you. Know your true inheritance — to be free, endowed with the full power, wisdom and love of the human divine spirit."

Izzy stared at The Keeper, waiting and wondering, and then finally asking, "How do I do that?"

"Have faith in the dominion of the divine life-force within," The Keeper explained. "Recall that once before you dove deep into the depth of your despair, faced your fears and found your true strength."

Izzy immediately felt the presence of Agnes, Robert and Jacob. When this dream first appeared to him, in Colorado, it had taught him to accept the loss of those he loved most dearly and to draw strength from the love that endured, even beyond death.

His eyes filled with tears reliving that moment of mourning and rebirth.

"Those tears are sacred, Isidor," The Keeper observed. "They have washed away despair, even as they water the fond memories that have made your spirit bloom again. They have left you cleansed. You have regained your faith in life, renewed the love of your heart and live once again in the light of joy."

Then, in wonder, Izzy received confirmation of what he had intuitively felt through his first days with the diary.

"But there is one thing left undone," The Keeper continued. "The earthly task of your lineage remains unfulfilled. In their time, your father and uncle also sensed this unfinished task, but it was not their fate to complete it. Now that destiny is yours to fulfill. You stand at the threshold of the generations. Soon the solar arc will reach its apex and align with the center eye of the great sky. This is your time."

The Keeper paused for Izzy to ponder the meaning of his words, then went on. "Long ago a treasure was buried. Look to Galileo's four moons of Jupiter. Find them, and you will be led unto the hallowed grounds of the eternal heart."

As he spoke, The Keeper placed his glowing hand over Izzy's heart. "Isidor, not only does the light of God's thought echo in these seed crystals before us, it resides within your own heart and, indeed, in every human heart. The heart is a diamond crystal that reflects the whole universe — all of creation, all of life. It holds the fullness of All-That-Is. But it lies undiscovered, waiting to be revealed. The moment will come — and you will know it."

Warmth surged through Izzy's body. Then light particles began to flow from The Keeper's hand. As the light began to pulse and increase in strength, Izzy looked down to see the light was entering his chest and he felt his heart flutter. He could feel the light expand his heart.

"Isidor, it is your time to move beyond the ordinary and glimpse the light of eternity. Hold its memory in your heart, as a reminder of this place." The Keeper tapped the center of Izzy's forehead and light flooded Izzy's mind and then enveloped his whole being.

Izzy could still feel The Keeper's touch, even as the form became indistinguishable from the light.

Izzy bolted straight up in bed. Moonbeams streaked across his chest and his eyes followed the light, astonished by his dream.

Then, instinctively, Izzy jumped out of bed and searched for something to write on. He must record the dream while the images were still vivid.

He had been tasked to fulfill his destiny. And in his dream The Keeper of Light had given him several clues. Izzy was now sure that Ethan's diary held more.

"Long ago a treasure was buried." The Keeper had said it, but what was the treasure? Of course Izzy's first thought was that it had to be Ethan's crystal. He had read about Ethan's work with the crystal. But could it be something more? Could Ethan have tapped into something intrinsic to the human experience that few people knew about? After all Ethan was an alchemist. And then there was The Keepers words to him "You stand at the threshold of generations."

Izzy's mind was ablaze and he resolved to review the diary again with fresh eyes, to find more details and look for hints that might explain the mysterious stone.

He recalled another phrase from the dream: Galileo's four moons of Jupiter. That was surely a significant clue.

Izzy looked at the time. It was three-thirty now. He longed to call Will Davenport and ask him about the moons of Jupiter, but it was far too early to contact him. And even if Will didn't mind, no doubt his wife would not appreciate a call so early.

Instead, Izzy went to his computer, emailed Will with his question and asked him to come to the shop first thing when he got into Grand Central.

Ian! Izzy dialed his cell and Ian's tired voice answered. "Are you awake? Where are you?"

"I'm at the gallery, Iz," Ian yawned. "Been looking at the box."

"Stay there! I've had a dream. I've got new clues. I'll be there as fast as I can get a cab."

Izzy paused, recalling his despair only hours before and now the voice in the dream: "You stand at the threshold of the generations."

Now he went to the kitchen and poured himself a glass of wine. With his first sip, Izzy toasted his father, his uncle and the Hawkins generations.

Chapter 31

Will and Nora

"Will, time to get up." Nora nudged him. A complaining moan let her know he was awake.

"I'm taking a quick shower. It's six-thirty. Coffee's made." Nora had been up for well over an hour, planning for her important meeting this morning.

As she disappeared into the bathroom, Will propped himself up and reached for his laptop on the night table. Amid the junk mail was a message from Izzy: "*Galileo's four Jupiter moons. Does that mean anything to you?*"

Even as sleep cleared, Will recognized the significance, though he couldn't imagine what prompted Izzy to wonder about Galileo's Jupiter moons. Still, he typed out his response:

"*In the 1600's, while viewing the four moons of Jupiter through a telescope, Galileo came up with a unique way of calculating latitude and longitude. But it only worked on land. At sea there were too many uncertainties, like the unsteadiness of a shifting deck, to make calculations via telescope reliable.*"

Will closed with a short, "*Why the interest?*" Then he hit SEND.

He received an immediate reply: "*Fascinating. Thank you. I want to know more. Meet me at Ian's gallery if you can this morning. I'll explain everything when I see you.*"

405

Will wrote back: *"Izzy, I'll be at Ian's as fast as I can."*

He'd been giving some thought to going out to see his parents today and talk to his dad about crystals. Will did a quick timetable in his head. If he got in before nine o'clock, he could spend the morning with Izzy and Ian Hillenbrand. Then he could run over to Penn Station, take the Long Island Rail Road and spend the afternoon with Robert and Olivia Davenport.

Will knew he was spending a lot of time with Izzy, helping him interpret the diary. Again today, he'd be a no-show at the university office. He imagined getting more hassle from Ken, who perceived Will's work habits as "lax." Yet that's the way it always was. Will had endured his brother's disapproval for years. But on the plus side, Ken, no doubt, would be glad he was going to see the folks.

Nora came out of the shower with a head of steam on, moving deliberately around the room, clearly absorbed in thought as she got dressed. Will recognized Nora's investigator's hat sitting firmly on her head. Her professional side was in full gear and he loved watching her mind at work. She was itching to dig her teeth into something.

"Hey, I think I'll try to go see my parents today on Long Island. What time is your meeting over? Think you can come with me?"

Nora had casually mentioned last night that she was taking an early train in this morning. But she'd kept the details brief. Will's invitation could be problematic. She knew she should go too — they hadn't seen Will's parents since they arrived in late February. But she wanted to keep her day open, for whatever might happen at the meeting set up by Jack Reed.

"You know I'd love to, honey," she began sweetly. "But I just can't do it today. My appointment's a follow-up to the one I had the day you were tracking down the diary. I'm not sure how long it will go — and I don't want to keep you from seeing your parents. Invite them for dinner, say, next weekend."

Will looked at Nora quizzically. "Sure, of course. What is this story, anyway? You haven't said."

Nora looked at her watch and was relieved to see that it was after seven o'clock. She could push this conversation off for at least a bit. "Look, I'm taking the seven forty-six train," she explained. "If you're taking the same train, you'd better get to it. I'll tell you on the way in."

Once on the train, Will was distracted googling everything he could about Galileo's discovery.

Nora welcomed Will's preoccupation, to further prepare for Jack Reed and the PAGA member. Her plan was to work Jason DeWitt into the conversation — to see how the PAGA person might respond and what might shake loose about DeWitt's involvement.

She was deep in thought when Will suddenly asked, "So what's this story that has you so wound up?"

The train car was crowded, far from ideal for discussing the story — and a good excuse for keeping the details minimal. Nora plunged ahead, leaning in close to Will and whispering, "A possible act of eco-terrorism."

Will's eyes grew wide and his voice rose. "What!?"

"Shhh!" Nora warned. "This group is allegedly planning to shut down the electrical grid to make a point about global warming and corporate irresponsibility."

"Whoa, Nora! When were you going to tell me about this?"

"Shhhh! I'm not even sure it's real."

"But what if it is?" Even in a whisper, Will's voice was full of concern. "You're poking around something very dangerous!"

"Look, Will, you know my process by now. I have to find out if they're legitimate — if the story has validity. I'm far from convinced that it is."

Will had to acknowledge that his wife had no fear when it came to following her nose to expose a truth.

"My contact has set up the meeting," Nora continued. "It's downtown, at Brookfield Place, a very public location. You know I'm always careful." Nora gave Will a smile and a quick kiss on the cheek, hoping Will didn't press her for further details.

"Alright Ace, just keep in touch by text … please." Will responded knowing once Nora made up her mind to pursue something, not much was going to stop her.

But even though this was a familiar conversation between them, Will had never gotten comfortable with some of Nora's journalistic requirements — prerequisites, she'd say, to ensure high quality investigative reporting.

Nora still did not reveal the Jason DeWitt connection. It was way too premature. She needed more evidence. If it turned out to be nothing, she didn't need to take Will down the rabbit hole with her.

The train pulled into Grand Central Station and they followed the crowd up the platform, holding hands. "You don't have to walk me to the subway, like it's our first date," Nora laughed.

Will pulled her to the side, out of the way of others. "Oh yes I do," he smiled, wrapping her in his arms and giving her a passionate kiss. "That's to remind you to text me and to be careful. I want you home safe with me tonight!"

Nora nodded. "If that's a promise of more to come, you can be sure of it! And *text me* when you head to Long Island. Give your parents my love."

Soon after they said their goodbyes, each on a mission that seemed worlds apart.

"So Izzy, Jupiter's four moons — where did you find that?" Will asked the second he walked through the door of Hillenbrand's gallery. Izzy and Ian were in the back, huddled around the diary.

"Amazingly, it came to me in a dream vision," Izzy explained. "I emailed you as soon as I awoke."

Will had come to expect the unusual from Izzy. Besides, the same curiosity that inspired his scientific exploration, made him also embrace the idea that there were unseen forces in the world — other states of consciousness that conveyed meaning. There had been plenty of times his hunches, plucked from who knows where, panned out in the lab. And now he had to consider whether Izzy's dream reference of Galileo's Jupiter moons could be a significant piece of the puzzle. If Galileo's method of calculating longitude were noted in the diary, it might lead to the location of the Hawkins treasure. It was sure worth a shot.

Ian turned over the diary to Will, who began searching for any indications he might find, direct or hidden, to Galileo's Jupiter moons. Will's previous reviews of the diary had only begun to reveal the scientific knowledge accumulated by Ethan and Benjamin Hawkins. There was a wealth of information, with charts and diagrams, and a host of descriptions and recipes for remedies. Most amazing to Will were the explanations of planetary movements and their influence on everything physical, from lunar cycles and when to plant seeds, to how planetary alignments affect life-force energy and using those optimal times for developing healing remedies.

"This is likely going to take some time, Izzy," Will explained. "But I have a sense that it's an important clue. Have you come across any other references to moons?"

Ian had been searching for a breakthrough of his own. From the first time he saw the diary, Ian was focused on the silver box, convinced the pastoral depiction of a man and woman pointing to a waterfall was more than mere decoration. "There are what look like stars here, but could they be moons instead?"

Will shook his head. "They don't appear to be moons, but it's worth considering. Let's keep that in mind as we move forward."

Ian nodded in response. "I've been spending hours on this box, looking for any markings hidden in the picture — examining it under the magnifier.

"Well keep at it, something may click," Will advised.

Izzy wasn't satisfied with their progress. "Ian, what about the other Newton letters? Anything?"

"I've tried to contact that SOB, Gabriel Hornsby!" Ian exclaimed. Clearly irritated with the lack of results so far, he turned to Will and explained. "Hornsby's a noted collector and an expert on great English philosopher's letters and manuscripts. He might know something. But the bastard has yet to respond to me, which annoys me no end!"

Will grimaced, mirroring Ian's expression. Then his face signaled a new thought. "Izzy," Will asked, "Do you have your Newton letter with you?"

"Of course," Izzy replied, carefully removing it from his satchel and handing it to Will.

Will quickly scanned the letter. "This passage: *'Should what you say be true, we may have, at long last, found the prize, the treasure of treasures, the very keystone that reveals the deepest secrets.'*

Could it be that the attributes of Ethan Hawkins' crystal be even more then we surmise? How can a crystal reveal the deepest secrets?" That question hug in the air for a few seconds and then, "I'm going out to see my dad today. He's an expert on crystals." Will's determination clearly written on his face.

Izzy's demeanor brightened.

"My father knows everything there is to know about crystals." Will explained. "His insights and knowledge just might spark something important that we are just not seeing."

"I like your thinking Will," Izzy responded.

Will then summarized where they were in the hunt. "Gentlemen, we basically still have three mysteries: what exactly is 'the treasure,' where is it to be found, and what are these secrets Newton and Fletcher speak about?"

Chapter 32

BROOKFIELD PLACE, MANHATTAN
MARCH 15
10:00 A.M.

Nora

Nora got off the subway downtown at Fulton Street and headed for the café at the Brookfield Place complex of stores, galleries and eateries. Weaving through the crowd, she had the distinct feeling that she was being watched.

She stopped to send Will a quick text, and then scanned the people around her. Everyone was walking at such a fast pace. All these people crowded together in a setting so different from home back in California. She stood observing, contemplating for a moment how quickly her life and Will's had shifted.

"Nora Martin."

She turned to see Jack Reed — Lester Edwards, though Nora had yet to learn his real identity.

"You said to meet in the café, Reed."

"I wanted to be sure you found us. There are several places that might qualify as a café."

Reed's oily manner repelled Nora. Her instincts not to trust him were stronger than ever.

"There, at that table." He pointed to a young woman in jeans and a lace and sequin blouse. "Expecting a firebrand extremist dressed in army fatigues?" His voice was mocking.

"I didn't expect anything," Nora lied. "I want to meet with her alone, Reed. Let's be clear. We follow my terms on this — or I leave now."

Reed's mocking voice again. "Of course. *I* wouldn't expect anything less from *you*, the consummate professional!"

As they walked to the table, the woman eyed Nora cautiously.

"I'm Nora Martin."

"I know. You can call me Grace."

Reed left, as promised and without fanfare, allowing Nora to get down to business. She took a seat next to Grace and pulled out her phone, to record the conversation.

"No recordings!" Grace was adamant.

"Grace, if you want me to tell your story, you're going to have to trust me."

"One step at a time, Ms. Martin."

"All right, we'll play it your way."

"Oh, we're not playing. The powers that run the world have gone too far, and we are going to end it, right here and now." Despite her soft appearance, Grace had a steely presence that impressed Nora.

"That sounds ominous," Nora observed.

"And so it is. But it has to be this way. There is no time left. Corporate greed has infiltrated every aspect of life so completely, there's hardly any space where people can think for themselves. They tell us that our lives are empty unless we buy what they're selling. From the moment we wake till the time we go to sleep, life is saturated with sleek, hypnotic messages. It's little wonder why we walk around like brainwashed sheep! They purposely addict us so our only worry is getting the next upgraded cell phone, or sharing stupid photos online or following what some celebrity had for lunch!..."

Graced paused, looked directly at Nora gauging her reaction. But

Nora's face was intentionally emotionless. Undaunted Graced took in a deep breath, and continued, her volume rising. "All the while our freedoms are being taken away! Governments spy on us, businesses prey on us, religious leaders victimize our children and politicians manipulate our fears, sending the flower of every generation off to war!"

Nora listened intently, waiting for mention of environmental concerns. At another pause, she jumped in. "Grace, excuse me, but I thought the environment was your greatest worry?"

"IT IS!" Grace was clearly offended. "Don't you get it? They're killing the planet we live on, dooming our future! Everything they do is toxic!"

"I hear you, Grace." Nora's voice was quiet, aiming to calm her contact. From experience, Nora knew a source that was too riled might exaggerate information. She needed to know that what Grace provided was sound. "But it's not as though people average people have no control, no choices."

Grace shook her head vehemently. "It's hardly a choice when billions of dollars are spent to program people to consume and consume! The latest trends send people rushing online to click away endless hours. All the while needless products are produced, blackening the skies of Mother Earth with the dark stain of fossil fuels. Global warming is denied, just so a little more money can line the pockets of the super rich as the spirit of the planet is sucked dry!"

As was her way, Nora wanted to push, play devil's advocate. It was not her role to agree. Though with Grace, Nora saw the need to be watchful of just how far she pushed. "But Grace...," she began.

"There are no buts about it!" Grace interrupted, her manner more and more ferocious. "Something has to be done to awaken the poor souls who have been put to slumber as automatons on this planet! Something — before it's too late!"

"Okay, so what are *you* going to do, Grace?" Nora asked, keeping her own demeanor calm and almost disinterested — the complete opposite of what she felt.

"We have to put a stop to it, NOW, and we will … and we are!" Grace declared, her eyes blazing.

"And how will you do that?"

It was the moment of truth for learning PAGA's intentions. Nora listened as Grace outlined the same plot to shut down the grid that Reed had revealed previously.

"Don't you think that shutting down the grid is extreme?" Nora replied. "Millions of people will suffer. Everyone will panic. Food supplies will rot; the sick in hospitals might die. Who knows what other lethal consequences there will be. It's a steep price to pay to save the planet."

Grace looked at her unmoved. "No, Nora, it's a small price to pay. Will people die? Maybe. Be uncomfortable? For sure. But the future of the planet and all of humankind is at stake."

Nora was struck again by what seemed to be the young woman's unshakable core. Grace's voice became calmer as she continued to speak. "Reed said you wouldn't let anything get in the way of truth-telling. What I just told you is the truth. Now will you help us get our side of the story out to the public?"

"What Reed told you is correct," Nora confirmed. "My job as a journalist is to expose the truth and inform the public of what they need to know."

"So you'll help us?"

Nora wasn't about to become part of the story. She needed for Grace to understand the terms.

"If 'by help' you mean to present your position, why you've become radicalized, yes. But I am not a party to your plot, Grace. In fact, I'm agreeing to write this story to demonstrate that there are ways to make your points *without* violence and disruption. However, to tell your story, there is much more I need to know. And that means I need for you to place your plans on hold, while I gather more information."

"I won't promise that, Nora, not indefinitely."

"But I need some time," Nora pressed. "Our interview today is not enough."

Grace paused, then nodded. "We'll give you a week, two weeks at the most, while you get the story together — *but* that's all. We're not going to wait forever."

Nora was relieved. "Understood," she answered. "Can you can give me some leads? Names of people I should contact or investigate?"

Grace shrugged. "If you're trying to determine whether or not we're legit, I can assure you we are. Other than that, I can't help you."

"Here's a name Reed mentioned to me when we met: Jason DeWitt. Do you know him?" Nora asked, undeterred and keeping her voice casual.

Grace nodded. "His greedy rich family has been some of the biggest polluters! He's just the kind we want to bring down!"

Nora had to be sure. "So he's not working with you?"

For the first time in their meeting, Grace let out a laugh. "Working with us? That's a joke. Most definitely not! But there's something coming his way when the smoke clears."

With that auspicious prediction, the meeting ended.

From a distance Lester Edwards watched the interview end as he had viewed the entire conversation — with amusement. Grace was so vehement! Nora Martin, intent, professional, sincere!

He could see that neither realized they were just pawns in his game. Theirs was an exercise in pointlessness. He was calling the shots.

Chapter 33

Will, Robert & Olivia Davenport

Robert Livingston Davenport's warehouse was located in the town of Freeport on the south shore of Long Island, down by the water. Will took the hour long train ride from Penn Station, wondering what his parents, and especially his father, would say. He hadn't seen them since his Party Girl debacle. And he hadn't seen the warehouse since its grand opening, which he and Nora had attended right after they were married.

Originally located in California, Robert and Olivia Davenport moved Meraki Minerals to New York for personal and professional reasons. They wanted to be closer to Ken's two young kids. "Grandchildren are like a magnet," Olivia explained. And there were the museum opportunities that had first come through Ken's advisory work, and then to Robert directly. Interest in crystals of all kinds had captured the public's imagination like never before, and his experience as a preeminent geological explorer was suddenly in great demand.

The move took place in the summer of 2012. Unfortunately, when Hurricane Sandy hit at the end of October, not much more than a week after the opening festivities, the Atlantic paid its visit, flooding the first floor of the warehouse.

Robert was initially shocked at the turn of events. He considered selling his remaining inventory and getting out of the business. But Olivia would hear none of that talk. Partners from the beginning, she handled all the accounting and financial aspects. They had always made a great team. And when she secured the funding necessary to weather the storm, Robert took Olivia's lead and Mother Nature's calling card as a challenge to redouble his efforts. The result was one of the most diverse and exotic collections of crystals, minerals, fossils and petrified woods in the United States.

Now husband and wife, mother and father, waited at the train station for the arrival of their younger son. The train was late, per usual, which only increased the intensity of their greeting.

"There he is!" Olivia opened her arms wide to Will.

"Let's have a look at him," Robert chimed in. "And," addressing Olivia, "He looks good. I told you there's nothing to worry about."

"I'll be the judge of that," Olivia remarked, inspecting Will's face, searching for any signs that would raise her concern.

"Nora sends her love. She was going to come, but she got called into a last-minute meeting — a lead on a story."

"Already! No grass grows under that girl's feet," said Robert admiringly of his daughter-in-law.

"Sorry it took me so long to get out here," Will added. "Nora wants you to come for dinner. How's next Saturday?"

"Of course. I'll put it on our calendar," Olivia nodded.

"Now that's settled, we're off to the warehouse," Robert directed, as all three got into the elder Davenports' SUV. "Lots of changes, Will. And I want to show you my latest finds."

When they reached the warehouse, Olivia headed for the office, first reminding them of the afternoon plans. "I've made a reservation for a late lunch at our favorite seafood place, so you two have about an hour," Olivia instructed. "Don't get too lost!" she laughed.

Meraki Minerals was no ordinary warehouse. It was more like a vast showroom, and Will was duly impressed. "The shelves are loaded! You've been doing a lot of buying," he admired.

"And selling too," Robert confirmed. "The large pieces are moving out of here at a pace I've never experienced — they're selling like hotcakes. Between the museums and the interior decorators, I cannot get enough."

Looking over it all, Will could see why potential buyers had a field day in this place. His father had set up display counters filled with rare specimens from Brazil, Uruguay and even the Himalayas. Fossils of ancient animals and sea creatures lined glass shelves. There were installations of large crystal geodes of amethyst and citrine. Then beyond that, row upon row of shelves filled with every shade and cut of crystals and minerals, petrified woods, Peruvian pyrite, agate slices and druzy quartz.

"Take a look at this one!" Father led son to a five-foot-tall quartz crystal with polished terminated points. "This beauty is from the Himalaya Mountains. Quite unique. You don't see something like this every day."

Robert ran his hand along the plane of one side of the crystal. "Think of it, Will. This is millions of years old. It most certainly has seen the dawning of humanity and may well be here beyond our days."

Both paused, taking in that unfathomable concept. "It's simply staggering how elements of the cosmos came together to manifest these beautiful crystals," Robert mused. "And they're all part of the earth."

Will had heard his father speak this way since he was a child, yet today those words hit him differently. It was precisely why he had come to visit now.

For as long as Robert Davenport could remember he had a deep affinity for minerals. He felt each crystal had unique qualities. Though they appeared fossilized, they were anything but — to him, they were alive.

"By the way, Will, did you see that a group of scientists were able to record Earth's vibration at the bottom of the ocean? It's like Earth has a heartbeat!" Robert waited to hear what Will had to say. He was excited to have his younger boy nearby. They'd lived on opposite coasts for the better part of a decade, and he now looked forward to spending time together, exchanging ideas and getting to know his son again.

Will was quiet, still considering the image of the crystal before him, millions of years old, watching over human history, chronicling the collective human narrative. It occurred to him that, in some elegant and sublime way, he too was millions of years old. DNA codes, whole biological systems and functions that have evolved over eons, all were operating within him. He recognized the impossibility of calculating all the neurological reactions and muscle movements, all the body function happening beyond his conscious awareness.... Awareness! That word kept popping up over and over again and Will wondered. *Where does my awareness actually begin? Is it also millions of years old?*

"What do you think, Will? Imagine, Earth's vibrations. Do you think we actually feel it without realizing what it is?" Robert was trying to engage his son, who seemed off in another world. "Hey, Earth to Will, come in Will Davenport."

Earth vibrations… crystals… awareness… is there a connection? Will wondered.

"Say, Dad," he began. "Tell me about crystals…."

An hour later, Olivia was seeking them out. "All right, you two! You're late. We've got to hustle to get to the restaurant."

Will and his parents had lunch in a restaurant down by the docks. Olivia did her best not to pester him too much. Her motherly intuition told her Will had turned a corner. His eyes sparkled as he described the thrilling pace of New York City.

She then turned her attention to her other son. "So you're seeing a lot of Ken. How are you finding your brother?" Olivia asked. "And who's this Molly McQuire he mentions so often? Such an unusual name! We haven't seen him in weeks. What's going on?"

Will chuckled to himself, recalling how Ken had bugged him to come out here. Probably wanted some pressure off himself, Will now realized.

"Ken seems Ken, Mom," Will insisted. "Molly's an assistant. She's been great helping me settle in. And," he added, knowing his parents would want to hear it, but feeling it genuinely too, "Ken has been great. He got me the office, a fantastic place to work on my manuscript."

"Something tells me she's more than an assistant," Olivia responded.

But Will wasn't touching that comment with a ten-foot pole.

From there the conversation veered to his work. Will offered a brief outline of what he hoped to accomplish with his book. He decided to keep his interest in Newton and the Hawkins diary quiet for now. He'd wait for further developments.

All in all, it was a successful visit. And his father had told him some interesting details about crystals that Will had not anticipated — information that could turn out to be very helpful in the search for Ethan's treasure.

And to Will's surprise, it was a unique experience that led to Robert Livingston Davenport completely devoting himself to collecting Earth's crystals and minerals many years ago.

"It started innocently enough," he told Will. "It was before you and Ken were born."

And all the way back to Westchester, Will replayed his father's story. Since he was a boy, Will always like hearing tales about his father's history. Then they were a window into his father's life, and now it was no different.

Robert Davenport had been buying minerals in South America

for an industrial research firm in California. He had quickly gained a reputation with the locals as someone with a discerning eye for the qualities and characteristics of different stones, and an expert evaluator of unique materials. One day he was called in by a small mining facility to analyze an underground rock formation that had deposits of an unknown glass-like substance. They wanted to know if it was worth mining.

"I expected it to be something ordinary. It almost always was in these cases." Robert recalled. "And when I went into the mine and saw the rock formation I thought it was as I suspected, a familiar stratum of common crystal. But when I looked closer, I saw veins of clear blue running through it. In awe of its beauty I ran my hand on the rock formation... and I had a vision. At least I think it was a vision. It's hard to explain. For sure it was a communication of a different kind."

Spending time with Izzy, Will was not surprised by uncommon occurrences. But this was his father — and what his father had told him next, took his breath away.

"I swear to you, Will, it was as if the blue veins ran down deep into the earth, and through them the Earth spoke to me. But it wasn't so much that, if that isn't odd enough. It was the message that struck me — loud and clear as if broadcast for all the universe to hear, if it dared.

"I'll never forget it — a sentient transmission that is *still* playing in my ears." Robert paused, listening, almost as if he was checking to hear if the message was there.... He then proceeded to share it with his son.

"With my hand still on the blue crystal vein, I envisioned the Earth spinning around circling the sun, and this is what was communicated to me:

"'I have been evolving since my birth, embodying the fullness of my being. The enormity and responsibility and the power to be born a planet is a singular experience. To have all the living systems depend on me is an obligation I took on long before my birth. I have seen much joy, and much sorrow, and still I persevere. Many will come and many will go. The fullness of what I AM is undefinable and yet still to be. But my destination will not be deterred.'"

Then his dad had told Will something he knew Izzy needed to hear.

"Suddenly, a vibration from the blue veins in the rock formation entered the palm of my hand, and rode the blood vessels straight into my heart and spoke directly to me. 'You too are made of the cosmos. The fusion of the stars form universes in your very being. Be not afraid. Ride the wave and be free.'"

The rest of the train ride, Will focused on the end of his father's story. "Shortly after my experience, the mine had a cave-in. Fortunately, there were only minor injuries. But from that day on, I considered that cave sacred ground not to be disturbed. And when I told the owners that in my opinion the blue veins in the crystal were common, not worth pursuing, they decided not to reopen the mine.

"Naturally, I couldn't tell them of my 'vision,' whatever it was. Nobody would believe me anyway. But I always took the cave in as a sign that the message that day was for my ears alone. And I've never taken that experience for granted. It's with me always. I didn't think there'd be more to it. But somehow Will, whatever you're working on, whatever is going on in your life, I think there's a message in it for you, too. It's up to you to figure it out!"

Will couldn't get his father's experience and the message he received out of his mind. Especially his father's belief that there was a message in it for Will.

Newton's letters, Ethan's dairy, the crystal — what did it all mean and how was he to figure it out?

Chapter 34

BOSTON
MARCH 15
8:00 P.M.

Levi Rhodes

On the day he relinquished the diary to Izzy, Levi ultimately canceled his five o'clock appointment with Gabriel Hornsby, breaking the news by phone instead. Though disappointed, Hornsby took the turn of events in stride. In his world, there was always another prize to acquire. The hunt was what Hornsby loved. If someone beat him to the prize — *c'est la vie.* Granted, of course, that Hornsby lost nothing tangible, and certainly not cash.

Since he turned over the Hawkins diary to Izzy, Levi had also been on an emotional roller coaster, struggling to sort out his feelings. At first he blocked any thought of Izzy. He went back to his high finance and his secret project for Victor Strong and tried to resume his life as it had been, before the call from Hornsby that had set in motion the diary chase.

But he was only partially successful. His iron-will held at work, but at night, when he was home alone, Levi frequently found himself thinking of Izzy. Part of Levi felt a kind of relief from having revealed the truth, finally, about their father's death and from letting go of that terrible secret.

However, that sense of being unburdened was short lived. When he recalled Izzy's reaction — his brother's confusion, hurt and anger — Levi felt a profound sense of guilt. He had not only stolen the letters, but he had robbed his brother and himself of their father's presence. And Levi had destroyed their mother's happiness, too. She was never the same after Elijah's death.

Levi began to face the depth of the damage he had caused. But he could not yet accept the full blame for all that had occurred. Guilt turned to anger as he lashed out at Izzy in his mind. *He should have left well enough alone. Izzy caused this whole mess! Why was Izzy so obsessed with the Hawkins family legacy?*

He blamed not only Izzy for his emotional anguish, but his father too. *None of this would have happened if only you had given me the money! It was just until the market turned around!*

Eventually though, after Levi blamed everybody but himself, he could avoid the truth no longer. He was a realist, after all, and he knew the length and breadth of his own actions. He had done what he needed to do at the time. And with that admission, the mental armor that had protected him from the full force of the consequences of his behavior, melted away. His emotions lay bear before him.

Now it was a week past Teterboro. Levi had come home from the office early and had been shut up in his library, the fireplace roaring, with a bottle of excellent scotch, which had gone from full to half empty.

As the expensive clock on his expensive mantle chimed the eight o'clock hour, Levi heard each toll of the bell as a judgment knell.

He had created the tragedy that ruined his family. And with the attempted theft of the diary away from Izzy, he had compounded that tragedy. How would Izzy respond, knowing his father's death had been caused by his own brother, whose lying, stealing and brazen behavior had brought about such enormous destruction?

Levi's deepening despair wrapped around him in a shroud of guilt and blame. An emotional storm raged within him and, with a sudden ferociousness, tears flowed down his cheeks. The inevitable came to rest at his doorstep and he accepted its pronouncement.

He had not cried since his mother's death. Now he wept openly, fully acknowledging what he had done.

And when his tears finally passed, surprisingly, Levi felt as if a spell had broken. His head suddenly clear, he emerged with one desire, to make amends. And he set his path toward atonement.

He had scarcely looked at the poem that had fallen from the silver box since the day on the plane. Now he withdrew it from his desk drawer and began to read it once again.

Over and over, the lines of the poem ran through his head. And over and over, he struggled to interpret the lines. That the poem was together with the diary suggested to him that it had a special significance. Unlocking the message hidden in the poem was his best way, perhaps his only way, of winning Izzy's trust and rebuilding their relationship as brothers.

But he was stumped. Unable to decipher the poem, he knew he needed help. And he knew just where to go — the other Newton-Fletcher letters, which might hold clues to the poem's hidden meaning. And that required another call.

"Gabriel, it's Levi…," he began.

Chapter 35

BOSTON
MARCH 25
5:00 P.M.

Levi

Ten days later, Levi was on his way to meet Gabriel Hornsby with the promise of another prize for his collection. All that was needed was for Levi to see the Newton-Fletcher letters.

Levi arrived at Hornsby's grand home on Beacon Hill, the heart of old guard Boston. Hornsby's longtime assistant guided him to the "Collections Room," with its choice framed images of Newton and other luminaries whose writings and thoughts Hornsby gathered as his own. In response to Levi's request, the assistant poured scotch into an exquisite crystal glass. Then he offered Levi a seat at a magnificent desk on which sat a portfolio, the cover engraved with "Newton-Fletcher" in gold leaf. It was not the portfolio he had delivered to Hornsby forty years earlier. This was museum quality, with thick leather and the highest-grade archival materials for optimum preservation.

Then the assistant produced a set of fine cotton gloves. "If you please, Mr. Rhodes, for reviewing the pages. Mr. Hornsby will join you eventually. He is detained at present."

Levi suspected the old goat was not "detained" but probably in the next room, listening — or watching through a peephole. But he could care less, as long as he had access to the Newton-Fletcher letters.

He downed the scotch in a few sips, grateful for the fortification. He was feeling the impact of seeing the letters again — among the last things his father and uncle ever read, ever touched — the letters that were a turning point all those years ago, and perhaps could be again.

Settling in, he began to read.

∞

Dear Isaac,

I know you are most disappointed that Ethan Hawkins' diamond stone, as well as his valued diary, went off to the New World with his son Benjamin. Under the circumstances, if you were in my place, no doubt, you would come to the same conclusion — the stone's destiny is with Benjamin.

Yet fear not Isaac, all is not lost. Last night I had a visitation of the most unusual kind. It propels me to an unexpected undertaking. My eldest son, Jacob, and I shall make you a visit in Cambridge, for I seek your wisdom — and may I venture, dear friend, confirmation of my own suspicions of the crystal, and what next I must do.

The heavens play an interesting game with the fate of men. It appears all is as it is meant to be. I'll explain my assumptions when I see you. The diamond stone, the diary, the Hawkins family, you and I spin at the behest of a cosmic self, a life-force that knows us all. The diamond, too, has a destiny fixed in the heavens. It leads to wealth of an unexpected kind.

If all goes well, we shall arrive to you within a fortnight. Until we meet,

Be well, my friend,
Daniel Fletcher

When Levi had gone through every correspondence in the collection, it was this letter that stood out, the one with the clearest evidence of a treasure still to be found.

It was also a letter that Hornsby had obtained through another source. All of the Newton letters Levi had sold him were written by Newton *to* Fletcher. Clearly, this letter was *received* by Newton.

Even Father and Uncle Samuel never saw this letter! Levi reasoned. And in some twist of fate, perhaps finding this letter might be, in one of life's ironies, the proverbial silver lining to the dark clouds of the past.

A few moments later Hornsby had joined him and was listening as Levi interpreted the all-important Fletcher letter.

"You, see, Gabriel, there it is, *'wealth of an unexpected kind',*" Levi confirmed.

Hornsby waved away the phrase. "Ah, Levi, that may be. But a mere crystal? Even if it's a diamond, it doesn't really interest me. I leave diamonds to my wife to collect, at which she's quite the expert. The monetary value of this Hawkins stone, whatever it is, while worthwhile to some, is not to me," he plainly stated, dismissive of Levi's find.

"I know it holds a family significance for you," Hornsby added. "But, honestly, I'm tiring of this Newton-Fletcher-Hawkins triangle."

He rose from his chair and walked toward the door, ending the conversation. "You're welcome to remain for as long as you choose. My man will see you out when you're ready. I have other business to attend to. It's a pity there wasn't a greater prize to find. But perhaps, Levi, another time."

Levi had hoped to come to Izzy with more. No doubt Hornsby was right. It was a big fuss for what, a crystal? The treasure Newton mentions surely must be something else.

There was little reason to continue looking, yet before he left, Levi took a photo with his phone of the letter Fletcher wrote to Newton. No telling whether Hornsby would give him access again, and the wording of the letter might be useful. Who knew?

Levi returned to his office just before nine o'clock that evening. Victor Strong was gone.

He unlocked the top drawer of his massive mahogany desk and withdrew a leather portfolio containing the poem he found on the floor of the plane.

Leaning back in his thickly padded chair, he swiveled to look out at the lights of Boston Harbor. He knew not where Benjamin Hawkins had arrived in "the New World" — whether other Hawkins family members, maybe Fletchers too, had followed. Perhaps they sailed upon the very waters he looked out on. And if not this harbor, then doubtless New York.

Levi read the poem silently, pausing after the first words:

"Here, in this place, dwells the pleasure that only heaven knows."

Levi could only wonder where that place might be. And he wondered too about his own place. Everything was changing. Where he was just a few days ago was gone. And in it's place, who knew.

He recalled his father and uncle in the shop on West 86th Street and their excitement that night in the hotel in Denver. He thought of Izzy at Grand Central, filled with passion for the pursuit of the diary.

In the span of a month, Levi had lost his purpose. The golden luster of his life was tarnished beyond recognition. Yes, he had been proud of his success but, truthfully, in hindsight his methods and practices felt slimy at best. Even now, his latest assignment from Strong, working for that ass, DeWitt, reeked — something was off.

He looked down at the poem again. There was a time he'd have had no interest in these words. But now … he reread it for the umpteenth time.

Another line struck him: *"When the solar arc reaches its apex and aligns with the center of the great sky."*

What could that mean?

Levi took in the full moon rising over Boston. *Where was "the center of the great sky"?* His "center" had always been making money. But he had more money than he would ever need. At this moment it gave him no comfort. *It's time to put things right with Izzy.*

He didn't know how, except that he wanted another chance with his brother. Certainly helping Izzy realize "the family legacy" might go a long way toward making amends and achieving a reunion.

Levi resolved to take a gamble. He would fly to New York in the morning. No calling Izzy in advance. No request for a meeting. He would show up, with the poem in hand, the text of the Fletcher letter too — and he'd hope for the best.

Chapter 36

Nora, Will & Lester Edwards

Nora arrived home to a dark house, thinking, *Thank God! Will isn't here. I don't know how I'm going to tell him. If I don't get a handle on this, it could all blow up in my face, and fast.*

She'd been in the city for a second meeting with Grace and had again not told Will. That the meeting was filled with landmines was an understatement.

When Nora received the text from Jack Reed the previous Friday — "Grace wants to meet with you again" — she was glad for another opportunity to speak with her. Nora's research on PAGA, People for A Green America, was still turning up basically nothing. Either the members were smart enough to keep their major activities offline — or their website was a ruse and there was no such group. In which case, what was Grace, or Jack Reed, up to? Nora could only hope to answer those questions by meeting with Grace again.

As well, Nora was still highly motivated to discover the role of Jason DeWitt in the so-called PAGA plot. Was he planning to double-cross PAGA, as Reed said? Or was the check for a hundred grand that Reed waved around during their lunch at Al Dente's, signed by DeWitt, another ruse? Where and how DeWitt fit into all of this was still a mystery. And Nora's journalistic gut told her there was something here.

But as Nora had time to think over the weekend before her Monday meeting, a question began to nag at her. *What did Grace have to gain with another meeting?* Grace had been clear in the first meeting that she wouldn't provide names or other leads. Nora tried to put herself in Grace's head and came away empty, unable to come up with a motive.

And now after today's meeting, Nora was furious. *How could I let myself be caught so unprepared?* Grace had been insistent in her expectation that Nora be sympathetic to her cause. And then Grace explained why — because of Will and his statements about the vulnerable U.S. electrical grid and his worldview on the seduction of modern life, as presented in his Congressional testimony. Grace had told Nora that Will's views were in lock step with the overall goals of the PAGA.

Nora knew that Reed had to be behind Grace becoming aware of Nora's connection to Will. Grace insisted she had done her own research, eventually linking Nora Martin and Dr. Will Davenport. And Nora could see Grace's delight in telling her, realizing the opportunity.

Why didn't I recognize this could be a risk? God forbid Will was pegged as the inspiration for an attack on the New York City electrical grid! But what to do to prevent it?

Nora had shared little with Will about the meeting the week before — just enough to assure him she was not getting drawn into something dangerous. And Will knew to expect that. Nora always kept a lid on her story research until there was reason to share it — with an editor she was working with or with her husband.

For his part, Will had spent the previous week with plenty to keep him busy. He and Izzy huddled together with Ian Hillenbrand just about every day, searching for clues to solve their Ethan Hawkins mystery. In fact, he'd been so focused on the task at hand that he was completely satisfied with Nora's description of her first meeting with Grace, a passionate young woman with high ideals, not a gun-toting radical ready to take down the world.

But now, Nora recognized, the stakes had changed. *I have to tell him. But should I tell him about DeWitt too?* Reliving those bitter memories would make it impossible for her to continue to track the story. Will would fly off the handle and everything would spin out of control. *No,* Nora concluded, *not DeWitt — not yet.*

Two hours later and Nora was reminded of why she did *not* reveal many details of her work with Will, who was immediately up in arms. "Jesus! Shouldn't you just go to the police? Let me call Ken, he'll get Cooper in on this!"

"Will," Nora responded, trying to remain calm. "Look, certainly if I think these people are going to act, I will take action. But," she paused, coming to the punch line, "at this moment I want to get you out of the line of fire. I'm very concerned that you could get implicated some-how — even if the whole thing is phony. I don't want your reputation smeared as someone who even *potentially* could inspire eco-terrorism! I can threaten to pull out of the story, but I don't know for sure that it's *not* real. Right now I want to squash your connection. Tell me what I can say to Grace to convince her that she is taking your words wholly out of context."

Will stared at Nora, and then refilled his glass of red wine nearly to the rim. He just needed extra fortification for the battle he expected to come next.

"I don't think there's anything *you* can say. I think this needs to come from me. Set it up so I can meet her. We can do it together. I won't step on your journalist's toes. But let me convince her."

Nora shook her head vigorously. "That's not what I'm asking you to do! It's not so much stepping on my toes. I don't want to involve you, honey. I don't want you to be compromised by this story."

Will refilled Nora's wine glass, then sat down next to her on the sofa. "Look, if I'm honest with myself, I've been careless in a lot of ways in my career. I've done things that were foolhardy — *and* I've said things that I should have recognized could get twisted. I need to fix this. That I could have encouraged such destructive thinking...."

Nora listened, torn between her concern about Will meeting Grace — and Jack Reed yet understanding the logic of his reasoning and the emotion behind it.

"OK, let me text Reed, the contact. I'll tell him I want another meeting with Grace and that you'll be with me. I'm going to request we meet at Brookfield Place again."

Will raised his glass and gave Nora's a clink. "You're running the show, Ace. Whatever you say."

It was almost midnight. Nora lay in bed, listening to Will's steady breathing. They'd made love until they were both in blissed-out exhaustion.

Yet sleep wouldn't come for her — and she *had* to get some rest. She had to be ready for the meeting, now set for tomorrow.

Reed had responded fairly quickly for Reed. And he'd made no snide remarks, his usual MO. His mocking tone infuriated her, yet she'd come to expect it.

Nora flipped to her side, snuggling next to Will, her breasts feeling the warmth of his back. This story... when she'd agreed to pursue this story, it had never occurred to her that Will could get pulled into it. Unexpected consequences — that was a theme that kept popping up.

And what about the consequences she wanted to see? Nora thought again how she discarded her birth control nearly three weeks ago and the added intensity of their lovemaking since. It was too soon to know, of course … but let *that* have the intended affect, she prayed.

Lester Edwards sent off his text with a wicked smile. It was a cryptic message to Grace from Jack Reed's cell, to let her know that she'd be meeting the great Will Davenport tomorrow.

Oh, Reed was smooth as silk this time. Edwards was going to miss Jack Reed when this was over. He might even take on some of the Reed qualities permanently.

Naturally, Edwards had manipulated it all. He fed Grace information about Davenport and how it would "encourage" Nora Martin to support the PAGA line. He'd enjoyed watching Martin try to hide her shock as she realized her hubby had become a target. Edwards loved being the puppet master of this production.

He'd had a Plan B for getting Davenport literally in the picture, but Plan A had worked just fine. And now he intended for Grace to record the conversation. He'd give her a few pointers. Make sure she got graphic detail from Davenport on what the aftermath of an electrical grid explosion would look like.

Edwards would take care of the rest — and especially getting the *money shot* of Davenport on video. Edwards was a pro at manipulating recordings. He'd used the technique many times before. He would zero in on what he wanted, erase what he didn't, and produce a sound and pictures "greatest hits" of Davenport targeting the New York City electrical grid.

Then Edwards could do whatever he chose with the "evidence" — such as demonstrate his usefulness to DeWitt and why he deserved far more than he was being paid. And if DeWitt balked, he could remind the cheap bastard that with Nora Martin Davenport in his service, he could spill all kinds of beans — including revealing the nitty-gritty on DeWitt's role in trashing her husband.

But if his handiwork was rewarded appropriately, when Edwards created the explosion that DeWitt had in mind, the evidence to put Will Davenport in the crosshairs of suspicion would be ready to release to the world.

Edwards laughed, thinking about his many options, each very much to his benefit.

Chapter 37

GRAND CENTRAL
MARCH 26
8:30 A.M.

Levi, Izzy & Will

Levi's plane landed on time at Teterboro Airport, and from there it was a short drive to Grand Central Station and The Great American Timepiece. Looking at his watch, Levi expected to get to Izzy by around eight-thirty. For sure, his brother would be at the shop. He assumed Izzy opened the doors at seven o'clock every morning, the tradition started by their father and uncle.

What made Levi a success was his ability to execute a well-thought-out plan. Now he was flying by the seat of his pants, with one goal in mind — to offer Izzy the poem and hope it would light a spark of reconciliation.

How he would approach his brother was another matter. Uncharacteristically, he felt his nerves mounting as he entered Grand Central Station. In the maze of hallways and people, it took him a few minutes to arrive at the shop.

To Levi's surprise, when he reached the store it was dark, the glass door still closed. Yet he could see a form inside. It was Izzy, his back to the door. Uncertain, Levi began to knock.

"It's open!" Izzy yelled in response. He had arrived late and was turning the store lights on from a panel behind the display counter. At that hour, he expected to see Will standing at the door.

Izzy had been reading Ethan Hawkins' account of his twin sons and was eager to discuss them with Will. It was not lost on Izzy the parallels between Benjamin and Jeremiah and he and Levi. And what happened to Jeremiah Hawkins? That seemed another family mystery in the diary to unravel.

"Izzy…," Levi spoke quietly.

Perhaps it was the power of habit and expectation. Will had been stopping by to see Izzy every day before heading up to his office. So now with head down, fussing with the display case, Izzy addressed the voice that he heard as Will's. "From Ethan's telling, it's amazing how different the Hawkins twins were!"

"As different as the two of us, I suppose." Levi stood just inside the doorway of The Great American Timepiece, impeccably dressed in a cashmere coat over a Savile Row suit and tie.

Izzy looked up in complete surprise. This voice was his brother's. There stood Levi, flesh and blood.

"I told you I never want to see you again! Now get the hell out of MY STORE!" Izzy's voice boomed, loud enough in the relative din of Grand Central to attract the notice of people passing by the shop.

"Izzy…," Levi tried again, stepping further into the shop.

"You're a son of a bitch, you know that!" Izzy interrupted. "It takes a lot of nerve waltzing in here after what you did."

Will was now standing behind Levi, having arrived in time to hear everything. He watched as Levi stepped ever closer to Izzy, until he was only a foot or so from the display case, behind which Izzy still stood. For a moment Will was taken with the visual contrast between the two brothers — Levi's groomed and immaculate bearing next to Izzy's rumpled appearance, his jacket creased, tie askew and hair in need of a trim.

Then Izzy was out from behind the counter. "I SAID GET OUT!"

The brothers were nearly nose to nose.

"GIVE ME A CHANCE…!" Levi's voice matched Izzy's in volume.

"A CHANCE?" Izzy interrupted again, spitting out the words in disgust.

Will's attention turned to the murmuring of people outside the shop. The fight was drawing a crowd. Will stepped forward, placing himself within reach of Izzy and took his arm. "You might want to move this inside your office, Iz."

Izzy seemed to ignore Will's presence. "YOU BETTER HAVE A GOOD REASON FOR BEING HERE!" Izzy demanded of Levi, still shouting.

Levi nodded a silent thanks to Will and, in a flood of words, explained his unexpected presence. "Izzy, I have something you need to see! A poem. I found it on the plane. Maybe I should have come to you sooner, but I was hopeful I could decipher it first and then bring it to you."

The mention of the poem immediately silenced Izzy. He surmised Levi must have had it. He'd actually been preparing himself to go to Levi and confront him about it. Yet Levi's sudden appearance had been like a lightning strike, evoking feelings of rage, closing off Izzy's heart to anything that Levi had said.

Will watched Izzy, waiting, wondering in what direction this moment might turn. Should he intercede?

Instead, Levi took control, his manner contrite yet determined that his brother would hear him out. "Look Izzy, I understand your fury, and God knows I don't deserve your understanding, but let me show you what I've brought. Certainly not for my sake, but for yours and Dad's and Uncle Samuel's."

Then, looking at Will, Levi continued, "I think you'll find this fascinating too, Dr. Davenport. And with your understanding of the cosmos, I think you could be the one to unlock the meaning."

Izzy stared at Levi, not saying a word. Will found him impossible to read. But there was an opportunity here that should not be lost.

"Izzy…," Will's voice was infinitely calm. "We need the poem. Without it, we may never…."

Izzy held out his hand to silence Will. In the quiet that followed, the last of the small crowd that had stopped to watch a brewing fight drifted away.

"Will, can you stay a while?" Izzy asked as he walked to the shop door and locked it. Lucy would take over when she arrived.

Then, to Levi, "We'll go in the office. I'll call Hillenbrand to join us."

Moments later, the three stood together at Izzy's desk. As Levi withdrew the leather portfolio from his briefcase, a sense of relief gripped Izzy.

Finally, all of the pieces together! he thought. *Now we can find the answers!*

With that release, some of his wrath against Levi, justified as it was, fell away a glimpse, perhaps, of a reconciliation to come.

"Here it is," Levi explained, opening the portfolio.

"Take your coat off, Levi," Izzy directed. "Have a seat," he added, pulling out his desk chair. Then, still standing, in a voice that grew stronger with each line, Izzy read the poem aloud:

> *"Here, in this place, dwells the pleasure that only heavens knows.*
> *A man and a woman stand at the threshold, soon to be crossed, after the generations come and go.*
> *When the solar arc reaches its apex and aligns with the center eye of the great sky,*
> *A jubilation foretold by ancient ones will behold the diamond crystal stone restored.*
> *Taken in the hand it fills the palm, every facet will glow once more, a secret revealed, a throne*
> *beyond this world.*
> *Seek it my brethren, when the time is right, there where the headwaters fall.*

Fletcher knew it, Newton too.
But in Hawkins blood the key remains; unlock the secret in
*   our name, a treasure of truth, of glory*
and diamond glow."

"'*When the solar arc reaches its apex and aligns with the center of the great sky!*" Izzy repeated, aghast. "That line was in my dream! Will, what do you make of it?"

Will shook his head, acknowledging the significance. "It speaks to a moment in time when a cosmological sequences takes place. But when is that time? That's what we have to find out."

For the rest of the morning, Izzy, Levi and Will read and reread and discussed and compared what each line, each word, might mean. Ian Hillenbrand soon joined them, confirming triumphantly that it was, indeed, the poem that he had found concealed within the diary.

For Will, the poem was full of imagery that most certainly offered valuable clues, and if decoded, could lead to promising discoveries. He recognized that "solar arc" was a reference to an unusual planetary alignment — a configuration in the cosmic sky that would take place in the distant future of the poem's author. This key factor had to indicate a time when the sun was lined up with the galactic center — the black hole at the center of the universe.

But what was to take place then? Was it possible, that with this alignment, gravitation waves from the center of the galaxy would hit the sun in such a way that it would trigger some momentous event in human history? Had it happened already? Or was this alignment and event so significant that when it arrived the planetary influences would release a transformative cosmic energy that would affect all life on earth?

The reference was so general. And added to that, who was the author of the poem? When was it written? It was not signed or dated.

Will determined that much more information was needed. Ian suggested they analyze the paper and ink to try to date the poem. They could also compare the script with Ethan's handwriting in the diary. Comb through each page again. Perhaps there were notations from others in the diary that they missed — from Benjamin or even Jeremiah. Then they could match it with Izzy's Newton letter, just in case — to try to identify the poet.

As Will and Ian discussed, Levi and Izzy were quiet, each with his own thoughts.

For Levi, Izzy's acceptance of the poem was a beginning. Painful as it was, he had finally taken responsibility for what had happened and sought to make amends. With that he could feel the worst of the emotional storms of guilt — which he had done his best to suppress — were passing. He felt himself standing in a new place and, perhaps going forward, one where his brother was in his life again. What would that feel like?

For Izzy, each line of the poem struck a chord in his heart. It was confirmation of a truth that was there all along, hidden in plain sight. All he needed were clear eyes to see it. His life, with all its difficulties, had a noble purpose and his quest was riding on the waves of generations. Now his journey was about to reach new heights, as prescribed in the poem's last line: *"But in Hawkins blood the key remains; unlock the secret in our name, a treasure of truth, of glory and diamond glow."*

What was the secret? What could it be?

As the four men hovered around Izzy's desk, eager to understand the poem, the diary, the mysteries before them, each in his own way and for his own reasons felt a pause. It was a moment to savor the significance of their shared endeavor.

Shortly thereafter, Will's phone rang. It was Nora. "Absolutely. I'll meet you there at track 34," he confirmed. Then, turning to Izzy, "Nora's here in the city. She wants me to meet her. I'll check in with you later. This is getting interesting Iz! Let's see where all this takes us."

"Thanks, Will." Izzy responded.

Then Will began a quick round of handshakes. Izzy gave him a strong clasp, wanting to convey how deeply appreciative he was of the role Will was playing.

And when Will came to Levi, he added a slight nod to acknowledge the importance of what Levi had done for all of them.

In the process, Levi got a clearer look at Will than before. And when he had left, Levi asked, "Is that the same Will Davenport who was on television, the one with the scandal?"

"Yes, that's him," Izzy replied. "He's never said a word about it. I don't give a shit about that celebrity stuff, but having gotten to know him, I'm sure he was raked over the coals. One of these days, I'll ask."

"When the time's right, I suppose," Levi nodded.

And that thought — everything has a time and place — didn't escape either man's notice.

Chapter 38

Will & Nora

Will's thoughts were multiplying exponentially when he met Nora at the track entrance where her train had come in. And now he had to change gears for another critical meeting.

"Hi!" she greeted him. "What's going on? You've been at Izzy's this whole time — since you got in this morning?"

Will gave her a bear hug. "I have! I stopped by as usual. Couldn't tell you on the phone when you called, but Levi — you know, Izzy's brother — was there. He'd just arrived from Boston, out of the blue. And with the poem! The missing one from the Hawkins diary! We've been going over it for hours."

Nora registered the importance of what happened in Will's excited delivery. He'd shared plenty of what transpired between the brothers at Teterboro and the frustration since in interpreting the diary. "You look wiped. Are you okay?" she asked.

"It was intense, lots of fireworks, especially at first. It couldn't have been easy for Izzy, or Levi for that matter. I think it turned out all right — at least they're talking."

Nora gave Will another hug along with a kiss. "Sorry for the timing of this meeting, Will. I guess you won't make it to the university today."

He shrugged. "At this point, I don't really care. Sitting at a desk working on the book in *Ken's* office is becoming less and less relevant by the day. It's clear to me my time with Izzy is important field work — hands on research that I'm certain will reveal some astonishing insights that could be eye-popping. It's all so fascinating. And now this poem. I don't have all the ins and outs yet, but I'm certain that what Izzy and I are going to discover will offer proof positive that my overarching book thesis has validity."

Squeezing his hand, feeling his warmth, Nora said, "I have all the confidence in the world that it's going to come together for you. And I'm sure Izzy must be grateful to have your knowledge and insights."

Will squeezed back. "Oh, without a doubt he is. What we are doing together is interesting and important, remarkable really. But go try telling that to *my* brother."

"I'm sure Ken will come around," Nora assured him.

"Nora, I'm three weeks into this and he's riding me every step of the way. I was taking a bathroom break this morning when I got a text from Ken asking what the hell ever happened to me and my so-called book! There I am at the urinal, taking two seconds to pee after my umpteenth cup of coffee, in the middle of trying to analyze a poem that could be centuries old, and Ken's busting my chops! Jesus!"

Nora searched Will's face, trying to accurately read his expression. He was all amped-up from being with Izzy and the annoying message from Ken. *Could he settle down now and focus on Grace?* She wasn't sure.

"Seriously, honey, I am sorry for the timing. I can see you've been in it up to your ears today. I can't change the meeting now, but you don't have to go. I mean that. We've got time. Let's find a place to sit and you tell me what you want me to say. I can record it on my phone. I can play your explanation for Grace. She'll hear your voice — know it's coming from you."

Will shook his head. "Nice try, Mrs. Davenport. Look, I'm okay. Yes, it certainly hasn't been the day I expected. But I want to — I need to — meet this woman, be there to answer her questions, refute her arguments. I can tape an explanation but I can't anticipate what she might say in response, especially if she isn't thinking rationally."

He took Nora's arm, pointing them toward the great hall of Grand Central. "Come on. Let's get the subway."

Nora stopped and stared into his face, looking for certainty. "If you're sure…?"

Will cupped Nora's face with his hands and gave her a smooch. "Of course, I am!" he smiled. "In fact, I'm pumped!"

"That's what I'm afraid of champ. Take it down a notch or two — okay?"

Will snapped his fingers. "Not a problem. Just call me Mr. Cool."

Nora smiled at Will's imitation of "cool," though she was still uncertain he'd settle down in time for their meeting with Grace.

"If there are no delays down to Brookfield Place, we'll have time for a bite to eat, Mr. Cool."

"Great. A good debate always makes me hungry!" he added with a laugh.

∞

An hour later, post a sandwich and coffee, Will and Nora were at the appointed location for the meeting, watching as a young woman approached. "That's Grace," Nora whispered, standing to meet her. *Where was Reed?* Nora had expected him to be present.

Will, on his feet as well, stepped forward, hand extended. Grace hesitated, then accepted Will's hand and shook Nora's too.

Grace pointed to the chair where Nora had been sitting. "I want to be there. I don't want my back to the room," she demanded. "I need to see everything that's happening."

"Be my guest," said Nora, holding the chair out for her.

Will started the conversation. "Nora has told me about your

previous meeting and what was said. I wanted a chance to explain myself."

"Don't try to stop us!" Grace's expression went from serious to angry in a flash.

"I'm just here to talk, Grace," Will confirmed, his voice sincere. "I think you may have misinterpreted some of my public statements."

Grace shook her head vehemently. "No! We've watched you very closely — your media appearances. Your lectures are all over YouTube. Your Congressional testimony makes you a guiding light to our cause. There's no mistake."

Nora was alarmed. This was not going well. "Look, Grace…."

Before she could make her point, Grace interrupted. "Your husband's a hypocrite!" Then, looking Will straight in the eyes, "And a *traitor* too. You take a stand like some valiant knight, only to crumble at the sight of real action. YOU'RE ALL TALK!"

A few heads nearby turned in their direction. *We've got to get this conversation under control,* Nora thought.

"It's okay." Will's voice was calm and modulating, addressing Grace and Nora too. "I'm not here to backtrack. I've nothing to backtrack from. I used my platform in the public eye to sound the warning. I've always urged caution — but *only* caution. Ultimately, I have faith in our institutions to revitalize and reinvent themselves. That once a problem is pointed out, good people will eventually recognize that change is needed and initiate it."

Grace responded with an ominous smile. "You say you only sound the alarm, but do you remember this?" She had pulled a sheet of printed text from her tote. "This sounds more like *a threat* from Dr. Davenport!"

Nora could hear the echo of Reed's mocking tone in Grace's pronunciation of Will's name. *Meeting Grace again was a mistake. Started badly and getting worse!*

Grace was reading aloud. "'The lightening speed of technological change happening now is like nothing we've ever seen. If we are not careful we may find ourselves in a world where our personal freedoms are greatly diminished… A tsunami is coming. You cannot say you have not been warned.' A tsunami! You said it! And it's almost here!"

Grace laughed in a way that chilled Nora. *Was this young woman mad? She had not seemed so before … but now.…*

Will had immediately recognized fragments of his Congressional testimony. "Grace, I probably don't need to tell you that's not my full testimony. I stand by what I said that day — what I said before and what I will say again. But it's easy for words to get twisted. What you're proposing — to blow up an electrical grid in order to save humanity — Grace, there will be unintended consequences that you can't imagine."

Will observed this young woman intently, wondering what she was understanding, what tack would help him get through to her.

"Look," he continued. "Let's say you plant a bomb that explodes in a key location of the grid. New York City — more, the entire Eastern Seaboard — goes dark. *Anything, everything that requires electricity comes to a halt.* In the first moments, before backup generators kick in, critical patients die in hospitals and homes. Subways stop, elevators stall, people are trapped. Chaos reigns on streets and roads without traffic lights. Business comes to a standstill. As time passes, food spoilage leads to shortages to God knows what. The oldest, the youngest, the most vulnerable are at greatest risk. Yes, there's your tsunami, sweeping away every semblance of normal life. And just as tsunamis kill, *this will kill!* Hundreds, thousands. Loss of life, property, livelihood. *Yes, you'll make a statement that no one can ignore, but you'll also destroy any hope you have of changing things for the better, too!*"

Grace listened as the recorder Reed had given her captured every word. Contrary to Will's intent, the images he painted were thrilling to her. A tsunami. She could see it in her mind. Get people to pay attention, and then the elimination of the corrupt social structure.

And stationed strategically, Lester Edwards filmed his silent movie of the "brilliant yet troubled scientist," as Will Davenport would surely be described. Grace had placed herself and Davenport precisely where they needed to be. Edwards laughed each time he zoomed in to catch the urgency on Davenport's face, the way his arms opened expansively, his furrowed brow.

Oh, what a coup it would be when he could make this masterpiece complete by editing in select pieces of audio from Grace's recording. Edwards grinned. And to think Nora Martin, the equally brilliant yet soon-to-be very troubled reporter, had set it all in motion.

Chapter 39

WESTCHESTER, NEW YORK
MARCH 27
6:00 A.M.

Nora & Will

Morning had come early for Nora and Will after an uncomfortable late night. Both had concluded that the meeting with Grace left them unsure about what would happen next. It was this degree of uncertainty that, in turn, prompted Nora to reveal the Jason DeWitt connection and what she had learned so far about his relationship with PAGA. And that led to probably too much red wine and an almost ugly fight as Nora showed Will the research she'd compiled.

That Grace had used Will's Congressional testimony for her justification resurrected all the difficulties of the last few years. It was a scathing reminder to both Will and Nora of the dangers of any kind of public life.

And watching Grace as Will described the horrendous consequences of sabotaging the electrical grid, Nora had serious doubts about whether he had gotten through. In the end Nora tried to get Grace to promise not to do anything "rash," to let Nora continue her investigation. But Grace was noncommittal, saying only, "I'll report back to my group. I'm not promising anything beyond that. But rest assured we are not going to sit back forever."

Everything about the meeting with Grace had in many ways the opposite effect of what both she and Will had hoped. Also unsettling to Nora was why Reed hadn't shown up, nor had he texted or called to explain his absence.

When Nora had opened her DeWitt file, Will had been particularly surprised to see the photo of DeWitt with Senator Broderick, his nemesis from the hearing — and irritated with Nora for keeping it from him.

"I know you have this 'do it on my own' obsession," Will barked. "I get your reporter instinct. But I'm your husband — and this is about me! I'm the one who got screwed big time!"

"I know you did! But it affected me too, you know!" Nora answered. She hated it when Will seemed to forget she'd lived through it all with him.

"Yes, I know! But you didn't have a bastard like Broderick doing all he could to make you look like a flaming Cassandra. And then DeWitt, who just tried to make me look like a lunatic and a fool!"

Frustrated, Nora had poured herself more wine, yet knowing she should watch her drinking. She was trying to get pregnant, after all. And that had her asking *why on earth did I decide that now was the right time to try for a baby, in the midst of all this craziness.*

"Look, Will, all I was trying to do was see what else I could find out! More often than not leads don't pan out. Besides, you were just getting started on the book and I didn't want to throw you off. And don't forget how consumed you've been with Izzy's diary!"

"And what's wrong with that?" Will's tone was defensive.

"Nothing! Far from it! I haven't seen you so excited in over a year, and it's plain to see how important it is to you. But don't you *understand*, honey? When Reed showed me the check signed by DeWitt, I was stunned and I've been trying to see how it all fits together ever since! With so many balls in the air, I thought it was better to let everything settle first before I came to you."

Then both had paused, neither wanting a disagreement fueled by painful memories to get out of hand.

"Nora, it's been a hellava day. Let's hit reset on this."

"Gladly!" Nora agreed. "But there is one more thing I have to show you. I was doing another google search on DeWitt and this article popped up on the CNBC website. It's about DeWitt and a tech innovator, a woman named Charlie May Maddison. She was suing DeWitt for suspected corporate espionage. I want to contact her, see if she'll meet with me to talk about DeWitt. Her company is based in the city. Website says one of her chief assistants is a Jennifer Harrison. I thought I'd email her first."

Will took the article, shaking his head as he read. "You know, honestly, how did I miss so much about DeWitt when he was badmouthing me? I thought this guy was MIT, but he's a whole lot more. And why'd he go after me so hard? I know you said back then it was jealousy — but this is beyond jealousy."

Then, in a wish to put a happy ending to an otherwise exhausting day, Will let the article drop to the floor and reached out his arms to envelope Nora. "Of course that asshole DeWitt is jealous, he doesn't have the fabulous Nora Martin as a wife! That's reason enough for any man to be outrageously jealous of me...."

"Thank you, kind sir!" Nora hugged Will in return, and then wiggled out of his embrace. "I'm going to write that email to Harrison and save it as a draft. I'll review in the morning and then send it."

Sleep had been fitful and the email intended for Charlie May Maddison via Jennifer Harrison was on its way at dawn. The smell of coffee brewing was enough to wake Will and send him downstairs into the kitchen.

"How are you?" he asked, accepting a cup from Nora and offering a kiss.

"I'm a little queasy. These are probably the culprits." Nora held up two red wine bottles, one empty and one nearly so.

"That and the topic of conversation last night. I smell a rat named DeWitt," Will observed.

"I hate that saying, but I have to admit, DeWitt does stink to high heaven. And I have a nose for these things," Nora responded. They both laughed.

A breakfast of eggs and toast helped restore them. "I'd better get moving. Show my face to my brother today," Will grinned, "and check in with Izzy."

"I know Ken's been difficult and maybe the timing isn't the best. But why don't you work from here today," Nora proposed. "Take a break from the Hawkins *and* Rhodes *and* Davenport families for the day. Spend it with me. I've got my research to do, and of course you have yours. But I'd like you here, Will. Especially now that you know about the DeWitt and Reed and Grace connection, maybe you can see something that I've overlooked. All my instincts are telling me there's something really off with this story." While it was true Nora wanted Will to give fresh eyes to what she had uncovered so far, she really just wanted him close-by today.

"You don't have to ask twice, Ms. Martin! I'll text Ken — yes, I'm texting. Call me a coward. Then I'll phone Izzy. Find out what's new … if Levi is still in New York … if they discovered any leads to the meaning of Galileo's Jupiter moons and this Hawkins secret…."

As Will left the kitchen to retrieve his phone upstairs, Nora reflected on the dynamic of brothers. Will and Ken — Izzy and his brother, Levi. She thought again of her wish for a child. *How about a daughter?* she smiled.

Chapter 40

Charlie May Maddison

Fifty-year-old Charlie May Maddison stared out of the window of her farmhouse in New Paltz, New York. Even in March, when her apple orchards were weeks away from flowering, she loved the beauty of the place.

Charlie May had two other homes, one by the ocean in East Hampton on Long Island, and the other, a spacious New York City apartment overlooking Central Park West. But the farm was her favorite. And she was proud of the apples it produced.

It went without saying that Charlie May was very wealthy. She had inherited a sizable fortune from her parents when she was only twenty-five. They were killed in a freakish accident, when their private jet went down over Utah on a spur-of-the-moment ski trip. At the time, Charlie May was a graduate student in economics and computer science at Princeton.

The Maddison family had made their money from a chain of department stores — like Macy's and Bloomingdale's, known as Maddison's with an apostrophe *s* — that were concentrated in the Midwest. Charlie May's father, Joshua, had expanded a business that had its humble roots in the colonial era. The Maddisons were descendants of Abigail and Jeremiah Hawkins. Family lore described them as proprietors of a general store established in the late 1600's, in the early days of New York. Over time, along with the great American migration westward, Maddison's stores relocated, eventually becoming headquartered in Chicago.

Still, Joshua had made much of that founding history in advertising Maddison's as a legacy brand "as strong and reliable as America itself." And under Joshua's direction the business eventually went public on the New York Stock Exchange and doubled in size and success.

Proud as she was of Maddison's, heading a department store chain was never what Charlie May had in mind for her future. Soon after her parents' death, she sold her shares in Maddison's with the skill of a seasoned stock player. And having discovered she liked the game on Wall Street, she proceeded to parley those millions into over a half a billion dollars seemingly overnight. There were no short cuts or insider trading for Charlie May. She was scrupulously honest but was also diligent and shrewd. She did her research and she knew how to work the system. It didn't hurt that she had considerable skill with computer programming when very few people knew the value of high-frequency trading.

Charlie May became a celebrity in New York society circles. The press featured her financial success and noted her involvement in developing music and art programs for inner-city school children. Ever passionate about helping those less fortunate, she became a mover and a shaker on the Manhattan charity circuit, lobbying others for money and support. As with anything that Charlie May touched, she was hugely successful. She learned to navigate the world of political influence with charm, guts and, when necessary, guile.

As her fortune grew, Charlie May strategically invested in technology startups and acquired important patents that eventually became cornerstones in international industries — including those that strengthened national security. That led to Charlie May becoming a well-known presence in and around the nation's capital.

Her impulse was always for the common good, but not so everyone she came up against. Many times Charlie May went to battle to oppose corrupt and entrenched forces in industry and government. She made as many powerful enemies as friends.

She was a unique woman, a blend of steel nerves and great compassion. Although Charlie May never chose to marry, a relationship with a famous filmmaker gave her the child she desired. Eva, now twenty, was in her second year at the University of Chicago, having decided to go back to her mother's roots for college. Charlie May had lobbied for a school in New York, to keep Eva closer, but she accepted her daughter's choice, recognizing that her own independent-minded genes were alive and well in her child.

If there was anything that Charlie May missed, it was not having siblings or even close cousins. Perhaps it was why she especially loved spending time on her farm in New Paltz, located in the Hudson River Valley. It was where her bones felt a longing. From this place, she could hear her ancestors calling to her. She came from solid pioneer stock and was proud of it. She knew some of that history, thanks to its value to the Maddison's store franchise. It made her feel part of a larger epic.

Nonetheless, the story that was passed down was in some ways detailed, in others vague, including precisely how Abigail and Jeremiah, from their store in colonial Manhattan, came to have a connection to this area far up the Hudson. Charlie May viewed it all as the legend of Ethan Hawkins, an alchemist in England, and his twin sons Jeremiah and Benjamin. But whatever happened to Benjamin was not in the Maddison family history, and that always struck Charlie May as particularly sad. She knew something about loss. Her unique name was given in remembrance of her fraternal twin, who had died at birth.

On this particular day, Charlie May was more focused on the present than the past. She was awaiting the arrival of her research manager, Jennifer Harrison. Disturbing information had crossed Jennifer's desk that needed Charlie May's immediate attention. To heighten her concern, it involved Charlie May's longtime rival, Jason DeWitt.

Her business interests and DeWitt Technologies were often in competition. Charlie May didn't mind competition at all, but she objected strenuously to underhanded tactics, which were DeWitt's specialties. His companies frequently violated her patents or used surreptitious means to try to steal her technologies. Once when she refused his request to use one of her patents, a software virus invaded her hard drives. If it had not been caught in time, the program would have scrubbed her drives completely clean. She always suspected DeWitt.

When his attempts at corporate espionage didn't work, he spread false rumors. One that got a lot of notice was that her wealth came from insider trading. It was all over the business news, with continuing segments and talking heads speculating on Charlie May's future. She showed her savvy by not adding fuel to the fire with public pronouncements. Rather, she quietly provided documents that confirmed her honesty and uncovered the source of the rumors. Everything led back to DeWitt by way of the brokerage house Strong, Price, Applebaum and Goodwin. She filed a cease-and-desist lawsuit and that was the end of that episode.

But she was always ready for more and kept vigilant tabs on DeWitt. Now he was snooping around her newest innovation, a powerful encryption program. A host of institutions were clamoring to run trials, and there was universal interest in making it the new standard in computer security. Everyone from the NSA, to Wall Street firms, to major utility companies were interested in getting onboard. The need was obvious. Computer attacks were ever increasing, and Charlie May's software team had come up with the most powerful encryption software to date.

Charlie May had also heard rumors that DeWitt was close to perfecting a quantum computer. That he was enquiring about her encryption software signaled he was up to something. And if it involved DeWitt, it couldn't be good.

At a little past ten o'clock a Subaru Outback pulled up the long driveway. Jennifer Harrison briskly stepped out after the nearly three-hour drive from her Manhattan office. She was a woman on a mission. In fact, she wasted no time in getting to the point of her private meeting with Charlie May, when in other circumstances a phone call might do.

"We've got confirmation that DeWitt's quantum computer is operational, or almost so," Jennifer explained.

"Who's the someone, the source?"

"Still don't know that for sure. Seems to be someone deep inside DeWitt's software team. He or she doesn't like the way DeWitt operates."

Charlie May gave a skeptical wave of her hand. "That doesn't seem good enough. But let's say it's true. What does that mean for us?"

Jennifer nodded, expecting Charlie May's response. "Here's our best theory. DeWitt wants to do workarounds on our encryption software. He's making sure nothing interferes with the number-crunching speed of his quantum computer, ensuring our software is obsolete before it gets into trials. That way, he can sell his computer as the gold standard in computer security, without any competition from us."

"Knowing DeWitt, that could be the most benign reason," Charlie May replied with disgust. "My gut tells me there's something else going on."

Charlie May was not happy with the news. She had a lot riding on her new encryption project. Financially this program was a winner, but more importantly, her unblemished track record as a technological innovator was essential. It kept her as the go-to person for out-of-the box solutions. It was an image she enjoyed and didn't want usurped, especially by a thief like DeWitt.

"Good work, Jen. At least we have the broad strokes of the challenges we face. If DeWitt has an operational computer, we need to know what its capabilities are. It would be a disaster if he were the one to revolutionize the field. DeWitt's a thug and I hate to think where that power would take him."

"I'll keep digging," Jennifer confirmed, closing the old-fashioned reporter's notebook she'd been reading from — her sure-fire security against hackers. Then, reopening it, she flipped to another page.

"I almost forgot. It's probably just coincidence but I received an email from an investigative reporter named Nora Martin. She's inquiring about DeWitt — doing some research on him and found an article about you suing him. Her email came in about five this morning, so she's an early bird, but I didn't have a chance to check her out yet. Do you just want me to get rid of her?"

Jennifer knew that Charlie May didn't like people digging into her past. And it could be an attempt by DeWitt to find out about her encryption program.

"Let's look her up right now." With anything concerning DeWitt, Charlie May didn't need much to motivate her.

Taking out her laptop, Jennifer easily found Nora's profile. "Here she is, a freelance investigative reporter. She looks legitimate — awards, big expose on California power companies. She's married to Will Davenport. He's the science guy who got into trouble with a starlet."

Charlie May nodded. "I remember him. What a shame. So much promise."

Jennifer closed the laptop. "So how do you want me to respond to Nora Martin?"

"If she's checking on DeWitt, we should follow up. Maybe there's something there. Pieces of a puzzle can come from unexpected sources. Did you get her number?"

"Yes," said Jennifer, looking back into her notebook. "Cell and landline."

"A landline! Woman after my own heart," Charlie May laughed. "Let's get her on the phone right now and see what she wants."

Moments later, Jennifer Harrison had Nora on the line: "Hello, Nora Martin? I have Charlie May Maddison calling."

Chapter 41

Nora & Charlie May Maddison & Reed/Edwards

A busy morning for both Davenports was suddenly interrupted by the harsh *brringg!* of the landline. Will was closest and checked the ID.

"It's a cell, Nora — Manhattan area code."

"Great!" Nora rushed to answer. "Maybe it's ... hello ... Davenports ..."

A voice she did not recognize asked: "Hello, Nora Martin?"

"Yes, this is Nora Martin."

"I have Charlie May Maddison calling."

Nora's eyes lit up with anticipation. There was a slight pause and she could imagine the phone being transferred.

"Ms. Martin, I received your message that you're looking for information on Jason DeWitt. What's your interest in DeWitt?"

Nora could detect caution in Charlie May's voice. Based on what Nora had been learning about DeWitt, that was natural and good sense. Everything to do with this guy advised vigilance.

"Ms. Maddison, you may know my background. I'm an investigative reporter. I've been working on a story in which Jason DeWitt appears to have a key role."

Nora stopped momentarily. How much should she reveal? She

decided to press forward, to trust her instinct — that contacting Charlie May was the right move.

"My queries are personal too. DeWitt helped to discredit my husband, Will Davenport. You may have heard…."

"Yes, I recall the controversy around your husband," Charlie May stated. "He had such a promising career."

Nora appreciated the implied sympathy but was equally determined to set the record straight. "Still does, Ms. Maddison, he still does. And I think there's more to Jason DeWitt than is publicly known. But I'm not looking for dirt on DeWitt. I'm trying to get to the truth of who he is and, frankly, what he's up to. I'm turning up information that indicates he could be planning something on a grand scale that could end up hurting a lot of people."

From her dicey experiences with DeWitt, Charlie May knew what Nora Martin was describing rang true. Her concerns that Martin might be a DeWitt plant were quickly dismissed. Perhaps they might help each other.

"I've had my run-ins with DeWitt," Charlie May confirmed, "but you obviously know that. Can you tell me about DeWitt's involvement in this story you're working on?"

Nora debated how much to divulge. But she had done her homework on Charlie May Maddison. She had a reputation as a formidable, no-nonsense woman with high degree of integrity. It was this and her hunch about Charlie May that Nora decided to trust.

"Ms. Maddison, there's a lot I can't say. But a man named Jack Reed came to me about a possible plot involving environmental activists. He showed me a check made out to him from Falconer Energy Industries and signed by Jason DeWitt. If it's legit, DeWitt could be sponsoring possible extremism."

Charlie May listened carefully, recognizing the danger Nora Martin was trying to convey.

"Is Reed's name familiar to you?" Nora asked.

"I can't say that it is. But writing a check that would so easily lead back to him is careless and that's not DeWitt's style," Charlie May offered.

"Reed is probably not his real name," Nora agreed. "He reached out to me looking for an immunity deal, willing to blow the whistle on the main players, with DeWitt being at the top of the list."

"So there's more than one skunk here?"

"Yes, Ms. Maddison. We — Will and I — have been saying rat, but skunk fits too. It all smells bad!"

"Ms. Martin — Nora — please call me Charlie May. I think we'll have some business to do together — that I can give credence to your suspicions. For now, everything I say is off the record and only for background. Agreed?"

Nora nodded as she spoke. "Of course I'll honor that. What can you tell me?"

"I've recently come across information regarding a quantum computer that Jason DeWitt is likely behind. What you've learned about DeWitt's possible financing of terrorism may not be true, of course. *Or* it could be implying something bigger in the works. Leave no doubt, DeWitt is sleazy and he plays big time *and* he plays for keeps."

By now Will was beside Nora as she hurriedly took notes.

"You're right," Nora responded. "If it's real, it's a plot against the electrical grid in the city."

"And likely far beyond too," Charlie May added. "DeWitt is a ruthless bastard, Nora. Now you know why I insisted my statements are off the record! He's despicable and I put nothing past him."

Nora could feel both excitement and worry rising. If DeWitt was involved, this story was even more important and dangerous than she suspected. That DeWitt had targeted Will was even more disturbing.

"Charlie May, I'd like to meet," Nora proposed. "Could we arrange something? As soon as possible?"

Charlie May did not hesitate. "Absolutely, Nora. My office in Manhattan. On Park. What's your schedule look like tomorrow?"

"Anytime works for me," Nora confirmed.

"Excellent. Jennifer will email you with the time and our address."

After a mutual thank-you, Nora hung up. She felt slightly stunned at the sudden acceleration of her investigation and needed a moment to catch her balance.

"What'd she say? Give me the details! Judging from the look on your face, it's big!" Will exclaimed.

"You're not going to believe it…," Nora began. "You know that was Charlie May Maddison. Well, Jason DeWitt is…. oh shit…!"

Nora was interrupted by the chime of her cell on the counter, where it was charging. She waved it away. "Leave it … I want to tell you this!" Yet from habit she checked to see who it was.

The display read JACK REED.

"Damn, Will, it's Reed. I've got to answer," she explained as she accepted the call.

Will hated the kind of people Nora had to deal with in her work. This guy Reed was bad news.

"Reed," Nora answered, keeping her voice steady. "Where've you been? I expected you at the meeting yesterday."

"Oh, I was there. You didn't see me?" Lester Edwards asked, working to sound innocuous — to start — but laughing silently at what was to follow.

"Look, Reed, I'm not interested in your games, particularly hide and seek. What do you want?"

"Let's just say I've upped the ante on what I want."

His tone made Nora's skin crawl. TROUBLE – TROUBLE – TROUBLE! His words were like flashing lights and sirens wailing through her head. Yet she decided to give Reed a push. Maybe she could make him flinch, show himself.

"Look, Reed, I'm tired of being jerked around by you and by Grace as well. I'm still looking for proof to confirm what you've said and she's said. Right this moment I think you're full of it and that Grace is either your accomplice or your puppet. Bottom line, I'm not sure there's a story here at all."

Edwards could feel his Reed persona crumbling as he listened to Nora Martin's insulting tone. *Look, you bitch!* The words were on the tip of his tongue, but he caught himself. *Not yet, not yet!* And he did appreciate the reference to Grace as his puppet. Indeed she was — and so was Martin, as she was about to learn.

"We need to work together, you know, NORA," Reed answered. "And I've got something for you that I guarantee you'll be very interested in. It will show you just how serious all of this is. But it's for your eyes only. If hubby is there, I don't want him peeking."

Fatefully, Nora's go-it-alone instinct kicked in. She looked at Will's face, both curious and alarmed.

"Okay, Reed, not a problem. I understand," she answered calmly, to reassure Will.

"Good girl, Nora. I'm sending my message when we hang up. I'll count to ten, then I'll send it by text. So if you need to go somewhere private to enjoy it, you've got ten seconds — starting now."

Nora watched the screen darken as Reed clicked off. His condescending use of "girl" was alarming. *Stay calm!* she thought.

"What was that all about?" Will demanded. "I'm telling you Nora, this whole story…."

Nora quickly cut Will off with a kiss. "Sweets, don't worry. Reed's just a jerk. Look, I've got to pee then I'll tell you all about my call with Charlie May! I'm meeting with her tomorrow!"

Will reached out to hold her, but Nora quickly moved away. "Truly, honey, I gotta go! I'll be right back. Make us a fresh pot of coffee!"

Nora raced upstairs to the bathroom off their bedroom. She had to be out of hearing range. With seconds to spare, her phone announced the sprightly text alert. A video, she noted. *What could this be?*

When the video finished playing, Nora felt faint. Spots of light danced a hideous jig before her eyes. Then Nora could feel her stomach spasm and revolt. She raised the lid of the toilet as vomit spewed into the bowl. The sound of her text alert triggered another shockwave.

Nora leaned over the sink. She splashed her face with cold water and then brushed her teeth, trying to remove the awful taste in her mouth. Finally, summoning her grit, Nora looked at the text, certain it was from Reed.

"Cooperate and the video of hubby stays out of sight. I'll let you know what I want and when. Remember — cooperate."

Nora struggled to get her bearings. From downstairs she could hear Will's voice. "Hey, up there, you okay?"

Quickly she opened the bedroom door, telling herself: *Keep it together. He doesn't need to know. Not yet. It'll only make matters worse.* Nora cleared her throat and then called out, "Sorry, I'll be right down! I'm ready for another cup of coffee!"

She read the text again before she headed downstairs. *Cooperate? How? What the hell did Reed want?* Certainly the video of Will appearing to incite mass chaos through the destruction of the electrical grid was intended as blackmail. *Oh, God, this is trouble!*

She knew Reed expected her to negotiate his immunity. But why implicate Will? Something wasn't adding up. For now, she decided she would have to trust that whatever Reed wanted, it was in his interest not to reveal the video — or not yet. And that gave her what she needed: time.

Nora sent a one-word text back to Reed, all caps for emphasis: *UNDERSTOOD.*

Closing the bedroom door, she made her way downstairs to tell Will about Charlie May. Thoughts of their meeting tomorrow gave Nora a modicum of relief. With each step, mindful of her still queasy stomach, she made a vow: *I'll tell you what's understood — when Jason DeWitt goes down, Jack f***ing Reed does too.*

∞

Lester Edwards' exchange with Jason DeWitt had been even more satisfying. He could only imagine Nora Martin Davenport's reaction to the video and Reed's warning. Though he liked the brevity of her response. No arguing, no threats. She was a smart cookie. Edwards had recognized that about her all along. He'd only called her a "girl" to deliberately irritate her. She was one cool lady.

DeWitt, on the other hand, didn't realize right away that he'd been outfoxed. Edwards didn't have to pretend to be Reed with DeWitt. He could be the street fighter he was, more than capable of taking down a pampered pansy like Jason DeWitt.

That phone conversation had been so satisfying! Edwards could remember every word.

DeWitt had begun with his usual threats. "What the hell are you talking about, Edwards? Get your shitty self off the phone! I don't have time for you. I'm not giving you another cent. Got it? Not another penny!"

Edwards had been unfazed. "I think you might. I think you're going to want give me a LOT more! Like we're talking millions now, DeWitt. Check your cell, DeWitt. I got some pictures for you!"

The best part had been DeWitt's response and then the chance to set him straight.

"Jesus, Lester! This is fantastic! How did you get this? Will Davenport!" DeWitt had laughed hysterically. Edwards could hear the video playing.

"OK, this might be a worth a little bonus, Edwards, I'll give you that," DeWitt conceded. But just as quickly, his voice stiffened. "You'll get a couple grand more. But millions? Come on, it's not that good!"

So then, Edwards recalled triumphantly, he'd gone in for the kill. "I'm a fixer, DeWitt, not a filmmaker. Here's why it's worth millions — yeah, DeWitt, the price is two million — and you'll pay it. Because — ready — are you listening? Nora Martin has this video too. Nora Martin, investigative reporter. And guess who can give her all kinds of scoops on you, DeWitt? And she's got a BIG incentive to cooperate! 'Cause she loves her husband. She stuck by him through the bimbo fiasco. She's going to protect him. And when I tell her about you and all your dirty tricks, especially the ones you pulled on her husband, it'll win her the Pulitzer Prize."

The line went silent, though Edwards could hear DeWitt's heavy breathing. A sinister smirk spread across Edwards' face.

"DeWitt? DeWitt? You still there? Should I call 9-1-1?" he asked, with mock concern.

When DeWitt finally spoke, his voice was raspy, as though each word caught in his throat. "You're playing with fire, Lester," he threatened again. "You can get burned too."

"Two million, DeWitt. I don't give a shit about your threats. Save 'em for somebody else. The price of my silence is two mil. You've got a day to come up with it."

Edwards had clicked off, not waiting for DeWitt to respond.

Nah, he was no filmmaker, Edwards grinned. *He was a puppet master!*

Chapter 42

Nora, Charlie May Maddison & Jason DeWitt

"Jason DeWitt! This is Charlie May Maddison. I'm sure you remember me."

Charlie May could hear the slightest intake of breath on the other end of the phone line. Good, DeWitt was surprised, as she hoped he would be.

"What can I do for you, Maddison?" DeWitt was momentarily caught off guard, but he quickly regained his balance.

"Well, I'm in my office and I'm putting you on speaker, because I have an interesting guest. I'm sitting with Nora Martin, the investigative reporter. You know her? Will Davenport's wife?"

Martin! With Maddison? DeWitt's already heightened alert was immediately elevated further. Yesterday Lester Edwards had demanded a king's ransom for his silence, threatening to expose all the details of DeWitt's "activities" to Nora Martin. Now if Martin was in league with Charlie May, things could get out of hand in a hurry.

DeWitt's mind raced, but he kept his reply smooth and crisp. "Pity you have time to kill, Charlie May. Anything else you'd like to tell me besides who's on your calendar for today? Because *I am* busy."

Charlie May laughed, undaunted. "Oh, Jason, since we're getting familiar, yes, I called to share a coincidence I've just learned. It's not only my good name you've been busy dragging through the mud. But why the nasty vendetta against Ms. Martin's husband?"

"Poor Charlie May, have you just discovered it's a big bad world out there? Sorry to be the one to break it to you," DeWitt scoffed.

"True enough, DeWitt. Here's what else I know: you're up to something. When you went after me, you did me a favor. From that moment on, I've had a laser focus on you, because I knew one day you'd outthink yourself."

"And you think that day has come?" DeWitt was keeping his voice steady. "I'm flattered you think of me at all."

DeWitt was beginning to relax — working the conversation to find out what Maddison thought she knew.

Charlie May noted the change in DeWitt's voice. *Thinks he has the upper hand? Not quite.*

"Try this on for size, DeWitt," she continued. "I understand you have a quantum computer. Perhaps that's why my encryption programs are of such interest to you."

Corporate espionage was always a concern. But DeWitt had gone to great lengths to keep his quantum computer under wraps. That Charlie May Maddison knew meant others might too. DeWitt gripped the side of his desk.

Nora mouthed, "Is he still there?" Charlie May nodded affirmatively.

Charlie May had baited the hook and now was waiting for DeWitt to nibble — or if she was lucky take the bait, hook, line, and sinker. "I bet you're trying to figure out which one of your loyal minions has spilled the beans."

That DeWitt had not hung up meant he wanted to hear what else she might know. As the seconds of quiet ticked by, Charlie May considered what else to reveal. She'd offer another nugget.

"You know, DeWitt, Ms. Martin — Nora; she and I are getting quite friendly — has shared some other quite surprising details about you and your associate, Jack Reed. You seem to be very generous these days. Handing out checks with rather large numbers, signed by you. Reed made a point of showing one to Nora. It's all very interesting, DeWitt. Must be for something mighty important."

"I don't know any Jack Reed ... never heard of him. If some guy has a check signed by me, then he made it himself! I suggest you get your facts straight."

Charlie May gave Nora a reassuring grin. "DeWitt, I haven't shared all the facts yet. Like that Nora doubts *Reed* is his real name. Maybe you know him as someone else. Think about it, DeWitt. According to Mr. alias Reed, your money — *allegedly* — is funding a radical group ready to take down the electrical grid in New York City and beyond. And my guess is your quantum computer *and* encryption cracking are all mixed up in some elaborate, grand plot! But what would the motive be? What if it was something like shutting down the grid to prove the worth of your computer? Doesn't that sound like something you'd do, DeWitt? I know it does to me!"

Edwards had put him in the crosshairs. But it was Charlie May's guesswork that stunned him. Under different circumstances, he'd be impressed.

"Oh, Charlie May, what an imagination! No wonder you've been so successful!" DeWitt quietly pounded his slick leather armrest. Maddison and Martin knew too much already. He had to do something. *But what?* DeWitt's mind was quickly calculating options.

"We've been competitors for too long, Charlie May. Let's get together — and let's not wait. I have to be in New York tomorrow. Let me show you my latest research. I know you'll find it extremely enticing. It's time we put our differences aside and join forces. Imagine the good our companies can do together."

Silently Charlie May and Nora exchanged smiles. Just as they'd hoped — get a face-to-face meeting with DeWitt.

"That's a turnaround, DeWitt. I never think of 'doing good' as one of your priorities. But you know I can't resist an intriguing offer. Agreed. We'll meet in my office," Charlie May responded.

"Oh, no, Charlie May, let's make it a business lunch. You know, break bread together." DeWitt was not going to allow himself to be recorded, as Edwards had the Davenports.

Now Charlie May and Nora exchanged confused looks. What was DeWitt up to?

Nora quickly scribbled on her pad: Bryant Park? 42nd Street and Fifth. It was very near Charlie May's office.

Charlie May nodded in agreement. "Well, then, how about a cozy little picnic in Bryant Park, DeWitt? Say two o'clock tomorrow? It's still too cool for ants. But we can't promise there won't be cockroaches. You know they've survived for millions of years. That's why, personally, I never mind *squashing one.*"

DeWitt's face burned red with fury. *That bitch! To see her squirm, how pleasant that would be!* He swallowed hard before he spoke. "Excellent, choice, Charlie May. And so cultured, in the shadow of the great New York Public Library! Be sure to bring Nora Martin with you. I think she'd be interested in the story — two industrial giants discussing the possibility of unprecedented technological innovation, for the betterment of humanity."

"Not to worry, DeWitt. I wouldn't think of coming without her!"

DeWitt was scheming on the fly. He had to go to New York to deal with Lester Edwards' treachery. But Edwards might continue to be useful after all. It was obvious that Edwards would do anything for money, and DeWitt had plenty to offer. He'd pay off Edwards and have him remove Charlie May Maddison and Nora Martin from the equation as part of the deal. Then he'd have something happen to Edwards … and he knew just the person to call.

After that, everything would be back on track. Edwards had so usefully sent DeWitt a copy of his Will Davenport masterpiece. DeWitt could even come forward in the role of hero … share this mad scientist's rant with the world in a race against time to stop a plot that, sadly, in the end, would be all too successful.

The pieces of his plan were falling into place — some a little sooner than he expected. But no matter, the end game was the same.

Next call, Lester Edwards. DeWitt did not bother to say hello. "I'm coming to the city tomorrow."

"That's convenient," Edwards smirked.

"Whatever shithole you're in, get yourself a room at that hotel next to Grand Central on 42nd Street. I'll meet you there tomorrow, one o'clock. In your room, Edwards, not the lobby."

It was precisely DeWitt's contemptuous, condescending voice that made Edwards despise him. "For somebody in your *position,* you've got a lot of demands," Edwards growled.

"Just be there, and on time. I have another assignment for you. One you'll relish. It comes with a bonus. We've got an appointment nearby, at two o'clock."

DeWitt's last call was to Victor Strong. Charlie May's interference had accelerated the inevitable. As with Edwards, DeWitt wasted no words on pleasantries. "I need Doyle in New York tomorrow," he barked at Strong.

Timmy Doyle was Strong's enforcer. In fact, when DeWitt was putting his plan together, he initially tagged Doyle, not Edwards, to set up the Davenports. But Doyle was too closely connected to Strong and could too easily lead from Strong to DeWitt. Edwards was untraceable.

But now DeWitt had no choice. He would have to risk using Doyle to clean up the mess that Lester Edwards had created.

Chapter 43

Victor Strong & Timmy Doyle

Victor Strong, brows furrowed, stood squinting out the window of his twentieth-floor downtown Boston office. The afternoon sun was bright but he chose not to draw the curtains. Today he appreciated the light. It would be dark soon enough.

Strong checked his watch. It was just past four o'clock. Doyle was always prompt, unless it was beyond his control to be on time. The call he expected would go a long way to determine Strong's future.

As he followed the second hand making another sweep around the dial of his exquisite timepiece, Strong felt an unaccustomed nervous anxiety that sent him to the bottle of bourbon in the lower bottom drawer of his desk. Despite his other expensive tastes, no premium brand for Strong. He drank Jack Daniels straight up, decent enough booze. And not that he imbibed often — just to take the edge off now and then, when he needed it. Like now.

For some time Victor Strong had sensed that the wheels of fate were turning against him. He felt squeezed. Doyle's news could go either way — tighten the screws, or give him room to maneuver, to do what needed to be done.

Timmy Doyle, his chief of security, was meeting his contact, an informant in the U.S. Attorney General's office in Washington D.C. and was due to report in any minute.

Strong was ready for whatever the news would bring. In fact, he suspected his scheme to avoid ruin and most likely jail time was about to go into hyperdrive.

He had allied himself with Jason DeWitt for far too long.

The exact moment he got involved with DeWitt escaped him, but somehow all the years were coming to a climax. He was determined to free himself from the tangled web of lies and deceits that came along with this unholy, decades-old alliance.

Generations of Strongs had been at the helm of Strong, Price, Applebaum and Goodwin for well over a century. From the beginning, the firm had specialized in a broad spectrum of investments. But after joining up with DeWitt, Victor Strong's focus narrowed to the energy sector, and he marshalled all the firm's resources in an attempt to dominate the field — with stunning results. Whether it was bought, sold, collected, transported, used or stored, they were involved. It didn't matter if it was future derivatives, stocks, commodities, or you name it, Strong, Price, Applebaum and Goodwin controlled the market.

Acting with DeWitt, Victor had put together a consortium of millionaires and billionaires, all private capital bundled to sway the politics and economics of anything dealing with energy. Naturally, "old world energy" — oil, gas and coal was a crucial priority. But new paradigm energy, including solar, wind, geothermal and even out-of-the-box stuff like Tesla turbines and generators, work based on Nikola Tesla's designs, were all on the table — nothing with potential returns escaped their involvement.

Strong and DeWitt left no stone unturned. And all in an effort to control and profit from, and ultimately, to accumulate and unleash *power,* in all its forms and meanings. The kind of power that comes along only by holding the reins of the world.

Inherent in such an enterprise was risk, and sometimes risk bore losses. To hide those losses from his powerful investors, Strong had accumulated a bevy of accountants and lawyers that knew all the imaginative ways to cook the books. And they were good, no doubt about it. But he knew at some point in time it would all go up in flames. And that time had come. In truth, it was overdue.

The oil market had turned south big time and some of Strong's high-profile clients were enormously unhappy. They were questioning his business practices in no uncertain terms. And some were doing more than questioning. They wanted a full accounting and held their influence with the Securities and Exchange Commission as a hammer over the heads of DeWitt and Strong. The thing about having a world-class clientele is that when they are with you, their connections can move mountains. But if they turn against you — well, that saying about a woman scorned. Correction, hell hath no fury like a high-roller burned. And now a whole lot of disenchanted investors had the devil's own pitchforks pointed at DeWitt and Strong.

That's why Timmy Doyle's informant was so important. Strong was depending on that source for advance warning of impending government action, so he could plot a strategy — or, as required, hightail it to a paradise island with no extradition agreement with the USA.

Of course, DeWitt had his scheme to get them out from under. But Strong had no intentions of relying on that alone. Hence, Timmy Doyle, the mole and the island awaiting.

Then again, DeWitt's plan might work. Strong had executed his part of it flawlessly. And he was experienced at the financial market high-wire act, and for the most part, had always come out wealthier and with his tracks covered. Strong was ready for a repeat performance, to turn millions into billions, square things with their investors and have plenty left over for himself and DeWitt.

All the ducks were lining up. The mathematical genius of Levi Rhodes was going to be put to the ultimate test.

Levi had worked for the firm for decades. Strong had lost track of when Levi started but he'd never lost sight of Levi as one of the firms best hires ever. And though they paid Rhodes handsomely, the firm had gained tremendous financial leverage with Levi's ingenious computer-driven trades.

Levi Rhodes loved the thrill of a challenge. Strong valued that trait and had handed him his greatest test — DeWitt's quantum computer. Naturally, Levi had no idea about the computer's larger purpose. Strong and DeWitt were expert at parceling out the shreds of information that each player in their plots needed to know. Only Strong and DeWitt knew *everything,* the full scope of what they were planning.

Perhaps for that reason, neither trusted the other. Each was the greatest liability to the other, since each "had the goods," in noir language, on the other. Strong assumed the time would come when only one of them would be the last man standing — and he intended to be the one still on his feet.

Except, at the moment, DeWitt seemed to be holding all the cards. And that was keeping Victor Strong up at night.

DeWitt was in charge of creating a massive diversion so that Strong's high-frequency trades using phantom investors would go largely unnoticed. The world would be so aghast at the takedown of the electrical grid that it would take years, if ever, to unravel the financial heist.

DeWitt insisted that he had everything under control. But he refused to reveal to Strong how he was pulling off the grid catastrophe — and that created Strong's sleepless nights. DeWitt thought himself a genius. He was condescending to everyone, including Strong. And while Strong believed in honor among thieves, DeWitt would cheat his own grandmother — probably had.

DeWitt was also a skinflint, the type who would screw somebody for a dime. And in the world of payoffs, as Strong well knew, that was dangerous. Refuse people, deceive them, undercut and gyp them, and you create unnecessary enemies. And those were all typical DeWitt tactics, which made the current circumstance too uncertain for Strong's liking.

Strong also knew that DeWitt was a *goddamn liar*. He could easily have something up his sleeve to sell out Strong and ensure he, DeWitt, got all of the profits generated by his quantum computer. Or more importantly, if things went south, DeWitt would find a way to cover his ass by throwing Strong to the wolves.

But Victor Strong had an ace in the hole — in fact, a very formidable ace in Timmy Doyle. He had plucked Doyle from the heap of obscurity and been repaid with unwavering devotion.

Timmy Doyle was an Iraq War special-ops veteran who came home to a dead-end job standing guard at the bank that handled Strong's brokerage account. Doyle also came home to a wife with coronary disease and a tangled veteran's insurance program that moved glacially in the face of her dire condition.

Strong liked to play the benevolent millionaire and, upon learning of Doyle's situation, paid for the surgery, treatments and at-home nursing that saved Timmy's wife. What Strong hadn't expected was the depth of Doyle's gratitude, which he expressed in a pledge of lifelong service.

And Doyle had been true to his word. With his special-ops training, he was a cunning and formidable agent. He did whatever Strong requested, no questions asked, with only one set of restrictions — nothing physical against women and children.

Now, out of the blue, DeWitt had asked for Doyle's services. What was DeWitt up to? At first Strong was reluctant. But upon second thought, if the time came — *when it came* Doyle's loyalty would be to Strong only. Victor could stake his life on that.

His thoughts were interrupted by a brisk knock on the office door, a pause, another knock and then the presence of Mercedes Woods, Strong's longtime assistant. "Sorry to interrupt. Timmy Doyle is on the line for you."

"Put him through, Mercedes."

Seconds later, "Mr. Strong?" Timmy Doyle whispered.

"What's the weather?" Victor replied with their agreed-upon code.

"The sky over Washington is getting quite cloudy. It's going to rain anytime now," Doyle explained.

It was bad news. The Justice Department was getting ready to act. Strong's investors were losing patience and ready to turn the screws by way of the U.S. Attorney General's office.

"The sun is out here in Boston. Do you think the storm will come up the coast?" Victor asked, continuing to use their meteorological euphemisms to determine whether possible indictments from the Attorney General's office were imminent.

"It's looking that way. It depends on which way the wind blows," Doyle noted. His code words were saying it depended on whether the investors felt confident that the results Strong promised were immediately forthcoming. If not, the Attorney General was set to pounce.

"But one should be prepared to stay off the road if the downpour arrives," Doyle concluded. That was Doyle's warning to Strong to be prepared, in case the shit storm could not be avoided and headed his way.

"Okay, then, I'm leaving shortly and will be home early, if any updates come in," Strong finished. "But one more thing. A friend of ours has theatre tickets for you in New York City for tomorrow. It's a tale of betrayal and sacrifice. I'll text you the details."

Doyle grunted in response. "Am I expected by a certain time?"

"Make your way there as soon as possible," Strong explained. "Tonight if you can. You don't want to chance a delay and miss the show."

Another grunt. "Got it."

"And stay in touch, Timmy. I might want to see the show too, but I need to get your opinion first."

Strong hung up thinking, *Good.* DeWitt had requested Doyle in New York. Whatever DeWitt was up to, Timmy would get the details and report back to Strong.

In fact, Strong couldn't be happier than if he himself had arranged to have Doyle by DeWitt's side. He had a powerful suspicion there was a fly in the ointment of DeWitt's plan. And having Doyle's eyes on the ground to oversee DeWitt was an advantage not to be passed up.

He could absolutely count on Timmy Doyle to do his bidding — or, in a pinch, whatever Doyle reasoned would be best for Victor Strong. And, if necessary, Timmy would fade into the woodwork when the job was done. No questions asked!

Chapter 44

UPPER WEST SIDE, MANHATTAN
MARCH 28
4:30 P.M.

Will

Will had begun the morning worried about Nora and the meeting she was having with Charlie May Maddison. Something didn't feel right. Nora wasn't herself. And Will could pinpoint the time and place when it turned. After her call yesterday with that bastard Jack Reed, she'd been different. Oh, she tried to cover it up, whatever it was. She came back downstairs all chatty about the call with Maddison. But she'd thrown up — despite the toothpaste, he could tell.

Was it morning sickness? Might she be pregnant already? Will realized he was genuinely thrilled at that prospect — except his gut told him that wasn't it. In part because he expected that Nora would tell him the moment she suspected herself.

No, Will was more certain it had to do with Reed. That guy was a complete slimeball. *Well, when she does get pregnant, no more of the likes of Jack Reed,* Will promised himself. He'd insist on safer stories to pursue.

It was because of his sense of alarm that Will had taken a later train to the city today, so he could come in with Nora, who had a one-thirty appointment with Charlie May. Per usual, he planned to pop into Izzy's shop to discuss the latest on the diary. And when he did, at a little past one o'clock, Izzy was running around like a madman.

"Will, over here!" Izzy had greeted him. The store was the busiest Will had ever seen it. He moved closer to Izzy behind the counter, who whispered, "Crazy day! Lucy's in the back logging in a shipment of watches that's two days late. Malcolm's out."

After the concerns about Nora, Will was anxious for a distraction. To his disappointment, it appeared that Izzy was too busy for anything other than watches. "I thought we'd look everything over again, Izzy, especially that silver box. But if you're too busy today…."

Izzy cut him off. "Never! What are you thinking?"

Will was relieved. "Something tells me we're missing the obvious. I brought along a book from the university library on Galileo's theories. Your dream about Galileo's Jupiter moons has got to mean something, Izzy. I'm sure that's the clue we need."

"Let me get Lucy to take the counter and I'll meet you in the back," Izzy agreed.

In no time Izzy made his way to the back office and had the diary, silver box, poem and Fletcher letter spread out across his desk.

"Izzy, it's something hidden in plain sight," Will was certain of it.

Izzy shook his head in frustration. "I'm not one to give up, but we've been over everything a million times, Will. What could we be missing?"

"I don't know, Izzy, but we have to be able to solve this puzzle. Galileo's Jupiter moons, the phrase from your dream, was a method of locating a place. And the Fletcher letter that Levi found in Gabriel Hornsby's collection is proof positive. It seems clear we're chasing after the ancient crystal that Ethan Hawkins found and that Benjamin Hawkins brought with him to America. Benjamin brought the diary too. So what happened to the crystal? That's the location we're trying to find. At least we know what we're searching for."

Will started by inspecting the silver box. "This pictorial scene was created by certain kinds of markings. They are arranged in shapes to produce images that appear natural, like this waterfall. This crosshatching appears as water falling from a cliff and pooling into a pond. I know Ian has examined the box, but let's look at it again. You have a magnifying glass, right?"

"Will, you're in a watch repair shop. Name the magnification and we have it." Izzy handed Will a loop with high magnification.

"Just look at that!" Will was scanning the silver box. "to make this complex etching look like a waterfall is simply mind blowing."

Now Izzy took a turn with the magnifying glass as well and scanned another section. "These plants around the pond are made up circles," he explained. "Each plant has six circles around another, seven circles in all."

Izzy paused, looking at Will. "This reminds me of artists using mathematics to create illusions in their illustrations. Some are so intricate, one person can see one thing and another person sees something very different."

"I think we've been going at this all wrong!" Will declared. "I have a hunch. We should be looking for markings that are different from the rest. If your ancestors are sending us a message through this box, they may have etched them at a different time than the box was originally made."

Izzy continued looking over the box as Will took out the book about Galileo. He recalled a page.... And then ..., there it was, a table titled CASSINI'S JOVIAN MOONS ECLIPSES. Although Galileo was the main advocate of using the moons of Jupiter to plot location, another astronomer, Giovanni Cassini perfected the art of charting the Jupiter moons' movements.

Then the room practically shook. "Eureka!" Izzy shouted. "Take a look at these crude scratchings on the edge of the lid!"

"My God, Izzy, they're numbers!" Will yelled.

It was all coming together for them. Will took out his laptop. "These could be latitude and longitude!"

He plugged them in to search. It took a little trial and error, for it was difficult to read the numbers clearly. Fortunately, the errors were clearly errors — the location, for instance, was not likely to be in the Sahara Desert.

Still, it didn't take long to have an answer that was entirely plausible.

"KATONAH, NEW YORK! Practically in Nora and my backyard!" Will confirmed.

Will and Izzy exchanged a celebration hug. At last they had something to go on. A solid location.

"I've gotta go tell Lucy. She thinks we're crazy!" Izzy grinned.

Will had called Nora, hoping to catch her before her meeting with Charlie May began, and then sent a text. But she didn't respond to either. He assumed her phone was off. That was typical Nora, the pro. She gave her full attention to whoever she was interviewing. "People are so rude with their devices!" she often complained. "I won't be one of them!" Still, Will wished for once she'd just pick up.

Izzy returned with Lucy. "Okay, you two crazy men," she laughed. "I guess congratulations — and next stop, Westchester and the village of Katonah."

Shortly thereafter, Will took the subway to his university office uptown. Ken had given him such a hard time, now he wanted to share his good news — prove he wasn't wasting his time. It was a few minutes after four as he climbed up from the subway station closest to the university and sent Nora another text, to let her know where he was.

When Will got off the elevator in the geology building, he nearly walked into Molly, who was waiting to enter.

"Hi, Will!" she called cheerily. "Ken was looking for you this morning. He's in the office now. You might want to stop in."

"Thanks, Molly. He's just the man I want to see," Will responded. Moments later, he popped his head inside his brother's open office door. "Hey, Ken!"

"Hey yourself, Stranger. Where the hell have you been?"

"Doing research." It was the simple truth.

Ken was standing up now. "Come on, let's go to your office. I want to talk to you."

Despite his excitement, Will felt the chill in his brother's voice and had his usual thought in response: *Oh, shit, now what does he want?*

Will led the way and opened the door. The room looked empty except for a few of his research books he'd left on the desk.

"You know I had to pull strings to get you in here!" Ken was angry, though he kept the volume controlled. He didn't want to be overheard.

"I do know. I thank you! I'll thank you again and again. I appreciate everything you've done for me!" Will answered, trying to keep his voice low as well.

"You've always been this way, you know that, Will! So freakin' irresponsible!" Ken was seething now, digging up old grievances. "Everything comes so easy for you. I've had to work hard to earn everything I've built. Ever since we were kids, it's been 'watch out for your little brother.' I'm tired of cleaning up after your messes!"

But Will was tired of Ken's big-brother pestering, "Look, goddamn it! I didn't ask you for any of this! And I don't GIVE A SHIT what people think about how I work. I'm not going to twist myself into a pretzel to be the researcher that you or anybody else thinks I should be!"

Ken stood with his arms crossed. He was too furious to consider Will's point of view.

"Oh, screw this!" Will hissed.

In the silence that followed, both brothers took a breath. Will was the first to speak again. "Look, I hear what you're saying, Ken. And I DO appreciate having this office to work on my manuscript. The thing is, I'm working on something else that's also VERY IMPORTANT. It informs my theories. And the research on THAT frequently takes me away from this office right now. THAT's what's going on and why I'm not here everyday, or morning to night."

"Okay, I get that," Ken conceded. "So what is it? What are you working on?"

"Let's sit down." Over the next hour, Will described his exploits with Izzy and the hunt for the diary — and now the crystal stone — of Ethan Hawkins.

Chapter 45

Will & Nora; Jason DeWitt & Lester Edwards

"You're not going alone. I'm coming with you."

Will was insistent that Nora not meet DeWitt without him. They had been having this running argument since Nora told him of the meeting planned for today. Now they'd taken the train in together and were walking through Grand Central. And Will was reminded of the contentious quarrel he had with Nora, right here in Grand Central, almost the same spot, right before they boarded the train to go back home to Westchester the previous night.

Will had met Nora at Grand Central right after his difficult conversation with Ken — which thankfully ended on a high note. Ken now had a better picture of what Will was engaged in. The worst of Ken's fears, that Will was still floundering, was unfounded. And that, Will concluded, was cause to go out on the town and celebrate. So too was his call with Izzy. The two had made plans to continue their quest by going to Katonah and looking for the waterfall.

But his high spirits had fallen flat with Nora.

486

"Honey, I'm thrilled for you — but I can't go out tonight. I'm sorry, Will. I've got to prepare and be totally alert for my meeting with Charlie May and DeWitt in Byrant Park."

And that's how the evening played out — a quick and quiet dinner at home and then Nora went to her office to review her DeWitt file and then in bed by ten. Will had spent the evening researching the history of Katonah and its settlement, searching for accounts of early settlers, landholdings, historical and contemporary topographical maps, realtors representing properties for sale anything that might pinpoint where next to look for the Hawkins "secret."

It was well after midnight when Will crawled into bed. But sleep eluded him and he found himself thinking about his spat with Ken earlier in the day. As he looked at Nora, fast asleep beside him, Will considered how much Ken must have struggled since the divorce, and now, with seeing his kids so seldom. Ken's marriage had fallen apart while Will was dealing with the fallout from the Party Girl scandal, and he'd done little to support Ken.

But there was something else in his conversation with Ken that struck him. Recalling his exact words, Will heard himself again proclaiming that he didn't GIVE A SHIT what people thought about how he worked; that he wouldn't twist himself into a pretzel to be the researcher that Ken or anybody else thought he should be!

Those words were still ringing in his ears as Will realized that, in fact when he dug deep into his psyche and surveyed his feelings, *all his life* he had indeed been concerned about what people thought of him. His father and mother; Ken; Nora; later on, his colleagues; and then the vast general public out there, watching on television and following him on social media and online. It made him wonder what would it be like to have the freedom not to feel *the need* for validation, from anyone? Not to have to push ever forward, in order to attain that glorious feeling of success and glow of accomplishment. What would it feel like to know that the ultimate satisfaction comes from appreciating and living the

joy of one's own *uniqueness*? What would it feel like to be able to celebrate that, and to find peace in that, knowing deep in your bones that
being you is more than enough to derive contentment from one's life?

In the next moments, he let those thoughts roll through him as new
fundamental insights — seeds freshly planted, waiting to take root, and
to be nurtured as time went on.

But then more pressing thoughts captured his attention. The imme-
diacy of tomorrow came into view. He looked again at Nora and was
disturbed to see that even as she slept, she had a tense expression on
her face.

Will kissed his sleeping wife, beseeching her guardian angel to keep
her safe. If anything ever happened to Nora … he couldn't bear to
think about it….

Will's worries and Nora's understandable resistance had only ramped
up as the meeting time approached. They were standing off to the side
by the busy 42nd Street entrance, people moving in and out the doors,
with Nora trying to reassure Will.

"I'm going with Charlie May. We're in a public place. Nothing is
going to happen," Nora stated sharply, aiming to cut off any further
debate.

She was struggling to keep her voice calm, but Will was trying her
patience. "Look, honey, our plan is simple. We record our conversation
and get DeWitt to incriminate himself. If you show up out of the blue,
getting DeWitt to talk will be much harder. Think about it, Will, he'll
immediately expect a confrontation — or a trap. It's better this way.
Charlie May and I have everything under control."

Will was not convinced. "Charlie May already tried to get DeWitt
to reveal himself on the phone."

For the second time, Nora explained their strategy to her skeptical husband. "No! She was trying to *surprise* DeWitt, knock him off balance — *and she clearly did.* That was step one. Take it from me, when you meet someone in person, it changes the whole dynamic. DeWitt is such a smug son of a bitch that with a little baiting, he'll give himself away today. I'm sure of it."

Nora softened as she looked at Will's anxious face. "Sweetheart, please try to understand. Your presence could actually blow this. Trust me…. Look, I've got to get going. I told Charlie May I'd be at her office by one. Then we're going to Bryant Park together."

"I guess it doesn't matter what I say," Will finally relented.

"Of course it matters. But sometimes you've got to have faith that I have a good sense about these things." Nora kissed him softly. "Okay then!" Nora laughed, wiping her lipstick off his lips. "I love you!"

"Ditto," he called.

But Will wasn't on board with Nora's plan. *After all,* he thought. *I didn't technically agree.* He did trust her — but he didn't trust Jason DeWitt. And so there was no way he was going to sit idly by when Nora was walking into who knows what.

He'd make a plan of his own. He'd stop to see Izzy. Then make his way to the university by way of a side trip to Bryant Park.

Will was determined to be there, just in case he was needed.

As Will and Nora argued in Grand Central, Lester Edwards was next door, pacing around his luxury hotel room, waiting for DeWitt to show.

And as Nora made her way to Charlie May's office, at precisely one o'clock, Edwards answered the knock on his room door. DeWitt, briefcase in hand, entered briskly.

There was no mutual greeting, as each man measured the other.

"Let's get on with it, Edwards," DeWitt said curtly. "We've got things to do."

"As you wish. You have my money?" Edwards was as direct as DeWitt.

"You might say that." DeWitt opened the briefcase and pulled out several large blocks of bills, all hundreds.

Edwards raised his eyebrows and snorted, smelling a double cross. "This looks short to me, DeWitt. Where's my two million?"

"Calm down, Edwards, you'll get it all. First, I have to be sure you'll play this out to the end. When I hired you I thought you were a professional. Based on this charade, I can count on one thing — you'll do anything for money. So here's an incentive. You'll get your ransom money and another million when everything is done. All you have to do is get rid of two problems I have."

"Okay," Edwards responded, considering how best to test DeWitt. "How do you know I won't just take off with this ... leave you high and dry with your two little problems?"

"For starters, Edwards, a million dollars is a lot of money to leave on the table, and two million is even more. Let's say I have a high level of confidence that it's just not in your nature."

No, only an idiot would walk away from that kind of dough, Edwards reasoned. "So what do you have in mind?"

DeWitt eyed Edwards with contempt. Of course he'd been right about him. "I'm meeting with Nora Martin Davenport and Charlie May Maddison this afternoon in Bryant Park. And you're coming with me."

Edwards was intrigued. "You do remember I'm 'Jack Reed' to Martin? And who's Maddison?"

"A woman who has stuck her nose in where it doesn't belong," DeWitt answered angrily. Thoughts of Charlie May's insults and Edwards' questions made him want to lash out. "And I know who Nora Davenport thinks you are. Just shut up and listen! Those two bitches are going to push me to explain myself. They'll record our conversation to expose me. And I don't care if they do."

"And why's that, DeWitt?" Edwards' voice was smug. He hoped

to irritate the bastard further by holding back, not giving DeWitt any indication that he was on board with whatever DeWitt was planning.

"Because you'll be waiting in the wings. I'll signal as the meeting is nearing its end. I'm sure Ms. Martin, Mrs. Davenport — whatever name you choose — will be quite surprised to see you. Then you'll take over from there and I'll take my leave. The rest is up to you. Your job is to be sure I never hear their annoying voices again."

Edwards had always assumed the Davenports were expendable and this Charlie May Maddison had stumbled into where she didn't belong. Edwards did a quick assessment of the difficulty involved. "What about the husband?" he asked.

"No. Not yet. We still need him to play a starring role in the big show today."

Edwards looked at his watch — it was nearly one-thirty. "You haven't given me much time to figure this out, especially since you intend to just waltz off. Bryant Park is a very public place. Not so easy to operate there. What am I going to do? Stuff them in the trunk of the car with everyone watching?"

"I've done some thinking for you." DeWitt reached into his suit jacket and produced a set of keys. "I have access to a place in the Bronx, by the Westchester border. The building's secluded and empty."

"It still won't be easy handling the two of them," Edwards complained.

"What's next, Lester, are you going to cry? I thought you were a pro. Besides, it'll all be easier when all hell breaks loose after the lights go out. We're moving up that operation too."

DeWitt returned to his briefcase and pulled out a set of nondescript manila envelopes, each addressed to a major media outlet. *The New York Times* envelope was on top. "These are going out by messenger now. It's all arranged. We leave them with the concierge. Inside each one is your little video masterpiece, Edwards. So when they're looking for clues as to who made New York go dark, they'll have a name: Will Davenport."

For a brief moment Lester Edwards considered the distinct possibility that he had screwed himself. Had lost control of events? DeWitt was acting like he was running the show.

"So call your band of crazies. It's performance time, Edwards! Make sure they know where to set the explosion and when — five minutes before six o'clock. Precisely five-fifty-five today. Such a nice ring to it."

DeWitt had to look away to hide his satisfied grin. Everything was in its place now. Just before the power went off, accounts in three major brokerage houses would be hacked, with the money transferred to bogus offshore accounts. And once the electrical grid exploded, the world would recognize the necessity of the encrypted security that DeWitt's quantum computer could provide, which meant more money pouring in for Jason DeWitt.

And Edwards would never see any of that money, or even his piddling three million. Once Davenport and Maddison were out of the way, Timmy Doyle would eliminate Edwards.

As Edwards gave Grace the "go" signal, DeWitt thought contentedly, *Not bad. All in a day's work. And screw you, Edwards. In fact, screw all of you!*

Chapter 46

Will & Izzy; Nora, Charlie May, DeWitt & Edwards

"What's going on?" Izzy could see that Will was not his usual self. Yesterday he'd been brimming with excitement over the discovery of the Katonah location and all the possibilities it raised. Yet even as he shared the research he'd done last night on Katonah, Izzy could feel that Will's usual keen interest in their mutual mission was missing. He was only half listening to Izzy's responses, fidgeting and sneaking looks at his watch. As a student of people — and someone who had the gift of gab — Izzy knew the signs of someone who really wanted to be somewhere else.

With another quick check of the time, Will announced, "I've got to head out, Iz. Nora has a meeting today that has me worried. It's that story she's been working on and it's screaming 'bad news.' Her appointment is near here, at Bryant Park. My gut tells me I should get my ass over there in case she needs me. The thing is, if she sees me, she'll be upset. It's a long story...."

"Of course," Izzy responded, his instincts confirmed. "What do you plan on doing when you get there?"

"I thought I could hang in the background. Station myself where

Nora and the bastard she's meeting can't see me. All I really know is that I have to be there."

Izzy nodded. "Just wait one second." Then he opened the door to the back office and called out, "Malcolm, I need you to take over out here. And please grab my camera bag. It's hanging on my chair."

"No, Iz, you don't need to come with me," Will insisted.

"Will, I know this city better than you do, in every way. And my camera and long lens might come in handy. I get a sense there's more to this story, something you're not saying. It might help you to get your worries off your chest. We'll talk while we walk."

Malcolm emerged at that moment, camera bag in hand. With a quick nod of thanks from them both, Will and Izzy set off.

Had they exited Grand Central five minutes earlier, they might have observed Jason DeWitt and Lester Edwards getting into Edwards' car, brought up from the nearby hotel parking garage.

Instead, Will and Izzy made their way to the exit on 42nd Street and Vanderbilt Avenue — the short block named for Cornelius Vanderbilt, builder of railroads, whose statue stood in front of Grand Central. Bryant Park was just two avenues away.

Will took a deep breath as he and Izzy walked briskly. "Iz, there's another scientist, Jason DeWitt, who worked pretty hard to discredit all my research, and while he was at it, took a demolition ball to my hard won reputation in the sciences. Frankly, he was challenging everything about me. DeWitt's well-known, influential and very wealthy. The media pays attention to what he has to say. The bastard kicked me in the nuts, you might say, when I was already down. And that's the bastard Nora is meeting."

Izzy's voice was reassuring. "Will, I remember the unpleasant stories about you. I realized who you were the first time we met. But I never let someone else's opinion color my judgment. And fortunately for me, I've come to know the decent, engaging, dedicated and, yes, brilliant man you are and that I now call my friend. Say no more about it.... But tell me about DeWitt and your concerns."

Will gently grasped Izzy's arm, a warm gesture of gratitude for his words and support. "DeWitt's part of the story Nora's working on. It's something nefarious, but more than that, I smell desperation. The guy is very powerful and I'm worried if Nora is on to whatever DeWitt wants to keep secret…."

There was no need for Will to continue. Izzy understood. Whatever the reason DeWitt had originally targeted Will, the whole thing could be playing itself out now, putting Nora in danger.

Will was glad to air his concerns. Yet looking at Izzy beside him, he was starting to think practically what would happen when they got to Bryant Park. "Iz, you're a big guy. Nora's more likely to see you than me. I appreciate you coming along, but I think I should enter the park alone."

Izzy immediately offered an alternative. "Then how about this? I'll get Lucy and the car…."

"We don't have time for that!" Will interrupted, his anxiety showing in his impatience.

"We do. Let me finish," Izzy answered calmly. "She's nearby, at Ian's … made a delivery for me. She can meet us on the corner of 40th and Fifth. I've got my camera and long lens. We'll find a place where I can sit in the car and watch what's happening from one location. You can watch from another. We'll have Nora doubly protected. AND we'll have a car if we need it."

Charlie May and Nora were standing by the 42nd Street entrance to Bryant Park. It was 2:15 and no sign yet of DeWitt.

"He's obviously making us wait, hoping we'll get anxious and frustrated," Nora coolly observed.

"Does he really think that crap would work with us?" Charlie May responded, as steady as Nora.

In truth, Nora was feeling some butterflies, though not from fear.

She was worried that her emotions would get the better of her. She wanted to nail DeWitt and needed to stay focused.

"There he is," Charlie May whispered. "Every hair in place. That's Jason DeWitt!"

Nora stared, recalling his photo with Senator Broderick. His image was burned into her memory, waiting for the day she could *vindicate Will's good name*.

"Charlie May Maddison!" DeWitt announced. "How in the world did you get mixed up with the Davenports?" he snickered.

Charlie May put on her poker face. "Good fortune, I guess."

"Let's sit." Nora pointed to an empty table. It was one of those unpredictable late-March days that had started out sunny but turned threatening, apropos the meeting about to begin.

DeWitt opened with a ridiculous plea. "Charlie May, tell me you're not listening to Mrs. Davenport and all the nasty stuff she says I've done to her husband!"

"You forget, DeWitt," said Charlie May, "I've had my own experiences with you. I know firsthand what a snake you are."

Ignoring her insult, Dewitt continued. "When it comes to science, I have very high standards. Surely, Charlie May, you've read about Will Davenport's unscrupulous behavior. Face it Mrs. Davenport, your husband's a charlatan. And his favorite stars are pretty, young things...."

DeWitt intended to put a wedge of doubt between the two women or, at least, to unnerve Nora with a reminder of Will's straying with "party girl."

However, Nora was confident that Charlie May would see through DeWitt, just as she could. It was time to get down to business. "Who's Jack Reed and what's your association with him?"

For DeWitt, there was only one purpose to this meeting to get the two women in a place where Edwards could take over. Still, he wasn't beyond taunting his victims first by giving them his longed-for confession.

"Screw, Reed. He's not important! Don't you really want to know why I went after your husband so hard?"

Nora looked at him stone-faced.

"I'll take that as a yes. Will Davenport was riding high, so full of himself. You know what the Greeks warned about getting too close to the sun? No matter where you looked, there he was, spewing out his theories on this or that. And, by the way, your exposés on the power grid and fracking cost me a lot of money too, which only put your husband more firmly on my radar screen and made both of you quite the deserving targets! I don't remember precisely how it came to me. It may have been when Levi Rhodes delivered the good news that he had successfully concluded experiments on my quantum computer…."

Nora could see that Charlie May tensed at the mention of a quantum computer, and was thinking of her encryption codes. But what would a quantum computer have to do with Will? The reference to Levi immediately brought to mind Izzy and Will's involvement in deciphering the diary. But what would that have to do with DeWitt? Nora did not understand.

DeWitt was enjoying the look of confusion on Nora's face. *Not quite as smart as you thought, Mrs. Davenport?*

"Let me tell you more, Nora. I was instrumental in 'introducing' your husband to that bimbo, Vanessa Sotherland. She was so willing to get her face plastered all over the news, so willing to plant that big, juicy kiss on your husband's lips or do whatever else, for that matter….." DeWitt paused, leering at his own description and encouraging Nora to consider the possibilities.

"Your husband is a handsome guy," he continued, "and a no-talent like Vanessa needs all the publicity she can get. Too bad about what followed, but so predictable. Celebrities can get away with bad behavior like that, but not a serious scientist."

His swarmy smirk changed to a cold-eyed stare. "Bottom line, Nora. I don't like competition. Just ask Charlie May."

Despite herself, Nora was aghast. "You would do all that because you saw Will as a threat? To what?"

DeWitt shook his head in mock surprise. "I am disappointed in you, Nora. For one thing, given your own success, haven't you met anyone who resents it? I've always been top dog. I don't like to see somebody get ahead of me — for any reason. Isn't that right, Charlie May? Why so quiet?"

Charlie May had been listening intently, not wanting to interrupt DeWitt while he was, hopefully, digging his own grave. "Oh, don't let me stop you from talking, Jason. You said there was another reason you went after Will Davenport. Do tell…."

It was hard for DeWitt not to have a grudging respect for Charlie May Maddison. He'd miss her as an adversary.

"Well, Nora knows that answer," he explained, "since we both have an interesting video we've received lately. A very powerful speech by her husband inciting violence. Really, Nora! What's gotten into Will Davenport? To say all that on camera!"

Nora was stunned again — DeWitt had the tape too! She was feeling outfoxed, and this was a particularly dangerous development.

"To be honest, Nora, that was more than I could hope for," DeWitt chuckled. "I thought desperation might drive your husband to something that would benefit me — and it has! You can't plan everything, though I'm pretty adept at it. Right, Charlie May? I know where to go to get what I need — like, say, the best encryption software."

Alarm bells were ringing in Charlie May's head. DeWitt was revealing *too much* and in such a glib way. She didn't like the direction the conversation was going. But all she could do now was play along and hope his end game would soon be clear.

"So, the rumors are true, DeWitt," Charlie May replied. "You *do* have a working quantum computer. And that's why you're after the software my team developed. You want to test it against your computer.

You must have gotten a heads-up that the New York Stock Exchange was beta testing my codes system-wide."

"Bingo! Smart cookie that Charlie May!" crowed DeWitt. "Yes, that's my story, ladies. And now let me introduce you to a colleague."

Lester Edwards had moved forward stealthily and was positioned behind Nora and Charlie May.

Nora turned to look into a face she recognized. "Reed!" she declared.

"Of course, *Mrs. Davenport*, you know him as Jack Reed. His real name, or it could be just his *nom de guerre*, is Lester Edwards," DeWitt crowed. He nodded as Edwards moved next to him. "And since our meeting has ended, Edwards will be joining us. In case you have other ideas, he has a gun pointed at you. Yes, just like in the movies. Let's all go quietly. We've got a car on the corner."

"You have to be kidding!" Charlie May was defiant. "Why would we go anywhere with you? What are you going to do? Shoot us here in the middle of Manhattan?"

"People have. It's easier then you think," DeWitt growled. "But here's something that will encourage Nora to go along."

DeWitt pulled out his phone and began to play the video of Will at Brookfield Place. The volume was low, but Will's dire warnings could still be heard. The excitement in his voice that had meant to caution Grace and her followers, through Edwards' manipulation, sounded like maniacal calls to violence.

"Kudos again, Edwards," DeWitt nodded. Then, to Nora and Charlie May, "You two balk and you can watch this go out to every media outlet in this city, *and* to the NYPD and FBI. Given there's a surprise in store for NYC and beyond this afternoon, this is going to be of special interest to everybody."

Nora understood instantly. "Oh my God, the grid! You're going to do it!"

"There's a scoop that you can't use, Ms. Martin," DeWitt laughed.

"I'll just take your phones, ladies, since you won't be needing them." Dewitt took Charlie May's phone and pointed to Edwards to grab Nora's, not wanting to carry both.

Feeling trapped, both Nora and Charlie May complied. Within seconds they were walking toward a black car, with DeWitt strategically ahead and Edwards behind.

Will and Izzy had caught much of the meeting, though their spin as detectives had been less than successful. Will had stationed himself at a table a distance from Nora and Charlie May. He was certain Nora could not see him, but he could see Charlie May quite well and was trying to judge from her expression how the meeting was going. He noticed she seemed to be mainly listening. Then a large group — a family of tourists, probably took a table that completely blocked Will's view. Frustrated and worried about what he couldn't see, he left the park by an opposite entrance and joined Izzy and Lucy in the car. They were parked on the corner of Sixth Avenue and 40th Street, at the southwestern edge of the park. With Izzy's long lens, he could see Nora — except when people on the sidewalk and in the park got in the way, which was often.

Will was anxiously trying to gauge whether he needed to get involved. Nora looked angry and irritated, which was a little surprising. Her professional demeanor was usually in observer mode, trying to stay focused to glean every detail. But now at times she also looked confused and even stunned. Yet Will determined there were no signs so far of immediate danger. To interfere now, he thought, would only infuriate Nora.

"Look at that idiot!" Lucy exclaimed as a man in a black car double-parked on the far north corner next to the park, at 42nd Street and Sixth Avenue. "Asshole! Can't park there!"

"Lucy, your language, please," Izzy corrected.

The man stepped out of the car and entered the park. Another crowd obscured their view for seconds. When it was clear again, the man was standing next to DeWitt.

"Who's that, Will?" Izzy asked.

"I don't know. Let me take a look, Iz."

"This is weird. DeWitt's showing Nora and Charlie May his phone," Will narrated. "Jesus, Nora looks really upset!"

More people crossed his sightline and Will's view was blocked again. He completely lost sight of Nora. "Shit! I can't see them at all!"

Seconds later, Lucy was shouting, "There!"

All four, the unknown man included, were emerging from the park and headed for the black car.

Will jumped out of Lucy's car and dashed toward Nora, Izzy on his heels. "NORA!" Will screamed.

But Will had only seconds to cover a length of two blocks. And between the general din of horns and people, Nora couldn't hear his voice. She and Charlie May were hustled inside the black car, which pulled away quickly, to join the stream of traffic up Sixth Avenue. And then....Gone....

Chapter 47

DeWitt, Edwards, Nora & Charlie May;
Will, Izzy & Lucy

DeWitt was in the driver's seat of Edwards' car as they crawled up Sixth Avenue, but he had a creeping feeling that he was not driving the events as planned. He'd felt in control of the meeting in Bryant Park — up until Edwards appeared. Then it became clear that he could not make the clean exit he expected. Edwards couldn't manage both women alone. Nora Martin and Charlie May Maddison were each no shrinking violet. Together they posed a formidable challenge. It was Edwards' gun and their concern that no bystanders get hurt, and of course for Nora, Edwards' video, that convinced them to go along quietly to the car.

But then, what? In an instant DeWitt could see that he had no choice but to do the driving while Edwards got in the back seat with Martin and Maddison, his gun continuing to keep them under control — for now. But that gun also meant that Edwards had the equalizer, and that didn't make DeWitt happy. Yet he still had Timmy Doyle as his ace in the hole. *He'll solve any problems when we get to the Bronx,* DeWitt thought.

"Jesus, DeWitt! Watch it!" Edwards was screaming. "You almost rear-ended that car!"

Will had watched helplessly as Nora was whisked away. That Nora had not looked back, nor Charlie May either, made his spirits sink lower. They didn't even realize that he was there! But DeWitt hadn't seemed to notice him either, or the other man, whom Will instinctively thought must be Jack Reed.

Thankfully, it was only a few seconds that Will stood frozen on the sidewalk. And fortunate too that Izzy had cooked up the idea of watching the meeting from Lucy's car. Now Izzy was beside Will, tugging at his arm to turn him around. "Get back to the car, Will!" Izzy shouted.

Lucy was ready with the car running when Will and Izzy jumped inside. "They went straight up Sixth!" Izzy shouted. "Go, Luce!"

"Goddamnit! They can't think they're going to get away with this!" Will cursed.

"Desperate people do desperate things," Izzy concluded.

"Oh, shit!" Lucy bellowed. The light changed before she could get across 42nd Street.

Waiting for the light to turn green seemed like an eternity, but Lucy soon caught up and had sight of the car. "Ha! Who is this guy? He doesn't know how to drive!" scoffed Lucy, experienced city driver and proud of it.

"His name's DeWitt," mumbled Will.

"He lives in Boston, Luce," Izzy explained.

"Well, he's a shitty driver wherever he's from!" she declared.

They were at West 57th Street, a main thoroughfare, when DeWitt suddenly turned right. He was headed for the East Side.

"Damn this traffic!" Lucy yelled. At that moment a crosstown bus lumbered by.

"Careful, Luce," Izzy directed, pointing to the bus and a line of cars behind it.

"This app actually works!" Will suddenly exclaimed. He had pulled out his phone and was excitedly studying it. "I can't believe I forgot about this!"

"Forgot what? And what on earth are you doing?" Izzy asked, momentarily perplexed at Will being distracted by his phone.

"I've got them on GPS! Nora still has her phone or at least it's in the car!"

"How?" Izzy asked.

"It's a GPS phone locator app," Will explained. "I'm following Nora's phone! I put the app on both our phones because I was worried about the meetings she was having with this story! I can't believe DeWitt didn't throw away her phone! Not as smart as he thinks he is — thank God! And if Nora can check her phone, she'll know we're on their tail!"

"That's great!" Izzy and Lucy said in unison. "Where are they now, Will?" Lucy asked.

"They made a left onto Madison and they're headed north," Will narrated. "Now they've made another left and are headed for Fifth."

Then, moments later, "They're going through Central Park at 66th Street." Will continued to track them as they moved farther west through the city.

"That's weird," noted Lucy. "Why didn't they just go left at 57th? Seems like they went way out of their way for nothing."

"Because as you said Lucy, apparently DeWitt is a shitty driver. And he probably has a dumb-ass GPS system taking him to God knows where," Will declared.

"Stay close, Lucy," Izzy urged. "Even with this app thing. Better if we can see them."

"I got it and I'm on it!" Lucy exclaimed as she sped through the park drive.

"Yeah, get as close as you can Lucy, but not too close that DeWitt recognizes we're following. We don't want them to wise up or God forbid toss Nora's phone!" added Will.

∞

The drive, indeed, was not going smoothly for DeWitt and Edwards.

"DeWitt, where the hell did you learn to drive? You're gonna get us all killed!" Edwards yelled out as DeWitt swerved, just missing a pedestrian crossing the street. "This is New York. People and bicycles are everywhere — darting out into the streets every-which-way they please!"

"Shut up, asshole!" DeWitt hissed.

Edwards momentarily thought about taking over, but he wasn't about to give up the gun and control of all the players.

Nora looked at Charlie May, and both women were thinking the same thing. These two were already at each other's throats. It was something to capitalize on — if, indeed, they survived this car ride.

Charlie May was closest to the door. Nora was sitting closest to Edwards. She'd known him as Jack Reed. How to use that to turn them against each other?

"So … Lester Edwards … or is it Jack Reed?" Nora began. "What's DeWitt promising you? Whatever it is, you know he can't be trusted."

"Take it from me, Edwards! He's planning a double cross!" Charlie May chimed in. The two-women tag team was just getting started.

"Both of you, SHUT UP!" DeWitt fumed.

Nora watched DeWitt's eyes as he stared at Edwards in the rear-view mirror. Clearly she and Charlie May were in trouble. This was no joyride. But all her instincts once again confirmed that their best hope was the mutual contempt that Jason DeWitt and Lester Edwards held for each other.

Charlie May responded to Nora's subtle elbow in the ribs. She was equally aware of their predicament and of the dynamic between DeWitt and Edwards. Charlie May knew DeWitt to be a condescending prick. No time to waste.

She leaned forward to address Edwards. "What *is* he paying you? You know he's worth billions?"

DeWitt didn't wait for Edwards to answer. "Charlie May, shut that squealing hole of yours!"

Charlie May feigned shock. "DeWitt, with your silver-spoon pedigree! Certainly your mommy taught you to have better manners. And to be kind to the servants."

Nora could feel Edwards stiffen. Charlie May had hit a mark. Nora gave her an encouraging squeeze of the hand.

"And what about you, Jason?" Charlie May continued. "You think Edwards here is going to be content with the chump change you're giving him, when you and your friends are going to be raking in zillions?"

"And you have to know, DeWitt," Nora jumped in, "he'll be blackmailing you for the rest of your miserable life."

"BOTH OF YOU BITCHES, SHUT UP!" DeWitt was spitting fury, with saliva splattering the dashboard.

Nora and Charlie May exchanged furtive glances. The car went silent, but only for a moment.

"Edwards, DeWitt's no fool," Nora started again. "Just like he has the plan for us, I'm sure he's got something cooked up for you too."

Charlie May laughed sinisterly. "THAT you can take to the bank … the money he's paying you, not so much."

To their disappointment, DeWitt's response was matter of fact. "There's enough money for everyone. You don't have to worry about Edwards, ladies, he's getting what he asked for, and then some, as long as he completes his work."

Nora could feel Edwards relax some. *Damn,* she thought. But still, she and Charlie May had shown they could rattle DeWitt's cage and Edwards' too. There was more where that came from.

∞

Traffic had been stop-start, stop-start, ever since DeWitt turned north onto the West Side Highway. They were heading toward the Bronx. "Why are there so many goddamn people in this city?" DeWitt fumed.

He glanced quickly at his watch. He had to be out of New York well before 5:55. It was cutting it close. *Timmy Doyle better be waiting when we get there!* DeWitt thought and considered the order of things: *Doyle does the job, then we take the car and he can drive me back to Boston. That's the best plan. He probably knows every route....*

"The exit, DeWitt!" Edwards was shouting. "You idiot! Get over to the right!"

Horns honking, DeWitt veered right, cutting off more than one car as they made their way across lanes to reach the exit.

"Jesus, DeWitt!" Edwards muttered. "If there's ever a next time...."

DeWitt interrupted. "There won't be."

Nora said a silent prayer. *Keep it up, you two. Keep it up....*

From the signage they were in the Bronx. Now Nora and Charlie May felt less need to rile their adversaries, who were doing a great job on their own. Rather, the two women were focused on how they might escape and how to communicate the ideas they had to each other. They both knew the moment of truth would come when they stopped.

And then they did. DeWitt pulled in front of a small office building, burrowed into an isolated side street away from traffic. The windows appeared dark.

The sky was getting dark too. "Looks like it might rain, ladies," DeWitt announced. "You'd better go inside before the storm hits. Edwards, you show them the way."

Edwards jumped out, herding Charlie May and Nora out of the back seat.

DeWitt made another check of the time. It was almost five o'clock. The trip had taken nearly two hours from midtown. He was exhausted. But he was here. And it was almost over.... except that asshole Edwards was just standing on the sidewalk with the women...!

"Where's the key I gave you, Edwards?" DeWitt commanded. "Use it!"

Retrieving the key from his coat pocket, Edwards threw it at DeWitt. "Here! You do it! I'm busy! Can't you see?" With no one on the sidewalk, Edwards felt free to wave his gun, making sure it was clear he had the upper hand.

Why had DeWitt given Edwards the key? Nora exchanged a quick glance with Charlie May, willing her to read Nora's mind. *Was the original plan for Edwards to do this alone? Was it a sign DeWitt had set up Edwards?* Both were on the alert for a chance to escape.

"I own this building," DeWitt explained as he unlocked the main door. They entered a small lobby, with a single elevator. The building appeared to be completely empty.

Nora looked around, registering the eeriness of the place. "What did you use this for?" she asked.

"You'll see," DeWitt replied, moving ahead of the others. He pushed the *up* button and waited for the elevator to slowly ascend from the basement.

Edwards prodded both women forward. "Hurry it up!" he demanded.

Charlie May turned to face him. "Watch it, asshole…!"

"And what are you going to do about it…?" smirked Edwards.

"Knock it off and get inside," DeWitt grumbled. *Let's get this over with!*

They all got into the elevator, Charlie May and Edwards continuing to face off. Nora aimed to keep her reporter's persona and her wits sharp. Somehow she'd survive this, she vowed. *Victim* was not an identity she wished to take on.

DeWitt pressed the button for 5. The fifth floor housed a series of test labs, set up for experiments away from prying eyes at his main lab complex in Boston. It was deserted, no longer needed for what it was originally intended.

Now DeWitt had something else in mind.

∞

"They've stopped," Will reported, his eyes glued to his phone. "They're in the Bronx."

"Unless DeWitt woke up and disposed of Nora's cell," Izzy reminded them. "Why don't you call your brother and have him alert his detective friend?"

"No time for that! Nora needs us now!" Will answered. By the time he explained everything, it might be too late. And besides … "If the cops get there before we do, Izzy,…. I don't want DeWitt to be forced to react…."

"Step on it, Lucy," Izzy urged, understanding all of Will's worries.

"Heavy traffic, but I'm on it!" Lucy confirmed. "I'll take the exit up ahead."

Chapter 48

DeWitt, Edwards, Nora & Charlie May; Will, Izzy & Lucy

Will was ready to explode with anxiety. Lucy had gotten off the highway too soon and was now somewhere on the Grand Concourse, the Bronx's famous thoroughfare, inspired, it was said, by the Champs-Élysées in Paris.

"They've definitely stopped!" Will announced, his eyes still glued to his cell. "Nothing's changed so they've arrived to wherever it is that arrogant asshole, DeWitt's was going. That is unless he's tossed the phones."

"Give me the address and I'll punch it into my GPS!" Lucy was eager to make up the time lost after she took the wrong exit. And then … "shit, that's about twenty minutes away!" she exclaimed when the location and recommended route came up.

"Just do your best, Lucy!" Izzy said. Shifting his body, he gave Will a reassuring pat on the arm. "Have faith, Will, have faith. We are going to get there."

But the stakes were so high….

∞

The elevator doors opened to the fifth floor lab offices. There was a receptionist's desk, long unattended. There were two large windows in the reception area. A long hallway extended forward, with a few closed doors on either side.

"That room there, Edwards. To the left, open the door!" DeWitt commanded.

Lester Edwards was getting tired of DeWitt barking out orders. Two days ago he thought he had DeWitt in the palm of his hand. Now here he was, with DeWitt treating him like a piece of shit.

And what Martin and Maddison had said in the car was banging around in his brain. They were probably right. DeWitt had to have a plan to double cross him, cheat him out of his money — or worse.

But Edwards had the gun and, as long as he did, he was in control of the situation. He'd finished the job, tidy up DeWitt's problem women and — once he had his money — take care of DeWitt too. How he wasn't sure yet. That DeWitt had been forced to come with them to the Bronx had given Edwards more options. He could blackmail DeWitt … or reserve a bullet or two for the son of a bitch. It would depend on how the next few minutes went.

As Edwards opened the door, DeWitt stepped forward, turning on the lights. Charlie May followed, but Nora resisted. Edwards jabbed the gun into Nora's ribs, driving her into the room and locking the door behind them.

"Hey asshole, that hurt!" Nora yelled, rubbing her side.

Charlie May went to her and asked, "Are you all right?" Then, to Dewitt, "You're pathetic. You've always found some chump to do your dirty work!"

"That's the smart way, Maddison!" DeWitt laughed.

"I hope you're listening, Edwards. DeWitt agrees, you're his chump or should I say chimp?" Charlie May responded.

"Never mind about that," DeWitt answered. "Edwards knows where his bread is buttered, as they say." Then, motioning toward some dusty office chairs, "Just make yourselves comfortable, ladies."

As Charlie May and Nora complied, DeWitt looked again at his watch. It was five-thirty. Less than a half hour before the grid would go down.

A quiet settled over the room. Nora and Charlie May were sitting side by side, both watching carefully, whispering.

Charlie May broke the silence. "What are you going to do with us?" she demanded.

DeWitt took his time answering. Then, with a grin, "Let's just say it's for me to know and you to find out!"

In the pause before DeWitt spoke, Nora watched Edwards. He had been strangely aloof for a while. *What was he calculating?* Nora wondered.

Then it hit her. He was deciding when to kill them. And he was probably waiting for the blackout, for the confusion that was sure to reign.

Terrified as she felt, *it was time to do something!*

"It's obvious, Charlie May!" Nora responded. "DeWitt's tying up loose ends. You and I — and Edwards — we're all loose ends."

Charlie May was no fool. She recognized the odds against them and what Nora was trying to do.

"Absolutely, you're so right, Nora! Listening Edwards? We're all in the same boat. Nora, you and me. You're his pawn! Once you do his dirty work, I'm sure he's got something cooked up for you, too. You'll never see the money he's promised you."

"SHUT UP, YOU BITCHES!" DeWitt exploded. "I've had enough of your SHIT!"

He didn't bother to look at the time again. It was close enough. Martin was right. He was tying up all the loose ends.

"EDWARDS!" DeWitt commanded. "You want your money? TAKE CARE OF THIS NOW!" DeWitt turned toward the door, prepared to leave. He wanted no part of what was to come next.

Edwards watched DeWitt. *That slimy bastard. Martin-Davenport and Maddison called it. No way I'm getting my money!*

"Hold it, DeWitt!"

Edwards felt humiliated. He'd been out-schemed. *Do DeWitt's dirty work, and then he gets off scot-free? No way!*

"You're not going anywhere."

For the first time since Bryant Park, Lester Edwards turned the gun from Nora and Charlie May to DeWitt.

"There's a black sedan!" Izzy shouted.

It was in front of the address they were looking for.

Lucy pulled up and parked a distance away from the building. They couldn't risk being too obvious. Together they debated their next move.

"They must be in there," Izzy said. "There's a light on the top floor. The rest of the building is dark."

"Top floor, okay, let's go!" Will was opening the car door.

"Wait, Will! How are we going to get inside?" Izzy asked. "Break a window?"

"I don't know! Come on!" Will urged. "We've gotta find a way in!"

"Will, WAIT!" Izzy demanded. "I know you want to get to Nora. But we've got to take a minute to think this through."

"Should we just call the police?" Lucy asked.

"No time for that. We can't find a way in from here. Hell, I'm going to start by trying the door!" Will had waited long enough.

"Edwards, you ass! Get that gun off me or you won't see a dime!"

For all his brilliance, DeWitt seemed not to recognize the power of the gun pointed at his chest. Ignoring Edwards, he continued toward the door.

"I SAID STOP!" Edwards screamed, racing toward DeWitt to block his path. To Edwards' surprise, DeWitt fought back, reaching for the gun. Seconds later they were in a life-and-death struggle on the floor.

Nora and Charlie May saw their chance. Nora reached the door first and pulled. The lock was stuck!

Edwards had freed himself from DeWitt and was attempting to stand. "Charlie May!" Nora screamed.

Looking around frantically, Charlie May picked up a small metal chair and heaved it at Edwards. It hit hard, enough to make him stumble.

Still on the floor, DeWitt grabbed at Edwards' leg. Edwards responded with a sharp kick that made DeWitt wince in pain.

The distraction gave Nora the time she needed to free the stubborn door lock. With Charlie May beside her now, Nora opened the door, pulled Charlie May through and slammed the door behind them.

"Not the elevator. Find the stairs!" Nora directed.

Around the corner they ran, expecting to hear footsteps behind them. But nothing.

They scrambled down the stairs: fourth floor, third floor.

"Come on!" Nora whispered. "We've got to hurry!"

When they reached the second floor, they froze. There before them, climbing up the stairs, was another man! He wore a long beard, baseball cap and dark glasses.

Nora and Charlie May could feel each other's terror. Who was this man and what would he do? Then gunfire rang out from above… one shot … two. The man ran past them up the stairs.

Not wasting another moment, Nora and Charlie May raced down the remaining flights of stairs. As they reached the door to the lobby, Nora stayed Charlie May's hand. "Listen!" Nora whispered.

There were light footsteps. Someone was walking in the lobby. Then a voice, speaking so quietly… and yet ….

Will! Nora pulled open the door and was in Will's embrace in practically the same instant.

"Thank God!" Will repeated as he held Nora close.

"We've got to get out of here! They're upstairs!" Nora gasped, still catching her breath.

Izzy was already beside Charlie May, who was limping and winded.

Nora was still on high alert. "Did you hear the shots? They've got a gun! On the fifth floor! That's where we were!"

"Come on!" Will led the way out of the building. "Let's get out of here. No telling what's happened. They could be coming down after us."

Lucy ran ahead to get the car. As soon as she pulled up the foursome piled in and Lucy stepped on the gas. Will hit Ken's number on his cell.

"Ken!" Will's voice was quivering.

"Will! What's going on? Where are you? Something's happened here…," Ken sputtered.

"Call Cooper!" Will yelled into the phone.

The line went dead.

"Dammit!" Will shouted. "MY PHONE!"

They all looked around to see buildings going dark.

"Blackout … it's hit … probably cell towers knocked out by DeWitt's blackout," said Charlie May, exhausted.

Once again, in the back seat, Nora was in the middle. She held Charlie May's hand for reassurance as she clung to Will.

Nora felt traumatized but aware as well. Somehow she and Charlie May had survived. *But what was next?* Edwards' video of Will was out there somewhere. *What had happened to Edwards? Who else might have it? And if it was released, what might happen to Will? To both of them?*

Chapter 49

Timmy Doyle, Lester Edwards & Jason DeWitt

Timmy Doyle emerged from the stairwell on the fifth floor. The hall was dark, the lights off. He moved stealthily, uncertain what he would find, ready for anything.

He had arrived early, around four o'clock, and hidden outside. About five he'd observed DeWitt and Edwards herding two women into the building. Doyle had not expected to see DeWitt. Obviously something had gone wrong.

He decided to wait for DeWitt to reappear and leave the building before taking any action. But a half hour went by, and then another. After a while a car pulled up and parked a distance away.

When Doyle saw three people get out of the car, approach the building and try to get inside, it was time to act. He marked the trio as civilians. They were certainly not acting like undercover cops.

Regardless, he had a job to do and intended to do it. Doyle made his way into the building and slipped inside the stairwell. When he met the two women coming down, he was relieved. Whatever DeWitt or Edwards had done to each other, the women were unharmed. Doyle's disguise guaranteed they'd never know who he was. Then gunshots and he took off, bolting up the stairs.

When DeWitt had first arrived he watched and waited outside the building and noticed the lights on the fifth floor turned on. And now knew which floor to get out.

He stopped and looked out the windows of the reception area. He was watching the women and their rescuers get inside their car. Perhaps a minute passed and the car pulled out and flew down the street.

That meant only Lester Edwards and Jason DeWitt were still inside the building. Doyle was glad the women got away, but they were now free to summon the police. He needed to act fast....

Then another gunshot rang out from down the hallway. Somebody was still alive. But who?

Doyle gripped his gun and moved in the direction of the sound. He cautiously opened the door.

The room was only faintly lit from outside. Even so, Doyle could easily identify Lester Edwards kneeling over Jason DeWitt.

Blood was soaking DeWitt's starched white shirt. A pool of blood was spreading out from underneath him. Edwards was shaking DeWitt, trying to revive him. "I want my money, you bastard! You better not die on me!"

"He looks dead to me." Doyle was matter of fact.

Edwards reached for the gun next to him on the floor.

"Nope, I wouldn't do that if I were you," Doyle stated.

Edwards' hand hovered over the gun.

"You a cop?" Edwards asked.

"Get up and move over there."

"It was self-defense," Edwards offered, already playing the angles.

"Makes no difference to me." Doyle's voice was quiet and steady.

"You're not a cop," Edwards confirmed.

"No, I'm not."

"Not undercover?" Edwards was still trying to make sense of the disguise.

"I said I'm not a cop."

"You following DeWitt?"

"I was following both of you and the two women you brought here."

"They get away?" Edwards asked. He was getting right to the point, trying to figure out who this was, clearly sensing his own life was on the line.

"I wouldn't worry about them." Doyle wasn't about to give Edwards any information.

"Now what?" Edwards asked and then added his advice. "I think we should get out of here, before the cops come."

"No, not until you clean up this mess."

"What do you mean?" Edwards hadn't expected that response.

"You're gonna help me move him."

"Move him where?"

"You'll see. One step at a time."

"Well, I'd just like to know where I'm going."

"Then turn on the lights."

Edwards paused. *Did this guy not know? Who was he?*

"No lights in the whole goddamn city. Grid explosion," Edwards explained. "It was DeWitt's plan. You didn't know?"

Strong knew DeWitt was up to something, Doyle recalled. So it was this — a blackout. There would be chaos in the city now. Timing was everything. He'd use the confusion to his advantage.

Can't leave DeWitt's body here. Those two women and the three they were with all know about this building.... No, DeWitt has to be dumped in the Hudson, Doyle decided.

Edwards eyed Doyle, still trying to figure him out. *Could this guy be reasoned with?*

Doyle caught the look and pointed his gun at Edwards' head. He still commanded the room.

"Do as I tell you, Edwards, and I might let you slink back into the woodwork. Cross me and I'll make sure the police know exactly where to find you — maybe alive. Maybe not."

"You know my name! How?"

"I do, *Lester*. I was instructed by DeWitt to get rid of you. Then I had a second job to do later tonight — but, change of plans."

Edwards caught on fast. "I get it! You were going to kill DeWitt. That's why you don't care he's dead. I did your work for you."

"You know for a man in your position, you're doing a lot of talking. In fact, too much."

But Edwards was on a roll though. "I see now! You work for … what the hell is his name? That's right, Strong … Victor Strong! I heard DeWitt arguing with Strong over the phone. Well played. But why? I mean, DeWitt's a prick and all … but…?"

Because DeWitt had outlived his usefulness, thought Doyle. *He was getting more reckless with each passing day, Strong explained.*

"Forget the name Victor Strong, like pronto. Got that, Edwards?"

"And if I don't?"

"Lots of things can happen." Doyle held out his hands. "See," he pointed to his gloves. Then he picked up Edwards' gun and held it by the barrel.

"Very sloppy," Doyle scolded. "Do a job like this, even if it's your gun, you wear gloves."

Now Doyle slipped Edwards' gun into the deep pocket of his coat. "If you don't cooperate, I always have this little item, and it can show up at police headquarters at a moment's notice. Or, you never know, it might just go off."

Edwards prided himself on being tough, but he was also smart enough to recognize someone who was tougher. Go along. It was his best chance for survival.

How do you suggest we get DeWitt's body out of here?" Edwards asked.

"Find something to wrap it in. Leave the rest to me."

Edwards glanced around the room. "There's nothing here."

"Look for something!" Doyle commanded.

"I DID! I don't see anything!" Then, a sudden brainstorm. "But hey, I'll tell you where to take DeWitt!" Edwards offered. "Will Davenport's office."

"Who's that?" asked Doyle. "And why there?

"DeWitt pinned this whole grid explosion on Davenport. Will Davenport, you know — he's a scientist. His wife — younger of the two women — a reporter. They have a solid motive to kill DeWitt. He ruined Davenport's reputation as a scientist and set them both up big time with this blackout. I managed the whole affair. Doctored an incriminating tape of Davenport. DeWitt sent it to EVERYBODY — newspapers, TV."

Doyle listened, latching on to one detail. "You were going to kill the reporter? And the other woman! How do you kill a woman, Edwards? You make me sick."

Edwards thought about his gun in this crazy man's pocket. If only he could get to it, to protect himself. Instead, he had to talk fast.

"Hey, it wasn't in the plan until today. I wasn't gonna do it! That's why I fought with DeWitt!"

"Uh-huh," Doyle responded, skeptical.

"Look, it's true! And I don't know what Strong told you to do with DeWitt. But DeWitt was Strong's partner. It's not a stretch to think that Strong could take some heat, where Davenport's already in the crosshairs. It's a good plan and will ensure that Strong and you — *we* all stay out of it. And," Edwards couldn't help himself, thinking of the bonus money he'd lost now that DeWitt was gone, "I'm sure Strong would show his *appreciation* to me, right?"

Doyle offered no response, though the argument was making sense. He knew Edwards had been a handler for DeWitt. He also surmised that Edwards was deeply motivated by money or why else would he bring it up now. Not a bad way to keep Edwards in line. String him along.

Granted, planting DeWitt in Davenport's office would take some doing, Doyle recognized. But it was worth it to keep the heat off Strong.

"OK, so where do we take DeWitt?"

"There's an office Davenport uses," Edwards explained. "Uptown, at the big university. I've tracked him — just part of my work in following the reporter wife. Security's a joke in that place, especially with what's going on now with the lights out! In and out, no problem."

Doyle listened, his special-ops experience weighing the plan. "I like it," he confirmed. "No mistakes," Doyle paused, "and I'm sure Mr. Strong will show his appreciation. He's a very fair man."

"I just remembered…. I think there's a rug in the reception area," Edwards added, solidifying what he considered a deal. "Wrap up DeWitt like a sausage!" he laughed.

"Get it," Doyle ordered. "It's time to leave."

Chapter 50

Will, Nora, Charlie May, Izzy & Lucy

"Lucy, watch it! It looks like all of the traffic lights are out!" Izzy barked.

"I've got eyes, Iz! I think I can see that!" Lucy barked back.

The gravity of the situation had them all on edge. They had made their getaway from the building at high speed, but it was quickly clear that Lucy had to slow down. Most drivers were being careful — but not all, like the guy who'd gone barreling through the intersection in front of Lucy.

They were en route back to Manhattan, trying to choose side streets that might have the least traffic.

In the back seat, Will was thinking things through. He wanted to meet Ken and then Cooper to explain everything that had happened. But it would be dark soon and with the blackout Ken could be stuck anywhere — the office or even a subway, trying to get home. Besides going through the city now would be pure madness, even if they could somehow zigzag their way there.

"Lucy, you should turn around. We can't go back to the city. Head up to Westchester…."

Will's statement roused Nora. She'd been catching her breath, knowing she had to tell Will about the video but dreading it. She couldn't wait any longer.

"No, we definitely can't go to the city!" Nora agreed. Then, addressing Will, "But we can't go home either. That's the first place they'll look for us, so that's out!"

"What do you mean?" Will asked, confused, looking from Nora to Charlie May. "DeWitt and Edwards can't touch us now. The best thing to do is contact Ken as soon as we can. He'll get us in touch with his friend, Detective Cooper, NYPD. You two were kidnapped! Case closed. No, we'll go home. Lucy… "

"Will, I'm telling you: NO! We can't GO HOME!" Nora interrupted, her voice emphatic.

Lucy suddenly stopped, then pulled the car over to one side of street they were on. "OK! I've had enough of this. I'm not moving until we decide what we're doing and where we're going! And then….."

Izzy discreetly reached out his hand and tapped Lucy's arm, signaling her to be quiet. Nora's tension suggested that there was something worse about this already bad situation.

Charlie May had briefly seen the video of Will in Bryant Park. But the events that followed pushed it into the background. Now she too was sorting out the risk. "It looks like DeWitt was telling the truth about the power grid going down. There's no telling what's coming next."

Turning to Charlie May, not yet able to face her husband, Nora eased into the explanation she knew she could no longer avoid. "DeWitt is certain to put the blame on Will — probably me too."

"Look at me, Nora." Will's voice was perplexed, his brows furrowed with concern. "What on earth are you talking about? How are *we* to blame? Does this have to do with crazy Grace?"

Squeezing his hand, praying for courage, Nora took a deep breath. "Edwards doctored a video of our meeting with Grace that implicates us in her plot. It shows us egging her on, actually."

"What do you mean he 'doctored' a video?" Will demanded.

"He made a highly edited video that manipulates your words and makes it sound like you are glorifying eco-terrorism and encouraging Grace to implement an agreed-upon plan." Nora surprised herself at how succinct she sounded explaining this horrifying predicament.

"You mean all my words of caution got twisted? And it's on video?" Will's face registered alarm as the consequences unfolded before him. "Tell me this isn't happening! We're screwed… beyond screwed. After the hits I've taken, who's going to believe my story of what happened?"

Nora could only nod. Yes, everything Will was saying was true. And then, the question she was dreading.

"When did you find out about this video?" Disbelief was morphing into anger.

"Will, please. Just give me a minute and I'll explain everything. You won't like it," Nora acknowledged, "but I had good reasons."

Izzy had been sitting in silence. But now he sensed the situation was about to go into overdrive. Trying to diffuse the charged atmosphere, a somber Izzy turned and addressed Will directly. "There'll be time enough for that. We've all been through a lot. Let's first decide where the hell we can go to be safe. And then let's get the hell out of here."

The car fell silent now, as they all tried to grasp what had taken place — and what to do next.

Formidable Charlie May made the decision and took the lead. "New Paltz. We'll go to my home in New Paltz. We'll figure out what happened and determine our next move. And Izzy, you get in the back seat," she commanded. "I'll get in the front with Lucy, so I can be navigator."

Lucy let out a sigh. "Great, a plan! Sounds good to me!" Then, still irrepressible, eyeing Izzy and hoping for a smile, she announced, "And — except for Charlie May — I don't want to hear anyone else telling me where to go and what to do!"

Chapter 51

Victor Strong; Levi Rhodes & Mercedes Woods

Victor Strong sat in his office, watching the accounts he had set up accumulate funds from transactions executed by the programming genius of Levi Rhodes. DeWitt's quantum computer was running like a charm.

And New York was in darkness and futures markets around the world were in turmoil. So DeWitt had planned an excellent distraction after all — exquisite really.

Strong had to give him credit for that. Though he didn't appreciate the bastard keeping the details a secret. That's what made DeWitt dangerous. He was like a loose cannon, fuse lit, rolling on the deck of a ship, ready to explode and take down all on board.

But now, by the time the dust settled, Victor Strong's clients would be billions of dollars wealthier, while his own accounts would swell handsomely. All he needed was confirmation that Timmy Doyle had dispatched DeWitt to the seven seas — via the Hudson River, East River, Bronx River, New York Harbor. Strong didn't care which and didn't want to know. He had asked for no details from Doyle and he knew Doyle would give none. He was secure knowing that Doyle had his back and would protect his interests to the max.

Strong thought again, as he often did, that the money to save Doyle's wife had been one of the best investments he ever made.

DeWitt's request for Doyle had given Strong the idea and opportunity to dispatch his loyal agent for his own purposes. DeWitt had thought himself so clever using Doyle to clean up whatever mess he had gotten himself into. Thinking he could keep it from Strong was not so clever. Doyle, ever faithful, reported the details back to Strong. His task was to get rid of the handler DeWitt was using in New York, a guy named Edwards, in an abandoned building that DeWitt owned in the Bronx. That was fine with Strong. This Edwards was sure to be a loose end. Another loose end — DeWitt.

Dispose of both DeWitt and Edwards, Strong had instructed, explaining the growing danger DeWitt was posing to him.

That he hadn't heard from Doyle worried Strong not a bit. Doyle was as steady as they come. DeWitt and Edwards would make excellent fall guys when the truth about the grid explosion came out. And, conveniently, neither would be able to tell his side of the story. Victor Strong was safe. Timmy Doyle was making sure of that.

Both Mercedes Woods, Strong's assistant, and Levi Rhodes were also at the office late tonight. Strong had asked each to stick around because of "uncertainties around the blackout in New York," as he explained.

"Uncertainties" was the word, Mercedes had been thinking all evening. Now, in conversation with Levi, she whispered in ever-more-hushed tones. It was as if she feared the walls had ears that were leaning in closer and closer to hear what she was sharing.

Mercedes kept an eye on Strong's office door as she spoke. This might be her only chance to talk to Levi. But she couldn't leave her desk and she couldn't wait any longer. Rhodes was the only one she trusted enough to tell.

Remembering past Wall Street scandals, she was not about to be the sacrificial lamb in this affair — if her speculations were right.

Mercedes had been suspicious of Strong and DeWitt's activities for some time. "I've been setting up hundreds of new accounts on the quantum computer," she told Levi.

"Nothing unusual about that, Mercedes," Levi assured her.

"Okay, but here's the thing. All of the accounts funnel into one offshore account. Under the name S.J. Harris Oil Reserves. That was a holding company Victor set up almost thirty years ago, when I first started working for him." Mercedes paused, looking directly at Levi. "It had been dormant ever since, that is until now."

Levi nodded, urging her to go on. He needed to know more.

"All those years ago, I once innocently asked Victor about it. I'd noticed the ledger sheets had some unusual postings," Mercedes explained. "I told him that I found an accounting anomaly. He told me not to worry, that he understood I was new to the business. That it was easy to be confused by complex business finances. He took the ledgers from me. As I was leaving his office, I saw him put the ledgers in his private safe."

Levi shrugged. "That's not a crime, Mercedes. If you'd found something illegal, don't you think he would have fired you?"

With a steely-eyed look, Mercedes continued. "You might not realize this about me, Levi, but over the years I've learned a thing or two from my perch outside Victor's office. His response to me that day made me determined to learn everything there is to know about business finance and accounting. And I did — in more depth than anybody here knows. I'm sure that Victor and DeWitt have been siphoning money from the other partners and clients."

Levi was still skeptical. "Come on, Mercedes, how do you know that?"

"Listen, you're a computer-math genius. Turns out I'm an accounting genius, and pretty damn good at snooping. Let's leave it at that."

"So if you've known about it all this time, why didn't you ever say anything?" Levi challenged her. "And since you obviously didn't, why all the concern now?"

Mercedes nodded. "I understand how this looks. And I've compromised big time," she confessed. "I chose to keep this job and the very nice money I make, including the whopping bonus Victor gives me from his personal account. And there are other reasons too why I've kept my mouth shut."

Levi understood the reference. It was a not-so-secret secret that Mercedes and Victor had been having an on-again, off-again affair for years. No doubt that was one reason why Mercedes had kept Victor's pilfering under wraps.

And recalling his own recent dark night of the soul, Levi was not in a position to act as judge and jury. "Mercedes, I have my own personal demons. I assume everybody does. But why the change now? What's going on?"

Mercedes gave Levi a smile, acknowledging his understanding. That was one of the reasons she came to him. It was a leap of faith on her part, but intuitively she felt Levi could help.

"Granted, I shouldn't have been, but I was snooping yesterday," she confessed again. "I listened when Victor was talking to Timmy Doyle."

"Yeah, the security chief."

"Doyle's more than that, Levi. Victor sent Doyle to New York today — and now there's been an explosion and a blackout."

Levi waved away the connection. "That proves nothing, Mercedes. Doyle in New York is probably a coincidence. I was there myself a few days ago. Means nothing."

"But Doyle was calling from Washington yesterday, and he and Victor were talking in some sort of code."

"Talking in code?"

"Well, not like Morse code, Levi. I wrote it down." Mercedes dug into her large leather handbag and pulled out a sheet of paper covered in words and phrases. With another quick check in the direction of Strong's office, she handed the paper to Levi.

He took a brief glimpse. "As the saying goes, looks like Greek to me."

"Look, Levi, I don't think there's anything funny about this," she responded coldly.

Again she eyed Strong's door for any sign of movement. Satisfied it was firmly closed, Mercedes began to read. "Doyle told Victor something like 'the sky over Washington is getting cloudy. It's going to rain.' Victor responded, 'The sun is out in Boston.' Then he asked a question. 'Is the storm coming up the coast?' Doyle answered, 'It looks that way.' Those two never talk about the weather!"

Not wanting to offend, Levi's voice was deadly serious. "I can't imagine they would. But what do you think they were talking about? Do you have an idea?"

"Let's just say I know Victor like a book. I know what makes him tick."

"Mercedes, I don't doubt you know Victor, but I don't know what you think is going on, or what you want me to do about it. Despite your caution, given he's right next door, I recommend we continue this another time."

Mercedes shook her head violently, her voice a whisper. "No, no, no. There isn't another time. The shit is hitting the fan as we speak! Consider this. DeWitt asked Victor to help him with a big withdrawal — two million. I know because, now and then, Victor has me listen in on their calls. He doesn't trust DeWitt. And who would? So DeWitt came in this morning and picked up a suitcase of cash."

Gesturing to Levi to move closer, she continued, "And there's something else. Yesterday, Victor told Doyle he was *needed* in New York. He didn't send Doyle there on vacation, Levi. With DeWitt going to New York hauling a suitcase of cash and Doyle, Victor's henchman, following him, and then the blackout…. Something big is happening! Now Victor's in his office, watching his computer, smiling away…."

Mercedes' face was filled with anguish. "Victor is behind something terrible. I know it!"

Levi nodded, feeling a kind of empathy with Mercedes, who clearly still had strong feelings for Strong. But Victor Strong had also helped to make Levi's career. It was upsetting to consider that Strong was involved in something criminal, and possibly deeply so.

At the same time, based on what Mercedes had heard and observed, Levi recognized that he couldn't just dismiss her suspicions. Levi's own involvement with the quantum computer could implicate him, although indirectly. But if DeWitt was using it for something criminal … and Strong knew….

For now, Levi wanted to urge calm. "Yes, it's all very troubling, Mercedes, but none of it proves anything. Let's keep our eyes open. Keep each other posted."

Mercedes laughed bitterly. "Oh, Levi, this is beyond troubling, I fear. These two have done things in the past, shady things. They're in the shadows again, and this time I think it's deadly serious. Someone is going down. And it's not going to be me — and for your sake, I hope it won't be you either."

Chapter 52

Will, Nora, Charlie May, Izzy & Lucy

It was an excruciating drive to Charlie May's farm in New Paltz. What normally would have taken less than two hours from the Bronx took nearly four. By the time they arrived, they were all exhausted. The worries about what was happening, who had the video of Will and Nora, and how and when it might be released, added to the tension of the ride. Reception on the radio was spotty and often garbled. It was impossible to make sense of anything they heard.

Once they arrived in New Paltz, Charlie May, the gracious host, helped them all feel at home. The blackout had spread far beyond New York City, but with its own generator, her home had all the electricity they needed.

Now they could get the television news reports, which were a series of frenzied rumors and wild speculations and assumptions from talking heads. What really happened was beyond anyone's grasp. All sorts of theories abounded, from a terrorist attack to hackers, and even a major grid malfunction. So far no one had come forward to take credit for the explosion.

Listening to the reports, Nora was wrestling with more and more guilt. "I feel so responsible! Maybe I should have gone to the police from the start! But I couldn't get confirmation this was real. And if I'm going to be honest, I wanted to get DeWitt!"

"Maybe you should have, but as we all know, only hindsight is twenty-twenty," Charlie May responded in her forthright way. "And three things: one, if there's anybody who understands the desire 'to get' Jason DeWitt, it's me. Two, no question, you and Will were set up by DeWitt."

Charlie May paused, feeling protective of Nora given what the women had been through together.

"And what's the third thing?" Lucy piped up.

Charlie May laughed. Placing her arms around Nora's shoulders, she continued. "The third is that, Nora, you've been through enough for one day! Let's wait to hear what comes out, what the authorities know and reveal. And Will, maybe soon you can get through to your brother. Though I think for the moment even that call should wait until we know more."

Nora was grateful to Charlie May and returned her embrace. Certainly she'd been through the ringer today. Luckily, the video of Will had yet to appear in the news reports. Yet, tired as she was, Nora knew she had to continue the explanation that had begun in the car. She could feel Will was still bristling and she wanted him to understand.

So, with a glass of wine for fortification, she and Will made their way upstairs to the guest room where they were staying. Nora hoped they could have a quiet reasoned discussion, and not a big showdown.

She decided to start off in a conciliatory way. "You're right, Will, I should have let you know about the video from Reed … Edwards … whatever the hell his name is. I should have shown it to you the minute he sent it to me. But, honestly, honey, I was so shocked by it!"

Nora wanted to try to recreate the moment so she could clearly present why she did what she did. "Edwards stated that if I 'cooperated' he wouldn't reveal the video. My instinct told me he wanted it for some other purpose — that it was more about manipulating DeWitt than trying to get you."

However, Will's couldn't resist the frustration he felt from being cut out of the decision making. He'd had no control, then or now, over something that impacted him deeply. And that was the rub! "Nora, I get you're independent and competent. Those are qualities I love about you. I'm not asking you to change. But this involved me and I had a right to know! Yes, you should have told me — played the video for me — as soon as you got it!"

"I know, Will, I just admitted that! I don't know what else you want me to say!" Nora responded, her own frustrations were growing from her inability to make Will understand that she was doing it to protect him. Will's praise of her "qualities" felt hollow. She needed him to trust her, even if her decisions didn't turn out as expected.

"Look, I'm not saying my judgment is always the best…," Will began.

Nora could not resist a scoffing, "Yeah!" Considering his recent track record.

"OK!" Will conceded. "In fact, we know it's not. But you're not always right either!"

Nora felt her temper rising. "Maybe I'm not! But if YOU had used better judgment with Party Girl, YOU wouldn't have ended up so goddamn vulnerable! Ever since that moment I've felt the need to protect you … to protect US!"

Like a punch in the gut, Will felt the wind taken out of him. He immediately recognized the truth in Nora's statement. His voice completely changed. Reflective now, he grasped the enormous pressure Nora was dealing with — having to navigate though the churning waters of consequences that were not hers in the making. "You *are* right about that. Looks like my mistake just keeps rippling out. I'm so sorry, Nora, for what I've put you through."

His apology took her by surprise. It was the soothing balm she needed for her wounded and worried self. Nora put her arms around Will. "Thank you for saying that. You never know where the ripples will flow. But let's see if we can lead them to still waters, together."

Will reached out, enveloping Nora in a strong hug. After a long kiss, he spoke. "I don't know where I'd be without you. If there's a luckier man than one Will Davenport…"

Nora hugged him again and tears welled up in her eyes. Her happiness in that moment was both an emotional release she didn't expect, and the sudden realization that all that had happened between her and Will only strengthened their bond. "I'm so lucky to have you too," she responded.

Wiping the tears from Nora's face and with a gentle smile Will added, "We're lucky to have each other."

Chapter 53

Timmy Doyle & Lester Edwards

Timmy Doyle and Lester Edwards were carrying the body of Jason DeWitt, wrapped inside a dusty old rug, their destination almost at hand — Will's office at the university.

It was an arduous climb, up eleven floors. Edwards had not factored in no electricity, no elevator, when he suggested Davenport's office. Nor had he considered the darkness they encountered.

Doyle had no concerns about the pitch-black stairwell. He had night-vision goggles, which he always carried. *Habit,* he explained to Edwards. He'd used them to drive through the dark roads and streets on their stealth journey back to Manhattan, and now to lead them up the stairs.

They emerged from the stairwell into an equally dark hallway. And after meandering through multiple corridors, they stood before the locked door of Will's office.

Edwards proceeded to pick the lock. "Like I said, security is a joke," he smirked. "I've been here before, keeping tabs on Davenport for DeWitt. I can do this with my eyes closed!" Sure enough, they were inside the office in no time.

Edwards laughed loudly as they unrolled DeWitt's body. "And he was snug as a bug in a rug!"

"Shut up!" Doyle commanded. "You don't know who's around."

"It's pitch black. These college types are all curled up afraid of the dark," Edwards scoffed.

"Never mind them, Edwards. Get over here," Doyle whispered. "I want to set this near the window, so it breaks a lot of glass and creates a loud boom. I want it as dramatic as possible. Everybody needs to hear it and let the panic set in again."

They were setting the stage to cover their tracks with an additional stroke of genius, courtesy of Edwards.

Before they'd left the building in the Bronx, they'd scouted out the materials in DeWitt's idle lab. There were ample supplies available — apparently to get the lab up and running again at a moment's notice, should the occasion arise.

Consequently, it was easy to find what was needed to create a decent explosion. Edwards had bragged about his jack-of-all-trades knowledge of everything, including explosives. Doyle allowed him to ramble on until he'd had enough. Then he revealed his special-ops past, to remind Edwards once again that to challenge his authority would be a mistake.

Doyle set enough explosives to rock the office and break the windows, but not do further damage. His intent was to frighten, not to destroy. The evidence had to be found intact. Besides, there was no need for gratuitous violence. Use only the amount of force required to meet the objective. That was the guiding principle that had served him well over his years in the service and ever since.

"Now pick up the rug, Edwards," he directed. "We'll dump it someplace else."

"Why not just leave it? I don't want to carry this filthy thing again."

"Because I said so, that's why." In the pitch black, Lester Edwards felt only the brief stir of air before the gun butt smashed against his head.

After making his point, Doyle repeated his command. "I said pick it up. We don't want it to seem like the body was transported here." Doyle explained with a note of disdain for Edwards' lack of foresight.

This time Edwards complied without saying another word.

"I'm giving us a long fuse, Edwards," Doyle explained. "Plenty of time to get out. But you drag your ass and you won't make it," he warned.

Edwards only nodded.

"OK, move it." Timmy Doyle pointed in the direction of the stairwell that would take them out of the building.

Lester Edwards had no choice but to comply. He was no fool or wishful thinker. Strong's mystery henchman had been sent to kill DeWitt. And, he reasoned, most likely to kill him too. Edwards was sure his turn was coming.

If he stood a chance of escaping, he had to act swiftly and soon. His gut told him this guy would not kill him in the building. No, he'd do it where the body would not be easily found. Edwards had to watch for a moment on the way down the stairs. It might be his best, maybe his only, chance.

The stairs were cement, with a railing on each side. The only light was from a dim emergency sign at the top of each floor. But it was still almost impossible to see. Edwards went first, at Doyle's insistence. With his night-vision goggles, his gun in hand, and Edwards' gun still in his coat pocket, Doyle had all the advantages.

"Hey, pal, come on. Isn't it time you told me your name?" Edwards asked, trying to divert some of Doyle's intense focus.

"Not a chance." Doyle liked that Edwards would be in the dark about who killed him until the very end. And he wanted Edwards dead within the hour. It was time to wrap up and get back to Boston.

All Doyle needed was a place to dispose of Edwards, unheard and unseen. Get out of here, and get back to the car.

"Like I said before, Edwards, you talk too much. Just keep moving. I don't want to be here when the fireworks begin and this building is crawling with cops, and I don't think you do either, especially considering who put the bullet in DeWitt."

Without any doubt, Edwards knew he was a dead man. There were eleven floors to descend. He had eleven floors to make his move. *What and how and when?*

Edwards clung to the railing, struggling to carry the rug and keep his footing, while Doyle prodded him continually from behind. As they made their way ... ninth floor ... seventh ... fifth ... Edwards' rising fury at Doyle's insistent pokes and jabs, combined with the ferocity of his resolve to survive, were creating a combustible force just waiting to ignite.

At the top of the third floor, as Edwards was descending the first step, he felt the sharp slap of Doyle's hand atop his head. "Goddamn it, Edwards, you're as slow as molasses. What are you some kind of a pansy, afraid you might trip? NOW MOVE BEFORE I SEND YOU DOWN THESE STAIRS!"

To make his point, Doyle reached out his hand, poised to give Edwards a push.

Every instinct on the alert, every nerve on end, Edwards sensed that Doyle stood free at the top of the stairs. With his adrenaline surging, Edwards dropped the rug and turned with a cyclonic spin, grasping Doyle's hand and pulling with the explosive desperation of the last-ditch effort that it was.

In that moment, Timmy Doyle was fatefully caught off guard. He felt himself tumble forward, headfirst. He grabbed wildly for the railing but found only air. As his gun clattered down the stairs, he felt a jolting pain spike into his face and forehead as his night-vision goggles hit cement, and then the pain thrust on into the back of his head. Once, twice, three times, his head banged down the stairs. He gasped for air, unable to breath.

Losing his own balance, Edwards toppled after Doyle down the stairs. His body banged hard into Doyle, who cushioned Edwards' fall. It took mere seconds for both men to reach the landing below. In that final instant, Lester Edwards fell squarely on the head and shoulders of Timmy Doyle.

In the quiet and the dark, Edwards heard a groaning and assumed it to be Doyle. In another minute he realized they were his groans, coming from his body as it registered the fall. He rolled off Doyle, waiting for his response, certain Doyle would rise up at any instant, gun in hand, to shoot him.

Doyle was motionless. As Edwards' mind cleared, he inched closer. Doyle's head cocked at an unnatural angle. Peering still closer, Edwards saw a dark ooze filling Doyle's one exposed ear.

Broken neck. It had to be. *Damn, he'd done it. He'd killed the son of a bitch sent to kill him!*

Then reason took hold and reminded Edwards that he was still in considerable danger. There were now two dead bodies and an explosion about to ignite.

His gun, Edwards thought. He had to retrieve his gun. Fortunately, the adrenaline that had enabled him to fling Doyle down the stairs was still at Edwards' service. He lifted the dead weight of Doyle to reach his pockets and there it was, his gun — the evidence that would link him to DeWitt's murder. Doyle's gun had landed inches away. He stuffed that in his pockets too.

In his search, he found Doyle's wallet. *Why not?* Edwards thought. *It would take a second.* Riffling through, he found the driver license of his would-be killer. He could not resist taking the extra seconds he needed to make out the name.

In the heartbeat before he fled, Edwards whispered, "Nice to meet you, Timmy Doyle!"

Down to the second floor … the first … and now to find the outside door. There … the red exit light worked, even in a blackout.

Outside, another stroke of luck. He was in an alley behind the building. It was lined with dumpsters, into which Edwards wiped his fingerprints from Doyle's gun and wallet and quickly tossed, minus the cash. He'd count the money later.

As he debated in which direction to go, the explosion rang out. Immediately alarms were screaming from within the building.

Edwards could see shadows running toward him. *Security… Don't run.* He told himself… *You'll be suspicious. Hug close to the buildings.*

As he moved out toward the concourse that ran through the campus, Edwards saw a throng of frightened people. Many were young, probably students, running away from the explosion. Edwards slipped among the pack that was fleeing.

Got to get to the hotel. He still had the room. Edwards laughed at the realization that DeWitt had expected him to be dead by now.

"Sweet dreams, asshole," Edwards mouthed toward the commotion surrounding the scene of the explosion. He imagined DeWitt prone on the floor of Davenport's office. *Were they inside yet? Had they found DeWitt? How long before they would find Timmy Doyle?*

Edwards was walking briskly now, heading south. The prospect of walking seventy-some blocks to his hotel on 42nd Street was hardly appealing, but survival was still his guide and the options were few. No subways were running. No buses. Few taxis, and he didn't particularly want to be seen. Walking made the most sense.

Edwards was grateful for the dark city. He liked New York this way.

He could feel the impact of the fall the further he walked. His head throbbed and he felt pretty banged up, but he was certain nothing was broken.

Couldn't say the same for Doyle, with his neck askew, or DeWitt, with the holes in his chest. Well, they got it worse. And that had always been Edwards' motto. Make sure the other guy gets it worse.

Chapter 54

Will, Nora, Charlie May, Izzy & Lucy

Exhaustion had claimed both Nora and Will. They drifted off into a light sleep, arms wrapped around each other. Then, urgent knocking on their room door roused them both. It was Charlie May.

"Sorry. I thought you might be sleeping, but you'd better come see this. It's broken — the video is everywhere."

It was stunning how quickly, in the midst of the blackout, a case against Will was being built. There were excerpts of his testimony before Congress, his op-ed pieces, even his appearance on the Los Angeles station when he and Nora first met.

The caveat "alleged" was used a lot in terms of Will's connection to the blackout, but it did little to diminish the damning impact. There was Will predicting the dangers of solar flares and, most incriminating, the nation's lack of preparedness and protection for the grid. His comment that a disaster might be a needed wake-up call, when seen and heard in the context of the video, gave enormous weight to Will Davenport as mastermind of the blackout. And it was on an endless loop, echoing again and again: guilty, guilty, guilty.

Nora was also featured in the reports. A co-conspirator? Her involvement was under the microscope as well.

Will was flabbergasted by the video and how expertly Edwards had transformed a speech to Grace urging caution into one that was a call for destruction.

As they listened to the speculation and veiled accusations, Nora found herself glancing frequently at Charlie May, Izzy and Lucy, trying to use her reporter's eye to assess their reactions. Yes, they'd all grown close quickly. Yet, the truth was, they hardly knew her or Will. What if they had suspicions? Especially Charlie May. Might she be assessing the risk to her own reputation in sheltering them?

"We have to get a message to my brother." Will broke the silence. "Ken has to convince Cooper that we had nothing to do with the blackout!" At this point, Will thought reaching out to Ken was his only chance.

"How much do you think Ken heard when you called him from the car, as we were leaving DeWitt's building?" Nora asked. "You said, 'Call Cooper.'"

Will shook his head. "I heard Ken answer and say my name, so he knew it was me. But then the line cut out."

With another peek at Charlie May, Izzy and Lucy, who appeared sympathetic but remained silent, Nora pulled Will aside. "Call Ken, and then we have to head back to New York as soon as possible. We've got to tell the police what we know. We need to get to them before they come after us, and we lose complete control of the narrative. Once the grid is back up and running, the police will be under tremendous pressure to explain what happened and who's responsible. They'll come at us full throttle."

Will was not convinced. "Everything is going to be white hot. If we come walking in the door, with that video of me playing endlessly, they won't look any farther. Let's hold back and have Ken make the contact for us."

Nora's voice was an urgent whisper. "Look, Will, there's so much we don't know. I'm not sure how far the First Amendment protects me on this. And if I'm criminally liable for not reporting the plot, you definitely are. Plus, we don't know if DeWitt is dead or alive — if Edwards shot him or they killed each other."

"There've been no reports," Will noted.

"One thing is for sure. We have to get our side of the story out there. If DeWitt is still around, he'll be working hard to ensure that all signs point to us! I still think we've got to get in there, get a lawyer and attack this head on," Nora insisted. "Maybe we can get to Grace. I don't think Cooper's help, if we can even get it, will be enough."

Both Nora and Will were feeling time closing in on them. *What to do? What to do?* They read the same urgent question in each other's eyes.

Charlie May, Izzy and Lucy were watching the continuing news reports, all the while aware of Nora and Will's anxious discussion. Charlie May, indeed, was considering the risk they all faced now.

As was Izzy, who stood up suddenly, addressing Will and Nora. "I'm going to interrupt you two, because I want to make myself clear I don't believe any of this crap! I don't know how we're going to get you out of this, but what I do know is this: We have to take stock of our resources and pull together."

Charlie May was immediately beside him. "I concur. Now let's put our heads together. There's a solution here and we're going to find it."

From across the room, Lucy chimed in. "Count me in too!"

Nora looked at each with gratitude and relief. How foolish, she realized, to imagine that Charlie May, Izzy and Lucy might doubt them.

Now they all huddled together as Will and Nora shared their opposite thinking about what to do next. Charlie May listened, then offered her assessment. "Here's my take on the situation. Will, I think your insistence on calling Ken is a nonstarter at this instant. They'll trace your location immediately and the police will be here in no time. But, Nora, if you go back to the city, they'd arrest you — at least detain you — for sure. And before you go to the police, you need a savvy attorney at your side. You're too vulnerable. For now, I think you've got to stay out of sight."

Then, reacting to breaking news, Lucy gave them another reason to stay put. "Holy shit! … uh, sorry … an explosion! Listen…."

They all paused for the news report describing the explosion at the university … in the geology department building. Early reports traced it to an office of a professor on sabbatical.

"Oh my God, DeWitt *has* set you up!" Nora's voice was filled with fear.

As they continued to watch, an outdoor view of the blown-out window appeared. Harsh spotlights were illuminating the scene.

"That's the building," Will said quietly. "Jesus, I hope nobody was hurt. I wish they'd say." Then, looking at Charlie May, "I've got to call my brother!"

Charlie May shook her head. "No, Will, more than ever, you can't reveal where you are — not now. Let's see how this develops."

They watched into the wee hours of the morning. The reports at first offered some relief. The explosion was small, confined to the office. The main damage was the broken window.

But then the reports grew dire for Will and Nora. First came confirmation that the office was being used by the same scientist in the incriminating video. A university spokesperson, looking deeply uncomfortable, appeared at a police briefing to explain that it was understood Dr. Will Davenport was working on a book manuscript … that the university had no connection with him … that the temporary office had been arranged by Dr. Kenneth Davenport, a geology professor at the university, highly respected … longtime member of the faculty… and Will Davenport's brother.

"Ken's got to be feeling some heat, no doubt! And my parents…." Will could not finish the sentence.

Next, further reports revealed that Will had been using the office for less than a month and that he was often not there, raising questions about his real purpose. And why had he and Nora recently moved from California to New York? In a new frenzy of speculation, news anchors and their expert guests were creating any number of scenarios that put Will, and Nora by association, in the center of the grid explosion.

Then, around 3:30, came an unconfirmed report from a source inside the police department that a body had been found in the office.

Will felt immediate panic. "You don't think it could be Ken? What if he went looking for me?"

Nora shook her head. "Will, think about it. You're sure Ken heard your voice when you called around the time of the blackout. He knew you weren't on campus — that you had plans with Izzy. My guess is he's waiting to hear from you again. Probably at home." Nora reasoned. "Look, we've been manipulated from the start, and I'm worried this could be the grand finale of an elaborate setup. The body in your office is there by design."

"I'm afraid I agree." said Charlie May. "It could be Reed … Edwards … whoever he was. Or that man who ran by us in the stairwell…."

"Or DeWitt!" Nora shouted.

It didn't take long, about a half hour or so, for an identification of the body. There was a collective gasp from the group when Jason DeWitt's photo appeared on the screen.

"So that bastard got it!" Charlie May reacted. "Live by the sword, die by the sword!"

As much as she hated DeWitt, Nora felt only alarm. "Oh, Will, this is only going to sink us deeper!"

"Yeah, up next will be scenes of DeWitt blasting me in the media," he acknowledged in a weary voice.

Those clips appeared soon after, with the anchors and guests now speculating about motive. Had Jason DeWitt's criticism of Will Davenport ignited a feud that turned deadly? Everybody was weighing in on the possibilities.

"I've got to get to Ken!" Will insisted. "Find out what Cooper knows. I could send Ken an email."

"And it will become evidence," Charlie May stated. "They could take his computer. Your brother is certainly on their radar screen right now."

"I could take a message to him," Lucy offered.

"Excellent idea!" Charlie May confirmed.

Izzy had been silent until Lucy's offer. "No, I don't think so, Luce. Sorry, Will, but I don't want to see her mixed up in this."

"I think I already am, Iz. I did drive the 'getaway car'." Lucy had her say.

Charlie May stepped in again. "There are other ways we can do it. You don't have a company like mine in an industry like mine without employing specialists at making themselves invisible."

Then, addressing Will and Nora, "But let's talk about where you are. Okay, DeWitt is dead. Anything against you is circumstantial. He was shot. If they found the gun, no way your prints are on it. That's good. But your prints are in the office."

Exasperated, Will cut to the chase. "The bottom line is, how do we prove DeWitt set us up?"

"What about our phones?" Nora offered. "Edwards had mine. But DeWitt pocketed Charlie May's phone."

"My phone could still be on his body?" Charlie May offered." "If it is, I RECORDED THE MEETING IN BRYANT PARK!"

"Plus there could be texts between Edwards and DeWitt. Edwards had to send DeWitt the video he doctored someway," Nora added. "He texted it to me, so he could have texted it to Dewitt as well."

With that optimistic note, Will, Nora, Izzy and Lucy exchanged hopeful smiles.

Charlie May quickly made them all face facts. "Nora, the phone may be lost. Assuming Edwards killed DeWitt, he may have tossed it, smashed it. It could have been blown up in the explosion. Our phones could be anywhere."

Charlie May's sobering assessment sent a chill through the air. "But," she continued, "murderers make mistakes all the time. That's why prisons are full of them! The phone could still be on DeWitt. You two decide what you want to say and write it out. I'll alert Jennifer — she's my trusted go-between, as you know — and we'll get it to her and she'll get it to the right person. Probably better to go to both your brother's home and office, to be sure he gets it ASAP," she directed, completing the plan.

Nora looked at Will and shrugged. "I don't think we have a choice. We have to hope the police can find the phone. Though if we could also get to Grace that might help…. And if Edwards is caught…."

"Edwards may very well be dead too," said Charlie May, solemnly. "Maybe even your girl Grace. DeWitt pulled off closing down the grid. You can be sure he had sophisticated plans for that quantum computer of his. This thing isn't over yet!"

"Will, do you remember that photo of DeWitt, Senator Broderick and Victor Strong…," Nora began.

"Levi works for Strong," Izzy interrupted, surprised at the connection. "Levi's my brother, Charlie May."

"I know Strong," Charlie May replied, "and I've got some contacts in D.C. that might offer some insights on Broderick's connection. We have to look into every lead we can."

"I don't know anybody, but if you need an expert driver, I'm your woman!" Lucy exclaimed, giving them all a much-needed laugh.

"I think we've covered all the bases," concluded Charlie May. "And now, folks, I think it's time we all some got sleep. I can't speak for the rest of you, but I don't get kidnapped at gunpoint every day!"

A short time later, as Charlie May made the rounds, checking if anything was needed, she found Izzy inspecting a telescope set up by the balcony door of his guestroom.

"That was given to me by my father. It's been in our family for generations," Charlie May explained.

"It's in great shape. I couldn't resist taking a look through the lens."

"Maybe this will prompt you to take a second look," Charlie May smiled proudly. "It purportedly belonged to Isaac Newton."

"Newton! Seriously? And you keep it here, by the window, in a guestroom?"

"This room is not occupied very often. I like to come in on starry nights to use the telescope. To imagine looking at the world through, literally, the same lens as Isaac Newton."

Izzy gave the telescope a gentle pat. "I hope we can find some time to talk more about this. I think we've got some things in common, Charlie May — and not only the well-being of our friends, the Davenports."

Chapter 55

Lester Edwards

By the time Edwards reached the hotel, it had rigged enough power from its emergency generators for lighting, but there was only one elevator operational and it was going to the upper floors. Guests staying on the lower floors needed to use the stairs.

For once, Edwards didn't object to such inconvenience. After all, though battered, he felt himself a returning hero.

And now he was planning his next move. Get his money from the hotel safe and make his getaway.

First things first, he went straight to the front desk and the money.

"Sir, are you injured?" asked the concierge, squinting at Edwards to assess him more sharply.

Edwards considered the question, imagining splatters of DeWitt's dried blood on his clothing, the lump on his head from Doyle's gun, and the marks and bruises on his face from his plunge down the stairs.

For once, he could give an honest answer. "I'm okay. I just took a bad fall in the dark."

"If you're sure, sir. We can arrange to help you to a hospital, though you might have quite a wait. Limited service, you know. The blackout...."

Ironically, Edwards recalled Davenport's warning about how hospitals would be impacted. Of course that part he'd edited out. *The video ... what was happening?* he wondered. *Has it made its television debut?*

The concierge was still rattling on about the blackout....

"I want my briefcase from the safe," Edwards interrupted.

"That's what I was saying, sir. That if you have something in the safe, you should be able to retrieve it in the morning. We're sorry for the inconvenience, but it's the power source. We're working to bring it up ... electric locks...."

Under other circumstances, that news might have thrown Edwards into a tirade ... or panic. But after the events of the day, he took it in uncharacteristic stride.

"What time?" he asked. "You got a time when I can get it?"

"We're hoping by nine o'clock," answered the concierge. "That's what I've been told."

"Good enough," replied Edwards. "I'll be back then."

At last, safely in his room, Edwards took a shower and then stretched out on the soft bed. Thankfully, the pains in his head and aching body were subsiding some.

The hotel had enough power for the television to work. It was all news and all about the blackout. He watched, waiting for an update on the explosion at the university. When it came, there was no mention of a body, in office or stairwell — yet. Of course they'd found DeWitt. "Cops just haven't released it," he said aloud.

But no waiting for his video — there it was, again and again! Along with Will Davenport's history of "unorthodox" theories. The starlet scandal was getting plenty of mention too.

At about four in the morning, a breaking news alert delivered what he'd been hoping to hear. Edwards was half asleep at the time, but not for long: A body, found at the site of the university explosion, identified as Dr. Jason DeWitt, professor, wealthy Boston family, with a brief summary of how DeWitt had discredited Will Davenport and the promise of more details to come.

That part of his mission was accomplished. Police have their motive. "I'm almost there. Home free!" Edwards declared.

But where was "there"? Leaving the city was now his priority.

Of course! Edwards thought. *Right next door — Grand Central!* He could take a train north. Get a flight from Westchester Airport. Even better, Stewart Airport near Newburgh. There'd be fewer cops looking around, for sure.

Or he could get on an Amtrak train if he went to Poughkeepsie from Grand Central — make his way to *Boston.*

Whichever route he took, his next stop was a visit to Victor Strong to see what he could squeeze from DeWitt's accomplice.

Chapter 56

Will, Nora, Charlie May, Izzy & Lucy

First light slipped through the window in the bedroom where Izzy slept. From the growing brightness, he knew the sun would soon rise. He checked his watch. He'd barely slept two hours.

But he was hardly surprised, given the previous day's and night's events. Izzy was worried about how, or even if, Will and Nora could exonerate themselves. He suspected Charlie May was worried too. But he was determined to do all he could to help Will and Nora.

Then thoughts of his brief discussion with Charlie May came to mind and he glanced at the amazing telescope in the corner by the sliding glass door. *Isaac Newton's telescope, what are the odds?*

Sacrificing the possibility of more sleep to his impatient curiosity, he catapulted from the bed and went to inspect the telescope and this time to see if there were any morning stars to find.

He dared not move the precious Newtonian artifact and, instead, opened the glass door for a clearer view outside. Remembering Charlie May's words, he had the same sense of awe at staring through an instrument that might have been used by Newton to survey the *very* stars he was searching for.

As he looked through the lens, another astonishing thought occurred to him. Given Ethan Hawkins' tie to Newton, could one of Izzy's own ancestors have once gazed through it as well?

When they had time, Izzy was eager to hear how Charlie May's family had come by the telescope.

Will and Charlie May were already at the breakfast table when Izzy joined them. With the message to Ken safely dispatched, Nora was trying for a few more hours of sleep. She felt lousy, she told Will. No doubt it was all the anxiety from the horrific events of yesterday.

Lucy was also sleeping. The television was off. Charlie May had checked earlier and there was nothing new. Playing endlessly was the same recap of what was already known. They all needed a breather, she suggested.

Izzy saw the opportunity to introduce the topic of Newton. "Charlie May," he began, "I woke up with stars and the moon still glowing in the morning sky and had to took another look through your magnificent telescope."

Then, to Will, "It may have belonged to Isaac Newton."

"Newton? How amazing is that!" Will responded, feeling genuine excitement at the prospect. He was also grateful for any conversation that was not about his and Nora's precarious situation. "What's the Newton connection?" he asked.

"The telescope has been in my family for years — centuries, really. Based on family lore, the telescope was given by Newton to Jacob Fletcher. He's not a relative. It's an interesting story. Jacob's father was an alchemist who practiced with Newton. Will, you certainly know that history about Newton and his interest in alchemy…."

As Charlie May spoke, Izzy and Will exchanged stunned glances. Yet neither spoke, both needing a moment to process what Charlie May was actually telling them. The possibility seemed too extraordinary.

"Jacob's father … Daniel was his name … was also a friend of Ethan

Hawkins. His son, my ancestor, was Jeremiah Hawkins. Somehow the telescope ended up in America and with Jeremiah after he emigrated here. Why Jacob Fletcher, who also settled here from England, didn't keep it, I don't know. But its been in my family ever since — a remarkable gift from the past with a provenance that brings a smile to my face every time I think about it!"

Charlie May looked from Izzy to Will, trying to decipher the shock on their faces. "What is it?" she asked. "Do you know something I don't about the telescope?"

Izzy sat with his mouth open and eyes wide. Looking at him, Will was almost giddy. "Charlie May, it's not easy to strike Izzy Rhodes speechless, but you have!"

"Why? What is it?" Charlie May repeated, half smiling and waiting for an explanation to what had suddenly turned both Will and Izzy thunderstruck.

It was left to cosmologist Will Davenport to explain the inexplicable. "It appears that the stars have aligned in such a way that the Hawkins family descendants are about to take a wild ride into the sublime workings of the universe. Izzy is also related to a Hawkins — Benjamin, also a son of Ethan. Benjamin and Jeremiah were fraternal twins."

Will gave that a moment to sink in. Then he asked Charlie May, "Did you know about Benjamin?"

Lucy had entered the room in time to hear the revelation. "Oh my God, the two of you are related!" she squealed.

Charlie May, who also was rarely rendered speechless, stared at the group in awe.

"Just like Izzy, wordless," Lucy observed. "Maybe it's a family trait!"

Lucy's quip produced a hearty laugh from all. Given the drama of the previous twenty-four hours, this was exhilarating news that was lifting all their spirits.

"But how do you know this? How are you so sure?" Charlie May's curiosity was bursting.

"Where's your backpack, Izzy?" Will asked.

Since the lost-and-found of the diary and poem, Izzy took no chances. He carried them with him everywhere.

"I'll get it," Izzy replied. "It's up in the room."

Izzy faltered as he stood, sending Lucy to his side. Perhaps all the excitement was too much. "You okay, Iz? Let me run up and get your backpack," she urged.

"No, no" Izzy insisted. "Thanks Lucy, but I'm fine. I'll be right back."

In truth, Izzy needed a few minutes alone, to compose himself. It was the surprise that had him woozy. *How could this be?* That he and Charlie May found each other now and in such a way — was it simply happenstance, or was something greater at work?

He also thought about the brothers, Benjamin and Jeremiah, a family pulled apart, fractured, leaving their descendants unknown to each other. Yet here they were, Charlie May and himself, centuries later, discovering their ancestral connection. Then the image of Levi returning the poem appeared to Izzy. His brother had made an effort to reconcile. It suddenly occurred to Izzy that perhaps the discovery that he and Charlie May were family, was also a sign that maybe his relationship with Levi was not beyond repair. That even with the wide rift between them, he and Levi could begin down the road to bridge the gap.

The group soon moved from the kitchen to Charlie May's study, buzzing in speculation about Ethan, Benjamin and Jeremiah, about Isaac Newton and the Fletchers. As Izzy and Charlie May discussed their family history, and as they all considered the odds of the cousins meeting under such extraordinary circumstances, they echoed their astonishment again and again.

Charlie May glanced through the diary, eager to read every word.

She was particularly amazed by the dedication. To think that Newton had given Ethan Hawkins the diary — that Newton had taken such an interest in Ethan.

"How did you get this?" she asked Izzy, rubbing her hand lightly over the leather cover.

"My father and uncle dealt in artifacts and were keen investigators of our family history. And let's just say it was a dream of mine to find the diary," Izzy replied, smiling at his own oblique reference to his Colorado experience. That so much of what had transpired was set in motion by that dream, was still hard to comprehend.

Charlie May nodded. "We cared about family history too, certainly in a commercial way. I wonder if the Maddison stores had been in the East, rather than all in the Midwest, perhaps you might have heard the references to Jeremiah Hawkins in our advertising. We might have met before now."

Izzy shook his head. "Maybe. But there was so much I didn't know until I had the diary."

And he thought about the crystal and its secrets — the legacy still to be found. Now it was Charlie May's legacy too.

The television was on in the study, tuned to cable news, as Nora joined the group around ten. It was only a few hours of extra sleep, but she was definitely feeling better.

"What's all the excitement about?" she asked. "Have we heard from Ken? Was Edwards caught?"

Her disappointment was immediate when she learned the "big" news that Charlie May and Izzy were related. "That's amazing!" Nora smiled, working to conceal her true feelings. "Will, come with me while I get some coffee," she continued, her tone not giving him the option to decline.

"What about us? Any news?" Nora asked anxiously when they were alone. "What are you doing, Will? I know you've been on this diary quest with Izzy. But it can't take your attention now, not at this moment!"

Ever observant, Charlie May called out to announce her presence. "Hey, just checking if you've found the mugs." Then, stepping into the kitchen to join them, she held up the newspaper and pointed to a headline.

"'Noted Cosmologist and Journalist Wife Missing'," Charlie May read aloud. "You made the front page of *The Times*. And I predict someday you'll have this newspaper to show your grandkids," she declared.

Nora didn't share her optimism. "But what if DeWitt or Edwards *did* throw away the phones? Then proving our innocence will be almost impossible, and those grandkids you're talking about, puff!"

Charlie May was insistent. "There's nothing new on the television, Nora. Your messages were delivered to Ken's home and office. Hundred percent confirmed. And through Jennifer, I've put out some feelers in Washington, to find out who's nervous at DeWitt's demise. *We know* you're innocent. Trust me, it's just a matter of time. We never saw DeWitt toss our phones. And in all the confusion during our escape, and apparently what followed, *there is* a very good chance that my cell phone was still on him when they found his body. And I recorded everything."

Then, winking at Will, Charlie May gave Nora's hand a squeeze. "I know it's lousy timing, but *it is astounding* that Izzy and I are cousins. And the diary *is* an amazing find."

Taking his cue from Charlie May, and trying to strike a reassuring tone, Will gave Nora a hug saying, "Look, honey, we just have to sit tight. We've done what we can for the moment. Things are in motion. I agree with Charlie May. We have some good possibilities going for us. We have no option but to let them pan out."

Except that Will spoke too soon. A breathless Lucy announced the next development. "They found another body!"

"In the Bronx?"

"No, Nora, at the university."

"Same building?" asked Charlie May.

"Yeah, in the stairwell."

Now it was Will's turn with the sixty-four-thousand-dollar question. "Is there an ID on the body? Are they saying anything that's a clue?"

Lucy shook her head grimly. "Only that it's a man."

Charlie May looked squarely at Nora and Will. "It's not your brother, Will. It's either that other guy — or it's Edwards."

…beep…beep…beep. Will looked down at his phone.

Chapter 57

Lester Edwards

By ten o'clock the next morning, Edwards was finally in Grand Central, ready to make his escape. He was an hour behind schedule. He had expected to be gone by now, but the hotel safe had still not been "cracked," as promised by nine o'clock. *Clowns,* he'd scoffed.

Yet now, as Edwards walked through the terminal, his money from DeWitt was safely inside his duffel bag, along with a plastic laundry bag from the hotel stuffed with yesterday's stained clothing.

There was only limited service on the commuter lines, so Edwards had few choices. *Doesn't matter,* he thought. *I'll go anywhere. Just get me out of New York.*

He had to wait for the next train, but that was okay too. He still had some things to do.

Number one, get rid of the clothes. A trash bin in the men's room would work just fine.

Edwards had debated the risk if the clothing were found. But with all his aliases, he was sure there was no way to trace DNA back to him. And if they found DeWitt's blood — no big deal — Edwards would be long gone in an hour or so.

Making his way down to the lower level, taking the stairs — his head was throbbing again — Edwards entered the men's room and was pleased at what he found. *This should be a piece of cake. No one here except that homeless guy passed out in the corner.*

He stuffed the plastic bag in a near-empty receptacle. Even better to know the bag would soon be covered by layers of who knows what.

A quick glance in the mirror before he left shocked him. He looked like shit! He felt like shit too. The pounding in his head would not stop.

And perhaps it was his aching head that left him unfocused. Otherwise he might have noticed that the person he thought was sleeping was not, and through half-slit eyes, observed Edwards' deposit and watched him leave. Homeless, yes, but expert in street survival for sure. A rich man's garbage was a poor man's treasure.

What the hell is this? Blood? It wasn't the first time the homeless man had seen bloodstained clothing. It was that and way worse in Iraq. And now, back home in America, not great either.

There's blood everywhere. Something's not right here … gotta find Officer Johnston.

First mission accomplished, Edwards slowly climbed the stairs back to the upper level. Now there was a ringing in his ears too. *Shit! That fall was more than I thought. Need a place to sit…. Get some food in me… a cup of coffee… that will help steady things…I'll be all right….*

Then from the corner of his eye, he saw a cop. He was talking to someone, had something in his hands. And they were looking in his direction.

That homeless guy in the john. Shit!

Stay cool…. You know nothing…. It's that homeless piece of crap's word against yours.

But his head! What was ripping through his brain? *Shit! Shit! Shit!*

"Good morning." A voice was speaking to him … the cop.

Officer Thad Johnston was not taking anything for granted. Not today. Not since the blackout. Not with everyone and everything on high alert. "This man said he saw you throw these items in the trash."

"Really, officer?" Edwards managed to muster his most elegant voice. "Are you going to take this man's word over mine?"

"Tell me about these clothes, sir."

Edwards' eyes refused to focus and his ears refused to hear. Everything was a blur. It was the pain stabbing his brain.

"See, Johnston, he can't even answer you!" The homeless man was steadfast, relying on his friendship with the beat cop to be believed.

If I didn't feel so dizzy … if it wasn't so damn noisy in here…. I can't hear myself think…!

"I need to know your name," Johnston insisted.

"Sure… sure thing."

Edwards could feel the cop's suspicion. And the bum kept rambling on, "I know every coming and going in that bathroom!"

Edwards wanted to shut him up.

He felt trapped. *Get away…. Get away from the cop … the bum. How? Subway! Escape on the subway…. RUN!*

Malcolm Thornberry was turning the key to open The Great American Timepiece. Lucy had called to say she and Izzy were fine but not able to come in. Could Malcolm make it to Grand Central to open the shop, now that some of the electricity in Manhattan had been restored?

Malcolm was happy to have a good reason to leave his apartment. He set out on foot and reached Grand Central around ten-thirty, which he didn't think was too late, considering….

"POLICE, STOP!" The words came flying down the corridor.

Malcolm stopped and leaned into the corridor. *What was happening?*

"HOLD IT RIGHT THERE!"

He saw a man running toward him, his movements jerky, weaving from one side to the other. With the zigging and zagging, it was impossible for Malcolm to avoid him.

He felt a huge thud against his chest. And then he was on the floor, with the man on top of him. The guy tried to get up and was flailing his arms, but Malcolm held on to him for dear life.

"You're under arrest! Failing to obey an officer of the law!"

Edwards struggled to get away. But it was no use.

Officer Johnston and another Grand Central cop handcuffed Edwards, as a third officer helped Malcolm up.

"You okay, sir?" the cop asked. "Thank you for assisting."

Malcolm was pleased and embarrassed by the praise. He hoped Izzy and especially Lucy would believe his heroics.

"Good job, buddy!" The homeless man had come up next to Malcolm.

To Malcolm's surprise, the cops and the homeless man exchanged a salute.

In the capture of Lester Edwards, two people stood out. One was former Lieutenant Hank Rainy, once an American war hero, and a hero once again. The other was Malcolm Thornberry, watch repairman and now city hero.

The charges racked up for Edwards once a police search revealed his gun and the cash. And there were the clothes with the blood.

Later, after his arrest, technically for carrying a concealed weapon, Edwards wondered what might have happened if he'd never entered Grand Central Station. Might he have gotten away to parts unknown? Might he have blackmailed Victor Strong? That was where the big money was.

Clearly, he'd never know. Already detectives were badgering him about the cash. And it was only a matter of time before they linked his gun to the bullets inside DeWitt and the blood to DeWitt and Doyle.

But there were things Edwards knew — in fact, a lot of things. He knew who was behind the blackout. He could give the cops everything they needed to get to Grace and her group of crazies. The grid bombers could be known and arrested within hours.

And he knew all about Jason DeWitt and his dirty dealings. And he knew DeWitt was connected to Victor Strong and that big, big money had been their goal.

No need to worry. He had plenty of bargaining chips and the time was coming to cash them in. He'd admit it all — including how the video had been doctored, the bimbo kiss, all the ways that DeWitt had set up Will Davenport from the start.

It would be his gift to Nora Martin and her scientist husband. Edwards admired Martin. She had guts. Charlie May Maddison too.

Yep, time to get ahead of this rolling tsunami. *Time to make a deal. Talk and then walk — even if he had to pay with a few years first....*

Chapter 58

Nora, Will, Charlie May, Izzy & Lucy

For Nora, it was an exceedingly long and difficult day. Unlike the rest, she did not have the diary to distract her attention, though they all tried to draw her in. "Join us, Nora!" Izzy encouraged. "We could use your investigative skills."

But for Nora, the Hawkins' saga was impossible to consider when the saga of Will and Nora Davenport was so much in doubt. She watched the news endlessly, waiting for an update that would reveal the identity of the second body. When it finally came in the late afternoon, it offered one note of clarity: It wasn't Edwards. Rather, someone named Timothy Doyle was found in a back stairwell, and his wallet and a gun with his prints were found in dumpsters behind the campus building.

So Lester Edwards was still alive, as far as they knew. But where was he?

And what about her cell phone? And Charlie May's? What was Ken doing? And Cooper?

More than once she escaped outside to walk amongst Charlie May's apple trees. Nora wondered when the trees would flower this year, and when the apples would begin to grow. And what of the child she wanted to conceive? How could her life with Will and their desire for a family flower now? They were suspected of being terrorists, and worse, maybe murderers.

Nora wept freely on those walks, composing herself before she returned inside. Then she would try again to join the continuing conversation in the study, where the others were deeply immersed — transported even, back to England and New York and the Hudson Valley of the late sixteen hundreds.

After hours of constant discussions, their attention finally coalesced around the mysterious lost crystal.

"Do you know about the diamond stone?" Izzy asked Charlie May.

She nodded, then qualified what she knew. "My Grandfather Maddison told the 'Jeremiah' story, basically. There was a magic crystal found after a terrible storm in the roots of an upturned oak tree. It sounds like a movie, doesn't it?" Charlie May noted ironically.

"That discovery led to a series of tragedies," she continued. "And eventually Jeremiah came to New York on the same ship as the woman he would marry, Abigail. They had a store in lower Manhattan with Abigail's sister and her husband. I knew Jeremiah had a brother, Benjamin, but I didn't know what happened to him. My grandfather insisted that something terrible broke the family apart. But a lot of our history of Jeremiah and Abigail was oral. There was no diary like this."

Then, with a clear tinge of sadness, Charlie May asked, "What caused the rift? How could a stone be the reason, unless it was a real diamond? Is the answer in this diary?"

"It's all here, Charlie May," Izzy stated. "It's a saga of our ancestors and a mysteriously imbued crystal, which Ethan originally found and then threw away. It was Benjamin who discovered it the second time."

"And," Will added, "the crystal apparently held significant sway over all their lives, including Jeremiah's."

"What does the diary say about the crystal? Why was is it so special?" Lucy wondered aloud. In all these weeks, she realized, she'd never learned — or, had to admit, paid attention to — a lot of the details. "Was it worth a lot of money?"

"Let's have our resident scientist explain it," Izzy said, turning to Will's expertise.

Will eagerly detailed all he understood about the nature of the crystal and its vibrational power for those who could connect to it. Charlie May and Lucy were captivated.

"So for Jeremiah the crystal was dead," Will described. "Whereas, for Ethan and Benjamin, it was alive, infused with a force they could feel and discern. The way it's described in the diary, the stone could light up in their hands, and that connection allowed them to encounter their world in an uncommon way. The diary is quite detailed with the experiences of both Ethan and Benjamin," Will added. "Each of them describe vividly what they felt when holding the crystal — how it heightened their sense of sight and sound and sensation. And how the power of the crystal changed the way they interacted with the world. It was as if they could see beyond the veil of the ordinary."

Charlie May listened with Jeremiah in mind. "If it was an experience that Jeremiah couldn't and didn't share, I'm certain that would be enough to pull two siblings apart," she observed.

"Izzy, would you consider leaving the diary with me? I'd like the time to find out what I can learn about Jeremiah — what Ethan and Benjamin wrote about him. I so wish Jeremiah had written in the diary too," Charlie May added wistfully.

At first the request surprised Izzy. He hadn't expected to ever part with the diary. But if the last few weeks had taught him anything, it was to trust his instincts to an even greater degree than before. And to allow events to unfold on their own, without projecting fear onto an imagined result. It was as if he was learning a new vocabulary that would inform his life.

"Of course," Izzy complied. "It's your heritage as well as mine." As he spoke he was surprised how much affection he had for this woman whom he had met only the day before. *Was it the shared DNA that created this immediate link?* Izzy wondered.

Charlie May held the diary reverently. "To think this belonged to our, what, how many great grandfathers ago? Thank you for trusting me with it. Maybe you want to take the telescope for a time?"

"Say yes to that, Iz!" Will instantly spoke up. "I'd love to examine Newton's telescope!"

"Consider it done!" said Charlie May. "With what you've told me, how do you think Jeremiah could have gotten the telescope via Jacob Fletcher? How do the Fletchers fit into all this?"

Izzy opened the diary to the inscription page. "It starts with Daniel Fletcher and his friendship with Newton. Both Newton and Fletcher were mentors to Ethan. There's a great deal about Daniel from Ethan and from Benjamin. And it was Daniel who helped Benjamin get to America. When Benjamin first takes over the diary, he thanks Daniel. There's also a cryptic reference to a fatal fight with Jeremiah. Then Benjamin declares remorse at his father's death."

That description stunned Charlie May. "My God, could the fight have *caused* Ethan's death?"

"It's not stated anywhere, so we may never know," Izzy answered. "There are letters between Daniel Fletcher and Newton. I have one, with tantalizing details."

Izzy paused, debating how much to reveal about Levi and the tragic history of the letters. "There's so much we don't know," he continued, "although there are other Newton-Fletcher letters that might fill in some of the details. They were sold years ago to a collector."

"Izzy, we have to find those letters!" Insisted Charlie May. "Let's see if they're available. And if it's about money, I'm happy to pay! We can't pass up the chance to learn more about our family, we owe it to ourselves to find out. Seriously, do you know the name of the collector who owns the letters?"

Izzy thought hard on that statement. Might he at last have the letters that his father and Uncle Samuel had sought — that they'd held for such a brief time? Ian Hillenbrand suspected it was Gabriel Hornsby. And Levi knew for sure....

"You've got the diary, Iz. The letters could hold some answers too," Will advised and then revealed, "Charlie May here's the best part. We think we know where the crystal is...."

But before Charlie May could respond, the antique ring of Will's cell phone rang out. And then ... "IT'S KEN!" he shouted. "NORA! It's KEN!"

Nora, who'd been in the living room, listening for news updates, raced into the study.

"Unbelievable! Hang on, Ken... just a second. I'm putting you on speaker." Will reached out to Nora, to hold her close as Ken's voice boomed into the room.

"I just heard from Cooper," Ken began. "Lester Edwards is alive and in police custody. He's making a full confession. He spilled the beans, on DeWitt, the grid blackout *and* the bombing in Will's office. The whole enchilada, baby! It was all linked to some big money scheme with an investment guy in Boston named Strong. It hasn't been announced to the public, not officially yet. But it's coming and Cooper gave me the okay to let you know...!"

Nora listened, holding her breath, waiting to hear the confirmation she could really trust. At last....

"And Nora, they found your cell phone on DeWitt! Confirmed everything. You and Will are in the clear. IT'S OVER!"

Tears rolled down Nora's cheeks as Will held her tightly. Both were too overcome with relief to speak.

"Hey, you two still there?" Ken shouted.

"I can't thank you enough, big brother," Will managed to say. "You really came through — *again*!"

Then Ken added more details. "Edwards was also part of DeWitt's slimy work discrediting you, Will. He paid the starlet for the infamous kiss… Little brother, I think there's going to be some serious crow-eating in certain circles."

As Ken signed off, the room was filled with noisy excitement and relief. Izzy, Charlie May and Lucy surrounded Will and Nora in a giant hug.

"Oh, Will, I can't believe it's over… finally over… really over!" Nora cried, a smile beaming through happy tears. "Vindication, finally! Party Girl and all!"

"YES!" Will cheered. "It's over, dear, and we have our lives back!"

"And I have just the thing to celebrate with!" announced Charlie May. "Champagne!"

As the champagne flowed, they toasted Nora and Will again and again. But even in his delight for the Davenports, Izzy had to step back and consider Levi and his involvement with DeWitt and Strong.

Lucy noticed first. They were in the kitchen, taking a break for water. "What is it, Izzy? What's up?"

"Nothing." Izzy waved a hand, dismissing her attention.

"Iz, I know you too well."

"I can't hide anything from you, can I. It's Ken's remark about the money scheme. Levi works for Strong. You know that. I'm wondering if he's mixed up in this."

"What's happened to the party?" Charlie May appeared.

"Ask your cousin," Lucy explained, giving Izzy a gentle nudge.

"What is it?" questioned Charlie May. "Anything I can help with?"

"You're family now … and you should know…." With that lead-in, Izzy gave a brief history of Levi, his successful career built on the stolen letters, the diary theft and Levi's recent return of the poem and offer of the Fletcher letter.

"I know he's trying to make amends," Izzy concluded. "He and I have a very long way to go. But I hope he's not mixed up in this thing with DeWitt and Strong."

"Wow, Izzy," Charlie May began. "Clearly, this has been a trial for you. I can only imagine how you've felt with all these twist and turns…. Look, I have many contacts in Boston and Washington. If Levi was part of the dirty deeds, he'll have to pay for that. But if he's not — and we'll hope he's not — I'm sure I can help."

Izzy's eyes welled and he nodded his thanks.

"Now come on!" Charlie May herded them out the kitchen. "Let's get back to Nora and Will, and the champagne. I want to hear about the crystal and where you think it might be!"

Nora was only too happy to let the conversation turn completely to the diary and the crystal. "Yes, these two have been on a treasure hunt ever since they met," she mused, raising her glass to acknowledge Izzy and Will.

"It's the silver box that holds the diary," Will explained. "We think these are longitude and latitude coordinates scratched here on the lid."

Charlie May passed her finger over the numbers. "How do you suppose they came up with the numbers?"

"Well, I've been thinking about that and I have a theory…It wouldn't be out of the realm of possibility that they used your Newton telescope!" Will answered, seeing the obvious connection and amazed at the prospect.

"But then, was Jeremiah part of all this at some point?" quizzed Charlie May. "Could he have met with Benjamin here in America? I'm still trying to understand how he fits in with the diary and crystal … how he ended up with the telescope!"

"Maybe Charlie May, the only true explanation for all of this rests in the mysterious ways of divine providence," Izzy proposed. His dreams of the Palace of Light, more vivid than ever, came to mind. So did his notion that cosmic forces were at play — streams of unknowable power were balancing a drama that swept across the mystical nature of time. Whatever it was that had brought them all together, to Isidor Rhodes it felt so right.

"I take it you've plotted the coordinates," asserted Charlie May. "Where is this place?"

"Incredibly, it's not far: Katonah, about an hour south of here."

"I know Katonah! I've been there plenty of times! Let's find out who owns the property."

"We have. It's for sale," Will verified. "We found out the day before. Izzy and I originally planned to visit yesterday…." Then he grinned. "But as you know, we've had a little detour!"

All welcomed the chance to laugh at the harrowing previous days. Charlie May shook her head in wonder. "Amazing? Katonah! I'm not necessarily a believer in divine providence. But, Izzy, after this, I might have to change my mind."

Izzy pointed to the scene on the silver box. "Will and I think this depicts the place where we'll find the crystal stone."

Charlie May admired the engraving. "That's beautiful."

"Show her the poem that Ian found in the lining of the diary," Lucy suggested.

Izzy began to read: "*Here, in this place, dwells the pleasure that only heavens knows….*"

When he finished the poem, Charlie May sat in silence, letting the meaning sink in, before she spoke. "It takes a lot to astonish me, Izzy, and you've done it."

"There *is* always the possibility that it's just a picture and just a poem," Will noted, throwing caution into the mix.

"Of course," Charlie May agreed, "but we have to find out. We've got to see this place…."

Will looked at Izzy, pumping his fist in triumph. Then, eyebrows tilted at Nora, Will looked for her okay. Stepping closer, she signaled her approval with a kiss. "Honey, I'm all in!"

"And you have to have a driver!" Lucy declared.

"Then it's official!" Will affirmed. "Next stop, Katonah!"

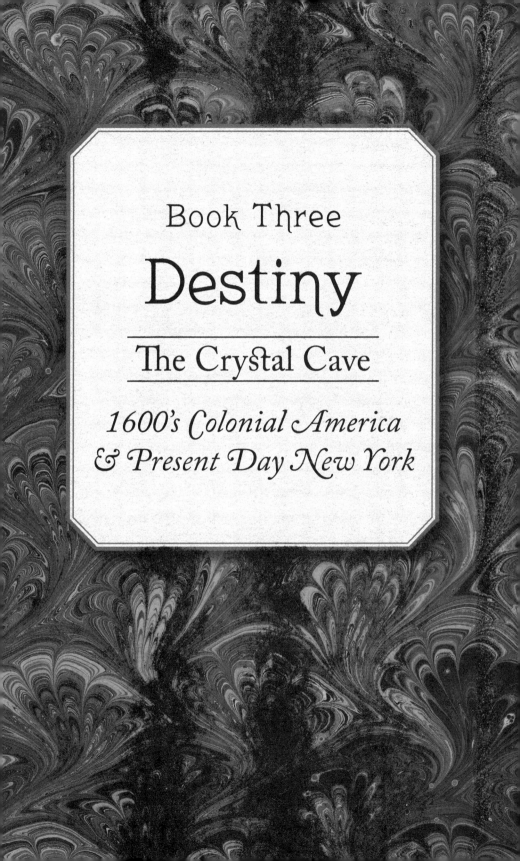

Book Three

Destiny

The Crystal Cave

1600's Colonial America & Present Day New York

Prologue

Hunstanton, England
APRIL 1691

Ethan Hawkins

Final diary entry

*G*ood stewards of this Earth, Newton's gravity holds us to her skin as we spin with the great spheres of influence traveling through the seasons of time, marked by the stars in the night sky.

Our life-force streams through us and emerges all around us. It is alive with a mystery that is more than it seems to the ordinary eye. Our senses flow with signs and powers that when opened wide, give way to limitless imagination. Are not all things possible?

Each heartbeat unfolds the light of eternal bounty. As within, so without; as without, so within. The great spheres, near and far, racing through space, tell the heart to unfurl her eternal glory, and the heart beholds itself.

The secret is held in the blood that flows in the veins of every man and woman. For together, humanity, bound to the wheel of Earth's dominion, in time will transform all dimensions, separate no more. One unified symphony, vibrating from the highest octaves, will give flight with *majesty from on high. No veils remain. The eye of pure awareness is opened.*

Good stewards of this Earth, the task spans the generations, and then the moment is at hand. The heart opens to the eternal and kisses the night sky. A stream of milk and honey unlocks the riddle of life. Ever-living waters reflect the beauty of the world, and an everlasting current flows from the unknown to the known, ever and forever.

Chapter 1

Hudson Valley
AUGUST 1694
Third week, First day

Hawkins Families & Daniel, Alfredo & Jacob

Even as the serenity of the rolling green hills and a sun-filled breeze warmed the air, Benjamin and Catherine Hawkins felt uneasy, waiting patiently for the arrival of Captain Alberto Alfredo with Daniel and Jacob Fletcher. Alfredo had expected they would reach New York in August. Now the month was half gone, and still no word, no sign that they had actually made the voyage.

"Benjamin, no doubt it is very likely that any minute now, Alfredo will be knocking at our door with a broad smile, as always," Catherine stated confidently.

"I wish it so, *dear wife,* but I was hoping for a note from Alfredo that they've landed in New York and were beginning the journey up the Hudson. That way, at least their arrival and the worry associated with their coming would not hang so far over our heads."

Catherine knew what troubled Benjamin. "We've discussed this and I know your fears. Have faith that Daniel's purpose in coming is a happy one. From every story of Daniel you've shared, he loved your father and he loves you. And you can trust that whatever changes have occurred in both your lives will be mutually accepted with kindness and good tidings."

Benjamin wanted to desperately believe in Catherine's optimism. But even as he returned her hug, her growing belly a tender sign of the ever-stronger bonds between them, he could not shake the apprehension that had plagued him for weeks. Would Daniel understand how the diamond crystal that had torn the Hawkins' family apart was no longer an everyday part of his life? That perhaps all the suffering — Jeremiah's, their father's, Daniel's at his friend's death and Benjamin's own — all had been for naught?

Would Daniel be forgiving? What if he was not? And whether he was angry or kind, would Daniel want to take the stone for his own?

As one brother worried, so did the other, though for very different reasons.

Since sunrise, Jeremiah, never one for idle talk, had grown nearly silent. According to Alberto, they would reach his land and Benjamin's cabin by midday. *And then what?* Jeremiah agonized. *What would Benjamin do?* As far as he knew, Benjamin had no warning of his impending approach.

And what would he do when he faced Benjamin again? Could he be certain that all his feelings of revenge and anger were behind him? *The crystal … where was it now?*

Uncertainty had traveled with Jeremiah since he'd agreed to this trip. Their pace had been leisurely by Alfredo's standards. The captain had recognized that a journey on the river and then over land with Abigail and Jeremiah's baby in tow could not be hurried. And Jeremiah had welcomed every opportunity to delay the inevitable moment when he would see Benjamin again.

Abigail understood her husband's mood and let him be. Occasionally she patted his arm to reassure him that he was doing the right thing. Or she pointed out the beauty of their sleeping Elizabeth Rebecca — to remind him of the riches he had in their darling girl and of the bright future they shared together.

Riding ahead by several lengths, with Jacob driving their wagon, Daniel and Alberto quietly spoke now and then of what might be ahead. With so much unresolved between the brothers, and the crystal stone presumably still with Benjamin, they sat on the razor's edge. Yet they felt this moment was something perhaps written in the stars. Each brother having been brought to this crossroads — a crucible of doubt, yet also, perchance, a vessel for redemption. "I've witnessed many an adventure and it never ceases to astound me, the field of emotions men plow," Alfredo mused.

"This life is never short of drama," Daniel agreed. "All our dreams and desires dance together, with so many twists and turns on our earthbound stage. Each of us hears the song of life and adds our own unique voice. And we're all the better for it."

As Daniel spoke, they reached the top of a ridge. "Ah, there it is!" Alberto pointed to a clearing in the distance, marked by plowed fields waving with tall cornstalks and the small cabin beyond. Daniel savored the moment. Though the outcome of this visit was anything but certain, he was excited to see Benjamin again, to meet his wife and young son. Looking down at the fields below, illuminated by golden sunshine, he thought again of the crystal. And not simply that it was still in Benjamin's keeping, but that he might hold it once more and feel its power. Those thoughts filled Daniel with a desire that he couldn't deny. Yet they troubled him too, for if he had such longing for the crystal, might Jeremiah as well?

Benjamin was in the cornfield, picking the ripe ears. He moved rhythmically, using a knife to slice and then snap off each ear from its stalk. The only sounds he heard were the buzzing of insects — until suddenly

Catherine was standing next to him, holding their son Alexander by one hand and Benjamin's gun in the other.

"Travelers!" she pointed toward the ridge above. "Perhaps it's Alfredo and Daniel — I cannot tell — but I brought this in case," she explained, handing him the weapon.

Benjamin didn't answer, watching in the next few moments as a wagon and two horsemen came closer and clearer into view. "No need for this!" Benjamin exclaimed as he turned the gun toward the ground. "That's Alfredo, with Daniel Fletcher and Jacob! Back to the house, so we can give them a proper welcome."

He scooped up the full basket of corn and led the way, his emotions a swirling mix of joy, anticipation and dogged worry. "Catherine, say nothing about the crystal," Benjamin advised. "I need to explain to Daniel in my own time."

Catherine nodded, acknowledging his request, and then called out in surprise. "Benjamin, look! There's a second wagon now. It follows in the same path as the other."

There was no reply as Benjamin peered into the distance, shading his eyes from the sun. But he didn't need to see who it was; his gut told him.

"There's a woman in that wagon," Catherine described, "and a child and…"

"And my brother!" Benjamin completed the sentence, his voice choked with bewilderment and concern. "What in God's name is he doing here? And why would Daniel Fletcher be the one to have brought him?"

Jeremiah spotted Benjamin immediately. "He looks bigger than I remember," he said, speaking his first thoughts aloud. Hard physical labor had filled out his brother's form. Jeremiah knew the telltale signs — he recognized himself in his brother's changed form.

"That must be his wife," Abigail noted. She had not thought much about Catherine Hawkins until this moment. Now Abigail prayed they would get along, to soften the way for their husbands reunion.

"Remember, my dearest," she continued, "let not the pains of the past enslave your thoughts now. You are your own master, your own captain. You can decide what this meeting will be. Whatever choice your brother makes in how he greets you, how he treats you, you can choose the way of peace."

Can I? Jeremiah wondered. *What if Benjamin challenges me?*

He took in Abigail's wise words, but his thoughts, like his brother's, were the same swirling mix of anticipation and worry. Jeremiah maneuvered the horse carefully to follow the wagon ahead, moving closer step by step.

"Jeremiah! Why is he here?" Benjamin's voice was filled with apprehension. Catherine looked on with even greater concern. She well knew the tortured history of the brothers.

Memories flashed in Benjamin's mind. Jeremiah flying in the air, landing on him. His father's bed crashing beneath him. The crystal stone rolling away.

Then another scene: his father bursting through the cottage door, yelling Benjamin's name. The fire in the hearth roaring with heat and flame. Jeremiah at his throat, he at Jeremiah's and their father separating them with such force.

He and Jeremiah … each fuming with rage at the other… and then their father on the floor, his life's blood pouring out….

"Benjamin!" Catherine spoke sharply, shaking her husband's arm. She recognized the far-off look that signaled he had gone deep into the past or to the mysterious place beyond this realm. But she needed him to be present, in the here and now.

"Benjamin! The wagons draw near!"

Catherine moved Alexander behind her, letting her long skirt shelter her little one-year-old from what might come. She watched anxiously as Benjamin stepped forward and the visitors approached….

As he waited, again Benjamin flashed back to the past, fleeing from the cottage, expecting to hear Jeremiah's footsteps, to feel his hands pulling him back. Then he was in Daniel's cottage, in the windowless room, listening to Jeremiah demand to know where he was.

Now he was about to face his brother. *So Jeremiah, you have found me.*

The past had caught up with them both. Whatever it would be, a resolution, good or ill, was near.

Jeremiah could see the stunned look on Benjamin's face. *What must he be thinking?*

Abigail too saw the surprise in Benjamin's expression. She put her hand gently on Jeremiah's arm, hoping to steady him, yet feeling the tension in his muscles.

Daniel, Jacob and Alfredo were the first to arrive. Tears welled in Benjamin's eyes as he returned Daniel Fletcher's hearty embrace. Then with sweeping smiles, he and Alberto Alfredo held each other by the shoulders.

"Jacob!" Benjamin offered Daniel's son a welcoming embrace as well.

Before Daniel could explain, Jeremiah's wagon was arriving. Daniel looked at Benjamin, and then at Jeremiah, trying to anticipate the minutes ahead, silently beseeching a blessing on them all.

As they approached, Abigail smiled and nodded in Catherine's direction.

Jeremiah tugged on the reins and commanded the horse to halt. He stood up, reins still in hand, looking large and entirely formidable.

No one spoke a word.

Jeremiah jumped from the wagon and then helped Abigail, who held Elizabeth Rebecca.

Daniel looked on, recognizing the moment of truth was upon them. Where once he was Benjamin's protector, here there were no sides to take. The brothers must find their own way forward — together, or forever apart.

Alfredo stood at the ready, if intervention was needed. While his loyalty and friendship to Benjamin were his overriding concern, he had come to appreciate Jeremiah. He had a steady hand in the wilderness, an admirable sense of fairness and an obvious deep tenderness for his wife and child.

Catherine stepped forward to greet Abigail. "I'm Catherine and this is Alexander, named for my father. Welcome to our home."

"I'm happy to meet you, Catherine. And this is Elizabeth Rose, named for their mother," Abigail explained softly, nodding first at her husband and then at his brother.

Another long pause, and then, as though silently agreed, with sure steady strides, each brother reached out for the other, each with a hand open and extended.

They grasped hands, tentative at first, and then shoulders. And then, unable to resist the power of unspoken emotions swelling their hearts, the brothers embraced. Without a word between them, they wept in each other's arms. They grieved for their father, and they grieved for themselves, for what had been lost between them. Though what would happen next was still uncertain, in that moment they were both driven by an inexplicable need to let go of a painful past and be released from the chains that bound them.

Watching the brothers, Daniel Fletcher bore witness to the capacity of even the most wounded to heal. "Though we struggle, the heart teaches us peace," he whispered to his son, with gratitude to the heavens.

Chapter 2

Hudson Valley
AUGUST 1694
Second day

Benjamin and Daniel

Startled, Benjamin opened his eyes and was relieved to find himself in his bed next to Catherine. His dreams had taken him far away, leaving him with a churning in the pit of his stomach that defied explanation.

"What are you thinking?" Catherine asked, now awake and watching her husband stare at the rough logs that fashioned the ceiling of their small bedroom.

"My mind is spinning. I have no idea what to say to Jeremiah. Or to Daniel either," Benjamin confessed.

Embracing his brother had been instinctual — an impulse that came from a place that neither of them could grasp. Yet there, simmering within each, twin emotions spiraled together — unresolved fear and unspoken love, bound to the story they shared. While they both had moved well beyond the lives they knew together, there was still a past to reckon with. Was it a haunting that could easily slip from memory into the present without warning?

"You must find a way to resolve the heartache between you and Jeremiah," Catherine stated, quietly yet firmly. "It's good that Daniel has come, and that he encouraged Jeremiah to come too. It gives you and Jeremiah an opportunity to resolve what lays hidden below the surface. Look into the depth of your heart, Benjamin. It will show you the way."

"Maybe so. But the crystal hangs tightly around my neck, forcing me to make unwelcome choices. Though yesterday they didn't say, it is very probable that Jeremiah has come for it, or even Daniel."

"The crystal? I thought you let go of the stone," Catherine countered, concerned. "Oh, Benjamin, do not let it take hold of you again. You are a different man now, opened hearted and brave. Let not wariness and suspicion be your guide."

"Catherine, I do not want you to worry. It's only that I've thought to keep the stone near, should I feel called by its power again. Sometimes I think of it as waiting for me." Benjamin looked in the direction of the trunk, where the crystal lay dormant.

Leaning into Benjamin, Catherine gave him an adoring kiss. "You will feel your way through, as you always do," she assured him.

Yet both looked into the other's eyes not at all certain of what would happen next.

The previous day, after their embrace, Benjamin and Jeremiah made an attempt at cautious talk. But it fell to Abigail and Catherine to ease the way forward. Catherine suggested that Benjamin waste no time in showing Alfredo the progress they were making with the land. Daniel went along, marveling at Benjamin's fields of herbs and other healing plants, and at the remedies Benjamin described, drawn from the strength of each plant.

Seeing Jeremiah hesitate at joining Benjamin's tour of the land, Abigail enquired about a fishing stream, so they might contribute to the meal. And she well knew that doing something useful would channel Jeremiah's anxious energy. Jacob, who had always been sympathetic toward Jeremiah, the less-favored Hawkins son, opted for fishing too.

Then it was only Catherine, Abigail and the children at the cabin, the women's bond growing as they got to know each other.

Later, both parties of men returned, Benjamin and Daniel each with an armload of plants, and Jeremiah and Jacob with a line of stout fish.

That first evening, after cooperating to prepare a fine dinner, Catherine and Abigail had introduced conversation about their husbands' heroics. It had begun naturally enough, with Daniel's praise for Benjamin's remedies. Catherine was soon describing how Benjamin had saved her father's life in the fire at the fort and healed his burns with a nearly miraculous ointment. In turn, Abigail proudly narrated how Jeremiah had saved her sister from irreparable harm on their crossing to America — pointing out the admirable qualities that the brothers shared.

The treachery aboard ship reminded Alfredo of Benjamin's courage in thwarting the would-be mutiny of his crew. He smiled at the memory, but thought it not the time to recount that story.

Daniel found a way to reference Jeremiah and Abigail's store in New York, with its well-stocked inventory and congenial service. And so the conversation ended with both brothers shining equally in the spotlight.

Abigail and Catherine had successfully navigated the first day of the reunion. Daniel felt ever more grateful that Abigail had come along and delighted that Benjamin had found such a perfect companion in Catherine.

Now Benjamin began the second day feeling unsure of what to do. Daniel Fletcher was awake and standing in the doorway, looking out onto the morning scene.

"There," Daniel said, pointing toward Jeremiah. He had walked a distance from the cabin and was standing with his arms held wide, greeting the sun.

Benjamin felt a flash of familiarity. His father had welcomed the morning in much the same way, and Benjamin too began his day many times in a similar position.

He started toward Jeremiah, intending to share the ritual with his brother. But Daniel, sensing Jeremiah's need for solitary communion, intervened and suggested Benjamin should wait. "Best to leave your brother alone right now."

Being restrained by Daniel had a jarring effect on Benjamin. He felt a surge of anger at the uninvited presence of Daniel Fletcher and the brother he expected to never see again. Though he was unable to discern exactly why, all he knew was in that moment he wanted Jeremiah gone. And uncertain of Daniel's reason for being there, he wanted him gone as well.

That hostile feeling seemed to linger in the air. Benjamin considered heading straight to the fields, to get away from everyone. But then, staring at his brother, seeing him delight in the morning sun without reservation, Benjamin's irritation gave way to recognition: the crystal was at the root of his anger. Yes, he had given up working with it, yet the stone still had an allure capable of seizing control of his reason. The prospect of Jeremiah or Daniel taking the crystal from him held jealous sway over his mind.

That realization frightened him, with the terrifying reminder of the tragic history spawned by the crystal. *Why can't I give it up willingly?* Benjamin heard his mind ask. *Why do I still want to possess it solely for myself?*

Daniel could feel the tension in Benjamin's body and thought he suspected the cause. "What is it?" he inquired. Already the brothers had come such a long way toward each other. Daniel did not want to see jealousy, envy and greed rise up to again split them apart.

Little did Daniel realize that his own presence was also fueling Benjamin's upset. "What is it?" Daniel repeated. "What is it, Benjamin? Please do speak."

With each word Daniel uttered, Benjamin's worry grew into a

full-blown fever. "Why have you come here, Daniel? Why would you cross the ocean now?" Benjamin's voice rose louder. "Did you and Newton determine that my time with the crystal is over? HAVE YOU COME TO TAKE THE CRYSTAL FROM ME?"

Benjamin was immediately embarrassed to have shouted such accusations at his one-time protector. His face turned red and he averted his eyes to avoid Daniel's searching gaze. He had let his emotions get the best of him.

Indeed, Daniel looked at Benjamin, first with surprise and then, as the meaning of the young man's words sunk in, with understanding. Not knowing Daniel's intent for coming, Benjamin had grown suspicious. And it had carried his mind to a dread-filled place. Knowing the crystal's power and the history with Jeremiah too, Daniel could see how Benjamin might conjure up distorted visions of why both were here.

"No, Benjamin," Daniel began, "I did not come to *take* the stone. Rather, it was a most unusual visitation *about the crystal* — an experience I thought vital to share with you in person — that prompted me to come to America and seek you out. Then when I found Jeremiah in New York, which was fully unexpected, I knew fate was leading my way."

Benjamin nodded, attempting to regain his emotional balance. "Forgive me, Daniel. I confess that ever since I received Alfredo's letter, with notice of your impending visit, I've been overcome with growing dismay. And now I've allowed my fears to come between us."

He paused, carefully considering his next words. "I put the crystal aside a year ago, soon after Alexander was born. I learned all that I could from it, and I knew it to be true as its light dimmed in my hand. Yet, at the same time, I realized that I didn't need it for healing any longer. Ever since, I've relied on the innate gifts given to me by birth and honed with experience. In hindsight maybe I would never have known my own inner strength if I didn't put the crystal aside."

Daniel listened silently to this momentous news. When he spoke, his words were grave yet filled with genuine curiosity, acknowledging the deep significance of what had occurred. "If the crystal no longer has the same importance, what made you so fearful when you learned I was coming?"

"Oh, Daniel, what can I say? And seeing Jeremiah, too…. I am so filled with… I know not…." Benjamin struggled to give voice to what he felt impossible to say aloud.

"What, Benjamin?" Daniel coaxed.

"Shame! I feel a deep shame!" The word spilled out, and with it Benjamin felt a deep release. "It's been within me, hiding in the shadows, ever since Father and I began working with the crystal and concealed it from Jeremiah. How could I have wanted my father and brother to be gone, just to be with a stone? And then they *were* gone — Father dead and Jeremiah alone, as I ran away with Captain Alfredo. And here I am, all over again, thinking the same thoughts, wanting the stone all for me! Why does it plague me so?"

Benjamin stopped for a moment and when he spoke again, his voice was filled with anguish. "What kind of man am I?"

Daniel let the question hang in the air, as he summoned an answer to help Benjamin find a way out of his pain. "Each of us, as we live, we learn," Daniel began. "That is the nature of our lives on this good Earth. But it is what we learn about ourselves that will determine the life we create going forward."

Then, putting his hands on Benjamin's shoulders, he looked squarely at the young man. "You and Jeremiah are writing a new story. It began with your embrace when you met again. The next chapter will be very different from what came before. You are not the same boy who ran away three years ago. And recognize that Jeremiah is not the same either. What an impossible situation you and your brother and your father were in! But that is over. You can start again."

Benjamin listened with hope. Yet could he really move beyond the shadow that darkened his way? "I should gladly give you the stone!" he insisted. "You've done so much for me!"

"Follow me, Benjamin." Daniel walked out into the sunshine, his arms spread wide. "We are our own jailers. Release the boy who ran away with the stone. Release the chains that bind you to that which no longer serves you. Know peace, Benjamin. You have lived the story of jealousy and shame. You have learned from it… and now you can be free of it."

Benjamin felt the warmth of the sun surrounding him. It overflowed his heart with truth and understanding. As it did, his mind eased … the grip on his thoughts loosened…. And there, shining brightly without the specter of worry or doubt, he saw himself anew. In order to dwell in that freedom, he needed to forgive himself and let it all go.

"Thank you, Daniel," he said quietly. "As always, thank you for your wisdom."

"Benjamin, wise words often fall to the ground, discarded or simply unheard. It is the wise man who is able to hear them and make them his own."

Benjamin nodded in agreement, grateful again for this dear old man, a true and faithful friend.

And then, with eyes flashing, he recalled Daniel's mention of the real reason for the long journey to America. "When will you tell me of your visitation, Daniel — what has brought you here?" Benjamin asked.

"All in good time," Daniel replied. "But first, I am ready for breakfast!"

"And you'll have it soon!" Catherine called from the doorway, where she stood with Alexander. Abigail appeared as well, searching for Jeremiah and satisfied when she saw him off in the distance, walking now with Alfredo and Jacob.

"After breakfast then?" Benjamin asked again. "I am eager to know."

"Yes," Daniel promised. "All in good time."

∞

As the second day continued, a natural rhythm developed among the group. Catherine and Abigail's comfortable rapport made for light and easy conversation as they cared for their children and worked together to finish the daily household chores.

After breakfast, Daniel excused himself to survey the medicinal plants collected the day before. Jeremiah and Jacob willingly joined Benjamin in harvesting the corn, and the trio worked well in unison to clear the field. In the late afternoon they went together to the fishing stream, to wash away the dirt of their good day's work and try their luck at catching another evening's meal.

Alfredo spent most of the day looking over his land and considering when he might choose to leave the sea and settle permanently in this valley. Daniel accompanied him for a portion of the trek and together they searched, though fruitlessly, for the waterfall depicted on Jeremiah's silver box — the one he received from Emma Wells. When Alberto first saw the box, he'd been certain it depicted his own piece of the Hudson Valley. Now he wondered if his mind had played tricks on him, confusing the scene with some far-off landscape from a long-ago voyage.

The sun was low in the sky as all of the men returned to the cabin, the three younger with another string of trout for a bountiful meal. A smile spread across Daniel's face as he watched Benjamin and Jeremiah, with Jacob between them, walk together with far greater ease than the previous day. All three joined in a laugh now and then, with the brothers occasionally leaning forward to address each other directly.

It was time, Daniel thought. The possibility of deep healing had been set in motion for Jeremiah and Benjamin, and today's work together had kept it moving on a path that was open and wide.

Daniel could only hope that the crystal would not lead them astray. Rather, as his mysterious visitor revealed, let it be an agent of reconciliation and renewal that would continue through generations of Hawkins to come.

Chapter 3

Hudson Valley
AUGUST 1694
Second evening

Jeremiah, Benjamin & Daniel

That night the ale flowed and a meal of fish, fresh corn and other vegetables from Catherine's garden near the cabin was consumed over stories from Alberto Alfredo of life on the high seas. Then, as Alfredo and Daniel recalled how they first met in Woolsthorpe, the talk inevitably turned to Ethan Hawkins and Daniel's stories of Ethan as an orphaned stable boy.

Benjamin found himself watching Jeremiah's reaction to these stories of their father's early life. Ethan had shared snippets of his boyhood with his sons, but now Benjamin realized there was so much more he wanted to know about his father. And it occurred to him that while he had the diary to fill in some details, not so Jeremiah. *It's been unfair of me to keep the diary to myself,* Benjamin concluded. *Jeremiah needs to read our father's thoughts and feelings too.*

For his part, as Jeremiah listened to the stories, and as a husband and father now, for the first time he considered what his own father had gone through in losing his wife, and having twin sons not yet two years old to care for. As much to himself as to the rest, Jeremiah spoke aloud. "He was a good man. I wish he'd told us more about his life, and about our mother. I'm sure he tried his best after she died. He could never have expected to raise us alone."

Daniel looked toward Benjamin and watched for his response. Did he read the signal? Benjamin quietly left the room.

Daniel's heart began to pound. Pray he had understood his visitor's vision. Pray he was an instrument of fate, bringing Benjamin and Jeremiah together as they were meant to be. The brothers had embraced; they had worked together in the fields today. Yet Daniel was sure that what had sundered them so violently remained wrapped in emotional turmoil, hidden inside both of their hearts. Daniel further prayed that the moment of profound healing was truly at hand. That in their willingness to face each other and look deep within themselves — in confronting their fears and accumulated hurts — Benjamin and Jeremiah could bind their wounds and give each the gift of forgiveness, and allow reconciliation to take seed and flower.

Benjamin returned with a leather satchel that Daniel immediately recognized. He was brought back to Benjamin's hurried escape from Hunstanton, in April 1691.

Catherine and Abigail had heard only snippets of the conversation as they cleaned up from supper and put the children to bed. Now they gathered with the men around the fire. Seeing Benjamin with the leather satchel, she held her breath. Abigail sensed Catherine's concern and became apprehensive too. *The crystal?*

Jeremiah watched and waited as well. He felt it in the marrow of his bones — the time had arrived. And he searched his heart for the jealousy that had once consumed him.

Benjamin made no explanation, for none was needed. He opened the satchel and retrieved an object wrapped in an old scrap of burlap.

The diary. Jeremiah recognized it immediately and his emotions shot to the surface. Struggling to contain himself, Jeremiah was transported back to his last glimpse of his father's diary. It was in Benjamin's hand, as his brother fled their cottage, with their father dead on the floor.

Still silent, Benjamin held the diary out to Jeremiah. Without hesitating, he accepted it. Jeremiah unwrapped the cloth and fingered the cover, longing for his father.

"There is an entry I want you to read," Benjamin said quietly.

Jeremiah looked to Abigail, who nodded confidently, urging him on. He handed the book back to Benjamin, who quickly found the entry, for he knew it well.

"Here it is." Benjamin pointed to the passage as he handed the book back to Jeremiah.

With Abigail standing at his shoulder, Jeremiah read aloud:

> *"Today, I went down to the sea, as I do every morning. But this day is different from any other. For today Jeremiah and, on his heels, Benjamin, were born. My dearest Elizabeth, my treasure beyond all treasures, struggled mightily to bring these new souls into the world. She and I are charged with shaping their young lives. There is much to teach them, although it may be their lot is pre-ordained in the great halls of light. I do not see the where, the why or the how, yet the light of their lives shines brightly in my mind's eye. As the waves of the ocean roll in and roll out, each kissing the shoreline and whispering the law of truth — I AM — so too Jeremiah and Benjamin will sing a song of love and be transformed. It is no accident they are born together. Each will make his own mark, yet what they learn from each other will, in their time, set them apart from others. May I, as their father, always keep that in mind.*

"My heart is full. While the mystery of life alludes me, of this I am sure. The glory of All-That-Is has bestowed divine grace upon Elizabeth and me, and life will never be the same."

Tears welled in Jeremiah's eyes and then rolled down his cheeks. Benjamin reached out to place a hand on his brother's shoulder. "Father loved you, Jeremiah, from the day you were born."

"And I him. The guilt I hold at his death will be with me until the end of my time," Jeremiah replied.

"It is a guilt we share. And I ran away, leaving you to face his death alone. It's a burden you should not have had to shoulder entirely yourself," Benjamin confessed.

"My jealousy was so easily ignited." Jeremiah looked straight into his brother's eyes.

Benjamin met his brother's gaze. "But Father and I should not have kept the crystal a secret from you."

"It was not only the crystal, Benjamin. I never felt myself your equal in our father's eyes. Perhaps the same was true with our mother, though I have no memory of her. What happened with the crystal confirmed that belief." Jeremiah spoke with an honesty that made Abigail weep for her husband. Even Daniel felt again his own guilt at having favored Benjamin as the boys grew up.

Then Benjamin retrieved a second object from the satchel. He unwrapped its burlap cover and held it in the palm of his hand.

"My time with the crystal stone is over," Benjamin explained. "It's yours, if you want it. Perhaps it can be a healing stone for you. Or, if you choose, rid yourself of the burden, if that's what it still represents."

Daniel watched with eyes wide, remembering the power of the diamond crystal and feeling its presence. Despite himself, the thought of Jeremiah tossing the stone away was alarming....

Jeremiah stared at the crystal. The sight of it ignited his fear. If he held it, would the stone light up for him, as it once had for Father and Benjamin?

Just as quickly, Jeremiah resolved to let those feelings go. He shook his head with irony, thinking of how his inability to make the crystal glow had gripped him so tightly. Yes, he wanted to hold the crystal again, but not to show his worth. He simply wanted to hold this object that had felt his father's touch.

Jeremiah cupped his hands and Benjamin placed the crystal in his brother's palms. Jeremiah felt its weight but nothing else. But he allowed his curiosity to take hold and he closed his eyes, imagining the stone in his father's hand.

Then the slightest surge of emotion shivered inside of him … and then another…and still another … until a stream of feeling swept through him.

But his first thought was not jealousy or fury, as in the past, but sorrow that traveled from his palms through his arms and into his heart. Sorrow for the collective tragedy the stone had unleashed. His hands began to tremble as the waves of unresolved emotions rolled through him. Now the jealousy and fury that still resided within, reappeared. And Jeremiah felt the crystal cleansing the wounds that hid in the caverns of his heart.

"You feel it, don't you?" Benjamin asked. "The vibration?"

"Yes," Jeremiah answered, his voice faint. "What is that?"

"The power of the crystal's life-force moving through you. It is gathering and releasing the healing forces within you."

Jeremiah could see his hands enveloped in light and when he opened them, the crystal was glowing. He marveled at the stone's transformation, as did everyone looking on. Then Jeremiah closed his eyes again, to experience the crystal's full strength.

He could feel his heart beat, and with each beat his being was expanding. His nostrils flared and his breathing deepened. As he inhaled, the image of diamond light filled his mind and it was like breathing in the starlight that filled the night sky. His vision became illuminated with a glowing purple-blue light. He could feel his own life-force flow from his fingertips.

Then the whispering voices in the room receded far into the distance, and now Jeremiah felt transported to a field of wild flowers, all purple, red and yellow. A stream glistening with the light of a midday sky ambled beside him. He heard the gentle song of a robin as she flew overhead. He looked up to see a waterfall cascading from a cliff above, the water pooling below with a golden mist that filled the air.

Jeremiah climbed the rocks to find the source of the water. But when he was nearly there, his eyes were diverted by water falling in streams of rainbow colors. He found a path around the water and crossed the threshold into a cave; yet inside, instead of darkness, everything before him was lit in sunlight. The cave walls sparkled and when Jeremiah placed one hand on the wall, it vibrated like the diamond crystal. He touched another part and it did the same. The floor of the cave began to undulate beneath his feet in warm waves of oscillating pulses.... and then, suddenly, he was back in Benjamin's cabin.

"You left us," Daniel confirmed.

Jeremiah could not speak.

"Jeremiah?" Abigail reached out to touch him, but he did not respond. "What has happened to him?" she asked in alarm. "What has the crystal done to him?"

Still silent, Jeremiah stood up and left the room, the crystal in his hand. Abigail ran after him.

Benjamin looked at Daniel, unsure of what was to come. *Where was Jeremiah going? Would Jeremiah return as himself or had some fundamental change occurred? And…he had the crystal in his hand!*

∞

Tension built as those within the cabin awaited the return of Jeremiah and Abigail. As though distressed by her parents' absence, Elizabeth Rose awoke with a loud wail. Catherine went to soothe the babe and, for long minutes more, they all wondered what was happening outside.

At last Jeremiah and Abigail reappeared. Abigail ran to scoop up her daughter. Jeremiah walked slowly toward Benjamin, and then handed him the silver box. "I saw this place. Just now, as I held the crystal," he explained.

The familiar scene on the box stunned Benjamin. "Where did you get this?" he asked.

"From a woman peddling ale and reading fortunes. Her name was Emma Wells."

Benjamin was surprised and, yet, somehow not. He turned to address Catherine. "Remember the woman I told you about my first night at the fort?"

"Of course, the one who left you the card." Catherine went to a desk and retrieved it. Holding the card next to the box, one was the perfect image of the other.

Alfredo was suddenly animated as he looked from card to box and back again. "Daniel, I know why I couldn't recall where this is! I know it from above, where the water begins to fall. My trapper-guide showed me when I was first given this land. He talked of a Native myth around the waterfall, but I paid him no mind, having no interest then in myths or waterfalls. But now…." Alberto had no need to finish. They were all sensing the hand of providence upon them.

"Isn't *now* the moment to tell us what brought you here, Daniel?" Benjamin asked. "You said it was a visitation."

Daniel nodded and smiled. "Yes, it is indeed time." He looked at Jacob, who knew the tale from their visit to Newton. "Jacob, if I forget any details, please remind me."

Then Daniel began to recount the experience that brought him to Alfredo's valley and Benjamin's doorstep. "One night I was sitting by the

fire, alone with my thoughts, when a knock came upon my door...."
Daniel told them about the man who had traveled from the Himalaya
Mountains. That he stumbled upon a crystal cave and, there, Daniel's
visitor had a vision. "He saw Ethan, your father, standing on the shore,
and then wading into the water, where he found the diamond crystal
stone. He saw the day you two were born. In this picture, your father
looked out to sea, with the crystal in his hand and he could see the
dance of generations to follow. It was as if Ethan's internal eye traveled
to a future time."

Daniel paused, willing both Jeremiah and Benjamin to listen with
open hearts. "And then my visitor saw another cave far away, where two
brothers stand together, as providence guides them to complete a task."

Everyone listened intently, mesmerized by Daniel's tale. "Before my
visitor left, I asked what he wanted of me, why he had told me this
tale. He said, 'The future is to be written. Search your heart and go
find your place in it.' So I sought the wisdom of the great Isaac Newton, your father's first teacher, and he agreed that surely the message
was meant for you, the sons of Ethan Hawkins. I sailed to find you,
Benjamin, and found you, Jeremiah, as well. Then I surely knew Fate
was leading my way."

They were all silenced by the confluence of events that had brought
them together.

Jeremiah was first to speak. "This has to be the same cave I saw in
my vision," he declared. "It lies behind the waterfall. I saw it as I held
the stone." Jeremiah looked at the crystal still in the palm of his hand.
Its diamond light was a prism of colors, refracting around the room.

"Father always said the crystal would glow in your hands one day,"
Benjamin confirmed, feeling genuine joy for his brother.

"It's something I wanted so desperately," Jeremiah sighed. "I'm so
glad to have experienced it."

"It's yours to work with if you wish," Benjamin reminded his brother.

Jeremiah stared at the crystal as the fire crackled inside the hearth.

For the briefest moment, he saw the crystal tossed among the flames, as it had been years before. But swiftly the image faded.

Then Jeremiah stood and retrieved the burlap that had covered the crystal. And as he carefully wrapped the stone, for another instant, he was transported back to the cottage in Hunstanton, the day he searched frantically for the crystal. As the memory dissolved, the crystal's hold on him was released as well, and he gladly returned the stone to Benjamin.

His face an expression of quiet contentment, Jeremiah went to Abigail and Elizabeth Rebecca, wrapping his long arms around them. "My life is full. As brief as it was, I have come to know the beauty of our father's crystal and gained all I needed. I'll leave its mysteries for others to know."

Chapter 4

Izzy, Will, Nora, Charlie May & Lucy

A gentle early morning rain gave way to bright sunshine, and with that change in the weather, consensus was reached to make an early afternoon visit to Katonah. Now that Will and Nora were no longer suspects in the blackout or in Jason DeWitt's demise, they were all eager to view the property that they hoped was the site of the waterfall depicted on the silver box.

After a hearty breakfast, they readied themselves for what they were certain would be a much less chaotic and harrowing experience than they'd been through in the previous days.

It was a mere one-hour drive from Charlie May's farm in New Paltz to the real estate office in Katonah. They were still in the beautiful Hudson Valley, moving closer to what might have been the land settled centuries earlier by Benjamin Hawkins. They would know soon.

With Lucy's able driving, they arrived precisely on time for Charlie May's two o'clock appointment with Frank and Bonnie Hammerstein, husband, wife and real-estate partners.

Frank had worn many hats during his seventy years on the planet, from hotel manager to art dealer. But real estate was his passion. Bonnie was a former history teacher who enjoyed digging into the past of the houses they sold. And now, as a world traveler who savored experiencing different places and cultures, she also loved telling stories of the neighborhoods that she and Frank represented. Each brought a unique brand of real estate wisdom to the table.

"I see you've brought the whole family!" Bonnie welcomed them at the door, introducing herself and Frank.

"Yes, friends and family," said Charlie May. "Izzy and I are cousins. And these are our dear friends, Will, Nora and Lucy."

"I think you're going to love this property. It's been in the Walker family for generations," Frank explained.

"The farmhouse is charming! It predates the Revolutionary War," Bonnie noted.

"Why is the owner selling, after all these years?" asked Charlie May.

"You know, timing is everything." Frank had a ready answer. "I think he's decided that it's the right moment to live a different life. But he's not looking for any buyer."

"No? What kind of person is he looking for?" Charlie May was intrigued.

"It's all about appreciating the land. It's been so good to all the Walker generations," Bonnie explained.

"Can we meet Mr. Walker?" Will inquired, hoping he could be a source of more information about the Hawkins family.

"Let's first see if you like the house," Frank suggested. He was always acutely aware of a seller's time and wouldn't bother one with less-than-serious buyers.

"How well do you know the property?" Izzy asked.

"We know it quite well. Wouldn't you say, Frank?" Bonnie responded. "We've been friends with the present owner, Colt Walker, for many years, and have been to the house many times."

Izzy removed the silver box from his backpack and held it up for Frank and Bonnie. "Does this look familiar? Is there a cliff like this one? And a waterfall?"

The Hammersteins appeared dumbfounded.

"Where did you get this?" Frank asked.

"It's a family heirloom," Izzy answered.

Bonnie turned to Frank. "That engraving is very similar to the large drawing over the mantle in the library, don't you think?"

"You're right, Bonnie. And if I remember correctly, Colt showed me that very spot once. It's not far from the farmhouse. I never put the two together before now."

"I am interested in buying the property," Charlie May announced, "but we need to confirm this site exists and is part of the sale."

Frank and Bonnie were used to meeting all types in their line of work, but these people had so many odd questions and connections. This seemed anything but a straight real estate deal. Were they after something from Colt Walker? The Hammersteins had a sterling reputation. They protected their clients from "snoops and kooks," as they liked to say. And they didn't want their good name tarnished.

Charlie May recognized the sudden air of caution and wanted to clarify. "Let me explain. Even though the Walkers have lived there for generations, we have reason to believe that our ancestors are part of this property's history too."

Frank and Bonnie were immediately more at ease. "Oh, we understand that. Everyone's searching for their ancestors," Bonnie agreed. "Frank just sent in his DNA to see where his family comes from."

Everyone smiled. If Frank and Bonnie could only know the lengths to which Izzy had gone in search of his family connections....

"Well, the only way we'll know for sure is to go find out!" Frank declared, never one to turn down a possible sale, no mater how peculiar the circumstance.

He ushered everyone to their cars, promising, "It's short ride. Follow me!"

As they arrived at the old farmhouse, Izzy and Will exchanged a silent nod that conveyed a mutual thought: *Well, this is it!* Then, with a large open meadow before them, they started walking with an anticipation that was palpable.

"Wouldn't you like to see the house first?" Bonnie asked.

"Let's see the land before we show them the house," Frank advised, reminding his wife of what mattered in this sale.

"During the summer this is all covered in tall, lush grass," he noted, starting his sales pitch. "Colt mows it to create a variety of paths that lead to different parts of the property."

As they approached a wooded area, there were remnants of stone walls that Bonnie said had been there since colonial times. Tall trees of maple, oak, white and black birch stood together. They were surprised to see a path that clearly cut through the dense woodlands.

"I don't remember this path," Frank said. "But then, to be honest, we haven't come this far out from the house to show the property since Colt listed it with us."

"How far do you folks want to walk?" Bonnie asked, checking her watch. "I guess we've got plenty of time before the sun sets."

They had walked about a mile or so when they began to hear water.

"It must be over there," Izzy pointed. They left the path and walked a few yards to a clearing. As each of them emerged from the woods, they gazed at an astounding scene.

"It's just like the engraving on the silver box!" Nora confirmed.

"And after all these years, still the same," Will added in wonder.

"Just like Colt's drawing in the library," Bonnie whispered to Frank.

Izzy was in awe of the moment. "If only my father and Uncle Sam could be here now…."

Lucy grabbed hold of Izzy's arm. "For sure, I always thought you were a little obsessed with your family stories, Iz," she admitted, "until now."

"My grandfather enjoyed describing Jeremiah's historical importance to our family business. But he always wanted to know more," Charlie May acknowledged. "I wish he could be here too."

"Let's climb the waterfall and see what we can find!" Will proposed, trotting off in the direction of the water.

"Oh, I don't think that's such a great idea!" Bonnie replied, voicing her concern. "It looks wet from the water. What if someone falls?"

"Yes, we can't let Colt be liable," Frank stated firmly.

"Don't worry. We'll take full responsibility," Izzy yelled, taking off after Will.

Nora and Lucy were immediately on Izzy's heels, calling out for Will to wait.

Charlie May gave the Hammersteins a confident smile and then followed the rest toward the waterfall.

Bonnie and Frank hung back, not sure what to do....

Chapter 5

Hudson Valley
AUGUST 1694
Third day

Daniel, Jeremiah & Benjamin

When Daniel Fletcher left England to sail to America, he had only his instinct and the encouragement of Isaac Newton, whom he respected more than any other man, to guide his way. And even when he arrived in New York and discovered Jeremiah, in all the wide world a mere few days journey from his brother, Daniel was not fully certain of his task. Was the crystal's time with the Hawkins family complete? Had the time come for he and Newton to take possession of the crystal and to experience its power and unleash its secrets?

Now though, after the events of the previous night, Daniel understood completely that the crystal's legacy was meant to be passed on to a Hawkins generation in another time. He wished Newton was here with him, to see that they were keeping faith with the future.

It was early morning when Daniel, Jeremiah and Benjamin greeted the sun together in the open field near Benjamin's cabin. As they walked back to prepare for the task ahead of them, Daniel expounded on the alchemist's journey — a code intended for the glorification of both man and God.

"Alchemy is understanding that all substance is God's mind materialized," he explained. "There will come a time when our eternal life-force will flow in its full glory through our physical form — a form that will evolve and unfold through time, as Earth makes her way through the cosmic sky. A river of creative power from the source of all things will channel through us like never before, when what we become will be beyond the boundary of today."

Neither Jeremiah or Benjamin responded with words, but as the pair entered the cabin, both felt inspired by Daniel's portrayal of the future world and its possibilities.

"The cosmic clock of the great celestial bodies is aligned to assist you in fulfilling your purpose with this crystal," Captain Alfredo observed as he joined the three men at the breakfast table.

When Jacob was also seated, Abigail and Catherine brought out platters of food for their first meal of the day. Afterward they all lingered, to make the necessary plans.

"We know the ideal place for the crystal to rest," noted Catherine. "From Daniel's visitor, to Jeremiah's vision, to Emma Wells' silver box and Benjamin's card, to Captain Alfredo's land, the waterfall calls to us so she may fulfill her destiny."

Jacob, who had been silent through much of the meal, asked a most pertinent question. "If the crystal is intended to have a new purpose in the future, how will this happen? What is to ensure that it's found and at the appointed time?"

"Excellent questions, Jacob," Daniel stated. "We need to leave a clue — something that is not too obvious — to ensure that only the rightful souls find it."

Benjamin was surveying the diary. "I have an idea. Let's devise a lyric for the ear and eye of a future Hawkins to decipher. If this man or woman be true to the task, the heavens will see to it that the diamond crystal is found. Just as the stone came to Father, as I found it later by the uprooted tree and, now, as it has spoken to Jeremiah to guide us with his vision."

"Agreed," said Jeremiah.

"But how can we be certain the verse will reach the right person?" Pragmatic Jacob still questioned the plan.

Benjamin pointed to the diary. "We'll hide it inside."

"Here." Jeremiah tapped on the cover. "This leather has sufficient thickness. We'll slice it open and place Benjamin's lyric inside."

"So the diary will be separate from the crystal?" Jacob asked. "Who will keep the diary?"

For a moment they all paused. If one brother kept it, would the other be jealous?

"You keep it, Benjamin," Jeremiah offered. "I'll hold no ill will."

Benjamin thought for a moment and then, looking at Jeremiah and Abigail, spoke from his heart. "For my family to keep the diary would not be fair to you and yours.... But what if Daniel Fletcher shall keep it secure in his possession and, in time, he will give it to Jacob? In turn, Jacob, you will give it to your children, and they to theirs. And each Fletcher generation shall receive the same set of instructions: to seek out the rightful Hawkins generation and return the diary."

Jeremiah concurred. "Yes, we'll pass it on to the Fletchers. Daniel, Father thanked you as much as he did Newton for giving him the diary. And now we thank you and Jacob for keeping it."

"But how will the right generation be found?" Jacob asked, considering his new obligation and even more confounded by it. "This seems a most difficult task to complete when it will happen perhaps far into the future."

"My visitor offered clues to the future time line of restoration," Daniel assured them. And then, as he recalled the visitation, he took a deep breath and welcomed images that accumulated in his mind. When Daniel spoke, it was from deep within, from beyond memory, beyond intellect, beyond intuition. His words gave rise to the poem, with phrases and promises to inspire the future.

"When the moon is full and eclipsed by the sun, as it reaches its solar arc, it will align with the crystal cave. Then cosmic winds from the center of our galaxy will blow a divine influence that will strike a chord in the human heart and bring about an unfolding. The earth crystal will be caught by the cosmic wave and bestow blessings that now sleep in the mind of humanity. A new man and a new woman will emerge with traits and abilities that have lain dormant in the human form, yet they will be of kind and courageous heart. Their trials will be many, but they will emerge stronger with a clear vision of what is good and decent in this world, and in service of its cause."

When the poem was complete, Catherine wrote it out in a final form, for she had the most beautiful script among them.

"We must remember to provide the coordinates, so when the time is right, it helps navigate the way to the cave," added Alfredo. "Bring Newton's telescope, and let's make sure it's in order."

Jacob agreed, immediately retrieving his prized procession from the wagon.

"When shall we leave?" Catherine asked, never considering that only the men would go.

"Tomorrow," said Benjamin. "We'll find the cave, all of us, to conceal the diamond crystal stone." He looked at Jeremiah and the brothers nodded in unison, sealing the agreement.

Then it would be done. And it did not go unnoticed by any of those present that this journey together would define them for the rest of their days and that of the generations to follow.

But even as the decision was made, a doubt entered the mind of each brother and of Daniel Fletcher too. When the moment arrived, could they really let go of the crystal's power and influence? Might it speak to one of them in such a way that a different future would take hold?

Chapter 6

Hudson Valley
AUGUST 1694
Fourth day, late morning

Hawkins Families, Daniel, Jacob & Alfredo

"There it is, the pool of water, and the waterfall above," Alberto Alfredo called out as they reached the ridge overlooking their destination. There was a natural path lined with colorful wild flowers that led down to a pool of crystal clear water.

They had headed out early that morning, and reach this secluded corner of Alfredo's land before the sun reached its noon spot in the sky. Now the horses and wagon followed the path to a lush grazing spot beside the water. The entire party, adults and children, would make the climb up the side of the waterfall on foot. But before beginning their ascent, they rested a moment. The water reflected a blue sky and the sound of the waterfall flowing from the rocks above was a soothing presence.

Without a word, they started up the rise. Each reverent step they climbed gave them a sense that they held the future in their hands.

"I see it," Alfredo said, leading the way. Behind the waterfall was a footpath that led into a cave. At the entrance there was a sweet powerful scent of rose. "How odd," Abigail whispered to Jeremiah and they both looked for the source, finding none.

The mouth of the cave was dark and somewhat narrow. Jeremiah had a lantern, which he now lit and passed to Alfredo, who was still in the lead.

"Well, that's a sight!" Alfredo bellowed out.

As they assembled in what was a large vaulted room, they were astonished to see light flooding the walls. They gazed in rapture at the glowing quartz crystals around them. Shafts of sunlight from an opening above spilled onto the floor, sending waves of splendor throughout the cave. A prism-like rainbow flashed colorful rays of light all around the space.

"Look at that!" Benjamin said, as he passed his hand on the side of the cave, which glittered green, blue, red and white. Where he touched, Benjamin could feel the wall vibrate. Without a doubt, this was no ordinary cave.

Jeremiah looked around, amazed to see images that were familiar from his vision. He took hold of Abigail's hand and whispered, "My vision has come true in the here and now."

"This is exactly how my visitor described the cave that he stumbled upon!" Daniel confirmed. He had always believed his visitation was an otherworldly experience, though he sometimes questioned whether it might have been all a dream. He knew of ancient tales of traveling into the past and future during dreamtime. But standing here, Daniel was astonished at how real it was. And dream or not, there was a purpose — to bring Benjamin and Jeremiah together in this place — to fulfill their destiny and that of the crystal stone.

In the silence of the cave, all that could be heard was the waterfall thundering outside. Inside everyone was held spellbound by the waves of light that cascaded down the walls and onto the floor. Their senses opened wide and they drifted away, musing about how had they arrived at such a place:

> Abigail imagined the first time she and sister Bess
> saw Jeremiah sprawled out in the alley, so badly beaten
> he was lucky to be alive. They nursed his poor soul back
> to health. At the time she wasn't sure which was more

severe, the wounds to his body or the emotional gashes that lined his face. She had felt so drawn to him. And when he joined them on the voyage to America, her own heart stirred with gladness. Aboard ship, when he saved Bess from certain hell, she knew that this man would be a blessing in their lives. He awoke the love that had been buried in her heart after her short time with Miles Briar, God rest his soul. She was devoted to Jeremiah, so courageous in body and spirit, and she reveled in their love and for their daughter in her arms.

Catherine's imagination flew back to the night when a raging fire engulfed her family home. Without hesitation, Benjamin ran into the flames to save her father, who was passed out and trapped inside. In Benjamin's daring and selflessness, she saw his nature. But, even before that, the young man who arrived at the fort had an irresistible twinkle in his eye that intrigued her. They touched each other's hearts beyond words, and she knew that their destiny together would run the length of their days. And with young Alexander, and God willing, a second healthy babe to come, their happiness would also grow beyond measure in the years ahead.

Captain Alfredo returned to his first voyages from England to its young colonies and the gratitude of the crown that gave him this promising land in this extraordinary valley. His thoughts recalled the letter from Daniel asking him to take a young lad in trouble onboard his ship. Unschooled in the ways of the world, and naive to the harshness that dwells between men, Benjamin had a quiet faith, even as sorrow hung about him like the yoke on an ox. And then, when that young man saved the captain from mutiny and certain death, he felt a kinship with Benjamin and was determined to keep an eye on his march through the years, by inviting him to settle this remarkable land.

Jacob considered the opportunities that had come to him as his father's eldest son and how his fate was shifting from what he had expected growing up in Hunstanton. The chance to go to Cambridge and meet Isaac Newton, and now the experience of traveling to America with his father and Captain Alfredo, opened his eyes to new possibilities for his life. Perhaps the New World was meant to be his world too, as Benjamin and Jeremiah had discovered. Perhaps a wife for him, a future for him, was to be found here and not in England.

Daniel remembered his friend Ethan. Here Daniel was, finally having reached America, as he and Ethan had intended to do decades ago before illness — or was it fate? — determined they would go no farther than the North Sea. They had both found happiness, he in Hannah, Ethan in Elizabeth. Yet Ethan had also found the diamond crystal, which had been a blessing and a curse. Ethan's death was a blow that still echoed in his heart. It was left to him, as he kept faith with his beloved friend, to ferry Benjamin out of harm's way. And then with Benjamin safely away, he tried but failed to guide Jeremiah from the torment that vexed his soul. Yet Daniel had come to understand that everything had its time and place — which had led to bringing the brothers together here in this moment.

Jeremiah and Benjamin, in a bond that only those born at the same time could know, remembered their cottage by the North Sea and their father Ethan. How the three of them had lived a life of rhythms that blended days of carefree joy and complex struggles too. Who knows how they would have lived out their days if Benjamin had not found the stone by the upturned tree? When he took the crystal in his hands and watched it glow, the light of the life they knew faded away. The trouble that ensued led to their father's death and rent the fabric of their humble lives. Yet now in finding each other, sharing their sorrows and regrets, forgiving the hurt they inflicted on each other, and binding those wounds with the love each still held for his brother, Benjamin and Jeremiah could see a way toward a greater peace — a blessing on them both and on the memory of their father.

As they stood in the cave, caught in the grip of reverie, each sensed that the cycle of change was upon them. One story was coming to a close and a new one was about to begin.

Chapter 7

Izzy, Will, Nora, Charlie May & Lucy

Fortunately, the trail beside the waterfall had a gentler slope than might be expected, even as the water made a roaring dive into the natural pool below. Before long they were all well over halfway up the rock outcrop. Will was the first to spot the entrance to a cave. He waited for the others to join him.

"There's actually light in there," Will said to Izzy, the next to arrive.

"Must be sunlight coming through from an opening above," Izzy proposed.

"We'll find out," Will answered, as he led the group inside.

Not far within they were surrounded by a spectrum of colors.

"I can't believe what I'm seeing. This cave is made of quartz crystal!" Will announced. He was reminded of his father's warehouse filled with crystals.

"The light is bouncing everywhere! It's incredible," Nora added.

Charlie May's eyes sparkled. "It's beautiful."

"Izzy, this is amazing!" Lucy looked for Izzy's reaction. But he didn't answer. "Izzy, is there anything wrong?"

Izzy stood in the center of the cave, not moving, awestruck by what he saw.

As Lucy, Will, Charlie May and Nora gathered around Izzy, each in turn slipped into another state, as Izzy had, brought on by the light and vibration of the crystal cave. With the waterfall filling their ears with nature's song, they had heard the call to enter an uncommon world — and when each walked through the door they experienced the moment differently:

Charlie May felt the depth of her heritage rising from her soul. Something had lay dormant there. Now, in the crystal cave it was coming alive. The Hawkins family story was one of challenge, mystery and redemption. She was living proof, centuries in the making, of how time crosses beyond boundaries to fulfill an evolutionary destiny written in the stars. As she and Izzy, descendants of Jeremiah and Benjamin, experienced this moment together, Charlie May realized that the ordinary state of mind was only the tip of the iceberg of reality. She could feel her essence, the power of her life-force, expanding beyond any boundaries. All of life's mysteries felt infinitely inspiring.

Nora's eyes filled with light and her mind was quiet with the grace of peace. Her life for many years had been a race with an unrelenting purpose. She found success as a journalist, an exposer of truths hidden in the crafted corners of deceit. She had triumphantly climbed that ladder. Will's fall was devastating but now it seemed to have been a blessing in disguise. She felt free, ready for a new phase of her life — to let go of what was, of old beliefs she had lived by, and to fill her life with new beginnings. To her joy, she felt the promise of having a child would be fulfilled, and her heart swelled with love and gratitude for Will and the love they shared. Their journey so defined for such a long time, now turned to empty pages yet to be written, foretelling new wonders to discover, new secrets to reveal.

For Lucy, her journey with Izzy was the core of her life so far. When Agnes died, Izzy was a soul adrift in despair. As they discovered, life brings people together in unusual ways. She had helped him heal and learned from him too. Her heart blossomed with happiness and satisfaction watching Izzy realize his long-held dream. But even as she took delight in his joy at recovering the Hawkins family legacy, she could feel an ending and a new beginning too. In this moment her mind was lit with excitement. The time was ripe to seek new vistas of self-discovery. Yes, in some way she and Izzy would forever be traveling together, but she needed to discover herself anew. She could feel the rhythm of her heart beating out a passion for life yet to be explored.

Will was a dreamer, a student of the night sky, impassioned by the whole cosmic universe. His quest to understand the world led him to devote his life to modern science, to ponder the nature of reality and how it worked. And while he appreciated the need to define and classify, he quickly understood that defining something can never approach experiencing its essence. Rather than adhering to conditioned scientific orthodoxy, he left the door wide open for his imagination to roam the mysteries behind everything he considered. Now as he stood beside Nora, the woman he loved with ever fiber in his being, and beside Izzy, the man whose destiny had entangled Will's own, he felt the vibration of the crystal cave encompass him. It was unlike anything he had ever experienced. There was no need to explain or categorize it. Rather he allowed it *to be*. He relaxed his body, his breathing eased and it was as though he were inhaling light itself. And he understood that the truth of this moment would stay with him forever and change his life in ways he could not yet know.

Izzy stood in wonder of all that was around him. And as the sun shifted in the late afternoon sky, a shaft of light streamed into the cave from an opening above. A cove on the far wall was lit up in shimmering diamond light. It reminded Izzy of his epiphany in Colorado, when he floated to the Palace of Light. Once again Izzy recalled his dreams within that grand palace and saw the shining light on a pedestal. And he felt himself drifting back there....

"So my friend, you have found what you sought," whispered The Keeper of Light. "You have come a long way, many lifetimes, to be here in this moment."

Chapter 8

Inside the Crystal Cave
1694

A streak of sunlight illuminated the farthest wall from the entrance. There a natural cove was grooved into the wall. Without speaking, as if they had lived this moment before, rehearsed from another time, Benjamin and Jeremiah walked forward together. Benjamin removed the crystal from a wool sack he carried and handed it to Jeremiah, who unwrapped the burlap cover.

Then Jeremiah placed the stone in the indented space and Benjamin checked it in turn, to ensure it was secure and to give the crystal a parting touch. They stayed there for a while, each remembering the crystal's influence on their lives. For both, there was amazement mixed with gratitude that this was where the family journey with the crystal would end. That after all the years of angst, it was possible for the crystal to be the center of such an act of communion.

The sunlight grew stronger, as if the sun and diamond crystal were alive and speaking to each other. The crystal grew brighter and brighter in its new home, until sparkles of blue plasma filled the air.

"Benjamin, do you feel that?" Jeremiah whispered in wonder.

"Yes," Benjamin responded.

"Father's presence! I can feel him!" Jeremiah's voice was thick with emotion.

"I as well," Benjamin confirmed.

Tears wet their cheeks as the brothers were surrounded by their father's love.

"Forgive us, Father," they recited in unison.

Their words of contrition seemed suspended in the air, and then a language of light filled their ears with a familiar tone. "Forgive me, as I forgive you, my darling sons. Each of us has learned from the others. The glory of life unfolds in unimaginable ways, and we discover we are more than we thought we were or could be."

Benjamin and Jeremiah took deep breaths, letting that blessing sink into their souls....

Then distracted by a familiar fragrance, Jeremiah turned to his brother, "Roses! Benjamin! Do you smell the roses?"

"I do, but where do you suppose the scent is coming from? There are no roses here."

Both brothers closed their eyes and took deep, steady breaths. With each inhalation the bouquet became stronger and stronger. Immediately images of roses filled their inner vision — red, white, and pink, too. And from above a woman with long flowing robes appeared to them. With an outstretched arm she held a gilded winged staff, shimmering in a stream of golden light.

Jeremiah instantly remembered the first time she appeared to him in the cottage in England. That time he had turned away from her offering, her blessings. But now would he?

Benjamin, who was accustomed to other-worldly images, was awed by the sight nonetheless, and waited expectantly, uncertain what this vision could mean.

Then she gazed upon their faces, her eyes overflowing with kindness. With a sweep of her arm she touched each brother upon the heart with her golden staff. As she did so, she proclaimed, "Blessings to you. Blessings and great love, my boys of light. From my womb you entered the world of flesh and bone. Though born at the same time, each of you is a sacred soul consecrating the earth with his uniqueness. Each of you is a joy to me forever."

Jeremiah and Benjamin stood motionless as the air became filled with glorious sound.

Then she opened her arms wide, her hands hovering over them. With her chest gleaming brightly, golden light came pouring from her heart.

In that instant their hearts flew open and Jeremiah and Benjamin knew Elizabeth, their dear mother. Not yet two years old when she died, all their lives they wondered who she was. Now she came to them and they felt the totality of her being. And a lifetime of a mother's eternal love, ever-present, inscribed this moment forever on all their hearts.

"Love and blessings," those words echoed in their ears as the image of their mother began to fade and then…she was gone.

It was over. All that they had been, all that they were, all that they would be, was framed in a new light. Jeremiah and Benjamin opened their eyes and looked at each other neither able to speak yet. But they could see peace and contentment in each other's eyes.

Now they turned to beckon the others, and together all formed a semicircle around the stone where it sat in the wall of the cave.

"Fortunate are they who transcend the ordinary to glimpse the world beyond the world," Daniel murmured.

Yet this was not a moment of truth and restoration for Jeremiah and Benjamin alone. The crystal cave offered insights to all that were present, as their hearts became flooded with the churning waters of the unresolved — all frustrations, anger, anxiety, and resentments that they had experienced in their length of days. Their minds stood transfixed taking it all in, a cosmic instance that opened wide the gates of time. The fullness of the human drama — love and joy, fear and hardship, the nature of life itself — filled the light in their eyes.

Then the cave grew brighter still, until the whole cavern was in diamond white light. And the brightness flooded their bodies with wisdom bathed in the light of loving kindness and compassion, and their hearts were drained of the pains and fears of the past. All their thoughts were still. No idea entered their minds, no barriers, no borders, nothing to measure or define — only the flow of life from the fountain of all life.

And their spirits descended to fill every part of their bodies, and their entire beings were enlightened, shining brightly in *The One.*

In that moment they transcended all time and space, and everything they ever experienced blended together into *is-ness* and ineffable wonder was upon them.

In the midst of his own epiphany, Daniel felt a familiar presence. It was the visitor who had sent him on his journey to seek out Benjamin.

In his mind, Daniel asked, *"Who are you?"* And the answer came in a flash of diamond light that anchored in his heart.

"I am The Keeper of Light. It is the light that shines without beginning or end. It shines brightly, always and forever, beyond time and space, from *The Eternal Heart.* It dwells in every heart, and fills all things. It is the essence of life itself."

Daniel listened, watching for a form within the brilliant light.

"I am that light of pure awareness," The Keeper continued. "You are that light of pure awareness too. All is from *The One.* All is One. I am in your heart, as you are in my heart. From the heart of a grain of sand, the heart of a drop of water, the heart of the windswept breeze, to the heart of the earth, the heart of the sun, moon and stars, to the heart at the center of the galaxy — all diamond light — ever connected, the essence of awareness lit by the boundless light of eternity."

And the old alchemist, Daniel Fletcher, found his philosopher's stone. It was there all along, alive with every beat of his heart.

The moment of profound insight passed and it was as though they all awoke, once again back in the earthly plane, as when they first entered the cave, before the light and vibration moved them to a different place.

It was time to depart. Each felt it intuitively.

"The crystal stone has found a new home. Its destiny remains to be fulfilled in another time," Daniel confirmed.

"Our work is done," Alberto Alfredo added with finality.

One by one they exited the cave. Benjamin was the last to leave, and as he looked back at the crystal, still glowing in brilliant light, he whispered, "Thank you."

Then they slowly made their way down the path beside the waterfall, feeling the heat of the day and the wider world after the coolness and mystery of the cave. When they reached the pool of water below, a hummingbird hovered among them and chirped for their attention.

Daniel caught Benjamin's eye. They both knew the symbolism of the hummingbird.

"Ah, how fitting!" exclaimed Daniel. "The hummingbird comes with the message for us to enjoy the sweetness of life and to express love more fully throughout the day. Our little friend here is capable of the most amazing feats despite its small size, traveling great distances and even flying backwards. The hummingbird invites us to recognize our ability to adapt and be resilient, all the while being playful in spirit."

Alexander suddenly broke from his mother's hand as he tried to reach for the bird, which was away in a flash. Taking a tumble, he quickly picked himself up, and then seeing the assembly all focused on him, sat down amid a bed of flowers and began to laugh.

"I think Alexander has the right idea," Jacob observed. "To enjoy life and always remember to laugh."

With smiles but few words, they walked to the wagon and horses. As they made their way back to the cabin of Benjamin and Catherine, contentment was a common bond among them.

Chapter 9

Inside the Crystal Cave
Present Day

"So my friend, you have found what you sought. You have come a long way — many lifetimes to be here in this moment." With those words whispered by The Keeper of Light, Izzy felt himself inside the Palace of Light, once again standing before the eternal crystal that vibrated humanity's common destiny with Earth.

"Your journey is everyone's journey," The Keeper of Light explained. "The diamond light shines love from *The One Heart* that lights everyone, everything, everywhere. It is a light of unfoldment that reveals all of existence. From the most refined vibration to the most dense there is but one substance — divine light. When the light of pure awareness is lived in the heart of humanity, the boundaries of time and space disappear, and the fear of death and separation no longer hold sway."

Izzy listened to the ethereal being before him describing the light that resides in all hearts, that heals all emotional wounds, that transforms all fear-driven thought and renews the body, so it can encompass the light of *All That Is*.

"From this moment, every cell within you will be set aglow with new purpose. Your senses will expand beyond all boundaries. You will hear color and see sound; your lungs will breathe the breath of ethereal white diamond light; you will know the essence of all things. You will travel the endless universe, creating with a loving heart, worlds of wonder as you go, residing in the highest states of consciousness. You will encompass the light of *All That Is*."

Izzy listened to this prophecy with awe, and when The Keeper had finished, Izzy could no longer hold back his curiosity. "Who are you?" he asked.

"You and I are one being. I am you and you are me — in spirit, in soul, in body — encompassing the experience of many lives that have dwelled in the past and the present, and will dwell in the future. I have been with you before time — a *Self* that has always been and always will be. Search your heart for the truth."

Izzy could feel the truth in The Keeper's answer. He took a deep breath and focused on his heart. As he did, diamond light filled Izzy's chest and the most sublime feeling of elation and beauty filled his body. With each beat of his heart, the glory of his being pulsed through his veins. He dove into the essence of himself. His awareness traveled, transcending time and space, and grace of the highest order descended upon him and he knew the totality of who he was, is and will always be.

Then the Palace of Light faded and disappeared. The ethereal being was also no longer before him. Those images no longer resided outside of him but now merged within as one. Izzy felt as if he had returned home.

"Izzy?" Lucy and Will called softly in unison as they stood by his side.

Then Izzy spoke as he pointed toward the crystal. "Lucy, Will, there it is."

"I know. It's the crystal, so beautiful. Are you okay, Izzy?" Lucy asked as she placed her arm around his shoulders. "You stopped speaking, Iz. You seemed to be in another world."

Izzy adjusted his eyes, seeing that he was still in the crystal cave. He looked around at his faithful Lucy, at Will and Nora, at Charlie May.

"Of course," Izzy confirmed. "Never better," he added in words of pure truth.

They waited as Izzy remained in place seemingly not wanting to move yet… and then finally Will asked, "Aren't you going to hold the crystal?"

Izzy looked astonished at the suggestion. His reverence for what they were experiencing had almost numbed his mind to that possibility.

"It's been over 300 years since a Hawkins has held it." Will reminded him. "It's your birthright."

Izzy took a deep breath. He looked first toward Charlie May. It was her birthright too.

Charlie May motioned for him to go ahead. This was Izzy's journey to complete. Intuitively she knew her time with the crystal would come soon enough.

Izzy smiled and nodded yes, to Will and Charlie May, and walked toward the cove where the crystal was perched.

As he approached the stone he felt a wave of energy reach out to him. A peace for all the ages seeped into his bones.

As he touched the crystal everything he ever was instantly slipped away. Everything he thought or felt about himself — the way he experienced himself, was gone….

In utter silence *IZZY* came to rest…. the life he had lead was now in repose — all his striving hushed in the twilight of yesterday. …. And in the next moment, from *a place inside* himself that he didn't recognize, he could feel the emergence of a divine sovereign self. And he waited…

… and then… *THE DEPTH OF HIS SPIRIT BURST ALIVE IN THE FUILLNESS OF ITS EVERLASTING GLORY* …. There were no words, no images, no thoughts, no past, no future. Only *the diamond light of newness from beyond time.* And there he stayed….

…Until…

…The sound of his own familiar voice rose in his ear. "Return to the world. There's more yet *to be*…."

… And Izzy instantly knew he would visit *THIS PLACE* often to explore the promise of a new horizon….

Then, as though offering a benediction, he spoke with an uncommon tenderness. "It's time to go home."

Chapter 10

Hudson Valley

AUGUST 1694

Fourth day, late afternoon

Hawkins Families, Daniel, Jacob, Alfredo & Emma Wells

"**W**ho's that?" Catherine asked as they approached the cabin. It had been a quiet return journey from the crystal cave, with everyone deep in thought. Even as Catherine's curiosity was aroused, she hoped that nothing would intrude on the peaceful afterglow that continued to resonate from their experience in the crystal cave. She knew that strangers in the wilderness might bring unexpected and unwelcome news.

Abigail was sitting beside her. She shielded her eyes against the sun, low in the sky, to see better. "Looks like a tinker's wagon," she noted. "Seems familiar…."

About then, Jeremiah, driving the wagon, and Benjamin, seated beside him, each let out a holler. "Emma Wells!" they said at the same time, beaming at each other.

Jeremiah picked up the pace, as he and Benjamin delighted again and again at Emma's timely appearance.

As they greeted Emma in her covered wagon, Daniel, Jacob and Alfredo, on horseback, were reaching the cabin, with growing interest about this unexpected visitor.

"I see that the two lost brothers have found each other!" Emma announced, grinning from ear to ear.

"Emma! What are you doing here?" Benjamin asked.

"Checking up on the two of you," she declared.

"How did you know to find us?" Jeremiah added.

"I have my ways. I thought you knew that," Emma replied with a knowing smile, the air of mystery still hovering around her.

Catherine and Abigail watched this unlikely reunion, both knowing the significance of Emma Wells. "I remember her," Abigail whispered. "She was entertaining in front of our store."

"I remember her too," Catherine confirmed. "Intriguing she should show up here … now … of all times."

The brothers introduced their families, the women nodding to acknowledge each other. "Yes, of course I remember Catherine, Colonel Steward's daughter. I am still a frequent guest at the fort," Emma confirmed.

Then Benjamin introduced Daniel and Jacob. Emma was duly impressed. They each possessed such grace.

Captain Alfredo was the last to step forward. He had been holding back, still basking in the experience of the crystal cave and not wanting to change his state of mind.

"And who is this handsome fellow?" Emma asked, not waiting for an introduction. She was instantly captivated by Alfredo's exotic appearance.

"Captain Alberto Alfredo, at your service, madam."

"Emma Wells," she said, extending her hand. Alberto had the distinct impression that Emma was kissing him with her eyes. He was not the least bit disturbed by the attention and to show his delight, he bowed low, to place his lips on the top of her hand.

That evening as the sun descended behind the highlands around them, the home of Benjamin and Catherine was filled with good cheer. While the future was unknown, the past seemed cleansed and the moment was free, overflowing with love and with the satisfaction of fulfilling a task appointed to them.

Even the uncanny presence of Emma Wells seemed fitting to the successful conclusion of Benjamin and Jeremiah's extraordinary journey.

Daniel Fletcher leaned over to catch the ear of Alfredo, sitting beside him at the table. "Life is forever a mystery, is it not, Alberto?"

In response, Alfredo let loose with a hearty laugh. "Indeed, sometimes we are so sure of what will happen … only to find that what seemed inevitable never comes to pass. And then we watch in wonder as what we think is impossible appears in stunning surprise!"

Later, with Elizabeth Rose asleep, Jeremiah slipped outside and Abigail followed, watchful as always of her husband and his deep well of feeling. When she caught up with him, out near the field, he was looking up at another night sky sprinkled with stars.

"Where are you?" Abigail asked. "You look so far away."

"I am here. I am in the cave. I am back in my old cottage in Hunstanton," Jeremiah answered softly. "I always hoped that I would see Benjamin again, though my dark heart, before I met you, was intent on revenge. But that it would happen like this…. I am so glad and so grateful and still filled with the wonder of it all."

"Life often takes us in unplanned directions," Abigail affirmed.

"It does! But all this is as much mystery to me as the good fortune that brought me to you, and that brought us Elizabeth Rose. I never expected to feel the diamond crystal, to have a vision — to know the power that my father and Benjamin felt. I understand now why they were so compelled to possess the stone."

"And you, my dearest? You gave it up when you could have had your time with it. Why?"

Jeremiah answered by first wrapping Abigail in his arms. "Years ago, it would have been different. Then it would have affected me, as it did them. But not now. I meant it when I said it holds no sway over me. It is where it should be, waiting for its future."

Then he paused, not sure how to explain himself. "There was a part of my vision I did not share. I saw others in the cave, in garments I didn't recognize, and they too were there for the crystal."

Abigail immediately understood his meaning. "Jeremiah! Perhaps you traveled to another time and place and saw those in the future who will find the crystal? Oh, my dear, no wonder you gave it up so willingly."

Jeremiah hugged her tighter. "Besides. I have my own diamond light. I have you, and Elizabeth Rose, and our lives together."

Then looking up, he raised his hand, open to the sky. "I'm ready to dream new dreams, with you, reaching for the stars. And…."

As Jeremiah paused, Abigail asked, "And what?"

"I have my brother. Wherever our paths lead now, we have found peace together."

Sleep eluded Daniel Fletcher that night as he pondered his life. He reflected on how he and Isaac Newton, alchemists both, went in search of the greatest mystery of all — how the physical world, in all its multiplicity, materialized from spiritual ether.

Inevitably, Daniel thought back to how he and his dear friend Ethan had set out for the New World, all those many years ago. And now the wonder that he was in that world, in America, with Ethan's sons, having helped to bring them together again.

Yet he understood that it was ultimately the courage of Jeremiah and Benjamin that delivered them to a hard-won destiny. Each discovered the strength to reach beyond the anguish in his life, and to climb out of the depths of jealousy and hatred. And in doing so, to hear the love song still playing in his heart and that of his brother.

Daniel truly appreciated how far Jeremiah and Benjamin had traveled. How it was the illumination of love that led them through a winding path, from difficulty and loss, to experience divine grace. He recognized it as a universal, redeeming gift to all of humanity, with the power to heal and reconcile every heart. In that moment Daniel wished every man and every woman could feel love's flow, lifting the mind and heart to new vistas, to see the world in new ways.

Those thoughts brought him back to his visitor, The Keeper of Light. In their first meeting, in England, the visitor had foretold of a new time to come…. "*In the course of human affairs, cosmic winds from the center of our galaxy will blow a divine influence that will strike a hidden chord in the human heart. It will bring about an unfolding. A new man and a new woman will emerge with traits and abilities that have lain dormant in the human form. The earth crystal will be caught by the cosmic wave and bestow blessings that now sleep in the mind of humanity.*"

Then Daniel recalled a long-ago discussion with Newton about the nature of Earth's core and whether it might be of crystal. Certainly the cave was proof of Earth's crystalline nature. And as Earth sped through the galaxy, cosmic forces would surely influence her properties, and that in turn would alchemize the life of every man and women on its surface — a transformation of flesh into spirit.

Daniel was sure the "Earth crystal" that now slept in the cave beyond the waterfall was destined to "bestow its blessings in untold ways that his imagination had yet to grasp."

At last Daniel drifted off to sleep, and in his dreams his mind opened to a vision of a magnificent meadow. Morning dew on green grass glistened in the sun and wild flowers smiled as he walked a path that led to a shimmering Palace of Light.

∽

There were others about that night, awake and exploring the meaning of an encounter that seemed guided by the stars. As those within the cabin and those bedded down outside welcomed soothing sleep, Alberto went to Emma in her wagon. She was waiting for him, ready to discover a new beginning — one they both saw in each others eyes the moment they met.

Chapter 11

Hudson Valley
AUGUST 1694
Fifth day

Hawkins Families, Daniel & Jacob, Alfredo & Emma

The following morning Benjamin was sitting in the shade of the front porch, with the diary in his lap. It was turned to Ethan's last entry, which was written the evening before he died. Jeremiah, Daniel and Jacob were just coming back from a morning walk.

"Good morning, Benjamin," Jeremiah greeted his brother.

"And a fine day it is," Benjamin replied.

"What are you reading?" Daniel asked.

"Father's diary — his last entry. "I could never make complete sense of what he was trying to say in this entry," Benjamin admitted.

"Read it to us," Jeremiah suggested. To which Benjamin softly smiled and complied.

> "*Good stewards of this Earth, Newton's gravity holds us to her skin as we spin with the great spheres of influence traveling through the seasons of time, marked by the stars in the night sky.*
>
> "*Our life-force streams through us and emerges all around us. It is alive with a mystery that is more than*

it seems to the ordinary eye. Our senses flow with signs and powers that when opened wide, give way to limitless imagination. Are not all things possible?

"Each heartbeat unfolds the light of eternal bounty. As within, so without; as without, so within. The great spheres, near and far, racing through space, tell the heart to unfurl her eternal glory and the heart beholds itself.

"The secret is held in the blood that flows in the veins of every man and woman. For together, humanity, bound to the wheel of Earth's dominion, in time will transform all dimensions, separate no more. One unified symphony, vibrating from the highest octaves, will give flight with majesty from on high. No veils remain. The eye of pure awareness is opened...."

Everyone was listening intently, feeling Ethan's inspirational words. Benjamin stopped to take a deep breath before he read the last lines:

"Good stewards of this Earth, the task spans the generations, and then the moment is at hand. The heart opens to the eternal and kisses the night sky. A stream of milk and honey unlocks the riddle of life. Ever-living waters reflect the beauty of the world, and an everlasting current flows from the unknown to the known, ever and forever."

Benjamin's voice faded to quiet and, together, Jeremiah, Benjamin, Daniel and Jacob allowed Ethan's words to wash over them.

Then Jacob, normally the last to speak, took the lead. "I think I know what Ethan was trying to tell us."

"Go on," Daniel urged, eager to hear what his son would say.

"We are wed to this Earth and our destinies arise together with hers. We are like convergent waters — Earth streaming in a sea of planets and stars, and humanity a river of life-force flowing through this world. And we each play a part in the fate of the other. When the time is right, our currents will blend in such a way as to form a new stream of life. What will emerge is our mutual transformation, when a new light will shine. We and our good Earth will pass on to a new plane of existence, where the veils of separation are no more. And life, ongoing and everlasting, is a continuous cycle that renews itself, transforming our experience from a world that is unknown and mysterious, to one waiting to become known and witnessed. And all that is needed is to become aware."

"It's a unique way of looking at the stars and planets. How did you come by it?" Jeremiah asked, intrigued by Jacob's impressions.

"Newton's telescope. He gave it to me before we left for America and I've been studying the stars ever since."

Benjamin was also struck by Jacob's interpretation. "You seem to have learned a great deal with the telescope."

Jacob waited, eyeing his father, who still seemed to contemplate his words. There was more that he wanted to say, and yet he hesitated, wanting to find the right moment. Something had been brewing in Jacob's mind since the experience in the crystal cave. He had a request, one that he felt could prove pivotal to his future. He had not spoken of it with his father. But sensing that now *was* the moment, Jacob summoned his courage.

"Benjamin, I have something to ask you," he announced.

"Anything, Jacob," Benjamin responded.

With that opening, Jacob turned to address Daniel. "I'm sorry, Father, that I have not discussed this with you first." Then, to Benjamin, "Instead of returning to England, I would like to stay with you and become your student. Will you teach me about the plants you grow here and the healing remedies you make from them?"

And then, to Jeremiah, "And perhaps after, I could come to New York and work in the store with you and Abigail? In that way I might learn commerce and shop keeping. Perhaps then I can determine my place in the world and what my future might hold."

Daniel was astonished at Jacob's request. Why had his son never come to him, seeking his ample knowledge of plants and healing remedies?

"Jacob, I could teach you, in England," Daniel proposed.

"Of course, Father. But I feel something for this place, for America. It's a land of adventure. My heart stirs here."

Though Daniel had been unprepared for Jacob's sudden request, he quickly understood his son's wisdom. Jacob was a young man ready to strike out on his own and America could offer choices not found in Hunstanton.

Benjamin and Jeremiah remained silent, watching the unspoken emotions between Fletcher elder and younger. Both were sympathetic to Jacob's request, yet both also knew the power of a father's hold on a son.

Daniel reached out to grasp Jacob's hand. "My son, my wish to hold you close momentarily blinded me to your desire. You have my blessing for whatever path you follow."

"Thank you, Father!" Jacob beamed, his voice animated with excitement.

Benjamin welcomed the chance to pass along the knowledge he had gained and to repay Daniel's kindness by helping his son. "Jacob, you are more than welcome to stay with Catherine and me," he confirmed. "I will teach you all I know and guide you in discovering your own gifts."

"I would say the same," echoed Jeremiah. "And Henry Rodgers will be pleased to have another strong back in the store!" he laughed.

"But one request, Jacob," Daniel added. "You must promise to write your mother as often as your time allows. And if you can, return to England, if only to visit. I will help your mother understand the richness of this wilderness and the many prospects for a young man like you."

"And you do not mind making the voyage without me?" Jacob asked, making certain all considerations were covered.

Daniel smiled. "I am old, son, but not so old. Besides, I will have Alfredo for company."

Now all were standing, shaking Jacob's hand to seal their agreements. "And Catherine will not mind?" Jacob asked.

Catherine, Abigail and the children were coming out with freshly baked bread and more coffee for the men and heard the last of their conversation.

"Indeed, Jacob, you are welcome here! Benjamin can use the extra hand and of course we will make room for you," Catherine answered. Then, placing one hand on her blooming belly, she added, "Though it may be wise to build your own cabin off yonder, unless you can sleep through two crying babes at night!" And as if on cue, Alexander began to wail, demanding his own slice of bread.

"My own cabin sounds like a very good idea," Jacob concurred, and they all laughed.

"Abigail, Jacob also intends to work beside us in the store," Jeremiah explained, "to learn our trade."

"We can always use more able help! That will suit me just fine!" Abigail agreed.

"Father?" Jacob inquired, for final approval.

"Yes, Jacob, it's settled all around," Daniel smiled, giving Jacob a confirming hug.

Alfredo and Emma Wells returned from riding about Alfredo's land to find everyone gathered around the table, gobbling down the warm bread and enjoying their last sips of coffee.

Talk of the store had reminded Jeremiah of the time that had passed. "We must begin our way back tomorrow," he announced.

"I shall be sorry to say goodbye. I feel as close to you as my own sister," Abigail declared, giving Catherine a warm hug.

"And I dare say your sister, Bess, will be delighted to hear it, Abigail. She was most happy about your visit here," Emma confirmed.

"How in the world do you know that?" Abigail asked, confused. She had been skeptical of Emma's fortune-telling but perhaps....

"She told me herself," Emma explained, "when my travels took me back to your bustling city of New York. I stopped by Rogers & Hawkins and there I learned that you and Jeremiah had joined a party going to find Benjamin in the Hudson Valley. Bess and Henry were most helpful in explaining how I might reach the land of Captain Alberto Alfredo."

Whatever had brought Emma into the lives of Benjamin and Jeremiah at auspicious times, everyone was thankful for the part she played in channeling the forces of peace and goodness, to bring Benjamin and Jeremiah together again.

But no one was happier than Alfredo, for what he and Emma had begun the night before had continued to deepen on their ride through his acres. The captain had considered when it might be time to leave the seas and settle ashore. As to Emma, she had expected the day would come when her constant travels would end. And as so often happens in life, change is signaled when it's least expected. Now both imagined a different time ahead.

Chapter 12

Izzy, Will, Nora, Charlie May, Lucy & Colt Walker

As the group slowly descended the path beside the waterfall, the Hammersteins were waiting below. A younger man had joined them as well.

"Did you get what you came for?" the stranger asked.

"Yes, and then some," Will offered.

Frank and Bonnie quickly made introductions, singling out Charlie May as the prospective buyer.

"Colt Walker," he repeated as he shook hands all around. Then, to Izzy and Charlie May, "I understand you're the cousins."

"Yes," said Charlie May. "The Hawkins family, two brothers. I'm descended from Jeremiah and Izzy is descended from Benjamin."

"This land has been in my family since before America was a nation," Colt proudly stated.

"That's remarkable — to stay in one family all this time, especially since people move around so much," Charlie May responded.

"Ironically, my first ancestors were both constantly on the move until they settled here together," mused Colt. "Frank and Bonnie probably told you. I've been waiting for the right moment for some time. I wasn't sure I was ever going to see this day."

"The right moment to sell the property? Is that what you mean?" Charlie May inquired.

"Actually, what I meant is I've been expecting *you*…," Colt clarified and immediately held everyone's attention. "Come to the farmhouse and let me explain. I know you've experienced the cave. When Frank and Bonnie told me of the beautiful silver box you have with the image and that you were climbing the waterfall — well, I knew I had to meet you now."

"Then lead the way," Izzy said, considering all that had happened already, anything was possible now.

"What I have to tell you will put some things in perspective," Colt explained. "Besides, there's something I need from you and I'm certain you need from me," he noted, looking directly at Izzy and Charlie May.

When they arrived at the farmhouse, Colt graciously welcomed everyone. "This home has seen a lot of life. It's been on this very spot, in one form or another, since the year 1696. In fact," speaking directly to Izzy, "I'm sure your ancestor, Benjamin Hawkins, visited here many times."

Izzy's eyes lit up in wonder as he walked through he door.

"What of Jeremiah?" Charlie May asked.

"Honestly, I can't say," Colt replied. "What I do know is that Benjamin and Catherine, his wife, also lived on this land, though a distance from here. This house seemed to be deliberately situated near the waterfall."

Colt showed them to a large open room. "Everyone, please make yourselves comfortable."

Izzy came straight to the point. "How is it that you came to 'expect' us? What's your connection to the Hawkins family?"

And Colt began to explain. "For as long as I can remember, I've had a sixth sense about people, places and events. I can read the energy field around a person. I get a feel for who you are, where you come from and what your possible future might be."

"Are you telling us you're clairvoyant, and that's how you knew we were coming?" a skeptical Charlie May asked.

"No, no, not at all, not really — or, not in this case, anyway."

"Then what are you saying?" Izzy asked.

"My mother, Christina Walker, was adept with many spiritual gifts, including hands-on healing, which she passed on to me. It's an ability that seems to have come down through the generations and has to do with the nature of this place. When I was twenty-two and studying quantum physics at college, my mother became suddenly ill. Of course I rushed home. My older sister Chelsey, who was married and lived nearby, was caring for our mom. She left to take a break and briefly went back to her own house, leaving me alone with my mother. My mom suddenly took a turn and went into a semi-conscious state. I did the only thing I knew, which was to put my hand on her heart, hoping to channel my life-force to help her recover."

"Wow," Lucy interrupted, "that must have been tough for you!"

Colt acknowledged her with an affirmative nod, and then continued. "My mother awoke, determined to tell me something. She spoke softly and her words have never left me. 'Colt, I must leave you now. I have done the work I needed to do in my allotted time. Now it is up to you.' She pointed to her dresser and told me to pull out the bottom panel. 'Reach up, son. There is something you need to see.' I did so and retrieved a scrolled parchment hidden inside. It was an elaborate and colorful drawing, very old, and signed by Emma Wells, who was married to Captain Alberto Alfredo. I am their direct descendent. It was Alfredo who first owned this property. He passed it down to his sons and the generations to follow, down to my mom and to my sister and me."

"That's amazing. And what was the drawing of?" asked Lucy, enthralled by the story.

"You've been there today." Colt watched their faces light up. "It was a portrait of the waterfall. My mother told me that there was a cave by the waterfall, closed off long ago. As you now know, it's the crystal cave, which I found and reopened. Then she directed me to her computer, to a file named *Seed Stone*, and assured me it would explain everything."

Colt paused, needing a moment. It was clear to everyone that he was feeling the emotion of his mother's passing, though some twenty years had gone by.

He pulled himself together and continued. "I put my hand on her heart again, but her breathing was becoming more labored. She took my hand and whispered, 'The book the man is holding is Ethan Hawkins' diary. Find it, Colt. The last entry tells you what you need to know.' I said to her, 'Okay Mom, I understand. Now relax. EMS will be here soon.' But she looked at me, squeezed my hand, smiled, and took her last breath."

"Oh!" Nora gasped softly, imagining the emotional pain of that moment.

"Thanks," Colt acknowledged, paused for a moment and then continued. "In the aftermath of her passing, I was so distraught I forgot about the computer file. I was young and my father had died the year before. But as I was going through her things, reviewing her life as I went along, I suddenly remembered to check the file."

Then Colt took two weathered sheets of folded paper from his pocket. "Here are the contents of my mother's Seed Stone file." He began to read aloud:

> *"Long ago our ancestors, Captain Alfredo and Emma Wells, were friends of the Hawkins and Fletcher families. They gathered here at a significant moment in each of their lives and set in motion a future destiny intended to light the minds of their progeny. Emma, a dealer in crafts during colonial times and an artist in her own right, recorded it for her family — our family. Her drawing depicts a time when an alignment in the night sky triggers an evolutionary*

unfoldment of the human drama. Humankind is part of a continuing process of becoming. And Emma has left this gift to our family, and I bestow its meaning onto my children, Colt and Chelsey.

"The image is filled with symbolism. The woman is pouring water onto the land and into the water simultaneously. The water represents the cleansing of the soul with the nourishment and nectar of life — liquid starlight that heals, renews and inspires the heart. Look closely and you'll see the water dividing into five rivulets on the land, which represent our five senses — smell, taste, touch, hearing and sight. The water from the container rippling into the pool below the waterfall is our emotional life and inner world. Here is the blending and balancing of everything we are — all gifts that are our rightful heritage. There is a phoenix above the waterfall, a symbol of transformation that lifts our earthly burdens and allows us to fly beyond the boundaries of limited thought to be reborn. There is a butterfly too that represents transformation from one state of being to another, where we live the octaves that are embedded deep within our life-force on the earthly plane. This state of being heralds a new life born into a higher realm.

"There are twelve stars around the one. The twelve represent our primary energy centers in the body that dissolve and blend into one, reflected in the purified heart that fills the body with the vibration of love. The man is pointing to the cave where lies the diamond crystal stone that Ethan Hawkins found, and which Benjamin and Jeremiah Hawkins placed in the cave behind the waterfall.

"To Ethan, the diamond crystal was a teaching stone. He discovered it could aid in opening the heart and mind to

the higher planes of existence. Benjamin Hawkins, his son, found it could transform all of his senses — physically, emotionally and spiritually — beyond the boundaries of time and space, beyond the constraints of his limited thought, to expand his awareness to a realm of peace and balance.

"The man is pointing to the cave with one hand and holding the Hawkins diary in the other. According to Emma, the last entry of that diary holds the secret key, the zenith of all of Ethan's work.

"What I've shared here comes from Emma's memory. She foretold a time when the rightful descendants of Ethan and Elizabeth Hawkins, of Jeremiah and Abigail, of Benjamin and Catherine, will search for their inheritance — the diamond crystal stone — and release the unfolding of their human spirit in flesh and bone."

As Colt finished reading, the room was silent. Then Izzy stood up abruptly. "Lucy, I need the car keys, please."

"I'll go," Lucy insisted. "The car's right outside."

"No, thanks. I'll be right back." Izzy walked out, keys in hand.

Will knew Izzy's mission, as did Lucy. A hushed conversation filled the brief time until Izzy reappeared.

It was the diary, of course, that Izzy had gone to retrieve. "Here you go, Colt. The diary of Ethan Hawkins, with entries by Benjamin Hawkins too," he confirmed, holding up the weathered volume. Then he turned to the specific page and handed the diary to Colt. "This is the last entry written by Ethan. He died the next day."

Colt began to read aloud: *"Good Stewards of this Earth...."*

Will had read Ethan's last entry before, yet hearing Colt read it now, after the experience in the crystal cave, Will's mind was filled with intuitive supposition. Ever since he was young, curiosity about human evolution spurred his imagination. Some people looked at humanity as a finished creation. Will believed that science was only scratching the surface of the potential of the human endeavor. He often speculated that everything we encounter influences our biology and consciousness, and holds the possibility of unlocking some unknown factor in the human saga.

"I believe I know what Ethan Hawkins was trying to tell us," Will began. "We live in a sea of vibrating frequencies. Everything vibrates with information — from nature all around us, to planetary influences. Everything from Earth's gravitational pull to solar flares that streak into our atmosphere. All have an undetermined impact on physical experience, which in turn influences our consciousness. Our bodies are designed to process frequencies whether sound, color or smell — even what we eat."

"You're losing me," Lucy admitted. "What does that mean?"

"All frequencies are available to us," Will continued. "As our inner awareness evolves and opens, we sync with the energy signatures that are around us, based on the signals that emanate from us. One attracts the other. One nourishes the other, and the result is the flowering of the human experience."

Using his own science background, Colt expanded the discussion. "I've heard it said that our very bone structure is actually crystal and in effect acts like a tuning folk, vibrating our internal signal — broadcasting who we are sonically at any given moment. As our physicality is made up of mostly a fluid-like substance electrically charged, some speculate that even every cell is crystalline in nature, biologically receptive to frequency, creating a field of life-force energy that interacts with everything that we encounter."

"And what we vibrate finds resonance with outside sources that support the frequency of our inner awareness," Will added. "A quantum scientist might say that everything exists as pure potential, and we collapse the wave form with our state of consciousness and consequentially create our own reality."

"Let me try to translate that one," offered Nora. "It means opening our hearts to feeling and expressing love is so crucial to our quality of life. In other words, when we vibrate love, love comes back to us."

Will loved Nora's poetic interpretation. It was as if he could feel Nora's love being broadcast from her body.

Then Colt brought the conversation full circle. "What if cosmic influences like gamma rays, solar flares and gravitational waves coming from space are of divine essence? What if they are divinely timed — an evolutionary spiral — to reach Earth at prescribed moments, to recalibrate the DNA/RNA structure in our biology so we can accommodate higher vibrations of light?" Colt proposed.

"Now that's an interesting thought," Will concurred. "As Ethan Hawkins said, things are constantly being revealed from the unknown to the known, shifting our points of reference and expanding our perception of reality."

Charlie May had listened throughout the conversation, fascinated at the theories, but also considering all that had transpired, and all she had discovered since the day Nora first called to ask about Jason DeWitt. Now she offered her hand to Colt. "But, if you don't mind my asking, why are you leaving this house and land now?"

Colt took a deep breath and then explained. "Ever since I reopened it, the energy in the crystal cave has been remarkably steady. Wonderfully soothing, peaceful and comforting. Then about six months ago something changed. The vibration heightened and the light grew incredibly vibrant. There was an intensity I had never experienced before. Intuitively, I knew something significant was happening. I decided to put the property up for sale hoping to push the process — to see if what I was feeling in the cave was an indication that Ethan's descendants would make an appearance. Putting the land up for sale was the only way I knew how to get people here on the property."

"And you're still interested in selling?" Charlie May asked.

"Before now, I had to wonder if this moment would ever come."

He smiled and looked at Izzy and Charlie May. "With your arrival today and your experience in the crystal cave, my time here has come to a close. I have fulfilled an obligation my ancestors took on centuries ago. Their lives were so instrumental and interwoven in the fate and very fabric of your family. I've come to understand all of this simply as keeping faith with the enduring truth and beauty that reveals the mystery embedded into all of life. I've always sensed that Emma Wells and Captain Alfredo have been ever present here with me. I've often imagined them not only roaming these lands in their day but no doubt exploring these hills and valleys with me down through the years.

"Leaving here is bittersweet. Yet my responsibility to my descendants, and especially the promise I made to my mother, has been completed. I'm ready for a new journey."

Colt paused. And then with a reporter's curiosity Nora couldn't help but ask, "Where will you go?"

"A few years after my mother died, my sister and her husband moved to the West Coast. I see her and her family, but not nearly enough. At this point in my life, I've decided I would like to join her on the other side of the country. And, I know I'm passing this land on to the people who truly belong to it, whose roots are here too."

Putting her hand on Colt's shoulder Charlie May full heartedly offered, "You'll always be welcome back here." And then turning to Izzy to confirm, "Right, Izzy?"

The sound of his name brought Izzy back from thoughts of his father and uncle. How he wished he could see their faces at what he was discovering.

He walked to Colt and holding him at arms length tenderly addressed him, "Colt it's impossible to express the gratitude I have to you and your family. Spanning the generations, each of us in our own way have somehow arrived at this moment that defies logic. But that's the point isn't it. Life shows us again and again that it is always more then it appears.... And I for one, am glad of it.

"I want you to know that the door here will always be opened to you and your sister's family. I have a feeling we will be seeing more of each other."

As Izzy embraced Colt the image of his uncle and father came to him again and he could feel the light of there smiles shinning down on him.

At that, Nora stood up. "Well Professor Davenport, I think it's time we headed home." She stepped forward to shake Colt's hand. "We're close enough that we can get a taxi."

"No, I'll take you," Lucy insisted. "We've come this far together! Charlie May, you don't mind, do you? Then we'll take you home, and Izzy and I will head back to the city."

"It's hard to leave, but I guess it's time," Will agreed. It had been a momentous day to say the least. "Colt, I'd love to speak some more," he added.

"I'd like that … Professor. Where do you teach?" Colt inquired.

"I'm not at the moment. Writing a book," answered Will. "And based on today, I see a whole new chapter — and maybe more."

"Thank you Colt." Charlie May said as they all walked toward the front entrance. "Can I call you tomorrow and arrange for the sale of the property."

"I look forward to it." Colt responded, and told each one, "It was a pleasure to meet you."

He watched them depart, and closed the door.

Chapter 13

Will and Nora

Will was at the breakfast table, finishing yet another cup of coffee. He had come in late the night before after a full day of appointments, including one with the dean of the science department at the university. Will had texted Nora with the good news — he had a publisher and was in line for a teaching position! Grateful to Ken for his continued support, Will had treated his brother to dinner.

As Will expected, Nora was already asleep when he got in. He went straight to bed, but awoke in the early morning with a flurry of ideas and was inspired to write. Will's scientific reasoning and his ability to translate it into compelling prose had been ablaze for months. Work on the book had proceeded at an amazing pace. It was as though the crystal's diamond light had illuminated new neurological pathways, triggering synapses across his brain with extraordinary swiftness.

Ever since Will went into the crystal cave five months ago, his imagination was firing on all cylinders. It was unlike any other moments of inspired revelation he had ever experienced. Of course he was curious as to why, but for now he was satisfied knowing that he had undergone an awakening that fundamentally changed the way his mind worked. It was as if the crystals in the cave transmitted some profound information. It wasn't so much a language in words. Rather, Will felt it as codes, symbols and signals wrapped in thought waves that could open the gates to higher awareness.

Over the last few months, Will found himself often thinking about his father's story and how he encountered the vein of blue crystal in the mine in South America — that it was a conduit to Earth's core that transmitted an unfathomable message — one that informed and enriched his father's life from that moment forward.

After discussing that experience with his father again, and also sharing his own story about the crystal cave, Will's core theories began to evolve again. It was a given that everything was comprised of energy, vibrating and alive. But now he was convinced more than ever that all things are constantly broadcasting information about their own existence — and an exchange of information is happening all the time between everything. Will further theorized when we reach a certain state of awareness our senses open and expand so we can assimilate this vibrating information in new and important ways beyond our current abilities.

Will's father had been right. Sharing his experience in South America with his son had given Will a framework in which to grasp his own experience in the crystal cave.

In need of more coffee to keep those brain cells humming, Will was pouring another cup when he heard footsteps coming down the stairs.

"Good morning, sleepyhead." He reached out to hug Nora, still yawning as she came into the room.

"You've been busy!" Nora took in the sheets of yellow legal pad spread across the kitchen table — Will's notes from another furious round of writing.

"Now that I have a publishing deal for my book, I'll be very busy to finish it on time!" he warned.

"I'm so happy for you, though I'm not surprised," Nora returned Will's hug. "So tell me about the meeting, with the publisher and with the dean."

"The editors are ecstatic about the Newton entries from Ethan's diary and the incredible story about how it was discovered. Izzy is helping me chronicle the details. I'm not sure who's more excited him or me. It's already creating a buzz in certain circles, especially with Ethan being a contemporary of Newton and describing some of Newton's theories as the great man himself is revealing them! And with the university deciding to endorse the publication, the book will have instant credibility in the scientific community." As he spoke, Will's pride was evident.

"But, I'll tell you, Nora I'm not sure the whole thing would have happened without your expose´ on DeWitt and Strong," he confirmed. "Your insider scoop read like a blockbuster suspense novel. The blackout, the attempted market manipulation, the FBI and Homeland Security. Murder and deception — trying to pin the blame on a well-known scientist — you had the whole country riveted. It certainly pays to have a partner with a detective's nose and a brave heart. Thank God for my talented dear wife!"

"You're quite welcome, my dear husband! And you're not so bad yourself!" she laughed. "But you know what surprised me? The statement from Senator Broderick following the explosion, endorsing your calls for greater protection of the grid. I have to say, even though I've gotten numb to corrupt officials, I was relieved that Broderick wasn't in league with DeWitt and Strong. He was tough when you testified simply because he disagreed with your thinking."

"He was pig headed, but at least he came by it honestly," Will added with a wry smile.

"That's one way of putting it," Nora smirked. "But how about those spineless shitheads at California Union offering you a position again!

Ken predicted that one correctly. Thank God you turned them down. I wouldn't think of leaving New York now. And when this whole thing started, I never thought this California girl would say that!"

"I'm glad you feel that way, given the offer from the university. I thought the dean only wanted to discuss my manuscript. But a full professorship, not bad. I guess it didn't hurt being vindicated in the national news and subsequently resurrected as a media darling." He laughed at his own self-portrayal.

About then Will realized that Nora sat at the table without her usual cup of coffee. "What, no coffee for you this morning." he asked, nodding toward the coffee pot. "How about I brew you a fresh pot?"

Nora had been waiting for the moment to share her own news. Will had offered the perfect opening.

"No coffee for me. Actually I'm just going to have to go decaf from now on." Then Nora smiled as she watched the quizzical look on Will's face. "I'm pregnant … it's official!"

"Oh my God!" Will jumped up and wrapped his arms around Nora's shoulders and squeezed her tightly. "When? Why didn't you tell me?"

"I went yesterday. I wanted to be sure. It was such a disappointment to both of us when I thought I was pregnant back in April. It was the shock of everything that had happened, or so the doctor said. She told me to relax. So I did, and now, voila. Perfect timing!"

"But I still don't get why you didn't tell me," Will insisted.

"I guess I also wanted to surprise you," Nora whispered.

Will broke into full-out laughter.

"What's so funny?"

"Old habits die hard. Forever with the surprises."

"Well, here's another one. You might want to sit down for this: we're having twins!"

"Oh my God, Nora!"

"Pleased?"

"Yes, I'm definitely pleased. But, wow! Twins! Boys, girls, both?"

"Too early for that, sweetie. In another month."

"But you went by yourself? I feel terrible about that!" Will's face showed genuine puzzlement.

"No, not to worry!" Nora comforted him. "Charlie May came with me. She was fantastic, as you can imagine, and so thrilled that we're having twins."

"So… we're expanding from two to four! I can't believe it!" Will declared eagerly.

"And talk about expanding, I'm going to be huge in no time," Nora grinned, rubbing what was already a bump on her slender frame.

"You'll be beautifully huge!" Will hugged her. "Davenport kids, wow! I wonder what they'll be like?"

"Oh, how about just strong, smart, loving, curious and kind!" Nora suggested.

But before Will could respond, a shadowy feeling inexplicably rose inside him. His aversion to the uncertainty this change would bring was arriving as an unwelcomed guest.

"You really think so?" He asked.

Nora could see she had a nervous husband on her hands. "Of course silly. Look, I've had a little more time to get used to the idea. Sure, even though we've been planning for a child, when you come right to it, when reality sets in, it's a big change."

"Sure is! And oh my God when I think of all the trillions of biological functions needed for everything to go smoothly, to create a human being." Will jumped right in, imagining more than a few sleepless nights.

"Slow down Joe scientist. Life happens, honey. If we've learned anything these past few months, being alive means change. Right? And besides, we've done alright so far haven't we. Nora's declaration came with a smile, her eyes soft and reassuring.

Will gave Nora a hug fully accepting her comfort. And something started to flow between them — a soothing sense of allowing what will be — to be. As they embraced they slipped the bonds of the ordinary into an intuitive leap of the heart. Here they were beyond shadow and light, and entered a place where life keeps faith with the mystery of love. And truth and beauty come to rest without *the need to know* — leaving one basking in its peace — as fleeting as it may be.

"I guess we're on a new journey now." Will said, now holding her at arms length.

"Sure are partner." Nora answered.

"As my dad is so fond of saying, explore the world, take in the experience, live it fully and express what you learn and share it with others."

"That sounds like something you may want to teach these babies I'm carrying."

"Good idea! And I think I'll had another "E" to the mix…. Evolve."

"And why's that?"

"It seems nothing stays the same. And I suppose that's the way it's meant to be. Life feels like it is always moving toward something. And while I think it's folly to assume we can understand all of life's mysteries, there has to be a reason for all of this. But the answers always seem beyond the realm of what we know — hidden in the shadows waiting for light to reveal them. Some days I feel *the need to know* everything there is to know. And yet there are some days I want to be free of all that. I just want to *let it be*…. More recently it seems that by easing up, life flows naturally, magically, and it's both exhilarating and restful at the same time."

"I feel that way too!" Nora said, closed her eyes and embraced Will tightly.

"We sure have come a long way together." Will then declared.

"Have we ever…. You know, in a weird way, I guess we have Jason DeWitt to thank," Nora proposed.

"How do you figure that?" Will stared, confounded by Nora's thinking.

"If it weren't for him and all his plotting, we never would have ended up in New York City. Despite Ken and your parents here, I doubt we would have left California. And then we never would have met Izzy and Charlie May and Lucy … or Colt … or Levi either. We never would have had the Hawkins adventure, or discovered the crystal cave. Who knows even about a baby? Actually, it was that moment in the cave that I knew we would have a child. I just didn't imagine we'd have twins, though given Benjamin and Jeremiah, maybe I should have."

"Let's be sure our twins are always friends!" Will cautioned.

"They will be. And besides, we have plenty of examples of how brothers, at least, can forgive and reunite…."

"You're right about that," Will said wistfully. And then, more brightly, "I can't wait to tell Izzy!"

"Yes, and while you're at it, you might ask him how he feels about us taking up residence in the Walker farmhouse," Nora added. "Charlie May suggested we might want to move in, at least for a year, to have more room for our new brood."

Will's eyes crinkled with excitement. "Oh, I know Izzy well enough to say he would never object! That would be amazing, to live so close to the waterfall, and the cave and the crystal…."

"I knew that would appeal to you. Charlie May has gone into the cave many times since our first visit and says it gets more and more amazing each time. You've got to see how excited she is. In fact, she wants to talk to you about what she is experiencing."

"You don't have to ask me twice, I'm in."

Nora and Will let the moment wash over them. In the turning of the world, in the unfolding of fate, Will and Nora rode a roller coaster of highs and lows and highs again — from fame and fortune, to depression and isolation, and ultimately to rebirth and renewal.

"I love you, Nora Martin Davenport. Have I told you that today?"

"Not in those words, sir! And I love you, William Conner Davenport," echoed Nora, "always have, always will."

Chapter 14

GRAND CENTRAL STATION
AUGUST 1
10:00 A.M.

Izzy & Levi

About the time that Nora and Will were celebrating the momentous prospect of Davenport twins, the Rhodes brothers were working their way back toward restoring the bonds of family.

Izzy was behind the counter of The Great American Timepiece, when Levi walked through the open door. They had not been alone together in Grand Central Station since the day in March when Levi arrived, similarly unexpected, with the Hawkins poem and the Fletcher letter. Now more than five months had passed.

"Hello, Izzy," Levi announced.

"Levi!"

"Did I catch you at a bad time?" he inquired, noting that Izzy had a preoccupied look on his face.

"No, I was just waiting to hear from Lucy — you know, my assistant. She's got a serious boyfriend now and wants me to meet him. We're having dinner tonight. She's calling with the place and time. I don't know. I just hope he's a nice guy. You know she's like a daughter to me."

"I'm sure she feels the same closeness. That's why she wants your approval."

The events of the previous months had changed Levi's view of his brother. Among the traits he had come to admire was Izzy's ability to deeply connect with the people in his life.

"So what's brought you here?" asked Izzy, ready to change the subject.

"I wanted to thank you personally for getting me in touch with Charlie May…."

Indeed, at the behest of Izzy, Charlie May had made good on her promise to help her newfound cousin Levi Rhodes — provided he was innocent of wrongdoing. Fortunately he was, and through her government contacts in Washington, she had helped to dispel any suspicion of him, aided by the information that he and Mercedes Woods could provide about Victor Strong's activities.

Both Levi and Mercedes had walked away from the imploding catastrophe at Strong, Price, Applebaum and Goodwin with a clear conscience, and legally unscathed.

Strong was now under indictment, the U.S. Attorney General's office and the Securities and Exchange Commission building a stronger federal case against him every day. Grace and her cohorts were headed to prison, having chosen to plead guilty to declare the rightness of their plan. And Lester Edwards had plea-bargained his way to a reduced manslaughter charge, with plans to emerge from prison in only a few years ready to try his hand again with new schemes of deception and intrigue.

"I still cannot believe Charlie May Maddison is our cousin … and a math and computer genius, no less," Levi mused.

"Runs in the family," Izzy observed.

"I owe her a lot," Levi continued, a reference to her putting her reputation on the line, defending him in quarters where it mattered. "Now

I'm doing consulting for Charlie May's company. I'm meeting with one of her programmers this afternoon. We're working on a government contract to establish a unified code for supercomputers. That way no one can have a monopolistic stranglehold on the technological advances in computer sciences, like what DeWitt attempted," Levi explained.

He moved closer to Izzy, extending his hand. "We haven't spoken much … directly, that is. Charlie May has been a most effective go-between. But I thought it was time…."

Levi waited, watching his brother and holding the door to their relationship open — hopeful that in the days to follow he and Izzy could find a place of real understanding from which to start anew.

Izzy accepted his brother's hand. "Charlie May told me you were instrumental in clawing back the profits Strong received from the blackout scheme," Izzy declared. "A little computer magic she said, but didn't elaborate."

"Let me put it this way. I installed a back door into DeWitt's computer," Levi explained. "I didn't trust DeWitt and, over time, I started to have my doubts about Victor too. Even though he helped make my career, DeWitt's influence on him was corrosive. So I added a discreet entrance into DeWitt's quantum computer — a hidden program that could uncover information that DeWitt and Strong intended to keep secret. When Mercedes Woods, Victor's assistant, told me about bogus accounts she'd discovered, I knew how to unlock what they were up to and reveal what they'd stolen."

"Well, Levi, you've certainly landed on your feet. Especially now that you're working with Charlie May. Her company is top-notch."

"You probably think undeservedly so… and you'd be right," Levi said quietly.

"That might have been true when I found out about your involvement in Sam and Dad's death. Then I thought I'd never forgive you. But over the last few months I've learned a lot. My emotions have been discharged by the power of my recent experiences."

Levi nodded. "Charlie May told me about the crystal cave and Ethan Hawkins' diamond crystal. I always thought you and Dad were crazy chasing after some pie-in-the-sky treasure. Wow, was I wrong! But I'm happy for you, Iz. You've fulfilled Dad's quest and your own. That certainly must be satisfying."

"Yes, Levi, it is…." Izzy began. He wanted to tell Levi what was revealed to him in the cave … how his life had changed … that he had found a way to elevate his thoughts to be unified in *The One Light* … that his heart was filled with gratitude, and that being grateful was an actual frequency of light. He discovered that by breathing in gratitude, a band of energy was emitted that nourished not only himself but those around him as well. Izzy wanted to confide in Levi, so that he'd understand the full impact of what had happened. But at that moment he didn't know how.

And there was something else that was happening to Izzy that he shared with no one, though he knew eventually he would tell Will. A palpable metamorphous was coursing through his body. In hindsight, he now recognized that it actually began the day in Colorado when he collapsed in the field, lost consciousness, and rode an ethereal wave to the Palace of Light. A dimensional shift, an alchemy of the heart, was initiated that day.

Now, after the moment he stood transfixed in the crystal cave, he was experiencing unpredictable surges of cosmic life-force, prompting his DNA to release crystal diamond codes. Izzy felt it as the same force that upholds the entire cosmos — all dimensions — all timelines. He felt that everything that ever was, is, or will be, was naturally occurring eternally inside him — life force teeming with information, forever unfolding. He discovered that something as simple as taking a breath could attune his state of awareness. No longer just breathing in oxygen, now he inhaled a cosmic substance he imagined as solar plasma, carrying with it the fuel for restructuring his biologic state. His spine and skull felt crystal-like. Even his very skin felt like a crystal matrix — an information highway that resonated with rarefied frequencies.

When he closed his eyes he could feel wings of prismatic color of sky blue, rose red, emerald green and golden yellow, sparkling diamond light, emanating from his heart. Up and down his spine the colors streamed and then spread out, extending in wide sweeps to the left and right of him, way beyond his physical body. And the light of pure consciousness and pure light moved beyond his mind's command as he felt his heart revealing its blueprint, a portal that was unifying his entire being.

And it was that understanding of his evolving heart that assured Izzy the moment would come when he'd find the words to achieve a complete reconciliation with Levi. Love, Izzy knew, is often expressed in imperfect ways. Love is indefinable, yet can be intimately felt and lived. To open that gateway … to follow that path … and walk through the door … infuses every facet of life beyond measure.

For now, Izzy settled on something his father would have wanted, and that he wanted too. Something he could do, as Benjamin and Jeremiah had done, to begin to reconcile his life and Levi's, and to find resurrection in the bounty of brotherly love.

"One day soon, we'll go to the crystal cave together," Izzy proposed. "Charlie May and I own the property now. No doubt you know that. We've decided to leave Ethan's crystal in place. Benjamin and Jeremiah not only left the crystal there for us to discover, but they found its perfect resting place. The cave is a sanctuary, a place of reverence and homage to Earth's power as she rides the waves of the cosmos. And for us, what better place to commune and discover the essence of ourselves."

"I'm looking forward to seeing it. It's still amazing to me. What were the chances you would ever find that place!" Levi marveled.

Izzy chuckled at the odds, though he was certain chance had nothing to do with it. Something mysterious and undefinable had brought them all together. It was something that traveled the inner pathways from beyond time to enter their lives. It was something from deep within, something intimate yet unknowable.

"Yes, someday soon," he repeated, "the three of us — you, me and Charlie May — will make the trek up the waterfall and behold the legacy we all share. Levi, there is magic in the world. There is no need to grasp for the future or dwell in the past. Life is right here before us, in the present, filled with power and beauty. It's an alchemy that Ethan, Benjamin and Jeremiah discovered. And I've come to feel it too. Who knows what we can discover together in the days to come?"

…And at last, the generations of Ethan Hawkins had come full circle.

Chapter 15

Colonial New York – Hunstanton, England
AUTUMN 1694 & BEYOND

Daniel Fletcher & Isaac Newton

As a crisp fall day arrived in full light, Daniel Fletcher was in a room above the store of Rogers & Hawkins, reviewing a letter he had just finished to Isaac Newton of all that had happened in America. Daniel could not wait until he returned to England to share his experiences with his fellow alchemist. His encounter in the crystal cave had profoundly changed his sense of himself and the world as he knew it. Daniel hoped, once he returned to England, to meet with Newton again and discuss the deeper meaning of what he had discovered. But for now this letter would have to do.

In America, The Colony of New York
30ᵗʰ Day of September, 1694

Dear Isaac,
*   I have been through much since my arrival here in America, and I dare say, my good friend, I shall never view the world, or our work in it, the same again. Ethan's crystal stone was indeed a treasure. It served its purpose in our time — to shine as a guiding light — a portal to a realm of awareness that glows in great truth and beauty.*

But my new understanding shows me now that there are many such talismans all around us. Whether stone or star, our existence is immersed in a sea of entryways to the eternal lamp of being. The human spirit — our awareness and the very core of being — is one and the same. Once we recognize that great truth, our search enables us to go within and discover the glory that we exist — I AM … WE ARE. If we touch that presence with all that we are, our heart and mind, our body and soul, we find ourselves at home, in an ongoing, everlasting beauty. It is a beauty that glitters in mysterious joy and bestows the blessing of being at peace in experiencing the unknowable.

Why do we thirst to know what life is — the world and everything in it? After all these years of study, I see now that it is simple. We live to learn to love life, in all its unbound beauty and difficulty. We live to love one another, even as we recognize our differences, and we live to love ourselves, even when we misguidedly think ourselves lacking. Earth is the field in which we toil. But it is also the place that travels with us through time, a symbiotic relationship that causes the universe to take notice.

So in the end, Ethan's crystal was a reminder of the structure of our being and its eternal unfoldment. Like the caterpillar that turns into the butterfly, we too are in a continual process of transformation. And all the while, moving beyond everyday angst and fear, we learn to take wing, knowing and believing in the miracle that WE ARE — and coming to rest in faith that we have meaning, and in truth WE ARE MEANING.

My dear friend, we searched for a treasure that we had all along. In every breath we take, life dwells within us, an awareness that is eternal and immeasurable. Our heart,

a diamond that reflects the glory of The One Life and the
gifts bestowed to us, is a treasure for all time.
   Your loving friend,
   Daniel

Daniel Fletcher kept his promise to his dear wife Hannah and arrived in Hunstanton just ahead of the new year of 1695. But his return took far longer than expected, as the voyage was delayed many weeks. Alberto Alfredo's cargo of fur was slow in filling his ship. And rather than push the cargo masters in New York to deliver, the captain took the extra time to enjoy the company of Emma Wells.

Until the day they set sail, Daniel stayed with Jeremiah and Abigail. They talked much during those weeks about Ethan and Elizabeth, Jeremiah wanting to know every detail about his mother that Daniel could remember. Thus, Daniel was elated to finally have a deep relationship with Ethan's other son, to see qualities of Ethan and Elizabeth that were flourishing in Jeremiah as an adult, and with the wise and tender influence of Abigail. And when Daniel at last embarked for England, he did so knowing his work in America was done and that he had been instrumental in helping the Hawkins brothers find a long-sought happiness, together and apart.

Daniel's voyage home was Alberto Alfredo's last as captain of the ship. After a lifetime of roaming, two wanderers had found each other: Alberto the adventurer, navigating the deep waters of the Atlantic, and Emma, an empathic intuitive, traveling the dusty roads of the English colonies in the New World. It would not be long before Alfredo would give up the sea and Emma her peddler's wagon. Together they settled on Alfredo's land, built a grand house and raised a family whose descendants would live on that land and in that dwelling for generations to come.

Benjamin and Catherine remained on Alfredo's land for some ten more years. Alfredo made good on his promise to give Benjamin his own acres, but eventually Catherine saw new opportunities and more advantages for them in the growing city of Boston, in the Massachusetts colony. Her father was commanding British troops in Boston and Jane Steward was delighted to at last have her daughter and five grandchildren nearby. Benjamin's skill as a healer was always in demand, and he became noted for innovative therapies. He saved many from distress and illness, offering wise counsel and a gentle touch.

Eventually, in the city indelibly connected to the American Revolution, the Hawkins clan would grow into fierce patriots fighting for independence. Then, in the new United States, the Benjamin Hawkins generations moved in ways as diverse as the country itself. In the early twentieth century, a daughter of a descendant married into the family of Rhodes — and the unfolding of the Hawkins legacy began.

Before Benjamin and Catherine's auspicious move, Jeremiah and Abigail had made their own. In the year 1701, Henry Rogers was ready to expand once again and offered Jeremiah and Abigail a full partnership in all of Henry's Virginia holdings. Jeremiah and Abigail, with Elizabeth Rose and her three siblings by then, all moved south and settled in Williamsburg, where once again they prospered.

Only Elizabeth Rose would live to a ripe old age. With more than her share of the Hawkins courage, she and her husband joined the push of settlers heading ever west and settled in Kentucky, certain that a source of goods would always be needed. And commerce became the Hawkins and then Maddison family trade for centuries, with success the common trait.

Jacob Fletcher found his way in America, first as Benjamin's apprentice and then as Jeremiah's. Jacob had a deep reverence for Benjamin and rightly believed that his future would be steeped in learning the ways of a hidden world.

Still, Jacob felt a particular kinship to Jeremiah, who had developed a quiet wisdom that Jacob appreciated and shared. In an act of friendship, he gave Jeremiah the Newton telescope when Jeremiah left for Virginia, with the wish that the planets and stars would lead Jeremiah and his growing family to good fortune. And when Elizabeth Rose left for Kentucky, she too carried the telescope — and thus it made its way to Charlie May Maddison, along with an extraordinary fortune.

In time, Jacob Fletcher also kept his father's wish that he voyage to England, to see his dear mother and Daniel before they passed on. But it was only a visit. America was too deeply a part of Jacob now. And when he returned to America, he carried with him the Hawkins diary, which his father had entrusted to him. And when Daniel died, Isaac Fletcher, Jacob's brother, honored their father's wishes by sending Jacob the collection of letters between Daniel and Newton.

By then Jacob was a healer like Benjamin. In time, as America expanded, Jacob was a wanderer too. He traveled to the territories that were opening in Ohio, the diary and letters always in his possession. In fact, no better keeper of these Hawkins treasures could be found than in Jacob Fletcher. He took to heart the charge to safeguard the diary and the letters too, with their explanations of the crystal and of Ethan's observations on how the world works. Jacob faithfully kept the diary in the silver box and the letters in the leather satchel that had belonged to Daniel. And his children did the same.

However, Isaac Newton's fame gave the letters a far greater conventional value. They were sold – though by whom and when remained murky in the Fletcher family history. But the diary remained with the Fletchers. And although there was only a general sense of what should be done, it was enough for Timothy Fletcher to deliver the diary to Isidor Rhodes.

Daniel had long since returned to Hunstanton when at last a letter came from Cambridge. He opened the missive with anticipation, eager for the insights that Newton would share. Indeed, Daniel was not disappointed and kept the letter with him always.

> *Dear Fletcher,*
>
> *Your observations about Ethan's crystal and the power of awareness have led me to new questions and suppositions of my own. I have always viewed science and alchemy as pathways toward enlightenment. By investigating the natural world, we unlock unknown worlds and the secrets of nature. The universe is ours to behold, and when we uncover the inner workings of what we observe, we add our voice to the onward march of man's evolution.*
>
> *You and I have endeavored to understand the nature of how the world came to be. I am reminded of the alchemist's creed: "As above, so below."*
>
> *But I sense something else. What if the world is made manifest by a different axiom: "As within, so without?"*
>
> *Consider, our physical world is made manifest through the essence of eternal life that resides within all things. We live our lives in an ocean of inspired substance. All of life is creative plasma, a divine gift.*
>
> *Our states of awareness are powerful tools to manifest our world. As divine beings, do we, in fact, form all that we see? Do we collectively create the world into which we are born? Does the world we observe actually reflect who we are? Steeped in the power of awareness and by using our divine attention, can we realize a newer planet upon which to live?*
>
> *I do not yet have the answers to these questions, Daniel, but I believe that all things are possible. Your experience with Ethan's diamond crystal tells me that the nature of what we are is only beginning to unfold. What we are today*

will shift to the who and what we will be tomorrow. That
is an exciting adventure, indeed.

Salutations my friend, until the next time,
Is. Newton

Alas, Daniel's wished-for meeting with Isaac Newton never occurred. Newton remained as busy as ever, Hannah was loathe to let Daniel travel too far after his long absence and, over time, both men grew frailer in health. Yet they continued their correspondence, sharing their observations about the world and reveling in the mystery of it all, for many more years.

Daniel lived out his days with Hannah, and after she was gone, he continued to enjoy the quiet village by the North Sea. Often Daniel sat by a fire in the evening, sipping brandy, waiting for a knock on the door from an unknown visitor. He was never disappointed.

Epilogue

Ethan Hawkins

Ethan Hawkins looks out to the sea. He sees his life before him reflected in the sunlight dancing on the waves — crests revealing the brightness in his life and shallows exposing the darkness he must face. The wave of his life flows in all its glory, and he is astonished to see the distance his story travels.

He begins as an orphan, trapped in the stable of his uncle's tavern, until he meets Daniel Fletcher and Isaac Newton. They recognize unique qualities within him. Their friendship and encouragement help him unleash his passion — to know life's deepest secrets.

What can his existence mean? That quest has directed his steps beyond what he thinks is possible. Now his wife, Elizabeth, is about to give birth. He takes a deep breath and then another. His heart beats in deep gratitude. Elizabeth, his forever treasure, will be with him always.

Suddenly he finds himself in a place vibrating with pure essence, unbound by the constraints of time and space. His light expands and reaches into eternity. He imbibes the moment, letting it heighten and swell.

In the next instant everything shifts. He feels the presence of two grown men standing with him. They are weathered by the storms of life, but they stand tall and true, joyful in the love they have found.

Each has fulfilled his destiny in the appointed time and appear transformed. Ethan is pleased that the fruit of his days has gone beyond his own lifetime.

That image fades to be replaced by another. Ethan watches as he wades into the water. Looking down he sees a crystal stone. He knows this time and place very well. It is the moment that everything changes. The diamond crystal, glistening with the light of pure possibility, catches the wonder in his eyes.

Ethan senses within him a presence. It is a life beyond this life, an eternal life, an eternal witness of pure awareness, the very core of his being.

His heart is lit with the language of diamond light and he feels the glory of *The One Light*. All the stars in all the galaxies and every planet glow in unison — *One Heartbeat*, shared by all.

Ethan looks out over the glistening sea… life emerging, forever flowing, waves of light upon the shore. In the glory of his eternal being — a watchful witness of pure awareness — his heart is filled with the flame of truth, beauty and grace, burning bright…. And all his days, from all his lives, every moment, fly home now — and he shines in the full glory of who he is, free and unbound, and exalted in the light of love.

In Appreciation

I want to express my gratitude to those people who have helped me throughout the process of writing *The Alchemist's Lost Treasure*. It is with deep appreciation that I thank Nancy Hereford. Nancy is my editor and friend. Her devotion to this work is on every page. We shared countless hours brainstorming concepts, storylines and presentation – always delighting in how the right words find their way into being. Nancy, thank you for your grace filled guidance.

I consider myself fortunate to have found Deb Tremper of Six Penny Graphics. Her creative hand, from book cover to text design, artistically enriches the reading experience. I am privileged to have her vivid imagination arrive at my doorstep.

I would also like to thank Rebecca Humrich of Sheridan Books for shepherding *The Alchemist's Lost Treasure* through the printing process. Her watchful eye ensured the highest quality.

To all my friends who have encouraged my writing throughout the years, your support has meant the world to me.

The *Alchemist's Lost Treasure* would never have come about without the love and encouragement of my wife, Carolyn and son, Josh. They are always ready to read my musings, challenge my assumptions and offer their suggestions and ideas. They light up my life every day with joy, laughter, and a sense of well-being.

I want to thank my parents, Ed and Seena Liebling, whose love, wisdom, and strength are always with me. The music of their lives is forever in my heart.